The Year's Best

Fantasy a·n·d Horror

The Year's Best

Fantasy and Horror

ELEVENTH ANNUAL COLLECTION

Edited by
Ellen Datlow & Terri Windling

ST. MARTIN'S PRESS ❧ NEW YORK

To the fabulous Tucson crew,
with heartfelt appreciation:
Richard Kunz, Mardelle Kunz, and Bill Murphy
—T.W.

To Jack Womack, a friend indeed
—E.D.

Contents

Acknowledgments

I would like to thank Lawrence Schimel, Linda Marotta, Gardner Dozois, Bill Congreve, Jo Fletcher, Stephen Jones, and Richard and Mardelle Kunz for their recommendations. I'd also like to thank John Klima and June Miller who volunteered their time and energy to help me with the nongenre material.

Thanks Jim Frenkel, who annually shoves us gracefully toward the finishing line, to our in-house editor Gordon Van Gelder for his continuing support, and to Tom Canty for his unceasing ability to deftly transmute his dark imaginings into gorgeous jacket art and design. Finally, thanks to Terri Windling, my long-distance partner in this enterprise. I used the following references to help me with the overview of the year: *Locus* magazine, *Publishers Weekly, Washington Post Book World, The New York Times Book Review*, Mark V. Ziesing's catalog, the Dreamhaven catalog, the Overlook Connection catalog, PDW catalog, the DarkEcho Newsletter, *Horror, Necrofile*, and *Hellnotes*.   —E.D.

I am grateful to all the publishers, editors, writers, artists, booksellers, and readers who sent material and shared their thoughts on the year in fantasy publishing with me. *Locus, Science Fiction Chronicle, Publishers Weekly, The Hungry Mind Review, The Women's Review of Books, Folk Roots*, Hear's Music, Tucson and Amazon.com were invaluable reference resources. I am particularly grateful for the hard work and dedication of Richard and Mardelle Kunz, Editorial Assistants for the fantasy half of this volume (and other Endicott Studio projects); and to Bill Murphy, library scout extraordinaire. There are gems in this book that would not be here without them. (Submission information and other Endicott Studio news can be found on our web site: *http://www.endicott-studio.com/*).

Thanks are also due to Ellen Kushner and Charles de Lint for music recommendations, Ellen Steiber for deadline support, and to: Delia Sherman, Jane Yolen, James Minz, Thomas Harlan VII, Lawrence Schimel, Gardner Dozois, Andy Heidel, and Brian Stableford for help of various kinds. Special thanks go to our St. Martin's editor, Gordon Van Gelder, and his assistant, Corin See; to our packager, Jim Frenkel, and his assistants, Kristopher O'Higgins and Seth Johnson; to cover artist and pal Tom Canty; and to my amazing coeditor, Ellen Datlow.   —T.W.

Each year this huge project requires the efforts of more people. The efforts of our editors speak for themselves. Same goes to the indomitable Van Gelder. *Ad Astra*, Gordo. My greatest thanks go to Kristopher O'Higgins, my new right-hand man, and to Seth Johnson, who again pulled double duty this year, helping with late production as well as writing the comics column. Also invaluable are University of Wisconsin interns: Kate Allgeier, Mary Layzell, Natalie Maus, Melanie Orpen, Sally Sosnouski, and Eric Thomas. Without their hands and brains, this book would never get done on time or with so few errors. Also, thanks to all the authors, agents, and publishers who cooperate with us by granting permission to reprint material. And of course, the U. of W. Memorial Library Reference Desk is an invaluable resource. Special thanks once again to Jessica Frenkel for inspiration in conceiving the jacket. —J.F.

Summation 1997: Fantasy

by Terri Windling

Welcome to the eleventh edition of *The Year's Best Fantasy and Horror* annual collection. It is quite astonishing to me to look at the ten fat, previous volumes sitting on my desk and to realize we are entering our second decade with this series. Our mandate has not changed since the first volume, published in 1987: The purpose of these books is to collect and preserve the very best magical, mythic, surrealistic, and horrific fiction published each year . . . and to seek out far-flung publications that lovers of fantasy literature might otherwise miss.

For readers new to this series, let me explain that our definition of fantasy fiction (and its overlapping sister field of horror) is a broad and inclusive one, ignoring the strict genre boundaries so beloved by modern publishers. Due to the modern fetish for book labels and categorization, "fantasy" has come to mean swords-and-dragons books to all too many readers . . . but if you move past commercial labels and look at several centuries of world literature, you'll find that "fantasy" is simply a tool employed by a wide variety of writers to tell a wide variety of stories—both tales set in our world and those set in magical realms.

These days, when you walk into a bookstore you are as likely to find fantasy fiction on the mainstream shelves as in the genre section, for magical realism (popularized by Latin American authors like Gabriel García Márquez) has strongly influenced a whole generation of writers all around the world. Angela Carter, Joyce Carol Oates, A. S. Byatt, Steven Millhauser, Robert Coover, and other mainstream authors all work with the tropes of fantasy—myth, folklore, fairy tales, and elements of surrealist fantasia—while fantasists like James P. Blaylock, John Crowley, and Karen Joy Fowler have created fine magical realist works over on the genre shelves. In other words, thanks to excellent fiction published on both sides of the genre/mainstream divide, we're coming into a time of increasing acceptance of post-Realism in the literary arts, where genre boundaries are wisely ignored. You'll find serious literature and light entertainment side-by-side in every category of fiction, no matter what label a book wears on its spine, no matter what shelf it sits on. Thus, in this volume, we have made it our mission to track down the year's best magical fiction no matter where it may be found . . . and to point you in the direction of literary treasures no book lover should miss.

The stories and poems reprinted in the volume come, once again, from a variety of sources: genre collections and anthologies, mainstream collections, foreign works in translation, and magazines ranging from *Asimov's Science Fiction* to *The New Yorker, Prairie Schooner, Southerly* (Australia), and *Black Warrior Review*. This book contains a liberal mix of fantasy, horror, and everything in between. Readers interested only in fantasy should look for stories with my initials listed on the introductions; those interested only in horror should look for Ellen Datlow's initials—although we encourage you to explore both the dark and light of fantastic fiction. (It pleases me that the majority of readers I talk to or receive correspondence from—even those favoring one form over the other—enjoy this opportunity to sample the best of both.) Inevitably, there are stories that fall in the shadow realm between fantasy and horror—in which case you'll find both our initials on the story introduction (with the editor who acquired the story for the volume listed first).

While both Ellen and I strive for a diversity of tales (to reflect the diversity of the field), please bear in mind that we are limited by what was actually published last year. For instance, the last decade has seen a modern renaissance of adult fairy tale retellings, originally sparked by Angela Carter's brilliant fiction, and fostered in-genre by the market for such work. Thus you'll find a high number of fairy tale retellings in these annual volumes, since many top writers are experimenting with this form—in contrast, say, to swords-and-sorcery stories, a form that is not currently attracting the best talent in our field (as it did back in the Pulp era). One thing I can't help but notice over ten years of reading for this series is how rare it is to find truly first-rate traditional fantasy short fiction (i.e., imaginary world fiction of the Tolkien or Le Guin sort). I've come to believe that this is because the invented-world type of fantasy is most successfully evoked at novel length (and usually in a fat novel at that, or even a whole series of novels), although there are some wonderful exceptions, such as the fine Peter S. Beagle story in this volume. (Mind you, even Beagle's story is set in a landscape first created in greater detail in his novel *The Innkeeper's Song.*) Brian Stableford (in his generous, insightful review of our series in *Necrofile* 26) points out that "*short* fantasies are mostly mutated folktales and surrealized slices of life; they have not the space to indulge in the more ambitious kinds of world-building which are almost definitive of modern genre fantasy. In horror, too, the restriction to shorter length favours the kind of *conte cruel* which deals in shocking revelation or in mocking black comedy at the expense of sustained exercises in paranoid crescendo." For this reason, if you're looking for a true overview of the fantasy field in 1997, don't stop with the short stories included in this volume, but look also at the novels (and other works) recommended below.

As I look back over the past year in fantasy publishing, there are several things that stand out above the general publishing din.

First, I'm both amazed and delighted by the number of strong first novels that appeared in 1997 (many of which, despite distinctly magical elements, came out as mainstream publications). There were also several good second novels, both inside the genre and in the mainstream. We're seeing a new generation of writers emerging here, which is exciting indeed (. . . and a bit unnerving for those of us who came into the field in the 1980s, and are used to being the "new kids" ourselves. Time certainly marches on).

Second, I've noticed that the 1997 novels that struck me most forcefully (and continue to haunt my dreams) were all coming-of-age tales by writers using magic symbolism to tell powerfully personal stories: Seamus Deane's *Reading in the Dark*, Heinz Insu Fenkl's *Memories of My Ghost Brother*, Will Shetterly's *Dogland*, Brian Hall's *Saskiad*, and Martha Brooks's *BoneDance*.

Third, I'm pleased that despite the manifold attractions of the magic realist brand of fantasy, this "new generation" of writers isn't abandoning the traditional fantasy form altogether. J. Gregory Keyes, Patrick O'Leary, Sean Russell, Candas Jane Dorsey, and others have given this form of literature a much-needed transfusion of healthy new blood.

Fourth, I'm pleased by the fresh vitality of "interstitial fiction"—that is, fiction that falls in the cracks between genres, defying labels or easy categorization. Books such as Paul Witcover's brilliant *Waking Beauty*, Sean Stewart's *Night Watch*, and Michael Swanwick's *Jack Faust* all ignore the boundary lines between fantasy, horror, science fiction, suspense, and mainstream fiction. Pat Mora's *House of Houses* and Heinz Insu Fenkl's *Memories of My Ghost Brother* blur the lines between novel and memoir, to powerful effect; while Chitra Banarjee Divakaruni's *Mistress of Spices* and Emma Donoghue's *Kissing the Witch* blur the lines drawn between oral storytelling, poetry, and prose.

In nonfiction, I'll remember 1997 as the year the landmark volume *The Encyclopedia of Fantasy*, by John Clute and John Grant, finally came out. It's an impressive achievement, and my hat is off to both these gentlemen. It was also the year Ellen Kushner's fascinating "Sound and Spirit" radio program (broadcast nationally by PRI) and Lewis Hyde's inspired book *Trickster Makes This World: Mischief, Myth, and Art* both helped to fill the hollow space left by Joseph Campbell's death, reminding us of the importance of myth, art, and spirit in our lives.

It was also the year my growing doubts about the health of the World Fantasy Awards coalesced into sheer disbelief when the judges failed to come up with a full ballot of award-worthy short fiction—despite our finding so many brilliant tales that we couldn't fit them all into the last volume of *Year's Best*. When books like Patricia A. McKillip's exquisite *Winter Rose* fail to get even a nod, it's time to start re-examining the way such awards are chosen.

It was a year in which my book-buying shifted almost entirely to the Internet (with its astonishing array of titles), while in the stores all I seemed to see on the shelves were brand-name authors and media tie-ins.

It was a year in which my publishing colleagues worried about an industry in flux, unable to predict what will happen next; in which a few writers got very rich and the rest were scrambling for contracts. Nonetheless, good books continue to be published. Magical imagery continues to be prevalent in all forms of book and media arts. Despite the problems of the book industry itself, fantasy literature is still flourishing, as evidenced by the books below. These recommended reading lists are drawn from the over four hundred books that crowded me out of my office this year. I think there were some gems among them. I hope you will agree.

Here are twenty "Must Read" novels of 1997 (in alphabetical order by author). An extended reading list of novels, short stories, art books, and nonfiction follows.

Spirits of the Ordinary by Kathleen Alcalá (Chronicle Books). Alcalá is a Mexican-American author who has published short fiction in both genre and mainstream venues. (Check out her terrific 1992 collection *Mrs. Vargas and the Dead Naturalist*.) This is Alcalá's first novel, and it's an impressive debut. Set in the nineteenth century, involving three generations in a Mexican-Jewish family, this story of a gold speculator who gets caught up in a bloody peasant revolt ranges from northern Mexico to the Casa Grandes cliff dwellings. Told in confident magic realist prose, Alcalá's book is a beauty.

Human Croquet by Kate Atkinson (Picador USA). When your first novel wins England's prestigious Whitman Book of the Year Award, how do you follow it up? With a wildly unconventional time-travel novel about an eccentric family in an English village (circa 1960)—a tale laced with fairy-tale allusions and an arch, distinctively British wit. *Human Croquet* is the story of sixteen-year-old Isobel Fairfax, daughter of a disillusioned grocer and a mother who has mysteriously disappeared. The *New York Times* wondered what to call it: "magical postmodern fiction? postmagical realism? postmodern magicalism?" Genre readers will have no such problem—they'll recognize it as fantasy (of the John Crowley sort).

Lava by Pamela Ball (W. W. Norton). "What if you lived in a world where you could wake the dead, where men had a shark jaw buried in their backs just as the shark god did when he stepped on the shore and became human? A place where scalding lava ran through the streets of the town and down into the hissing sea. Where women picked up guns and never put them down again, where it rained three days out of three, and ghosts drank from the rain gutters and huddled under the eaves of the wooden buildings. What if you lived in a town like that?" If, like me, you think this is one of the most beautiful opening passages you've come across in years, you'll love Ball's evocative tale of Hawaiian magical realism. Like the Alcalá book above, this is a highly memorable first novel.

Winter Tides by James P. Blaylock (Ace). You don't *have* to go to the mainstream shelves to find first-rate magical realism, as Blaylock proves with a dark and ghostly novel set on the California coast. This book will keep you thoroughly engrossed with its tale of identical twin sisters, and the man who was able to save only one of them from drowning. It's a novel about the ghosts of memory; about love, hate, and the nature of redemption. It's a page-turner, to be sure—but the power of the book lies in Blaylock's ability to get right inside his characters, bringing them vividly to life in all their human complexity.

Freedom and Necessity by Steven Brust and Emma Bull (Tor). This delightfully entertaining book—a collaboration by two writers from the Minneapolis "Scribblies" group—is a magical romp through the revolutionary politics of nineteenth-century England (who else but Brust and Bull would put Friedrich Engels in a fantasy novel?). Told in the form of letters and journal entries (incorporating actual contemporary documents), it's a tale chock-full of family intrigue, secret mystical societies, sword fighting, cross-dressing, puzzles within puzzles, romance, and revolution . . . what more can you ask for? If you're looking for a read that's simply lots of fun, while also smart and literate, this is the book.

Reading in the Dark by Seamus Deane (Knopf). Another first novel, this one—by an Irish poet—was short-listed for the Booker Prize. Deane's dark, violent, gorgeously poetic book is set in Northern Ireland, written in the autobiographical voice of a boy growing up in Derry in the middle of this century. It's an unforgettable coming-of-age story, haunted by ghosts, curses, family secrets, imbued with tales from Irish folklore. I read it months ago and I still can't get it out of my mind.

Trader by Charles de Lint (Tor). This is the latest in de Lint's Newford series, set on the streets of a modern (yet magical) city somewhere in North America. It's the tale of two men (a quiet, introspective guitar maker and a handsome, heartless rogue) who wake up in each other's bodies, plunked down in the middle of each other's lives. This intriguing premise is gounded in myths of a North American nature: the intermingled Native and immigrant lore unique to our continent. De Lint's work of recent years has gained a maturity of vision that makes this more than just another Newford book—welcome as that would be. He's forging his own distinctive brand of mythic fiction book by book, gaining a readership on both sides of the genre/mainstream divide.

The Mistress of Spices by Chitra Banarjee Divakaruni (Doubleday/Anchor). Another exceptional first novel—this one by the Indian-American author of the award-winning story collection *Arranged Marriages* (1995). The narrator of *The Mistress of Spices* is Tilo, born in a distant land, trained in a mystical healing art. When the novel begins, she has set up shop in Oakland, California, dispensing spices (for cooking and for healing) along with uncannily clairvoyant advice . . . until her work brings her into a magical conflict with the "old one," her teacher. This highly sensual story uses fantasy to explore the Indian-American immigrant experience and a clashing of vastly different cultures. The story is dreamlike, while still firmly grounded in its modern urban setting, and the ancient "art of spices" is conjured with passages of incandescent prose.

Memories of My Ghost Brother by Heinz Insu Fenkl (Dutton). Yet another unforgettable first novel (actually published in 1996, but not seen until this year) by a folklore scholar, and author of both mainstream and genre fiction. *Memories of My Ghost Brother* is a spellbinding coming-of-age tale about the son of a Korean black-marketeer and a German-American soldier, set in postwar South Korea . . . a land where fox demons haunt the countryside and ghosts drift through the dark city streets. Fenkl's poignant autobiographical book could be called a "magical realist memoir," woven through as it is with folktales and spirits. With its elegantly understated prose, its richly multilayered story, and its vivid portrait of the life of mixed-blood children, *Memories of My Ghost Brother* is one of the very best books I've read in years. Don't miss this one.

In the Land of Winter by Richard Grant (Avon). Grant's latest is the story of a modern day witch raising a daughter in a small Northeastern village—until hysteria generated by the Christian Right causes her child to be put in a State home. The protagonist is particularly well drawn: initially so ditzy you could shake her, by novel's end she has come into her own. I loved this book, with its passages of poetic prose, its humor, its all-too-believable characters, its magic—beautifully conjured from the winter woods and a mother's heart.

Here on Earth by Alice Hoffman (Putnam). Hoffman is one of the best American magical realists publishing in mainstream today—and her latest, while not as overtly fantastic as previous books (such as *Practical Magic* or *Illumination Night*), is a beauty nonetheless. It's the tale of a woman, her teenage daughter, and a handsome man with a twisted heart, set in a small New England town evoked with prose reminiscent of folk tales (or the works of Gabriel García Márquez). Like much of Hoffman's work, it's about the nature of love—in this case, love's dark underbelly. It's a hard-hitting book, filled with strong characterizations, woven throughout with the folklore of foxes. If you like James P. Blaylock's work, don't miss Alice Hoffman's (and vice versa).

Gate of Ivory, Gate of Horn by Robert Holdstock (Roc). One of the great mythic stories of our time is being created, book by book, in Holdstock's Mythago Wood sequence. All lovers of myth, fantasy, and fine prose should be aware of this masterwork of British fiction. The latest volume follows World War I vet Christian Huxley (son of George Huxley) into the depths of Ryhope Wood, a patch of primeval forest filled with myths, "mythagos," creatures of legend (from King Arthur to Cinderella), and ghosts out of history and dream. For readers familiar with Ryhope Wood, this gorgeous new book will not disappoint (despite its rather unattractive package). If you haven't journeyed into these woods before, don't start with this one—start with *Mythago Wood* or *Lavondyss*.

The Blackgod by J. Gregory Keyes (Del Rey). At this point you must be wondering whether there's any good "imaginary world" fantasy being written these days. While magical realism has indeed changed the nature of the fantasy field, claiming a number of its best authors, I'm happy to report that there are finally some good new writers of traditional fantasy—and Keyes is among the best of them. *The Blackgod* is the sequel and conclusion to a story begun in *The Waterborn*—so read these two fat volumes together for a thoroughly satisfying journey into a skillfully invented landscape, beautifully evoked, properly mythic, and convincing. The packaging makes *The Blackgod* look like just-another-Tolkien-redux-saga poised to hit the bestsellers lists, but don't let that deter you. Keyes has his own voice—smart, sly, wise and, genuinely original. Indeed, I hope Del Rey's garish packaging works, and the book gets out to a broad readership—because even readers of commerically slick fantasy deserve the real thing.

The Gift by Patrick O'Leary (Tor). Here's another book to restore your faith in the vitality of traditional fantasy fiction. Like the Keyes book above, *The Gift* is a second novel—and quite an impressive one. This magical coming-of-age novel (handsomely packaged with a Thomas Canty cover) begins aboard a ship, where stories are told, and stories within other stories, examining the nature of storytelling itself in a multilayered saga that makes excellent use of the tropes of high fantasy. I was reminded of the early books of Peter S. Beagle or Patricia A. McKillip—not so much because of O'Leary's style (which is very much his own), but because of that particular excitement you feel when you discover an author you know you're going to be reading for years to come.

The Moon and the Sun by Vonda N. McIntyre (Pocket). Even with all these talented newcomers around, it's still a pleasure to find oneself in the capable hands of a well-established writer—particularly a writer as fine as McIntyre and a book as good as this one. *The Moon and the Sun* is historical fantasy set in seventeenth-century France at the court of Louis XIV. The byzantine plot involves a captive mermaid, an ambitious lady-in-waiting, a Jesuit priest, a dwarf, and numerous other memorable characters; together, they create a unique tale as entertaining as it is enchanting.

Rose Daughter by Robin McKinley (Greenwillow). Twenty years ago McKinley made a name for herself with her first novel, *Beauty*, a gentle, romantic retelling of "Beauty and the Beast." Interestingly enough, the author found herself drawn back to the same tale two decades later, resulting in *Rose Daughter*, a completely new novel based on this material. If McKinley's prose weren't reason enough to recommend this quietly magical book, it is also fascinating to compare the two retellings. Some readers will prefer the first version; others will swear by the later one. Whichever you prefer, McKinley once again offers beautiful evidence of the enduring power of fairy tales to inspire fine modern fiction.

Earthquake Weather by Tim Powers (Tor). Another fast-paced, unpredictable, and utterly mad dark fantasy—a "road novel" racing through Powers's demented version of modern California. Set in a wasteland of ghosts, ghost eaters, unusual villains, and unlikely heroes, the plot of *Earthquake Weather* involves characters first met in *Last Call* and *Expiration Date*, drawing these two seemingly unrelated books together. Powers is a true original, and one of the most sharply inventive fantasists working today. To see the cutting-edge of the fantasy field (and of American fiction), check out this terrific writer's work.

The Subtle Knife by Philip Pullman (Knopf). This marvelous Young Adult novel (the middle book in a projected trilogy, beautifully packaged with cover art by Eric Rohmann) is the follow-up to Pullman's Carnegie Award–winning *The Golden Compass*. Set in an imaginary landscape rendered with exquisite detail, *The Subtle Knife* brings its young protagonists, Will and Lyra, into the "city of magpies" (where adults are absent and children run wild) in their search for Will's father and the Subtle Knife, an ancient magical tool. Pullman is creating an intricate, multilayered work of fantasy that is destined to be a classic of children's fiction.

The Stars Dispose by Michaela Roessner (Tor). In this sparkling Renaissance tale, based on the life of Catherine de'Medici, magic is practiced by the household servants of Florence's leading families, served up with the food, wound into ancient practices of table and hearth, underpinning Florentine society with spells and counterspells. Roessner has turned a delicious stew of magical ingredients into a fresh, utterly charming novel well steeped in Italian folklore.

Dogland by Will Shetterly (Tor). Here's another engaging coming-of-age story with magical realism at its core. Based in part on the author's own background, but not strictly autobiographical, the narrator is a young man growing up among the clashing cultures of Florida in the '60s while living in his family's roadside attraction, Dogland, a rather dubious venture featuring dogs of many different breeds. Shetterly has always shown great promise as a writer, particularly in his books for young adults, but with this wise, poignant story he has come into his own at last. I highly recommend it.

Also Recommended

Two excellent, hard-to-classify novels, not strictly fantasy (falling somewhere in the shadowy realm between science fiction, fantasy, and horror) are so good they deserve a special mention:

Jack Faust by Michael Swanwick (Avon), a retelling of Goethe's *Faust* set in the sixteenth century, involves a science fiction premise but has passages of pure magic too. Swanwick, like Powers, is a writer who likes to dance on the cutting edge of the field—so it comes as no surprise to discover his new book is a winner. *Waking Beauty* by Paul Witcover (HarperPrism) also defies easy publishing labels. Science fiction? Fantasy? Postmodern parable? Erotic adventure? No matter what you call it, Witcover's first novel is one of the finest, most thought-provoking books of 1997, exploring issues of power, gender, beauty, and survival with hypnotic prose, a dazzling plot, and powerfully complex characters.

Don't miss either of these books.

First Novels

In addition to the Alcalá, Ball, Deane, Divakaruni, Fenkl, and Witcover books listed above, all published as mainstream titles, two strong first novels also appeared in the fantasy genre this year. *The Art of Arrow Cutting* by Stephen Dedman (Tor) is magical noir suspense by one of Australia's hot new writers. This page-turner of a murder mystery weaves Japanese myth into the story of a photographer involved with the Japanese underworld of California. I recommend it highly. I also recommend *Black Wine* by Candas Jane Dorsey (Tor). Officially published in January 1997, Dorsey's unusual book appeared on the stands in late 1996 and won the William J. Crawford Award for the best first novel of that year. This dark, lyrical fantasy explores a variety of gender issues through the lives of five generations of women in a vivid imaginary world.

Other notable genre debuts in 1997: *The Harlequin's Dance* by Tom Arden (Gollancz), *The Seventh Heart* by Marina Fitch (Ace), and *The Stone Prince* by Fiona Patton (DAW). These are all writers to watch.

Oddities

The Best Peculiar Book distinction of 1997 is a three-way tie between the following: *The Bear Comes Home* by Rafi Zabor (W. W. Norton) is a hip, inventive novel about an alto sax–playing bear who becomes a jazz musician in Manhattan. It's overlong and a bit overblown, but if you stifle the occasional impulse to throw it out the nearest window, it's got some weirdly wonderful moments. When it works, it really works. *American Goliath* by Harvey Jacobs (St. Martin's Press) is based on a bizarre true event in American history: the faked discovery of the petrified remains of a giant in upstate New York (in 1869). Jacobs turns this actual event into a gonzo comic novel with magic realist elements. It's a raw, raucous portrait of post–Civil War America, involving P. T. Barnum, Cornelius Vanderbilt, Edwin Booth, and hucksters of every stripe. *Island of the Sequined Love Nun* by Christopher Moore (Avon) is pure farce, with the infectious humor of those screwball comedy films of the '30s and '40s. A hapless jet pilot ends up on a Micronesian island (populated by the Shark People), where he becomes involved with a mad doctor (selling the organs of ritual sacrifice victims to the Japanese), a sex goddess, a Filipino transvestite, and a talking fruit bat named Roberto. What can I say? It's unique.

Other oddities: *Capolan: Travels of a Vagabond Country* by Nick Bantock

(Chronicle) documents an imaginary land "more mysterious than Atlantis" in a box complete with a 48-page book, souvenir stamps, and fifteen postcards. Bantock's now-familiar work gets a little obscure here, lacking even the minimal story that held together *Griffin and Sabine.* Another Bantock project, *The Forgetting Room* (HarperCollins), is more successful. This is the story of a man who inherits a house in Spain from his grandfather, a surrealist painter. Traveling to Spain, he gradually uncovers the mystery of his grandfather's life and work. Bantock's text evokes a lovely sense of place, the volume is packaged handsomely, and the connection between art and story is more satisfying than in the above-mentioned book. Equally odd, but also handsome, is another Chronicle publication: *The Merchant of Marvels and the Peddler of Dreams* by the brilliant French book illustrator Frédéric Clément. This combines a surrealistic prose-poem with snippets of art that don't show Clement's work to best advantage. Nevertheless, it's nice to see a publisher willing to let an artist experiment.

Imaginary World Fantasy

The best traditional fantasy novels of the year (i.e., those set in imaginary landscapes) were the Keyes, O'Leary, and McKinley books above. In addition, here are other good reads that lovers of traditional fantasy shouldn't miss:

Beneath the Vaulted Hills by Sean Russell (DAW). Russell is one of the best of the new post-Tolkien, post–Le Guin generation of fantasists. His work is clearly influenced by both these writers, yet unlike so many cookie-cutter books clogging the fantasy shelves these days, Russell brings a fresh vision to the form, and genuine writing skill. The publisher is calling this one a prequel to the Moontide and Magic Rise books (*World without End* and *Sea without Shore*), for it's set in the same invented world some years earlier. *Beneath the Vaunted Hills* can be read and enjoyed without a familiarity with Russell's other books, but it's probably best appreciated by reading the Moontide and Magic Rise novels first. If you like to get lost in fat fantasy sagas, and roam through magical landscapes so real you can feel the earth beneath your feet, check out this writer's work.

Allamanda by Michael Williams (Roc). This sequel to last year's *Arcady* should definitely be read after the previous book, for it continues the arcane adventures of the extended Hawken family, who live in a haunted manor house on the border of a magical realm. Williams has created a literate and intriguing work of dark fantasy rooted in British Romantic poetry. Fans of *Arcady* won't be disappointed; this is a strong follow-up book.

Stalking Darkness by Lynn Flewelling (Bantam). Also a sequel, this one continues the story begun in *Luck in the Shadows.* Flewelling is another new writer bringing vigor back to the traditional fantasy form. In this highly engaging adventure novel, the most powerful magic is conjured out of friendship and loyalty. The author has a gift for creating characters you genuinely care about.

Future Indefinite by Dave Duncan (Del Rey). This novel concludes the Great Game trilogy. (*Past Imperative* and *Present Tense* were the previous volumes.) Okay, it's standard quest fantasy, but Duncan writes with unusual flair, drawing upon folklore, myth, and his gift for creating ingenious plots.

Assassin's Quest by Robin Hobb (Bantam). Hobb's latest concludes the Farseer trilogy. (*Royal Assassin* and *Assassin's Apprentice* were the previous volumes.) I'll read anything by this talented author, whether she's writing under the name Robin Hobb or Megan Lindholm. As Robin Hobb, her books seem to be more muscular and adventurous, yet still display the gift for strong characterization that distinguishes all her work.

The Mines of Behemoth by Michael Shea (Baen). Michael Shea's *Nifft the Lean* was the dark horse that carried away the 1983 World Fantasy Award. After disappearing from the publishing scene for more than a decade, he's back with a sequel to his award-winning novel, and I'm happy to report that it's a good one. This is pure swords-and-sorcery, yet a far cut above the mediocrity in which much of that fiction languishes these days. Shea's work is reminiscent of the best S&S from the old American "pulp" writers—Jack Vance, C. L. Moore, Fritz Leiber . . . a bit of Poul Anderson thrown in for good measure.

When the Gods Are Silent by Jane M. Lindskold (AvoNova). This is standard quest fantasy, unlike Lindskold's highly original *Brother to Dragons, Companion to Owls* (1994). Nonetheless, Lindskold is a talented writer and this tale of the adventures of a young warrior woman is worth picking up.

I recommend seeking out two omnibus editions that appeared last year (if the original publications aren't already on your shelves): *The Dreaming Tree* by C. J. Cherryh (DAW) reworks two darkly magical faery novels set in the enchanted forest of Ealdwood (*The Dream Stone* and *The Tree of Swords and Jewels*) into one long, satisfying saga. As always, Cherryh's work is intelligent, robust, and haunting. She makes skillful use of faery folklore, and completely avoids the twee airy-fairyness of other writers on this subject. *Avaryan Rising* by Judith Tarr (Tor) brings this author's terrific first "high fantasy" trilogy back into print. *The Hall of the Mountain King*, *The Lady of Han-Gilen*, and *A Fall of Princes* are all contained in one volume, handsomely packaged with a Robert Gould cover.

Other worthwhile reads, noted briefly: *Kar Kalim* by Deborah Christian (Tor), *King's Dragon* by Kate Elliot (DAW), *Ever: The War in the Waste* by Felicity Savage (HarperPrism), *The White Tribunal* by Paula Volsky (Bantam), and *Magister* by Jonathan Wylie (Orbit, U.K.).

Contemporary Fantasy

Nineteen ninety-seven was a good year for contemporary fantasy (i.e., magical novels set in the real world, published in the fantasy field). The very best were the Blaylock, de Lint, Grant, Powers, and Shetterly books mentioned above, but here are four more books of this type that I also recommend:

The Night Watch by Sean Stewart (Ace). This novel, by another talented writer from the new generation of fantasists, falls squarely on the fantasy/SF divide. *The Night Watch* takes place in the same enchanted near-future setting as Stewart's *Resurrection Man* (1995), a thoroughly modern yet magical world of gods, ghosts, haunted forests, rogue machines, lost children, all mixed together into a suspenseful, highly original tale.

Dry Water by Eric S. Nylund (Avon). Nylund is also a new writer to watch, and his latest is a real page-turner. Set in the small "reborn ghosttown" of Dry Water, New Mexico, the protagonist finds a landscape filled with spirits, ghosts, shamans, ancient legends, and water magic. Editorial assistant Richard Kunz came up with this succinct description: "Imagine Tony Hillerman writing like Tim Powers spiced with a touch of Warner Brothers cartoons."

Neverwhere by Neil Gaiman (Avon). I admit I had some resistance to reading this novel, based on a television show Gaiman created for the BBC. Despite its media origins, I needn't have worried—Gaiman is too skillful an author to turn in anything but a first-rate tale. The story is about a young Scotsman drawn into a subterranean world beneath the London streets—a dark, Dickensian landscape filled with monsters and murderers, angels and saints. This isn't *Beauty and the Beast* redux; it's pure Gaiman, and terrifically entertaining.

How like a God by Brenda W. Clough (Tor). Clough's new novel is the story of an ordinary man who discovers he has the power to read (and alter) other people's thoughts, a device the author employs to explore basic issues of human nature and familial relationships. It's an intriguing premise, well executed.

Historical Fantasy

The very best historical fantasy published in 1997 is the Brust and Bull collaboration mentioned above, while two other strong historical novels are by writers who came out of the same Minneapolis writers' group: *Bijapur* by Kara Dalkey (Tor) is the sequel to *Goa* (1996). The middle book in a series set in India in the sixteenth century, it's an exotic tale of an apothecary's apprentice searching for the secret of eternal life. *The Magician's Ward* by Patricia C. Wrede (Tor) is the sequel to *Mairelon the Magician* (1991)—a delightfully romantic story set in Regency England.

Two strong "alternate history" novels postulate a different end to the American Civil War: *How Few Remain* by Harry Turtledove (Ballantine) is an action-packed saga combining suspenseful storytelling with rigorous historical extrapolation. *Bring the Jubilee* by Ward Moore (Del Rey) is a classic work of alternate history, first published in 1953 and finally brought back into print.

Other historical fantasies of note: *Cross and Crescent* by Susan Shwartz (Tor) is a well-researched novel set in a magical version of eleventh-century Byzantium. *Queen of Swords* by Judith Tarr (Tor) is published as straight historical fiction, but readers of Tarr's fantasy novels will want to check out this enchanting tale of twelfth-century Jerusalem. *A Letter of Mary* by Laurie R. King (St. Martin's Press) is a clever mystery novel (#3 in King's popular Mary Russell Holmes series) that might also be called an alternate history of sorts, postulating that King's Oxford-educated American sleuth is the wife and partner of Sherlock Holmes. King's latest is an engrossing story involving an archaeologist/suffragist who may have found a letter from "Mary of Magdala" (an apostle of Jesus) before she was murdered . . . a letter whose existence threatens to turn the religious world upside down.

Arthurian Fantasy

The best of the Arthurian books I read this year was yet another first novel, *Albion* by Patrick McCormack (Robinson, U.K.). This Oxford-educated British author has created a gripping Celtic saga set in the Dark Ages, well grounded in both history and myth. The book is published as historical fiction, but it has enough mysticism around the edges to keep fantasy readers happy. I recommend it highly.

Merlin's Gift by Ian McDowell (AvoNova) is another book I strongly recommend. It's the sequel to McDowell's excellent first novel, *Mordred's Curse* (1996), a dark, introspective retelling of the Arthurian mythos from the perspective of Arthur's bastard son.

The Eagle and the Sword by A. A. Attanasio (HarperPrism) continues the saga begun in *The Dragon and the Unicorn*. The previous volume recounted the story of Uther Pendragon and Ygrane, parents of the child Arthor. Now the author turns to Arthor himself—and Merlin, and a sword named Lightning. Attanasio, an excellent writer, puts a fresh spin on familiar material.

The Eagle's Brood by Jack Whyte (Forge), the third in a series firmly grounded in Roman history, is an Arthurian novel that focuses on Merlyn, and his conflicted relationship with Uther Pendragon, who is destined to bear a son named Arthur. An original approach with great sweep and texture.

Enemy of God by Bernard Cornwall (St. Martin's Press). This muscular, very masculine Arthurian retelling is also set in the Dark Ages, without the streak of Celtic mysticism found in the McCormack book above. It's the middle book in a trilogy that began with *The Winter King*.

Lady of Avalon by Marion Zimmer Bradley (Viking). In contrast to Cornwall's book, Bradley's novel looks at the Arthurian mythos from a woman's point of view. *Lady of Avalon* is a prequel to the 1982 best-seller *The Mists of Avalon*. Unlike that page-turner of a volume, however, I was unable to finish Bradley's new book—the New Age philosophy here is rather heavy-handed. Still, if you loved *The Mists of Avalon*, you might want to check this one out.

Gawain and the Green Lady by Anne Eliot Crompton (Donald I. Fine). This tale of the Knights of the Round Table, drawn from Middle English poetry, dramatizes the clash between Druidism and Christianity in the British Isles. Like the previous volume (*Merlin's Harp*), it's a magical romance in both senses of the word.

The Seven Songs of Merlin by T. A. Barron (Philomel). In the second book of his Lost Years of Merlin trilogy (for young adult readers), Barron has created a coming-of-age tale focused on a teenage Merlin. It's a richly colored book filled with Celtic mythic lore and a subtle spirituality. I recommend this lovely series to readers of all ages. Another terrific Arthurian book for children (written for a middle-grade reading level) is *Merlin* by Jane Yolen (Harcourt Brace), the third book in her Young Merlin trilogy. This story draws upon myths of Merlin in the wildwood, told in the lyrical prose for which Yolen is justly famed.

Other Arthurian publications of note: *Chronicles of the Round Table* edited by Mike Ashley (Robinson, U.K.) is the latest in Ashley's series of anthologies of short Arthurian fiction—fat volumes filled with entertaining, informative tales (both reprints and originals). *The Arthurian Companion* by Phyllis Ann Karr (Chaosium) is a useful alphabetical guide to who's who in Arthurian myth and literature, published in a handy (if not particularly elegant) trade paperback edition.

Other Mythic Novels

The Saskiad by Brian Hall (Houghton Mifflin) is one of the very best novels I read all year—funny, insightful, vastly entertaining, beautifully written. There's no supernatural element in it, and thus it's hard to justify as a fantasy novel even under our inclusive definition of the term—otherwise I would surely have listed it among the "Twenty Best Books" above. Nonetheless, it's certainly a novel about myth, involving a myth-obsessed teenage protagonist (who reminds me, almost painfully, of many ferociously bright, bookish young fans of fantasy literature). Set on a commune in upstate New York, and among the eco-activists of Europe, it's the coming-of-age tale of the narrator, precocious Saskia, who lives her life as though she's a hero straight out of the great Greek epics. Don't miss this terrific book.

Meeting the Minotaur by Carol Dawson (Algonquin). This intellectual adventure tale is a modern-day retelling of Theseus and the Minotaur. The protagonist is a six-and-a-half-foot-tall cat burglar who goes off in search of his absentee father—and ends up in the middle of a drug smuggling ring and international corporate intrigue.

The God of Impertinence by Sten Nadolny (Viking). In this quirky, satiric German novel (translated by Breon Mitchell), the Greek trickster god Hermes is freed from two thousand years of imprisonment in a Greek volcano. He sets off through Europe and North America to try to come to terms with modern society.

Oedipus on the Road by Henry Bauchau (Arcade). A complex, erudite, highly textural novel postulating a new chapter in the Oedipus mythos.

Fairy Tale Retellings

Nineteen ninety-seven was another good year for adult fairy tale fiction. The Atkinson, Deane, and Fenkl books listed above all work skillfully with imagery drawn from classic fairy tales and world folklore; Robin McKinley's *Rose Daughter* is a straight (and poignant) retelling of Beauty and the Beast. In addition, I recommend a book that is neither a novel nor story collection, but falls somewhere between the two: *Kissing the Witch: Old Tales in New Skins* by Emma Donoghue (Joanna Cotler Books/Harper Collins). This brilliant book consists of interconnected stories, woven together to form a single, circular narrative. Each story is based on a traditional tale, re-imagined in lucent prose by one of Ireland's best young writers. Donoghue approaches folkloric material from a decidedly female-centered point of view, but any political agenda she may have never gets in the way of her storytelling. This is a satisfyingly magical book, firmly in the Angela Carter tradition. The writing is positively luminous and begs to be read aloud.

The Inland Ice and Other Stories by Eilis Ni Dhuibhne (The Blackstaff Press, Belfast). Another lovely book out of Ireland, this glittering collection of basically realist stories (about love and modern relationships) is stitched together with Irish folklore—which makes it of interest to fantasy readers. It's a beauty.

Fairy Tale by Alice Thomas Ellis (Moyer Bell Ltd). Published in 1996 in the U.K., coming out in early 1998 in America, I'm going to split the difference and call this a 1997 book. It's an odd but rather enchanting novel, drawing upon

Welsh fairy tales (particularly "fairy changeling" motifs) to tell the story of a woman and a mysterious baby in the hills of modern-day Wales.

Briar Rose by Robert Coover (Grove Press). Published in 1996, this one was mentioned here last year, but since it keeps appearing on 1997 lists I don't mind mentioning it again. Coover's short novel is a gorgeous, highly literary meditation on the Sleeping Beauty theme, as well as on the nature of desire, told in prose that is as dense and thorny as a briar hedge without being inaccessible. Recommended highly.

Black Swan, White Raven edited by Ellen Datlow and Terri Windling (Avon). Adult fairy tale retellings (see listing below, under Anthologies).

Fantasy in the Mainstream

There was certainly no shortage of magical fiction published in the mainstream this year, particularly in the fields of Chicano fiction and Spanish works in translation.

House of Houses by Pat Mora (Beacon Press). This shimmering magical realist tale is about a Mexican-American family in a house in El Paso, Texas—all seven generations of them, as the spirits of the dead go about their business side-by-side with the living. Like the Fenkl book listed above, this could be called a magical realist memoir, for the author blends autobiographical writing with passages of magical enchantment, as well as poetry, folk remedies, recipes, family jokes—all organized into chapters based on a gardener's calendar. Humorous, wise, sensuous—this one's a gem.

Perdido by Rick Collignon (MacMurray and Beck). This is the sequel to Collignon's impressive first novel, *The Journal of Antonio Montoya* (1996). Set in the same haunted northern New Mexican town as the previous book, the story involves ghosts, santos, and a dead girl hanging from Las Manos Bridge. It's pure magic.

The Chin Kiss King by Ana Veciana-Suarez (Farrar, Straus and Giroux). In this gently magical tale—about three generations of Cuban-American women in Miami—the story involves the brief life of a baby born with an extra chromosome. Told in language spiced with the cadence of oral storytelling and the traditional folkways of Cuba, Veciana-Suarez creates a memorable story of love and loss.

Vaporetto 13 by Robert Girardi (Delacorte). This sophisticated ghost story is set in Venice. A currency trader from Washington, D.C., finds himself in a city of mists, masks, disguises, and sinister folk traditions surrounding the Holiday of Death. Mysterious, well-written, and gorgeously descriptive, this one really pulls you in.

Mister Sandman by Barbara Gowdy (Steerforth). Gowdy's magical, frankly sexual fantasia about life in a family full of secrets is a tale of dark humor and incisive prose, with a surprising tenderness hidden at its heart. Margaret Atwood called it the Book of the Year. It's well worth seeking out.

Four Letters of Love by Niall Williams (Farrar, Straus and Giroux). This gentle work of Irish magical realism involves a painter in the West of Ireland, a family on a remote island off the shore of Galway, and the transcendent (but troublesome) nature of love in its many forms.

Masks of the Night by Mary Ryan (St. Martin's Press). Yet another Irish fantasy—a ghostly mystery set both at the turn of the century and in the 1960s, involving old diaries, carnival masks, and a haunted house.

The Three-Arched Bridge by Ismail Kadare (Arcade). Set in a small Balkan village in 1377, Kadare weaves history and folklore together into the story of a bridge built over a river called Ujana e Keqe (Wicked Waters)—a river that may be the last line of defense against the encroaching Ottoman empire. This unnerving, beautifully crafted novel (by a Pulitzer Prize nominee) is translated from the Albanian by John Hodgson.

A *Blessing on the Moon* by Joseph Skibell (Algonquin). This dark, mesmerizing novel about Polish Jews during World War II is leavened by earthy humor and passages of crystalline prose. The protagonists are a dead man (shot and thrown into a mass grave) and his village rabbi (shape-shifted into a talking crow) in their after-life pilgrimage through a postwar landscape. Not a light read, to be sure—but a rewarding one.

Timequake by Kurt Vonnegut (Putnam). This is the highly anticipated new book from a master of iconoclastic speculative fiction. Time bends, breaks, and repeats itself in the lives of the residents of a failing Rhode Island mill town. It's a good read, pure Vonnegut, and recommended.

Time on My Hands by Peter Delacorte (Scribner). Based on a rather loony time-travel premise, Delacorte's novel is surprisingly engaging nonetheless. A writer of travel guides is sent through time to prevent Ronald Reagan from becoming President—and finds that this is not as easy to accomplish as it first appears.

Santa Evita by Tomas Eloy Martinez (Knopf). Wild Latin American magical realism from an accomplished Argentinean-born writer, this terrifically strange novel is based on the fantastical life of Eva Peron.

In the Palm of Darkness by Mayra Montero (HarperCollins). The first of this Cuban-born author's novels to appear in English (translated by Edith Grossman), it's a marvelous, mystical story following an American herpetologist in Haiti and his native Haitian guide, as they search for an endangered species of frogs through an island thick with spirits.

They're Cows, We're Pigs by Carmen Boullosa (Grove/Atlantic). This darkly magical, action-packed novel of pirates in the Caribbean in the seventeenth century is by a popular Mexican writer (translated from the Spanish by Leland H. Chambers). A thirteen-year-old Flanders boy is kidnapped into slavery, then initiated into the mysteries of medicine by an African healer and a French surgeon. There are secrets to uncover as these two mentors are mysteriously murdered.

Salt by Earl Lovelace (Persea Books). This story about life in Trinidad opens with a Caribbean folktale. The magic of the novel lies in the descriptive passages rather than in Lovelace's plot . . . but it's powerful magic nonetheless.

Deluge by Albertine Strong (Harmony). This absolutely gorgeous novel by a Native American author is shot through with flashes of legend and myth. The narrative moves boldly back and forth through mythic and present time, following the book's protagonist—a modern part-Ojibwe storyteller—as she endeavors to come to terms with her heritage, her family, and her life.

The Night Remembers by Kathleen Eagle (Avon). I found myself annoyed with this novel for being somewhat predictable, and overly sentimental, and yet the story has haunted me despite these flaws. Eagle makes fascinating use of Native American trickster myths in this sensual, romantic tale of a woman running from the past, a fast-talking half-black/half-Sioux homeless boy, and a mysterious Sioux carpenter in the slums of Minneapolis.

The Dogs of Winter by Kem Nunn (Scribner). This unusual, well-crafted, suspenseful book is a dark fantasy/mystery about surfers in California. The magical element is a young Anglo woman's dangerous obsession with Native American witchcraft.

The Shaman's Bones by James D. Doss (Avon). Another murder mystery with elements of Native American myth, this one is part of the author's Shaman series—set on a Ute reservation in Colorado, and inevitably compared to Tony Hillerman's books.

My Soul to Keep by Tananarive Due (HarperCollins). This gripping dark fantasy/horror story is about an African-American family torn apart by supernatural forces. The magical elements in Due's story are deeply rooted in African-American history and culture, skillfully woven into the modern story.

On the Road with the Archangel by Frederick Buechner (HarperSanFrancisco). Buechner's mystical short novel was inspired by the apocryphal *Book of Tobit* from the second century B.C. This overtly spiritual book (by a Pulitzer Prize nominee) is the tale of two troubled families brought together by the archangel Raphael.

Milton in America by Peter Ackroyd (Doubleday). Ackroyd brings the poet John Milton to colonial America in 1660, where he becomes a despotic leader of the Puritan settlers. This historical fantasy is an erudite, satiric, and ultimately tragic look at early America.

Ingenious Pain by Andrew Miller (Harcourt Brace). Set in eighteenth-century Europe, Miller's novel follows the life of a boy physically unable to feel pain. Exhibited as a scientific freak, he grows up to become a successful, and rather ruthless, medical doctor—until his path crosses that of a woman with supernatural healing powers. This is a highly unusual dark fantasy by one of England's lauded new writers.

The Collector Collector by Tibor Fischer (Henry Holt). Fischer, another celebrated young English novelist, has been called the Tom Robbins of London (and indeed the book has a Robbins quote on the back). I have to admit I wasn't entirely won over by Fischer's peculiar story about a prophetic clay bowl, witness to great events in history and now sitting in the South London apartment of a lovelorn art appraiser.

Pfitz by Andrew Crumey (Picador USA). This one came out last year in England, but is now widely available in this country. It's a charmingly strange book about an eighteenth-century German prince obsessed with imaginary cities.

A Face at the Window by Dennis McFarland (Broadway Books). McFarland's new novel is a literary ghost story about a man and his mystery-novelist wife staying in a haunted hotel. The ghosts of the tale are not only the vivid supernatural creatures who haunt the building, but ghosts of the protagonist's painfully troubled past in the deep South.

The Calcutta Chromosome by Amitav Ghosh (Knopf). If you can imagine such a thing as a postmodern Victorian ghost story, this would be it. I'm not sure I can even begin to describe it, so I'm just going to recommend it.

Van Gogh's Bad Cafe by Frederic Tuten (Morrow). Tuten's short novel is a fantasia about Vincent van Gogh's imaginary last lover—a morphine-addicted nineteen-year-old photographer who steps through a crack in the wall of the Bad Cafe and ends up in present-day New York (East Village, of course). It's an impassioned, quirky and rather sad story about love and art.

Portrait of the Walrus by a Young Artist by Laurie Foos (Coffee House Press). Foos's second novel is an offbeat coming-of-age tale about a teenage artist trying to deal with her father's death, her mother's remarriage (to a bowling alley tycoon), and the demands of her muse—a walrus. The book is witty in its own weird way, a tad self-indulgent, but certainly unique.

Tropic of Orange by Karen Tei Yamashita (Coffee House Press). The publisher calls this surrealistic novel (by a young Japanese-American writer in California) "magical realism, noir, hip-hop and Chicanismo." I call it just plain odd, but it has its moments.

Tutor and the Balloonist by Debbie Lee Wesselmann (MacMurray and Beck). This mystery novel about a young woman hired to compile the biography of an artist in New England is a tale wound through with secrets, riddles, and slight elements of surrealism. The book has some genuinely suspenseful moments, although the protagonist—supposedly a literary academic—severely strains credibility when she wonders if "any academic has ever devoted time to the serious study of children's literature," apparently believing this is a new idea.

Circles of Stone by Joan Dahr Lambert (Pocket). This is a prehistoric fantasy of the *Clan of the Cave Bear* variety, with strong matriarchal elements.

I Who Have Never Known Men by Jacqueline Harpman (Seven Stories Press). The first of this writer's ten novels to be translated from the French (by translator Ros Schwartz), this is a dark, postapocalyptic, surrealist tale about forty women held prisoner in an underground bunker—part fantasy, part mystery, part science fiction, and rather Kafkaesque.

The Troika by Stepan Chapman (Ministry of Whimsy Press). Chapman's dreamlike, densely surrealist novel, published by a small press in Florida, is somewhat obscure as a whole, but has some lovely passages.

No-body: A Novel by Richard Foreman (Overlook). Like the Harpman and Chapman books above, this one's for hardcore fans of surrealism. It's a highly iconoclastic work by one of America's leading avant-garde playwrights.

Raining Cats and Dogs

For some reason, there have been several heavily promoted cat and dog fantasies in the past year or so. *The Wild Road* by Gabriel King (Del Rey), an epic cat fantasy written in collaboration by the talented team of Jane Johnson and M. John Harrison, is the book making the biggest splash—but since it's technically a 1998 publication, I'll cover it in more detail next year.

Mrs. Chippy's Last Expedition: The Remarkable Journal of Shackleton's Polar-Bound Cat by Caroline Alexander (HarperCollins) is written in the form of the personal journal of a cat on Sir Ernest Shackleton's expedition to the Antarctic in 1914, presented and annotated by a second cat, Lord Mouser-Hunt, F.R.G.S. It's a charming conceit, well executed, and I recommend it to cat lovers.

On the other hand, *The Book of Night with Moon*, by the usually dependable Diana Duane (Warner), is hard going even for die-hard feline fans. Duane invents a "cat language" which makes the text needlessly confusing, and the plot (involving wizards and dinosaurs) is a bit far-fetched even for this specialized sub-genre.

Lives of the Monster Dogs by Kirsten Bakis (Farrar, Straus and Giroux). The publishers gave a gorgeous package and a big advertising push to this unusual first novel, a canine fantasy published as mainstream fiction. The "monster dogs" are a race of dog-people concocted by a mad Prussian scientist attempting to create a race of superior dog soldiers. After revolting against their human masters, and living in isolation in the Canadian north, the dogs appear in twenty-first century Manhattan, where the protagonist of the novel becomes a journalist in order to document their story. I began the novel with great enthusiasm, and quickly became disillusioned by this young author's awkward prose and a plot chock full of big gaping holes. Bakis is trying to reinvent the wheel here—no one seems to have told her, or the critics, that fantasy writers have done all this already, and with greater skill. On the other hand, my coeditor, Ellen Datlow, loved the book, and she's no critical slouch. Reviews of *Lives of the Monster Dogs* have been equally divided between those who loved and hated it, so the best I can suggest is that you take a look for yourself. (But if you throw it at the nearest wall, as I did, don't say I didn't warn you.)

If you're still in the mood for magical canines after reading the Bakis book, try *The Mythology of Dogs: Canine Legend and Lore through the Ages* by Gerald and Loretta Hausman (St. Martin's Press), an exploration of the myths and legends surrounding over seventy breeds of pooches. And then, of course, there's *Dogland*, the excellent magical realist tale by Will Shetterly, listed above.

Briefly Noted

The following fantasy novels hit the bestseller lists in 1997. Beloved by large numbers of readers across the country, they deserve mention: *Running with Demons* by Terry Brooks (Del Rey), *Lord of the Isles* by David Drake (Tor), *Polgara the Sorceress* by David and Leigh Eddings (Ballantine), *Rage of a Demon King* by Raymond E. Feist (Avon), *Temple of the Winds* by Terry Goodkind (Tor), *A Crown of Swords* by Robert Jordan (Tor), *Into the Forge* by Dennis L. McKiernan (Roc), *The Soprano Sorceress* by L. E. Modesitt, Jr. (Tor), and *Legacy of the Darksword* by Margaret Weis and Tracy Hickman (Bantam).

In the field of science fiction there were several books with strong magical elements published in 1997 that fantasy readers may also enjoy: *Signs of Life* by M. John Harrison (St. Martin's Press), a darkly magical story about dreams, genetics, and a woman who longs to fly; *Glimmering* by Elizabeth Hand (HarperPrism), a dark near-future novel by one of the most intelligent and inventive writers in the field; *The Family Tree* by Sheri S. Tepper (Avon), a fascinating murder mystery set in twenty-first-century America in an overdeveloped city where nature has literally taken to fighting back; *Sewer, Gas and Electric* by Matt Ruff (Grove/Atlantic), a comic sf thriller involving Ayn Rand, Abbie Hoffman and the Tower of Babel (by the author of *Fool on the Hill*); *The War amongst the Angels* by Michael Moorcock (Avon), a brilliant, semi-autobiographical time-traveling adventure; *Donnerjack* by Roger Zelazny and Jane Lindskold (Avon), virtual reality sf with magic—and, sadly, one of the last books we're going to see from Zelazny; *As She Climbed across the Table* by Jonathan Lethem (Double-day), a delightful tale about physics and passion, with echoes of *Alice in Wonderland*; and *Cinderblock* by Janine Ellen Young (Roc), a first novel using elements of the Cinderella tale in a near-future Los Angeles setting.

Young Adult Fantasy

The top Young Adult fantasy novel of the year has to be *The Subtle Knife* by Philip Pullman (listed above)—but my own personal favorite was a small contemporary fantasy novel from Canada: *Bone Dance* by Martha Brooks (Orchard). It's a deeply mystical, romantic story about a headstrong teenage girl, the ghost of her Native grandfather, and a handsome loner haunted by the ancient spirits of a wintry landscape. If you love the work of Charles de Lint or Susan Power, don't miss this quietly gorgeous tale. A similar book, equally well written but set in lands much farther south, is *Johnny Voodoo*, a first novel by Dakota Lane (Delacorte). All right, I admit it—there's no real magic in this book and it's hard to justify listing it here, but it's so darn good I'm going to do so anyway. The plot involves a teenage girl from New York transplanted to Louisiana, and a mysterious Creole boy who lives out in the bayou. It's a haunted, and haunting, tale.

The Best of the Rest:

Daughter of the Sea by Berlie Doherty (DK Publishing). This small book by a Carnegie Award–winning British writer is based on the old "selchie" folktales of Ireland and Scotland. Doherty invokes the magic of the sea with the understated power of her simple, lucent prose.

The Iron Ring by Lloyd Alexander (Dutton). This master fantasist (author of the Prydain series) turns to the magic of Asia in this delicious tale of a young Indian King in a land of spirits, talking animals, and mythic adventures.

Sanctuary by Paul Monette (Scribner). The last book by Paul Monette (who died of AIDS in 1995) is a little gem—a modern fairy tale about the forbidden love of Renarda the Fox and Lapine the Rabbit. It's a fable, yes, but not a heavy-handed one, and reminiscent of the animal stories of Randall Jarrell. The illustrations by Vivienne Flesher are as lovely as the prose.

The Vampire's Beautiful Daughter by S. P. Somtow (Byron Preiss/Atheneum). This amusing story, set in modern California, is about a young girl who must choose between life as a vampire (like her father), or a mortal life with the boy who loves her. Somtow, as always, is a good storyteller, and Gary A. Lippincott's illustrations are a treat.

Blood and Chocolate by Annette Curtis Klaus (Delacorte). This contemporary teen-werewolf story is sensuous and genuinely magical—just as you'd expect from the award-winning author of *The Silver Kiss*.

Red Unicorn by Tanith Lee (Tor). This well-crafted fantasy adventure about two sisters in a magical world is the sequel to *Gold Unicorn*, also recommended.

For younger Middle Grade readers:

My favorite book for the 8-to-12 set is *Silverwing* by Kenneth Oppel (Simon and Schuster). This novel tells the story of a young silverwing bat, runt of the litter, who is swept away from his colony in a storm during their winter migration. It's an entertaining, suspenseful tale, filled with nifty bat lore. Also of note: *Real* by Felice Holman (Atheneum) is a sweet little time-travel tale about the son of a Hollywood stuntman who discovers the real West in the deserts of Southern California. *The Boggart and the Monster* by Susan Cooper (Simon and Schuster) is a delightful tale by the author of the Dark Is Rising series, telling the story of a faery creature from an ancient Scottish castle, and the Loch Ness monster. *The Trickster and the Troll* by Virginia Driving Hawk Sneve (University of Nebraska Press) brings the diverse cultural traditions of this author's family together in a tale of Iktomi the trickster (from Lakota Sioux legends) and a gentle Norwegian troll who loses track of his immigrant family as they travel across the Great Plains.

Single-Author Story Collections

The flat-out best story collection published in 1997 was *Kissing the Witch: Old Tales in New Skins* by Ireland's Emma Donoghue (see description above, under Fairy Tale Retellings), but there were other strong (primarily reprint) collections published as well.

Giant Bones by Peter S. Beagle (Roc), a volume of six excellent new "imaginary world" stories, gives ample proof of why Beagle is still an undisputed master of the fantasy form. Beagle fans might also check out *The Rhinoceros Who Quoted Nietzsche and Other Odd Acquaintances* by Peter S. Beagle, with an introduction by Patricia A. McKillip (Tachyon Publications, 1459 18th Street #139, San Francisco, CA 94107). This small-press collection mixes classic tales (such as "Come Lady Death" and "Lila the Werewolf") with new gems (such as the title story), early stories, and various nonfiction. Beagle's essay about D. H. Lawrence in Taos is worth the price of the book.

In the mainstream, here are two collections you don't want to miss: *Fado and Other Stories* by Katherine Vaz (University of Pittsburgh Press), a book of sensuous Portugese-American stories, is one of my favorite finds of the year. Boy, can this woman write! "The Remains of Princess Kailulani's Garden" (reprinted here) will give you a taste of the collection; "Undressing the Vanity Dolls," "My Hunt for King Sebastião," and other stories also contain strikingly unusual fantasy elements. It's well worth seeking out this award-winning small-press publication. *The Puttermasser Papers* by Cynthia Ozick (Knopf) consists of interconnected stories comprising the fictional biography of Ruth Puttermasser, a Jewish attorney in New York City, and her personal golem, Xanthippe. Ozick's clever, well-written tales range from realism to magical realism to pure fantasy.

Four reprint volumes published in 1997 collect stories by distinguished writers from the field of American speculative fiction: *Thunder and Roses:The Complete Stories of Theodore Sturgeon* (North Atlantic) is Volume IV in an ongoing project gathering the wide-ranging work of this celebrated author. *Slippage* by Harlan Ellison (Houghton Mifflin) is billed as a volume of "previously uncollected, precariously poised stories," marking the fortieth anniversary of Ellison's career with twenty-one fine tales and essays. *Driving Blind* by Ray Bradbury (Avon) contains previously uncollected fiction (and a few original pieces) by a multi-award-winning writer of classic science fiction and fantasy. *Exorcisms and Ecstasies* by Karl Wagner (Fedogan and Bremer, 3721 Minnehaha Ave. S., Minneapolis, MN 55406) is a memorial volume containing thirty-two stories (two of them original) by an author who devoted many years to the fantasy and horror fields. The book also includes photographs, and appreciations by Peter Straub, Ramsey Campbell, and others.

Also of note:

Tales from the Texas Wood by Michael Moorcock (Mojo Press, P.O. Box 140005, Austin, TX 78714). This terrific small press collection of stories and essays explores an award-winning English writer's "life-long love affair with the American West."

Fractal Paisleys by Paul di Filippo (Four Walls Eight Windows, 39 W. 14th St., Room 503, New York, NY 10011). This small press collection of ten wild sf and fantasy stories (two originals) is by one of the pioneers of "steampunk"—a type of speculative fiction mingling modern punk and nineteenth-century sensibilites. It's a delight.

The Pure Product by John Kessel (Tor). Although best known as a science fiction writer, Kessel includes some good "alternate history" fantasy in his new collection—with a typically satiric bite.

The Arbitrary Placement of Walls by Martha Soukup (DreamHaven, 912 West Lake St., Minneapolis, MN 55408). This handsome small press edition collects sf and fantasy stories first published in *Full Spectrum, Xanadu, Twists of the Tale,* and various genre magazines.

Apocryphal Tales by Karel Čapek (Catbird Press, 16 Winsor Rd., North Haven, CT 06473). These outrageously wonderful fables, parables, and allegories from an important Czech fantasist are published in English translation (by Norma Comrada) for the first time.

Love and Longing in Bombay by Vikram Chandra (Little, Brown). These wonderful, interconnected stories, each set in a different genre, are connected by their narrator, a civil servant sitting in a bar off the Sassoon Dock in Bombay.

The Embroidered Shoes by Can Xue (Henry Holt). A collection of ghostly, highly literary tales from one of the most interesting (and subversive) young writers in China.

The Blue Lantern by Victor Pelevin (New Directions). These are stories by a young Russian author with a taste for satire, mysticism, and a surrealism that is never obscure. Pelevin's tales are translated from the Russian by Andrew Bromfield.

People on the Prowl by Jaime Collyer (Latin American Literary Review Press). This is a powerful collection of stories (reminiscent of Borges's work) by an award-winning Chilean writer, translated from the Spanish by Lillian Lorca de Tagle.

Dangerous Virtues by Ana Maria Moix (University of Nebraska Press). This Spanish writer makes interesting use of fairy tale themes, magical realism, and surrealism in a collection translated from the Spanish by Margaret E. W. Jones.

Señora Rodriguez and Other Worlds by Martha Cerda (Duke University Press). In this collection of magical realist and surrealist tales by a popular Mexican writer, family anecdotes and stories are stitched together into a narrative whole.

Almost No Memory by Lydia Davis (Farrar, Straus and Giroux). This elegant reprint collection includes dark fables and magical realism first published in *Grand Street, Paris Review, Conjunctions*, and other literary journals.

The Celibacy Club by Janice Eidus (City Lights). This volume of tales, reprinted from the *Village Voice* and other venues, includes some notable magical realist work.

Woman in a Special House: Windows Between Reality and Fantasy, Sanity and Insanity by Geraldine Little (Fithian Press). This is an unusual, hard-hitting collection, with slight magical realist overtones.

Additional small press offerings, noted briefly: *Forest Plains* by Peter Crowther (Hypatia Press, Blue Moon Books, 60 W. First, Eugene, OR 97401)—a dark fantasy novella published in a signed, limited edition, with an introduction by Charles de Lint. *The Final Trick of Funny Man* by Bruce Taylor (Ministry of Whimsy Press, P.O. Box 4248, Tallahassee, FL 32315)—a collection of surrealist stories first printed in *Pulphouse, The Silver Web*, and other small genre magazines. *The Mortal Immortal: the Complete Supernatural Short Fiction of Mary Shelley* (Tachyon)—a slim, not particularly attractive volume, primarily of interest to Shelley fans, distinguished by an introduction from Michael Bishop. *Beyond the Wall of Sleep* by R. Andrew Heidel (MORTCO, P.O. Box 1430, Cooper Station, New York, NY 10276)—a collection of magical and surrealist works from a young Brooklyn writer. *The Drag Queen of Elfland* by Lawrence Schimel (Circlet Press; *ctan@circlet.com*)—a collection of traditional fantasy tales and magical realism by a young gay writer.

The best story collection for children published in 1997 was *The Lion Tamer's Daughter and Other Stories* by Peter Dickinson (Delacorte). Also recommended: *Twelve Impossible Things Before Breakfast* by Jane Yolen (Harcourt Brace); *Curses, Inc.* by Vivian Vande Velde (Harcourt Brace); and *The Book of Hob Stories* by William Mayne, illustrated by Patrick Benson (Candlewick Press).

Anthologies

Nineteen ninety-seven was frankly a lackluster year for fantasy anthologies. There were few anthologies publishing original stories above the ordinary, with a few sterling exceptions:

The Horns of Elfland edited by Ellen Kushner, Donald G. Keller, and Delia Sherman (Roc) would have been my top pick for 1997 even if I'd not had a story included in the collection—so I hope you'll excuse my personal bias and check out this well-constructed book (despite its unfortunate cover). Kushner is the host of a national radio program on music, myth, and spirituality ("Sound and Spirit"), so the theme of the volume—magical tales involving music—should come as no surprise. What is a surprise is the range of musical inspiration, from folk to rock to hip-hop to jazz to classical to shape note singing. Jack Womack, Susan Palwick, and editors Kushner and Sherman themselves contributed the strongest stories to the volume (the Womack is reprinted here).

Black Swan, White Raven edited by Ellen Datlow and Terri Windling (Avon). This is #4 in a six-volume series of modern adult fairy tales by the likes of Joyce Carol Oates, John Crowley, Karen Joy Fowler, Nancy Kress, Michael Cadnum, Jane Yolen, and Midori Snyder. I can't get past my bias here—you'll have to judge this one for yourself.

Bending the Landscape: Fantasy edited by Nicola Griffith and Stephen Pagel (White Wolf). This anthology of stories about gender and identity, written primarily (but not exclusively) by gay writers, has only a few fantasy pieces mixed in with the science fiction (despite the subtitle), but it's worth checking out for strong contributions by Richard Bowes and Jessica Amanda Salmonson, and the first-rate Ellen Kushner–Delia Sherman collaboration (reprinted here).

Marilyn: Shades of Blonde edited by Carole Nelson Douglas (Forge). I admit to being a bit tired of dead-celebrity theme books, but this one won me over. Like *Bending the Landscape*, the book has only a few fantasy stories in its mix of cross-genre fiction, but check out the tales by Lynne Barrett and Nancy Pickard (the latter reprinted here).

Of the mass market theme anthologies, most of which seem to be produced by Martin H. Greenberg, the best of the lot was *Tarot Fantastic*, edited by Greenberg and Lawrence Schimel (DAW), containing good work by Jane Yolen, Susan Wade, and Charles de Lint (the last reprinted here).

Turning to reprint anthologies, the following are notable editions published in 1997:

Fantastic Tales edited by Italo Calvino (Pantheon). This is a useful and elegant collection of classic nineteenth-century tales by Balzac, Gogol, Hawthorne, Sheridan Le Fanu, Poe, James, Kipling, and others, divided into two sections, "The Visionary Fantastic" and "The Everyday Fantastic." It also contains a good, but all-too-brief, introduction by Calvino, a master of Italian magical realism.

Modern Classics of Fantasy edited by Gardner Dozois (St. Martin's Press). We listed this strong anthology last year, but it seems to be appearing on the 1997 lists, so here's the listing again: A solid reprint collection (solid in both literary quality and sheer size) filled with stories that haven't been anthologized to death, ranging from classics by Avram Davidson, Roger Zelazny, and L. Sprague de Camp, to recent works by John Crowley, Lucius Shepard, Tanith Lee, James P. Blaylock, and Michael Swanwick. This is a great book to give to readers who seem stuck in pre-1980s fantasy (. . . and you know the ones).

Treasures of Fantasy edited by Margaret Weis and Tracy Hickman (HarperPrism). I prefer the above Dozois book to this wildly uneven volume with a swords-and-sorcery emphasis, but fans of adventure fantasy might want to give it a look. This rather odd collection mixes good "high fantasy" work in with tales by the likes of John Jakes, but if what the editors are intending to do here is introduce young "commercial fantasy" readers to writers like McKillip and Yolen, then more power to them.

An Anthology of Scottish Fantasy Literature edited by Colin Manlove (Polygon, U.K.). This collection of stories, poems, and extracts from novels and plays provides a survey of the fantastic in Scottish literature over the last thousand years.

The Mammoth Book of Fairy Tales edited by Mike Ashley (Carroll and Graf). A nice fat anthology of fifty-six stories (four of them original) from classic tales to modern writers such as Louise Cooper and Nancy Springer.

Chronicles of the Round Table edited by Mike Ashley (see listing under Arthurian fiction above).

Visions and Imaginings: Classic Fantasy Fiction edited by Robert H. Boyer and Kenneth J. Zahorski (Academy Chicago). Boyer and Zahorski (a hardworking team of academic anthologists) were almost as influential as Lin Carter (editor of the "Sign of the Unicorn" series) in shaping the modern fantasy field, for many of us in the field today cut our teeth on all those excellent Boyer and Zahorski collections: *The Fantastic Imagination Volumes I and II, Dark Imaginings, The Phoenix Tree* and *Visions of Wonder* (1977–1981). With the original volumes out of print, *Visions and Imaginings* is a welcome edition reprinting seventeen tales drawn from these important texts.

Alternative Alices: Visions and Revisions of Lewis Carroll's Alice Books edited by Carolyn Sigler (University Press of Kentucky). Sigler has compiled twenty Alice-inspired texts published between 1869 and 1930, demonstrating Carroll's influence on English writers of the period, many of them women. "Alice was appealing for women writers," Sigler notes, "because she made them feel authorized to write about women heroes." It's an interesting collection, with an informative introduction.

Erotic Fantasy

Most of the erotic fantasy that crossed my desk last year was uniformly dreadful. (Why do people write these things? And then why do they send them to me?) One exception was *Fermentation* by Angelica J. (Grove Press), a surrealistic little book set in Paris during a heat wave. J.'s short novel is a highly sensual exploration of dreams, desire . . . and cheese. Yes, cheese. It's odd, well written, and reminiscent of Anaïs Nin.

Another exception was *Urban Oracles* by Mayra Santos-Febres (Brookline Books). This is an excellent, strange collection of magical realism and surrealist erotic vignettes by an award-winning Puerto Rican author. (See the tale "Marina's Fragrance," reprinted in this volume, for a taste of this writer's work.)

Also of note: *Aphrodite's Daughters* edited by Jalaja Bonheim (Simon and Schuster) contains deliciously sexual stories by women drawing on mythic archetypes. *Dying for It* edited by Gardner Dozois (HarperPrism) is a volume of "sexual horror stories"—but some of the works included are dark fantasy, and all are extremely well written. Less professional in execution, but earnest in intent, is *SexMagick 2* edited by Cecelia Tan (Circlet Press), sequel to *SexMagick*, which has just been rereleased.

Poetry

There are several poetry volumes of particular interest to those who love fantasy and myth. I recommend highly:

An Intellect of the Heart by Bill Lewis (available from Lazerwolf, 66 Glencoe Road, Chatham, Kent, ME4 5QE, England). Lewis is a British poet, storyteller and traveling performance artist who often works with themes from European (particularly Celtic) and North American myth. This lovely chapbook is both magical and spiritual, with flashes of Trickster-like humor. (Two poems from the volume are reprinted here.)

Aunt Carmen's Book of Practical Saints by Pat Mora (Beacon Press). The latest collection from this award-winning Chicana writer contains poems written in the voice of eighty-year-old "Aunt Carmen," on the theme of saints, santos, and the Catholic folk traditions of northern New Mexico. It's a handsome edition, beautifully illustrated with images from the Museum of International Folk Art in Santa Fe.

A Snake in Her Mouth by nila northSun (University of New Mexico Press). Evocative poems deeply rooted in the language of Native folklore and myth by an acclaimed Chippewa-Shoshone storyteller. This one's a beauty.

Kinky by Denise Duhamel (Orchises Press). This wild, wry, insightful collection, by one of America's lauded young poets, is a sequence of poems on Barbie doll themes—and very, very good.

Bed of Sphinxes by Philip Lamantia (City Lights). This collection of new and selected poems contains many of Lamantia's marvelous early surrealist works.

I also recommend seeking out the Fall 1997 issue of *Raritan Review*, the literary journal of Rutgers University, which includes two long poems inspired by Greek mythology by the great Ted Hughes. I had hoped to include at least one of these extraordinary poems in this volume, but (as occasionally happens) the reprint costs were prohibitive.

The Magazines

Nineteen ninety-seven was not a sterling year for fantasy in the genre magazines; only one of the fantasy selections for this volume came from this source (the Howard Waldrop story, originally published in *Asimov's Science Fiction* magazine). This is not to say there weren't any *good* stories in *F&SF*, *Asimov's*, and *Realms of Fantasy* (see the Honorable Mentions list)—just few *great* ones. I have better hopes for *F&SF* in the year to come, now that its new editor, Gordon Van Gelder, is getting through the backlog of old inventory and more of his own choices are starting to appear. *Omni* (available only online now) and England's *Interzone* are dependable sources for good fiction, but both were weighted more to sf than to fantasy in 1997. *Realms of Fantasy*, I should note, continues to provide the best showcase for artists in the field (in their Gallery section).

The semipro 'zines were even more disappointing. The best of them, *Century* and *Crank!*, suspended publication in '97, and I regret to say that much of what I'm reading in the rest is barely up to publishable standards. Small press 'zines are important to this field as a place for new writers to hone their skills—we desperately need more 'zines edited with the critical rigor (and production values) of *Century*, *Crank!*, and those old *Pulphouse* hardback editions, to serve this necessary function. The editor of *Crank!* (Bryan Cholfin) and the team who produce *Century* (Meg Hamel, Robert K. J. Killheffer, and Jenna A. Felice) swear these magazines aren't dead and are promising new issues in 1998. Let's keep our fingers crossed. *Odyssey*, a new sf/fantasy magazine from England edited by Liz Holliday, began publication in 1997 with contributions from Vonda N. McIntyre, Colin Greenland, and Terry Bisson. The graphics aren't great and the fiction is uneven, but it's a new production so we can cut them some slack. I wish them every bit of luck. For more information, their web address is: *http://members.aol.com.bjeapes/odyssey*. Another debut was *Age of Wonder* edited by Paul Recchia, billing itself as "the speculative fiction magazine appealing to the higher senses" (whatever that means). For more information their web address is: *http://nebc.mv.com/fiction*.

Magical realism is still alive and well in mainstream magazines, both those on the newsstands and small press journals. You'll find selections in this volume from *The New Yorker, Prairie Schooner, Black Warrior Review, New England Review, Raritan Review, The Georgia Review, Bridge, Southerly,* and *The Alsop Review* (online).

It seems unfortunate to me that the magazine selections for this volume came overwhelmingly from out-of-genre sources, and I hope this does not mark a trend. At the moment, however, the best writers in the field (the McKillips and Blaylocks and Holdstocks and O'Learys) are either sticking to novel-length works, or selling short fiction to anthologies rather than to the magazines. Since *Realms of Fantasy* is primarily (not exclusively) geared to adventure fantasy, the digests to an sf audience, and *Omni* to those with Internet access, what we could really use is a serious, high-end magazine for fantastic literature and art, promoting cutting-edge work, mythic fiction, and magical realism from both sides of the genre/mainstream divide. (Any takers out there?)

Art

The very best art book of 1997 was, without doubt, *Cowgirl Rising: The Art of Donna Howell-Sickles,* with text by Peg Streep (Greenwich Workshop Press). I'd never seen the work of this Texan artist before. Now I'm completely smitten and I dare to predict you will be too. Howell-Sickles makes an icon of the "mythic cowgirl" in these exuberant, colorful paintings, many of them relating to legends of the West and Native America. This woman draws so very, very well that I am positively green with envy. Don't miss her amazingly beautiful book, whether you're a cowgirl fan or not. It costs a hefty $35.00—but is worth every single penny.

The other big art event of the year was the publication of *The Hobbit* by J. R. R. Tolkien, illustrated by Alan Lee (Houghton Mifflin)—the sixtieth anniversary edition of the book, and companion to Lee's lovely anniversary edition of *The Lord of the Rings.* Alan Lee is an English watercolorist whose work is every bit as good as that produced by the masters of England's "Golden Age" of illustration (Arthur Rackham, Edmund Dulac, Wm. Heath Robinson, et al.). This is a volume to save, cherish, and pass down to your grandchildren.

Other notable editions of 1997:

Visions of Life and Love: Pre-Raphaelite Art from the Birmingham Collection, with text by Stephen Wildman (Art Series International). The city of Birmingham, England, is home to an extensive collection of paintings by its native son Sir Edward Burne-Jones, and other Pre-Raphaelite masters. I recommend this beautiful and informative edition highly.

A Treasury of the Children's Book Illustrators by Susan E. Meyer (Harry N. Abrams). This handsome art book features illustrations by all the greats: Rackham, Dulac, Nielsen, Pyle, et al.

Mermaids: Nymphs of the Sea by Theodore Gachot (Raincoast Books). This attractive coffee table book collects mermaid imagery from a variety of sources.

The Complete Book of Flower Fairies by Cicely Mary Barker (Frederick Warne). This edition collects Barker's classic "flower fairy" paintings, first published in the 1920s. Her childlike fairies (posing with flowers, fruits, and tree blossoms) may be a little too sweet for some, but I think they're rather charming.

"Repent, Harlequin!" Said the Ticktockman by Harlan Ellison, illustrated by Rick Berry (Underwood). In this terrific small press edition, a classic Ellison story is well matched by art from a dazzling Boston painter.

The Dark Tower IV: Wizard and Glass by Stephen King, illustrated by Dave McKean (Donald M. Grant). Dave McKean is an artist, like Rick Berry, above, who brings fine-art sensibilities into highly original book illustrations, as demonstrated in the paintings for this small press edition of King's dark fantasy tale.

While I leave most comic book reviews up to my colleague Seth Johnson, there are two I just have to mention here. Even if you don't usually look on the comic book shelves, I recommend: *Stardust* by Neil Gaiman and Charles Vess (DC Vertigo). This comics series is pure "high fantasy" set in a village at the crossroads of Faery. Gaiman's text is enchanting, and the art by Charles Vess, reminiscent of Rackham's work, is utterly magical. *Ballads* by Charles Vess (Green Man Press, 152 E. Main St., Abingdon, VA 24210). This trade paperback collects the separate installments of Vess's lovely Ballad series under one cover. The text (by Neil Gaiman, Sharyn McCrumb, Jeff Smith, Midori Snyder, Delia Sherman, Jane Yolen, and Charles de Lint) consists of stories based on traditional folk ballads. Once again, Vess's illustrations are a treat.

Spectrum IV: The Best in Contemporary Fantastic Art edited by Cathy Fenner and Arnie Fenner, with Jim Loehr (Underwood Books). I'm noting the existence of this volume for the record, since I didn't actually see it this year.

Picture Books

Children's picture books are a wonderful showcase for magical storytelling and art. Here's a baker's dozen of the best to cross my desk in 1997 (in alphabetical order):

One Grain of Rice: A Mathematical Folktale written and illustrated by Demi (Scholastic)—an Indian tale with gorgeous paintings (glittering with gold) inspired by Indian miniatures.

The Day I Swapped My Dad for Two Goldfish by Neil Gaiman, illustrated by Dave McKean (White Wolf)—a rather offbeat tale (as one would expect from this duo), hilarious, and beautifully presented. I recommend it highly.

The Brave Little Tailor by Jacob and Wilhelm Grimm, translated by Anthea Bell, illustrated by Sergei Goloshapov (North-South Books)—a dark, perverse treatment of the tale conjured up by a master of Russian illustration.

A Ring of Tricksters: Animal Tales from America, the West Indies, and Africa by Virginia Hamilton, illustrated by Barry Moser (Scholastic)—a fine collaboration between an award-winning author and a major American book artist.

The Veil of Snows by Mark Helprin, illustrated by Chris Van Allsburg (Viking/Ariel)—the last book in the award-winning *Swan Lake* trilogy, a bittersweet story complemented with luminous art.

The Bootmaker and the Elves by Susan Lowell, illustrated by Tom Curry (Orchard)—a very funny version of the tale set in the American West, which will be of particular delight to cowboy boot fanatics. Also check out *Little Red Cowboy Hat* by Susan Lowell, illustrated by Randy Cecil (Henry Holt)—another book in the same vein.

Unicorns! Unicorns! by Geraldine McCaughrean, illustrated by Sophie Windham (Holiday House)—a poignant story about the unicorns who never made it onto Noah's ark, splendidly illustrated.

The Book of Little Folk: Faery Stories and Poems from Around the World by Lauren Mills (Dial)—an utterly charming edition. Also check out *Elfabet* by Jane Yolen and Lauren Mills (Little, Brown)—equally delightful.

The Great Kettles of Time by Dean Morrissey (Abrams)—another magical adventure from a man who paints like a cross between Winsor McCay and Norman Rockwell. This one passed the "try it out on kids" test with flying colors.

The Girl Who Dreamed Only Geese and Other Tales of the Far North by Howard Norman, illustrated by Leo and Diane Dillon (Harcourt Brace)—the very best of the bunch, combining ten Inuit tales (retold by an author who has spent decades collaborating with Inuit storytellers in Siberia, Alaska, the Canadian Arctic, and Greenland) with the distinctive, sophisticated art of this husband-and-wife design team.

Bearskin by Howard Pyle, illustrated by Trina Schart Hyman (Books of Wonder/Morrow)—a romantic tale with romantic new paintings by one of America's finest illustrators.

Rumplestiltskin's Daughter, written and illustrated by Diane Stanley (Morrow)—a wonderful original fairy tale with a feisty, clever heroine, and hilarious illustrations. This one's recommended highly.

Rapunzel by Paul O. Zelinsky (Dutton)—one of the most beautiful treatments of Rapunzel I've ever seen, with art inspired by Italian Renaissance paintings. It's simply stunning.

Briefly noted:

Nicholas Pipe by Robert D. San Souci, a merman story with haunting paintings by David Shannon (Dial Press); *Smokey Mountain Rose*, an Appalachian Cinderella retelling by Alan Schroeder with wry illustrations by Brad Sneed (Dial Press); *The King of Ireland's Son*, by the Irish poet Brendan Behan, with vivid watercolors by the acclaimed Irish illustrator P. J. Lynch (Orchard); *Enchantment in the Garden*, a magical story about a lonely girl in an Italian garden, written and illustrated by Shirley Hughes (Lothrop, Lee and Shepard); *Rhymes and Reasons: An Annotated Collection of Mother Goose Rhymes* by James Christensen (Greenwich Workshop Press): seventy-three classic rhymes along with annotations on the texts; *The Traveller: A Magical Journey*, written by James Keller, illustrated by Daniel Page Schallau (Greenwich Workshop Press), a marvelous "magical house" story; *Days of the Blackbird*, a folktale from northern Italy charmingly retold and illustrated by Tomie dePaulo (Putnam); *The Emperor's New Clothes*, retold by Naomi Lewis and elegantly illustrated by Angela Barrett (Candlewick Press); *The Three Little Pigs*, a fractured fairy tale by Steven Kellogg (Morrow); *Punia and the King of Sharks*, a Hawaiian folktale nicely retold by Lee Wardlaw, colorfully illustrated by Mexican artist Filipe Davalos (Dial Press); *Little Oh*, a sweet Japanese tale by Laura Krauss Melmed, gently illustrated by Jim LaMarche (Lothrop, Lee and Shepard); *The Paper Dragon*, a magical Chinese story by Marguerite W. Davol, with extraordinary paper cut-out art by Robert Sabuda (Atheneum); *The Monkey Bridge*, an Indian folktale retold by Rafe Martin, with illustrations based on Persian miniatures by Iranian artist Fahimeh Amiri (Knopf); *Brother Rabbit*, a lively Cambodian folktale retold by Minfong Ho and Saphan Ros, with wonderful woodblock art by Jennifer Hewetson

(Lothrop, Lee and Shepard); *The Cricket's Cage* (Disney Press), a Chinese folk-tale told and illustrated by Stefan Czernecki, who based his art on traditional Chinese paintings; *The Khan's Daughter*, a Mongolian folktale well told by Lawrence Yep, illustrated by Jean ad Mou-sien Tseng (Scholastic); *Señor Cat's Romance and Other Favorite Stories from Latin America*, retold by Cuban-American author Lucia M. Gonzalez, illustrated by Lulu Delacre (Scholastic); *Musicians of the Sun*, a retelling of an Aztec myth written and illustrated by Gerald McDermott of the Joseph Campbell Foundation (Simon and Schuster); and *Scary Godmother* by Jill Thompson, a Halloween tale written and illustrated by comic book artist Jill Thompson (Sirius).

Nonfiction

The most notable nonfiction event of the year was the appearance of *The Encyclopedia of Fantasy* edited by John Clute and John Grant (Orbit, U.K.; St Martin's Press, U.S.)—a massive reference volume, intelligently constructed and astonishingly thorough. We've needed a book like this for years, and no fantasy bookshelf should be without it.

The best of the rest:

Borgo Press released two good volumes of interest to fantasy readers: *Discovering Classic Fantasy* edited by Darrell Schweitzer and *Opening Minds: Essays on Fantastic Literature* by Brian Stableford (Borgo Press, P.O. Box 2845, San Bernardino, CA 92406-2845).

The Postmodern Archipelago by Michael Swanwick (Tachyon Publications, 1459 18th Street #139, San Francisco, CA 94107)—contains Swanwick's brilliant essay "In the Tradition" along with a controversial essay on science fiction. It's not a very handsome edition, but it's good to see this essay in print.

A House of Her Own by Judith D. Suther (University of Nebraska Press)—the first full-length biography of the American surrealist painter Kay Sage.

Automatic Women: The Representation of Women in Surrealism by Katharine Conley (University of Nebraska Press)—a fascinating volume, with a full chapter on the surrealist fiction writer/painter Leonora Carrington.

The Letters of Christina Rossetti, edited by Anthony H. Harrison (University Press of Virginia)—the letters of a poet at the edge of the Pre-Raphaelite circle, author of "Goblin Market."

The Collected Letters of William Morris edited by Norman Kelvin (Princeton University Press)—the letters of this major Pre-Raphaelite artist and Victorian fantasist.

The Flowers of William Morris by Derek W. Baker (Chicago Review Press)—an intriguing look at Morris's gardens, and their effect on his design work. If you're both a Pre-Raphaelite fan and a gardener, don't miss this one.

Re-Framing the Pre-Raphaelites: Historical and Theoretical Essays edited by Ellen Harding (Scolar Press)—a terrific, wide-ranging collection of new essays on the subject (but rather pricey at $75).

Oz and Beyond: the Fantasy Worlds of L. Frank Baum by Michael O. Riley (University Press of Kansas)—a concise analysis of the Oz books and other works by Baum; and the enduring influence of Baum's creation on American popular culture.

Mythology and Fairy Tales

The top mythology book of the year is one I cannot recommend too highly, for it's one of the most brilliant books I've ever read. *Trickster Makes This World: Mischief, Myth and Art* by Lewis Hyde (Farrar, Straus and Giroux) examines Trickster figures from legends all around the world, and the role of trickster in modern society and the arts. You needn't be a mythic scholar to enjoy this lively book, chock full of ideas that will change the way you look at art, creativity, and the world.

In addition to Hyde's book, several other texts on Trickster myths appeared in 1997. *Mythical Trickster Figures: Contours, Contexts, and Criticism*, edited by William J. Hynes and William G. Doty (University of Alabama Press), is the first important collection of scholarly essays on this topic since Raul Radin's *Trickster* (1955), exploring worldwide Trickster figures from Coyote of North America to Susa-no-O in Japan. *Yoruba Trickster Tales* compiled by Oyekan Owomoyela (University of Nebraska Press) is a marvelous collection of twenty-three Trickster tales from the Yoruba of West Africa. *Tales of Uncle Tompa* compiled by Rinjing Dorje (Station Hill Arts, *www.stationhill.org*) is a lovely slim volume of Tibetan Trickster tales, translated by a Tibetan storyteller. *Mercury Rising: Women, Evil and the Trickster Gods* by Deldon Anne McNeely (Spring Publications, 299 East Quassett Road, Woodstock, CT 06281) is an interesting but uneven volume full of fascinating nuggets of information, albeit from the idiosyncratic point of view of a practicing Jungian psychoanalyst.

Three new texts look at the role of gender in mythic material. *Athena: A Biography* by Lee Hall (Addison Wesley Longman) turns myth and legend into a narrated "life" of this Greek goddess, exploring the role of women in ancient myth, history, and classical literature. *The Body of the Goddess: Sacred Wisdom in Myth, Landscape and Culture* by Rachel Pollack (Element Books) is a highly readable exploration of the Goddess in myth, history, poetry, and art. Also in this vein, check out *When the Drummers Were Women: A Spiritual History of Rhythm* by Layne Redmond (Three Rivers Press).

Great Heroes of Mythology by Petra Press (Metro Books) is a lavishly illustrated coffee table book presenting hero tales from all over the world, divided into chapters by geographical region (the British Isles, Scandinavia, Australia, Africa, and elsewhere). It won't contain any surprises for readers well-versed in mythology, but makes a good introduction to those who are not. The "Myths of the World" series from Metro Books consists of handsome large editions that give an overview of the legends of each culture, nicely packaged with color photographs and art. The volumes I've seen so far are *Legends of Africa* by Mwizenge Tembo, *Legends of Native America* by Edward Huffstetler, and *Gods of the Maya, Aztecs and Incas* by Timothy R. Roberts. The full series will form a useful and concise mythic library. *The Sacred World of the Celts* by Nigel Pennick (Inner Traditions International) is a compendium of information on Celtic myth and theories on Celtic spirituality, presented in a handsome square gift-book format, full of color photographs and art. I found this a bit too New Agey for comfort, but if that doesn't bother you, check it out.

Happily Ever After: Fairy Tales, Children and the Culture Industry by Jack Zipes (Routledge) provides an in-depth analysis of this subject by one of the leading scholars in the fairy tale field. *Postmodern Fairy Tales* by Cristina Baccilega (University of Pennsylvania Press) explores gender issues in traditional tales, from the older oral tellings through modern literary retellings by Angela Carter, Robert Coover, Donald Barthelme, et al. (as well as in television and film). *The Tongue Is Fire* by Harold Scheub (University of Wisconsin Press) examines the ways South African storytellers have used folk tales, myth, and metaphor to preserve their cultural traditions and confront apartheid. *Yiddish Folktales*, edited by Beatrice Silverman Weinreich, translated by Leonard Wolf (Pantheon), gathers Jewish folk tales from small towns across Eastern Europe prior to World War II. *The Glass Mountain* by W. S. Kuniczak (Hippocrene Books) is a nice edition collecting twenty-eight folk and fairy tales from Poland.

Myths of Ancient Mexico by Michel Graulich (University of Oklahoma Press) is a thorough exploration of the myths of Mesoamerican cultures, translated by Bernard R. and Thelma Ortiz de Montellano. *Myths and Legends of the Pacific Northwest* selected by Katharine Berry Judson (University of Nebraska Press) is a good little edition collecting tales from the Klamath, Nez Percé, Tillamook, Modoc, Flathead, and other tribes of the Northwest coast. *Folklore of the Winnebago Tribe* by David Lee Smith (University of Oklahoma Press) presents tales from the oral tradition transcribed by a Winnebago tribal historian. *Echoes of the Elders: The Stories and Paintings of Chief Lelooska* edited by Christine Normandin (DK Publishing) is an attractive oversized edition of Kwakiutl tales from the Pacific Northwest, packaged with a CD of Chief Lelooska himself reading the tales. *No Word for Time* by the Mimac author Evan T. Pritchard (Council Oak Books, Tulsa, OK 74120) is my favorite of the books about Native American culture I've come across this year—an eloquent, open-hearted little book examining the stories, traditions, rituals, and deeply poetic worldview of an extended family of tribes in Northeast America and Canada.

Several good books presenting mythic material for children appeared in 1997. *Spider Spins a Story* edited by Jill Max (Rising Moon) collects fourteen Native American legends illustrated by five Native American artists: Benjamin Harjo, Baje Whitethorne, Robert Annesley, Redwing T. Nez, and Michael Lacapa. The "Landscapes of Legend" series from Children's Press features natural history, folklore, and legends from around the world on the following subjects: *Mighty Mountains, Fabulous Beasts, Sacred Skies,* and *The Water of Life,* all written by Finn Bevan, illustrated by Diane and Margaret Mayo. *Mythical Birds and Beasts from Many Lands* retold by Margaret Mayo, illustrated by Jane Ray (Dutton) is a beautiful book adorned by art reminiscent of Kay Nielsen's later work. *The Book of the Unicorn* by Nigel Suckling, illustrated by Linda and Roger Garland (Overlook), is a lovely book for older children, chock full of art and tales. For younger children, try *The Book of Fairies: Nature Spirit Stories from Around the World* retold by Rose Williams, illustrated by Robin T. Barrett (Beyond Words).

Music

The audiences for fantasy fiction and folk music overlap a great deal, probably because the old folk ballads (particularly in the Celtic tradition) are often based on the same mythic or folkloric roots as many fantasy stories. Contemporary world music working with traditional rhythms is the musical equivalent to modern mythic fiction: these creative artists (musicians and writers alike) are updating ancient themes for a modern age.

Three fine new releases are recommended to those who love Celtic balladry: *Aleyn* by the great British singer June Tabor (Topic); *Flesh and Blood* by Tabor's sometime-partner Maddy Prior (Park Records); and *Hourglass* by a new young singer, Kate Rusby (Pure). I also recommend *Vittrad* by Garmana, filled with magical balladry out of Scandinavia. (Boiled in Lead's Drew Miller had a hand in this one, apparently.) *Eliza Carthy and the Kings of Calicutt* (Topic) is a lively CD of English trad and new folk—and yes, Eliza comes from *that* Carthy family. For traditional Irish music, try *Made in Cork* by the ever-dependable Patrick Street (Green Linnet) and *Runaway Sunday,* the latest from Altan (Virgin). Matt Molloy (flute player for the Chieftains) has released a stunning solo effort, *Shadows on Stone* (Virgin), which includes a mystical fantasy called "The Music of the Seals" based on Irish selchie legends. *The Mystery of Amergin* by the Keltz (Lochshore) is a slightly New Agey but interesting piece based on the ancient Irish poem, mixing Celtic and Indian music with improvisational jazz. Singer Maura O'Connell has come back to traditional Irish songs at last with a haunting new CD aptly titled *Wandering Home* (Hannibal). *Rhythm and Rhyme* by the band Tamalin is uneven, but worth the price of admission for their versions of "Crazy Man Michael" and the Yeats poem "Gort Na Sailean." Scotland's acclaimed Capercaille have released a CD titled *Beautiful Wasteland* (Survival); Paul Mounsey's *Nahootoo* (Iona) mixes the Gaelic music of Scotland with Brazilian rhythms. *As Fadas De Estrano Nome* features Celtic music from Spain, performed in concert by the Galician band Milladoiro (Green Linnet). For progressive Celtic music try *It's About Time* by Sin E (Rhiannon)—a bit uneven overall, but mighty infectious. Better yet, try *Octoroon* by Laura Love (Mercury)—a completely wonderful mix of Celtic, jazz, zydeco, blues and just about anything else this extraordinary performer can come up with.

For music with a mystical bent, I recommend *African Spirit Music* by Thomas Mapfumo (WOMAD Select) or *Inner Knowledge* by Paban das Baul (WOMAD Select), featuring the mystic music of the Bauls, mendicant minstrels from Bengal. *Summoning the Spirit: Music in the T'boli Heartland* (Rykodisc) is another fascinating release, for the T'boli (of the Philippine Islands) summon spirits to enter into their music, made with bamboo zithers, lutes, fiddles, and percussion. *Tibet: The Heart of Dharma* (Ellipses Arts) is a transcendent work recording Tibetan chants. *The Sounds True Anthology of Sacred Music* (Sounds True) features everything from Irish mystical singing to the Sufi music of Morocco. Singer Marta Sebestyen has long been at the forefront of the Hungarian folk revival; you can sample her fine work on *The Best of Marta Sebestyen* (Hannibal). *Blues at Dawn* by Okros Ensemble (ABT) is a recording of eerie traditional songs from Transylvania. *On the Trace of Maneros* by singer Katerina Xirou (Thessis) presents an ancient form of music going back to the myths of Greece. Paulo Braganca is an avant-garde musician with his roots in Portuguese fado (a musical form of lamentation)—check out his strange, terrific CD *Amai* (Luaka Bop), mixing fado with flamenco, samba, hip-hop, and all kinds of other grooves. *Folk Roots Magazine* chose *Buena Vista Social Club* by Ry Cooder (World Circuit) as their album of the year—and it's hard to disagree; Cooder brought together some of the best musicians in Cuba for this stellar recording.

Native American poet Joy Harjo mixes music and the spoken word on *The End of the Twentieth Century* by Joy Harjo and Poetic Justice (Silverwave)—tribal jazz reggae with delicious poetry from this very fine writer/musician. For an introduction to new Native music, try *I Am Walking*, a lovely compilation CD from Narada Records—and for an absolutely beautiful CD of Native American women's music, don't miss *Walela* by Rita Coolidge, Laura Satterfield, and Priscilla Coolidge. Rounder Records's compilation CD *Divine Divas: A World of Women's Voices* is also enchanting, bringing together female singers and musicians from all around the world. *Fra Senegal Til Setesdal* (Grappa) is an unusual CD featuring performers of Norwegian traditional music and West African kora musicians; you'd expect the result to be a bastardized mish-mash, but it's actually wonderful.

Ellen Kushner, fantasy novelist and host of the nationally broadcast radio program "Sound & Spirit," offers the following recommendations: "*Zoom* by Alan Stivell (Disques Dreyfus/Keltia): he's the musician who led the 1970s revival of traditional music of Brittany, the Celtic province in France . . . and single-handedly re-created the lost sound of the Breton Harp. *Eileen McGann: Heritage, traditional songs of Ireland, Scotland, England and Canada* (Borealis/Dragonwing): I was afraid they weren't making them like this anymore! Clear, comfortable ballad singing, from sea chanteys to love songs. *Susana Baka* (Luaka Bop/Warner Brothers): a Peruvian singer of African descent, dedicated to the preservation of the history and culture of her people, singing a repertoire both old and new. *The Book of Secrets* by Loreena McKennitt (Warner Brothers): she is her very own genre—you might call it 'romantic neo-pagan world-folk.' This new release brings us a host of original songs inspired by her latest journeys to an Irish monastery, the hills of Tuscany, the palaces of Venice, the steppes of the Caucasus, and beyond . . . including her ten-minute setting of Alfred Noyes's classic poem, 'The Highwayman.' *Tarabu* by Malika, *Music from the Swahili of Kenya* (Schanachie): Popular music of East Africa in a style that mixes Arab, African, Indian, and even Latin elements. Malika is a fantastic singer, and her lyrics come from very beautiful Swahili poetry about life, death, the universe, and everything."

Charles de Lint is a fantasy writer whose books are steeped in folk music; he's also a professional Celtic folk musician. Here are his picks for the year: "My two favourite albums of last year were *End of the Summer* by Dar Williams (Razor and Tie) and Steve Earle's *El Corazón* (E-Squared). Neither is strictly world beat, or even traditional for that matter, but both artists write strong, evocative story-songs that will readily appeal to the readers of this book. In traditional Celtic music, old favourites released strong new albums: Déanta with *Whisper of A Secret* (Green Linnet), Dervish's 2-CD concert set *Live in Palma* (Whirling Discs), Altan's *Runaway Sunday* (Virgin), and *Sunny Spells and Scattered Showers* by Solas (Shanachie). A couple of other stand-outs came from Kathryn Tickell who, despite the loss of Karen Tweed from her band, came back with one of her strongest albums to date in *The Gathering* (Park Records), and the Canadian brother-and-sister act (nine siblings, all told!) Leahy with their self-titled, independent release. Whenever I hear (and especially when I see the video for) their tune "The Call to Dance," I'm transported to the city of Newford, which is only supposed to exist in my imagination. Vocal fans got a triple treat this year with a solo album from Solas's Karan Casey (*Songlines* on Shanachie), as well as the new releases by Kate Rusby and Loreena McKennitt (see listings above). This is the sound of angels singing. More adventuresome music seemed to have a Latin/Mediterranean flavour this past year with fascinating releases such as *Ancient Forces* by Celtarabia (Osmoys), *Monstruos y Demonios, Angels & Lovers* by Salsa Celtica (Eclectic Records), and *Rumba Angelina* by Radio Tarifa (Nonesuch). My own favourite was *La Llorona* by Lhasa (Les Disques Audiogramme), a Montreal-based singer who has taken the music of her native Mexico and recast it in an acoustic jazz setting."

Awards

The Mythopoeic Awards are chosen each year by committees composed of volunteer Mythopoeic Society members, and presented at Mythcon. The award is a statuette of a seated lion, evoking Aslan from C. S. Lewis's *Chronicles of Narnia*.

The Fantasy Awards honor current fantasy works "in the spirit of the Inklings" in two categories, adult and children's literature. The Scholarship Awards honor works published during the preceding three years that make a significant contribution to scholarship about the Inklings and genres of myth and fantasy studies.

Mythopoeic Fantasy Award for Adult Literature: *The Wood Wife* by Terri Windling; Mythopoeic Fantasy Award for Children's Literature: (combined with Adult Literature award); Mythopoeic Scholarship Award (in Inklings Studies): *The Rhetoric of Vision: Essays on Charles Williams* edited by Charles A. Huttar and Peter Schakel; Mythopoeic Scholarship Award (in Myth and Fantasy Studies): *When Toys Come Alive* by Lois Rostrow Kuznets.

The 1997 James Tiptree, Jr. Award went to *Black Wine* by Candas Jane Dorsey and "Travels with the Snow Queen" by Kelly Link.

Judges: Terry Garey (coordinator), Elizabeth Hand, Nalo Hopkinson, Jerry Kaufman, and James Patrick Kelly.

The 1997 World Fantasy convention was held in the Docklands of London, October 31–November 3, 1997. Both the World Fantasy Awards and the British Fantasy Awards were presented there. The World Fantasy Award winners were: *Godmother Night* by Rachel Pollack for Best Novel; *A City in Winter* by Mark Helprin for Best Novella; "Thirteen Phantasms" by James P. Blaylock for Best Short Fiction; *Starlight 1* edited by Patrick Nielsen Hayden for Best Anthology; *The Wall of the Sky, the Wall of the Eye* by Jonathan Lethem for Best Collection; Moebius (Jean Giraud) for Best Artist; Michael J. Weldon, for *The Psychotronic Video Guide* for Special Award—Professional; Barbara and Christopher Roden, for Ash-Tree Press for Special Award—Non-Professional; Madeleine L'Engle for Life Achievement and a convention award for Hugh B. Cave.

The 1997 British Fantasy Award Winners were: *The Tooth Fairy* by Graham Joyce for Best Novel (The August Derleth Fantasy Award); "Dancing About Architecture" by Martin Simpson for Best Short Story; *the Nightmare Factory* by Thomas Ligotti for Best Anthology/Collection; Jim Burns for Best Artist; *H. P. Lovecraft: A Life* by S. T. Joshi for Best Small Press; and a Special Award (the Karl Edward Wagner Award) to Jo Fletcher.

That's a brief look at the year in fantasy fiction, nonfiction, art, and music—now on to the stories themselves.

As usual, there are some stories and poems we are unable to include even in a volume as fat as this one. I consider the following pieces to be among the year's very best, and urge you to seek them out:

In alphabetical order:

John Crowley's "Lost and Abandoned," a powerful modern vision of Hansel and Gretel, published in the anthology *Black Swan, White Raven*.

Peter Dickinson's enchanting novella for young readers "The Lion Tamer's Daughter," in his collection *The Lion Tamer's Daughter and Other Stories*.

Czech writer Vilma Kadleckova's long gothic tale "Longing for Blood," translated by M. Klima and Bruce Sterling, in the January 1997 issue of *F&SF*.

Robert Stone's brilliant novella (working with themes from Native American myth), "Bear and His Daughter," in his collection *Bear and His Daughter: Stories*.

Ted Hughes's deeply mythic poem "Salmacis and Hermaphroditus" in the fall 1997 issue of *Raritan Review*.

Melanie Rae Thon's moving tale "The River Woman's Son" in *Ploughshares*, Spring 1997.

Katherine Vaz's dark fantasia "Undressing the Vanity Dolls" in her collection *Fado and Other Stories*.

I hope you'll enjoy the stories and poems that follow as much as I did. Many thanks to the authors, agents, and publishers who allowed us to reprint them here.

—T. W.
Devon/New York/Tucson
1997–1998

ℭummation 1997: ℌorror

by Ellen Datlow

News of the Year

The horror market is still in very bad shape. Although commercial publishers have been publishing a few anthologies and single-author collections, it's merely a trickle and I predict this trend will continue for the next few years as fewer anthologies have been and are being bought. The small press continues to take up some of the slack and the continued presence in the market of Stephen Jones's anthologies is somewhat reassuring, but the fact is, in the U.K., he is virtually the only person who *is* editing horror anthologies on a regular basis.

The early promise of White Wolf failed to be borne out, and as a result of major cutbacks and layoffs, the publisher's output of non-game-related material is tiny—the collected works of Harlan Ellison and the occasional anthology left in inventory; Tor is overstocked with anthologies; HarperPrism is only interested in publishing high concept/celebrity/media–related or erotic horror; DAW keeps churning out the mostly mediocre products of the Greenberg machine; the *Hot Blood* series published by Pocket Books seems to run on its own inertia; and there are few other major publishers hospitable to short fiction right now.

The return of the ghost story is the most significant trend in horror this year—two anthologies focused on them: *Gothic Ghosts* and *Midnight Never Comes*. The World Fantasy Award–winning Ash-Tree Press (publisher of the latter anthology) has been instrumental in introducing a host of obscure traditional writers of ghost stories to a new audience. No less than four stories in this year's volume are suffused with ghostly qualities.

There were some excellent stories and novellas that almost made the final cut but for various reasons (length, for one) did not: "Coppola's Dracula" by Kim Newman from *The Mammoth Book of Dracula*; "Everything's Eventual" by Stephen King from *F&SF*, October/November; "Outside the Gates" by Marni Scofidio Griffin from *Midnight Never Comes*; "Saved" by Andy Duncan from *Dying for It*; "The Country Store" by Virginia Baker from *Tomorrow SF #24*; "The End of the Pier Show" by Kim Newman from *Dark of the Night*; and "The Zombies of Madison County" by Douglas E. Winter from *Dark of the Night*.

Book Publishing

There were some high-level changes in book publishing that may have an influence on genre publishing, although probably not immediately.

- Penguin Putnam continued to consolidate, naming a new management team in early April, with the four top spots going to former Putnam employees. The consolidation of the sales forces resulted in the loss of about thirty-six sales reps, mostly from Penguin.
- In late October, Stephen King surprised everyone by turning down Penguin Putnam's offer for his new novel *Bag of Bones*. There was a week-long frenzy of offers by several publishers, and reports of a demand for $17 million plus 26% royalties for the book. It was announced on November 7 that Simon and Schuster/Scribner won King's novel, a collection of short stories, and a work on the craft of writing for about $2 million per book plus nearly 50 percent of the profits.
- Harold Evans, the high-profile president and publisher of the Random House Trade Publishing Group for the past seven years, resigned to become the editorial director and vice chairman of Mort Zuckerman's Publications Group. Ann Godoff succeeded him, retaining her title of editor-in-chief.
- HarperPrism, the HarperCollins sf and fantasy imprint, has been made a stand-alone division of HarperCollins U.S. John Silbersack was promoted to senior vice president of HarperCollins and publishing director of HarperPrism.
- In late June, HarperCollins announced it would not publish more than one hundred books already under contract. Although it was initially announced that all authors whose books were killed would receive their full advances, HarperCollins later demanded that authors repay advances if they resold their books.
- Random House, U.K., sold Legend, its sf/fantasy imprint, to Little, Brown, U.K., publisher of the Orbit science fiction line. The Legend list foundered with the departure of John Jarrold in 1996. He has since moved to Simon and Schuster, U.K., to start the "Earthlight" imprint.
- Headline, the sf/fantasy imprint of Hodder Stoughton, U.K., was closed down.
- TSR, the onetime major gaming publisher and most recent publisher of *Amazing Stories*, suspended publication in 1997 and threatened bankruptcy. Wizards of the Coast took over the company and paid TSR's debts within five weeks of the takeover.
- Wired Books laid off six of its thirteen employees, prompting the resignation of its publisher. The beleaguered company failed in two public stock offerings in 1996 and is in the midst of a financial restructuring after posting a $35 million loss last year. WB published ten titles, including a series of cyberpunk reprints by Bruce Sterling and Rudy Rucker. By the end of the year it was still limping along.
- Turner Publishing, founded in 1989, has closed down. The company's future had been up in the air since its parent company, Turner Communications, was acquired by Time Warner, which expressed lack of interest in integrat-

ing the Atlanta-based book unit into its own operation. The company primarily published illustrated books, including the very successful *Dinotopia* by James Gurney.

- Jim Turner, former editor and packager of Arkham House for more than twenty years, started Golden Gryphon Press, a new specialty house that will concentrate on science fiction and fantasy. The first title of the new line is *Think like a Dinosaur and Other Stories* by James Patrick Kelly.
- Kitchen Sink, publisher of alternative comic artists such as Charles Burns, Robert Crumb, and Will Eisner, announced in late May that it was likely to be shut down. Eighteen people were laid off at that time. Kitchen Sink's publisher plans to start a new, smaller company, or form a book packaging company, if it does shut down. It was still publishing at the end of the year.

Magazines

- Will Blythe, the literary editor of *Esquire*, resigned in February over the executive editor's decision to pull David Leavitt's story "The Term Paper Artist" (since published in his collection) from the April issue. The story contains explicit homoerotic scenes and "vulgar anatomical references." According to executive editor Edward Kosner, the decision to pull the story was made weeks before the issue was to go to press because the piece "was not an appropriate story." Blythe, who had been at *Esquire* for ten years, said the decision was made practically as the issue went to press, out of fear that corporate advertisers would object to the content.
- Steve Propisch, former publisher of *Bloodsongs*, the Australian horror magazine, resigned his position as fiction editor after publication of one issue under the U.S. publishing regime of *Implosion*. Propisch cited "artistic differences."
- Mark Rainey, along with the partners of Malicious Press, decided to cease publication of *Deathrealm* after the magazine's thirty-first issue. Rainey cited problems with distributors and his realization that the magazine was eating too much of his personal finances and time. He decided he would rather put his creative energies into his writing career. *Deathrealm* was one of the best of the small-press horror magazines published during the '80s and early '90s.
- *Stygian Articles*, edited by Jeremy Johnson, shut down with its eleventh issue.

General News

- In a seven-to-two ruling, the U.S. Supreme Court struck down the Communications Decency Act, holding that the provisions in the Internet anti-smut statute banning "indecent" and "patently offensive" digital transmissions violated the First Amendment. The decision affirmed a lower court ruling earlier in the year by a federal court in Philadelphia.
- H. R. Giger has protested to Twentieth Century–Fox the use of his alien designs for *Alien Resurrection* without credit.
- At the Horror Writers Association banquet, the Bram Stoker Awards, for superior achievement in horror for 1996, were given to: Novel: *The Green Mile* by Stephen King; First Novel: *Crota* by Owl Goingback; Novelette: "The Red

Tower" by Thomas Ligotti; Short Story: "Metalica," by P. D. Cacek; Collection: *The Nightmare Factory* by Thomas Ligotti; Nonfiction: *H. P. Lovecraft: A Life* by S. T. Joshi; Life Achievement: Ira Levin and Forrest J. Ackerman.

Novels

The Club Dumas by Arturo Pérez-Reverte, translated by Sonio Soto (Harcourt Brace), is a dark, literary thriller about a man hired to find a rare occult book that can summon the devil. An exuberant mystery brimming with erudite antiquarian booklore, the complex story includes tantalizing bits about a missing chapter of *The Three Musketeers*. Accessible and entertaining, this book deserves the attention and success of Umberto Eco's *Name of the Rose*. Highly recommended.

Spares by Michael Marshall Smith (Bantam) expands upon one of his sf/horror stories published a few years ago. A burnt out former soldier/cop is assigned caretaker to a farm where "spares," i.e. clones, are kept for use as spare parts by their rich counterparts. The story slides back and forth between the present and the past as the protagonist recalls "the Gap," a place that feels somewhat like Vietnam but is far stranger. Although Smith, repeatedly an award winner for his superb short horror, is still not quite in tune with novel structure—shifts in time and place occasionally jar—the writing is crisp and rich in detail, the voice is interesting, and the author isn't afraid to throw in a few grisly bits when necessary. Highly recommended.

Reliquary by Douglas Preston and Lincoln Child (Tor/Forge) is the page-turning sequel to *Relic*. Two mysterious skeletons are found in the Hudson River. One is that of a missing socialite, the other is unknown and unclaimed, possessing grotesque physical abnormalities. Are they related to the genetic monster that wreaked havoc in the Museum only eighteen months before? The authors are at their best with the authenticity they bring to their depiction of a particular area of Manhattan. My only quibble is that I didn't believe in the villain for a minute.

Sacrifice by Mitchell Smith (Dutton) is the fifth novel (under his own name) by the author of the classic prison thriller *Stone City*. A tough ex-con tries to settle into the calm of normality but is unable to resist one last score. After a successful but deadly bank robbery he learns that his daughter has been murdered. The rest of this gritty novel follows Pierce as he tracks down the killer and tries to elude the law. Smith is expert at creating likable, believable characters that you want to have happy lives (although you know some won't). Look for Smith's first novel, the unusual police procedural *Daydreams*, as well as *Stone City* and his dark mainstream novel, *Due North*.

Cimarron Rose by James Lee Burke (Hyperion) is not part of the Robicheaux series but is as richly detailed and textured nonetheless. In Deaf Smith, Texas, a lawyer and former Texas Ranger defends a teenager accused of the rape and murder of a girl he picked up in a bar. The lawyer's guilt over the death of his best friend (who appears to him as a ghost) and his unacknowledged fathering of the accused make for moral complications and ambiguities—the keynotes of Burke's best work.

Signs of Life by M. John Harrison (Victor Gollancz/St. Martin's Press) is a beautifully told story of a man, who, drifting through life, falls desperately in love with a woman much younger than he. The novel is about the complications that ensue from following her yearnings to fly (literally), and although it has the feel of a mainstream novel, it contains elements of science fiction, fantasy, and horror. Throughout, there is a sense of imminent disaster as the five principals meet, clash, mix, and come apart. Highly recommended.

Lives of the Monster Dogs, a lovely first novel by Kirsten Bakis (Farrar, Straus and Giroux), also has a mainstream feel to it although its Frankensteinian elements bring it solidly into the realms of the fantastic. In the late nineteenth century, a quintessential mad scientist dreams of creating an army of "monster dogs" with artificial voice boxes, hands, and boosted intelligence. Although he dies before his dream comes to fruition, his followers continue his work. Told in bits and pieces from diaries, notebooks, and journals of the scientist, as well as one of the dogs and their human chronicler, this is a weird, wonderful, and terribly sad book.

The Church of Dead Girls by Stephen Dobyns (Metropolitan Books) is one of the best horror novels of the year. Dobyns's last excursion into the realm of darkness was *The Two Deaths of Señora Puccini* (released as a movie with Sonia Braga a couple of years ago). *The Church of Dead Girls* is an absorbing study of a small town in upstate New York several years after a grisly murder. Now young girls are disappearing and suspicion is rampant. The confrontation between a small-minded bully and a smug, self-absorbed Marxist professor triggers a series of events that destroys the town. Dobyns terrifyingly depicts a town being eaten from within.

The Magician's Tale by David Hunt (Putnam) is a fine pseudonymous mystery told by a woman photographer who becomes friends with one of the young male hustlers she is photographing on the streets of San Francisco. His brutal murder echoes a series of gay murders twelve years earlier that the photographer's policeman father investigated. The personal resonances force her to take action, and by becoming immersed in life on the strip, she treads dangerous ground. Magic, twins, and kink.

Asylum by Patrick McGrath (Random House) is about a dangerous sexual obsession seen through the eyes of an unreliable narrator with his own agenda. I had hoped McGrath would break out of this stylistic dead end, but he hasn't quite. Although there are a few surprising twists and turns, that's not enough. Few of the characters come alive because of the flatness created by the veil through which we see the story.

In the Palm of Darkness by Mayra Montero (HarperCollins) could, I suppose, be called magical realism. Although based on certain facts—the inexplicable worldwide disappearance of frogs and toads leading to what seems to be mass extinctions of entire species—the story itself (about a professor searching Haiti for a supposedly extinct frog) veers into magic and horror. Montero's Haiti is filled with political violence and supernatural fears—a place where the living dead walk and must be hunted down by men specially trained to do so.

The Tooth Fairy by Graham Joyce (Signet, U.K./Tor) is a frightening, beautifully rendered coming-of-age story about three boys growing to maturity in a small English town during the '60s. Joyce immediately hooks his readers with a small sharp shock and holds the attention with engaging characters and an air of menace. This tooth fairy is not the kindly creature who leaves money in exchange for unwanted baby teeth but is mischievous and destructive, representing our own worst aspects.

Fog Heart by Thomas Tessier (Gollancz, U.K./St. Martin's Press) does something unusual for the genre—it takes a common horror trope and creates something fresh and beautiful merely in the writing of it. Tessier's eighth novel centers around two sisters, one a genuine psychic, and the two couples that elicit their help. The woman in each couple is haunted. The man in each couple is a real creep, jarring the balance of the novel a bit. Tessier's writing forces the reader's suspension of disbelief in the supernatural not only by his crisp language but with a reasonable (if tenuous) plausibility. Good show.

Nightmare Syndrome by William Marshall (Mysterious Press) gives me an occasion to mention a mystery series I've been avidly reading since its inception in 1975. The series follows the travails of a group of policemen in Hong Kong's imaginary Yellowthread Street precinct. The books have a wicked sense of humor and there is often a dark, even horrific element to the various mysteries. In *NS*, people are dying grisly, seemingly natural deaths—the deceased have all scratched out their own eyes and have a look of unspeakable terror on their faces. Is the murderer supernatural? Is he related to the death years before of Detective Chief Inspector Harry Feiffer's father? Frantic, funny, and frightening. Start with this one and then find the earlier novels in the series.

The Universal Donor by Craig Nova (Houghton Mifflin) magicks a beautiful and terrifying love story out of an unlikely premise. In the middle of the L.A. riots, an emergency doctor is faced with a race against time to save the woman he loves. She has been bitten by one of the venomous snakes she works with, and the only person in the hemisphere with her rare blood type is an escaped criminal. Interesting structure swings the story to the past and back again.

Glimmering by Elizabeth Hand (HarperPrism) is an exquisitely told story of the coming end of the world. As a result of the confluence of man-made and natural circumstances, a vast hole is ripped in the ozone layer, causing flashes of spectral color to stream across the skies, not to mention the disruption of life as we know it. As humanity faces the apocalypse, the publisher of an obsolete literary magazine faces his own tragic circumstances—he is dying of AIDS and has watched his personal world crumble. A memorable cast of characters populate this frightening scenario that combines sf and horror.

Dispossession by Chaz Brenchley (NEL, U.K.) is a fine, neatly constructed dark mystery about a man who awakens from a car crash with amnesia of the past three months of his life during which time he finds he has acquired a new wife, a new lifestyle, and a new boss—a crime lord. As he tries to unravel the various strands of strangeness, he discovers that his life may be in danger. Much of the action is realistic and down-to-earth—except the existence and participation of Luke, a fallen angel, who plays a very important part in the protagonist's fortunes.

True Crime by Andrew Klavan (Crown) is a page turner about an absolute prick of a newspaperman who drinks too much and compulsively cheats on his wife with all the wrong people—one boss's daughter, another boss's wife—but he *is* a crack reporter. At the last minute he takes over the coverage of a scheduled execution and comes to believe that the prisoner is innocent, and he has less than twenty-four hours to save the man's life. *True Crime* is thrilling and terrifying as one realizes just how easy it is to send the wrong person to his death.

The Dealings of Daniel Kesserich by Fritz Leiber (Tor) is the book publication of the long-lost novella that first appeared on *OMNI* Online in 1996. It feels like horror but is in fact a science fiction story.

Novel Listings

The Twilight Child by Elizabeth Harris (HarperCollins, U.K.); *The Chalice* by Phil Rickman (Macmillan, U.K.); *The Short Cut* by Mark Pepper (Hodder and Stoughton, U.K.); *Double Delight* by Rosamund Smith (Dutton/A. William Abrahams Books); *Blood Debt* by Tanya Huff (DAW); *Bright Shadow* by Elizabeth Forrest (DAW); *Tainted Blood* by Andrew Billings (Jove); *The Lost and Found House* by Michael Cadnum with illustrations by Steve Johnson and Lou Fancher (Viking Children's); *Shackled* by Ray Garton (Bantam); *Jumpers* by R. Patrick Gates (Dell); *Longbarrow* by Mark Morris (Piatkus, U.K.); *'48* by James Herbert (HarperPrism); *Outcry* by Harold Schecter (Pocket Books); *Wolf Moon* by John R. Holt (Bantam Spectra); *Somewhere South of Midnight* by Stephen Laws (NEL, U.K.); *Writ in Blood* by Chelsea Quinn Yarbro (Tor); *Meg* by Steve Alten (Doubleday); *Daughter of Darkness* by Steven Spruill (Doubleday); *Plague Tales* by Ann Benson (Delacorte); *Dracula: The Undead* by Freda Warrington (Penguin, U.K.); *The Stone Circle* by Gary Goshgarian (Donald I. Fine); *Shadows* by Jonathan Nasaw (Dutton); *Symphony* by Charles Grant (Tor); *The God Game* by Gerald Suster (NEL, U.K.); *Drawn to the Grave* by Mary Ann Mitchell (Leisure); *Slave of My Thirst* by Tom Holland (Pocket); *The Chosen Child* by Graham Masterton (Heinemann, U.K.); *Tooth and Claw* by Graham Masterton (Severn House); *Circle of Nightmares* by Malcolm Rose (Scholastic, U.K.); *The Devil on May Street* by Steve Harris (Gollancz, U.K.); *Bad Chili* by Joe R. Lansdale (Warner); *The Art of Arrow Cutting* by Stephen Dedman (Tor); *My Soul to Keep* by Tananarive Due (HarperCollins); *Disturbia* by Christopher Fowler (Warner, U.K.); *Furnace* by Murial Grey (Doubleday); *Prisoners of Limbo* by David Ratcliffe (Tanjen, U.K.); *Violin* by Anne Rice (Knopf); *The Beasties* by William Sleator (Penguin/Dutton); *The Vampire's Beautiful Daughter* by S. P. Somtow (Atheneum); *Deliver Us from Evil* by Tom Holland (Little, Brown, U.K.); *Into the Black* by David Aaron Clark (Eros, U.K.); *Superstition* by David Ambrose (Macmillan, U.K.); *Light Errant* by Chaz Brenchley (Hodder and Stoughton, U.K.); *Big Thunder* by Peter Atkins (HarperCollins, U.K.); *Shades of Pale* by Greg Kihn (Forge); *The Ruby Tear* by Rebecca Brand (Tor/Forge); *Carnivore* by Leigh Clark (Leisure); *A Face at the Window* by Dennis McFarland (Broadway); *Music from the Dead* by Bebe Faas Rice (HarperPaperbacks); *The Blackstone Chronicles* by John Saul (Ballantine/Fawcett); *The Carver* by Jenny Jones (Scholastic); *Out of Body* by Thomas Baum (St. Martin's Press); *The Green Mile* (the collected six volumes of the serial) by Stephen King (Penguin/Signet); *The Dancing Floor* by Barbara Michaels (HarperCollins); *Night People* by Maggie Pearson (Hodder Children's Books, U.K.); *The Ignored* by Bentley Little (Penguin/Signet); *Houses* by Bentley Little (Headline, U.K.); *Bloodsong* by Karen Marie Christa Minns (Bluestocking Books); *The Black Cat* by Robert A. Poe (Forge); *Angry Moon* by Terrill Lankford (Forge); *A Dry Spell* by Susie Moloney (Delacorte); *Execution of Innocence* by Christopher Pike (Pocket Books/Archway); *Miles and Flora* by

Hilary Bailey (Simon and Schuster, U.K.); *The Butcher of Glastonbury* by David Bowker (Gollancz, U.K.); *After Midnight* by Richard Laymon (Headline, U.K.); *Winter Tides* by James P. Blaylock (Ace); *I'll See You in My Dreams* by Helen Cooper (Viking YA); *The Powerhouse* by Ann Halam (Orion/Dolphin); *Fragments* by James F. David (Tor/Forge); *Room 13* by Henry Garfield (St. Martin's Press); *Vaporetto 13* by Robert Girardi (Delacorte); *The Prodigy* by Noel Hynd (Kensington); *The Darker Passions: Carmilla* by Amarantha Knight (Masquerade); *The Dark* by Andrew Neiderman (Pocket); *God's Gift* by John Evans (Arrow, U.K.); *Burning Bright* by Jay Russell (Raven, U.K.); *The Dark Lagoon* by Simon Shinerock (Ripping Publishing, U.K.); *Black River* by Melanie Tem (Headline, U.K.); *Recluse* by Derek Fox (Tanjen, U.K.); *Thorn, An Immortal Tale* by Frances Gordon (Headline, U.K.); *Mesmer* by Tim Lebbon (Tanjen, U.K.); *A Gracious Plenty* by Sheri Reynolds (Harmony); *Night of Broken Souls* by Thomas F. Monteleone (Warner Books); *Esau* by Philip Kerr (Henry Holt); *Meeting the Minotaur* by Carol Dawson (Algonquin Books of Chapel Hill); *The Poison Tree* by Tony Strong (Delacorte Press); *Murder Book* by Richard Raynor (Houghton Mifflin); *Deja Dead* by Kathy Reichs (Scribner); *Blood* by Jay Russell (Raven); *Ingenious Pain* by Andrew Miller (Harcourt Brace); *Skin Deep* by Diana Wagman (University Press of Mississippi); *Easy Peasy* by Lesley Glaister (A Wyatt Book for St. Martin's Press); *Bad Karma* by Andrew Harper (Kensington); *The Angel of Darkness* by Caleb Carr (Random House); *The Art of Breaking Glass* by Matthew Hall (Little, Brown); *The Salesman* by Joseph O'Connor (Secker and Warburg, U.K.); *The Bell Witch* by Brent Monahan (St. Martin's Press); *Guide* by Dennis Cooper (Grove Press); *The Dumb House* by John Burnside (Jonathan Cape, U.K.); *Dead Game* by James Neal Harvey (St. Martin's Press); *Girls* by Frederick Busch (Harmony Books); *Count Me Out* by Russell James (Foul Play Press); *In Awe* by Scott Heim (HarperCollins); *Blind Pursuit* by Matthew F. Jones (FSG); *Prelude to a Scream* by Jim Nisbet (C&G); *Gypsy Hearts* by Robert M. Evers (Grove Press); *Impossible Saints* by Michele Roberts (Little, Brown); *Class Trip* by Emmanuel Carrere (Metropolitan Books); *The Keepsake* by Kirsty Gunn (Atlantic Monthly Press); *The Stranger* by Eric James Fullilove (Bantam Spectra); *Prayer-Cushions of the Flesh* by Robert Irwin (Dedalus, U.K.); *The Beach* by Alex Garland (Riverhead Books); *Confessions of a Flesh-Eater* by David Madsen (Dedalus, U.K.); *An Irish Eye* by John Hawkes (Viking Press); *Fermentation* by Angelica J. (Grove Press); *Stone Cowboys* by Mark Jacobs (Soho); *Bunker Man* by Duncan McLean (W. W. Norton); *Soon She Will Be Gone* by John Farris (Forge); *Man Crazy* by Joyce Carol Oates (Dutton); *The Echo* by Minette Walters (Putnam); *Twitchy Eyes* by Joe Donnelly (Michael Joseph, U.K.); *Nazareth Hill* by Ramsey Campbell (Forge); *Slow Chocolate Autopsy* by Iain Sinclair and Dave McKean (Phoenix House, U.K.); *Acts of Revision* by Martyn Bedford (Doubleday); and *Renaissance Moon* by Linda Nevins (A Wyatt Book for St. Martin's Press).

Collections

Just an Ordinary Day by Shirley Jackson (Bantam) was probably the most anticipated collection published in 1997 (the book began appearing in stores late '96). It is a retrospective of Jackson's short fiction and includes a batch of stories recently found by her children. Unfortunately, the way the book is organized does Jackson an injustice. Always a versatile writer, Jackson wrote everything from light domestic pieces to dark classics. The new stories might have been better organized by type, but they are in no particular order and lack headnotes, which would have provided a context in Jackson's *oeuvre*. There are three or four little chillers here but none to rival her classics "One Ordinary Day, with Peanuts" or "The Lottery."

Six Stories by Stephen King (Philtrum Press) is a signed, limited trade paperback edition of 1,100 copies (sold out). The book includes two originals: the tour-de-force piece "Autopsy Room Four" and the excellent mainstream story "L. T.'s Theory of Pets," plus the award-winning "Lunch at the Gotham Café" and "The Man in the Black Suit," and the previously uncollected "The Lucky Quarter" and "Blind Willie."

Slippage by Harlan Ellison (Mark Ziesing/Houghton Mifflin) collects stories, essays, and teleplays published by Ellison since 1986 including the novella "Mefisto in Onyx." Ellison's introductory matter is, as always, riveting. The Ziesing edition is designed by Arnie Fenner with jacket art by Jill Bauman and has 30,000 words more than the HM edition.

Publish and Perish by James Hynes (Picador USA) collects three horror novellas connected neatly by characters who overlap from one story to the next. Hynes dishes academia with relish and if the actual plots aren't particularly original, it barely matters. "Queen of the Jungle" is about a man and his wife's cat; "99" is about a self-professed lady killer anthropologist who is too dim to live, and "Casting the Runes," an acknowledged pastiche of M. R. James's various works, is so funny in spots that I laughed aloud reading it on the subway.

Tales of H. P. Lovecraft: Major Works Selected and Introduced by Joyce Carol Oates (Ecco Press) collects ten stories with an incisive introduction by Oates. Also, *The Annotated H. P. Lovecraft* edited by S. T. Joshi (Dell) with four stories (all of which are in the Oates book) annotated with an appendix, index, and biographical introduction by Joshi is illustrated with photographs and art depicting Lovecraft's life and work (but strangely, contains no table of contents).

Best Ghost Stories by Bram Stoker (Dover) collects fourteen stories and has an introduction by Richard Dalby, who coedited the volume with Stefan R. Dziemianowicz.

The Mirror of the Night by Roberta Lannes (Silver Salamander Press) collects some of the more sexually explicit horror fiction of this talented short story writer. In this combination of reprints and originals, the stories are visceral and unflinching in their depiction of aberrations and the humans who perpetrate and/or endure them. The cover art is by Lannes, a former art director. There are three editions of the book, all signed by the author, two numbered. Also from the same press: Lucy Taylor's new collection *Painted in Blood* with six original stories and seven reprints ranging from flesh-eating and fucking zombies to a violent, brash, and fun wrestling jaunt. Taylor has undeniable talent, but occasionally her pieces are interesting conceits more than satisfying stories. It was published in both deluxe and trade limited editions.

Leavings, published in paperback by new publisher StarsEnd Creations is the first collection of stories by P. D. Cacek. Cacek is a crackerjack storyteller, and her best work is powerful and often moving. Her chilling Bram Stoker Award–winning story "Metalica" is in this collection.

In a Foreign Town, in a Foreign Land by Thomas Ligotti is a small, gorgeous clothbound book with a CD to read it by, published by the U.K.'s Durtro Press. The four original stories are related, with odd, overlapping inhabitants. The cover illustration and frontispiece are by Steven Stapleton; Durtro Press also reissued *The Book of Jade*, originally published anonymously (by David Park Barnitz) in 1901. It is a book of decadent supernatural poems dedicated to Baudelaire. It includes some writings not included in the original and has an afterword by Thomas Ligotti on "The Joys of Collecting Decadent Poetry."

Things Left Behind (CD Publications) is the excellent debut collection of the versatile Gary A. Braunbeck, reprinting some of his best stories and adding several new ones, a few of which will be published in upcoming anthologies. It's available in two hardcover editions, with cover art and interior illustrations by Alan M. Clark.

The Throne of Bones by Brian McNaughton (Terminal Fright Publications) is the first offering from Ken Abner's (former publisher of *Terminal Fright Magazine*) new publishing company, and it's an impressive beginning. McNaughton is a true original. Influenced by Clark Ashton Smith, his personable ghouls are crucial to his quirky tales of sword and sorcery, revenge, and violence. Not really my cup of tea, but unignorable. This collection will be on the Stoker and perhaps even the World Fantasy Award ballot. Illustrated by Jamie Oberschlake.

Screamplays edited by Richard Chizmar (Del Rey) publishes excellent never-before-published teleplays by Richard Matheson, Stephen King, Ed Gorman, Harlan Ellison, and Joe R. Lansdale. Dean Koontz provides some acerbic anecdotes about his experiences in the screenwriting biz.

Fedogan and Bremer published *Don't Dream*, a collection of sixteen mostly horror and fantasy stories, prose poems, essays, and marginalia by Donald Wandrei. Two of the stories and ten of the miscellany are original to this volume and there is an introduction by Helen Mary Hughesdon and an afterword by D. H. Olson. It is illustrated by Rodger Gerberding.

Also from Fedogan and Bremer is *The Door Below* by Hugh B. Cave, a twenty-five story retrospective of horror stories from the 1930s to the '90s. Cave, who was recently honored with the Lifetime Achievement Award from the World Fantasy Convention, also wrote the preface and biographical commentary. The book is illustrated by Alan M. Clark.

Exorcisms and Ecstasies (Fedogan and Bremer) by the late Karl Edward Wagner is edited by Stephen Jones, and has cover and interior art by J. K. Potter. The volume is divided into four sections—the first is the collection Wagner put together shortly before he died; the second consists of his uncollected Kane stories; the third is a fragment of an abandoned novel called *Satan's Gun*, plus two short stories about the main character from the novel; and the final section gathers up the remainder of his uncollected tales, including some early juvenilia.

The Vampire Stories of R. Chetwynd-Hayes (Fedogan and Bremer) edited by Stephen Jones, collects fifteen tales from 1973–1997 (one original). The collection has an introduction by Brian Lumley, an interview with the author, jacket art by Les Edwards, and interior illustrations by Jim Pitts. All Fedogan and Bremer titles are published in trade and limited editions.

Edgeworks 3 by Harlan Ellison (White Wolf) is an omnibus of *The Harlan Ellison Hornbook* and *Harlan Ellison's Movie*, with a new introduction by Ellison.

Borderlands Press published a thirty-year retrospective of Whitley Strieber's short fiction, *Evenings with Demons*, in a limited and a trade edition. Some of the stories are original to the collection but it's impossible to tell which, as the copyright information is incomplete. The stories range from his early work through his critically acclaimed "Pain."

From the Dark Regions "selected works" series: *Murmerous Haunts* by Bentley Little showcases nine stories, two of which are new, by this novelist and short story writer. A limited edition of 250 copies was signed by the author and artist. *Writhing in Darkness Part I and Part II* showcases some of Michael Arnzen's dark poetry. A limited edition of 125 copies was signed by author and artist. Dark Regions also published *Horizon Lines* by Jeffrey Osier, his second collection, with an introduction by Elizabeth Massie and cover art by the author. The book collects seven horror stories published between 1987 and 1992, with one original. Various editions are available.

Macabre, Inc., published *Endorphins*, a collection of two previously unpublished stories by Nancy Kilpatrick. The chapbook is simple but attractive, with two poems by Fabrice Dulac and illustrations by Chad Savage.

Argo Press published a collection of Albert J. Manachino's weird and macabre Madonna-Moloch stories, most originally published in the late magazine *Argonaut*. *Noctet* contains one original story, a "prelude" by the author, and illustrations by Larry Dickison.

Space and Time published *Animated Objects*, a first collection of thirty-six mixed-genre stories and poetry by Linda D. Addison. The introduction is by Barry N. Malzberg, and there are hardcover and paperback editions available.

Marietta Publishing released *The Dog Syndrome and Other Sick Puppies*, a chapbook by Tom Piccirilli with six stories, all but one original to the collection. The cover and each story is illustrated by a different artist and each of the 500 copies printed is signed by the author and artists.

Ash-Tree Press continues to publish its reprint series of collectible hardcover editions of neglected ghost stories: Amyas Northcote's rare 1921 collection *In Ghostly Company*; a beautiful hardcover edition of Terry Lamsley's first, self-published World Fantasy Award–nominated collection, *Under the Crust*, with jacket art by Douglas Walters; *Imagine a Man in a Box*, H. R. Wakefield's 1921 classic, augmented with previously uncollected tales by Wakefield; *Unholy Relics* by M. P. Dare; *Someone in the Room: Strange Tales Old and New* by A. M. Burrage features all the tales in *Someone in the Room*, five stories from *Between the Minute and the Hour* not collected in either of Burrage's volumes of tales, plus more rare and new stories and was edited by Jack Adrian; Richard Dalby edited *The Haunted Chair and Other Stories* by Richard Marsh. It collects eighteen stories of horror and the supernatural from 1898 to 1902 from an author whose work, when it was first published, created a greater stir than *Dracula*. Dalby provides an in-depth introduction to the life and work of this author, who was the grandfather of the late, great Robert Aickman.

The British Fantasy Society published the chapbook *Shocks*, a handsome, signed collection of four stories by the venerable Ronald Chetwynd-Hayes—the first in a series designed to collect obscure or out-of-print stories by well-known authors.

Tartarus Press and Caemaen Books published the first British edition of Arthur Machen's *Ornaments in Jade*. Although written in 1897, the book couldn't find a publisher until 1924 because the stories were considered too "decadent and risqué." It has an introduction by Barry Humphries. Tartarus also published *Tales of Horror and the Supernatural* by Arthur Machen, containing thirteen of the best of Machen's short stories and novellas with an introduction by Roger Dobson. A *Night with Mephistopheles* by Henry Ferris, also published by Tartarus, is a selection of six of the Irish supernaturalist's ghost stories and three essays, including a story previously attributed to Sheridan Le Fanu. It was edited by S. T. Joshi who also wrote the introduction. These small printings of classic works are attractively produced and extremely collectible.

Caliban is a new U.K. imprint devoted to "rare works of supernatural, fantasy and decadent literature." Its first title is a reprint of C. D. Pamely's *Tales of Mystery and Terror*, originally published in 1926. Illustrated by David Fletcher, it has an introduction by Brian Stableford and an afterword by Richard Dalby.

The Xothic Legend Cycle: Selected Mythos Fiction of Lin Carter was edited by and has an introduction by Robert M. Price (Chaosium); *The Scroll of Thoth* by Richard Tierney (Chaosium) collects twelve tales featuring Tierney's Simon Magus, mixing the Cthulhu and Hyborian myth cycles; *The Loved Dead and Other Revisions* by H. P. Lovecraft (Carroll and Graf), and *Short Stories 1895–1926* by Walter de la Mare with forty-two stories, fourteen previously uncollected. Volume Two will contain short stories written between 1927 and 1956, and Volume Three will collect his short stories for children (Giles de la Mare Publishing/ distributed by Faber).

The Monkey's Paw and Other Tales of Mystery and the Macabre by W. W. Jacobs (Academy Chicago Publishers), compiled by Gary Hoppenstand, collects eighteen stories in an attractive new edition with a brief introduction and selected bibliography.

Haunted Library Publications released *The Shell of Sense: Collected Ghost Stories of Olivia Howard Dunbar*, edited by Jessica Amanda Salmonson. The book collects four stories and two essays by Dunbar concerning ghostly fiction in the 1920s and earlier, and has a dust jacket and interior illustrations by Wendy Wees. It is the first in a projected series of volumes reprinting obscure, forgotten writers of supernatural fiction.

Necro Publications brought out *Inside the Works: A 3-Way Collection of Hardcore Horror* by Tom Piccirilli, Gerard Daniel Houarner, and Edward Lee. Ed Gorman introduces Piccirilli's five stories, Bentley Little introduces Houarner's novella, and Wayne Allen Sallee introduces Lee's novella. It is available in limited hardcover and trade paperback signed and numbered editions.

Necropolitan Press brought out a chapbook of W. H. Pugmire's *Tales of Sesqua Valley*, a mix of reprints and originals with illustrations throughout.

Cyber-Psychos AOD published *Snuff Flique*: six stories (three original) by Michael Hemmingson. Jacket art and interior illustrations are by Richard A. Schindler.

New publisher Meisha Merlin brought out a three-story collection, with one original story by Storm Constantine called *Three Heralds of the Storm*. The chapbook is signed by the author and the cover design is by Larry Friedman.

Fiends by Richard Laymon (Headline, U.K.) collects thirteen dark fantasy and thriller stories, including the original novel *Fiends*. The introduction is by Dean Koontz.

DreamHaven Books brought out *On Cats and Dogs*, a chapbook of two tales by Neil Gaiman, one original. It is illustrated with photographs of Lisa Snelling's sculptures.

Curses, Inc, and Other Stories by Vivian Vande Velde (Harcourt Brace) is a young-adult collection of ten stories, seven original; *The Hitchhikers* by Joy Cowley (Scholastic) collects twelve YA horror stories, most of which were originally broadcast by the "Ears" program of Radio New Zealand.

In His Own Write: Brian Lumley: Necroscribe is a collection of three stories with Lovecraftian elements published by Necronomicon Press.

Tanjen, U.K. published *Scattered Remains*, Paul Pinn's collection of reprints and originals to celebrate the 750th anniversary of the Royal Bethlehem Mental Hospital, the original source of the word *bedlam*.

Collections with Some Horror

Tiger Eyes Press published Michael Swanwick's *Geography of Unknown Lands*, collecting the versatile author's more recent short fiction, including two award-winning stories and one original stunner; *Barnacle Bill the Spacer and other Stories* by Lucius Shepard (Orion/Millennium U.K.) collects seven novellas and stories by this brilliant author of sf, fantasy, horror, and mainstream, including "A Little Night Music," reprinted in our *Year's Best* series; *The Martian Chronicles* and *The Illustrated Man*, both sf classics by Ray Bradbury, have been reissued in attractive new hardcover editions by Avon. These two collections, long embraced by the sf community, deserve a look by horror aficionados, as there is some very dark material in both books; and for more recent work by Bradbury, try *Driving Blind* (Avon Books), which collects four reprints and eighteen original stories by the master fantasist. At least three of the stories are dark enough to consider dark fantasy or horror; *Kissing the Witch: Old Tales in New Skins* by Emma Donoghue (HarperCollins/Joanna Cotler) is a YA collection of thirteen twisted retellings of fairy tales; *Foggy Mountain Breakdown* by Sharyn McCrumb (Ballantine) contains a couple of originals by a writer known for her (sometimes supernatural) mystery series based on Appalachian ballads and for her sf mystery novel, *Bimbos of the Death Sun*; *Perverts, Pedophiles & Other Theologians* by Clifford Lawrence Meth (Aardwolf Publishing) illustrations by Gene Colan; *The Final Trick of Funnyman and Other Stories* by Bruce Taylor (Ministry of Whimsy) is the first collection by a surrealist whose work has been published in several volumes of *New Dimensions*, and in *Twilight Zone, Pulphouse, On Spec*, and other magazines. It is attractively packaged with wonderfully appropriate cover art by Scott Eagle. Also, *Feeding the Glamour Hogs* by Mark McLaughlin (Ministry of Whimsy), the *No Frills Chapbook #2* reprints eight pieces of strangeness by the editor of *The Urbanite*; *The Skull of Charlotte Corday and Other Stories* by Leslie Dick (Scribner) is an interesting collection published as mainstream but with appeal to fantasy and horror readers, particularly the title story, reprinted herein; *The Reality Machine* by Cliff Burns (Black Dog Press) showcases a writer whose fantasy stories and vignettes have been published all over the field, including in an earlier volume of *The Year's Best*; *Ocean Eyes* by Stuart Hughes (Peeping Tom Books), by the editor of *Peeping Tom Magazine* contains ten reprint stories from a variety of U.K. small press magazines, and one original; *The Bridal Suite* by Matthew Sweeney (Cape Poetry U.K.) is a fascinating book of mainstream poetry full of dark themes; *The Arbitrary Placement of Walls* by Martha Soukup is beautifully designed by Robert T. Garcia and Rick Berry (who also did the cover art) and is the author's first collection of sf and fantasy, sometimes with a dark edge (DreamHaven Books); *Stealing My Rules* is a thirteen-story collection by Don Webb (Cyber-Psychos AOD) with some horror and a lot of weirdness. Illustrations and cover art by Christian Patchell and introduction by Paul Di Filippo; *Scared in School* by Roberta Simpson Brown (August House) is a collection of seventeen YA stories; *Distorture* by Rob Hardin (FC2) presents razor-sharp lyricism and experimental riffs about dark contemporary experience; *Future Fright: Tales of High-Tech Terror* by Don Wullfson (Lowell House Juvenile) is an original collection of six sf horror stories for young adults; *Poetic Dementica* by Darrell Schweitzer (Zadak Allen) collects thirteen poems, three original to the collection, and is illustrated by Thomas Brown; *Saul's Death and Other Poems* by Joe Haldeman (Anamnesis Press) collects thirty-two poems, including the Rhysling Award–winning title poem; *Ghost Seas* by Steven Utley (Ticonderoga Publications) is a first collection, bringing together fourteen stories written over a twenty-seven-year period, with introductions by Michael Bishop and Howard Waldrop; *Virtual Unrealities* by Alfred Bester (Vintage) is a collection with a wee bit of horror from the late, great author of *The Stars My Destination* and *The Demolished Man*. The stories range over his entire career, with one previously unpublished; *Think like a Dinosaur* by James Patrick Kelly (Golden Gryphon) is mostly science fiction, but Kelly's work occasionally veers into dark territory. The title story won the Hugo Award; some of Nebula Award–winning John Kessel's short work over the past decade is collected in *The Pure Product* (Tor). Kessel writes cross-genre fiction that, like Kelly's makes forays into darker territories; *The Din of Celestial Birds* by Brian Evenson (Wordcraft of Oregon) collects seventeen reprints and originals that feel quite a bit like magical realism; and *Twelve Impossible Things Before Breakfast* by Jane Yolen (Harcourt Brace), for children, has, among other things: trolls, sea monsters, an Alice in Wonderland story, a Peter Pan story, and a new take on an urban legend.

Anthologies

Love in Vein II edited by Poppy Z. Brite (HarperPrism) seems to be thrown together with considerably less care than the first volume. There are no author bios or introductions, and although there are a few powerful selections, overall the book is a disappointment, particularly because the first volume was so good.

The Hot Blood Series edited by Jeff Gelb and Michael Garrett (Pocket) chugs along merrily with two entries during 1997: *Kiss and Kill* and *Crimes of Passion*, providing another bunch of good, bad, and indifferent stories, as the editors continue their mission to titillate and horrify.

Revelations edited by Douglas E. Winter (HarperPrism), called *Millennium* in the U.K., is an experiment that works, to a degree. Winter, editor of *Prime Evil*, didn't want to repeat himself, so as a tribute to the coming millennium, he commissioned novellas from various writers, each assigned a different decade, from 1900 to 1999. Clive Barker provides a moving wraparound piece. The other contributors (there are several collaborations) pick a touchstone of each decade: the hurricane that destroyed Galveston, the great influenza epidemic, the flapper era, etc., and weave a history of the twentieth century. My qualm is that while the overall book is a brilliant depiction of our century, and quite entertaining, most of it isn't horror—there are horrific elements here and there but there's no terror—it doesn't give the reader a feeling of dread or impending doom that good horror must in order to succeed. So in Winter's own terms—if horror can be defined as an emotion, as he has argued—the book fails as horror. The Charles Grant novella is reprinted herein.

The Mammoth Book of Dracula edited by Stephen Jones (Robinson) is large and varied, as befits a centenary tribute to the greatest vampire of them all. The book, subtitled "Vampires for the New Millennium," has some nicely creepy (and some amusing) stories in which Dracula adapts to changes over the last century up through and past the new millennium. Jones has for the most part avoided the pitfalls of producing an anthology about one character. Also included is the long-lost prologue to a theatrical version of *Dracula* by Bram Stoker and some reprints, scattered among the originals. Nicholas Royle's story is reprinted herein.

Destination Unknown edited by Peter Crowther (White Wolf) is an interesting mixture of light and dark stories imbued with mystery and weirdness. I'm not exactly sure of the theme—possibly "strange travel" stories. But that doesn't really matter.

Tarot Fantastic edited by Martin H. Greenberg and Lawrence Schimel (DAW) contains a mixture of fantasy and dark fantasy, with some interesting stories in both genres.

The Fortune Teller edited by Lawrence Schimel and Martin H. Greenberg (DAW) is, unfortunately, so close enough to the anthology above that it's virtually impossible to tell them apart. I read them interchangeably and could not tell you now which stories were in which book. Not because either anthology was bad but because the themes are just too similar and six contributors overlap.

Dying for It edited by Gardner Dozois (HarperPrism) seems to be a collection of mostly original erotic ghost stories, but I'm not sure. The handful of science fiction stories don't feel well-integrated and hurt the overall mood. Despite this, there are some excellent pieces here.

Northern Frights 4 edited by Don Hutchinson (Mosaic—Canada) is the latest in this noteworthy series of original anthologies from Canada. It includes some fine stories about ghosts, vampires, werewolves, and serial killers, demonstrating that there's still blood in those old archetypes.

Palace Corbie Seven edited by Wayne Edwards is excellent, based loosely on the theme of personal terror. The minitheme anthology within, entitled "The Piano Player Has No Fingers" is a neat little experiment in commissioned short-shorts written to the title above, and generates some truly bizarre stories. Douglas Clegg's "I Am Infinite; I Contain Multitudes" is reprinted herein.

Gothic Ghosts edited by Charles Grant and Wendy Webb (Tor) is a noteworthy attempt to recapture the feeling of the classic ghost story. Despite a blandness to some of the stories there are also some very good ones, including the powerfully moving "Dust Motes" by P. D. Cacek, reprinted herein.

Dark Terrors 3 edited by Stephen Jones and David Sutton (Gollancz, U.K.) is the generally solid annual installment of that increasingly rare breed: the original non-theme horror anthology. There are some (American) names new to the series including Pat Cadigan, Ray Bradbury, Brian Hodge, Kathryn Ptacek, and Ray Garton. Caitlín R. Kiernan's and Christopher Fowler's stories are reprinted herein.

Monsters from Memphis edited by Beecher Smith (Zapizdat Publications) embarrassingly has five (!) stories by the editor (two under pseudonyms) and a minimal flavor of Memphis. Unlike New Orleans (now *that* would be a great regional horror antho), Memphis, at least judging from most of the stories, doesn't seem to have many identifying characteristics.

Scaremongers edited by Andrew Haigh (Tanjen) is an all-around excellent anthology with royalties going to the worthy cause of animal welfare charities. Its twenty-five stories include a few reprints but most are originals from a variety of famous and new British and American writers such as Joan Aiken, Ramsey Campbell, Ray Bradbury, Michael Marshall Smith, Dennis Etchison, Poppy Z. Brite, and Stephen Gallagher.

Midnight Never Comes edited by Barbara and Christopher Roden is the first original anthology from Ash-Tree Press and it's topnotch, with seventeen ghost stories by contemporary writers in the genre such as Jonathan Aycliffe, Terry Lamsley, John Whitbourne, Marni Scofidio Griffin, Rosemary Pardoe, and Simon Clark.

Dark of the Night edited by Stephen Jones from the newly formed Pumpkin Press is an excellent original non-theme anthology with many of the usual suspects. There is also a slip-cased limited edition available.

Love Kills edited by Ed Gorman and Martin H. Greenberg (Carroll and Graf Mystery) is a good, dark anthology of originals and reprints in the mystery/suspense genre, although most of the best stories are reprints. Worth a look.

Terminal Frights edited by Ken Abner is the editor's first foray into book publishing, changing his magazine into a very good anthology. The illustrations are by G. Wayne Miller.

Dark Dixie edited by Bruce Gehweiler calls itself an anthology series, but with three issues out in 1997 it looks to me like a magazine. There's no obvious reason for the title except that the magazine is produced in Marietta, Georgia. Each volume has three to four stories of dark fantasy, horror and science fiction. Pretty forgettable stories with a few exceptions.

Robert Bloch's Psychos edited by Robert Bloch (Pocket), long delayed (by the publisher and by the illness and death of Bloch) is the Horror Writer's Assocation's official anthology. I don't know how involved Bloch actually was in the selection process but the overall emphasis is unfortunately on the more obvious type of psychotic, with only a few stories that go into unexpected territory. One that definitely does is Gary Braunbeck's sad and terrifying story about mass murder, under a different title and in a different version in his collection, *Things Left Behind*. "Safe" (the *Psychos* version) is reprinted herein. A limited hardcover edition was published by CD Publications.

Urban Nightmares edited by Josepha Sherman and Keith R. A. DeCandido (Baen) is an amusingly nasty bunch of stories based on urban myths such as the spider in the hairdo, the hook, alligators in the sewers, and others.

Return to Lovecraft Country edited by Scott David Aniolowski is the first fiction project from Triad Entertainments and it's a pretty varied, mostly original anthology. But the cover art by H. E. Fassl and the design made me think it was a Chaosium book.

Chaosium continued its publication of Lovecraftian influenced anthologies with *Singers of Strange Songs: A Celebration of Brian Lumley*, eleven originals and reprints selected and introduced by Scott David Aniolowski with excellent cover art by H. E. Fassl and interior art by Allen Koszowski; *The Hastur Cycle*, introduced and with prefaces by series editor Robert M. Price, reprints thirteen tales by writers such as Ambrose Bierce, H. P. Lovecraft, Karl Edward Wagner, and Ramsey Campbell; *Bad Dreams* edited by Wendy Cooling (Dolphin, U.K.) is six original YA horror stories by authors including Ann Halam (Gwyneth Jones); *Spine Chillers* edited by Wendy Cooling (Dolphin, U.K.) is six original YA ghost stories; *Haunted Kansas: Ghost Stories and Other Eerie Tales* by Lisa Hefner Heitz (University Press of Kansas); *The Outer Limits, Volume 3* edited by Debbie Notkin (Prima/Proteus) is four stories, one reprint, three based on episodes of the original and new television series; *Bruce Coville's Book of Nightmares II* edited by Bruce Coville (Scholastic) is an illustrated YA anthology of eight originals and reprints by authors including Al Sarrantonio and Bruce Coville.

Mainstream, Sf, and Fantasy Anthologies with Some Dark Stories

Wild Women edited by Melissa Mia Hall (Carroll and Graf) features Lucy Taylor, Joyce Carol Oates, Lisa Tuttle, Pat Cadigan, Margaret Atwood, and others; *The Best of Interzone* edited by David Pringle (St. Martin's Press) collects stories published in the British magazine from 1990–1995; *Tesseracts 5* edited by Robert Runte and Yves Meynard (Tesseract Books 1996) gives an excellent cross-section of Canadian sf, fantasy, and horror writing; *The Year's Best Australian Science Fiction and Fantasy* edited by Jonathan Strahan and Jeremy G. Byrne (HarperCollins, Australia/Voyager) with an introduction by the editors discussing the history of Australian sf. Stephen Dedman's "Never Seen by Waking Eyes," reprinted in *The Year's Best Fantasy and Horror: Tenth Annual Collection* is included; *New Altars* edited by Dawn Albright and Sandra J. Hutchinson (Angelus Press) consists of nineteen sf/fantasy stories and two poems, most original, about spirituality and religion.

Reprint Anthologies

The Ash-Tree Press Annual Macabre 1997, edited by Jack Adrian, inaugurates a new series of hardcovers that will present stories by writers whose supernatural output is small, and those not generally associated with writing in the genre. The annual volumes will be published between Halloween and Christmas. The first volume's theme is weird stories by women writers, and reprints four obscure supernatural ghost stories by Patricia Wentworth, Jessie Douglas Kerruish, Carola Oman, and Molie Panter-Downes; *Selected Ghost Stories*, edited by Giles Gordon (Bloomsbury, U.K.) contains thirteen classic ghost stories; *The Best of Weird Tales: 1923*, edited by Marvin Kaye and John Gregory Betancourt (Wildside Press/Bleak House); *The Killing Spirit: An Anthology of Murder for Hire*, edited by Jay Hopler (The Overlook Press), has stories by T. Coraghessan Boyle, Patricia Highsmith, Joyce Carol Oates, Andrew Vachss, and Ian McEwan; *An Anthology of Scottish Fantastic Literature*, edited by Colin Manlove (Polygon), contains stories, verse, and extracts from novels and plays over the last one thousand years; Oxford University Press launched a new series of titles under the heading "Oxford Twelves." Each book combines "both familiar and rare stories, and [are] designed to appeal to the newcomer and enthusiast alike." The first two titles released are *Twelve Tales of the Supernatural*, edited by Michael Cox, which includes stories by Mrs. Riddell, A. N. L. Munby, and others, and *Twelve Victorian Ghost Stories* edited by Michael Cox, which includes stories by Vincent O'Sullivan, Amelia Edwards, Rhoda Broughton, and Margaret Oliphant, among others. Oxford University Press also published *The Vampyre and Other Tales of the Macabre* edited by Chris Baldick and Robert Morrison, with fourteen tales first published in London and Dublin magazines between 1819 and 1838 under its World Classics imprint; *Bodies of the Dead and Other Great American Ghost Stories* edited by David G. Hartwell (Tor) reprints thirteen classic literary ghost stories; *The Year's Finest Crime and Mystery Stories: Sixth Annual Edition* edited by Joan Hess, Ed Gorman, and Martin H. Greenberg (Carroll and Graf) didn't use anything outside of the genre magazines this time around, except for a *Playboy* story; *The Best American Mystery Stories 1997*, guest edited by Robert B. Parker (series editor Otto Penzler) (Houghton Mifflin), collects stories from a diverse group of writers including James Crumley, Elmore Leonard, Joyce Carol Oates, and Andrew Klavan; *Southern Blood: Vampire Stories from the American South* edited by Lawrence Schimel and Martin H. Greenburg (Cumberland House); *American Gothic* edited by Elizabeth Terry and Terri Hardin (B&N); *Vampires: The Greatest Stories* edited by Martin H. Greenberg (MJF Instant remainder); *Blood Lines: Vampire Stories From New England* edited by Lawrence Schimel and Martin H. Greenberg (Cumberland House) had one original story; *Sisters of Gore: Seven Gothic Melodramas by British Women, 1790–1843* edited by John Franceschina (Garland); *Classic Werewolf Stories* edited by Charlotte F. Otten (Lowell House Juvenile); *The Vintage Book of Ghosts* edited by Jenny Uglow (Vintage, U.K.) collects ghostly appearances from literature, myth, fable, and folktale, and excerpts from the Bible, A. S. Byatt, and William Hope Hodgson; *The Vintage Book of the Devil* edited by Francis Spufford (Vintage, U.K.) collects short excerpts from historical works about the nature, history, appearance, and habits of the titular personage; *The Nyarlathotep Cycle: Stories about the God of a Thousand Forms* selected and introduced by Robert M. Price series editor (Chaosium), includes sixteen stories and poems; *A Century of Horror 1870–1979* (MJF Books) is an anthology of twenty-one stories by Richard Matheson, Michael Bishop, Tanith Lee, and David Morrell, among others; *Grave Passions: Tales of the Gay Supernatural* edited by William J. Mann (Masquerade/BadBoy); *Weird Tales: Seven Decades of Terror* edited by John Betancourt and Robert Weinberg (B&N) reprints twenty-eight stories originally published in *Weird Tales* 1920–90, arranged in chronological order; *Girls' Night Out: Twenty-nine Female Vampire Stories* edited by Stefan R. Dziemianowicz, Robert E. Weinberg, and Martin H. Greenberg (B&N) reprints twenty-nine female vampire stories from E. F. Benson and Robert Bloch to K. W. Jeter and Pat Cadigan; *Haunted Houses: The Greatest Stories* edited by Martin H. Greenberg (MJF

Books); *One Hundred Fiendish Little Frightmares* edited by Stefan R. Dziemi-anowicz, Robert E. Weinberg, and Martin H. Greenberg (B&N); *Vampires, Wine and Roses* edited by John Richard Stephens (Berkley), an interesting mix of vampiric stories and excerpts ranging from the lyrics to "Moon Over Bourbon Street" by Sting and a story by F. Scott Fitzgerald, to excerpts from *Romeo and Juliet* by William Shakespeare and *The Wasteland* by T. S. Eliot, and a piece performed live by Lenny Bruce; *Blood Thirst: One Hundred Years of Vampire Fiction* edited by Leonard Wolf (Oxford University Press) does the same with an overlap of only two pieces, those by Anne Rice and Woody Allen; *The Best American Short Stories 1997* guest edited by E. Annie Proulx, series editor Katrina Kenison (Houghton Mifflin); *Murder and Other Acts of Literature* edited by Michele Slung (A Thomas Dunne Book/St. Martin's Press); *Restless Spirits: Ghost Stories by American Women, 1872–1926* edited with an introduction by Catherine A. Lundie (University of Massachusetts Press) collects twenty-two stories by well-known and little-known women of the period and, in an extensive introduction, discusses the differences of subject matter between them and their male counterparts; *The Mammoth Book of Best New Horror* edited by Stephen Jones (Robinson/C&G) reprinted twenty-four stories and novellas with remarkably little overlap with *The Year's Best Fantasy and Horror: Tenth Annual Collection*. Only one story is in both volumes. Jones does a recap of the year in horror and includes a necrology; *Razorblades* edited by Darren Floyd (RazorBlade Press, U.K.) selects stories from *Raw Nerve*, a Welsh magazine with which I'm unfamiliar. It contains stories by Tim Lebbon, Rhys Hughes, Stuart Hughes, and D. F. Lewis.

Magazines and Newletters

Note: Subscription prices are given for only those periodicals not readily found on newsstands.

As most small-press magazines do not come out on a regular schedule, and most fail after an average of about four issues, I'd advise readers to buy single issues where possible rather than subscribe.

The big difference between professional and nonprofessional magazines is that you would never read an editorial criticizing a rival in a professional magazine. Editors can complain all they want—in private—about how their magazine has not been nominated for this or that award and how a rival magazine isn't doing a very good job, etc. Save it for your friends if you want to be taken seriously.

Artists with notable work in magazines: Paul Swenson, Harry O. Morris, Kevin Kuder, Jay Brown, Jason Hurst, Mark McLaughlin, Augie Weidemann, Richard Dahlstrom, Piggy, Alan Casey, Sean Tan, Cathy Buburuz, Madeleine Finnegan, Rob Kiely, Dreyfus, Paul Mavrides, Alan M. Clark, H. E. Fassl, David Walters, Rodger Gerberding, Scott Eagle, Christine Boyka Kluge, Ian Brooks, J. K. Potter, Russell Morgan, GAK, D. L. Sproule, Lee Brown Coye, J. D. Garrison, W. Frazier Sandercombe, Douglas Walters, Charles Fallis, Tom Simonton, Don Wild, Gerard Gaubert, Richard Corben, Earl Geier, Kandis Elliot, Bob Crouch, Paul Lowe, Nick Maloret, Chris Whitlow, Eric Turnmire, Vera Nazarian, Daniel

Goods, Jim Burns, Steven Denton, Wendy Down, Mark Maxwell, Renate Muller, and Sam Dawson.

Tangent, edited by David A. Truesdale, is the only forum that reviews exclusively short fiction in the sf and fantasy field. *Tangent* also regularly runs (usually) astute criticism of short horror by Lillian Csernica, an unfailingly incendiary column about sf and fantasy by Paul Riddell (although Riddell has announced his "retirement" from criticism), along with interviews and genre news. A one-year subscription (four issues)is $20 (foreign, $28). Single issue: $5 (foreign, $7) payable to David A. Truesdale, 5779 Norfleet, Raytown, MO 64133. Recommended highly for anyone with an interest in short stories.

Horror edited by John B. Rosenman and Joe Morey is the horror field's equivalent of sf's *Locus*, although the magazine has not yet stuck to its quarterly schedule. The editors did manage to get out three issues in 1997 and promise to reach their goal in 1998. *Horror* is always chock full of interviews, market reports, reviews of magazines and books, and articles. The only down side is that even if it keeps to a quarterly schedule, much of the "news" is dated by the time of publication. Nonetheless, it is a must for the horror professional and readers interested in the field. A one-year subscription is $12 payable to Dark Regions Press, P.O. Box 6301, Concord, CA 94524.

DarkEcho edited by Paula Guran is a free weekly online newsletter of the horror field. A pioneer in this area, it's in its fourth year of publication. It covers news of the field in detail, but with a personal touch; e.g., describing Guran's experiences at BookExpoAmerica with an eye toward its importance to horror readers/publishers/writers. *DarkEcho* also publishes reviews, market reports, and news of the field. This is sent via e-mail and some of the material can also be found at her website. For information e-mail her at *Darkecho@aol.com*. Guran was nominated in 1997 for a World Fantasy Award in the Special Award—Non-Professional category for her work on *DarkEcho* newsletter and website.

Hellnotes edited by David B. Silva is a new weekly horror newsletter with interviews, news of the field, upcoming releases, and market reports. Available by subscription in print ($40), e-mail ($25), and fax ($49) versions payable by check or money order to David B. Silva, *Hellnotes*, 27780 Donkey Mine Road, Oak Run, CA 96069. For information e-mail him at *dbsilva@shasta.com*.

The Gila Queen's Guide to Markets edited by Kathryn Ptacek is the best, most reliable, and most professional-looking print market report around. Ptacek takes turns providing in-depth coverage of different genres and subgenres of fiction and nonfiction markets: children's markets, history and military, sf, fantasy, and horror, poetry, etc. There are also regular advice columns by Nancy Holder and others. It's published about every six weeks and costs $34 for a twelve-issue subscription payable to Kathryn Ptacek, P.O. Box 97, Newton, NJ 07860-0097.

Scavenger's Newsletter edited by Janet Fox is a monthly marketing newsletter for sf/fantasy/mystery/horror writers and artists interested in the small press. This is the oldest of the monthly newsletters. $21 (first class) or $17 (bulk rate) for a one-year subscription payable to Janet Fox, 519 Ellinwood, Osage City, KS 66523-1329.

Heliocentric Network edited by Lisa Bothell is an informative bimonthly newsletter for clients of the independent press. It contains market reports, news of the genre, mini-reviews, and advice on workshops though it sometimes goes overboard in the design department. Three dollars for a sample, $18 a year (six issues) payable to Lisa Bothell, 17650 1st Avenue South, Box 291, Seattle, WA 98148.

The Genre Writer's Newsletter edited by Bobbi Sinha-Morey is published bi-annually by the Genre Writer's Association. U.S. dues are $25 a year, payable to Dark Regions Press and addressed to the Genre Writer's Assocation, c/o Bobbi Sinha-Morey, PO Box 6301, Concord, CA 94524.

Severed Head: The Journal of the Australian Horror Writers edited by Aaron Stern was an invaluable source of information: news, market reports, articles, etc. on the state of horror in Australia and in general. The quarterly, available free to Australian Horror Writers members, has unfortunately ceased publication.

Necrofile is the only American critical magazine specializing in horror literature. Anyone interested in the field should subscribe to it. It is published by Necronomicon Press. Other publications from Necronomicon Press include *Cthulhu Codex* and *Midnight Shambler*, both edited by Robert M. Price, and both specialize in publishing original fiction based on Lovecraft's mythos. Although these quarterlies are mostly filled with lightweight (but fun) pastiches, something serious occasionally shows up. They're each $4.50 per issue. *Lovecraft Studies* edited by S. T. Joshi offers a serious forum for the study of Lovecraft's life and work. This biannual generally features articles, essays, reviews, and occasionally letters and news items about what's happening in "the Lovecraft world." Subscriptions are $12 a year. Address at the end of this essay. *The New Lovecraft Collector* is a quarterly newsletter devoted to informing subscribers about new and recent Lovecraft publications, films, and other miscellaneous items pertaining to Lovecraft. One year subscription $5. *Studies in Weird Fiction* edited by S. T. Joshi is a biannual journal designed to promote criticism of fantasy, horror, and supernatural fiction since Poe. Each issue features a number of essays, reviews, and brief notes covering recent offerings in the genre. $12 a year. All payable to Necronomicon Press. *Crypt of Cthulhu*, a quarterly edited by Robert M. Price, publishes fiction and nonfiction on Lovecraft and Lovecraftian themes. Also, the Cryptic Publications imprint has been revived by Robert M. Price and is being distributed by Necronomicon Press. *Tales of Lovecraftian Horror* came out quarterly in 1997. Address at the end of this essay.

Gauntlet: Exploring the Limits of Free Expression edited by Barry Hoffman is the only magazine exclusively devoted to this important issue and as such is worthy of your support. Semiannual, for $18 a year, payable to *Gauntlet*. Address at the end of this essay.

Mystery Scene edited by Ed Gorman is more for the mystery enthusiast than the horror reader but there's occasional overlap for those who enjoy dark suspense. This bimonthly provides news, interviews (with Patricia Cornwell and Tony Hillerman, among others), reviews, and regular columns by authors on the writing of their books.

Nova Express edited by Lawrence Person is a lively, irregularly published semi-pro 'zine out of Austin, Texas, that always has something interesting to say about horror, although it mostly covers fantasy and sf. The one issue I saw in 1997 had interviews with Bradley Denton and William Browning Spencer and lots of reviews of all kinds of books. $12 (four issues) payable to P.O. Box 27231, Austin, TX 78755-2231.

Video Watchdog edited by Tim Lucas is a bimonthly dedicated to meticulously detailing alternate versions of videos from their original commercial release and other video/laser disc versions. Its fascinating attention to detail makes it fun to read even if you haven't seen the actual movie. It has nice layouts with good reproduction of b&w movie stills. Lucas covers *everything*.

Psychotronic Video edited by Michael J. Weldon continues to entertain quarterly with its brief descriptions of hundreds of horror and exploitation movies, its reviews, and its necrology. It also contains profiles and interviews with people like director/producer Monte Hellman and Ernie Anderson, who played the character Ghoulardi, a popular horror host in the mid-1960s.

Scarlet Street edited by Richard Valley is a glossy quarterly with articles about and reviews of classic mystery, sf, and horror films. It often has excellent interviews (for instance, one with Patricia Neal about *The Day the Earth Stood Still*—she thought it hysterically funny and could barely keep from laughing throughout—and other films she's made over the years).

Fangoria edited by Anthony Timpone comes out ten times a year and is for the younger set. It concentrates on the contemporary, large studio-produced horror film with lots of splashy (and often gory) photographs of special effects.

Bare Bones edited by Peter Enfantino and John Scoleri snuck in to make the deadline with its December debut. The new quarterly is the reincarnation of the much-missed *The Scream Factory*. The 48-page digest-sized nonfiction magazine specializes in "unearthing vintage and forgotten horror/mystery/sci-fi/weird paperbacks-film-pulp-fiction-video." Check it out for $4.50 (single issue ppd) or take a chance at $15 (four issues) payable to Bare Bones, PO Box 2808, Apache Junction, AZ 85217.

The Magazine of Fantasy and Science Fiction, with a new editor, Gordon Van Gelder, was responsible for some very good short dark fiction during 1997, much of it probably from the inventory left by former editor Kristine Kathryn Rusch. Van Gelder has hired an excellent group of reviewers to alternate: Elizabeth Hand, Douglas E. Winter, Robert K. J. Killheffer, and Michelle West. (Gordon is Terri Windling's and my editor at St. Martin's Press for this volume.)

Interzone edited by David Pringle is the major science fiction monthly in the U.K., occasionally publishing sf/horror, or even just "horror." It often showcases new talent and is always literate. IZ also publishes several regular review columns by John Clute, Paul McAuley, Gwyneth Jones, and other notables in the field. *Interzone* has published first or early stories by Americans Richard Kadrey, Michael Blumlein, and Scott Bradfield. It is worthy of your support. $60 payable to *Interzone*, 217 Preston Drive, Brighton BN1 6FL, U.K. Molly Brown's "The Psychomantium" is reprinted herein.

Cemetery Dance edited by Richard Chizmar is the closest thing we have to a professional horror fiction magazine so it deserves your support. *CD* is slowly getting back onto its quarterly schedule. The fiction is always readable and often quite good, and there's a good mix of generally fine and/or provocative columns by Charles Grant, Bob Morrish, Poppy Z. Brite, and Tom Monteleone. Ed Bryant, Bill Sheehan, and other reviewers take on all kinds of horror-related material. It's well worth the $15 for a one-year subscription (four issues) payable to CD Publications. Address at the end of this essay.

The Third Alternative edited by Andy Cox has instituted the policy of having one artist illustrate an entire issue, giving each issue a lovely continuity. This quarterly is looking better and better with a strong, simple, readable design and format, excellent art, and really good short fiction. Issue 11 had a profile of Geoff Ryman and an interview with Chris Kenworthy. Issue 12 discusses the horror of Ian McEwan. Issue 13 had pieces on J. G. Ballard, Russell Hoban, and Patrick McGrath. All four issues are excellent. A year's subscription is $22, payable to TTA Press, 5 Martins Lane, Witcham, Ely, Cambs CB6 2LB, U.K.

Lore edited by Rod Heather missed its schedule and the magazine's first 1997 issue was delayed until the summer. The quality of issue #7 made the wait worth it with some very nicely written traditional horror. Four dollars per single issue or $15 for a four-issue subscription payable to Rod Heather, P.O. Box 381, Matawan, NJ 07747-0381.

Tales of the Unanticipated edited by Eric M. Heideman is a consistently entertaining mix of fiction. Only occasionally are there stories that could be called horror but those few are usually very good. Sponsored by the Minnesota Science Fiction Society, the magazine has relied on money raised at Minicon. Unfortunately, because of a shortfall, the schedule will be changing (temporarily, I hope) from about every eight months to an annual. It's a worthy magazine to support. The cost is $15 payable to *Tales of the Unanticipated*, Box 8036, Lake Street Station, Minneapolis, MN 55408.

The Urbanite: Surreal and Lively and Bizarre edited by Mark McLaughlin is exactly what's advertised, and sometimes there's even horror in it. With its clean and inviting design, the magazine is always worth a look. Five dollars for a single issue and $13.50 for a three-issue subscription payable to Urban Legend Press, P.O. Box 4737, Davenport, IA 52808.

Talebones: A Magazine of Science Fiction and Dark Fantasy edited by Patrick and Honna Swenson has readable type, and attractive and readable design. All four issues were very good and there was a smattering of horror throughout the year. A one-year subscription (four issues) costs $16 (add $1 per issue, Canada; $2 per issue, elsewhere) payable to *Talebones*, 10531 SE 250th Place #104, Kent, WA 98031.

Midnight Graffiti returned with a winter/spring 1997 issue. This erratically published magazine always looks good and this issue is no exception, with an H. R. Giger cover and visually attractive and readable interior layouts, excellent reviews, news section, and an exceptional interview with Neil Gaiman. Only the fiction falls short—three stories: one an unreadable experiment, one a reprint, and one entertaining but slight piece. Jessie Horsting is the editor. Per issue, $5.95+$3.00 postage payable to *Midnight Graffiti*, 22469 Domingo Road, Woodland Hills, CA 91364.

All Hallows: The Journal of the Ghost Story Society edited by Christopher and Barbara Roden is a *must* for anyone interested in the ghost story. It is published thrice-yearly in February, June, and October for members of the Ghost Story Society. The journal contains news, essays, reviews, and fiction relating to the ghost story. Highly recommended. Membership to the society is $23 payable to The Ghost Story Society, P.O. Box 1360, Ashcroft, British Columbia, Canada VOK 1AO. For more information contact the editors via e-mail: *ashtree@ mail.netshop.net*.

Ghosts and Scholars 23 edited by Rosemary Pardoe is an exceptionally good issue with excellent fiction choices. This is *the* publication for news and criticism of M. R. Jamesian–type horror and dark fantasy. The U.S. agent is Richard Fawcett, 61 Teecomwas Drive, Uncasville, CT 06382.

Peeping Tom edited by Stuart Hughes usually has an excellent selection of original and reprinted (although rarely credited) horror fiction. It's one of the consistently best horror magazines around. Issue 28 was particularly good. A four-issue subscription to this quarterly is £8, payable to *Peeping Tom*, Yew Tree House, 15 Nottingham Road, Ashby de la Zouche, Leicestershire LE65 1DJ, U.K.

Funeral Party edited by Shade Rupe is a beautiful-looking perfect-bound magazine about death, sex, and putrification (often combined). If you like to look at and read about these things in an elegant design, then this might be your cup of tea. It contains original fiction by Lucy Taylor, John Shirley, Rob Hardin, Jack Ketchum, and others.

Space and Time edited by Gordon Linzer came out with its thirtieth-anniversary issue, and an excellent one it was. The magazine has gotten progressively better and more professional-looking over the years, and biannually provides readers with a variety of sf, fantasy, and horror. A single issue is $5 + $1.50 handing charge. Subscriptions are 2/$10 payable to *Space and Time Magazine*, 138 W. 70th Street 4B, New York, NY 10023-4468.

Wetbones edited by Paula Guran is the new incarnation of the short-lived (one issue) *Bones* that debuted last November. Two issues came out in 1997. It's got excellent b&w illustrations, a good mix of dark fiction columns by John Shirley and Phil Nutman, film, music, and book reviews. Single issue: $4; three-issue subscription: $12 (add $1 Canadian; $2 overseas) payable by check or money order to DarkEcho, P.O. Box 5410, Akron, OH 44334.

Pirate Writings edited by Edward J. McFadden publishes a mix of fantasy, horror, sf stories, and poetry. The magazine regularly publishes interviews and reviews and a column on the weird and unexplainable. The format is readable and the layout attractive, but most of the art is awful. $15 for one year (four issues) payable to Pirate Writings Publishing, P.O. Box 329, Brightwaters, NY 11718-0329.

Not One of Us edited by John Benson has been a staple of the small press for several years now, publishing semiannually. Benson also publishes a one-off each year. A single issue is $4.50 ppd and a three-issue subscription is $10.50 payable to John Benson, 12 Curtis Road, Natick, MA 01760.

Psychotrope edited by Mark Beech has some good fiction, but has more of the surreal than horror this time around. A four-issue subscription is $20 payable to Psychotrope, Flat 6, Droitwich Road, Worcester, WR3 7LG, U.K.

Aurealis, with *Eidolon*, are the major sf/fantasy magazines in Australia. They publish horror only occasionally. *Aurealis* is edited by Dirk Strasser and Stephen Higgins. There were a few good dark stories in issue 18. Subscriptions are available only in Australian dollars or by credit card: Chimaera Publications, P.O. Box

2164, Mt. Waverley VIC 3149 Australia. *Eidolon: The Journal of Australian Science Fiction and Fantasy* edited by Richard Scriven, Jonathan Strahan, and Jeremy G. Byrne didn't publish much horror in 1997 except in the late issue 25/26, which will be considered for 1998.

Back Brain Recluse Number 23 edited by Chris Reed is one of a handful of mixed-genre magazines that publish excellent stories of all types. Some of its design is beautiful and some is just terrible. Two stories, in fact, are so over-designed as to make them unreadable, doing a grave injustice to the contributors and the readers. *BBR* can be ordered through the New SF Alliance. See address at the end of this essay.

The Silver Web edited by Ann Kennedy is a semiannual magazine that mixes sf, fantasy, and horror fiction and is always beautifully and carefully designed. Issue #14 has an extraordinarily revealing and tortured interview with artist Rodger Gerberding by Poppy Z. Brite and another good one with Jonathan Carroll. It contains smart, opinionated reviews by Cliff Burns and, as usual, good fiction. Two issues are $12 payable to BuzzCity Press, PO 38190, Tallahassee, FL 32315.

Weirdbook 30/Whispers combines two small press magazines important to the world of horror and dark fantasy into one final magazine. *Weirdbook* edited by W. Paul Ganley has published "weird" fiction in the tradition of the old *Weird Tales*, and this issue contains stories by the modern purveyors of such work— Jessica Amanda Salmonson, Darrell Schweitzer, and Brian McNaughton, among others. Ganley, in ill health, intends to terminate his publishing activities "in an orderly fashion" before he can no longer do so. *Whispers* edited by Stuart David Schiff was started in 1973 and specialized in dark fantasy. In this final issue Schiff presents the best of the twenty or so stories left in his inventory, including what may be the last story sold by Joseph Payne Brennan before he died, and stories by the late Avram Davidson, Hugh Cave, David Drake, Chet Williamson, and Ken Wisman. Both magazines will be sorely missed.

Tomorrow Speculative Fiction edited by A. J. Budrys printed its last issue (#24) and went on the web exclusively. Although mostly sf and fantasy, there's the occasional odd—and very good—horror story. *www.Tomorrowsf.com*, $23 for six issues.

Realms of Fantasy edited by Shawna McCarthy is a glossy bimonthly that, although better known for its fantasy, occasionally throws some excellent dark fantasy into the mix.

Albedo One (no editorial credit) is one of the few genre magazines from Ireland. I just began receiving it in 1997 and its mixture of sf, fantasy, and horror is worth a look. Irregularly published ("future issues of *Albedo One* are to be expected when you see them"), a subscription of four issues is $30 airmail to the U.S., payable to *Albedo One*, 2 Post Road, Lusk, Co. Dublin, Ireland.

Nasty Piece of Work edited by David A. Green is a cleanly designed little horror magazine with generally good illustrative work inside and a reasonable mix of the disgusting and illuminating. As the year went by, the quality of the fiction seemed to improve. A single copy is $4 and four issues are $15 payable to David A. Green, P.O. 20 Drum Mead, Petersfield, Hants GU32 3AQ, U.K.

Odyssey is a new magazine out of the U.K. edited by Liz Holliday. The first two issues look terrific, with sharp covers by Jim Burns and newcomer Daniel

Woods, slick paper, interviews and lots of nf and fiction. It contains a wee bit of dark fiction. Five issue subscriptions $35 payable to Partizan Press, 816-818, Leigh-on-Sea, Essex SS9 3NH, U.K.

Nonfiction Film Books

Weirdsville USA: The Obsessive Universe of David Lynch by Paul A. Woods (Plexus) is a must for anyone intrigued by the beautiful grotesqueries of *Eraserhead, Blue Velvet, Twin Peaks,* and *The Elephant Man.* Woods combines biographical information, work habits, and explication of Lynch's movies from his early student films through *Lost Highway.* It contains b&w stills throughout plus filmography; *Lost Highway* by David Lynch and Barry Gifford opens with a short interview by Chris Rodley about the genesis of the movie (Lynch had a dream with some of the opening images) and the process of collaborating with Barry Gifford on the screenplay. The rest of the book is the screenplay; also, *Lynch on Lynch* edited by Chris Rodley (both books from Faber and Faber U.K.) is an in-depth look at Lynch's movies, his continuing interest in photography and painting, and his musical collaborations—through interviews and interstitial material by Rodley.

Mondo Macabre: Weird and Wonderful Cinema Around the World by Pete Tombs (Titan Book/St. Martin's Press) is a profusely illustrated oversized paperback (in teeny-tiny type) of some really bad movies from Mexico, Argentina, Hong Kong, the Philippines, Turkey, Indonesia, and other exotic lands; *Bizarre Sinema!: Horror all'italiana 1957–1979* by Antonio Bruschini (Glittering Images) is about Italian cult movies and has a foreword by Barbara Steele; *Boris Karloff* edited by Gary and Susan Svehla (Midnight Marquee) provides analyses and b&w photographs of thirty-three films that helped make Karloff famous; *Tall, Dark, and Gruesome* by Christopher Lee (Victor Gollancz, U.K.) is a memoir with sixteen pages of pictures; *Dracula: The First Hundred Years* edited by Bob Madison (Midnight Marquee) is a collection of essays and photographs exploring the myth of Dracula in film and popular culture. It includes pieces by author Chelsea Quinn Yarbro, directors John Badham and John Landis, and actor Nicolas Cage; *Musclemen and Scream Queens: An A–Z of Exploitation Stars* by Philippe Rege (Titan, U.K.); *Aliens: The Special Effects* by Don Shay and Bill Norton (Titan, U.K.); *The Hammer Story* by Alan Barnes and Marcus Hearn (Titan); *Paul Blaisdell* by Randy Palmer (McFarland); *Lucio Fulci Beyond the Gates* by Chas. Balun (Blackest Heart); *Lugosi* by Gary Don Rhodes (McFarland); *Burton on Burton* edited by Mark Salisbury (Faber and Faber, U.K.) allows the visionary creator of *Beetlejuice, Edward Scissorhands,* and *Ed Wood* to discuss his work. It includes b&w photos, illustrations, and cartoons by Burton and a foreword by Johnny Depp; *Vamps* by Pam Keesey (Cleis) is a book on the femme fatale in film from Theda Bara to Sharon Stone. It contains illustrations and filmography, videography, and an index; *The Men Who Made the Monsters* by Paul M. Jensen (Twayne Publishers) is a detailed chronicle of the careers of five movie directors and special-effects men who specialized in making horror movies: James Whale, Willis O'Brien, Ray Harryhausen, Terence Fisher, and Freddie Francis. Extensive bibliographies and filmographies of each man are included. An accessible, enjoyable read; *The Films of Peter Greenaway* by Amy

Lawrence (Cambridge University Press) covers this distinctive director's work between 1980 and 1989, beginning with the mock-documentary *The Falls*—just as he was being noticed by the public at large—up through *Prospero's Book* (although not in chronological order). In the introduction, the author briefly covers Greenaway's short films. There are illustrations and photographs throughout; *Fritz Lang: The Nature of the Beast* by Patrick McGilligan (St. Martin's Press) is a biography of the director of such classics as *M*, *Dr. Mabuse*, and *Metropolis*.

Nonfiction Books

Nightmare on Main Street: Angels, Sadomasochism, and the Culture of the Gothic by Mark Edmundson (Harvard University Press) is exactly the kind of academic hogwash that readers of horror fear. The author firmly lays the blame for everything wrong with contemporary society on an increased interest in horror and the gothic. He argues that the public's so-called embrace of such true-life gothic "romances" as O. J. Simpson, Lorena Bobbitt, the repressed memory syndrome of purportedly abused adults, etc., is symptomatic of a depressed, neurotic, self-hating society (that part I might not argue with). Edmundson's assertion that the 1990s have seen a boom in horror film and fiction (using Anne Rice, Stephen King, and R. L. Stine as his only examples in the literary area) shows the author's ignorance of the field he's condemning to carry some very heavy baggage.

Blood Read: The Vampire as Metaphor in Contemporary Culture edited by Joan Gordon and Veronica Hollander (University of Pennsylvania Press) is a splash of fresh water after the above trashing of the genre. This absorbing and accessible book of essays explores the "domestication" of the vampire in literature and cinema—that is, its transformation from the monstrous outsider to a creature with which we can often empathize, if not sympathize. The essays are by scholars and three writers of vampire fiction: Brian Stableford, Suzy McKee Charnas, and Jewell Gomez.

Gothic: Transmutations of Horror in Late-Twentieth Century Art edited by Christoph Grunenberg (The MIT Press/The Institute of Contemporary Art, Boston) is a really interesting companion volume to an exhibition of twenty-three artists including Cindy Sherman, Alexis Rockman, and others who produce horror. It includes essays by Joyce Carol Oates and Patrick McGrath on the gothic in literature and a story by Dennis Cooper. It is profusely illustrated with photographs, fine art, etc.

Blood and Volts: Edison, Tesla, and the Electric Chair by Thomas Metzger (Autonomedia) is a fast, entertaining read about the rivalry between Edison and Tesla to dominate the technological future of the U.S. with different types of electrical current, and concurrently, the development of the electric chair. Metzger embroiders the facts, creating a wonderfully evocative account of the era, but I wouldn't mistake him for a historian.

Clive Barker's A–Z of Horror, compiled by Stephen Jones (BBC Books, U.K./HarperPrism), is the companion volume to the BBC television series of the same name, with commentary and illustrations by Clive Barker. It begins with "American Psycho"—devoted to the true story, with sidebars about fictional interpretations, of serial cannibal Ed Gein—and ends with Zombies. Although mostly a book about movies, there's a generous sprinkling of quotes from authorial luminaries of the field and from related works of literature.

Holy Terrors: Gargoyles on Medieval Buildings, by Janetta Rebold Benton (Abbeville Press) presents colorful photographs of gargoyles, accompanied by an intelligent and lively text by an art historian who obviously is a great admirer of these fantastical/grotesque, but utilitarian, waterspouts. The text places the artistry and creation of gargoyles into the context of medieval life. Also included is a guide to gargoyle sites throughout western Europe.

Kinky Cats, Immortal Amoebas, and Nine-Armed Octopuses by Raymond Obstfeld (HarperPerennial) is a fascinating exploration of kinky animal courtship rites, domestic abuse, homosexuality, incest, sex changes, etc.—in the animal world.

Nonfiction Book Listings

Cannibals: The Discovery and Representation of the Cannibal from Columbus to Jules Verne by Frank Lestringant, translated by Rosemary Morris (University of California Press); *Victorian Ghosts in the Noontide: Women Writers and the Supernatural* by Vanessa D. Dickerson (University of Missouri Press); *The Complete Book of Spells, Curses and Magical Recipes* by Leonard R. N. Ashley (Barricade); *The Grim Reader* edited by Maura Siegel and Richard Tristman (Anchor), an anthology about death and dying with contributions by Sigmund Freud, Bertolt Brecht, Colette, Monty Python, and others; *Dracula: The Connoisseur's Guide* by Leonard Wolf (Broadway) covers—in text and illustration—Gothic literature, precursors to Stoker and Stoker's life and works, and stage and screen adaptations of the novel; *The Anne Rice Reader* by Katherine Ramsland (Ballantine) collects entries by scholars, journalists, and fans and includes two previously uncollected short stories by Rice; *In the Shadow of the Vampire: Exploring the World of Anne Rice* by Jana Marcus (Thunder's Mouth Press) with text and photographs by Jana Marcus and an introduction by Katherine Ramsland; *Final Exposure: Portraits from Death Row* edited by Michael Radelet (Northeastern University) successfully brings together photographs by Lou Jones and interviews by Jones and Lori Savel that are meant to show that "even the worst criminals are human"; *The Dark Fantastic: Selected Essays from the Ninth International Conference of the Fantastic in the Arts* edited by C. W. Sullivan (Greenwood Press) is a critical anthology of twenty-one essays on dark themes in sf and fantasy selected from presentations made at the 1988 IAFA; *Grave Matters: A Lively Look at the Ways People Around the World Confront Death* by Nigel Barley (Henry Holt/A John Macrae Book); *The Salem Witchcraft Trials: A Legal History* by Peter Charles Hoffer (University Press of Kansas); *Field Guide to Mysterious Places of the Pacific Coast* by Salvatore M. Trento (Owl/Henry Holt); *The Passion of David Lynch: Wild at Heart in Hollywood* by Martha P. Nochimson (University of Texas); *Prisoner 1167: The Madman Who Was Jack the Ripper* by J. C. H. Tully (Carroll and Graf); *Fangoria: Masters of the Dark: Stephen King and Clive Barker* edited by Anthony Timpone (HarperPrism) collects interviews from the magazine *Fangoria; I Have Lived in the Monster* by Robert K. Ressler with Tom Shachtman (St. Martin's Press) chronicles serial killer hunter/profiler Ressler's career since he left the FBI; *An Evil Love* by Geoffrey Wansell (Headline, U.K.) is a biography of serial killer Frederick West; *Mosig at Last: A Psychologist Looks at H. P. Lovecraft* by Yozan Dirk W. Mosig (Necronomicon Press) is a collection of essays examining Lovecraft and his work; *Dean Koontz: A Writer's Biography* by Katherine Ramsland (HarperPrism); *Writing Horror: A Handbook by the Horror Writers of America* edited by Mort Castle (Writer's Digest); *Killer Cults* by Brian Lane (Headline, UK) is illustrated; *Anne Rice: A Critical Companion* by Jennifer Smith (Greenwood Press) is a critical guide of Rice's nonerotic supernatural fiction; *Dracula: Authoritative Text, Contexts, Reviews and Reactions, Dramatic and Film Variations, Criticism* edited by Nina Auerbach and David J. Skal (W. W. Norton) is an annotated critical edition of Bram Stoker's classic vampire story, gathering critical essays and reviews; *A Subtler Magick: The Writings and Philosophy of H. P. Lovecraft* by S. T. Joshi (Borgo Press) is the second edition of a critical guide to the works of Lovecraft, completely revised and expanded from the 1983 edition published by Starmont House; *Running from the Hunter: The Life and Works of Charles Beaumont* by Lee Prosser (Borgo Press); *Seven by Seven* by Neal Wilgus (Borgo Press) collects seven interviews (most dated from the early 1980s) with American sf/fantasy/horror writers of the West and Southwest, including Suzy McKee Charnas and Fred Saberhagen; *Corpses, Coffins, and Crypts* by Penny Colman (Library Guild) is a children's book about the history and purpose of traditions surrounding death, funerals, embalming, etc.; *Death Investigation: The Basics* by Brad Randall, M.D. (Galen) is a textbook for forensic pathologists; *The X-Files Book of the Unexplained Volume II* by Jane Goldman (HarperPrism); *Gods of Death* by Yaron Svoray with Thomas Hughes (Simon and Schuster) is a supposedly factual account of the investigations of an Israel journalist into the "Ultra-secret business of sex and death," a.k.a. the snuff film. It reads like fiction, and in such a cocky, action-oriented fashion that it seems utterly untrustworthy. However, the conclusion seems to be that the author never did find evidence of a "snuff film" industry; *Monsters in the Closet: Homosexuality and the Horror Film* by Harry Benshoff (Manchester University, U.K.) examines the historical figure of the movie monster in relation to medical, psychological, religious, and social models of homosexuality; *Offbeat Museums* by Saul Rubin (Santa Monica) covers everything from the Museum of Questionable Medical Devices to the Museum of Menstruation; *In a Desert Garden: Love and Death among the Insects* by John Alcock (W. W. Norton) is a serious bug book by a professor of zoology at Arizona State University who loves what he finds in his backyard; *Happily Ever After: Fairy Tales, Children, and the Culture Industry* by Jack Zipes (Routledge) is a collection of essays about fairy tales, including their relationship to the Disney films made from some of them. Zipes is *the* contemporary expert on fairy tales; *The Shadow Below* by Hugh Edwards (HarperCollins, Australia) is a totally absorbing and personal book about sharks by an Australian marine photographer who has been involved with them for more than forty years; *Dark Thoughts: On Writing* by Stanley Wiater (Underwood Books) collects fifty interviews that were originally published in *Dark Dreamers: Conversations with the Masters of Horror*, *Dark Visions: Conversations with the Masters of the Horror Film*, and *Comic Book Rebels: Conversations with the Creators of the New Comics* (the last coauthored with Stephen R. Bissette) plus some new material; *Dancing with the Dark* edited by Stephen Jones (Vista/Cassell, U.K.) collects true stories and opinions of the paranormal by writers such as Ramsey Campbell, Stephen King, Clive Barker, Vincent Price, Anne McCaffrey, Arthur Machen, Richard Matheson, et al.; and *The Body Emblazoned* by Jonathan Sawday (Routledge), tracing the culture of dissection in the English Renaissance, is dense and serious and not really for the casual reader.

Children's Books

When Chickens Grow Teeth retold from the French of Guy de Maupassant by Wendy Anderson Halperin (Orchard Books) is a good-natured tale of a big, jolly café keeper with a skinny, sour wife who raises chickens. When the husband is bedridden after a fall, Madame forces him to hatch eggs under his arms. Not dark, but a prettily illustrated book.

The Day I Swapped My Dad for Two Goldfish written by Neil Gaiman and illustrated by Dave McKean (White Wolf) is a charming book for children or adults. Dad sits behind a newspaper and isn't all that interesting, so when a friend brings a pet goldfish to visit, the unnamed narrator happily offers to swap his dad. Unfortunately, mom is a bit less happy when she gets home to discover her husband gone so she sends the boy and his sister to get their dad back. This book amply demonstrates that the creative team behind the brilliant graphic novels *Violent Cases* and *Mr. Punch* are equally at ease with children's books.

To Market to Market by Anne Miranda, illustrated by Janet Stevens (Harcourt, Brace and Company) is a silly and sweet illustrated rendition of the popular children's rhyme showing a fat pig draped over a hapless shopper's cart, a duck seated on her head, and quite a menagerie once she gets them all home.

Edward Lear's Nonsense Songs illustrated by Bea Willey (McElderry Books) gives colorful interpretation to "The Owl and the Pussycat," "The Jumblies," "The Pobble Who Has No Toes," and others to excellent effect. A must for children and collectors of illustrated books and Lear's work.

The Brave Little Tailor by Jacob and Wilhelm Grimm, pictures by Sergei Goloshapov (North-South Books) is basically a tale of deception and broken promises. You know it: a tailor kills seven flies then boasts that he "killed seven in one blow." This boast brings him trouble and adventures (he *is* clever) until the king of the land notices him and promises half his kingdom and a daughter if the tailor succeeds at certain tasks. The tailor does, the king and his daughter go back on their word until outwitted by the tailor once again. The illustrations are eye-popping but is this really the story you want your kids to learn from?

William Wegman's Farm Days (Hyperion) is the newest installment of the series by photographer Wegman and his weimaraners in which the dogs play dress-up and are given human hands to very odd effect. Perfect for kids.

Why Lapin's Ears Are Long and Other Tales from the Louisiana Bayou adapted by Sharon Arms Doucet and illustrated by David Catrow (Orchard Books) is a collection of three stories about Lapin, a rabbit trickster character. This is a fine rendition of the folktales with a very goofy-looking Lapin doing his thing.

The Five Fingers and the Moon by Kemal Kurt and illustrated by Aljoscha Blau (North-South Books) is a clever tale about the land of Elsewhere and how its rulers solve a problem—the moon has suddenly stopped moving in the sky.

Mr. Semolina-Semolinus is a Greek folktale retold by Anthony L. Manna and Christodoula Mitakidou and illustrated by Giselle Potter (Atheneum). A hard-to-please princess creates her own beautiful and kind man and he is immediately stolen away by an evil queen (hey, why shouldn't she want the perfect man too?). Anyway, the princess searches all over the world for her guy. Very much in the format of a traditional western fairy tale with odd-looking humans with sticklike limbs. Very nice; perfect for the kiddies.

Noah's Ark adapted by Heinz Janisch and illustrated by Lizbeth Zwerger (A Michael Neugebauer Book/North-South Books) was first published in Switzerland. The English translation is utterly straightforward—and flat. This is Zwerger's showcase (her last book was last year's recommended *The Wizard of Oz*). Noah wears an odd-looking high hat, and the animals are drawn with the precision of a naturalist. But here and there are those who were left behind, proving that Noah didn't take *all* the animals.

Cinderhazel: The Cinderella of Halloween by Deborah Nourse Lattimore (Blue Sky/Scholastic) is a winner—illustrated wittily and retold with spirit, this is *not* a Cinderella that mama would approve of: she's a witch, and she loves dirt. But the only important thing here is how does she win her Prince Alarming? Read this to kids (if you're too embarrassed to read it to yourself) and find out.

The Bootmaker and the Elves by Susan Lowell with pictures by Tom Curry (Orchard Books) is the classic fairy tale transported with verve to the American West. Cowboy boots is what we got here—beeyootiful ones of lizard and leather and all different colors (I can certainly appreciate them, as I've got my own collection)—made for a "rootin' tootin' cowboy from the back of beyond," a rodeo queen, and other assorted customers.

A Noteworthy Tale by Brenda Mutchnick and Ron Casden and illustrated by Ian Penney (Abrams) is a sweet book about two worlds: one with music named Rhapsody and one without named Slurr. The story is nothing special but the illustrations are colorful, and detailed with lots of musical details.

There Was an Old Lady Who Swallowed a Fly by Simms Taback (Viking Press) makes an old folk rhyme fresh by using the fun device of showing everything in the old lady's tummy, getting awfully crowded in there. Kids will love it and so will their parents as Taback, with mixed media and collage, creates twenty-three different kinds of flies on the back cover, and numerous birds and dogs inside.

The Emperor's New Clothes by Hans Christian Andersen, translated by Naomi Lewis, is given new life by the colorful and witty illustrations of Angela Barrett (Candlewick Press), shifted from the mid-nineteenth century of the original to 1913, a time of early motor cars, biplanes and sumptuousness among the many kingdoms of the world.

The Viewer by Gary Crew, designed and with illustrations by Shaun Tan (Lothian-Australia), is an eerie collaboration about a teenager who finds a box crammed full of treasures. The best treasure of all is what seems to be a viewmaster with three discs. The boy is drawn deeper and deeper into their mysteries by his curiosity.

Velcome written and illustrated by Kevin O'Malley (Walker and Company) is a very silly book of scary stories for children told by an ugly little man with bad taste and a lousy sense of humor, continually undermined by his dog.

The Reptile Ball by Jacqueline K. Ogburn with pictures by John O'Brien (Dial

Books for Young Readers) is a delightfully poetic tale of various types of reptiles and amphibians attending a gala with loads of dancing (the horned toad two-step and the alligator stomp) and yummy food (gizzard gumbo with octopus hearts).

A Ring of Tricksters: Animal Tales from America, the West Indies, and Africa retold by Virginia Hamilton and illustrated by Barry Moser (Blue Sky/Scholastic). Moser's sense of humor shows through his watercolors and helps provide the perfect visual complement to tales about Bruh Rabby and Bruh Gator, Anansi the spider, and Cunnie Rabbit (who is in fact a small gazelle, not a rabbit).

Raising the Dead by Daniel Cohen (Cobblehills/Dutton) is the perfect way to introduce children to the macabre in real life, in literature, and in the movies. The first nine chapters are about the Frankenstein monster, zombies, walking mummies, grave robbers, immortality, and other related subjects. The last chapter describes ten classic films, including such gruesome fare as the original *Night of the Living Dead*.

The Roald Dahl Treasury (Viking Children's) is a nice, chunky collection of the late fantasist's work in several different areas. It includes stories, memoirs, unpublished poetry, and letters. With an introduction by his daughter and illustrations throughout by Quentin Blake, it also has some illustrations by others artists such as Ralph Steadman, Raymond Briggs, Patrick Benson, and my personal favorite, Lane Smith (from *James and the Giant Peach*).

True Horror Stories by Terrance Dicks (Robinson's Children Books) doesn't soft-pedal the stories about sharks chewing off limbs of unfortunate victims, assorted disasters, and terrorist acts but it does include such dubious "true" accounts of space aliens, werewolves, and vampires.

Small Press and Limited Editions

Note: Only some limited editions are seen by me. Lettered editions (never seen by me) are usually very expensive and come in a tray case with many bells and whistles not available in the other editions. Many are sold out by the time this volume is published, so always check for availability with the publisher or a bookstore. Some are first editions of the work, others are not.

CD Publications published the Douglas E. Winter anthology *Revelations* in a deluxe limited, numbered edition and a deluxe lettered edition. Both editions are signed, bound, and slip-cased in full cloth, with full-color dust jacket, ribbon page marker, and illustrated endpapers with original artwork by Clive Barker; also, the first hardcover edition of Ray Garton's classic erotic vampire novel *Live Girls* comes with a CD with a musical score by Scott Vladimir Licina and dust jacket art and b&w interior illustrations by Jeff Pittarelli. It is available in numbered and lettered editions; in addition, CD Publications brought out Gary Braunbeck's collection *Things Left Behind*, which is mentioned under "collections." Also available are limited editions of Dean Koontz's new novel *Fear Nothing* and Richard Laymon's *Cellar*.

The long-awaited Stephen King novel *Wizard and Glass*, fourth in the *Dark Tower* series, was published by Donald M. Grant, designed and illustrated by

Dave McKean with eighteen beautiful full-color paintings and seven b&w drawings. Two editions were printed: a deluxe signed and slipcased two-volume set first offered to owners of the *The Dark Tower III: The Wastelands* (the remainder offered by lottery), and a limited trade hardcover edition. This is a collectible for both King and McKean fans.

Wordcraft of Oregon published Thomas E. Kennedy's novel *The Book of Angels* in trade paperback format as #15 in the *Speculative Writers Series*. Cover designed by Brian C. Clark.

Subterranean Press brought out three signed, limited edition chapbooks of short stories: "Between Floors" by Thomas F. Monteleone, attractively illustrated by Roger Gerberding and cleverly designed by Timothy K. Holt; "Website" by Ray Garton with cover art by Scott Vladimir; and "Bloodbrothers" by Richard T. Chizmar with cover art by Keith Minnion. Subterranean also published a collection of early stories and commentary by Joe R. Lansdale called *The Good, the Bad, and the Indifferent*. About half the stories are unpublished "warm-ups" that Lansdale used as a prep to write something more ambitious, others were written for his own amusement; with cover art by Mark A. Nelson, cover design by Bob Morrish, and an introduction by Norman Partridge. Available in hardcover trade and limited editions.

Sovereign Seal Books published Brian A. Hopkins's novella "Cold at Heart."

The Ministry of Whimsy published *The Troika*, a very well-received first novel by Stepan Chapman in a classy trade paperback edition with an unusual and beautiful color jacket painting by Alan M. Clark.

New U.K. publisher Pumpkin Press published *Dracula: or The Un-Dead: A Play in Prologue and Five Acts* by Bram Stoker. Edited and annotated by Sylvia Starshine, this is the first time the full text has been in print. A slipcased limited edition is also available.

Gauntlet Press published several books, including a signed, limited edition of publisher Barry Hoffman's novel *Hungry Eyes* with an introduction by William F. Nolan and an afterword by Rick Hautala; a signed and numbered futuristic noir novella by Ed Gorman and Richard Chizmar called *Dirty Coppers*, with cover and interior illustrations by Enrique Villagran; and a beautiful new edition of Ray Bradbury's classic *October Country*, in honor of the collection's fortieth anniversary. The latter's signed and numbered, limited edition has front and back jacket art by Ray Bradbury and b&w interior illustrations by Joe Mugnaini. It also has an introduction by Dennis Etchison, a preface by Bradbury, and an afterword by Robert R. McCammon; and a new limited edition of William Peter Blatty's influential novel *The Exorcist*, in honor of the book's twenty-fifth anniversary, with cover art by Kirk Reinert, introductions by F. Paul Wilson and Matthew R. Bradley, and afterword by Paul Clemens and Ron Magid.

Cyber-Psychos AOD published Jeffrey A. Stadt's original novella "Stigma: Afterworld" as an attractive chapbook illustrated by t. Winter-Damon, and S. Darnbrook Colson's "Hanging Man" with cover and illustrations by Alex Seminara. At $5 a pop you can't beat this value if you're fans of the authors' work.

Overlook Connection Press brought out a special edition of Michael Marshall Smith's British Fantasy Award–winning novel *Spares*, with cover art by Alan M. Clark, foreword by Edward Bryant and introduction by Neil Gaiman. It includes the original first chapter of the novel, not used in the trade editions, three previously published stories that contain elements from the novel, and an afterword by Smith. Three versions—lettered edition of 26 copies, Sterling edition of 100 numbered copies, 500-copy edition signed by all contributors—are available.

Ozark Triangle Press brought out "Nice Guys Finish Last," a chapbook by Gary Jonas in a 200-copy signed and numbered edition.

Marietta Publishing's Dark Dixie imprint brought out a collection of three excellent stories written and illustrated by Jeffrey Thomas, *Black Walls, Red Glass*. From the same publisher comes a signed and numbered chapbook of three stories by William A. Walker, Jr., called *Dystopia*, with cover and interior illustrations by Donald R. Owen III.

Mojo Press published a signed edition limited to 500 copies of Joe R. Lansdale's *Bad Chili*, and also a graphic novel collection of six Ambrose Bierce stories titled *Occurrences: The Illustrated Ambrose Bierce*, adapted and with biographical introduction by Debra Rodia and art by various artists.

The Bighead by Edward Lee (Necro Publications) has a sell line calling it "the grossest book you'll ever read"—need I say more? It was published in two editions, a 100-copy signed and numbered hardcover and a 400-copy signed and numbered trade paperback. Cover art is by Alan M. Clark.

Obsidian Press published *Shifters*, a new novel by Edward Lee and John Pelan in two limited editions. It has an introduction by Jack Ketchum and artwork by GAK.

Dennis Etchison and Ramsey Campbell put together an interesting package called *Talking in the Dark*—two audio tapes recorded at the Jazz Bakery in L.A., reading their own stories. It is signed and limited to 100 copies.

Art Books

Spectrum 4: The Best in Contemporary Fantastic Art edited by Cathy Fenner and Arnie Fenner with Jim Loehr (Underwood Books) is the fourth annual artistic overview of the fantasy field and it's a must for the fantasy enthusiast's library. The beautifully produced volume provides a broad variety of style ranging from the snazzy comic art of Charles Burns and Moebius through the eerily surrealistic images of Rafal Olbinski and David Bowers, and metallic sf-looking multimedia works of Rick Berry to the sexy, often dark work of John Jude Palencar. On the down side, the section on "dimensional work" stands out like a sore thumb. Also, the reader should be aware that although *Spectrum* regularly showcases excellent work, it is presenting an "overview," *not* necessarily the *best*—artists pay a fee to submit each piece of art. There is a lot of fine fantasy and horror art that the judges never see.

Stars by Kruger (Morpheus International) is an oversized hardcover showcase of the grotesque caricatures (or is that a redundancy?) by Sebastian Kruger of musicians, movie stars, writers, and artists such as Mick Jagger, Robert Johnson, Al Pacino, Bette Davis, William Burroughs, and Pablo Picasso. Colorful and amusing. Also from Morpheus comes *H. R. Giger's Retrospective: 1964–1984*, an excellent introduction to this dark fabulist's work. He is, of course, the creator of the "alien" and this book chronicles Giger's artistic accomplishments through 1984: the record jacket covers for the rock groups Emerson, Lake, and Palmer and Blondie; "alien" babies; N.Y.-inspired mechanistic paintings, and erotica. It's filled with beautiful, erotic, disturbing images. Another book by Giger, *wwwHRGiger.com* was published by Taschen (not seen by me).

The Sacred Heart: An Atlas of the Body Seen through Invasive Surgery by Max Aguilar-Hellveg (Bullfinch) is a gorgeous, unsettling book that's not for the sqeamish. With an introduction by Richard Seltzer, M.D. (author of *Mortal Lessons* and *Confession of a Knife* (nf books), and an afterword by photography critic A. D. Coleman, the book consists of full-page color photographs of all kinds of surgery, from removal of eye cataracts and organ transplants to the separation of newborn Siamese twins and skin grafts. The interspersed commentary by Aguilar-Hellveg would have better served the whole if it were used as an introduction or afterword, as it doesn't reflect or explicate the photographs at all. The reader/viewer must flip back and forth between the index, which *does* explain the surgery, and the photographs in order to understand what she is seeing. Despite this cavil, *The Sacred Heart* is *the* art book of the year for those who can stand it.

Michiko Kon: Still Lifes (Aperture) features the surreal products of this Japanese photographer's vivid imagination. In her studio, she fashions objets d'art from fish, flowers, and inanimate odds and ends, then photographs these temporary impossibilities. Some examples: the seeds of a sunflowers consist of sardine eyes; an ornamental clock is fashioned out of a Bluefish head and some freesia coming from its mouth; fish heads suspended among baby's breath make a beautiful still life. Her early work was exclusively black and white; now she uses color (red specifically). Ryu Murakami, author of *Coin Locker Babies*, introduces the book with a surreal short story. There's also an afterword by art historian Toshiharu Ito. Kon's work engages the senses in ways you might not want to think about. Always startling, often disturbing, this is the kind of art that you really must see to appreciate.

The Diary of Victor Frankenstein by Roscoe Cooper and Timothy Basil Ering (DK Ink) purports to be a diary started by Victor as a young medical student, proving that Mary Shelley's character was real. The book consists of journal entries, drawings, anatomical sketches, news clippings, etc.

Delirium (Aperture, summer 1997) was guest edited by W. M. Hunt and features photographs that (according to the editor) capture delirium on paper. Many of the photographs do indeed depict what looks like delirium, whether it be terror, panic, ecstasy, or joy. Others are inexplicable in their inclusion. The fall issue titled *Dark Days: Mystery, Murder, Mayhem* is really, really good, with photographs and essays on violence and death by Michael Lesey and E. Annie Proulx, fiction by Lynn Tillman, and a piece by Joel-Peter Witkin discussing two of his photographs and how he came to create them. For this itself, if you are an admirer of Witkin's work, this issue of the trade paperback journal is a must.

"Repent, Harlequin!" Said the Ticktockman, the classic story by Harlan Ellison, is given a classy new presentation by Underwood Press. This collectible hardcover coffee-table book, in trade and limited editions with jacket painting and interior illustrations by Rick Berry, is designed by Arnie Fenner.

Guyana, by Alexis Rockman (Twin Palms Publishers), is a beautiful, oversized coffee-table book of lush color paintings of the flora and fauna inspired by the artist's expedition into Guyana's tropical rain forest in 1994. All the creatures he depicts were seen by him, but Rockman's often larger-than-life views makes monsters out of insects. Katherine Dunn provides a thoughtful afterword.

Fabulous Beasts by Malcolm Ashman and text by Joyce Hargreaves (Overlook Press) is a colorful compendium of fantastic creatures from myth and legend. This oversized trade paperback is divided into four sections: Birds, Dragons and Serpents, Half Human, and Animals. There are some unusual visual interpretations of familiar creatures, such as a truly hideous rendition of Medusa and an almost reptilian Cyclops, plus many unfamiliar creatures.

Freak Show by Bernie Wrightson (Houthaven Netherlands) is a limited edition volume reprinting the horror comic "Freak Show" and a set of illustrations for Stephen King's novel *The Stand* (not seen).

Dust Covers: The Collected Sandman Covers 1989–1997 (DC Comics) collects the fruits of one of the most successful collaborations between writer and artist of the decade—the portfolio of Dave McKean's beautiful dark visions for Neil Gaiman's *Sandman* series. It includes a short story/introduction by Gaiman and genial comradely introductory material by McKean and Gaiman about each cover. All I can say is Wow!! If you love McKean's work (I do) you must have this book. If you're not familiar with his work, then shame on you! Run out and buy this book.

Houghton Mifflin published a brand new artistic interpretation of J. R. R. Tolkien's *Hobbit* by Alan Lee, in honor of the influential fantasy's sixtieth anniversary. It sports a luscious gold-foil cover with a resting dragon, twenty-five full color prints and more than thirty-five b&w drawings. Destined to be a classic edition.

Grimm's Grimmest illustrated by Tracy Arah Dockray (Chronicle Books) is a new version of nineteen stories collected by Jacob and Wilhelm Grimm in the nineteenth century. The brothers revised the original ribald, outrageous, and often gruesome tales over and over through the six successive editions published during their lifetimes until the stories were squeaky clean and salable to the children's market. This new edition, lavishly illustrated in color and b&w, features the tales as they appeared in the first three editions of *Kinder- und Hausmarchen* (*Nursery and Household Tales*).

Microcosmos: The Invisible World of Insects by Claude Nuridsany and Marie Pérennou (Stewart, Tabori and Chang) is a coffee table–appropriate companion volume to the wonderful documentary of the same title screened last year. The movie was eerie and had a very relaxing air as it filmed mating dances, meals, and the birth and death of all kinds of insects. The book presents some of the same events as stunning still photographs, with plenty of text and a chapter on the making of the film.

Haunter of Ruins: The Photography of Clarence John Laughlin (Bullfinch) collects sixty-five ghostly black-and-white images by the self-taught New Orleans photographer dubbed "Edgar Allan Poe with a camera." Laughlin's funereal images of cemetery statuary and gravestones, the vieux carré (old section), and the Louisiana landscape are quite memorable. Laughlin was a major influence on J. K. Potter.

Odds and Ends

The Registry of Death by Matt Coyle and Peter Lamb (Kitchen Sink Press—late 1996) tells a bleak and gruesome tale in graphic novel form of a man whose job is "eliminator"—he kills illegals. Given no explanation for why his victims must die, he performs his job without question until one assignment changes his life. Then he himself is hunted down by his former colleagues. Much of the action takes place in a slaughterhouse. The b&w drawings are finely rendered. A short introductory story by Poppy Z. Brite was inspired by the work itself.

Batman Black and White (DC Comics) is a gorgeous collector's item: an over-sized hardcover edition of the anthology series *Batman Black and White*, with illustrations and writing by some of the best in the field including Ted McKeever, Bill Sienkiewicz, Kent Williams, Richard Corben, Neil Gaiman, Archie Goodwin, and Howard Chaykin. It has a beautiful color cover painting by Jeffrey Jones and a special tip-in plate by Jim Steranko.

Vertigo published a very clever and moving one-shot collaboration between horror writer Christopher Fowler and artist John Bolton called *Menz Insana* about a happy couple living on the mental plane of insanity while their bodies languish in the "normal" physical world.

It's Dark in London, edited by Oscar Zarate (Serpent's Tale/Mask Noir), a '96 book, is an excellent compilation of noir stories about London by Neil Gaiman, Alan Moore, Iain Sinclair, and others illustrated by Dave McKean and other artists with whom I'm not familiar.

The Borden Tragedy, the second volume of the Rick Geary graphic novel series *A Treasury of Victorian Murder* (NBM Publishing), tells the tale of Lizzie Borden from the point of view of a friend of Borden's. Nothing new here but nicely told and illustrated.

Paradox Graphic Mystery Series from Pocket Books came out with two novels: *A History of Violence* written by John Wagner with art by Vince Locke and *Green Candles* written by Tom De Haven with art by Robin Smith.

The Kiss: A Memoir by Kathryn Harrison (Random House) is a tough, painful book to read despite its short length and beautiful language. This is Harrison's tortured account of the obsessive incestuous relationship between her twenty-year-old self and the father she barely knew (she met him two times before the titular "kiss" took place). In her great novel *Exposure* she transmuted her pain into art by using some of the material obliquely. Here, she sends it out into the world raw, revealing and scouring herself with self-mortification, creating an ultimately moving memoir.

The Merchant of Marvels and the Peddler of Dreams by Frédéric Clément (Chronicle Books) is a magical book of fantasies and phantasms that is beautifully designed and exquisitely detailed with text and illustrations. In it, the merchant of marvels is trying to find the perfect gift for his friend who has everything.

Capolan: Travels of a Vagabond Country by Nick Bantock (Chronicle Books/Art Box) is a gimmick, but a very clever gimmick! Capolan has supposedly existed for six and a half centuries, its people apparently nomads wandering even more than gypsies. This little box contains an inventive booklet about the mysterious country that no longer exists physically (the choice of the natives), and exotically beautiful stamps and postcards commemorating the roving country's various incarnations. This makes a great gift.

The Melancholy Death of Oyster Boy and Other Stories by Tim Burton (Rob Weisbach Books/William Morrow) is one of the first books published by the high-profile Weisbach imprint. I'm sure it sounded like a good idea—get a personality known for his oddball work and do it up in an inviting package and see what happens. It worked with comic Steve Martin's wonderful *Cruel Shoes* (although Martin's self-published version was much more effective than the flashy commercially published edition). This book is cute, macabre, and nicely produced with wonderful drawings by Burton. Unfortunately, there are only two or three real stories; the rest are vignettes or rhymes that for the most part lack the wit or grace of the best of Edward Gorey. The eponymous Oyster Boy is the best of the lot.

Ninety-nine More Unuseless Japanese Inventions by Kenji Kawakami, original and translated text by Dan Papia (W. W. Norton), provides as many chuckles as the first volume on the art of Chindogu, published a couple of years ago. The rules are laid out in the first few pages. These objects cannot be for real use but must actually work, are not for sale, must be made in the spirit of true anarchy not just for a laugh, etc. Some of the best ones are "a last bite bar" so that you can finally clean your plate with one eating implement; "extra step slippers"— plastic cups that can easily be snapped onto the bottom of slippers for us short people who need help reaching household items; a "portable lamp post" that will ensure that you never have to walk down a dark alley; and "baby mops" attached to the front of that little outfit baby wears so she can clean your floor while she crawls.

Goblin Market: A Tale of Two Sisters by Christina Rossetti with an afterword by Joyce Carol Oates (Chronicle Books) is a beautifully packaged reissue of the erotically suggestive poem about a young woman seduced by the fruits of the Goblins. Oates's essay examines some of the mysteries of the poem.

The Lovecraft Tarot by David Wynn, designed by D. L. Hutchinson (Mythos Books), is a *must* for collectors of Lovecraftian material. The 78-card deck comes with an instruction booklet/key that gives information about each card in the Major and Minor Arcana and the four suits. The oversized black-on-blue cards are lovingly illustrated with pictures of characters and places found in Lovecraft's novels and stories. My only quibble is that the contrast of the black-on-blue makes it difficult to read the name of the card.

Furtive Fauna: A Field Guide to the Creatures Who Live on You by Roger M. Knutson (Ten Speed Press) is a jaunty oddity in the tradition of the naturalist classics (well, I consider them classics) *Flattened Fauna* (also by Mr. Knutson) and *What Bird Did That?*

The Miseries of Human Life by James Beresford, adapted by Michelle Lovric (St. Martin's Press/A Thomas Dunne Book), is an adaptation of a book published in early 1806 listing daily annoyances about traveling, dining, miseries of town and country, et cetera, many of which are as apt today as they were then. It is a hardcover the size of a paperback with colorful amusing illustrations and cover by George Cruikshank, and has a ball and chain bookmark.

The Rat: A Perverse Miscellany collected by Barbara Hodgson (Ten Speed Press) does for the rat what last year's book *The Compleat Cockroach* did for that ubiquitous brown invertebrate. Lavishly illustrated with photographs, drawings, cartoons, etc., and full of scientific and literary lore about rats. A great book for dipping into.

Texas Death Row, photographs by Ken Light, essay by Suzanne Donovan (University Press of Mississippi). Recognizing that the most powerful images of death row come from our cinematic past, Donovan and Light's collaboration helps to humanize those waiting to die by order of the state, without excusing their violent acts. This book bears witness, illuminating a scene most of us will never experience.

An Inordinate Fondness for Beetles by Arthur V. Evans and Charles L. Bellamy with photography by Lisa Charles Watson (Henry Holt), is a coffee-table reference book that is an ode to the diversity and beauty of beetles. In accessible and inviting language, the two expert authors explain the anatomy, behavior, and habitat of each species. The lovingly rendered color close-ups throughout make some of the bugs look almost jewel-like.

Bodies of Subversion: A Secret History of Women and Tattoo by Margot Mifflin. Tattooing has been around for five thousand years and there have been numerous books on the subject, but this is the first history of women's tattoo art and it is as entertaining as it is illuminating. Loads of illustrations. *Concrete Jungle* edited by Mark Dion and Alexis Rockman is a "pop media investigation of death and survival in urban ecosystems." It includes an interview with an exterminator who loves his job, the memoir of a man who has been trapping and killing feral cats in Australia for forty years, essays on roadkill and recipes for cooking it, a whole chapter on rats, another on parasites, and so on. Lots of photographs and illustrations.

Dangerous Drawings edited by Andrea Juno collects extensive interviews by Juno with some of the more outré contemporary comix and graphix artists such as Julie Doucet, Chester Brown, Aline Kominsky-Crumb, and Dan Clowes. All three are published by Juno Books, the new solo effort by Andrea Juno, copublisher of the late, cutting-edge publisher of pop culture, Re/Search.

Torn Wings and Faux Pas: A Flashbook of Style, a Beastly Guide through the Writer's Labyrinth by Karen Elizabeth Gordon (Pantheon) is a marvelous handbook of common language usage with whimsical illustrations of real and mythical creatures by Rikki Ducornet interspersed throughout. Gordon has the knack of making grammar and style entertaining by using fantasy and dark fantasy images as examples. In *Torn Wings* she explains and gives examples of words and phrases that sound similar but have different meanings and usages. Check out her classics *The Deluxe Transitive Vampire* and *The New Well-Tempered Sentence*. The thing is, she makes grammar fun.

In the Bag by Samuele Mazzo (Chronicle) is one of a series (you might remember *Cinderella's Revenge*, about shoes) containing enchanting essays by Mazzo, Maurizio de Caro (curator of the exhibit the book seems to be based upon), and others about the meaning of the handbag, the shoulder bag, the back pack, and the suitcase—with photographs of antique and new purses, many fanciful and to be admired rather than used.

No Angels: Women Who Commit Violence edited by Alice Myers and Sarah

Wight (HarperCollins U.K.) explores society's attitudes towards women who commit violence against men. There are chapters about Ruth Ellis, the last woman hanged in England, Winnie Mandela's rise and fall in the public's opinion, Lorena Bobbitt, the suffragettes, and others.

Don't Do It!: A Dictionary of the Forbidden by Philip Thody (St. Martin's Press) is a a fun book to dip into for bits about taboos of all types from food to words and ideas.

A *Cabinet of Medical Curiosities* by Jan Bondesman (Cornell University Press) looks at such real and spurious phenomena as spontaneous human combustion; the occurrence of frogs, insects and snakes in stomachs; the "lousy disease" from which lice were believed to be spontaneously engendered from tumors on sufferers (and it gets worse than *that*); cases of human tails, etc. A serious and entertaining read.

Morpheus International 1998 Calendar of Fantastic Art boasts gorgeous images by Ernst Fuchs, Yacek Yeka, Judson Huss, Wayne Barlowe, and two artists unfamiliar to me: Arik Brauer and Zdzislaw Beksinski. It is a beautiful, collectable, annual calendar for art lovers.

H. R. Giger 1998 Calendar is as eerie, grotesque, and beautiful as ever. There are some picks from Giger's design work on Jodorowsky's ill-fated movie of *Dune*, sculptures, drawings, and paintings. The calendar is not for writing on, given its black background.

Small Press Publisher Addresses

Anamnesis Press, P.O. Box 51115 Palo Alto, CA 94303, e-mail:
  anamnesis@compuserve.com
Borgo Press, P.O. Box 2845, San Bernardino, CA 92406-2845
CD Publications, P.O. Box 943, Abingdon, MD 21009
Chaosium, 950 56th St., Oakland CA 94608
Cyber-Psychos AOD, P.O. Box 581, Denver, CO 80201
Dark Regions Press, P.O. Box 6301, Concord, CA 94524
Donald M. Grant, 19 Surrey Ln., P.O. Box 187, Hampton Falls, NY 03844
Fedogan and Bremer, 3721 Minnehaha Ave. S., Minneapolis, MN 55406,
  e-mail: *fedbrem@visi.com*
Gauntlet Press, 309 Powell Rd., Dept. L, Springfield, PA 19064
Greenwood Press, 88 Post Rd. West, Box 5007 Westport, CT 06881
Marietta Publishing, 1000 Arbor Forest Way, Marietta, GA 30064
Ministry of Whimsy, P.O. Box 4248, Tallahassee, FL 32315,
  e-mail: *jeffvan@freenet.scri.fsu.edu*
Mojo Press, P.O. Box 140005, Austin TX 78714, email: *mojo@eden.com*
Mosaic Press, 85 River Rock Dr., Suite 202, Buffalo, NY 14207
Mythos Books, 218 Hickory Meadow Ln., Poplar Bluff, MO 63901
Necro Publications, P.O. Box 540298, Orlando, FL 32854-0298,
  e-mail: *Necrodave@aol.com*
Necronomicon Press, P.O. Box 1304, West Warwick, RI 02983
Obsidian Press, 37800 38th Ave. South, Auburn, WA 98001,
  e-mail: *mjobsidian@aol.com*
Ozark Triangle Press, 305 N. Beaumont, Owassa, OK 74055

Pumpkin Books, P.O. 297, Nottingham NG2 4GW, England,
e-mail: *pumpkinbooks@netcentral.co.uk*
Silver Salamander Press, 4128 Woodland Park Ave. N., Seattle, WA 98103,
   e-mail: *jpelan@cnw.com*
Space and Time, 138 West 70th St. 4B, New York, NY 10023-4468
Subterranean Press, P.O. Box 190106, Burton, MI 48519
Terminal Fright Publications, P.O. Box 100, Black River, NY 13612,
e-mail: *kenabner@gisco.net*
Underwood Books, P.O. Box 1609, Grass Valley, CA 95945
Wordcraft of Oregon, P.O. Box 3235, La Grande, OR 97850,
e-mail: *wordcraft@oregontrail.net*
   Some British and U.S. magazines can be ordered through the New SF Alliance,
Box 625, Sheffield, S1 3GY, England. For a free catalog send an sase to NSFA,
% Chris Reed. For information online: *http://www.syspace.co.uk/bbr/nsfa-cat.html*

—E. D.

Ḣorror and Ḟantasy
in the Ṁedia: 1997

by Edward Bryant

Bright Lights, Big Screen

Much on film in 1997 could be called a trip back into the nostalgic days of yesteryear. There's a verity in written literature: A book you haven't read is a new book to you. Canny filmmakers and merchandisers are applying the same principle to the movies.

The year saw some genuine originality; but it also registered a plethora of disaster movies, big-critter monster flicks, and slick horror features that broke little new ground but still found an audience. That's because the young, affluent movie-going crowd keeps turning over, and there is no institutional memory. If you haven't seen it before, then it's *new*, and there was plenty of material familiar to the older viewer that knocked the youngsters' Adidas off.

Writer Kevin Williamson is the best example of my theory. Two years ago, the surprise Christmas season hit was *Scream*. When *Scream II*, along with *I Saw What You Did Last Summer*, hit big in 1997, it wasn't a surprise that both Williamson pictures did huge box office. Major ticket sales were registered by young adult viewers, many of whom don't know or care diddly about *Psycho*, but do know a great squeeze-and-shriek date movie when they see it. There are a variety of recycled shocks here, but they're done expertly, and often double as homages to earlier films that only older viewers twig to. Parlaying his success, Kevin Williamson's the creative force behind *Dawson's Creek* on Fox, the series *Buffy the Vampire Slayer* now leads into. It's good coming-of-age material, not really in the realm of the fantastic, other than the eponymous character being a young man hell-bent on becoming the next Spielberg.

And then there were the monster movies....

I grew up with 'em. I'm old, see. I saw *The Thing from Another World* and *Them!* and *Tarantula* (with Clint Eastwood in a brief cameo) first run at my small town movie house. As the fifties went on, I caught Val Lewton's sensationally moody b&w *Cat People* as a midnight feature locally, as well as a variety of sf and horror thrillers on the single, snowy, TV channel broadcast from 70 miles to the south in Cheyenne. Big bug flicks and Hammer films—I loved them

And so did Guillermo Del Toro, a little later, when he was growing up in Guadalajara. Del Toro so loved that variety of movie entertainment, he energetically built one of Mexico's biggest effects houses. Then he turned to directing. Nineteen ninety-two saw the release of *Cronos*, a quirky nontraditional look at immortality and vampirism. It was cleverly executed and even made good use of Ron Perlman. It was also enough, once it modestly succeeded as an art house release in the U.S., to get Del Toro a shot at the big time.

Thus we come to the summer of 1997 and *Mimic*. It's a monster movie, a big-bug melodrama, with a great cast (especially Charles Dutton as a transit cop) and wonderful execution. It's got one big problem, but more about that later. Based on a short story by Donald Wollheim, adapted by Del Toro and Matthew Robbins, *Mimic* possesses a wonderful look. A near-future New York City starts losing thousands of children to a terrible disease spread by roaches. No countermeasure works until genetics researcher Mira Sorvino blends some termite and mantis DNA and creates a "judas breed," a new bug that exterminates the roaches and then dies out itself after one generation. Well . . . you know what has to happen, or there wouldn't be a plot.

To raise the ante, the new breed is growing in size, somehow evolving non-insectile lungs to avoid the square-cube law about breathing and size, and also adapting to modern urban living. The bugs learn to mimic their most dangerous predator—people. These critters don't morph, and that's one of the nicest touches in the picture. When the bug stands upright and pretends to be human, it's still not a reassuring image. It looks like a tall, gaunt dude in an overcoat, with a face reminiscent of Nosferatu on a good day. When predatorily passing for human, the bugs tend to stand around in the shadows on rainy Manhattan nights. Del Toro loves puppetry, and uses that effect expertly blended with digital animation. There's a crackerjack scene that shows mimic-to-bug transformation, capped with one of the critters making off with Mira Sorvino from a deserted subway platform. Cool.

Okay, so *Mimic* has suspense, a few shocks, plenty of atmosphere, a great deal of craft, and some potentially interesting characters. So where does it go wrong? Maybe by not going right enough. Ultimately the director fashions a loving and faithful tribute to the big bug flicks he loved as a kid. And that's pretty much where the movie stays. Fun as the film is, it never pushes the envelope. There's nothing new here—at least for movie fans who know the lineage.

New, younger viewers with no historical background in this kind of low-budget terror fest will probably be knocked out. Just as they were with this year's big snake monster flick, *Anaconda*. If you've never seen this kind of filmmaking before, you'll be enormously more struck than if you're experienced and still recall your grounding in the cinema of rampaging ants, spiders, mantises, grasshoppers, and the like.

So *Mimic* is pretty cool—but don't expect anything revolutionary. And don't ask embarrassing questions like whatever happened to Mira Sorvino's neat punkoid assistant who just vanishes in mid-plot? And what about the little kid-savant who can mimic all sorts of sounds and emulates the bugs' clicking language with a pair of spoons? You could swear there was a whole lot going on there . . . but it feels like either the script or the running time itself was untimely clipped.

If so, too bad. Wait for the director's cut. . . .

I mentioned *Anaconda*. It's great to see contemporary B-movie skills turned toward following a funky expedition of misfits and loons as they travel into deepest, darkest South America in search of the wily, giant anaconda—or at least some serpent that's so large and hungry it serves as a god for the natives. Jennifer Lopez, Ice Cube, and the rest make for the classic mix of true-blue and venal types. Jon Voight not only contributes a truly over-the-top characterization to his comeback push, but he also garners the memorable scene in which he's devoured by the titular snake, then reappears thanks to the fascinating mechanism of reverse peristalsis. It was guaranteed to elicit a chorus of "yuk" and "grrr-osss" from the matinee crowd.

Starship Troopers, directed by Paul Verhoeven from Ed Neumier's script after Robert A. Heinlein's novel, was a big-budget, effects-laden sf epic. It was also a monster movie. Of the big bug variety, to be precise. Heinlein's classic novel was primarily an extended civics lesson, lengthily outlining the concept of a human society in which full citizenship—including the right to vote—had to be earned through military service. True, there was *some* bug-fighting, mostly in power suits, but the action scenes were the least memorable part of the book. The movie inverts that, but without forgetting the classroom lessons. Michael Ironside makes a great vet-turned-teacher, just as Clancy Brown does fine as a boot camp DI. Most of the young folks who play the Mobile Infantry grunts and pilots are newcomers, though it was interesting to see Doogie Howser reincarnated as a young intelligence officer.

Some critics roasted Verhoeven for simply building a movie out of bits and pieces of old World War II pictures. They were onto something there, but I think they were missing the primary point. *Starship Troopers* is a nonstop action movie supported by equally pervasive irony. Verhoeven's old enough to be a child of the Second World War in the Netherlands. It shows in this film. The human federation allied against the intelligent arachnids shows a distressingly fascist side, whether in political approach or in their choice of uniforms. The script even suggests that the arachnids may not truly be the aggressors here. The swearing-in scene for new recruits is reminiscent of the Nazi propaganda film *Triumph of the Will*. The narrative is effectively broken up with expository lumps cleverly disguised as contemporary news clips and classic propaganda spots. It's all actually nastily funny.

The locations were filmed primarily in Wyoming and South Dakota to capture a real sense of alien planetscapes. The CGI work with the varieties of alien bugs was exquisite. Likewise the human military ships and hardware. Few viewers seemed to give the film credit for what it actually appeared to be to me—not a pro-war bug-shoot, but rather a satirically edged screed *against* war.

Alien Resurrection was, of course, another monster flick. For the fourth time, we venture to that grungy future, hamstrung between corporate pragmatists and cynical military creeps, where huge forces are jockeying to obtain H. R. Giger's (inexplicably uncredited here) nasty alien critters to use for urban pacification and other worthy planetside roles. Sigourney Weaver's splendid Ripley is back, this time through cloning. Unfortunately for Ripley, she's now got some alien DNA mixed into her through the process. Joss Whedon's script unfortunately plays a bit too strongly with anachronistic humor, but otherwise crackles along, astutely wiring Ripley back into the temptations of motherhood and parental responsibility. Winona Ryder gets a late start, but quickly picks up the pace with her relationship with Weaver.

Alien Resurrection's helmed by the wonderful *City of Lost Children* and *Delicatessen* co-director Jean-Pierre Jeunet. The movie is chock-full of striking images; scenes such as the lab still storing the unsuccessful cloned versions of Ripley, and the underwater chase sequence in which aliens fluidly swim after humans in a flooded portion of the ship. The only problem with this whole enterprise is that virtually nothing is new. This is the *Alien* template movie we've watched and loved three times before. This version is good, but it's all too familiar.

Perhaps next time, with Ripley returned at long last to Earth, something will have come with her. . . .

And now for something completely different. Indiana writer/director Neil LaBute made *In the Company of Men* for something like $200,000. It's a wonderful monster movie. No big bugs here, but indulge me anyway. This is a tale of human monsters in which there is no graphic sex or violence. It's a tale of very bad and extremely flawed men at a nameless corporation who spend part of their time surviving and maneuvering the corporate shark tank—and part of their time setting up a cruel hoax to victimize an innocent deaf female office worker, all in the name of "avenging" men who have been screwed over by bad women.

Aaron Eckhart plays Chad, a Compleat Sociopath, a layered malign loon whose duplicity reaches levels we don't even suspect until the film's end. Matt Malloy plays his friend Howard, a man closer to humanity, but not close enough. Stacy Edwards is Christine, the woman who is at first victimized, but who ultimately shows herself in an ending grace note as the only character here who has the strength and guts to move beyond the malign human snares and corporate maelstrom that figure in most of the film.

No feel-good movie this. And believe me, this is probably the least promising first-date film ever. It's a movie to trigger intense discussion among viewers afterward. There are critics who think it's anti-woman; others who make a brief for it being anti-man. Everybody can agree it's intensely anti–corporate life.

But it is a beautifully crafted, tight and tense analysis of some of the least admirable facets of human behavior. And ultimately it's got surprises, in terms of both plot and the artistic mirrors it holds up to beholders. Note too that there's no musical score—just some frenetic percussion bridges in between day-by-day sections of the film.

So it's perhaps exaggerated—maybe not—but it's hardly fantastic. And I'd call it one of the best, most effective, most completely chilling monster movies of the year.

Here are three treats for the eye in terms of absolute visual strangeness. David Cronenberg's adaptation of J. G. Ballard's *Crash* did a spectacularly provocative job of portraying twisted Canadians seeking out the perverse sexual titillation embedded in car wrecks. James Spader, Debra Unger, Holly Hunter, Elias Koteas, Peter MacNeil, and Rosanna Arquette all did fine as the ultimate machine-age hedonists. While the film was reasonably graphic, it also cast a cold, cold eye on all the fun and games. The lone funny bit was a fine scene in which Spader and a highly handicapped, much-prosthetized Arquette visit a luxury car dealership, much to the consternation of the sales staff. I enjoyed the courage, the supercooled passion, the viscerally disturbing imagery, and the nasty edginess of *Crash* quite a lot. I will make no summary remark using the term autoeroticism.

Peter Greenaway's films are invariably visual masterpieces, though the stories range from the relatively conventional and accessible—for example, *The Cook, the Thief, His Wife, and Her Lover*—to the devastating but rather denser stuff of *The Baby of Macon*. In his new visual feast of the fantastic, *The Pillow Book*, Ewan McGregor and Vivian Wu offer a Japanese introduction to the concept of the human body as yet another element in graphic communication and language. Greenaway's lead characters customarily appear nude at least once, and then proceed on to terrible ends. *The Pillow Book* is a somewhat gentler Greenaway film than most, but only by comparison with what's gone before.

David Lynch's *Lost Highway* looked great on the surface; spectacular, in fact. Lynch and Barry Gifford collaborated on the script. Bill Pullman's a jealous jazz musician suspected of killing his wife. But then there's a remarkable personality (and maybe lifeline and reality stream) transposition that throws everything into quite a tenuous state of being. The cast is wonderful: Patricia Arquette, Balthazar Getty, Gary Busey, Robert Loggia, Henry Rollins, Jack Nance, Richard Pryor, Marilyn Manson, and others. Robert Blake appears very un-Baretta-like as a mystery man made up in the tradition of Klaus Kinski in *Nosferatu the Vampyre*. Generally with Lynch, even if the surface plot makes no sense whatsoever, the movie will work fine on the intuitive level. You *feel* that it's right. Not here. *Lost Highway* never seems to cohere in either the brain or the heart. One leaves the theater sure that something is missing. I suspect that's not the mystery Lynch intended.

Woody Allen's *Deconstructing Harry* gave us a mordant comedy about a writer beginning to lose his reality moorings as the scenes and characters from his novels take on an all-too-real life of their own. Poor Harry eventually takes his own personal journey to hell, discovering that Billy Crystal makes for an appropriate Satan. Without visual comment, the camera pans across a crowd of all the people Harry's known in his life, fictional and otherwise, never hesitating when it traverses a Mia Farrow lookalike. Both genuinely biting and unexpectedly funny, *Deconstructing Harry* is another film to add to the homework viewing list of any aspiring artist.

The best dark fantasy of the year was a genuine sleeper called *Eve's Bayou*. First-time writer/director Kasi Lemmons created a gorgeously textured and shot film with a spectacular ensemble cast on a shoestring budget. Envision an old Louisiana black family living in the same big house, on the same land, for close to three centuries. Samuel Jackson plays a small-town doctor with a roving eye whose wife, Lynn Whitfield, is at a loss in terms of what to do to save her family. It's an extended family in residence, including the aging mother and Jackson's sister, a troubled psychic. And then there are the three kids, living and playing in a darkly enchanted fairyland of a swamp. Without self-conscious fanfare, the movie folds in ghosts, second sight, curses, and voodoo. Call this a soulful potpourri of Southern gothic magical realism. It's splendid.

Not nearly so artfully done, but still a highly enjoyable fantasy, is *Wes Craven's*

Wishmaster. Since the incredible success of *Scream*, horror movie director Craven has become something of an instant franchise. This one he produced. Robert Kurtzman directed from a solid script by the *Hellraiser* series' Peter Atkins. It's a marvelously old-fashioned melodrama of ancient curses reflecting as evil doings in the modern world, something of a dark *Arabian Nights* tale. Robert Englund appears herein, along with cameos by the likes of Tom Savini and Tony Todd. Plenty of fun and thrills.

The fun was there most of the time, but so was predictability in *Devil's Advocate*. Al Pacino convincingly evoked the conceit of Old Nick being the perfect prototype of a successful lawyer.

The feature film of Todd McFarlane's super-antihero comic book *Spawn* wasn't exactly a groundbreaker, but the effects for the title character's rippling supernatural cloak were mindboggling. Mark Dippé's film possessed a startlingly beautiful look, but little content. John Leguizamo put his own talented stamp on the role of Satan's henchman here on Earth, while Michael Jai White at least lent some substance to Spawn himself.

As dark fantasy franchises go, the *Batman* series may have bottomed out. *Batman and Robin* boasted a high-priced cast and a surfeit of special effects, but it never engaged the viewer. Call it a movie without soul. The first twenty minutes are an extended action scene in which nothing in particular happens and the viewer at some point thinks, hmm, why am I staring at this silly meringue? George Clooney as the latest Batman and Chris O'Donnell as Robin are at least adequate. Arnold Schwarzenegger numbs as Mr. Freeze. Alicia Silverstone is a loss as Batgirl. About the only actor to come out of this with some honor is Uma Thurman, delicious as Poison Ivy. Oh, and one should not forget Michael Gough as the Bat butler.

For even lighter fantasy, one could see TV's Hercules, Kevin Sorbo, as Robert E. Howard's *Kull the Conqueror*. There was plenty of swordplay and dialog lite. Late in the production game, highly regarded *Conan* novelist Sean A. Moore was brought in to make some uncredited script tuneups. Even that did not help. The movie perished ignominiously at the box office.

For out-and-out horror, I'd need to recognize a film that was particularly shocking because of its literal reality. *Sick* was an astonishing documentary, the story of the life of Bob Flanagan, self-styled "Super Masochist." Flanagan, long-time sufferer from MS, used finely honed techniques of piercing, cutting, and other directed pain to keep himself in touch with his body as he slowly died over the years (and he is, indeed, fairly recently deceased). The movie is genuinely affecting, and just as genuinely painful to see. It's not even the sequences such as the one in which Flanagan nails his penis to a plank that get to the viewer; the real pain comes through in the minute or so montage of Bob Flanagan coughing his lungs out. What ultimately comes through is not the shock of spectacle, but rather the human tale of a man with dreams and family and relationships, attempting to persist through art—art in the most persistently extreme forms devisable. Tonally, *Sick* fits into the general area staked out by such equally tough-minded documentaries as *Crumb*, the filmed life of underground cartoonist R. Crumb.

Not everything was so grim, of course. The big summer hit was the slick and funny *Men in Black*. As deep-cover government agents attempting to regulate and deal with alien visitors here on Earth, Tommy Lee Jones and Will Smith made a solid comedic team. This was another sf movie with big bugs, though the leggy critters were primarily played for laughs.

For serious sf in 1997, the best example would have to be *Gattaca*, a debut directorial stint for Andrew Nicoll. Forget the misleading promotional trailers suggesting *Gattaca* was some sort of rip-off cloning melodrama. Like any genuine science fiction, the picture was about sober technological extrapolation and the interface with humanity. The issue here was genetic testing, and the effect this will ultimately have on both industry and human society in general. Ethan Hawke stars as a young man doomed by his less-than-optimal genetic predispositions, who devises ways to circumvent the stifling closed system he's born into. Uma Thurman's the perfect female who draws his attention. The special effects are there, but always secondary to the human drama. The tone is cool and a bit distant, but then that's the sort of world that has evolved. The picture deserved far more attention than it actually got. Footnote: the obscure title was cobbled up after it was discovered that the original title, *The Eighth Day*, had already been claimed by a highly regarded Belgian film.

The other sf film of major seriousness for the year cost a lot more than *Gattaca*, but was, for the most part, rather less successful in achieving its ambition. Adapted from Carl Sagan's novel, *Contact* gave Jodie Foster a meaty role that she made thoroughly her own. The supporting cast was impressive, but didn't come across as effectively as one might hope. Matthew McConaughey played an attractive man of the spirit one wished could be a worthy sparring partner for Foster's attractive woman of the intellect. Didn't happen. James Woods was just plain wasted as a two-dimensional government dude. This first-contact drama had much the same level of ambition as Kubrick/Clarke's *2001*, not to mention the realization, right down to the psychedelic journey to a destination of supreme illusion. Alas, the wonder of it all never really came across. And the ultimate God factor never really feels like the true spirit of Carl Sagan.

A bit down the level of intellectual aspiration, Luc Besson's *The Fifth Element* captured the look and spirit of comic book sf in a way that predecessors such as *Judge Dredd* never approached. The story was supremely silly; Bruce Willis was stolidly heroic; and Gary Oldman played his villain over the top to a degree not seen since his turn in *The Professional*. But it was the look—the lovingly textured surface appearance of the glittering future cities and worlds—that made things work.

The year's major disappointment in sf was probably Kevin Costner directing and starring in *The Postman*, adapted from the famed novel by David Brin. Beautifully shot and highly sincere, this tale of rebuilding civilization after an unspecified cataclysm was also long (three hours plus) and slow. I must say I have an affection for this production, but lord did it sometimes plod! One of Costner's major challenges, as the future everyguy who discovers a dead letter carrier's uniform and finds himself mistaken for a harbinger of a new rise of civilization, was to make the whole conceit affecting without lapsing into silliness. I could buy it. Evidently a lot of people couldn't.

Event Horizon, with Sam Neill as the loony scientist villain, appeared virtually unheralded, but made a tidy profit at the box office. This deep-space melodrama about a ship dispatched to Neptune orbit to investigate the mysteriously depopulated first interstellar expedition was essentially a haunted-house plot with some very Clive Barkerish design details.

John Woo's *Face/Off* was a slick near-future sf thriller with plenty of his trademark Hong Kong–style action. As mixed-up criminal/cop personality transpositions, Nicolas Cage and John Travolta went through their paces well.

One must not forget Steven Spielberg's spring crowd pleaser: *Jurassic Park: The Lost World*. The acting and story? You saw it, such as it was, back in the original *Jurassic Park*. This year you went to see the newest generation in dinosaur animation. The dinos looked great, though, ultimately, none made the final cut for best actor in the Oscar race.

Speaking of creatures of the late cretaceous, one might suppose that no one could ever replace Fred MacMurray. Robin Williams, however, executed a game try in *Flubber*, Disney's remake of *The Absent Minded Professor*. The flubber effects made the grade—imagine armies of little Pillsbury Doughpersons made of shimmering lime gelatin—and the level of humor (the sequence in which the villain ingests and ultimately expels some flubber, for example) commends itself magnificently to fourth graders of all ages.

The first DreamWorks SKG feature was *The Peacemaker*, a so-so high-tech thriller about revenge in the nuclear age. But DreamWorks also released, for Christmas, the unevenly received *Mousehunt*, starring the incomparable Nathan Lane and the fine British comedian Lee Evans as brothers who inherit an old house. The house could become something quite lucrative, save for the preternaturally competent mouse that presently inhabits it. The physical comedy occasionally capsizes, but most of this dark confection is keenly edged.

And surely you didn't miss *George of the Jungle*, the live-action feature version of the cult-classic animated TV series? I'm not sure whether it's a compliment to say that Brendan Fraser was the perfect George . . . but he was. He captured all the subtleties.

What about animation? Disney followed up its rerelease of *The Little Mermaid* with a new animated feature, *Hercules*. One has to call this a very loose translation of classical Greek mythology. The hip dialogue sailed most of the way to the *Xena* level. On the other hand, I do have to say that giving the Greek chorus a black gospel treatment was an effective innovation.

Fox is leading the way to giving the Mouse factory some real competition in the animated feature arena. Don Bluth and Gary Goldman's *Anastasia* had the look of classic Disney, but then animator Bluth first made his chops under the Sign of Mickey. Beautiful to look at, *Anastasia* played all too free and easy with actual history. The songs were forgettable. But the lasting impression came from the superb appearance.

There were few if any films in the year that didn't depend to some degree on special effects. Computer-generated imagery is almost ubiquitous. As effects master George Johnson has pointed out, the state of the art now is such that most of the time, the audience doesn't consciously notice the effects unless the director wishes to point them out. Probably the most expensive and largest collection of effects was displayed in James Cameron's *Titanic*. Remember the quarter-billion-dollar project that the naysayers predicted would tank? Hardly anyone these days will cop to having voiced that opinion. Not being female or teenaged, I saw the movie and shrugged at the Leonardo DeCaprio/Kate Winslet romance. But the ship itself and what befell her, now *that* was indeed impressive. For days after I saw the film, images returned to haunt me. For sheer breathless horror, it'll be hard to top the ship's broken stern section embarking upon its final, accelerating plunge into the icy North Atlantic. For another view of memorable special effects, one must change gears and visit *Boogie Nights*, that anti-paean to the Hollywood porn scene of the '70s directed by Paul Dale Anderson. In the final scene, Mark Wahlberg, playing a none-too-bright but lovable kid who's found his niche starring in blue movies, gives a close, bemused, ultimately approving inspection to the single asset that has enabled his success. The audience generally murmurs at this point. I expect that there will come a day when Wahlberg's, uh, adjunct will auction at some charity event for the same level of riches assigned to such memorabilia as *Citizen Kane*'s Rosebud sled, or Dorothy's ruby slippers from *The Wizard of Oz*.

Natural disaster movies are always fun. 1997 featured two volcano flicks, the first being *Dante's Peak*. Pierce Brosnan tries to save an ill-fated Northwestern mountain community and discovers how unreliable rubber tires can be while driving through boiling lava. Probably because it was released first, *Dante's Peak* beat the pants off Tommy Lee Jones in *Volcano*. The latter may have appeared much too self-absorbed to some of the audience, since it hypothesized that a volcano might actually grow out of the La Brea tar pits, right there in the heart of the movie capital, Los Angeles. Along with good effects and Tommy Lee, *Volcano* at least had one of the year's best marketing buzz-phrases: "The coast is toast." On the other hand, *Titanic*'s promotional phrase was "Collide with destiny." *Thunk*. One failed at the box office; the other soared. Go figure. Maybe it says something about the ultimate value of advertising phrasemakers.

One can't get through the year without pointing out a few of the interesting loony psychos in their particular subgenre of popular filmmaking. My favorite was an underplayed Steve Buscemi in *Con Air*. His role as a milder, gentler Hannibal Lecter was delicious. The most ambitiously affecting, though ultimately failed, psycho characterization was Samuel L. Jackson's disintegrating high school teacher in *187*. Kevin Reynolds directed this drama of a New York ghetto teacher terribly injured by a student who, following his long recovery, relocates in Southern California. It rapidly becomes apparent that psychological recovery is significantly lagging the physical. Jackson and costar John Heard do fine. The crunch comes when the script goes haywire at the end.

Severely dysfunctional personalities also fueled the engine for *Grosse Point Blank*, one of the year's sharpest black comedies. John Cusack was fine as the hit man back in town for his high school reunion (and a final professional job), who reconnects with Minnie Driver, the girl he left behind at the prom.

Properly speaking, *Chasing Amy* isn't sf or fantasy, but it still needs to be mentioned. This latest feature by *Clerks* writer-director Kevin Smith stars Ben Affleck and Joey Lauren Adams as New Jersey comic book creators. It's rapidly and hilariously clear that Smith knows his comics field. The main push of the film, ego conflicts and gender politics, isn't bad either. *Chasing Amy*'s funny and poignant.

For adventure thrillers that push so hard, they might as well be granted honorary fantasy status, first there was Pierce Brosnan, back as James Bond in *Tomorrow Never Dies*. The bonded gadgets and pace were familiar; the real show-stealer was athletic and charismatic Michelle Yeoh as a mainland Chinese intelligence operative. Then there was Jackie Chan's *Operation Condor*, an absolutely pulp-era madness about good guys sent to the Sahara in search of Nazi gold. A martial arts sequence in a huge underground Nazi wind tunnel (don't ask) is worth the price of admission.

Finally, I'd like to suggest an Oscar for the best, and indeed, most endearing, product placement in a 1997 movie. I quite enjoyed *Jackie Brown*, Quentin Tarantino's adaptation of the Elmore Leonard novel *Rum Punch*. It was good indeed to see both Pam Grier and Robert Forster working again, and working at a high level of achievement. There is a scene in the film in which Pam Grier is packing contraband into a flight bag; as part of the stage business, she covers what she wants to hide with clothing and a paperback. The book's cover appears quite clearly in frame; it's sf/fantasy novelist Peter Emshwiller's *Short Blade*.

Pushing books through movies. What a concept.

TV or Not TV

There was a time when I joined the fashionable trend of sneering at television. Actually I *still* sneer at a lot of TV, but I also have to admit I watch regularly. There is a tremendous amount of fiction of the fantastic on the tube—both series and made-for-cable movies. And some of it's good. I know it'll stereotype me, but I regularly tune in *Millennium*, *The X-Files*, *Buffy the Vampire Slayer*, *King of the Hill*, and *La Femme Nikita*. I'd be a devoted *South Park* fan if only my cable system received Comedy Central. Heck, I even checked out the final *Beavis and Butthead* segment, though I was disappointed to discover that the boys didn't actually buy the farm as the promos had suggested.

I want to speak briefly to the issue of female empowerment on the tube. I'm still a partisan of Lori Singer's late, lamented Fox sf series (and, if the truth be known, also a wonderful accomplishment for sometime story consultant John Shirley), *VR5*, which can still be seen in syndication on the Sci-Fi Channel. Singer played very well a young, smart, attractive, competent, and highly troubled woman, a computer geek immersed in a gigantic electronic conspiracy. Her character was smart, attractive, and very human.

On a different plane, you can still catch Lucy Lawless kicking anachronistic butt as *Xena: Warrior Princess*. Or the occasionally troubled goodness of *Sabrina the Teenage Witch*. I don't think I'll add to the discussion of Paramount's none-too-subtle approach to highlighting the consummate mammalness of *Star Trek: Voyager*'s new Borg crewperson, other than to suggest that Jeri Ryan's character, Seven of Nine, provides a fascinating adjunct to the previous ambitious push made by the series to suggest a gender-blind, egalitarian future.

But I do want to comment on *Buffy* and *Nikita*. *Buffy the Vampire Slayer* is a thoroughgoing delight. Joss Whedon spun this WB series off from his feature film version telling the story of the young woman chosen to be this generation's lone representative trained to kill vampires specifically, and to defend our world from the forces of darkness in general. For my money, the TV version functions far better, in part because it has the space to allow the characters and their ever more complicated relationships to evolve.

The first thing that makes the series work is creator Whedon's simple, ineluctably accurate conceit: high school *is* a horror show. Things *will* go badly. Demons, vampires, revivified mummies, robot versions of traditional '50s daddies, predatory roving packs of hyena-possessed teens, a girl turned literally invisible by the disregard of her classmates: the metaphors beautifully capture the anguished reality of teen life.

The second thing that works is the cast. Sarah Michelle Gellar bemusedly, wryly, reluctantly functions as humankind's only hope against Evil—even though she's only sixteen, stuck in a new high school, needing to deal with classes as well as staking night's predators, and really wishing she had a prom date. As the first and second seasons progressed, she fortunately found allies. There's Willow, the shy, spunky, very smart computer geek; Xander, the confused but game guy who's infatuated with Buffy, but still hormonally attracted to anything female; Cordelia, the finely bitchy and consummate social elitist, who proves to possess a core of courage. There's Rupert Giles, the librarian, Buffy's "watcher," her mentor, a guy who is turning out to have a variety of major secrets in his past as well. He's played by Anthony Stewart Head, the hunky mini–soap opera star Michael in seven years of Taster's Choice TV commercials. As the season progresses, he's orbiting closer and closer to the techno-pagan computer instructor. And then there's Angel (David Boreanaz), the 232-year-old vampire whose soul isn't quite damned yet, a charismatic creature trapped in the body of a young man, and who is gravitating toward being Buffy's boyfriend. Talk about March-December matchups!

The third successful element is the writing. Most of the scripts are quick, smart, funny. The action moves right along, and it's almost possible to believe that Sunnydale, California, is the center for resurgent Satanic activity here on earth. Would that it were true. Evil would be easier to combat.

The women in this show have good, adroitly shaded, powerful roles. Heck, so do the men.

Then there's *La Femme Nikita*, based on the 1990 Luc Besson film with Annie Parillaud as the condemned young woman forced by ruthless government forces to become an intelligence operative and assassin. The movie was remade in Hollywood in 1993 as a pretty awful all-slick-surface-no-guts-beneath production with Bridget Fonda as the woman of the hour. Who could have guessed that a third incarnation filmed in Canada for the USA cable network would click?

Well, click it has. The exquisite Peta Wilson's gained international stardom now for her anguished portrayal of a good person trapped in an incredibly hideous world. Imagine a contemporary nation in which unscrupulous forces use ultra-violence, sexual seduction, and torture both physical and mental to obtain their goals. They've got a variety of near-future sf technologies to implement their nefarious plans. These are the Good Guys. Poor Nikita. She's effectively in bondage to Section One, an anti-terrorist force she describes this way: "Their ends are just, but their means are ruthless." Played in a world of slightly futuristic technology and filmed in the Great White North, this is something of an intriguing political wet dream—what could the Canadian government accomplish if they possessed Real Power in the form of Section One?

Intriguingly, Nikita's portrayed and played as a highly trained, extremely capable, utterly competent operative who is still a pawn moved about the board by her bosses. Peta Wilson's portrayal is of a decent, conscientious young woman who desperately wishes to be part of a good, supportive, loving, and altogether accepting family. Unfortunately her surrogate clandestine government family is about as coldly dysfunctional as one could fear. Poor Nikita is constantly being betrayed by her own people, whether her bosses or her colleague and prickly passive-aggressive ally Michael (played with almost no change of expression by Roy Dupuis—you saw him last year in *Screamers*).

You think *The X-Files* is a poster-child for paranoia and cynicism? Set it beside *Nikita* and it looks like *Touched by an Angel*. Part of *Nikita*'s considerable appeal is its nastiness. What *will* Section One do next? And to whom? And how will poor Nikita get roped into another difficult moral quandary? How will she get out—or will she?

At the end of the most recent season, Nikita's apparently escaped from Section One. But don't believe it. Remember poor Patrick McGoohan as *The Prisoner*? And what happened to him when he escaped? Besides, *Nikita*'s ratings are too high.

In this series, Peta Wilson's character is a highly empowered woman—but it gets her no further than personal strength gets any other character. *Everyone* is a pawn of the system. It makes for an intriguing and surprisingly complexly textured show.

You know better, but you watch each episode wondering if this is the time Nikita will beat the odds. It's a tribute to the cast, the intermittently brilliant writing (especially the touches of utterly black humor), and prurient curiosity that viewers like me get sucked in every time.

So what else is happening on TV?

Well, there was big news in *Babylon 5*'s highly promoted move from the Warner Bros. to TNT. TNT not only introduced the fifth (and presumably climactic and final) season with both a made-for-TV *B5* feature and a documentary to help bring new viewers up to speed, but proceeded to strip the first four seasons' episodes in order, on a daily basis. It was a pretty heavy investment of money and promotional enthusiasm. The series itself continues to prove its mettle as a remarkable five-year maxiseries, essentially a long, long visual realization of an epic sf novel. Much of the traditional sf TV audience seems to be—almost grudgingly—switching its allegiance over from the *Star Trek* series. Sf fans have had to be tied to a chair in front of their first episode of B5; thereafter they love it.

Writer/producer/creator J. Michael Straczynski has shown there's still room in Hollywood for a lone, stubborn, compulsive-obsessive talent who can argue, cajole, negotiate, and muscle his dream vision into spectacular reality. So far that vision has been realized to the tune of more than $100 million, and the end is barely in sight. If all goes well, Straczynski shortly will launch *Crusade*, a spin-off series, as well as other projects. The man's creative energy is absolutely astonishing!

On the other side of the galaxy, *Star Trek: Voyager* and *Deep Space Nine* have continued to chug along. If you've liked them in the past, you'll continue to watch. Every once in a while, the Borg turn up to raise a little hell and trigger some excitement—or to add a pneumatic new crew member to *Voyager*.

Back on Earth, NBC's *Dark Skies*, the nostalgically written and produced '60s period piece about alien invasion, crashed and died. Some might speculate that its surface appearance as something of an *X-Files* prequel clone didn't really help out.

And speaking of Chris Carter, both his shows weathered the season well. *The X-Files* continues to develop the lovingly friendly, but sometimes still a little prickly, relationship between FBI agents Mulder and Scully. The show's apparently good for another couple seasons. Spring of 1998 will see the big budget *X-Files* movie. The producer swears one will not have to be a fan of the series to understand and enjoy the film.

The X-Files continues to pursue two primary approaches for its episodes. About half are moderately linked chapters in the ever more complex and paranoid plot thread dealing with alien visitation, alien abduction, and alien invasion. Poor Mulder continues to follow up frustrating clues about what happened to his presumably abducted sister, Samantha. But he keeps running into fakes, clones, and other plot difficulties. Poor Scully has her own problems, particularly dealing with the cancer connected with the alien implant buried behind her ear—except *maybe* the implant is actually U.S. government hardware. The complications just keep pyramiding.

The other episodes are stand-alone pieces that can cover everything from sf to the supernatural. I certainly liked the contemporary vampire tale that carefully balanced on dual narratives—one from Scully, one from Mulder. But my favorite episode of the season was probably the story called "The Postmodern Prometheus." The show was filmed in black and white and ably evoked an unholy combination of the Boris Karloff *Frankenstein* with the Cher/Eric Stoltz vehicle, *Mask*. Pop music was integral to the plot. So were the Southern California–style tents used to cover houses during fumigation. The whole thing was a stitch.

After a shaky beginning a year earlier, *Millennium* started getting its sea legs during the second season. It had been all too easy to dismiss the show initially as a serial-killer-of-the-week melodrama, although beautifully appointed with Lance Henriksen as the somewhat psychic investigator, Frank Black, and plenty of stylishly dark production touches. Even with a seemingly endless supply of similar plots, the show still beat NBC's *Profiler* all hollow.

In the second season, *Millennium* started working more elements of the fantastic into the scripts. In an episode guest-starring Brad Dourif, we encountered strangely similar, supernaturally bright children genetically engineered for a highly idiosyncratic purpose. We discovered that certain religious artifacts—the Holy Grail, the True Cross, all that stuff—are going to play a crucial role in the nasty events coming up at the turn of millennia. While some of the characters have psychic visions triggered by crime scenes, others have started seeing angels—or at least something that *could* be an angel. Producer Chris Carter complicated Frank Black's life by having him become estranged from his wife and daughter. No more perfect little family. The remarkable Christmas show had Frank alternating attempting to buy his daughter the perfect gift—and constantly fouling it up until giving up and consulting an officious team of young toy store yuppie sales staff—and dealing with literal ghosts from his childhood. One of the most memorable episodes was an echo of the "José Chung's from Outer Space" show from *The X-Files* in which Charles Nelson Reilly played an ambitious best-selling writer investigating the weird. Reilly brought his character to *Millennium* in a seriocomic episode in which the ever-serious Frank Black was caught going over the edge as a platinum-blond manic dream-version of himself. The bottom line really is that *Millennium* has developed some nice variety. Still not a ratings leader, it's snaffled another year's renewal from Fox.

ABC abortively launched *Prey*, a weird little concept that suggested that Homo superior—naturally inimical to all us normal sapiens—has been created by global warming. Grabbing high ratings, however, seems to be even more difficult than conquering the world.

In the animation department, Fox's *Simpsons* and *King of the Hill* continued to draw healthy, enthusiastic audiences. Comedy Central gave a shot to *South Park*, a truly weird and genuinely tasteless vision of Colorado's mountain culture. The Christmas shows were especially wonderful. If the episode with Mr. Hankie, the Christmas Poo, and such great musical selections as "I'm Just a Lonely Jew at Christmas" weren't enough to set most viewers' teeth on edge, the "Jesus versus Santa Claus" show probably did the trick. Imagine the Son of God using his halo in the manner of Oddjob utilizing his bowler.... Very cool—and incredibly funny. One of the show's prime movers is Trey Parker, mentioned here a while back for his direction of the great '50s musical *Alferd Packer: The Musical* (also shown on Cinemax as *Cannibal: The Musical*). In truth it's a '90s spoof of the *Paint Your Wagon* genre, but much, much funnier—and with plenty of tasteless ultra-violence to leaven the musical-production numbers.

HBO took a stab at adult animation with a miniseries adapted from Todd McFarlane's comic book *Spawn*. It looked great. But between the scripts and the artist-creator's sententious introductions, the impact wasn't that major for adults.

Highlander: The Series, the French/Canadian syndicated coproduction, is winding down its tenure with hero Adrian Paul. Lately the show's apparently been "trying out" a variety of female action star possibilities, though they've mostly all involved virtually the same revenge-plot script. So far the only actress to show real zest in the role is Claudia Christian, late of *B5*.

Kevin Sorbo and Lucy Lawless still have jobs. *Hercules* and *Xena: Warrior Princess* continue foraging through a Southern California of the spirit, and slaying pop culture monsters. Both shows are admittedly still amusing, but the gimmick of the contemporary cool-speak of the dialogue is beginning to wear a mite thin. Too bad, because the basic adventure frameworks of each are still diverting.

Fox started up *Roar*, a Shaun Cassidy brainstorm that initially showed great promise. After all, Cassidy's *American Gothic*, a ratings failure for ABC, was an innovative and effective enterprise. Unfortunately *Roar* manifested as something of a *Braveheart* with supernatural magic but little humor. Dull, I'm afraid.

As a companion piece to *Tales from the Crypt*, HBO gave us *Perversions of Science*. The animation heading up each show, the sequence introducing us to the sexy female robotic narrator, was the most effective part of the episode. The stories themselves were simply dreadful. Not to be outdone, Showtime produced *The Hunger*, an anthology series of erotic horror under the rubric of the Scotts—Ridley, Tony, and Jake. Most of the episodes were adaptations of perfectly good stories by known writers, all sorts of folks ranging from Brian Lumley to Harlan Ellison. Trouble is, a bunch of guys sitting around juggling high concepts about what constitutes erotic horror—well, that's cruising for trouble. It's too bad because this series had a great deal of promise.

Among made-for-television/cable movies the range of ambition and success (or lack thereof) was a wonder. On one end of the spectrum was Showtime's *Snow White: A Tale of Terror*, in which Sigourney Weaver starred as a magnificently terrifying wicked witch. HBO's *Second Civil War* eerily prefigured the later-in-the-year theatrical release *Wag the Dog*. It unevenly portrayed the governmental maneuvering and media management in a near-future America in which Idaho threatens to secede. Not always successful in its considerable ambition, when it did manage to cut with a satiric blade, the wound genuinely hurt.

Probably the most impressive small-screen project was the springtime ABC miniseries adaptation of Stephen King's *Shining*. Directed by Mick Garris, it was very faithful to the original, but then King wrote the script and was on location for the filming. Thanks to CGI, unlike the Stanley Kubrick movie, this time the hedge animals actually moved. The woman in the tub was there too, and she was properly ghastly. The cast was great (Steven Weber, Rebecca De Mornay, and Courtland Mead did fine work as the troubled Torrances), the family relationships resonated, and the intensity of the ultimate violence and horror was fairly extreme, particularly for a network production. All concerned should be proud of the result.

Mel Ferrer played the anti-hero in an adaptation of Stephen King's story *The Night Flyer*. First you have to accept that a very traditional sort of vampire is flying his light plane up and down the Eastern Seaboard, stopping at small airports to refuel and chow down. Ferrer did a great job. In *Quicksilver Highway*, Mick Garris wrote and directed a quick-and-dirty omnibus of stories by Stephen King ("Chattery Teeth") and Clive Barker ("The Body Politic"). It was solid entertainment. Then there were TV features such as *Escape from Atlantis*, mythology presented with the light deftness of a Biggie-sized order of fries; and *Target Earth* which was enough to give invaders a bad name.

It's Got a Great Beat and You Can Dance to It

Before I get to the music, I want to mention two interesting and worthwhile spoken-word albums; one from fantasy and science fiction, the other representing undiluted horror.

Even the Queen and Other Short Stories happens to be a beautifully produced audio album on which Connie Willis reads Connie Willis. Issued as the debut offering by a start-up audio publisher called Wyrmhole (6877 Marshall Dr., Boulder, CO 80303, $21.99, 180 min.), it bodes well for the company's future. Those of you who have had the pleasure of hearing Willis perform as toastmaster or read her works live know well that she's among the minority of writers who should be allowed to speak in public. She's neither Ellison nor Lansdale in terms of oral interpretation, but she's certainly ahead of the rest of the pack. *Even the Queen* reprints five of her stories, filling 180 minutes on two audio cassettes. Remember, these are readings of text, as opposed to dramatizations. The publisher has laid in some stock musical bridges and a very few audio effects, but the burden of communication throughout is laid upon the capable shoulders of the author. Humor, whether broad (at least as broad as Willis gets) or deadpan, is the common thread. The collection is mostly familiar stories, but presented with the added dimension of sound, much like having Connie Willis as a welcome houseguest for three hours. This album's a keeper.

Nightscape (Terminal Fright Audio, 117 Racetrack Rd, Box 169, Fort Walton Beach, FL 32547, $18.95, 120 min.) is effectively a single-author original story collection in audio format. This is a compilation of six horror stories by Ronald James, dramatized with sound effects, original music, and digital sound. The nice thing about audio albums is that I can check them out in my car. Can't usually do that with those great hulking paper texts. The trouble came when I was in an Arby's parking lot, squeezing Horsey sauce onto my take-out beef-'n'-cheddar, when the tape unexpectedly got to the scene in the title story of *Nightscape* where the two main characters are locked in tight embrace, and where they graphically start disassembling each other's faces. A reviewer's life is tough. I survived—and I enjoyed most of the album. *Nightscape*'s tone reminds me of classic potboiler radio drama. Much of that effect may come from the stark keyboard music riffs. Though the approach to these productions is essentially narration rather than heavy-duty dramatization, they work well. At two hours, the tape delivers a substantial diversion.

Novelist and filmmaker S. P. Somtow composed and recorded a remarkable score for a ballet piece that debuted at a royal command performance in Bangkok on July 25, 1997. For those interested parties who couldn't make it to Thailand for the $1,000-per-seat charity performance, the music's available for considerably less on a CD from Imaginary Records (P.O. Box 66, Whites Creek, TN 37189, $15, 73 min.). This is the score for *Kaki*, twenty pieces weaving the fabric of a danced tale of classic Buddhist myth. At angles to much of Somtow's post-serialist avant-garde musical reputation, *Kaki* is a lush, melodic production a bit suggestive of what Prokofiev might have done had he been scoring modern filmed fantasy epics. There's additional interest to his album in that Somtow produced and recorded the entirety in his home, via a "virtual symphony orchestra."

Something quite different, from another premier dark fantasist moonlighting in music, is John Shirley and the Panther Moderns' *Red Star* (Weathered Leather Records, 550 Shotwell St., San Francisco, CA 94110, $15, 60 min.). Here are eleven dark cuts, some dark indeed but still inextricably plaited with sinuous romance. My favorite may be "See You in Black," a key lyric being "I'd like to see you in black, makes me feel like your husband's dead." You don't think that's a love anthem for the '90s? Works for me. "Dominant Impulse" is a mordant story piece, the narrator leaving a slightly tentative phone message for the sister of the woman he just witnessed being murdered in a car compactor. And so on. Solid lyric-driven rock.

Prima Canadian dark fantasist Tia Travis is the bassist for an unforgettable Calgary group called Curse of Horseflesh. Horseflesh has got a self-titled mini-album out on cassette. For price and availability, write Alan Wayne, P.O. Box 64252, Calgary, Alberta, Canada T2K 6J1, or call (403) 276-5519. The five album cuts are more or less divided between new material and standards such as "Old Joe Clark" and "Wreck of the Old 97." Curse of Horseflesh has developed a rompin' stompin' fusion of berserk traditional country and high prairie surf music. Quentin Tarantino needs to hear this! So do you.

I want to express great appreciation to writers and music scouts Trey Barker, Gary Jonas, and Mark Barsotti for turning me on to a great variety of weird stuff. Loreena McKennitt's CD *The Book of Secrets* (Warner Bros.) is her usual exquisite Celtic-influenced collection. "The Highwayman" is her interpretation of the Alfred Noyes poem, and it's a nicely dark Irish Gothic sort of piece. On B. B. King's *Deuces Wild*, "There Must Be a Better World Somewhere" is a solidly world-weary (no surprise, true?) old New Orleans stomp boogie tune on which King teams with Dr. John. Are things ever gonna get better? What do you think? Very *noir*.

Johnny Cash's *American Recordings*, released in 1996, includes a number of songs involving murder or vague occult happenings. Murder's the staple in "Delia's Gone," the old folk tune in which the narrator can do nothing but to shoot her in order to keep her. Glenn Danzig's composition "Thirteen" dissects the number thirteen, the apellation given the narrator by the otherwise nameless "they" when he's born.

Check out the hefty Hawaiian singer Israel Kamakawiwo'ole on his release, *Facing Future*. There's a tune called "Maui Hawaiian Sup'pa Man," about a Hawaiian version of the Man of Steel coming to save the Hawaiian people. Also there's "Hawai'i '78" in which the gods come back to see what "progress" has wrought on the islands since Captain Cook found them in 1778. The song's eerie, and suggests the gods might well be pissed in a major way.

On Joe Ely's *Letter to Laredo*, "Run Preciosa" gives us a woman who had a baby by a man the narrator describes as a real hellraiser. Now that he's dead, she wanders the graveyard with the child, listening to the voice of her deceased lover . . . and maybe seeing him too. Nobody does energized fusion country death rock like Ely. No one.

The More Things Change, the More . . .

Well, you know the rest.

The rollover of nostalgia that I mentioned at the beginning of this essay will continue in 1998. If you haven't already seen the finished features, you've no doubt viewed the trailers for *Godzilla* and *Mighty Joe Young*.

If it worked once (or twice, or thrice, or sixteen times), Hollywood thinks, it'll probably find a whole new audience. Indeed, the retread's sometimes about as good as the original tire.

But at the same time, pray that independent production companies and irreverent new directors and writers will disdain tilling the same spent vineyards, and continue scrabbling to reach a new horizon or two. After all, *someone* has got to devise something new today so that someone else can spin it off or remake it tomorrow. It's too easy to forget the dialectic.

Comics: 1997

by Seth Johnson

In the right hands, comics can be a vehicle for powerful and wonderful story-telling. So if you know someone who thinks the wretched movie *Batman and Robin* represents what's to be found in comics, the first step in deprogramming them and opening their minds might be to put some of the following books into their hands:

Some terrific writers and artists turned their talents to fantasy in the last year. Kurt Busiek, who has already more than proved his chops in the superhero genre, wrote the wonderful *Wizard's Tale* (Homage), in which an aging and inept evil sorcerer finds himself thrust into the unlikely role of hero, with comic consequences. Neil Gaiman and Charles Vess, the writer/artist team who produced the only comic so far to win the World Fantasy Award, reteamed for *Stardust* (DC), a four-issue series following the adventures of Tristran Thorn, questing to prove his devotion to his beloved by retrieving a fallen star—a task that is both aided and made more complicated by its falling into the mystic land of Faerie.

Other award-winning fantasists worked on comics projects this year. Another issue of *Harlan Ellison's Dream Corridor* (Dark Horse) appeared, and Michael Moorcock lent his support to a Dark Horse Comics series by P. Craig Russell chronicling the adventures of Elric while also writing *Michael Moorcock's Multiverse* for DC Comics' Helix imprint.

Not to be overlooked are several creators who, while perhaps not well known outside of comics, are producing works of the fantastic that are garnering a great deal of attention within the field. Linda Medley's *Castle Waiting* (Olio) is a rising star, the author's own art illustrating a wonderful, lovingly crafted tale of a mystical land inhabited by a host of appealing characters, including a few familiar faces from folklore and fable. John Riley and Garrett Berner's *Lost Stories* (Creative Frontiers) follows a young boy as he is pulled into a world slightly askew from our own, on a quest that may lead to his long-lost father.

Two comics that are continually the best fantasy in modern comics are Jeff Smith's *Bone* (Cartoon Books) and Mark Crilley's *Akiko* (Sirius). Both follow the first rule of great storytelling: tell stories about Important Things like love, honor, and betrayal—and do so in a way that kids will enjoy, with action, comedy, and memorable characters. Parents who start reading these comics to their children will quickly find they've discovered a wonderful monthly installment of pre-bedtime reading—and both parents and children will wish that new issues came out more often.

Finally, before we move along I'd like to mention the work of one of my favorite creators, Francois Schuiten. Not much of his work made it over to the U.S. in 1997, but some of what has in the past is reprinted here by NBM Publishing in its *Cities of the Fantastic* line. Schuiten's tales are wonderfully moving and intelligent, and are crisply illustrated with a clean style that accentuates every fold in a piece of cloth and every plinth and arch of the surrounding architecture. Whether it's *The Walls of Samaris*, telling of a traveler's journey into the heart of a labyrinthine metropolis, *Fever in Urbicand*, in which an Orwellian city planner's designs are upset by a strange artifact, or *The Tower*, where one of its caretakers seeks the secrets that lie deep inside, Schuiten is an amazing writer/artist who doesn't have half the audience he deserves.

When it comes to horror, if you know someone who is a big fan of R. L. Stine, Stephen King, or Clive Barker but doesn't think there's anything they'll enjoy in comics, there are plenty of horror comics to stick in front of them. Gone except in reprints are the days of *The Vault of Fear* and *Tales from the Crypt*, where murderers and thieves met grisly four-color fates. But some horror titles have been resurrected, albeit in altered forms—such as Marvel's *Journey into Mystery* and DC's *House of Secrets*—and new titles have taken up elements of the old. The story of the crones who hosted *The Witching Hour* is being recrafted in James Robinson's occasional *Witchcraft* miniseries, and Cain and Abel, caretakers of the House of Mysteries and the House of Secrets, appear in *The Dreaming*, a spinoff of *The Sandman*, where they were reintroduced.

There are other characters whose stories have been continuous over the years yet have changed in nature until they began to follow darker paths. Much like Neil Gaiman's reconstruction of *Sandman* and Alan Moore's deconstruction of *Swamp Thing*, Jon Ostrander's new take on *The Spectre* (DC), the mystic crime-fighter of the fifties, recasts him as a fallen angel, God's Angel of Vengeance tied to the balancing force of his human host Jim Corrigan. Though the series came to an end in 1997, it's well worth digging out of back-issue boxes.

An ongoing series and a pair of graphic novels worth attention: *Desperadoes* (Image) by Jeff Mariotte with detailed, cinematic art by John Cassaday, follows a posse across the Old West in pursuit of a killer with dark powers and a darker purpose. *Scary Godmother* (Sirius) by Jill Thompson is less comic book than storybook, a library-ready hardcover full of beautiful illustrations of a touching story in which a young girl learns that despite what her brother tells her, there's nothing to fear from the monsters hiding in the shadows of Halloween Eve—thanks to the help of her scary godmother. *Occurrences: The Illustrated Ambrose Bierce* (Mojo Press) is a collection of terrific adaptations of Bierce short stories by artists including Michael Lark, Richard Case, and John Ricketts. The variety of styles these artists employ suits the variety of manners in which scripter Debra Rodia adapts stories from several of Bierce's modes—war tale, horror tale, tall tale—and all are done well.

. . .

Even if your potential subject for deprogramming isn't a fan of fantasy or horror, your arsenal is far from empty. Try some of these titles:

Terry Moore's *Strangers in Paradise* ran through a miniseries and two short-lived series before Moore finally returned to self-publishing under his Abstract Studios imprint. There's not a cape in sight in this tale of a tangled web of relationships, and while Moore has been releasing trade collections once or twice a year, regular readers will soon find themselves waiting at the newsstand for the next monthly issue.

A comic that draws from a different storytelling tradition is *Terminal City* (DC) by Dean Motter and Michael Lark. Imagine a Brave New World where the technological wonders *Popular Mechanics* promised in the 1950s came to pass, and you have a good picture of Terminal City. Add in stories that put together the best of pulp adventure with a biting wit and you get an idea of what this wonderful series is like.

In its first year *Transmetropolitan* (Helix) has shown itself to be one of the strongest titles in DC's sf line. Writer Warren Ellis follows the adventures of gonzo journalist Spider Jerusalem as he returns from a hermitage in the wilderness to the urban jungle of the next century. Spider's rapier wit, lack of decorum, and complete disrespect of authority fired down the barrel of a column on the city's largest newsfeed is a dangerous weapon, and Spider/Ellis takes no prisoners as he wages war on politics, religion, and ignorance. It's a rant that will leave the reader as breathless as the orator, an E-ticket ride that's well worth the price of admission.

Grant Morrison's *Invisibles* (DC) pulls the scales from readers' eyes to reveal a surreal underworld where conspiracy is only the first layer of complexity. With beautiful artwork by Phil Jimenez, Morrison draws on a multitude of threads from pop culture to academia to weave his convoluted plot, and does so with style and skill. A series that will appeal to the same audience is the *Big Book* series published by DC's Paradox Press imprint, beginning with *The Big Book of Conspiracies* and plunging through other topics ranging from Freaks to Hoaxes to Death. Illustrated by a stunningly diverse array of artists pulled from mainstream comics, alternative comics, and sources outside the medium, the books are a subversive and gleefully irreverent look at the darker side of life.

Speaking of the darker side of life, what if your milkman was also a rowdy drunk who was more interested in his favorite television show chronicling the daily life of a coma patient than delivering dairy products? That only begins to describe *Reid Fleming, World's Toughest Milkman* (Deep Sea Comics), David Boswell's surreal tale of love, hate, and dairy products. Actually, though the two titles are completely different, that's also a pretty good description of Evan Dorkin's *Milk and Cheese* (Slave Labor). The self-proclaimed "dairy products gone bad" are whirlwinds of vengeance directed against . . . well, just about everyone. Read *Milk and Cheese* long enough and you're bound to be offended, but in the grand tradition of Peter Finch—"I'm mad as hell, and I'm not gonna take it anymore!"—you'll also find yourself cheering for this cynical social satire.

Finally, the atom bomb for use in deprogramming of comic book naiveté, a title that proves that not only can comics be a medium for powerful storytelling but that superhero comics can too. In *Kurt Busiek's Astro City* (Homage) the titular writer, with the assistance of artists Brett Anderson and Alex Ross, continued to surpass himself in 1997, telling stories that were inventive and involving, and packed the cracks in the superhero world with real people and deep emotion, from the moving single-issue "The Nearness of You" to the epic "Confessions" storyline that ran for most of the year. *Astro City* should be required reading to remind people that capes aren't at all silly when worn by real heroes.

The comics in this essay should be available at your local comic shop, along with many other wonderful titles there wasn't room to mention. If you don't frequent a comic shop you can find one by checking the Yellow Pages or by calling the Comic Shop Locator Service toll-free at 1-888-COMIC-BOOK.

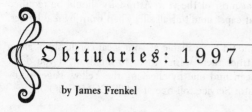

Obituaries: 1997

by James Frenkel

Each year, as with the cyclical death and rebirth of nature, creative individuals leave the stage as new people begin to contribute their own uniqueness to the constantly changing alchemy of imaginative arts. Last year was no exception, with notables from all the arts felled by accidents, the ravages of disease, or old age.

William S. Burroughs, 83, was the world-famous author of such experimental and electrifyingly different works of fiction as *Naked Lunch* and *Nova Express*. His work was fraught with a level of explicit violence and sex hitherto unseen in fiction; he was one of the major "beat" writers who pushed the definitions of fiction in work that defied middle-class expectations and actively sought to shock readers out of their complacency. Burroughs' work influenced several generations of writers and creators in other fields, redefining the language of fiction. **Allen Ginsberg,** 70, was sometimes referred to as the Poet Laureate of the Beat Generation. In addition to his rebelliously outrageous and intriguing poetry, perhaps best personified by "Howl," Ginsberg was also known as a person who flouted convention with his very public acts of nonconformity. He was known as a practicing homosexual well before it was socially acceptable. **Amos Tutuola,** 77, a renowned Nigerian writer, based much of his work on Yoruba folklore and tales of the supernatural. His novels included *The Palm-Wine Drinkard* and *Feather Woman of the Jungle,* among others.

James Laughlin, 83, was the publisher of New Directions, a fiercely independent and outstanding book company that championed the works of some of the greatest writers of the twentieth century, including such diverse talents as Djuna Barnes, Dylan Thomas, Ezra Pound, and Vladimir Nabokov. He took risks that few others dared take, looking first to publish what he believed in, rather than worrying about how he would profit from it. Starting in 1936, he charged low prices for his books, eschewing easy profits while pursuing authors he felt were worth the trouble to publish regardless of commercial appeal. He was able to do this because his family was extremely wealthy. He was exceptional, using his money to aid and abet literary art.

Judith Merril, 74, was an editor, critic, and writer of science fiction and literature of the imagination. In the 1950s and 1960s, she was one of the most influential critics in the field, in part because of her energetic and wide-ranging *Year's Best SF* anthology series. Her definition of "science fiction" was considerably more inclusive than that of most critics. In fact, she advocated use of the term "speculative fiction" instead, both in her anthologies and in columns she wrote regularly for *The Magazine of Fantasy and Science Fiction*. Merril was oft quoted by and also wrote articles for magazines outside the bounds of genre, and for many years was perhaps the most effective proponent of gender equality in the speculative fiction field. An iconoclast throughout her career, Merril was sui generis, allowing nobody to pigeonhole her, whether it be feminists with whom she disagreed, narrow-minded sexists, or reactionaries in the field who felt threatened by her openness and flexibility. Wherever she was, she inevitably was the youngest, most energetic person present, a constant whirlwind of activity who energized all those who came in contact with her. She had no patience for blind conformity, or for a lack of imagination.

Carl Jacobi, 89, was an American writer of fantasy, dark fantasy, and science fiction. His work was published primarily in the pulp magazines of the 1930s and 1940s, though he continued to write and was published as recently as 1994. His work was highly evocative and unusually good at the subtle scare. His stories were collected in volumes such as *Revelations in Black* and others. **V. S. Pritchett**, 96, was a distinguished man of letters and a master of the short story. He wrote a number of fine supernatural tales, and many nonfiction works, including biographies of several giants of nineteenth-century literature. **Eleanor Cameron**, 84, actually died in 1996 but by typographical error was mislisted. All but one of her novels were written for children, her best known work being *The Wonderful Flight to the Mushroom Planet*. Though the majority of her work was science fiction, it contained strong elements of fantasy, and a gentle whimsy that made it extremely approachable for young readers and equally appealing to adults. Many readers cut their teeth on her *Mushroom Planet* books.

Donald R. Bensen, 70, was a science fiction and fantasy editor for many years. As editor in chief of Pyramid Books, a mid-size mass-market house, from 1957 to 1968, he shaped one of the best and most eclectic lists of sf and fantasy of the era, publishing dozens of good books, both original and reprint, in a distinctive format that allowed readers to recognize instantly the Pyramid line. He also was a vital catalyst in creating the Dell sf/fantasy list in the late 1970s, helping to acquire a solid list that he coedited with me. His own work included editing two anthologies, *The Unknown* and *The Unknown Five*, both containing choice reprints from the great fantasy magazine. Bensen started out working for Ian Ballantine at Bantam, spent several years at Berkley, and edited the Beagle Books imprint for Ballantine in the early 1970s. He also wrote a comic sf novel, *And Having Writ . . .* , as well as a number of works of western and historical fiction. He was a gifted editor with a keen eye for the commercial and a brilliant copywriter, able to turn out snappy, succinct cover copy with remarkable speed. He was also one of the flat-out nicest people in the publishing business. Another member of the Dell editorial staff in the 1970s, **Lou Stathis**, 44, died this year. His first publishing job was as an assistant editor for *Amazing* and *Fantastic* magazines. After working as an editorial assistant for Dell, Stathis went on to work as a freelance writer, an editor at *Heavy Metal* magazine, where he first edited comix, and eventually to DC's Vertigo comics imprint. A man of diverse and daring taste in fiction, art, and music, Stathis was an original, both in writing and editing, a fresh and insistent champion of groundbreaking work. **Terry Nation**, 66, a British screenwriter, wrote countless television scripts for such series as *The Saint*, *The Avengers*, *Blake's Seven*, and most notably *Dr. Who*. He also wrote a Young Adult fantasy novel, *Rebecca's World*.

James Stewart, 89, an Oscar award–winning star of dozens of films, created a number of characters who became memorable screen presences, from the mercurial and ultimately decent George Bailey of *It's a Wonderful Life*, to the confused but amiable Elwood P. Dobbs of *Harvey*. His characters always seemed to have a certain dignity and the touch of the common man, and many say he was just playing himself. **Robert Mitchum**, 79, was an actor best known for his portrayals of tough but tender men. Ruggedly handsome, his powerful presence allowed him to play the quiet hero or the menacing villain. His best-known thriller roles were in *The Night of the Hunter*, in which he played a crazed, homicidal preacher with the words *Love* and *Hate* tattooed on his knuckles, and *Cape Fear* in which he played a sadistic killer bent on revenge. **Burgess Meredith**, 89, was a Broadway star, a pop icon (for his turn as the Penguin in *Batman*), a blacklisted victim of the McCarthy hearings of the fifties, and above all a consummate professional, capable of playing leads and character roles with equal skill on stage and in film. He received an Oscar nomination for his turn as the gruff trainer in *Rocky*. **William Hickey**, 69, was a stage actor, a character actor in various films, and an acting teacher in New York. He also played in live TV drama in the 1950s and 1960s. He received great acclaim for his role as the dying Don in *Prizzi's Honor*.

Donald I. Fine, 75, was an editor and publisher who helped redefine the way books are published. At Dell Books he founded Delacorte Press, the first hardcover imprint designed specifically to provide hardcover publication for books that would subsequently be reprinted in mass-market paperback by the same publisher, paying authors an unprecedented full share of hardcover and paperback royalties. He published many major authors at Dell and at the independent houses he later founded, Arbor House and Donald I. Fine Books. **Liz Knights**, 41, was the publisher of Victor Gollancz, a major publisher of sf and fantasy in England. She was instrumental in steering the formerly independent company through the shoals of two ownership changes, as the firm was sold first to Houghton Mifflin and then to French publisher Cassell. **Robert P. Hoskins**, 60, died, apparently in 1993. Hoskins was an editor and writer who worked for Lancer Books from 1969 to 1972, and then became a freelance editor and writer, editing a number of fantasy and science fiction anthologies, and writing gothic horror, suspense, teleplays, and other various novels. **Kit Denton**, 68, an Australian writer, radio broadcaster and film producer/director, was best known for *The Breaker*, basis for the film *Breaker Morant*. He wrote a number of stories of fantasy and science fiction, some of which were collected in *The Burning Spear*. **Ursula Torday**, 85, was a British novelist who wrote, under several names, a number of fantasy and horror novels. Her main pseudonyms were Charity Blackstock, Charlotte Keppel, and Paula Allardyce. Among her better-known works are *Witches' Sabbath* (Allardyce), *The Ghosts of Fontenoy* (Keppel), and *The Exorcism* (Blackstock). **Toby Lelyveld**, 85, was an academic who became an expert in the stage history of Shakespeare's plays. **Walter Sorell**, 91, was an erudite critic of dance, theater, and culture. He also translated several important novels from German, including *Steppenwolf* by Herman Hesse. **Anna Balakian,** 82, was a scholar in the fields of Symbolism and Surrealism. **Penelope Wallace,** 73, was a writer of many short works of the supernatural and the fantastic. She was the daughter of famous author Edgar Wallace. **Sam Moskowitz,** 76, was a fan, editor, and critic of sf and fantasy. Most of his work pertained to science fiction, but he also edited and wrote about fantasy literature in the fifties and sixties, when there was precious little being written about the field.

Ellis Rabb, 67, an actor and director, was a champion of repertory theater on Broadway, founding the Association of Producing Artists, which produced a marvelous variety of plays in the 1960s. **Irving Schneider,** 80, produced a number of plays on Broadway, most notably *Bell, Book, and Candle.* **Samuel Peeples,** 79, was a writer-producer and author who worked extensively in television in the 1950s and 1960s. He helped Robert Bloch get his first screenwriting job, and was influential in shaping of the concept of the first *Star Trek* series. **Tomoyuki Tanaka,** 86, was the head of Japan's Toho studio and produced over two hundred films, including the world-famous *Godzilla* series. Mexican screenwriter **Jose Maria Fernandez Unsaun,** 77, wrote over 200 films, including *The Ship of Monsters* and *Museum of Horror.* **Harry Essex,** 86, was a screenwriter whose credits include *The Creature from the Black Lagoon.* **Charles O'Neal,** 92, a film and TV writer, wrote *The Cry of the Werewolf,* among other scripts. **William S. Roberts,** 83, wrote the screenplay for *The Wonderful World of the Brothers Grimm* and other films. **Alexander Salkind,** 75, produced many films, including *Superman* and its sequels. Mexican director **Gilberto Martinez Solarez,** 90, was responsible for more than 150 films, including fantasies such as *World of the Dead.* **John Rawlins,** 94, a veteran director, worked on *Arabian Nights* among many other films. **Mark Patrick Carducci** wrote the script for *Pumpkinhead* among other film and TV works.

Mae Questel, 89, was the actress who created the cartoon voice of Betty Boop; she was also the voice of Olive Oyl and Sweet Pea, all Max Fleischer cartoon creations. She was also an actor of stage and screen. **Dawn Steel,** 51, a film producer and head of production at Paramount and then Columbia Pictures, was the first woman to head a major studio. Among the films she brought to fruition were *Flashdance, Ghostbusters II,* and *Flatliners.* **Juzo Itami,** 64, was the Japanese producer/director of some wonderfully strange films, including *Tampopo* and *Minbo, or the Gentle Art of Japanese Extortion,* the latter of which was famous for the violent reaction of several Japanese mobsters whose ilk were portrayed in the movies. He brought a rapier wit to the follies of modern life, sparing nothing from his searing vision. **Edward Mulhare,** 74, born in Ireland, was a debonair leading man who acted on stage, screen, and television. He was best known as the eponymous ghost of *The Ghost and Mrs. Muir* television series. **Morey Bunin,** 86, was a puppeteer who pioneered the form in the early days of television. In addition to his series "Lucky Pup" he appeared on many other shows. **William Alland,** 81, was a producer and actor who worked primarily in radio and film. Starting with Orson Welles's Mercury Theater, he acted in dozens of films. **John Beal,** 87, was an actor of film, theater, and television. He appeared in dozens of plays, films, and television productions, including *Our Town* by Thornton Wilder, among many others. **David Doyle,** 67, was a veteran character actor of stage and television. He played the avuncular Bosley, assistant to Charlie's Angels, on that series. He played many roles on Broadway as well. **Jack Nance,** 53, starred in David Lynch's *Eraserhead* and in the series *Twin Peaks*. Actor **Donald Curtis,** 82, appeared in a number of films, including fantasy and horror films such as *The Spiritualist* and *It Came from Beneath the Sea*. British character actress **Rosalie Crutchley,** 77, appeared in various fantasy and horror films including *The Keep* and *The Haunting*. **Elizabeth Brooks,** 46, starred in *The Howling*, and appeared in other fantasy films. British actor **Don Henderson,** 65, appeared in films such as *The Adventures of Baron Munchausen* and *The Ghoul*. Actress **Carol Forman,** 78, appeared in many serials, including *The Black Widow*. **Adriana Caselotti,** 80, was the voice of Snow White in the Disney film, and played in other fantasy films. **Jesse White,** 79, was a character actor who appeared in countless stage, film, and television productions, including stage and screen versions of *Harvey* and many *Twilight Zone* episodes. British character actor **James Cossins,** 63, appeared in numerous film and TV productions, including *The Lost Continent*, among other fantasy works. **Carey Loftin,** 83, a veteran stuntman, also appeared in many films as an actor, including many fantasy and horror films. **Howard Morton,** 71, was a character actor who appeared in many TV productions. British actor **Mike Raven,** 72, appeared in various films, including the fantasies *Crucible of Terror* and *Disciple of Death*. **Anthony Bushell,** 92, a British character actor, appeared in *The Ghoul* among many films. **Brian Glover,** 63, a British actor, had supporting roles in *An American Werewolf in Paris* and other films.

Kathy Acker, 53, was a wildly gifted performance artist, writer, and poet. She wrote a novel, *Don Quixote* (1986), a surreal fantasy. She was involved in the creative process in many forms. **Willem de Kooning,** 92, was a Dutch-born Abstract Expressionist painter considered by many to be one of the greatest of his school. He was also known for his generosity in helping young artists. **Roy Lichtenstein,** 73, was an extremely well known artist whose use of comic-art imagery earned him great recognition among the American public. His work was instantly recognizable, full of wit and bright colors. He saw himself as a provocateur, challenging the art establishment to redefine itself in a fast-changing world. **Roland Torpor,** 59, was a French writer and macabre cartoonist. Roman Polanski's film *The Tenant* was but one of several films based on Torpor's work. **Roy Gerrard,** 62, was an artist whose whimsical and colorful drawings and the stories he wrote to accompany them appealed to children of all ages. Set in the Middle Ages and Victorian and Edwardian England, his best known works may have been "The Favershams," "Sir Cedric," and "Sir Francis Drake." **Winslow Mortimer,** 78, was a longtime comics illustrator. He worked for many years for DC Comics and more recently worked at Continuity Graphics, and as an editorial cartoonist.

Stephane Grappelli, 89, was a great jazz violinist, and a master of improvisation whose career spanned eight decades and several continents. **Johnny Coles,** 71, was a trumpeter and fluegelhornist who played with some of the greatest jazz ensembles of the 1950s and 1960s, shining with a warm, lyrical improvisational style. **Burton Lane,** 84, was a composer whose songs included the scores for such fantasy musicals as *Finian's Rainbow, On a Clear Day You Can See*

Forever, and other shows. **Derek Taylor,** 65, was a rock-music publicist and author; he wrote *The Making of Raiders of the Lost Ark.*

Owen Barfield, 99, was a writer whose work influenced C. S. Lewis and J. R. R. Tolkien. His first novel, *The Silver Trumpet*, was fantasy. He wrote several other novels, and various scholarly works. **Shin'ichi Hoshi,** 71, was a seminal sf and fantasy writer responsible in some measure for the burgeoning of Japanese fandom, wrote a number of short stories and several novels, including the fantasy/ sf novels, *Target of Nightmare* and *Net of the Voice*. **William Rotsler,** 71, wrote science fiction and was an accomplished sculptor, but he was best known for his warmth and generosity and for his cartoons, seen throughout the field in fanzines, at conventions, and books. **Ingrid Zierhut,** 66, was a bookseller and then a friend and business manager for Andre Norton. In the mid-1980s, she helped the famous writer organize her business affairs and sell rights to many of her books overseas. She was an invaluable help to Norton in making her more productive than she had been in many years. **James M. Carey,** 36, was cofounder, with Peter Glassman, of Books of Wonder bookstore and publishing house, the latter producing handsome reprints of many classic children's books. **David P. Usher,** 57, was the cofounder and chairman of the Greenwich Workshop Press, which produces fine art prints and books, including the phenomenally successful *Dinotopia* by James Gurney. **Mervyn Wall,** 88, was an Irish author of fantasy and mainstream fiction and drama. His best-known works were probably his Fursey books, begun with *The Unfortunate Fursey*, a satiric fantasy. **Cathy Macdonald,** 48, was a New Zealand–born fantasy and science fiction writer. Her writing won many awards; perhaps her best-known fantasy is *Secret Lives*. **Paul Edwin Zimmer,** 54, the brother and occasional co-author of Marion Zimmer Bradley, also wrote solo fantasy, including *King Chondo's Ride* and *A Gathering of Heroes.*

And lastly, in the reality-is-stranger-than-fantasy department, **Johnny Vander Meer,** 82, is dead. He performed a feat that no baseball pitcher has ever duplicated, and which is unlikely ever to be done again. In 1938 he pitched two consecutive no-hit games for the Cincinnati Reds in shutout victories against, respectively, the then Boston Braves and Brooklyn Dodgers. His accomplishment was so singular that ever since, Vander Meer has been the true legend that challenges every pitcher who has ever hurled a no-hitter.

—J. F.

Emma Donoghue

The Tale of the Skin

Emma Donoghue, born in Dublin in 1969, has made a name for herself as one of the finest young writers in Europe. She is a playwright, novelist, historian, and the editor of Poems between Women: Four Centuries of Love, Romantic Friendship and Desire. *Her novels, published in several languages, are* Hood *and* Stir-fry.

"The Tale of the Skin" comes from Donoghue's gorgeous new book, Kissing the Witch: Old Tales in New Skins—*a collection of interconnected stories retelling classic fairy tales with an Irish feminist twist.*

—T. W.

See this leaf, little girl, blackened under the snow? It has died so it will be born again on the branch in springtime. Once I was a stupid girl; now I am an angry woman. Sometimes you must shed your skin to save it.

There was a king, there was a queen. He was as rich as she was beautiful. They were as good as they were happy. They lived in a palace on the edge of a vast forest where the leaves never fell. They were wrapped up in each other like a nut in its shell.

The only strange thing about this king was that his favorite, of all the splendid beasts that snorted and tossed their heads in his stables, was a donkey with lopsided ears. The princess was allowed to stroke the creature's ears on feast days, but never to ride her.

When I say the princess, I suppose I am referring to myself, though I have come such a long way from that little girl that I can hardly recognize her. I remember that I had golden hair, lily cheeks and ruby lips, just like my mother. I know I used to run in the garden and muddy my ankles. I liked to slip out of the palace grounds and visit a cottage in the evergreen forest. An old woman lived there who earned her bread by her needle, and by gathering herbs for medicines. I used to call her my flower-woman because her face was dry like a flower pressed in a book.

When the queen took sick, as good queens do, the king sent for physicians from east and west, far and wide. I overheard the maids talking about it. I asked to look at my mother but they told me to go and play.

By the time the physicians arrived, through the first drifts of snow, she was past hope. My father's knees were planted at her bedside like pine trees. I saw him through a crack in the door.

Snow fell on the palace like a shroud that night, and in the spring the lilies stood tall on her grave. The king was still locking himself away every day to lament. He had his favorite donkey brought to him, and wept into her hide until it was soaked; he slept between the animal's legs each night. His courtiers breathed through their mouths.

Fearing his mind was disturbed, they urged him to find a new wife. For the sake of his subjects, for the sake of the princess, for his own sweet sake. He shook his head from side to side as if to shake grief loose. No one could compare to his queen, he bellowed at them: where would he find again such golden hair, such lily cheeks, such ruby lips?

Finally he let them bring in the portraits. He stared at Flemish princesses and Spanish infantas, English duchesses and even an empress from beyond the sea. But though one had yellow hair and another white cheeks and another red lips, not one of them had all these at once, so the king smashed each picture in turn against the walls of his room. The donkey brayed in panic, and stove in the side of the throne with her hooves. The king tore the hair from one canvas, the cheeks from a second, the lips from a third, and squeezed them together in his hand.

The mingled howls of man and beast traveled along the corridors. The cowering courtiers held perfumed handkerchiefs to their noses so as not to catch the king's madness. His food was set on a gold tray outside his door.

After the death of my mother, I grew paler and taller. My curves prickled as they swelled; my limbs hurt from stretching. Not all the flower-woman's herbs could make me sleep through the night. One day I was walking through the palace when I heard a moan. I stared at the door and remembered that the king was my father. I picked up the heavy gold tray and brought it in to him.

The king was as hairy and grimy as the donkey asleep beside him. He looked up as if the heavens had opened.

I cleared my throat. Here is your dinner.

He peered closer. To think that all this time, the answer was under my nose, he whispered.

I gave him a doubtful smile.

Tell me, do you love me?

Of course.

The words barely had time to leave my mouth. I have been waiting too long, cried my father, and then he dashed the tray from my hand and pressed his mouth to mine. Bowls spun like snow, goblets shattered like hail. I knew that something was very wrong. He pleated me along the length of his body in a way no one had ever done before. He held me at arm's length and said, Such ruby lips, such lily cheeks, such golden hair is all my heart desires. You will be mine again, and more than ever before.

By the time I got out of the room, my dress was torn in three places. I smelt of dirt, and fear, and something I didn't understand. I wrapped myself in a cloak and ran to the flower-woman's cottage.

The courtiers had it proclaimed that the king's mind was unhinged; in a sort of waking dream he thought himself to be young again and the princess to be her mother in virgin form; a natural mistake. They urged me to stall, to let him court me while they sent for better physicians from farther afield; it could do the poor man no harm. They spoke of compassion, but I knew they were terrified.

Each afternoon I would be called to the king's chamber, with a maid for a chaperone. Some days he called me daughter; others, lover; others, his beauty. He sometimes let me comb the lice from his hair. His starving lips would make their way from the tips of my fingers to the crease at my elbow. He would serenade me on his knees, fawn over my forehead and weep in my lap. His words, sometimes in languages I had never heard, filled up the room till I couldn't breathe.

So matters continued for a month. If I loved him, the king whimpered, why would I not lie down in his bed? The courtiers insisted that I continue to humor him. The flower-woman told me how to win myself a little time. I had never played the petulant princess, but I set my mind to it now.

I told him, You have torn my dress. I need another before I marry you; would you take me for a beggar? I will have one as gold as the sun.

The king laughed out loud. He sent his courtiers to inquire through the whole kingdom. The only needle that could make such a dress belonged to the flower-woman. She worked with such meticulous detail that another moon passed, and I was still safe.

On the day the gold dress was finished, I put it on and danced a waltz for the king. The donkey brayed in time with the music. But when he would have let down my hair, I backed away and told him, I need another dress before I marry you; would you take me for a vagabond? I will have one as silver as the moon.

The king clapped his hands. He sent his courtiers back to the flower-woman. She worked with such tender care that another two moons passed, and I was still safe.

On the day the silver dress was finished, I put it on and danced a polka for the king. The donkey flapped her lopsided ears in time. But when he would have seized me in his arms, I backed away and told him, I need another dress before I marry you; would you take me for a woman of the roads? I will have one as glittering as the stars.

The king caused a fanfare to be blown. He sent his courtiers back to the flower-woman. She worked with such infinite slowness that another three moons passed, and I was still safe.

On the day the glittering dress was finished, I put it on and danced a mazurka for the king. But when he would have lifted my skirt, I backed away. I had one last request, and then I would marry him. Give me a cloak, I said, made of the hide of this donkey.

His face fell into itself, crumbled like a rotten pine cone. I almost softened.

Winter is tightening its grip on the palace, I cried. Would you have me colder than this dumb beast? Would you grudge me what the least of your brute subjects wears? Would you have me go naked against the wind?

My father hung his head.

I wept into my pillow that night, from relief. The kingdom might be turned upside down, but I would be safe now. I listened to the far-off scream of the wind.

The king came to my room at first light, and spread the skin before me, still warm with blood. His grin hung in folds as he said, Tomorrow shall be our wedding.

All that day I stayed in my room. I clung to the blanket and said to myself, You're a grown girl now. Worse things happen in the stories. There must be worse husbands. He is not a goblin, or a bear, or a monster. He is only your father, and mad.

And then I shuddered and thought to myself, he could kill me. I belong to him as surely as that donkey did. He could skin me like he has skinned his beloved beast, and who could stop him? I bent my head and wept until the blanket ran with rain.

But my old flower-woman came to me in the night, as I lay awake. You must fly now, she whispered, alone, in disguise, into some distant land where no one knows your name. She blackened with soot that cursed golden hair, those lily cheeks and ruby lips; she showed me how to rub dirt under my nails. I took my three bright dresses, my mother's wedding ring, and the donkey skin, wrapped round me to ward off curious glances.

It smelt of blood and shit, but it kept me warm. Lying curled up in ditches and caves, night after night, I hoped the predators would take me for a rotten carcass. The stars looked down on me and laughed. Was this freedom, I wondered? Was this better than a throne?

As I drifted from my father's kingdom into the next, following the caravan of days, I shed every layer of pride. Hair began to grow in unexpected places. It hung about my face like a thornbush; seeds and insects clung to my head. I began to learn the lessons of the ass. Eat anything that doesn't move. Snatch any warmth going. Suffer and endure.

I kept moving only because I had nowhere to stay. Children in tiny villages threw old boots at my head, called me Stinking Donkeyskin. I lived on what I begged or stole. I had meant to sell my dresses, but I found I couldn't part with them; they were the only brightness I had left. The first month of winter, my shoes felt like iron; by the third, they had worn out. I didn't notice losing them on the road at last; my feet were as hard as the scraps of shoe leather by the time they slid off. I had never felt so ugly, or so faint, or so strong.

I had lost count of the moons by the time I came to a strange kingdom where the trees were not green. The first time I saw the turning of the leaves it bewildered me; I thought it might be the end of the world. Not even the flower-woman could make a dress as bright as this destruction. I thought some invisible fire must be burning each leaf from the outside in; I could see the green veins retreating before the crisp tide of flame. When leaves fell on me I staggered out of their way. More colors than I had names for covered my feet as I walked. At night I slept on piles of crackling leaves, strangely comforted that all things were sharing in my fall.

My last night of vagabondage, or freedom, felt like any other. I curled up in a hollow tree to keep out of the wind. I was woken at dawn by the jangle of the hunt. Catch it alive if you can, came the cry. The dogs had sniffed me out. The huntsmen wept with laughter when I limped into the light. They carried me through the crackling forest, over the river, as a living trophy for their prince.

Now I was back in the land of the living, I could smell my own lowliness. Who are you? asked the prince, glancing up from his leather-bound book.

A poor donkey without mother or father.

What are you good for?

Nothing but to have boots thrown at my head.

He was the most handsome man I had ever seen. He seemed amused by my answers, and rewarded me with a corner in the kitchen. In return for washing dishcloths, peeling turnips and raking ashes, I had the right to sleep. The animal in me was glad of the fire, but I hated to hear the heavy bolt slide home, last thing at night. The turnspits joked so coarsely I could barely understand them. One of them with a face like a cabbage tried to find out what was behind that hairy hide of mine, but I brayed like a mad donkey and he backed away.

At last it was spring, and the air softened. There came a feast day when I was released from my duties. I wandered through the empty kitchen after dinner. A round-bellied copper pot hung on the wall; I caught sight of my own face in it, and flinched.

Down by the river I dropped my heavy skin and rinsed the past away. The comb hurt me but I was glad of its teeth. My mother's wedding ring slid easily onto my thin finger. I drew the golden dress from my pack, shook out its creases, and danced for my own reflection till it seemed the sun had come up twice. Next I tried the silver dress, spinning to make the birds think it was moonrise. Finally I slipped over my head the dress that glittered like the stars. Even without looking I knew myself to be beautiful. My fair hair flowed bright as the river. I was a princess again, right down to my slim toes in their shining slippers. From the castle, music enticed my footsteps.

No one challenged me when I entered the ballroom: the dress's magic opened every door. The prince followed me with his disbelieving eyes, and asked me to dance, three times in a row. It seems to me that we have met before, he said, but I only twirled faster. There is something so oddly familiar about you, he said, and yet you are unique, a swan among these common ducks.

I laughed, and began to tell him stories of my own kingdom. It was like a miracle to be speaking aloud again, to say more than three words at a time.

I slipped away when he wasn't looking. Down by the river I dressed myself in rags again and muddied my face and nails. I couldn't stop smiling.

The next day I expected to be the last of my time of trial. With a light heart I threw bones to the dogs and scrubbed fat from the floor; behind my donkey skin I walked like a queen. I knew the prince must be searching every room, every inch of the castle, for his missing beauty. The kitchen was bubbling over with gossip about the stranger's golden hair, lily cheeks and ruby lips. I knew exactly what would happen; my ears were pricked for the royal step on the stair.

It was evening by the time the courtiers reached the bottom of the castle. I had gravy and flour on my cheeks, but fanfares in my heart. I did not even look up as the royal party made their way through the kitchens, lifting their robes above the dirt. As I knew he would, the prince stopped and said, Come here, girl.

His eyes must have fallen on my mother's wedding ring, a thick band of gold that no amount of soot could hide. I looked up at him with a hint of amusement.

Who are you?

A poor donkey, I repeated.

What brought you into this kingdom?

Fear and need.

He was staring now, as if trying to see past the layer of grime. I smiled, to make it even easier for him. My features had not changed since yesterday; my voice was as sweet as ever, if he could only hear it. Inside my head I said, look at me. Make me beautiful in your beholding.

The prince's eyes narrowed.

Was he drugged, that he couldn't hear my heart calling to his? Surely he would know me all at once, any minute now, and burst out laughing at the absurdity of all such disguises?

He shook his head, as if collecting his wits, and turned back to his courtiers.

Was I tempted to cry out, to declare myself? It never seemed to me, thinking about it afterward, that there had been any chance, any time, anything worth saying.

I listened as courtiers ascended the stairs, discussing which kingdoms their prince should send messengers to in search of the mysterious princess. I swayed yet stood. When everyone else had finished their work and left the kitchen, I remained, a hollow tree refusing to fall.

My ring I dropped in the royal soup bowl for him to choke on. The gold and silver and starry dresses I left scattered by the river; let him think his lost beauty drowned. The donkey skin I pulled tightly around me as I set out for home.

Not on the whole length of my journey would I see any man half so handsome. Through the long nights in ditches and hollow trees I could not help thinking of him. I knew by now he would be sickening for love. The physicians would be ordering the cooks to prepare rare delicacies, but all in vain.

If he guessed his mistake, if he wanted me back, I thought, let him suffer and work for it as I had worked and suffered. Let him follow me over a mountain of iron and a lake of glass, and wear out three swords in my defense. But at my truest, lying awake trying to count the stars, I knew my prince would not follow. In my mind's eye I saw him in his palace, stroking the gold and silver and starry dresses which were fading now like leaves in winter, weeping for a spotless princess who did not exist, who had drowned in the river of time.

The king I had once called father had died childless and frothing, I learned over a beggars' campfire. The throne was now occupied by a distant cousin.

The flower-woman was standing outside my cottage that winter day, as if expecting me. She was a little older, but still smiling.

She gave me a drink to clear my head; she washed me in scented water; she put on me a new dress of homespun wool. She took me to the king's grave;

there we spread the donkey skin, cracked and frayed. I didn't need it any longer; let it keep him warm.

These were my feet, balancing like a cat's. This was my hand, the color of a rose. I looked down and recognized myself.

Jaimes Alsop

Beauty and the Beast

Jaimes Alsop, born and raised in England, has been a resident of the United States since the early Seventies. His poems and short stories have appeared in numerous magazines, and he is the publisher of The Alsop Review, *an on-line literary page* (http://www.hooked.net/~jalsop/). *Alsop and his wife, writer and choreographer Wendy Overin, live in San Francisco, California.*

The following sensual poem is based on a familiar tale indeed. It comes from Alsop's Internet magazine, The Alsop Review. *The poem was also published in the collection* Small Lies *(Monkshood Press, Colorado).*

—T. W.

1. The Beast

Knowing how you loved the birds
I fixed them to the trees
so they wouldn't fly away.
So you would stay.

And you remained silent
and never questioned my bloody palms
or reproached me the birds
because they didn't sing.

It couldn't last, of course.
No new birds came and those crucified
were taken by small animals or simply
disappeared from the nails.
I was sure then that you would leave me.

Finally I confessed.
Trembling, I brought you the hammer
and showed my broken fingers.
Leaves and branches in my hair,
the diagrams of Autumn
on the sky.

And you smiled and said it didn't matter
about the birds
and drank at my tears
like a rare and fragile wine
that they too would not be wasted.

2. Beauty

I came to you so carelessly
there were those who thought I had not been warned.
I could only point to the false lovers who carried marks
where you had pressed coins into their palms
and admit I was impatient for your scars.

The rumors followed us as easily
as if you murdered me every night;
hemlock in my evening wine,
a loosened bannister on the stair.
The dull villagers and daft princes
waited still and at distances
for grave news and relentless
until I could only point again
at their jealous eyes and whisper
I had discovered why you handled me
as though I were made of glass.

I know they want to know about our bodies.
Our virginity confuses them
and they are reduced to words and silences.
What shall we allow them to believe?

We are a thousand years old, no histories
and nothing to confess.

John Kessel

Gulliver at Home

John Kessel is an award-winning writer known for his satiric fiction examining popular culture, alternate history, and modern American life. He is the author of the novels Good News from Outer Space *and* Corrupting Dr. Nice; *his short fiction has recently been collected in* The Pure Product. *Kessel is also the coeditor of* Intersections: The Sycamore Hill Anthology. *He lives in Raleigh, North Carolina, where he teaches English at the University of North Carolina.*

"Gulliver at Home" is based on one of the most famous satiric fantasies of all time: Jonathan Swift's Gulliver's Travels *(1812). Kessel deftly reimagines Swift's story from a fresh (and poignant) point of view in the following fantasy reprinted from* The Pure Product.

—T. W.

For Karen Joy Fowler

No, Eliza, I did not wish your grandfather dead, though he swears that is what I said upon his return from his land of horses. What I said was that, given the neglect with which he has served us, and despite my Christian duties, even the best of wives might have wished him dead. The truth is, in the end, I love him.

"Seven months," he says, "were a sufficient time to correct every vice and folly to which Yahoos are subject, if their natures had been capable of the least disposition to virtue or wisdom."

There he sits every afternoon with the horses. He holds converse with them. Many a time have I stood outside that stable door and listened to him unburden his soul to a dumb beast. He tells them things he has never told me, except perhaps years ago during those hours in my father's garden. Yet when I close my eyes, his voice is just the same.

His lips were full, his voice low and assured. With it he conjured up a world larger, more alive than the stifling life of a hosier's youngest daughter.

"I had no knowledge of the deepest soul of man until I saw the evening light upon the Pyramids," he was saying. "The geometry of Euclid, the desire to transcend time. Riddles that have no answer. The Sphinx."

We sat in the garden of my father's house in Newgate Street. My father was away, on a trip to the continent purchasing fine holland, and Mother had retired to the sitting room to leave us some little privacy.

For three and a half years Lemuel had served as a surgeon on the merchant-man *Swallow*. He painted for me an image of the Levant: the camels, the deserts, the dead salt sea, and the dry stones that Jesus Himself trod.

"Did you not long for England's green hills?" I asked him.

He smiled. Your grandfather was the comeliest man I had ever seen. The set of his jaw, his eyes. Long, thick hair, the chestnut brown of a young stallion. He seemed larger than any of my other suitors. "From my earliest days I have had a passion to see strange lands and people," he told me. "To know their customs and language. This world is indeed a fit habitation for gods. But it seems I am never as desirous for home as when I am far away from it, and from the gentle conversation of such as yourself."

My father was the most prudent of men. In place of a mind, he carried a purse. Lemuel was of another sort. As I sat there trying to grasp these wonders he took my hand and told me I had the grace of the Greek maidens, who wore no shoes and whose curls fell down round their shoulders in the bright sun. My eyes were the color, he said, of the Aegean Sea. I blushed. I was frightened that my mother might hear, but I cannot tell you how my heart raced. His light brown eyes grew distant as he climbed the structures of his fancy, and it did not occur to me that I might have difficulty getting him to return from those ima-ginings to see me sitting beside him.

You are coming to be a woman, Eliza. But you cannot know what it was like to feel the force of his desire. He had a passion to embrace all the world and make it his. Part of that world he hoped to embrace, I saw as I sat beside him in that garden, was me.

"Mistress Mary Burton," he said, "help me to become a perfect man. Let me be your husband."

Little Lemuel, the child of our middle age, is just nine. Of late he has ceased calling on his friends in town. I found him yesterday in the garden, playing with his lead soldiers. He had lined them up, in their bright red coats, outside a fort of sticks and pebbles. He stood inside the fort's walls, giving orders to his toys. "Get away, you miserable Yahoos! You can't come in this house! Don't vex me! Your smell is unredurable!"

The third of five sons, Lemuel hailed from Nottinghamshire, where his father held a small estate. He had attended Emanuel College in Cambridge and was apprenticed to Mr. James Bates, the eminent London surgeon. Anticipating the advantage that would be mine in such a match, my father agreed on a dowry of four hundred pounds.

Having got an education, it was up to Lemuel now to get a living as best he could. There was to be no help for us from his family; though they were prosperous they were not rich, and what estate they had went to Lemuel's eldest brother John.

My wedding dress? Foolish girl, what matters a wedding dress in this world?

My wedding dress was of Orient silk, silk brought to England on some ship on which Lemuel perhaps served. My mother had labored over it for three months. It was not so fine as that of my older sister Nancy, but it was fine enough for me to turn Lemuel's head as I walked up the aisle of St. Stephen's church.

We took a small house in the Old Jury. We were quite happy. Mr. Bates recommended Lemuel to his patients, and for a space we did well. In those first years I bore three children. The middle one, Robert, we buried before his third month. But God smiling, my Betty, your mother, and your uncle John did survive and grow.

But after Mr. Bates died, Lemuel's practice began to fail. He refused to imitate the bad practice of other doctors, pampering hypochondriacs, promising secret cures for fatal disease. We moved to Wapping, where Lemuel hoped to improve our fortune by doctoring to sailors, but there was scant money in that, and his practice declined further. We discussed the matter for some time, and he chose to go to sea.

He departed from Bristol on May 4, 1699, on the *Antelope*, as ship's surgeon, bound for the south seas, under Master William Prichard.

The *Antelope* should have returned by the following spring. Instead it never came back. Much later, after repeated inquiries, I received report that the ship had never made its call at Sumatra. She was last seen when she landed to take on water at the Cape of Good Hope, and it was assumed that she had been lost somewhere in the Indian Ocean.

Dearest granddaughter, I hope you never have cause to feel the distress I felt then. But I did not have time to grieve, because we were in danger of being left paupers.

What money Lemuel had left us, in expectation of his rapid return, had gone. Our landlord, a goodly Christian man, Mr. Henry Potts of Wapping, was under great hardship himself, as his trade had slackened during the late wars with France and he was dependent on the rent from his holdings. Betty was nine and Johnny seven, neither able to help out. My father sent us what money he could, but owing to reverses of his own he could do little. As the date of Lemuel's expected return receded Mr. Potts's wife and son were after Mr. Potts to put us out.

I took in sewing—thank God and my parents I was a master seamstress. We raised a few hens for meat and eggs. We ate many a meal of cabbage and potatoes. The neighbors helped. Mr. Potts forbore. But in the bitter February of 1702 he died, and his son, upon assuming his inheritance, threatened to put us into the street.

One April morning, at our darkest moment, some three years after he sailed on the *Antelope*, Lemuel returned.

· · ·

The coach jounced and rattled over the Kent high road. "You won't believe me when I tell you, these minuscule people, not six inches high, had a war over which end of the egg to break."

Lemuel had been telling these tales for two weeks without stop. He'd hired the coach using money we did not have. I was vexed with the effort to force him to confront our penury.

"We haven't seen an egg here in two years!" I said. "Last fall came a pip that killed half the chickens. They staggered about with their little heads pointed down, like drunkards searching for coins on the street. They looked so sad. When it came time to market we left without a farthing."

Lemuel carefully balanced the box he carried on his knees. He peeked inside, to assure himself for the hundredth time that the tiny cattle and sheep it held were all right. We were on our way to the country estate of the Earl of Kent, who had summoned Lemuel when the rumors of the miniature creatures he'd brought back from Lilliput spread throughout the county. "Their empress almost had me beheaded. She didn't approve my method of dousing a fire that would have otherwise consumed her."

"In the midst of that, Betty almost died of the croup. I was up with her every night for a fortnight, cold compresses and bleeding."

"God knows I'd have given a hundred guineas for a cold compress when I burned with fever, a castaway on the shores of Lilliput."

"Once the novelty fades, cattle so tiny will be of no use. There's not a scrap of meat on them."

"True enough. I would eat thirty oxen at a meal." He sat silent, deep in thought. The coach lurched on. "I wonder if His Grace would lend me the money to take them on tour?"

"Lemuel, we owe Stephen Potts eleven pounds sixpence. To say nothing of the grocer. And if he is to have any chance at a profession, Johnny must be sent to school. We cannot even pay for his clothes."

"Lilliputian boys are dressed by men until four years of age, and then are obliged to dress themselves. They always go in the presence of a Professor, whereby they avoid those early impressions of vice and folly to which our children are subject. Would that you had done this for our John."

"Lemuel, we have no money! It was all I could do to keep him alive!"

He looked at me, and his brow furrowed. He tapped his fingers on the top of the cattle box. "I don't suppose I can blame her. It was a capital crime for any person whatsoever to make water within the precincts of the palace."

Last night your grandfather quarreled with your uncle John, who had just returned from the Temple. Johnny went out to the stables to speak with Lemuel concerning a suit for libel threatened by a nobleman who thinks himself the object of criticism in Lemuel's book. I followed.

Before Johnny could finish explaining the situation, Lemuel flew into a rage. "What use have I for attorneys? I had rather see them dropped to the deepest gulf of the sea."

In the violence of his gesture Lemuel nearly knocked over the lamp that stood on the wooden table. His long gray hair flew wildly as he stalked past the stall of the dappled mare he calls "Mistress Mary," to my everlasting dismay. I rushed forward to steady the lamp. Lemuel looked upon me with a gaze as blank as a brick.

"Father," Johnny said, "you may not care what this man does, but he is a cabinet minister, and a lawsuit could ruin us. It would be politic if you would publicly apologize for any slight your satire may have given."

Lemuel turned that pitiless gaze on our son. "I see you are no better than the other animals of this midden, and all my efforts to make something better of you are in vain. If you were capable of logic, I would ask you to explain to me how my report of events that occurred so many years ago, during another reign, and above five thousand leagues distant from this pathetic isle, might be applied to any of the Yahoos who today govern this herd. Yet in service of this idiocy you ask me to *say the thing that is not*. I had rather all your law books, and you immodest pleaders with them, were heaped into a bonfire in Smithfield for the entertainment of children."

I watched Johnny's face grow livid, but he mastered his rage and left the stable. Lemuel and I stood in silence. He would not look at me, and I thought for a moment he felt some regret at his intemperance. But he turned from me to calm the frightened horses. I put the lamp down on the table and ran back to the house.

Johnny was ten when Lemuel returned from Lilliput. He was overjoyed to see his father again, and worshiped him as a hero. When other of the townschildren mocked Lemuel, calling him a madman, Johnny fought them.

The Lilliputian cattle and sheep, despite my misgivings, brought us some advantage. Following the example of the Earl of Kent, Sir Humphrey Glover, Lord Sidwich, and other prominent men commanded Lemuel to show these creatures. Johnny prated on about the tiny animals all day, and it was all I could do to keep him from sleeping with them beneath his bedclothes, which would have gone the worse for them, as he was a restless child and in tossing at night would surely have crushed the life out of them. He built a little stable in the corner of his room. At first we fed them with biscuit, ground as fine as we could, and spring water. Johnny took great pains to keep the rats away.

It was his idea to build a pasture on the bowling green, where the grass was fine enough that they might eat and prosper. Lemuel basked in Johnny's enthusiasm. He charmed the boy with the tale of how he had captured the entire fleet of Blefescu using thread and fish-hooks, and towed it back to Lilliput. Johnny said that he would be a sea captain when he grew up.

As if in a dream, our fortunes turned. Lemuel's uncle John passed away, leaving him five hundred sterling and an estate in land near Epping that earned an income of about thirty pounds a year. Lemuel sold the Lilliputian cattle for six hundred pounds. He bought our big house in Redriff. After years of hardship, after I had lost hope, he had returned to save us.

We had been better served by bankruptcy if that would have kept him beside me in our bed.

You will find, Eliza, that a husband needs his wife in that way, and it can be a pleasant pastime. But it is different for them. Love is like a fire they cannot control, overwhelming, easily quenched, then as often as not forgotten, even regretted. Whenever Lemuel returned from these voyages he wanted me, and I do not hesitate to say, I him. Our bed was another country to which he would return, and explore for its mysteries. He embraced me with a fury that sought to extinguish all our time apart, and the leagues between us, in the heat of that moment. Spent, he would rest his head on my bosom, and I would stroke his hair. He was like a boy again, quiet and kind. He would whisper to me, in a voice of desperation, how I should never let him leave again.

Two months after his return, despite the comforts of my arms, he was gone again. His wild heart, he said, would not let him rest.

This time he left us well set. Fifteen hundred pounds, the house in Redriff, the land in Epping. He took a long lease on the Black Bull public house in Fetter Lane, which brought a regular income.

We traveled with him to Liverpool, where in June of 1702 he took ship aboard the *Adventure*, Captain John Nicholas commanding, bound for Surat.

It was a dreary day at the downs, the kind of blustery weather Liverpool has occasion for even in summer, low leaden clouds driven before a strong wind, the harbor rolling in swells and the ends of furled sails flapping above us. With tears in my eyes, I embraced him; he would not let me go. When I did pull away I saw that he wept as well. "Fare thee well, good heart," he whispered to me. "Forgive me my wandering soul."

Seeing the kindness and love in his gaze, the difficulty with which he tore himself from my bosom, I would have forgiven him anything. It occurred to me just how powerful a passion burned within him, driving him outside the circle of our hearth. Little Johnny shook his hand, very manly. Betty leapt into his arms, and he pressed her to his cheek, then set her down. Then he took up his canvas bag, turned and went aboard.

It is no easy matter being the wife of a man famous for his wild tales. The other day in town with Sarah to do the marketing, in the butcher's shop, I overheard Mrs. Boyle the butcher's wife arguing with a customer that the chicken was fresh. By its smell anyone past the age of two would know it was a week dead. But Mrs. Boyle insisted.

The shop was busy, and our neighbor Mr. Trent began to mock her, in a low voice, to some bystanders. He said, "Of course it is fresh. Mrs. Boyle insists it's fresh. It's as true as if Mr. Gulliver had said it."

All the people in the shop laughed. My face burned, and I left.

One June morning in 1706, three long years after Lemuel was due to return, I was attending to the boiling of some sheets in the kitchen when a cry came from Sarah, our housemaid. "God save me! Help!"

I rushed to the front door, there to see an uncouth spectacle. Sarah was staring at a man who had entered on all fours, peering up, his head canted to the side, so that his long hair brushed the ground (he wore no periwig) as he spied up at us. It was a moment before I recognized him as my Lemuel. My heart leapt within my breast as I went from widow to wife in a single instant.

When he came to the house, for which he had been forced to enquire, Sarah had opened the door. Lemuel bent down to go in, for fear of striking his head.

He had been living among giants and fancied himself sixty feet tall. Sarah had never met Mr. Gulliver, and thought him a madman. When I tried to embrace him, he stooped to my knees until I was forced to get down on my own to kiss him.

When Betty, your mother, who was then sixteen, ran in, holding some needlework, Lemuel tried to pick her up by her waist, in one hand, as if she had been a doll. He complained that the children and I had starved ourselves, so that we were wasted away to nothing. It was some weeks before he regained his sense of proper proportion.

I told him it was the last time he should ever go to sea.

It wasn't ten days before a Cornish captain, William Robinson, under whom Lemuel had served on a trip to the Levant some years before we were married, called upon us. That visit was purely a social one, or so he avowed, but within a month he was importuning Lemuel to join him as ship's surgeon on another trip to the East Indies.

One night, as we prepared for bed, I accosted him. "Lemuel, are you considering taking up Robinson on this offer?"

"What matter if I did? I am the master of this house. You are well taken care of."

"Taken care of by servants, not my husband."

"He is offering twice the usual salary, a share of the profits, two mates and a surgeon under me. I shall be gone no more than a year, and you will see us comfortably off, so that I might never have to go to sea again."

"You don't have to go to sea now. We have a comfortable life."

He removed his leather jerkin and began to unbutton his shirt. "And our children? Betty is nearly of marriageable age. What dowry can we offer her? Johnny must go to Cambridge, and have money to establish himself in some honorable profession. I want to do more for him than my father did for me."

"The children mourn your absences." I touched his arm. The muscles were taut as cords. "When you disappeared on the *Antelope*, we suffered more from the thought that you were dead than from the penury we lived in. Give them a father in their home and let the distant world go."

"You are thinking like a woman. The distant world comes into the home. It is a place of greed, vice, and folly. I seek for some understanding I can give to cope with it."

"Lemuel, what is this desire for strange lands but a type of greed, this abandonment of your family but the height of folly? And your refusal to admit your true motives is the utmost dishonesty, to the woman who loves you, and whom you vowed to love."

Lemuel took up his coat, pulled on his shoes.

"Where are you going?"

"Out. I need to take some air. Perhaps I can determine my true motives for you."

He left.

A week later, on the fifth of August, 1706, he left England on the *Hope-Well*, bound for the Indies. I did not see him again for four years.

. . . .

The only time I can coax him into the house is when he deigns to bathe. He is most fastidious, and insists that no one must remain on the same floor, let alone the same room, when he does.

I crept to the door last week and peeked in. He had finished, and dried himself, and now stood naked in front of the mirror, trembling. At first I thought he was cold, but the fire roared in the grate. Then he raised his hands from his sides, covered his eyes, and sobbed, and I understood that he was recoiling in horror from his own image.

When he left on the third voyage I was five-and-thirty years old. In the previous seven years he had spent a total of four months with me. I had no need to work, I was not an old woman, and my children had no father. When Lemuel did not return in the promised year, when that year stretched to two and the *Hope-Well* returned to Portsmouth without Lemuel aboard, I fell into despair. Captain Robinson came to the house in Redriff and told the tale. Stuck in the port of Tonquin awaiting the goods they were to ship back to England, Robinson hit on the plan of purchasing a sloop, giving command of it to Lemuel, and bidding him trade among the islands, returning in several months at which time, the *Hope-Well* being loaded, they might return. Lemuel set off on the sloop and was not heard from again. Robinson supposed that they might have been taken by the barbarous pirates of those islands, in which case Lemuel had undoubtedly been slain, as Christian mercy is a virtue unknown in those heathen lands.

I cannot say that I was surprised. I was angry, and I wept.

Being the wealthiest widow in the town, and by no means an old woman, I did not lack for suitors. Sir Robert Davies himself called on me more than once. It was all I could do to keep from having my head turned. "Marry me," he said. "I will be a father to your daughter, an example to your son."

"Johnny is about to go off to school, and Betty soon to be married," I told him. "One wedding is enough to worry about right now." Thus I put him off.

In truth I did lose myself in your mother's wedding; Betty was giddy with excitement, and your father, her betrothed, was about continually, helping put the house in order, traveling with Johnny to school. So it was I kept myself chaste.

The townspeople thought I was a fool. My mother commended me for my faithfulness, but I could tell she regretted the loss of a connection with nobility. Betty and Johnny stood by me. I don't need another father, Johnny said, I have one.

My reasons? Wherever he went Sir Robert carried a silver-headed cane, with which he would gently tap his footman's shoulder as he instructed him. I was mistress of my own home. I had given my heart once, and still treasured a hope of Lemuel's return. There are a hundred reasons, child, and there are things I cannot explain. Lemuel did return, and despite his ravings about a flying island and the curse of immortality, I felt that all my trouble had been justified. He seemed weary, but still my husband, the love of my youth come again. The joy of our meeting was great. Within three months he had got me with child.

Within five he had left again.

. . .

And so he came back, five years later, from the longest of his absences. He was aged five-and-fifty, I five-and-forty. He saw his son Lemuel for the first time. His daughter, married and a mother herself; his son, grown and an attorney. His wife, longing to hold him again.

No, I have not, Eliza. He shudders at my touch. He washes his hands. He accuses me of trying to seduce him.

"Are you ashamed of the touch that got you your sons and daughter?" I once asked him. "That got us poor Robert? That gave us young Lemuel, to be our comfort in our old age?

His face registered at first revulsion, and then, as he sat heavily in his chair, fatigue. "I can't regret our children if they be good, but I most certainly regret them if they be bad. There are Yahoos enough in the world."

We had long given him up for dead. I had made my peace, and held in my memory the man who had kissed me in my father's garden.

At first I thought that he had caught some foreign disease. As thin as a fence post, he stood in the doorway, his face a mask of dismay. It was the fifth of December, 1715. Three o'clock in the afternoon. I ran to him, kissed him. He fell into a swoon that lasted most of an hour. With difficulty we carried him to his bed. When he awoke, I put my hand to his face: he pulled away as if his skin had been flayed.

And so we live by these rules: "Save for the sabbath, you may not eat in the same room with me. You may not presume to touch my bread. You may not drink out of the same cup, or use my spoon or plate. You may not take me by the hand. That I might bear the reek of this house, fresh horse droppings shall be brought into my chambers each morning, and kept there in a special container I have had fashioned for that purpose."

My father's house, in Newgate Street, was not far from the prison. Outside, on the days of executions, straw was scattered on the street to muffle the wheels of passing wagons, in deference to the men being hanged inside. Here we scatter straw over the cobbled courtyard outside the stables because the noise of the wheels troubles him.

As a young man his heart was full of hope, but his heart has been beaten closed, not only by the sea and the storms and the mutinies and the pirates— but by some hard moral engine inside of him. He would rather be dead, I think, than to abide his flesh. Perhaps he soon will be. And I will have to go on living without him, as I have learned to do over these many years.

Might it have been different? I could say yes, but some thing I saw in his eyes that first afternoon in Newgate Street rises to stop me. He was a man who looked outward while the inward part of himself withered. He was drawn to the blank spaces outside the known world; we are too small to make a mark on his map. To Lemuel ordinary people are interesting only as we represent large things. He asked me to make him a perfect man. In seeking perfection he has gulled himself, and the postscript is that he spends four hours every day attempting to communicate with a horse, while his children, his grandchildren, his wife wait in his well-appointed home, the home they have prepared for him and labored to keep together in his absence, maintaining a place for him at every holiday table, praying for him at every service, treasuring him up in their hearts and memories, his portrait on the wall, his merest jottings pressed close in the book of memory, his boots in the wardrobe, maps in the cabinet, glass on the sideboard.

At Christmas, when we can coax him to eat with us, I sit at the other end of twelve feet of polished mahogany table and look across at a stranger who is yet the man I love.

During our conversation in the garden thirty years ago, Lemuel told me a story. The Greeks, he told me, believed that once there existed a creature that was complete and whole unto itself, perfect and without flaw. But in the beginning of time the gods split this being into two halves, and that is how man and woman came into the world. Each of us knows that we are not complete, and so we seek desperately after each other, yearning to possess our missing halves, pressing our bodies together in hope of becoming that one happy creature again. But of course we cannot do it, and so in frustration we turn away from each other, tearing ourselves apart all of our lives.

His book has been a great success. It is all they speak of in London. It has made us more money than his sixteen years of voyages.

He accuses us of enticing him into writing the wretched thing, and deems it a failure because it didn't immediately reform all of humanity. He told his story to the world in the hope that he would magically turn it into something perfect. I tell you mine, Eliza . . . I tell you mine because . . . bless me, I believe I've burned my hand on this kettle. Fetch me the lard.

That's better.

Soon you'll come of age to choose a husband, if your parents give you leave to choose. I don't doubt you tremble at the prospect. But remember: it is the only choice a woman is given to make in her life, save for the choice of clothes for her funeral.

And now, help me carry this soup up to him; help me to cover him, and make sure he is warm for the night.

Nancy Pickard

It Had to Be You

Nancy Pickard is best known as the author of the Jenny Cain series and other murder mysteries, for which she has won the Agatha, Anthony, Shamus, American Mystery, and Macavity awards. Her most recent novel is Twilight. *Although she is a regular in various Year's Best compilations in the mystery field, this story marks her first appearance in* The Year's Best Fantasy and Horror.*

"It Had to Be You," a departure from Pickard's usual subject matter, is a fantasia about Marilyn Monroe written for the anthology Marilyn: Shades of Blonde, *edited by Carole Nelson Douglas. I approached this story reluctantly when it was recommended by editorial assistant Richard Kunz, for its theme— a mysterious appearance on Mount Rushmore—seemed too close to Kristine Kathryn Rusch's Mount Rushmore story, "Monuments to the Dead," reprinted in Volume Eight of this series. Then I read Pickard's strange and wonderful tale, and my reservations melted away. It is clearly one of the year's very best, and I'm delighted to include it here.*

—T. W.

I've kept this secret for years, but I'm telling it now: My sister, Crystal, was possibly the first person to see Marilyn Monroe's image appear on Mount Rushmore.

Remember that incredible week?

You *don't* remember, do you?

It's the strangest thing, how I seem to be the only person in America who remembers. It's as if we suffer national amnesia. Ask any American, "Do you remember when Marilyn Monroe appeared on Mount Rushmore?" and they'll laugh at you, and say, "Are you crazy? That's a tabloid story, like Bigfoot and Nessie. I suppose you believe in *them*, too?"

Americans don't seem to comprehend that the story of Marilyn Monroe on Rushmore is only treated like a tabloid fabrication *here*; in other parts of the world, people remember it as the actual, astonishing event it really was. Their media run "Marilyn Retrospectives" every year on the anniversary of her appearance. In Japan, she's nearly a religious icon. Believe me, *she's* the reason— not the presidents—why thousands of foreign tourists stream into South Dakota, like pilgrims to Lourdes.

Americans think they're fools, those Marilyn-worshiping foreigners, but they're fools with money. We're delighted to sell them little Indian tom-toms (made in Korea) to take back home to their kiddies, but they search in vain for souvenirs of MM on Rushmore. They come, in their rented cars and tour buses, hoping to find photographs and commemorative books and souvenir paperweights so they can hold her in their hands, along George, Tom, Abe, and Teddy, but all they ever find are the presidents. They don't find any record of her appearance at Rushmore. You know that's true, if you've ever been there. Think about it: Have you ever seen any Marilyn souvenirs sold in the "trading posts" beneath the monument?

No, the event has vanished from *our* national memory, just as she eventually vanished from the face of the mountain.

But I'm telling you—I'm *reminding* you—she was there! For that all-too-brief but magical week, *she* was there. I really do think my sister saw her first, so it's possible I saw her second. But I'm getting ahead of myself.

I remember it all, even if nobody else in this country does.

It took us a couple of endless days to drive from Kansas City, Missouri, to the campground on a pine-forested ridge east of Mount Rushmore: two sweltering, interminable days of driving through Missouri, Nebraska, and South Dakota in ninety-degree heat without air conditioning, and one night in a tacky motel, with Mom and Dad either arguing or not speaking to each other most of the time.

In the car, Crystal and I ate the peanut butter and cracker "sandwiches" that Mom had packed, and drank lukewarm water from the Thermos—because Mom thought Cokes gave me pimples—and sang as many popular songs as we could remember the words to, and stared out the windows of the back seat of the Chevy the rest of the time.

Crystal looked miserable, and I was bored out of my skull and wondering how we were all going to be able to stand being cooped up together for two whole weeks on the road.

I had recently earned my driver's license, and my parents had promised to turn the wheel over to me now and then, once we got out of the heaviest of the summer tourist traffic. But that hadn't happened yet; it seemed as if the entire southern half of America was driving toward the northern half of it. So I was stuck in the back seat with my ten-year-old sister. Our ultimate destination on that year's vacation trip was supposed to be Dad's sister's family in Seattle.

We never made it past Mount Rushmore.

The morning when Marilyn Monroe began to appear on the monument, Mom and Dad woke up fighting, before dawn's early light, even. Maybe they'd never slept, it's entirely possible that they only held it down—the noise and the nasty words—during the night to enable Crys and me to sleep, and then as soon as they heard me slip out to the campground bathroom, they started in again, lying there in their separate bedrolls on the canvas floor of our tent. They probably figured Crystal would sleep through their furious whispering, where I wouldn't. They knew that if they woke me up, I'd fly out of the tent and run off into the night, and they were scared of that possibility, especially now that I could drive by myself.

I had run off once before, on a family camping trip to the Lake of the Ozarks just three weeks earlier. It had scared them both half to death when they couldn't locate me for several hours—they thought I'd drowned, or some hillbilly had captured me—and it made them start to look with wary eyes at me if I was in the room when they would start to argue, after that. (I'd been perfectly safe the whole time I was gone, having stumbled down a country road to the highway, where I sat on the stoop of a Dairy Queen in the sun for hours, getting a tan and flirting with the boys who drove in for burgers or Cokes. I got burned from the sun and also got poison ivy from my furious plunge through the thick Ozark foliage surrounding our tent, but it was worth it.)

So it wasn't as if they didn't love us, or ever think about us.

They did, but they got distracted by their own heat and noise. What did they fight about? What time to get up in the morning, where to eat breakfast, what to eat for breakfast, when to stop for bathrooms, which road to follow on the map . . . and private things, in angry whispers in their bed and bedrolls, things I absolutely did not want to overhear.

This time, however, it was Crystal who ran away, only she was a quiet little thing who just slipped out without them even noticing at first. None of us knew she was gone.

As I said, I was off in the campground ladies room, getting a shower before the hordes of other women and girls trooped in, holding their toothbrushes aloft like flags to stake their claim to their places in line for the showers. It was worth forcing myself to roust before sunup, just to have the bathroom to myself.

Basically, I hated camping, I hated being on vacation with my parents, and I hated them. Well, what can I say, I was sixteen. I loved my little sister, though, and had long considered it my job to shelter her from the acrimony between our parents. I didn't want her to feel as bad about it as I had during those five years before she came along to keep me company in the misery.

After Crystal was born, it was easier for me to tell Mom and Dad to shut up—or run away from them—because then I had somebody besides myself to do it for, to protect. I felt guilty about leaving Crystal behind that time in the Ozarks when I ran away, but it had seemed at the time as if everything was closing in on me, even my responsibility toward her, when all I really wanted was to be left back home, on my own with my friends, in Kansas City.

As of that summer, I was even beginning to resent Crystal—how much I thought she needed me—and to feel guilty about feeling that way, and naturally I hated *those* feelings, too. I was a mess of self-pity and self-righteousness, and Marilyn healed me, and not only me.

What I'm telling you, this story, I've adapted from the diary (we'd call it a journal now, I suppose) which I kept on that trip. If at times I sound a bit young in the telling, it's because I was, then. We were all younger then, we Americans.

Perhaps that's why it's hard for people to recall, because children change and grow, but they don't always remember the moment, the place, or the reason.

I kicked rocks coming back from the bathroom, feeling fresh as the piney air around me. Ten steps from the flap of the tent, I heard *them* arguing, and I seriously considered not going back in. But I stuck my head in anyway, kind of to see what they'd do, and sure enough, Mom and Dad looked at my face, then looked at each other, and then silently turned their backs and pretended to return to sleep. I felt suddenly, pleasantly, powerful, because my mere presence was enough to silence them.

Crystal's bedroll was empty.

"Where's Crys?"

"Bathroom," Mom said, sounding muffled by bedding.

I knew that wasn't true, or I'd have seen her myself. It was just barely light out, and I didn't like the idea of a ten-year-old girl wandering around the campground alone in the almost-dark. I also felt suddenly afraid that she'd picked up from me the idea of running away.

When I found Crys, she was sitting on a huge rock on the ridge overlooking the Black Hills and the monument and the valley below. We'd arrived late the night before, so we hadn't seen anything but the campground yet. I was really relieved to find her. She was staring—her knees drawn up to her chin, her arms hooked around them—spellbound into the distance.

I came up behind her and crawled onto the rock to sit beside her.

It was pretty impressive, the sight of those four huge faces.

The first thing I said to Crystal was, "Do you think Thomas Jefferson can hear Mom and Dad yelling at each other?" I wanted to let her know she wasn't alone in her distress, and I wanted to make her laugh.

"They woke me up," she said. "I wanted to scream at them."

"I know."

"Who's the other one?"

"The other one?" On the mountain, she meant. "Well, to our far left, that's George Washington, and of course you know he was our first President . . ."

"We already studied him," she agreed, impatiently.

"And next to him is Thomas Jefferson, and then there's Theodore Roosevelt, and the one on our right is Abraham Lincoln." I wanted to be either a writer or a history teacher when I grew up, which is why I was keeping a diary, and why I frequently took it upon myself to read travel books about the places we visited, and then to educate my little sister. "The sculptor was a man named Gutzon Borglum. He worked on them from 1927 until he died in 1941. Originally, he was going to carve them down to their waists, but he died before he could do all that. The heads, alone, though, are sixty feet high! And the reason they look so real, like they're looking right at you, is that the pupils of their eyes are actually these three-foot long posts carved out of the granite, and—"

"Who's the *other* one?"

"The other one?"

"Her! I never knew we had a woman president. Who is she?"

"What are you talking about, Crystal?"

And then I saw it: a faint outline on the mountain just to the left of George Washington, in the blank space where the sculptor had originally planned for Roosevelt to be. Only it wasn't blank. I could just barely see it at first, but even so, it was most definitely an outline of a female form. Most definitely. Not just a head, either, but a whole body, down through the spaghetti straps, the tight bodice and skirt of her dress, to the high-heel shoes. High-heel shoes? The outline was getting darker, too, as the rising sun shone fuller and fuller about it. Upon her. Now it looked like an etching. Now it was filling in, like an Etch-A-Sketch, so we could begin to see how bouffant her hair was, how wide her eyes, how full her lips, how round her curves. It wasn't a sculpture, like the presidents, but more like a painting in stone.

"Oh, my God," I whispered, and then I jumped up on the boulder, nearly losing my balance in my excitement. "Oh, my God! Crystal, this is impossible, but that's Marilyn Monroe!"

"Be careful!" Crys yelled at me, and pulled at the bottom edge of my shorts, trying to get me to sit down with her again. "What's going on? I'm getting scared! You're scaring me! What's happening? Who's Marilyn Monroe?!"

"It's a miracle!" I shouted to the valley.

Mom and Dad didn't think it was a miracle, when we dragged them out of the tent—away from an argument over whether or not the milk in the cooler was still fresh enough to pour over cereal—and out to the ledge. We wouldn't tell them why we were pleading and begging and insisting, because we knew they wouldn't believe us, not until they saw her themselves.

Once Mom recovered from her first astonishment, she said, "It's a trick of light."

But Dad's opinion was, "No, somebody's projecting it from somewhere in back of us, from an airplane, maybe. It's an advertising gimmick."

Crys and I turned to look up at the pale blue sky, but it was empty of everything including clouds.

"Oh, please," Mom was scathing, and didn't even bother to look. "An airplane? How about a flying saucer, while you're at it? What airplane could hold an image still for so long?"

"A helicopter," he retorted. "A Harrier jet."

"Oh, stop. It's a trick of light, that's all."

Before they could really get into arguing about *that*, I said in a hurry, "Let's get in the car and get closer! Let's see if we can still see her from any direction! Please?" I was, myself, determined to go chasing that image if I had to steal the keys from my mother's purse, and take off with Crystal and the car.

"It's only an advertising gimmick," Dad grumbled.

But he was curious enough to indulge us, and so we all ran back and piled into the car and started driving around the area. We found out that she was, indeed, visible from any angle, and from anywhere you could see the monument. Uphill, downhill, there she was; daybreak, noontime, and twilight, there she still was!

As each amazing hour passed, and more and more people noticed her, her image became clearer and clearer upon the mountain, until there was no longer any chance of anybody denying that she was there. There was one time of day when George Washington's face cast a shadow that covered her face, but you still couldn't miss the hair, or the rest of her body. She was more than five hundred feet tall, for heaven's sake! Her voluptuous figure was turned slightly toward the presidents, but the full and radiant incandescence of her smile was directed toward the land below the monument, where all of us were staring back up at her.

She was there all that first night, too, in the lights which came on every evening to illuminate the presidents. In the spotlights, her tight, spaghetti-strap dress sparkled like sequins.

Crystal and I squatted on our rock, like Indians, for hours in the darkness, until Mom came out and put her foot down, insisting we come into the tent and go to bed. We could hardly bear to wait until morning, to see if *she* was still there.

And that was the first day.

The second day of Marilyn Monroe's presence on Mount Rushmore was the beginning of pandemonium. When people woke up and looked outside their travel trailers and their motel rooms and their tents, like us, and realized her image was still smiling down at them from beside George Washington, they went nuts.

We drove right into town, or what I called "town," although it was really just the big area of parking lots and "trading posts" and information centers for the monument, and hung around there all day, where the action was. Before you could say "Good Morning, America," the television network news shows had crews landing at the airports at Rapid City and Sioux Falls, and then helicoptering out to the monument. Soon, it seemed as if every single one of us tourists from out of state got interviewed at least once by some reporter from some rinky-dink station or newspaper from somewhere in the country. By late afternoon, the international media was on the scene, too, until you could hardly hear yourself think for the whup-whup of helicopters dipping and twirling all around the monument and the parking lots, trying for the best photographic angle.

And you wouldn't have believed how fast some folks could set up a booth to sell "Marilyn Monroe on Mt. Rushmore" T-shirts! That was just the beginning, too. Dad joked that there must have been five factories in Taiwan, just waiting to get the word to put a rush on Monroe salt-and-pepper shakers and little ceramic statues of her with the wind blowing her skirt up, and copies of that nude calendar photograph of her, you know the one. But all of that came later in the week, most of it arriving at the worst possible time, as things turned out.

In the meantime, on that second day—when we were supposed to be well on the road to Seattle—Crystal and I wandered around on our own. We kept walking on the heels and stumbling into the backs of people who would be walking normally in front of us one minute, and then stopped dead on the sidewalk the next minute, staring up at *her*, as if they'd all at once been turned to stone, themselves.

Crys and I got to giggling about all the open mouths and wide eyes, until we had to lean against a stranger's Toyota and laugh until we were crying. We pleaded with each other, as we each kept making jokes about it, to "Stop, oh, please, stop!"

Too late, I realized the Toyota was occupied, only the owner wasn't inside the car, she was seated, cross-legged on its hood. I quickly pulled Crystal to her feet, and both of us moved away from the vehicle.

The woman on the hood, who was pretty obviously a Native American, was staring back at us.

"Some kind of religious hysteria?" she asked me.

"What?" I didn't know what she meant. She looked quite a bit older than I was, but younger than Mom. She had been wordlessly sitting up there—her black hair hanging way down her back and her bold nose pointed toward the monument—like a hood ornament. Now the dark Indian eyes that had been looking at *her* were observing the antics of my sister and me.

"It's a sacred mountain," she said, and pointed with her right arm to the monument. "We've been trying to tell white people that for centuries. So I guess it figures that a goddess would appear on it. I just never guessed it would be one of *yours*." She laughed in a way that managed to sound indignant, sad, and amused all at once. She didn't seem to be upset that we'd leaned on her car, however, so I tugged Crystal a little closer to the front of it, so we could hear her better. I didn't know how she could stand sitting on the hot metal, until I saw she had a plaid blanket under her.

"We Lakota believe the entire range of hills is our sacred mother from whom comes our food and our shelter," she said then, speaking directly to Crystal, who was clinging to me and looking shy. "Or, at least, it used to provide all that, until you guys took it away from us." She said it with more resignation in her voice than rancor, but I looked down at the ground, feeling vaguely guilty, anyway. But then she commanded my attention again by saying, "Look, you can see the shape of her in the line of the hills. She's lying down. There is her head—"

"I see her shoulders!" Crys let go of me and jumped up and down, thrilled. I understood that we weren't talking about Marilyn now, but rather about a much, much older—even ancient—female spirit that Native Americans attributed to the Black Hills.

"There's the curve of her bosom." The Indian woman pointed, and I thought that I saw it. "The mounds of her belly and her hips."

"I see her legs!" Crys looked up at me. "Do you see?"

I saw the dark, reclining form, all right, of a woman lying on her side, gazing our way. She was a lot bigger than Marilyn's image, because she was the profile of all the hills put together, and she was horizontal, where Marilyn was—for once, as my own father had joked—vertical.

"These hills are womanly," the woman on the car told us.

I thought I could actually feel the Black Hills at that moment, and they felt like a cool embrace on that hot day. I imagined I could feel the pull and attraction of them, and I remembered the way my eyes couldn't stop looking at them when we were driving toward them, the way I couldn't turn away for very long and look at anything else, and the desire that was getting stronger and stronger in me to get as close to them as I could, to walk into that mysterious darkness and let it enfold me. I thought I smelled something in the hot summer air—part baby powder, part some yeasty doughy aroma like bread cooking, part Shalimar perfume, part evergreen, and also something that smelled like my own body, and made me feel embarrassed and excited all at the same time.

Whether it was Marilyn I was smelling, or the sacred mountain mother, or the real live Indian woman beside us, or my own hot, sweaty self, I couldn't tell. Everything was getting confused in my mind as the woman talked to us, and I was beginning to have a hard time telling what was real.

It was real, all of it. And it was unreal, too.

Beside me, Crystal whispered, "Can we go up there?"

The Native American woman and I looked at each other.

"It is a miracle, isn't it?" I said.

She shrugged. "It's a sacred mountain. I'll say this for her: At least she just appeared on it without hurting it; she didn't carve herself into the very flesh of our mother."

"But what about Crazy Horse, down the road?" Crys asked her.

I thought it took some guts for Crystal to ask the Indian woman about that sculpture-in-progress, seventeen miles to the southwest. What Crys meant was: If it's not okay to carve a president into the mountain, why is it okay to carve an Indian chief?

"He never wanted an image to be made of him," the woman told us. "He wouldn't allow paintings or photographs while he was alive."

So it was *not* all right, she was telling us.

But I got the distinct impression that having Marilyn on the mountain was okay, even with her.

That night, the evening of the second day, the story was broadcast all over the world, and front-page photographs displayed the image to millions of people, some of whom believed it was true, and some of whom didn't.

Some of the ones who didn't began to arrive on the third day.

But so did hundreds, thousands, of the ones who did—and that's when the healings began.

The morning of the third day dawned quiet in our tent.

At the time, I didn't recognize that as an early sign that something fantastic was about to happen—a phenomenon that would be even more amazing than an image of a dead movie star appearing on a national monument.

After Crys and I had returned from checking out the view from the ridge (*she* was still there, and her smile competed with the sun, for wattage), for our break-fast of cereal in plastic bowls, we found Mom and Dad not speaking to each other while they were drinking their plastic cups of coffee. But it was a different kind of not-speaking, a kind that seemed peaceful and relaxed, for a change. I held my breath, waiting for the first word of dispute between them.

"More coffee, hon?" my father asked her.

"No, thanks, sweetie," Mom replied, smiling at him.

Crys and I exchanged glances. *Hon? Sweetie?*

"Don't you want some cereal?" Mom asked him.

"No, I think I'll wait for lunch."

I saw Crystal clench her jaw. Here's where it would start, the sarcastic retort from Mom that would poke a withering response out of Dad. Here's where she would say something like, "Great, so we get to look forward to being in the company of a hungry grouch all morning." And then he would say something like, "So? I get to enjoy the company of a grouch *all* the time!"

"Okay," my mother said.

Crystal's eyes widened, as she looked over at me.

Neither of us said a word; we were afraid to break the mood.

What finally moved us out of that idyllic space was an eerie, electric, yet strangely comforting sound, emanating from inside the tent next to us. Crystal heard it first, and she looked up from her Cap'n Crunch and said, "What's that?" With her leading the way, we all four trooped next door to "knock" and to be admitted by our "neighbors," a young couple from New Jersey. There, on their TV, we watched the news of the "Marilyn Miracle," as the reporters were now calling it.

At the moment, the cameras were panning the crowds below the monument, and picking up the noise from down there.

The eerie sound was coming from the crowds.

"Are they chanting?" Mom asked.

"No, listen," the young woman urged us.

And then we could hear that it wasn't *om* the crowds were humming.

It was *MMMMMMM*.

"They say there've been healings," the young woman told us, her eyes as wide as Crystal's had been earlier, when Mom and Dad were courteous to one another. "Sexual healings."

Mom cast a quick glance at Crys and me, and I tried to look bland.

"What's a sexual healing?" my sister blurted out.

Nobody answered her, though I wished somebody would, so I'd know, too! We stayed in their tent long enough (before Mom shooed us out) to get a hint not only of what that meant, but also of what the rest of the world was saying about "us."

"The vision, itself, appears to be a bonafide miracle, accompanied by actual physical miracles," attested one of the people being interviewed. "It is clearly on the order of Fatima or Lourdes, but is even more astonishing and believable, because it has been witnessed, and continues to be seen, by millions of people, if you include those watching it on television." The expert smiled, ever so slightly. "It is certainly not, however, a sighting of the Virgin."

"What's a virgin?" Crys whispered to me.

You, I thought, *and me.* But I put my finger to my lips.

"It's an illusion," claimed a man who was reputed to be an expert in unmasking fraudulent "miracles." "It's a spectacular magic trick to dupe the gullible."

"It is not!" Crystal shouted at his face on the screen. She may not have known what "gullible" meant, but she knew what the man meant. Dad said, "Shh, honey," and pulled her into a hug, and kept her there.

"Heresy," pronounced a high church official. "Blasphemy, for anyone to call this a religious experience!"

From the political right came similar, heated opinions: "It's a national disgrace, having that woman up there with our most beloved and respected presidents!"

But from down below the monument, the interviews were of a different tone, entirely: "She's so beautiful up there," said a man from North Dakota. And a woman from Minnesota was crying, as she said, "I can't stop crying. When I look at her, I can't stop crying, and yet I feel so happy. I can't explain it." And a man from Arizona said, "I loved Monroe in *Some Like It Hot,* and I love Monroe up there, but . . ." He bent down and kissed the forehead of the woman standing beside him, and smiled, as he said, ". . . I love *her* most of all."

"Oh," sighed the young woman from New Jersey. "Isn't that sweet?"

Mom made us leave their tent when medical experts started talking about the normal incidence of cures of impotence in an average population of men, and the statistical likelihood of instantaneous changes in the sexual responses of previously nonorgasmic women.

Down among the "trading posts" and parking lots that day, we drove into the atmosphere that could only be described as part religious revival, part movie star festival.

Clones of Marilyn (not all of them female, by any means) were arriving by the plane and bus load, accompanied by men dressed up like Tony Curtis, or Jack Lemmon, or Clark Gable, or any one of the male movie stars with whom Marilyn Monroe had appeared in pictures.

People were carrying around little statues of Marilyn, and holding them to their lips, and kissing them. Lots of people were kissing each other, too, which should have been excruciatingly embarrassing, especially for Crystal, but for some reason, it wasn't. As the lady from New Jersey had said, it was sweet. There was a sweetness to that crowd, and a tender courtesy in the way that many men and women were treating one another, a tenderness that only grew as the day progressed from warm to hot by late afternoon.

We heard men saying "please."

And women saying "thank you."

We saw people move back from doorways and murmur, "after you," and we saw shoppers wait patiently in the long lines, and we heard them speak respectfully to waiters and waitresses and sales clerks. We saw people with their arms around each other, and people laughing, and a lot of people crying, for no apparent reason.

As we strolled—carrying our own Marilyn souvenirs—my father held my mother's hand. By afternoon, they each had an arm around the other's waist. Crys and I tagged along all day, unwilling to break away from the feeling of affection that seemed to surround our parents. My sister and I had stopped staring at Marilyn on the mountain by that time; instead we stared at those linked arms, as if *they* were miracles, too.

And that was the third day, when you would have sworn world peace was at hand, not to mention peace in the war between the sexes.

On the fourth day, all hell broke loose.

For us, it started nearby, right after cereal.

Both the young couple in the tent to the left of us and the family of five in the tent to the right of us had portable televisions, which they seemed to have turned on, watching the news, more than they actually spent down in "town," or even watching the monument. Maybe that's why a fracas broke out between them—because their experience of *her* was so indirect—and wouldn't you know it began as a religious war?

From the tent to the right, we heard a TV preacher inveighing against Marilyn and her image. They had it turned up loud as it would go, clearly hoping all of us heathens would listen, and heed!

"Heed not the Queen of the Realm of Illusion!" shouted the hoarse-voiced preacher. His voice ripped into the tranquility of the morning. "Turn your eyes from the Whore of Babylon! Turn back your eyes to the Queen of Heaven, to God and Our Lord Jesus and His holy Mother! Drop to your knees this instant, and beg God's merciful forgiveness for so much as glancing at this evil image that has arisen steaming from the foul bowels of Hell! God, forgive us who repent, and punish those who persist in their iniquity! Hear us, believe us, that we who are gathered in Thy Name this day, do not love the Harlot! We do not accept the works of the Whore! We plead for the scourge of Thy Fury across the world, to whip the sin from the backs of the lovers of the Harlot! Blind them! So they cannot see her! Deafen them! So they do not hear her! Cripple them! So they bend their knees at last to Thee! Cast the Whore off Thy mountain! Kill, kill, kill the Harlot, and strike down the wicked who follow her!"

Crystal started looking confused and scared.

"Mom?" she said. "What does that mean?"

Dad was furious, at the noise level, if nothing else.

"I'm going over there and give them a piece of my mind," he fumed, which would once have been Mom's perfect cue to say something like, "That's why you're such a moron! You give so many pieces of your mind away!" But now she only placed both of her hands gently against his chest, and said, "Let's get in the car, and go back to town. Don't you think it might be best to get the girls away from those crazies?"

We were hurrying to do just that, when the couple from New Jersey burst out of their tent and started yelling at the people in the other tent to turn their "damned idiot preacher off!" Which brought out the man from that tent to shake his fist and yell back at them that they were "going straight to hell for worshiping that bitch of Satan!"

It was worse, if possible, in "town."

The forces against the miracle were gathering, even as more "healings" were being reported. Grim-faced people with pamphlets appeared in front of the "trading post." Men carrying large crosses started marching up and down between the cars in the parking lots. Women stood on street corners with their children and yelled Scripture at passersby.

Around lunchtime, there was a rumor that somebody had gone into one of the "trading posts" and had attacked the Marilyn souvenirs with an axe.

Unfortunately, truck after truck of mementos were pouring into the area that day (possibly from those factories in Taiwan Dad had joked about), just as the anti-Marilyn people began arriving in big groups, too. Of course, the sight of all of those bosomy little dolls just fueled the religious and political outrage and determination of some people to "do something about her." We heard several people say, in fact, that they were "going to do something about her."

"What can they do?" Mom wondered, out loud, to us.

"I don't think *they* know," was Dad's opinion.

We, ourselves, actually saw two men shove a man dressed up as Marilyn. The guy in the sequined dress stumbled in his high heels, which caused him to fall against a wall and scrape his bare shoulder. And we heard somebody hiss, "Whore," at a woman who was dressed up to look like Marilyn in the number "Diamonds Are a Girl's Best Friend" from *Gentlemen Prefer Blondes*.

When Mom heard that, she insisted on gathering us up and returning to the campground that minute. When we got there, our neighbors on both sides were quiet, but Dad said to start dismantling our tent, which Crys and Mom and I did, while he went off to try to locate another site for us. I was scared: I didn't want to get hurt, but I didn't want to leave Marilyn, either. I was afraid that if we left Mount Rushmore, our parents might revert to their old ways. The preachers might be screaming about Hell, but the last day and a half had seemed like heaven, to me.

"There's no other space for us here," Dad reported when he returned, and then he looked at all of us, in turn. "Should we go home?"

"No!" Crystal said, and tugged at him. "No! No!"

Dad glanced at me, and I shook my head.

Finally, he took Mom's vote. She didn't say yes or no. Instead, she said, "Let's find a place off by ourselves, in the woods." And that's how we came to move so much closer to *her*, so that we were right where we needed to be in order to become bit players in the final dramatic scene of her last appearance on earth.

By that night, it was—if you'll pardon the pun—crystal clear that somebody was going to have to explain some things to the ten-year-old. Our parents apparently assumed that I'd do the dirty work, as I usually did, but the problem with that convenient theory was that I didn't understand a lot of what was happening any better than Crys did!

It seemed that the healings that hundreds of people were attributing to the apparition were complete cures of an extremely specific sort: All of them were related somehow to sexuality. Some were physical healings of medically confirmed ailments such as ovarian or testicular cancer, while other cures seemed to be more of an emotional or psychological nature. Supposedly, there were men who confessed to having been child molesters, and who now claimed to have no further longings in that direction. In New York City, a convicted rapist was reported to have fallen to his knees in the middle of a prison exercise yard, and to have wept for his victims.

In addition, women who thought they were infertile were finding themselves suddenly pregnant. And women who desperately *didn't* want a baby were discovering their wombs to be mysteriously, blissfully empty! Women who'd always suffered from menstrual cramps were experiencing pain-free periods, and people who had been hiding sexual addictions were publicly declaring themselves liberated from compulsion!

As for me, I just wanted to be hanging around when Mom or Dad explained to Crys the meaning of phrases such as "sustained erection" and "multi-orgasmic"!

Our new campsite was miles closer to Mount Rushmore, close enough so that the lights that illuminated Marilyn and the presidents also cast a soft glow over us.

By suppertime, Crystal's questions were thick as ticks on a leaf.

"Mom, I heard people are getting cured of herpes," Crystal said, over baked beans and hot dogs under the fragrant pines. "What's herpes? I know what AIDS is. Is it true people are getting cured of that, like we heard?"

"I hope so," Mom replied, carefully answering the second question.

"What are genital warts?" Crystal, irrepressibly, asked next.

Dad nearly squirted his hot dog out of its bun, when he heard that.

"Oh, gross!" I blurted, and wished I could disappear.

"Crystal," said my mother, who looked as if she desperately wanted to laugh, "your sister will answer all your questions, after we eat."

"Mom!" I objected, loudly.

"Won't you?" she asked me.

"No! That's your job!"

I didn't want to tell her I didn't have all the answers.

She glanced for help toward Dad, but he only grinned, and said, "Right. That's definitely your job, sweetheart."

"Okay, Crystal," Mom said later, as the two of them sat cuddled together by our campfire. I was right inside the door of our tent, with one ear practically glued to the canvas. Dad had disappeared, on the pretext of gathering firewood. Poor Mom got stuck with the job. I listened for all I was worth, as she stumbled on with her explanations about the facts of life and miracles. "To understand what's going on, you need to understand about Marilyn Monroe."

"She was a movie star," Crys interrupted, in a knowing voice.

"Yes, but a very special one, and there has never been anybody quite like her, either before or since. She was what people call 'sexy.' That meant she was really attractive to the opposite sex—men, I mean—because she was so . . . so . . . uh, well, you know how last year you thought Danny Francis was so cute in your class?"

"Yeah, but Mom, that was last year!"

"I know, honey, but how you felt . . . that, in a great big way, is how millions of men felt about Marilyn Monroe. And not just men. A lot of women thought she was attractive, too. I loved her, for instance. I thought she was kind of embarrassing, because she wore these revealing clothes that made her look practically naked, and she was always flouncing around and wiggling her butt—"

Crystal and Mom giggled, together.

"But even so, I thought she was cute and pretty and funny and adorable." Mom paused, and the campfire filled that quiet moment with the hissing and crackling sounds of its burning. "And now I realize she was also powerful. And intelligent. I can see that in her now, when I look at her old movies. And that power and intelligence, that's all part of being sexy, too. Anyway . . ."

Mom's voice rushed on, before Crys could ask more questions.

"Sex is a powerful feeling of attraction between two people. It's part of what makes people fall in love. It brings people together to have babies. It's perfectly normal. But it can be used in healthy or unhealthy ways. Just like money can, or food, or anything else you can think of. Sex can cause good things to happen to people, or bad things."

Mom's words were coming slower now, as if she was choosing them ever more carefully, or maybe just thinking about what they meant as she said them.

"For some reason that none of us understands, this vision of Marilyn on the mountain is causing good things to happen to people, in regard to sex, and it's also undoing some bad things that have happened to them in regard to sex."

"Why?" Crystal asked.

The fire sang while I, too, waited for Mom's answer.

"Because we needed it, I guess," she said, so softly I barely heard her. "And maybe it had to be her, because she knew what it was like to need—to need so very much—to be healed."

"She?" Crys said.

"Marilyn."

"I love her," Crystal declared.

"I love her, too, honey."

Inside the tent, I thought, *Me, too.*

That was the moment I realized that I didn't hate the vacation or my parents, and that I didn't resent my little sister, not anymore. I felt good, better than I'd ever felt before in my life. I knew what it was like then to feel whole. Complete. Young. Hopeful and happy. *Thank you, Marilyn,* I whispered. I closed my eyes, and pictured her on Mount Rushmore. *Thanks very much.*

By the dawn of the fifth day, many of the people who believed the apparition was an abomination had, with seemingly incredible swiftness, formed themselves into a loud, aggressive coalition.

Dad went into "town" by himself early that morning, and came back talking of rumors of dynamite, of "blowing her off the mountain," of the National Guard being sent in to disperse the crowds and maintain order, of incidents of violence in the crowds, overnight, and of beatings and arrests, and of people being shipped off to jails wherever there was room to hold them in the little towns of South Dakota. He said he didn't know how much of what he'd heard was true. But Dad said he did know this was no longer a happy place to be, and that if there wasn't trouble now, there soon would be.

"I want to get you and the girls out of here," he told Mom.

But she looked thoughtfully at Crystal and me and then astonished me, at least, by saying, "The girls and I aren't ready to leave." She ordered me to take Crys for a walk in the woods "while your father and I sort this out." But before I could turn away, she said to me, "What's that on your face?"

My left hand flew to an itchy spot on my lower left cheek, where I felt something bumpy and kind of rough, and I immediately thought, *Damnation*, how come other people get cured of cancer, but I still get pimples?

Mom drew me close to her and squinted at the thing.

"It's a mole," she pronounced, and then she drew back from me . . . looked up at Marilyn on the mountain . . . looked back at me . . . looked over at Dad . . . and breathed, "Oh, my God, do you know what this is?"

It was a beauty mark, exactly like *hers*.

Mom called it a stigmata—which she explained was like Christ's wounds appearing in the hands of saints and martyrs. But Dad said she'd better not use that word loosely, especially not in "town," what with all the religious fanatics gathered there, and every one of them just looking for any excuse to be offended, and to strike out against the offender, which in this case would be me.

My sister looked at me doubtfully. "A saint?"

I kept touching the beauty mark, until Mom pulled my hand away from it.

"We have to talk," she said to Dad.

As we plodded off together onto our assigned walk in the woods, Crystal muttered, "It's not fair. I want one."

"Maybe when you're older," I told her, smugly.

She thwapped me with the back of her hand, and I laughed, feeling extraordinarily special and pleased with myself.

We stayed, and we even made a brief foray into town that fifth day, though I received stern instructions to keep my head down. Dad wanted to make me wear a head scarf, but Mom said that made me look even more like Marilyn during the period when she was married to the playwright. They compromised by sticking a bandage on my face, which made me feel embarrassed to be seen in public. Protesting did me no good; they said it was for my own safety.

Once in "town," however, we discovered I was not the only one to have received what the agitators were already calling "the mark of Marilyn." Girls and women all up and down the streets, and in the parking lots and "trading posts," were sprouting similar beauty marks, and some of the females wearing them were furious about it, because they were among the agitators. Dad said we were lucky that was the case, because the fact that it was also happening to them was probably the only thing that kept them from actually calling it the "mark of the Beast."

I felt let down, that I wasn't the only one.

People who felt as we did had almost disappeared from the congested area below the monument, because it was getting too dangerous to be there. If you were seen carrying a Marilyn souvenir, or wearing a Marilyn costume, you were accosted by people accusing you of being a traitor to America, or a blasphemer against God, or both, and you stood a risk of having your souvenir jerked out of your hands, or your costume torn off of you, and of being shoved, or worse. People who'd come like pilgrims hoping to be healed were shown on television as they stood weeping in disappointment, some of them, still at the airports in Rapid City and Sioux Falls, afraid to venture any further down the road to Mount Rushmore. At the "trading posts," the merchants swept the Monroe sales items off their shelves and put the presidents back in their front windows.

Mom and Dad hurried us away almost as soon as we arrived, but not before we saw the huge demolition machinery moving into "town," and not before we heard more of the rumors about "pinpoint explosives."

"Why do they hate her?" Crys asked, and asked, and asked. She was hyper with too much energy, bouncing up and down on the back seat of our car and chattering, chattering, chattering, until she drove us all crazy, and we all snapped at her. "Mom? Dad? Why do they hate her? Why do they want to kill her? Why do they call her those names? What's *wrong* with her?"

"Crystal, sit *down*," Dad finally told her.

"And be *quiet* for five minutes!" Mom said, sounding frantic herself.

"*Please!*" I chimed in.

Of course, Crys burst into tears. Feeling awful and guilty about taking it all out on her, I turned my face to the car window. Out of their sight, I gently rubbed my beauty spot, over and over, with the first two fingers of my right hand.

According to the news bulletins we heard on our car radio, the U.S. government truly was sending in the National Guard to keep order, but nobody seemed to think they could mobilize in time to save Marilyn, not that that was their objective, anyway. Their mission was to maintain law and order, and to protect the presidents.

"How," asked a talk-show deejay sympathetic to the apparition, "can they stop a dedicated cadre of explosives experts, anyway? In that wilderness around the monument? No way! Listen, folks, the bad guys are probably already on their way, armed to the teeth with dynamite, or nitroglycerin, or plastic explosives, or whatever it takes to slice our girl off the mountain. Talk to me, Callers! What's your opinion?"

At our tent, with the Ponderosa pines guarding our privacy like sentinels, we got more and more quiet as the day progressed, even Crystal, who kept breaking into convulsive little bursts of tears, and needing Mom or Dad to give her a hug and stroke her hair and lie to her and tell her it was all going to be all right.

"How can you tell her that?" I whispered, furiously, to Mom.

"Honey," she said, so gently it made me feel even more angry, "it *is* going to be all right. We'll go back home. You'll go back to school. Life will go on as usual. We'll forget all about Marilyn."

I touched my beauty mark. "I'll *never* forget her!"

Mom tried to hug me, but I wouldn't let her. I stalked off a little way into the woods, and my head filled up with the words, *I won't . . . ever . . . forget . . . you!*

At least, we got over making Crys the family scapegoat.

Nobody snapped angrily at her anymore. I came back into camp, my anger spent on hurling pine cones into space, and we just all walked around, or lounged around, like zombies, turning on the car radio every so often, and getting more discouraged and feeling more hopeless as the sun crossed over the monument and slid down the other side of it.

The spotlights came on, illuminating Washington, Jefferson, Lincoln, Roosevelt, and Monroe, for the last time.

The chanting started around 11 P.M.

It floated through the woods to us, winding around the pines, scooting along the ground and carried with the cold breeze of that summer evening. It woke us up, one by one, in our tent, and pulled us by our curiosity out into our little clearing.

"What in the world?" Dad murmured.

Crys and I had slept in our jeans and T-shirts, Mom and Dad had pajamas on, and we were all barefoot and rumple-haired and sleepy. For some reason, Mom ran back into the tent and put on her own jeans and T-shirt and a jacket, and even her socks and hiking boots. She threw jackets out at Crys and me, and then she insisted we both put shoes on.

She didn't say anything to Dad, so he just stood there, listening.

By the time Crys and I got back outside, the chanting was louder, and coming near us.

MMMMMMMMMM

That's all it was, a humming of that letter of the alphabet, and it sounded like a melodious, resonant, high-pitched wave rolling toward us, some of it sung in soprano, some in alto, for it was all women and girls who were chanting, and marching across the plain toward the monument. Within minutes, they reached us, and Mom took one of Crystal's hands and one of mine, and the three of us melted into the pines to become notes in the moving melody.

Dad started to hurry back into the tent to change clothes, but Mom stopped him with a softly voiced, "No, sweetheart." And when he then moved as if he'd join us, pajamas and all, she tugged her hand free from mine, blew him a kiss, and called back to him, "Somebody needs to stay here and guard the fort!"

I caught a glimpse of my father, standing there with the breeze whipping the ankles of his pajamas, and he staring at us, looking so worried, as if he were afraid he'd never see us again.

But he didn't follow us.

We left him behind, and joined the other women, dozens, hundreds of women, and more, all of us merging easily into a cadence with one another with every bold and quiet stride we took, softly humming as we marched along together to the base of the monument.

"Others are coming from above," one of the marchers told us.

From the Black Hills, from the west, she meant.

I looked for the Lakota woman, and thought I glimpsed her once, among the trees.

By morning's light, we were fully assembled: hundreds of women and girls, stationed at the base of Mount Rushmore; hundreds more of us lining the top of the monument, standing at the very edge that overlooked the plains and the "town" below.

Through a telescope or binoculars, or from an airplane or helicopter, anyone who saw us could read the words on the banner that some of the women draped over the apparition of Marilyn's hair.

It said, in big, black letters:

IF YOU DESTROY HER, YOU'LL KILL US!

And that's the sight that greeted not only the valley, but everybody who switched on a morning television news show. And there we remained, successfully defending *her*, all that sixth day and all of the sixth night, while the monument lights illuminated all of us: Presidents, Marilyn, living women and girls.

Food materialized from somewhere, and water as we needed it, and somehow there were bedrolls for the children, who organized their own games to play.

No one dared to touch her as long as we remained.

I think we could have stayed, if not indefinitely, then certainly a long, long time, because reinforcements, other women and girls, began arriving by the morning of the seventh day. But as it turned out, we didn't have to stay, because *she* took matters into her own hands.

The word came first to us from observers below.

"They say she's fading!" someone yelled.

We couldn't tell from where we stood and guarded her. We were too close to the image to be able to judge whether it appeared as dark and clear upon the mountain as it had all week.

"She's leaving the mountain!" the word came down.

And she was. Slowly, over the course of the seventh day, she took her leave of us, having drawn out of us our courage and our independence, having been protected by us when we believed she most needed it. Now she freed us by vanishing as mysteriously as she had come.

By the time the lights came on that night, she was gone.

As you know, the Crazy Horse monument was never finished.

Some people thought he'd gone chasing after her. If that's true, I'd call that a *really* Happy Hunting Ground! But I think he had too much dignity for that. Personally, I think she pulled his image away with her as a favor to a great man, knowing he would never have wanted to be there in the first place. How could she do that? Well, you know her magnetic appeal! She didn't take the presidents with her—obviously—and, to me, they look incomplete now, without her voluptuous, vibrant, incandescent femininity to balance them.

However, if you compare photos of them now with pictures of them before *she* appeared, you'll swear there has been a softening of the presidential brows, a loosening of tension in Tom's lips, a twinkle in George's stern glance. Abraham looks as if his load's been lightened, he looks encouraged and comforted, I think, and a little ashamed of himself for hanging up there on the Lakota's sacred mountain. None of those four had very enlightened attitudes toward the native peoples, after all, and Abe was no better than he had to be, in that regard. I know I'm reading a lot into stone, but over time even stone changes, doesn't it? The most dramatic transformation I detect is in Teddy, who used to look as if he were only peering over the plains for the biggest stag to shoot. Now I believe there's a hint of awe and tenderness in his gaze, as if he's deeply moved and even humbled by all he surveys. Any woman who could humble Teddy Roosevelt was a saint, in my book!

Everybody has forgotten, except the rest of the world and me.

Maybe, when she left, she took America's memory with her, because the important thing was not the conscious memory of her apparition, but the unconscious changes she wrought in us. We women are different now—stronger, more straightforward and honest—and so are our men, many of them just plain nicer people than they were before.

So maybe it doesn't really matter if everybody's beauty mark faded, except mine, evidently, or that even Crystal thinks I'm crazy when I try to remind her of our astonishing vacation to the Black Hills when she was ten years old.

It's not that I'm lonely with this memory. After all, I've got the rest of the world to remember it with me. It's just that I'd like her to get the credit, that's all.

So, now, can you see *her* there, on Mount Rushmore?

Are you beginning to remember?

Leslie Dick

The Skull of
Charlotte Corday

Leslie Dick is an American writer who lived in England from the age of ten. In 1988 she returned to the United States and currently teaches in the visual arts department at the California Institute of Arts. Her work has appeared in Bomb, Semiotext(e), Interview, Sight and Sound, Errant Bodies, and ANY. She is the author of two novels, Without Falling and Kicking. She divides her time between London, England, and Los Angeles, California.

In "The Skull of Charlotte Corday," Dick explores the story of Charlotte Corday, who, during the beginning of the Great Terror, assassinated French revolutionary leader Jean-Paul Marat while he was bathing. Corday's skull was preserved after her execution and was eventually passed along to Princess Maria Bonaparte, a descendant of Napoleon and an authority on psychoanalysis. This story comes from Dick's latest collection, The Skull of Charlotte Corday and Other Stories.

—E. D.

Dismembered limbs, a severed head, a hand cut off at the wrist . . . feet which dance by themselves . . . all these have something peculiarly uncanny about them, especially when, as in the last instance, they prove capable of independent activity in addition. As we already know, this kind of uncanniness springs from its proximity to the castration complex. To some people the idea of being buried alive by mistake is the most uncanny thing of all. And yet psychoanalysis has taught us that this terrifying phantasy is only a transformation of another phantasy which had originally nothing terrifying about it at all, but was qualified by a certain lasciviousness—the phantasy, I mean, of intrauterine existence.[1]

Skull of Charlotte Corday (Fig. 1)

1: 1889

Controversy at the Universal Exposition in Paris, on the centenary of the Revolution, as rival craniologists examine the skull of Charlotte Corday, kindly loaned for exhibition by Prince Roland Bonaparte, great-nephew of Napoleon and noted anthropologist, botanist, and photographer.

Professor Lombroso, criminal anthropologist, insists (after a brief examination of the skull) that specific cranial anomalies are present, which confirm his theory of criminal types, or 'born criminals'. He subsequently uses three photographs of the skull of Charlotte Corday, in his book *La Donna Delinquente, la Prostituta e la Donna Normale* (Turin, 1893, co-written with Guglielmo Ferrero, translated into English and published in 1895 as *The Female Offender*) to demonstrate that Corday, despite the pure passion and noble motive of her crime, was herself a born criminal, and therefore in some sense destined to murder:

Political criminals (female).—Not even the purest political crime, that which springs from passion, is exempt from the law which we have laid down. In the skull of Charlotte Corday herself, after a rapid inspection, I affirmed the presence of an extraordinary number of anomalies, and this opinion is confirmed not only by Topinard's very confused monograph, but still more by the photographs of the cranium which Prince R. Bonaparte presented to the writers, and which are reproduced in Figs. 1, 2, 3.

The cranium is platycephalic, a peculiarity which is rarer in the woman than in the man. To be noted also is a most remarkable jugular apophysis with strongly arched brows concave below, and confluent with the median line and beyond it. All the sutures are open, as in a young man aged from 23 to 25, and simple, especially the coronary suture.

The cranial capacity is 1,360 c.c., while the average among French women is 1,337; the shape is slightly dolichocephalic (77.7); and in the horizontal direction the zygomatic arch is visible only on the left—a clear instance of asymmetry. The insertion of the saggital process in the frontal bone is also asymmetrical, and there is a median occipital fossa. The crotaphitic lines are marked, as is also the top of the temples; the orbital cavities are enormous, especially the right one, which is lower than the left, as is indeed the whole right side of the face.

On both sides are pteroid wormian bones.

Measurements.—Even anthropometry here proves the existence of virile characteristics. The orbital area is 133 mm.q., while the average among Parisian women is 126. The height of the orbit is 35 mm., as against 33 in the normal Parisian.

The cephalic index is 77.5; zygomatic index 92.7; the facial angle of Camper, 85°; the nasal height, 50 (among Parisians 48); frontal breadth, 120 (among Parisian women 93.2).[2]

'The skull of Charlotte Corday herself'—Charlotte Corday, the 'angel of assassination', the beautiful virgin who fearlessly killed Marat in his bath, and calmly faced the guillotine, certain of the righteousness of her act. Corday becomes the paradigm of Lombroso's theory of innate criminality, simply because in every other respect she was so pure, so devoid of criminal characteristics. According to Lombroso, atavism in the male reveals itself in criminality; by contrast, the atavistic female is drawn to prostitution. Corday's virility is thus confirmed by her virginity.

The 'criminal type', or born criminal, is central to Lombroso's theory of anthropology. W. Douglas Morrison, Warden of H. M. Prison, Wandsworth, writes in his 1895 introduction to *The Female Offender*:

> The habitual criminal is a product, according to Dr Lombroso, of pathological and atavistic anomalies; he stands midway between the lunatic and the savage; and he represents a special type of the human race.[3]

Lombroso himself generalizes with ease about the female criminal type:

In short, we may assert that if female born criminals are fewer in number than the males, they are often much more ferocious.

What is the explanation? We have seen that the normal woman is naturally less sensitive to pain than a man, and compassion is the offspring of sensitiveness. If one be wanting, so will the other be.

We also saw that women have many traits in common with children; that their moral sense is deficient; that they are revengeful, jealous, inclined to vengeances of a refined cruelty.

In ordinary cases these defects are neutralized by piety, maternity, want of passion, sexual coldness, by weakness and an undeveloped intelligence. But when a morbid activity of the psychical centres intensifies the bad qualities of women, and induces them to seek relief in evil deeds; when piety and maternal sentiments are wanting, and in their place are strong passions and intensely erotic tendencies, much muscular strength and a superior intelligence for the conception and execution of evil, it is clear that the innocuous semi-criminal present in the normal woman must be transformed into a born criminal more terrible than any man.[4]

In 1889, as part of the Universal Exposition at Paris, numerous scientific congresses were held, and it was possible to attend three or four at a time. That summer, simultaneously there took place the International Congress of Physiological Psychology, the International Congress of Experimental and Therapeutic Hypnotism (participants included Freud, Myers, James, and Lombroso), and the Second International Congress of Criminal Anthropology. Many years later, Lombroso referred to that summer in Paris as that grievous or wretched time ('*dolorosa*'),[5] and this wretchedness was due, at least in part, to the violent arguments that took place between Lombroso and the French craniologists, notably Dr Paul Topinard, over the skull of Charlotte Corday. Lombroso recalled that the only truly happy moment of his stay in Paris was when he was permitted to examine the skull itself, which was entrusted to him by Prince Roland Bonaparte.

Lombroso was particularly thrilled to find, on the skull of Charlotte Corday, the median occipital fossa, upon which his theory of criminal atavism rested. Nineteen years before, in 1870, '*in un fredda e grigia mattina di dicembre*'—'on a cold, grey December morning',[6] Lombroso performed an autopsy on the skull of Villella, a thief, and discovered this cranial anomaly, which he believed related directly to the skull formations of apes. Lombroso kept the skull of Villella in a glass case on his desk for the rest of his life, and in 1907, he wrote: '*Quel cranio fin da quel giorno divenne per me il totem, il feticcio dell'antropologia criminale.*'— 'From that day on, this skull became for me the totem, the fetish of criminal anthropology.'[7] It was the median occipital fossa that proved to be the bone of contention, so to speak, at the Second Congress.

Turning to *L'Anthropologie*, volume 1, 1890, we find, on the very first page of this first volume, the text referred to by Lombroso as 'Topinard's very confused monograph', entitled 'A propos du Crâne de Charlotte Corday'. In this work, Topinard implicitly criticizes Lombroso's techniques of measuring cranial anomalies, but more importantly, rejects Lombroso's interpretations of these measurements. Topinard insists there is no determining connection between the shape of the skull and the psychology or behaviour of the human being:

> Our project is not to describe the skull as if it were that of a known person, with the objective of comparing craniological characteristics with the moral characteristics historically attributed to this person. We merely wish to take the opportunity for a study which could be carried out on any other skull, its object being to place before the eyes of our readers a summary of the manner in which, in our view, given the current state of the science, an isolated skull should be described, inspired by the methods and the very precise procedures of our illustrious and late lamented teacher, Paul Broca.[8]

Topinard goes on to emphasize the importance given by the school of Broca to averages, and therefore the relative insignificance of a single skull. On the other hand, he writes, with a very precious skull, it is correct to photograph and measure it, carefully, so that our grandchildren can make use of this data later, when science has progressed further. Topinard's description of the skull itself is vivid:

> The skull, before my eyes, is yellow like dirty ivory; it is shiny, smooth, as, in a word, those skulls that have been neither buried in the bosom of the earth, nor exposed to the open air, but which have been prepared by maceration [soaking], then carefully placed and kept for a long time in a drawer of a cupboard, sheltered from atmospheric vicissitudes.[9]

Topinard goes on to emphasize that, above all, the skull is normal, symmetrical, 'without a trace of artificial or pathological deformation, without a trace of illness',[10] etc. It is the skull of a woman, 23 to 25 years old (Corday was 24 when guillotined), and there follow twenty-four pages of close technical description, eschewing any overt moral or sociological commentary. In conclusion, Topinard clearly disagrees with Lombroso:

> It is a beautiful skull, regular, harmonic, having all the delicacy and the soft, but correct curves of feminine skulls.[11]

For Topinard, the crucial fact is that, quite apart from exhibiting the appropriate delicacy and softness of normal femininity, this skull is an average skull, typical of European females. Topinard admits there are a few minor asymmetries, but insists these are insignificant, merely 'individual variations'[12] on the norm. Topinard's polemic quietly but insistently defends Charlotte Corday's reputation, denying the virility, pathological asymmetry, and abnormality attributed to her by Lombroso.

Ironically, on p. 382 of the 1890 volume of *L'Anthropologie*, Topinard is obliged to insert a belated Errata to his essay on the skull of Charlotte Corday. He notes that it is a rare exception that a text so full of numbers should appear without some errors of transcription or typography. He himself spotted one such error, and 'M. Lombroso' caught another. Nevertheless, he writes, these slight changes do not affect in any way the terms of his polemic. It is easy to imagine Lombroso's satisfaction upon discovering these slips.

Clearly, the disagreements between Lombroso and Topinard went deeper than techniques of measurement. Yet Lombroso, who was Jewish and a Dreyfusard, wrote a book on anti-Semitism in 1894. He was against nationalism, militarism, and colonialism, and was the very first socialist candidate elected to the town council of Turin in 1902. His research into pellagra, a skin disease that ravaged the peasant population, was controversial, but accurate, and he struggled for many years to have his findings recognized and acted upon. Nevertheless, Lombroso's primary scientific project of criminal anthropology depends on the construction of a hierarchy based on genetic characteristics, and on theories of atavism and degeneracy. (In 1892, Max Nordau dedicated his extremely influential and pernicious book on degeneracy to Lombroso.)

By contrast, Topinard, reviewing an anonymous polemic that proposed the forcible deportation of all seven million black Americans to Africa, in order to avoid racial disharmony, writes:

> The solution is original, but impossible to realize . . . Instead of indulging in such a utopia, wouldn't the anonymous author do better to say that if the black and white races do not mix in his country, this is due to the inveterate prejudice of the Americans, who create an intolerable situation for the blacks, pushing them into an isolation in which they can only see them [the whites] as the enemy, a class which humiliates them, abuses its intellectual advantages, and refuses them an equal chance in the struggle for existence.
>
> There is only one significant fact in the state of things revealed by this book: this is that the blacks, in the United States, after twenty years of emancipation, remain pariahs . . . Here it is the question of the workers, the Jewish question, the Chinese question. The Negro question is of the same kind: anthropological notions of race have no bearing on it whatsoever.[13]

Lombroso's scientific socialism would probably have come under the heading of what Gramsci later dismissed as 'Lorianismo', after Loria, the political theorist whose most striking proposal was that everyone should have their own aeroplane, a utopian vision of Los Angeles freeway urbanism long before Los Angeles existed.[14] After a lifetime spent fascinated by the skulls of people of genius, political criminals, and anarchists, Lombroso became, in his later years, a fanatical spiritualist. His death, in 1909, was marked by obituaries on the front pages of daily newspapers in Russia, the United States, and Japan. The disposal of his corpse is noteworthy; Giorgio Colombo's recent book on the Museum of Criminal Anthropology in Turin, founded by Lombroso, includes a large photograph of Lombroso's head, beautifully preserved in alcohol in a glass jar. Colombo explains:

> Among the papers of the illustrious professor, his family found three different wills, made at three different times, with small variations of a familiar kind. But one disposition, constant in all three wills, clearly indicated an explicit desire of Cesare Lombroso, which his relatives must strictly observe. This required that his body be taken to the laboratory of forensic medicine, to undergo an autopsy by his colleague Professor Carrara—this was to reply, *post mortem*, to those who had accused him of only working on the bodies of the poor. His skull was to be measured and classified, and then mounted

on the rest of his skeleton; his brain was to be analysed in the light of his theory of the relation between genius and madness. Whether Carrara carried this out is not known; today the skeleton hangs in a glass case in the museum, the brain in a glass jar at its feet. In another case nearby stand the receptacles containing the intestines and the face itself. What remained of the body was cremated, and the ashes are to be found in an urn in the cemetery, between the painter Antonio Fontanesi and the poet Arturo Graf.[15]

The face of Cesare Lombroso in its jar, with his squashed and moustachioed features pressed against the glass, is a sight that, once seen, is not easily forgotten.

2: 1927

Marie Bonaparte, also known as Her Royal Highness Princess Marie of Greece and Denmark, was the only child of Prince Roland Bonaparte, owner of the skull of Charlotte Corday. She was seven years old in 1889, and later vividly remembered the inauguration of the Eiffel Tower and the Universal Exposition. She remembered also the reception that was given by her father for Thomas Edison, a very large party that included among the guests a group of American Indians in war paint and feathers. A number of different nationalities appeared as ethnographic and anthropological displays at the Exposition, imported especially for the event, to be measured by the anthropologists, and photographed by Prince Roland.[16] The 'Peaux-Rouges', however, were represented in Paris by Buffalo Bill Cody's troupe of performers, Sioux Indians from Dakota, most of whom politely refused to allow the scientists to measure their heads and bodies. These were the guests at the Prince's reception, in honour of Edison as an American. Marie remembered asking her father for permission to attend the party, if only for a little while. He refused. She wrote to him: 'O Papa, cruel Papa! I am not an ordinary woman like Mimau and Gragra. I am the true daughter of your brain. I am interested in science as you are.'[17]

In 1923, during the long hours spent at her beloved father's bedside, as he battled with terminal cancer, Marie Bonaparte discovered Freud, through reading his *Introductory Lectures on Psychoanalysis*, which had just been published in French. As a child, Marie was particularly vulnerable to her father's frequent absences, prohibitions, and general unavailability, because her mother had died only a few days after giving birth to her. In the year of his final illness, Prince Roland could no longer leave her, and they spent every day together, taking lunch and dinner by themselves. Her father finally died in April 1924, the same month Marie Bonaparte's pseudonymous article on the clitoris appeared in the journal *Bruxelles Médical*.[18]

Marie Bonaparte was fascinated with the problem of female frigidity, a condition she herself suffered from, and her 1951 book *De la Sexualité de la Femme* (translated into English in 1953 as *Female Sexuality*) is reminiscent of Lombroso in its constant appeals to an ideal of normal femininity. In 1924, her article, 'Considerations on the Anatomical Causes of Frigidity in Women', argues that while certain types of frigidity are due to psychic inhibition, and are therefore susceptible to cure by psychotherapy, others can be attributed to too great a

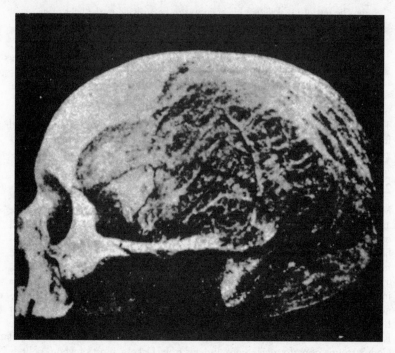

Skull of Charlotte Corday (Fig. 2)

distance between the clitoris and the opening of the vagina. Having come up with this anatomical theory, Marie Bonaparte was delighted to discover Dr Halban of Vienna, a surgeon who had developed an operation which consisted of moving the clitoris closer to the urethral passage. In the 1924 article, signed A. E. Narjani, Marie Bonaparte wrote that five women had been operated on, with positive results. Later, she was forced to admit that the operation was not always one hundred per cent successful.

In December of 1924, after a long illness (salpingitis, or inflammation of the Fallopian tubes), which struck immediately after her father's funeral, and an operation to remove an ovarian cyst, which kept her in bed for three months, Marie Bonaparte (who had virtually unlimited wealth, inherited from her mother's family, the Blancs, who owned the casino at Monte Carlo) imported the plastic surgeon Sir Harold Delf Gillies from London, whom she had met through King George V the previous summer. Gillies performed two operations: first, to 'correct' her breasts, and then, to retouch a scar at the base of her nose, a scar she'd had surgically adjusted twice before. At this time, Marie Bonaparte was forty-two years old and sexually very active, having had a series of passionate love affairs since her marriage to Prince George of Greece and Denmark, who was a closet homosexual, in love with his uncle, Prince Waldemar.

On February 21, 1925, Marie Bonaparte invited Drs René Laforgue and Otto

Rank to dinner, to discuss psychoanalysis. She received them in bed, still recuperating from her operations. In April, at Marie Bonaparte's request, Laforgue wrote to Freud, inquiring if he would accept her as a patient for psychoanalysis. In May, she was taking a cure in the south of France for persistent pains in the lower abdomen, pains she and Laforgue believed to have a psychological origin. (These pains seem to have been associated with her chronic pelvic inflammatory disease.) In June, Marie Bonaparte wrote directly to Freud for the first time. In September 1925, in Vienna, she began her analysis with Freud.

They got on like a house on fire. Freud quickly acceded to her request for two hours of his time daily. He enjoyed the *'Prinzessin'*, and maliciously confided: 'Lou Andreas-Salomé is a mirror—she has neither your virility, nor your sincerity, nor your style.'[19] It was not long before Marie Bonaparte decided to become a psychoanalyst, and gradually she became close friends with Ruth Mack Brunswick (who later became a junky) and Anna Freud. Marie Bonaparte showed Freud her breast, and discussed his personal finances with him. She gave him a chow, and thereafter the aged Freud became a fervent dog lover. The dogs functioned as a kind of extended family across Europe: puppies were exchanged, dogs were mated, and their deaths lamented. In 1936, Freud wrote to Marie Bonaparte of the 'affection without ambivalence . . . that feeling of an intimate affinity, of an undisputed solidarity', which he felt for his chow, Jo-fi.[20] And in 1938, together with Anna Freud, he translated Marie Bonaparte's book, *Topsy, Chow-Chow au Poil d'Or*—'Topsy, the Chow with the Golden Hair'.[21]

In July 1926, in Vienna (after six months of analysis with Freud), Marie Bonaparte had her first consultation with Dr Halban. In the spring of 1927, she had Halban sever her clitoris from its position and move it closer to the opening of her vagina. She always referred to this operation by the name 'Narjani'. The origins of this pseudonym are obscure. The operation, performed under local anaesthesia and in the presence of Ruth Mack Brunswick, took 22 minutes. Freud disapproved. It was 'the end of the honeymoon with analysis'.[22] In May Marie Bonaparte wrote to Freud that she was in despair over her stupidity. Freud, stern but forgiving, it seems, encouraged her to look after her seventeen-year-old daughter, Eugenie, who had been diagnosed as suffering from tuberculosis. Marie Bonaparte felt Freud was reproaching her for her narcissism. In June 1927, the very first issue of the *Revue Française de Psychanalyse*, financed by Marie Bonaparte, came out, and in 1928 she began to practise as an analyst, with Freud himself giving postal supervision.

Marie Bonaparte's conduct of psychoanalysis was from the beginning almost as unorthodox as that of her great enemy, Jacques-Marie Lacan. She would send her chauffeur in a limousine to pick up her patients, to drive them to her palatial home in Saint-Cloud for their sessions. In fine weather, the hour was spent in the garden, with Marie Bonaparte stretched out on a chaise longue behind the couch. She always crocheted as she listened, indoors or out. In later years, whenever possible, she would take her patients with her, as guests, to her houses in St Tropez or Athens, thus inventing the psychoanalytic house party.

In April 1930, Marie Bonaparte visited Vienna, in order to consult Dr Halban again. The sensitivity in the original place from which the clitoris had been moved persisted. (During this period, Marie Bonaparte was involved in a long affair with Rudolph Loewenstein, was later to become Lacan's analyst, and also analysed her son, Peter.) Halban proposed further surgery on the clitoris, in combination with a total hysterectomy to finally eliminate her chronic salpingitis. Ruth Mack Brunswick was again present at the operation, which took place in May.

In February 1931, Marie Bonaparte had her clitoris operated on by Halban for the third and last time. Throughout this time, of course, Freud was suffering from cancer of the jaw, and undergoing regular operations. Her daughter's health was also very bad during this period, and Eugenie had to have an extremely painful operation on a tubercular cyst in her leg in May 1931.

From very early childhood, Marie Bonaparte was fascinated by murder. Servants' gossip vividly presented the probability that the impecunious and unfeeling Prince Roland, conspiring with his scheming mother, Princess Pierre, had, so to speak, hastened the end of the young heiress, Marie's mother. Marie Bonaparte's very first contribution to the nascent *Revue Française de Psychanalyse* was an essay on 'Le Cas de Madame Lefèbvre',[23] an upper-middle-class woman from the north of France, who had shot her pregnant daughter-in-law in cold blood, while out for a drive with the young couple. Marie Bonaparte's second psychoanalytic essay, published the same year, is entitled: 'Du Symbolisme des Trophées de Tête', or 'On the Symbolism of Heads as Trophies'. The essay investigates the question why the cuckolded husband traditionally wears horns, when otherwise horns are a symbol of virility and power, in both animals and gods. She argues that the relation between castration and decapitation is always played out in terms of the Oedipal drama, and the ridiculous figure of the betrayed husband reconstructs this drama in fantasy, where the laughing spectator unconsciously identifies with the lover, the unfaithful wife stands in for the mother, and the cuckold represents the father. His totemic horns ironically invoke his paternal potency, while the childish wish to castrate (or murder) the father, to turn this threat against him, is sublimated in laughter and derision.[24]

Marie Bonaparte is perhaps most admired for her efficient arrangement of Freud's departure from Vienna in June 1938, after the German invasion of Austria in March of that year. She enlisted the help of the Greek diplomatic corps, and the King of Greece himself, in smuggling Freud's gold out of Austria.[25] On the 5th of June, Freud and his family spent twelve hours in Paris, at Marie Bonaparte's house at rue Adolphe Yvon, sitting in the garden and resting on the long journey from Vienna to London. Freud had not set foot in his beloved Paris since 1889, the summer of the Universal Exposition celebrating the centenary of the Revolution. Marie Bonaparte was also personally responsible for saving Freud's letters to Fliess, a correspondence which Freud himself would have preferred to suppress.[26]

In *Female Sexuality* (1951), Marie Bonaparte wrote at length about the practice of clitoridectomy in Africa, and about the operation that she here called 'the Halban-Narjani operation',[27] in the last section of her book, 'Notes on Excision'. In this text, she once again presents her theories on frigidity in women. Total frigidity, she suggests, where both vagina and clitoris remain anaesthetic, is 'moral and psychogenic, and psychical causes [including psychoanalysis] may equally remove it.'[28] For this reason, she writes: 'The prognosis for total frigidity in women is generally favourable.'[29] Not so the cases of partial frigidity, in which the woman experiences clitoral pleasure, but no vaginal orgasm. Marie Bonaparte considers whether the cultural prohibition on infantile masturbation works in the same way as the practice of clitoridectomy, as an attempt to 'vaginalize' the woman, to internalize the erotogenic zone, and intensify vaginal sensitivity. She concludes that neither method succeeds in 'feminizing' or 'vaginalizing' the young girl, and sees such physical or psychical 'intimidation' as cruel and unproductive.[30]

Earlier in *Female Sexuality*, Marie Bonaparte writes specifically about Halban's operation, referring once again to five cases. Two of these cases could not be followed up, two showed 'generally favourable, though not decisive results',[31] and one was unsuccessful. It is difficult to identify Marie Bonaparte herself among these five cases, although one cannot help suspecting the last. In this case, after the operation, the woman 'had only been satisfied twice in normal coitus, and then only while the cut, which became infected, remained unhealed, thus temporarily mobilizing the essential feminine masochism. Once the cut healed, she had to revert to the sole form of coitus which had so far satisfied her: the kneeling position on the man lying flat.'[32] Marie Bonaparte comments: 'This woman's masculinity complex was exceptionally strong.'[33]

3: 1793

In July 1793, Charlotte Corday travelled alone to Paris from Caen, in Normandy, in order to assassinate Marat. Passionately attached to the cause of the Girondins, she firmly believed the death of Marat would restore order and bring peace to France. She intended to kill Marat on the Champ de Mars on July 14th, at the Fête de la Liberté, the fourth anniversary of the storming of the Bastille. She later wrote that she had expected to be torn to pieces immediately by the people. She soon learned, however, that Marat was too ill either to take part in the festival or to attend the Convention. Corday was reduced to subterfuge in order to gain admittance to Marat's house.

On the 12th of July, Corday wrote her testament, a passionate justification of assassination, and pinned it, with her baptismal certificate and *laissez passer*, inside her dress. Very early the next morning, she put on a brown dress and a tall black hat, in the typical fashion of Normandy, and carrying her gloves, fan, and handbag containing watch, keys, and money, she left her cheap hotel to buy a kitchen knife. The heat was already intense.

At nine o'clock she took a cab to Marat's residence, No. 20, rue des Cordeliers, where he lived in cramped quarters above the press of his journal *L'Ami du Peuple*. The concierge asked Corday what she wanted, and she turned away without a word, walking quickly down the street. Corday returned at about half past eleven, managing to get past the concierge without being seen. She rang the bell, and Marat's partner, Simonne Evrard, and her sister, Catherine Evrard, together refused her entry. Marat was too ill to receive anyone.

Corday returned to the Hôtel de la Providence, and wrote Marat a letter, telling him she wanted to see him in order to give him information about the Girondist plots in Caen. She posted this, and then sat down to wait for a reply. In the late afternoon, she wrote a second letter, again appealing to be allowed a short interview. She ended this letter with the words, '*Il suffit que je sois bien Malheureuse pour avoir Droit à votre bienveillance.*'—'My great unhappiness gives

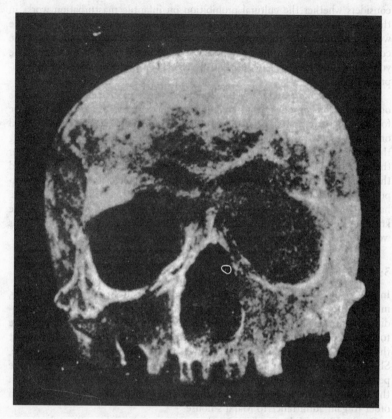

Skull of Charlotte Corday (Fig. 3)

me the right to your kindness.'[34] She posted this second letter, but Marat was dead before it was delivered.

Corday returned to the rue des Cordeliers at about seven in the evening, hoping to arrive shortly after her second letter. She had spent the afternoon having her hair done; she sent for a hairdresser to come to the hotel, he curled and set her hair, and powdered it lightly. She also changed her outfit. Thinking of Judith of Bethulia, she surmised that Marat was more likely to grant her an audience if she was seductively dressed. She wore a loose spotted muslin dress with a fichu of delicate pink gauze. She tied green ribbons around her high black hat, and once again took a cab to Marat's house.

At the door, Corday argued, first with the concierge and then with Simonne Evrard, until Marat, in his bath, called out to his companion, who went in to him. He would see Charlotte Corday.

Marat was in a tiny room, between the passage and his bedchamber, that was lit by two windows onto the street. He was sitting in a shoe bath, naked, with an old dressing gown thrown across his shoulders. A slab of wood rested across the bath, to serve as a desk, and on this were placed paper, pen, and a bottle of ink tilted by a small bit of wood. His head was wrapped in a cloth soaked in vinegar.

He was near death, as a result of his illnesses, which were various; he suffered acutely from eczema, migraines, herpes, diabetes, arthritis, and neurasthenia. His gastric troubles required him to consume only liquids, and in order to sustain his furious writing practice, Marat drank a minimum of twenty cups of coffee a day. The sores and lesions that covered his body were a horrifying sight; people were often reluctant to sit next to him in the Convention. One expert described his disease as *'l'affection squammeuse et vésiconte'*,[35] a sort of generalized scaly eczema. His body deteriorated quickly after his death, although this was partly due to the extreme July heat.

Admitted to his closet, Charlotte Corday talked to Marat briefly about the Girondists at Caen, her fan in one hand and her knife in the other, and then stabbed him, plunging the knife straight downwards into his naked breast. Marat cried out, *'À moi, chère amie, à moi!'*[36] Charlotte Corday was shocked to see Simonne Evrard's distress. There was a tremendous amount of blood, and he died almost immediately. Simonne Evrard and the cook dragged Marat's body out of his bath and tried to put him into bed. Charlotte Corday ventured into the corridor, but the street porter drove her into the salon, where he hit her over the head with a chair. A dentist appeared, followed by a doctor and the commissioner of police for the *'section du Théâtre Français'*. At eight o'clock Corday's second letter arrived; Guellard the police commissioner carefully wrote on it: 'This letter was not delivered . . . it was rendered useless by the admission of the assassin at half-past seven, at which hour she committed her crime.'[37]

David's extraordinary painting, *Marat Assassiné*,[38] shows the Friend of the People dead in his bath, holding in his left hand the letter dated 13 July 1793, with the words clearly legible: *'Il suffit que je sois bien Malheureuse pour avoir Droit à votre bienveillance.'* On the packing case next to the bath lies an *assignat*, or promissory note, with a covering letter from Marat, evidence of his generosity: 'Give this *assignat* to your mother.' The blood-stained knife lies on the floor; Marat's limp right arm hangs down, still grasping his quill pen. On the packing case itself, in Roman capitals, the text: *'À MARAT. DAVID. L'AN DEUX.'* These various texts, in simultaneous juxtaposition within the painting, tell the whole story, David's version of the story. Marat's skin is flawless and very pale.[39]

Historians argue over Charlotte Corday's beauty, the colour of her hair, and even what she was wearing when she committed the murder. After carefully weighing the different accounts, it seems she brought three outfits to Paris with her: the brown dress (before the murder), the spotted muslin (during), and a white dress (after), this last the dress she wore to her trial. To these outfits must be added the red chemise, which she wore to the guillotine, traditional execution dress for murderers, arsonists, and poisoners. On the subject of her hair, it seems to have been 'chestnut', and the tradition that holds her to have been *'blonde cendrée,'* or ash-blonde, was misled simply by the light powder that the hairdresser, M. Person, applied the afternoon of the murder. As for her beauty, it is generally agreed that her chin was very large, a classic sign of degeneracy in Lombroso's theory, though by 1889 the skull was missing its lower jaw, so he never knew this. The only objective account of Charlotte Corday's physical appearance comes from the *laissez passer*, issued at Caen for her trip to Paris. She is described as: 'twenty-four years old, height five feet one inch (*cinq pieds un pouce*), hair and brow chestnut (*châtains*), eyes grey, forehead high, nose long, mouth medium, chin round, cleft (*fourchu*), face oval'.[40] Her height is another area of uncertainty; often described as tall and striking, perhaps '*un pouce*' means two to three inches. Or possibly her traditional Normande hat, with its tall conical crown, added to her stature.

Immediately after the murder, the revolutionary press depicted Corday as a monster: '*une femme brune, noire, grosse et froide*'—'*malpropre, sans grâce . . . la figure dure insolente, érysipèlateuse et sanguine*'.[41] To the Gironde, needless to say, she was indescribably beautiful, an angel. Ironically, Corday's murder of Marat was a bloody turning point in the Revolution; it was arguably the event that precipitated the Terror. In 1836 Marat's sister, Albertine, declared: 'Had my brother lived, they would never have killed Danton, or Camille Desmoulins.'[42] Michelet notes his belief that Marat would have 'saved' Danton, 'and then saved Robespierre too; from which it follows that there would have been no Thermidor, no sudden, murderous reaction'.[43]

On the 16th of July, the funeral of Marat took place. In charge of the design, David passionately wanted to display the corpse of Marat arranged in his bath exactly as in his painting. Unfortunately, the corpse was in such a state of corruption that, despite the valiant efforts of the embalmers, this was not possible. The body was placed in a sarcophagus of purple porphyry taken from the collection of antiquities at the Louvre; a huge tricolour drapery, soaked in alcohol, was wrapped around the body; the alcohol was renewed at regular intervals, in the hope of retarding the bodily decay which, as David noted, was already far advanced.

A right arm was carefully placed, the hand holding a pen, to hang over the edge of the sarcophagus. The eyes and mouth of Marat were wide open, impossible to close, and the tongue, protruding in his death agony, had been cut out. The vast funeral procession began at the club of the Cordeliers, and wound through the streets of Paris, the chariot on which Marat's body was displayed being pulled by twelve men, while young girls in white, carrying cypress boughs, walked alongside. Thousands followed the cortège. As evening fell, torches were lit. At midnight, the procession returned to the garden of the Cordeliers. Speeches, revolutionary hymns, and elegies continued until two in the morning. One unfortunate enthusiast rushed forward to kiss the hand that held the pen, and the arm came off. One of David's special effects, the arm did not belong to Marat. Finally Marat was buried beneath a granite pyramid (designed by Martin), although the removal of his remains to the Panthéon was already planned. The funeral became a saturnalia that went on all night.

In prison, Charlotte Corday passed the 16th of July writing a long letter to Charles Barbaroux, the Girondin activist at Caen. In this letter she gave a complete account of her trip from Caen to Paris, the days of uncertainty at the hotel, the murder, and the aftermath. Her tone is elated: 'A lively imagination, a sensitive heart, promised me a stormy life; let those who regret me consider this and let them rejoice to think of me in the Elysian Fields with some other friends.'[44] On the 15th she had asked for a painter to come to the prison and paint her portrait: *'Je vous en prie de m'envoyer un peintre en miniature.'*[45] Corday wrote to Barbaroux that she always intended to remain anonymous, expecting to be torn to pieces immediately after the murder. Yet she pinned her identity papers and her manifesto inside the bosom of her dress, and in prison she both requested a portrait painter and had a hat made—*'faite à Paris selon la mode du temps'*[46]—a white bonnet which she wore to the scaffold.

At the trial, on the 17th, an ex-pupil of David and captain of the National Guard, Hauer, made a drawing of Charlotte Corday. She moved her head to afford him a better view. When the guilty verdict came through at mid-day, Hauer accompanied Corday to her cell, in order to improve his drawing. As he worked, she made suggestions and posed for him, placing her hands folded on her breast.

The executioner Sanson appeared at about three o'clock. In his memoirs he recalled that when Corday saw him come in, holding a pair of scissors in one hand and the *chemise rouge* in the other, she inadvertently exclaimed, *'Quoi, déjà*—'What, already!'[47] However, she soon regained her equilibrium. As Sanson was cutting her hair, she took the scissors from him and cut off a long lock to give to Hauer.

Usually worn by men, the red chemise hung low on her breast. Corday refused the chair offered by Sanson, preferring to stand in the tumbril, facing the insults and admiration of the crowd. Thousands turned out to see her go to the scaffold, in the Place de la Revolution (now the Place de la Concorde). It poured with rain for three quarters of an hour, as the cart moved slowly through the thronged streets, and the *chemise rouge*, soaked through, outlined her body, moulding her breasts. She paled slightly at the sight of the scaffold, but recovered by the time she got to the top of the steps. Sanson writes that he attempted to place himself in such a position as to block her view of the guillotine. Corday made a point of looking, commenting: 'In my position, one is naturally curious.'[48]

She tried to address the people, but was given no time; her fichu was torn off her neck, and in a moment, it seemed, her head rolled on the ground. Immediately one of Sanson's assistants, a follower of Marat called Legros, ran his knife up the severed neck and held the head high to show it to the crowd, whereupon he gave it a slap, or possibly two or three slaps. The face was seen to blush— not only the cheek that was slapped, but both cheeks, exactly as if she were still able to feel emotion. The spectators were appalled; Michelet writes: 'a tremor of horror ran through the murmuring crowd'.[49]

Much discussion ensued on the likelihood of sensation remaining after decapitation. Scientists entered into elaborate disputations on the *force vitale*, and on whether the head blushed from shame, grief, or indignation. Sanson wrote a letter to the newspaper, condemning the action; he considered it one of the most shameful moments of his career. Legros himself was thrown into jail.[50]

Immediately after the execution, an autopsy was carried out on the body, principally to determine Charlotte Corday's virginity. At the trial she'd been asked how many children she had, and the revolutionary press claimed she was four months pregnant. Perhaps the heroic and virginal figure of Jeanne d'Arc was behind this compulsion to prove Corday promiscuous. In any case, David himself, as a member of the National Convention, attended the autopsy, believing or hoping that 'traces of libertinage' would be found.[51] To his chagrin, her virginity was confirmed. There exists a vivid description of a drawing of this scene:

> The body lies outstretched on a board, supported by two trestles. The head is placed near the trunk; the arms hang down to the ground; the cadaver is still dressed in a white robe, the upper part of which is bloody. One person, holding a torch in one hand and an instrument (some kind of speculum?) in the other, seems to be stripping Charlotte of her clothing. Four others are bending forward, examining the body attentively. At the head we find two individuals, one of whom wears the tricolour belt; the other extends his hands as if to say: 'Here is the body, look.'[52]

Historians generally agree that Charlotte Corday's body was buried in Ditch No. 5 in the cemetery at the Madeleine, rue d'Anjou-Saint-Honoré, between Ditch No. 4, which held the corpse of Louis XVI, and No. 6, which would soon receive the bodies of Phillipe Egalité and Marie Antoinette. Chateaubriand was responsible for exhuming the royal remains in 1815, and left a vivid account, in his *Mémoires d'outre-tombe*, of how he recognised the skull of Marie Antoinette, from his recollection of the smile she gave him on one occasion at Versailles in early July 1789, just before the fall of the Bastille:

> When she smiled, Marie Antoinette drew the shape of her mouth so well that the memory of that smile (frightful thought!) made it possible for me to recognise the jaw-bone of this daughter of kings, when the head of the unfortunate was uncovered in the exhumations of 1815.[53]

It remains a mystery, however, precisely how the skull of Charlotte Corday came to be in the collection of Prince Roland Bonaparte. Dr Cabanès, celebrated collector of historical gossip and author of such valuable works as *Le Cabinet Secret de l'Histoire* (1905), *Les Indiscretions de l'Histoire* (1903), and *Les Morts mystèrieuses de l'Histoire* (1901), carried out extensive and thorough research on the provenance of this skull. He learned from Prince Roland that he had acquired it from M. George Duruy, 'who said he would not be sorry to get rid of this anatomical item because it terrified Mme Duruy.'[54] Duruy himself told Cabanès he'd discovered the skull at his aunt's, Mme Rousselin de Saint-Albin; a wardrobe door was standing slightly open, and Duruy spotted the skull sitting on a shelf inside. Mme de Saint-Albin told him it had belonged to her late husband, who was himself convinced it was the skull of Charlotte Corday. Indeed, Rousselin de Saint-Albin had gone so far as to write 'a sort of philosophical dialogue' between himself and the skull, in which they discuss her motives for the crime.[55] Saint-Albin claimed to have bought the skull from an antiquary on the Quai des Grands-Augustins, who had himself bought it in a sale. Cabanès speculates on the likelihood of the sale in question being that of the *'célèbre amateur'*, Denon, which took place in 1826, but notes that the catalogue of this sale does not mention a skull.[56]

Duruy himself believed that Saint-Albin was in a position to take possession of the skull immediately after the execution, since Saint-Albin was Danton's secretary, and therefore could have obtained the necessary authorization. Cabanès returns to the evidence of the anthropologists who examined the skull at the Universal Exposition of 1889, Bénédikt, Lombroso, and Topinard, who agreed that the skull 'had been neither buried in the earth, nor exposed to the air'.[57] Was the skull dug up immediately, or was it perhaps sold by the executioner, Sanson? Cabanès suggests that the story that is always denied most vehemently is likely to be the true account: that after the autopsy, *'la tête aurait été préparée par quelque médecin et conservée comme pièce curieuse'*—'the head was *treated* by some doctor and preserved as a curiosity'.[58]

Finally, Cabanès includes, as an appendix to his investigation, a long letter from M. Lenotre, 'the very knowledgable historian of *'Paris révolutionnaire'*,[59] to his friend G. Montorgueil, which was written in the full awareness that the letter would be passed on to Dr Cabanès. In this letter, Lenotre ventures his opinion that the skull is authentic. He argues that there was a thriving trade in body parts and hair of the victims of the guillotine, and points to the later wealth of the Sanson family as evidence that Sanson was 'in a good position to render certain services, to make deals, to traffic a little in the guillotine'.[60] Lenotre goes on to recount an anecdote of the period:

> If (Sanson) didn't sell heads, who did? For there's no question they were sold! One evening in 1793, a woman fainted in the rue Saint-Florentin; she fell; a package she was carrying in her apron rolled into the gutter: it was a head, freshly decapitated ... She was on her way from the cemetery at the Madeleine, where a grave-digger had supplied her with this horrible debris.[61]

Lenotre's most striking contribution to the discussion, however, is a description of a dinner party *chez* Rousselin de Saint-Albin:

> One evening, during the reign of Louis Philippe, Saint-Albin invited to dinner a group of friends who were curious about the history of the Revolution. He promised them a sensational surprise. At dessert, a large glass jar was brought in, and removed from its linen case. This was the surprise, and how sensational it was, you can judge, for the glass jar contained the head of Charlotte Corday. Not the skull merely, you understand, but the head, conserved in alcohol, with her half-closed eyes, her flesh, her hair ... The head had been in this condition since 1793; lately Saint-Albin had decided to have it *prepared*—excuse these macabre details—and wanted, before this operation, to allow his friends the spectacle of this thrilling relic.[62]

Once a head, preserved in alcohol; then a skull, to hold in one's hands, to measure. Now all that remains of Charlotte Corday, the last vestiges of the 'thrilling relic', are three photographs of the skull itself. And yet, how evocative these photographs seem, how poetic, these emblems of castration, perhaps, *memento mori* of the Revolution, these shadowy traces of secret exhumation.

> He (Freud) was indignant about the story of the sale (of the Fliess correspondence to Marie Bonaparte) and characteristically gave his advice in the

form of a Jewish anecdote. It was the one about how to cook a peacock. 'You first bury it in the earth for a week and then dig it up again.' 'And then?' 'Then you throw it away!'[63]

Notes

1. Sigmund Freud, 'The Uncanny', *Standard Edition* XVII (1919) p. 244.
2. Cesare Lombroso, *The Female Offender* (with Guglielmo Ferrero, London, 1895), p. 33–4.
3. Ibid., p. xvi.
4. Ibid., p. 150–1.
5. See: Gina Lombroso-Ferrero, *Cesare Lombroso: Storie della Vita e delle Opere* (Bologna, 1914), and Luigi Bulferetti, *Cesare Lombroso* (Turin, 1975).
6. Giorgio Colombo, *La Scienza Infelice: Il museo di antropologia criminale di Cesare Lombroso* (Turin, 1975), p. 45.
7. Ibid., p. 45.
8. Dr Paul Topinard, 'À propos du Crâne de Charlotte Corday', *L'Anthropologie* (1890), vol. I, p. 1.
9. Ibid., p. 1.
10. Ibid., p. 3.
11. Ibid., p. 25.
12. Ibid., p. 3.
13. Dr Paul Topinard, 'Le problème des Nègres aux Etats-Unis et sa solution radicale', *L'Anthropologie* (1890), vol. I, p. 382.
14. For Lorianism, see the poetry of Raymond Landau (aka Alexander Task), in Peter Wollen, 'The Mystery of Landau', *Readings and Writings* (London, 1982).
15. Giorgio Colombo, op. cit., p. 57.
16. See: J. Deniker and L. Laloy, 'Les Races Exotiques à l'Exposition Universelle de 1889', parts 1 and 2, *L'Anthropologie* (1890), vol. I, p. 257–294, p. 513–546, which includes sixteen extraordinary photographs by Prince Roland Bonaparte.
17. Celia Bertin, *Marie Bonaparte: A Life* (New York, 1982), p. 39.
18. A. E. Narjani, 'Considérations sur les causes anatomiques de la frigidité chez la femme', *Bruxelles Médical*, April 27, 1924.
19. Celia Bertin, op. cit., p. 155.
20. Letter from Sigmund Freud to Marie Bonaparte of December 6, 1936, No. 288 in Ernst L. Freud (ed.), *Letters of Sigmund Freud* (New York, 1960). I am indebted to Anne Friedberg for drawing my attention to the dogs.
21. Marie Bonaparte, *Topsy, Chow-Chow au Poil d'Or* (Paris, 1937), Sigmund and Anna Freud's translation published in Amsterdam, 1939.
22. Celia Bertin, op. cit., p. 170.
23. Marie Bonaparte, 'Le Cas de Madame Lefebvre', *Revue Française de Psychanalyse* (1927), vol. I, p. 149–198.
24. Marie Bonaparte, 'Du Symbolisme des trophées de tête', *Revue Française de Psychanalyse*, (1927), vol. I, p. 677–732.
25. See: Ernest Jones, *The Life and Work of Sigmund Freud* (New York, 1953), vol. III, p. 227.
26. See 'peacock anecdote' below, Ernest Jones, op. cit., vol. I, p. 288.
27. Marie Bonaparte, *Female Sexuality* (London, 1953), p. 202.
28. Ibid., p. 202.
29. Ibid., p. 202.
30. Ibid., p. 204.
31. Ibid., p. 151.
32. Ibid., p. 151.

33. Ibid., p. 151.
34. Joseph Shearing, *The Angel of Assassination* (New York, 1935), p. 201.
35. Dr Cabanès, 'La "Lèpre" de Marat', in *Le Cabinet Secret de l'Histoire* (Paris, 1905), p. 164.
36. Dr Cabanès, 'Le Coup de Charlotte Corday', in *Les Indiscretions de l'Histoire* (Paris, 1905), p. 119.
37. Joseph Shearing, op. cit., p. 213.
38. Jacques-Louis David (1748–1825), *Marat Assassiné* 1793, Brussels, Musées Royaux des Beaux-Arts de Belgique.
39. Jean Starobinski, *1789: The Emblems of Reason* (Rome, 1973, trans. Barbara Bray, Cambridge, Mass., 1988), p. 118–119.
40. Dr Cabanès, 'La Vraie Charlotte Corday—était-elle jolie?', in *Le Cabinet Secret de l'Histoire* (Paris, 1905), p. 181.
41. Joseph Shearing, op. cit., p. 230.
42. Jules Michelet, *History of the French Revolution*, (trans. Keith Botsford, Pennsylvania, 1973), vol. VI, Book 12, 'Anarchic Rule of the Hebertists', p. 169.
43. Ibid., p. 169.
44. Joseph Shearing, op. cit., p. 236–7.
45. Ibid., p. 234.
46. Dr Cabanès, op. cit., 'La Vraie Charlotte Corday—était-elle jolie?', p. 188.
47. Dr Cabanès, 'La Vraie Charlotte Corday—Le Soufflet de Charlotte Corday', *Le Cabinet Secret de l'Histoire* (Paris, 1905), p. 198.
48. Christopher Hibbert, *The Days of the French Revolution* (New York, 1981), p. 309.
49. Jules Michelet, op. cit., Book 12, 'The Death of Charlotte Corday', p. 146.
50. Ibid., p. 146.
51. Dr Cabanès, 'La Vraie Charlotte Corday—L'autopsie de Charlotte Corday', *Le Cabinet Secret de l'Histoire* (Paris, 1905), p. 211.
52. Ibid., p. 209.
53. Francois-René [Vicomte] de Chateaubriand, *Mémoires d'outre-tombe* (Paris, 1964), vol. 2. I am indebted to M. Patrick Bauchau for drawing my attention to this reference.
54. Dr Cabanès, op. cit., p. 218.
55. Ibid., p. 219.
56. Ibid., p. 218.
57. Ibid., p. 220.
58. Ibid., p. 221.
59. Ibid., p. 222.
60. Ibid., p. 223.
61. Ibid., p. 224. For traffic in skulls, see also: Folke Henschen, *The Human Skull*, A Cultural History (trans. S. Thomas, London, 1966).
62. Dr Cabanès, op. cit., p. 222–3.
63. Ernest Jones, op. cit., vol. I, p. 288.

Douglas Clegg

I Am Infinite; I Contain Multitudes

Douglas Clegg was born in Virginia, lived in Los Angeles for eleven years, and has, for the past two years, lived in Connecticut. He has published the novels Goat Dance, Breeder, Neverland, The Dark of the Eye, The Children's Hour, *and under the name Andrew Harper he published* Bad Karma. *His short stories have been published in the magazines* Cemetery Dance, Deathrealm, *and* The Scream Factory *and in the anthologies* Love in Vein, Little Deaths, Twists of the Tale, Lethal Kisses, Best New Horror, *and* The Year's Best Fantasy and Horror.

Clegg is able to depict the most sordid and grotesque situations in a way that draws in the reader rather than repulses. That's quite a talent. "I Am Infinite: I Contain Multitudes" was originally published in Palace Corbie Seven.

—E. D.

First off, I'll tell you, I saw both their files: Joe's and the old man's. I had to bribe a psych tech with all kinds of unpleasant favors, but I got to see their files. I want you to sit through my story, so I'll only tell you half of what I found. It was about Joe. He had murdered, sure, but more than that, he had told his psychiatrist that he only wanted to help people. He only wanted to keep them from hurting themselves. He wanted to love. Remember this.

It makes sense of everything I've been going through at Aurora.

Let me tell you something about Aurora, something that nobody seems to know but me: it is forsaken. Not just because of what you did to get there, or how haywire your brain is, but because it's built over the old Aurora. Right underneath it, where we do the farming. I heard this from Steve Parkinson, *right underneath it* is the old Aurora. I saw pictures in an album they keep in Intake. It used to be a dusty wasteland. The old Aurora was underground. Back then they believed it was better, if you were like us, to never see the light of day, to be chained like animals and have your food shoved to you in a slot at the bottom of your door. Back then, they believed that nobody in the town outside the fence wanted to know that you were there. But that's not why it's forsaken. You will know soon enough.

There was a town of Aurora once, too, but then it was bought out by Fort Salton, and 'round about 1949 they did the first tests.

I heard, from local legend, that there were fourteen men down there, just like in a bunker at the end of the war.

They did the tests out at the mountain, but some people said that those men in Aurora, underground, got worse afterwards.

I heard a story from my bunkmate that one guy got zapped and fried right in front of an old timer's eyes. Like he was locked in on the wrong side of the microwave door.

The old timer, he's still at Aurora; been there since he was nineteen, in '46. Had a problem, they said, with people after the war. He was in the Pacific, and had come back more than shell-shocked. That's all I ever knew about him, before I arrived. You can safely assume that he killed somebody or tried to kill himself or can't live without wanting to kill somebody. It's why we're all here. He's about as old as my father, but he doesn't look it. Maybe Aurora's kept him young.

He was always over there, across the Yard. He knew everything about everyone. I knew something about him, too. Actually, we all pretty much knew it.

He thought he was Father to us all. I don't mean like my father, or the guy who knocked your mother up. I mean the Father, as in God The.

In his mind, he created the very earth upon which we stood, his men, his sons. He could name each worm, each sowbug, each and every centipede that burrowed beneath the flagstone walk; the building was built of steel and concrete and had been erected upon the backs of laborers who had died within the walls of Aurora; the sky was anemic, the air dry and calm; he could glance in any direction at any given moment and know the inner workings of his men as we wandered the Yard, or know, in a heartbeat, no, the whisper of a heartbeat, where our next step would take us. There was no magic or deception to his knowledge. He was simply aware; call it, as he did, hyperawareness, from which had come his nickname, Hype. He was also criminally insane by a ruling of the courts of the state of California, as were most men in Aurora.

I watched him sometimes, standing there while we had our recreation time, or sitting upon the stoop to the infirmary, gazing across the sea of his men. His army, he called them, his infantry: they would one day spread across the land like the fires of Armageddon.

The week after Danny Boy got out was the first time he ever spoke to me.

"Hey," he said, waving his hand. "Come on over here."

I glanced around. I had only been at Aurora for four months, and I'd heard the legends of Hype. How he only called on you after watching you for years. How he could be silent for a year and then, in the span of a week, talk your head off. I couldn't believe he was speaking to me. He nodded when he saw my confusion. I went over to him.

"You're the one," he said, patting me on the back. You couldn't *not* look him in the eye, he was so magnetic, but all the guys had told me not to look him in the eye, not to stare straight at him at any point. They all warned me because they had failed at it. They had all been drawn to his presence at one time or another. He was pale white. He kept in the shade at all times. His hair was splotchy gray and white and longer than regulation. His eyes were nothing special: round and brown and maybe a little flecked with gold. ("He milks you with those eyes," Joe had told me.) There were wrinkles on his face, just like with any old man, but his were thin and straight, as if he had not ever changed his expression since he'd been young.

"I'm the one? *The one,*" I said, nodding as if I understood. I had a cigarette, leftover from the previous week. I offered it to him.

He took the cigarette, thrust it between his lips, and sucked on it. I glanced around for an orderly or psych tech, but we were alone together. I didn't know how I was going to light the cigarette for him. They all called me Doer, which was short for Good-Doer, because I tended to light cigarettes when I could, shine shoes for one of the supervisors I'd ass-kiss, or sweep floors for the lady-janitors. I did the good deeds because I'd always done them, all my life. Even when I murdered, I was respectful. But since there was no staff member around, I couldn't get a light for the old man.

Hype seemed content just to suck that cigarette, speaking through the side of his mouth, "Yeah, you don't know what it means, but you're it. Danny Boy, he would've been it, but he had to pretend."

"You think?"

He drew the cigarette from his mouth, and held it in his fingertips. "He was a sociopath, you must've recognized that. He had to perform for his doctor and the board. He studied Mitch over in B—the one who cries and moans all the time. Mitch with the tattoos?"

I nodded.

"He studied him for three years before perfecting his technique. Let me tell you about Danny Boy. He was born in Barstow, which may just doom a man from the start. He began his career by murdering a classmate in second grade. It was a simple thing to do, for they played out in the desert often, and it was not unusual for children to go missing out there. He managed to get that murder blamed on a local pedophile. Later, dropping out of high school, he murdered a teacher, and then, when he killed three women in Laguna, he got caught. The boy could not cry. It was not in him to understand why anyone made a fuss at all over murder. It was as natural to him as is breathing to you." He paused, and drew something from his breast pocket. He put the cigarette between his lips. He flicked his lighter up and lit the cigarette. Although we weren't supposed to have lighters, it didn't surprise me too much that Hype had one. As an old-timer he had special privileges, and as something of a seer, he was respected by the staff as well as by his men. It's strange to think that I was suitably impressed by this, his having a lighter, but I was. It might as well have been a gold brick, or a gun.

He continued, "Danny Boy is going to move in with one of the women who works in the cafeteria. She's never had a lover, and certainly never dreamed of having one as handsome as Danny Boy. Within six weeks, he will kill her and keep her skin for a souvenir. Danny Boy would've been it, but he wasn't a genuine person. You are. You know that don't you?"

"What, I cry, so that makes me real?"

He shook his head, puffing away, trying to suppress a laugh. "No. But I know about you, kid. You shouldn't even be here, only you come from a rich family who bought the best lawyer in L.A. I assume that in Court 90, he argued for your insanity and you played along 'cause you thought it would go easier for you in Aurora or Atascadero than in Chino or Chuckawalla. Tell me I'm wrong. No? How long you been here?"

"If you're so smart, you already know."

"Sixteen weeks already. Sixteen weeks of waking up in a cold sweat with Joe leaning over your bed. Sixteen weeks of playing baseball with men who would be happy to bash in your head just for the pleasure of it. Sixteen weeks hearing the screams, knowing about Cap and Eddie, knowing about how all they want is the taste of human flesh one more time before they die. And you, in their midst," he seemed to be enjoying his own speech. "You're not a sociopath, son, you're just someone who happened to kill some people and now you wish you hadn't, and maybe you wished you were in Chino getting bludgeoned and raped at night, but at least not dealing with this zoo."

The bell rang. I saw Trish, the Rec Counselor, waving to us from over at the baseball diamond. She was pretty, and we all wanted her and we were all protective of her, too, even down to the last sociopath.

"Looks like it's time for phys. ed.," Hype said. "She's a fine piece of work, that one. Women are good for men. Don't you think? Men can be good, too, sometimes, I guess. You'd know about that, I suppose."

"What am I 'it' for?" I asked, ignoring the implication of his comment.

He dropped the cigarette in the dust. "You're the one who's getting out."

I thought about what the old timer'd said all day.

In the late afternoon, I was sitting with Joe on the leather chairs in the t.v. room after we got shrunk by our shrinks, and said, "I don't get it. If Danny Boy wasn't it, and 'it' means you get out, why the hell am I it?"

Joe shrugged. "Maybe he means 'you're next.' Like you're the next one to get out. That old guy knows a shitload. He's God."

Joe had spent his life in the system. First, at Juvy, then at Boy's Camp in Chino, then Chino, and finally some judge figured out that you don't systematically kill everyone from your old neighborhood unless you're not quite right in the head. But Joe was a good egg behind the Aurora fence. He needed the system and the walls and the three hots and a cot just to stay on track. Maybe if he'd been a Jehovah's Witness or in the army, with all those rules, he never would've murdered anybody. He needed rules badly, and Aurora had plenty for him. He had always been gentle and decent with me, and was possibly my only friend at Aurora.

I nudged him with my elbow. "Why would I be it?"

"Maybe he's gonna break you," Joe whispered, checking the old lady at the desk to make sure she couldn't hear him. "I heard he broke another guy out ten years ago, through the underground. That old man's got a way to do it, if you go down in that rat-nest far enough. I heard," Joe grabbed my hand in his, his face inches from mine, "he knows where the way out is, and he only tells it if he thinks your destiny's aligned with the universe."

I almost laughed at Joe's seriousness. I drew back from him. "You got to be kidding."

Joe blinked. He didn't like being made fun of. "Believe what you want. All's I know is the old man thinks you're it. Can't argue with that."

And then, Joe kissed me gently, as he always did, or tried to do, when no one was looking, and I responded in kind. It was the closest thing to human warmth we had in that place. I pulled away from him, for a psych tech was trolling in with one of the shrinks. Joe pretended to be watching the t.v. When I looked up at the set, it was an ad for tampons. I laughed, nudging Joe, who found nothing funny about it.

I wanted to believe that Hype could break me out of Aurora. I spent the rest of the day and most of the evening fantasizing about getting out, about walking out on the grass and dirt beyond the fence. Of getting on a bus and going up North where my brother lived. From there I would go up to Canada, maybe Alaska, and get lost somewhere in the wilderness where they wouldn't come hunting for me. It was a dream I'd had since entering Aurora. It was a futile and useless dream, but I nurtured it day by day, hour by hour. I could close my eyes and suddenly be transported to a glassy river, surrounded by mountains of pure white, and air so fresh and cold it could stop your lungs; an eagle would scream as it dropped from the sky to grab its prey.

But my eyes opened; the dream was gone. In its place, the dull green of the walls, the smell of alcohol and urine, the sounds of Cap and Eddie screeching from their restraints two doors down, the small slit of window with the bright lights of the Yard on all night. Only Joe kept me warm at night, and the smell of his hair as he scrunched in bed, snoring lightly, beside me, kept alive any spirit which threatened to die inside me. I had never been interested in men on the Outside, but in Aurora, it had never seemed homosexual between us. It had seemed like survival. When you are in that kind of environment, you seek warmth and human affection, if you are at all sane. Even if sanity is just a frayed thread. Even the sociopaths sought human warmth; even they, it is supposed, want to be loved. I knew that Joe would one day kill me if I said the wrong thing to him, or if I wasn't generous in nature towards him. He had spent his life killing for those reasons. Still, I took the risk because he was so warm and comfortable, and sometimes, at night, that's all you need.

The next morning I sought Hype out, and plunked myself right down next to him. "Why me?"

He didn't look up from his plate. "Why *not* you?" His mood never seemed to alter. He had that stoned look of one who could see the invisible world. His smile was cocked, like a gun's trigger. "Why not Doer, the compassionate? Doer, the one who serves? Why not you?"

"No," I said. "It could be any one of these guys. Why me? I've only been here four months. We don't know each other."

"I know everybody. I'm infinite. I contain multitudes. Nothing is beyond me. Besides, I told you, you don't pretend."

"Huh?"

"You don't pretend. You face things. That's important. It won't work if you live in your own little world, like most of these boys. You've got the talent."

"Yeah, the talent," I said, finally deciding the old fart was as looney as the rest.

"I saw what you did," he said. As he spoke, I could feel my heart freeze. In the tone of his voice, the smoothness of old whiskey. "I saw how you took the gun and killed your son first. One bullet to the back of the skull, and then another to his ear, just to make sure. Then, your daughter, running through the house, trying to get away from you. She was actually the hardest, because she was screaming so much and moving so fast. You're not a good shot. It took you three bullets to bring her down."

"Just shut up," I said.

"Your wife was easy. She parked out front, and came in the side door, at the kitchen. She didn't know the kids were dead. All she knew was her husband was under a lot of pressure and she had to somehow make things right. She had groceries. She was going to cook dinner. While she was putting the wine in the fridge, you shot her and she died quickly. And then," Hype shook his head, "you took the dog out, too. Who would take care of it, right? With everybody dead, who would take care of the dog?"

I said nothing.

"Who would take care of the dog?" He repeated. "You had no choice but to take it out, too. You loved that dog. It probably was as hard for you to pull the trigger on that dog as it was to pull it on your son. Maybe harder."

I said nothing. I thought nothing. My mind was red paint across black night. His words meant nothing to me.

He patted me on the back like my father had before the trial. "It's all right. It's over. It wasn't anything anyone blames you for."

I began weeping; he rubbed his hand along my back, and whispered words of comfort to me.

"It wasn't like that," I managed to say, drying my tears. Although we had been left alone, I looked across the cafeteria and felt that all the others watched us. Watched me. But they did not; they were preoccupied with their meals. "It was . . ."

"Oh. How was it?"

I wiped my face with my filthy hands. I was so dirty; I just wished to be clean. I fought the urge to rise up and go find a shower. "I wanted it to be me. I wanted it to be me."

"But you wanted to live, too. You killed your family, and then suddenly—"

"Suddenly," I said.

"Suddenly, your life came back into focus. You couldn't kill yourself. You had to go through all of them before you found that out. Life's like that," he said. "The bad thing is, they're all dead. You did it. You *are* a murderer. But you're not like these others. It wasn't some genetic defect or some lack of conscience. Conscience is important. You couldn't kill yourself. That's important. I don't want to get some fellow out who's going to end up killing himself. You need to be part of something larger than yourself. You need God. Tell me, boy: how do you live with yourself?"

I couldn't look him in the eye. I was trying to think up a lie to tell him. He reached out and took my chin in his hand. He forced me to look at him.

I remembered the warning: *he milks you with those eyes.*

"I don't know how," I said, truthfully. "I wake up every morning and I think I am the worst human being in existence."

"Yes," he said. "You are. But here's the grace of Aurora. You're it. You will get out. You will live with what you did. You will not kill yourself or commit any further atrocities." He let go of my chin, and rose from the table. "Do you love your friend?"

"Joe?"

"That's right," he nodded. "Joe."

"Two guys can't love each other," I said. "It's just for now. It's surviving. It's barely even sexual."

"Ah," he nodded slowly. "That's good. It would be hell if you got out and you loved him and he was here. You must be careful around him, though. He is pretty, and he is warm. But he has the face of Judas. He will never truly love anyone. Now, you, you will love again. A man, perhaps. Or a woman. But not our friend Joe. Do you know what he did to the last man with whom he shared his bed? Has he ever told you?"

I shook my head slightly.

"Ask him," Hype said. He walked away. From the back, he didn't seem old. He had a young way of walking. I believed in him.

"Tonight," Hype said to me during Recreational Time. "Two thirty. You must first shower. You must be clean. I will not tolerate filth. Then, wait. I will be there. If your friend makes trouble, stop him any way you can."

Joe could be possessive, but not in the expected way. He was not jealous of other men or women. He simply wanted to own me all the time. He wanted me to shower with him, to sit with him, to go to the cafeteria with him. Our relationship seemed simple to me: we had met about the third week in, when he caught me masturbating in the bathroom. He joined in, and this led to some necking, which led to a chill for another week. Then, I got a letter from my mother in which she severed all connections with me, followed by one from my father and sister. I spent two days in bed staring at the wall. Joe came to me, and took care of me until I could eat and stand and laugh again. By that time, we were tight. I had only been at Aurora for two months when I realized that I could not disentangle myself from Joe without being murdered or tortured—it was a Joe thing. I didn't feel threatened, however, because I had grown quite fond of his occasional gropings and nightly sleep-overs. In a way, it was a little like being a child again, with a best friend, with a mother and lover and friend all rolled up into one man.

That night, when I rose from my bed at two a.m., Joe immediately woke up.

"Doer?" he asked.

"The can," I said, nodding towards the hallway. Because Joe and I weren't in the truly dangerous category, we and a few others were given free rein of our hallway at night. Knowing, of course, that the Night Shift Bitch was on duty at the end of the hall.

"I'll go, too," Joe whispered, rising. He drew his briefs up—he had the endearing habit of leaving them down around his ankles in postcoital negligence.

I tapped him on the chest, shaking my head.

"Doer," he said, "I got to go, too."

I sighed, and the two of us quietly went into the hall.

In the bathroom, he said, "I know what's going on." He leaned against the shiny tile wall. "It's Hype. Word went around. This is the night. Are you really going?"

I nodded, not wanting to lie. He had been sweet to me. I cared a great deal for him. I would be sad without him, for a time. "I'll miss you," I said.

"I could kill you for this."

"I know."

"If you leave I'll be lonely. Maybe it's love, who knows?" He laughed, as if making fun of himself. "Maybe I love you. That's a good one."

"No you don't." I knew that Joe was fairly incapable of something so morally developed as love, not because of his sexual leanings, but because of his pathology.

"Don't go," he said.

"For all I know, Hype is full of shit."

"He's not. I've seen him do this before. But don't go, Doer. Getting out's not so terrific."

"I want freedom," I said. "Plain and simple."

"I want you." Joe seemed to be getting a little testy.

"Now, come on, we're friends, you and me," I said, leaning forward to give him a friendly hug.

I didn't see the knife. All I saw was something shiny which caught the nearly-burnt-out light of the bathroom. It didn't hurt going in—that was more like a shock, like hearing an alarm clock at five a.m.

Coming out, it hurt like a motherfucker.

He pressed his hand against the wound in my chest. "You can't leave me."

"Don't kill me, Joe. I won't leave you, I promise. You can come too." This I gasped, because I was finding it difficult to breathe. I felt light-headed. The burning pain quickly turned to a frozen numbness. I coughed, and gasped, "Get help, Joe. I think you really did me."

Joe pressed his sweaty body against mine. I began to see brief tiny explosions of light and dark, as if the picture tube of life were going out. Joe kissed the wound where he'd stabbed me, as blood pulsed from it. "I love you this much," he said.

Then, he drew his briefs down, a full erection in his hand. He took his penis and inserted it in the wound, just under my armpit. As I worked to inhale, he pressed the head of his member into the widening hole of the wound.

He pushed further into my body.

I passed out, feeling wave after wave of his flesh as he ground himself against my side.

⋅   ⋅   ⋅

I awoke in the infirmary three days later, barely able to see through a cloud of pain-killers. My stomach ached with the antibiotics that had been pumped through me. I stared up at the ceiling until its small square acoustic tile came into focus.

When I was better, in the Yard, I sought Hype out. "I tried to make it," I said.

He said nothing. He seemed to look through me.

"You know what he did to me," I said. "Please, I want to get out. I have to get out."

After several minutes, Hype said, "Love transformed into fear. It's the human story. The last man Joe befriended was named Frank. He grew up in Compton. A good kid. He tore off another man's genitals with his bare hands and wore them around his neck. His only murder. Sweet kid. Twenty-two. Probably he was headed for release within a year or two. He had an A+ psych evaluation. A little morbid. Used to draw pictures of beheadings. Joe latched onto him, too. Took care of him. Bathed him. Serviced him. Loved him, if you will. Then, rumor went around that Frank was getting some from one of the psych techs. Totally fabricated, of course. Frank was taking a shower. Joe knocked him on the head. Strapped him to the bed, spread-eagled. Don't ask me how, but he'd gotten a hold of a drill—the old kind, you know, you turn manually and it spins. He made openings in Frank. First, in his throat to keep him from screaming. Then, the rest of him. Each opening . . ."

"I know," I said, remembering the pain under my arm. Then, something occurred to me. "Where did he get the knife?"

Hype made a face, like he'd chewed something sour.

"The knife," I repeated. "And the drill, too. Everything's locked up tight. You're supposed to be God or something, so you tell me."

Without changing his expression, Hype said, "Joe gets out."

The enormity of this revelation didn't completely hit me. "From here?"

Hype nodded. "It's not something I'm proud of. I can open the door for about three hours, if I use up all my energy. Joe knows it. He was the first one I took out. But he didn't want to stay out. He only wanted out to get his toys. Then, he wanted back. He's the only one who manages to get back. Why he wants to, I couldn't say." For the first time ever, I watched worry furrow the old man's brow. He placed his hand against his forehead. A small blue vein pulsed there, beneath his pale skin's surface. "I created the world, but it's not perfect."

"Joe knows how to get out?"

"I didn't say that. I can get it open. I just can't keep him from going back and forth. And then, it closes again."

I wasn't sure how to pose my next question, because there was a mystery to this place where men got out. I had figured it to be down in the old underground, where Hype would know the route of the labyrinthine tunnels. "Where does it go?"

"That," Hype sighed, "I can't tell you, having never been through it. I just know it takes you out."

. . .

Back in my own bed that night, trying to sleep, I felt his hand. Joe's hand. On my shoulder. He slipped swiftly between the covers to cradle my body against his. "Doer," he said. "I missed you."

"Get off me." I tried to shrug him away. He was burning with some fever. A few drops of his sweat touched the back of my neck.

"No," he tugged himself in closer. I could feel his warm breath on my neck. "I want you."

"Not after what you did."

He said nothing more with words. His mouth opened against my neck, and I felt his tongue heat my sore muscles. All his language came through his throat and mouth, and I let him. I hated him, but I let him.

Afterwards, I whispered, "I want out."

"No you don't."

"Yes. I don't care if you stab me again. I want out. You going to get me out?"

I waited a long time for his answer, and then fell asleep.

I was still waiting for his answer three days later.

I cornered him in the shower, placing my hands on either side of him. I could encompass his body within my arms. I stared straight into his eyes. "I want out."

He curled his upper lip; I thought he would answer, but first, he spat in my face. "I saved you. You don't even care. Out is not where you want to be. In here's the only safe place. You get fed, you got a bed." He leaned closer to me. "You have someone who loves you."

I was prepared this time. I brought my fist against his face and smashed him as hard as I could. His head lolled to the side, and I heard a sharp crack as his skull hit the mildewed tile wall. When he turned to face me again, there was blood at the corner of his lips. A smile grew from the blood.

"Okay," Joe said. "You want out. It can be arranged."

"Good. Next time, I kill you."

"Yeah," he nodded.

As I left the shower room, I glanced back at him for a second. He stood under the shower head, water streaming down—it almost looked like tears as the water streamed in rivulets across his face, taking with it the blood at his lips.

An hour later, Hype found me out by the crude baseball diamond we'd drawn in the Yard, under the shade of several oak trees which grew just beyond the high fence.

"Your lover told me we're moving up the schedule. Shouldn't do this but once every few years. You should've gotten out that night. Joe shouldn't have stopped you. Any idea why he did?"

I kicked at homeplate, which was a drawing in the dirt. Aurora was a funny place that way—because of things being considered dangerous around the inmates, even homeplate had to be just a drawing and not the real thing. The real things here were the fences and the factory-like buildings. "No," I said. "Maybe he's in love with me and doesn't want to lose me. I don't care. He can go to hell as far as I'm concerned."

"I once tried to get out," Hype said, ignoring me. "It was back in the early fifties. I was just a kid. Me and my buddies. I tried to get out, but back then, there was only one way—a coffin. Not a happy system. I didn't know then that I'd rather be in here than out there."

"Make sense, old man," I said, frustrated. I wanted to kick him. The thought of spending another night in this place with Joe on top of me wasn't my idea of living.

"A little patience'll go a long way, Doer," he said. It felt like a commandment. He continued, "Then they started doing those tests—bombs and all kinds of things, twenty, thirty miles away. Some closer, they said. Some this side of the mountain. We lived below back then. Me and Skimp and Ralph. Others, too, but these were my tribe. We were shell-shocked and crazy and we were put in with the paranoid schizophrenics and sociopaths and alcoholics—all of us together. Some restrained to a wall, some bound up in strait-jackets. Some of us roaming free in the subterranean hallways. Skimp, he thought he was still on a submarine. He really did. But I knew where we were—in the furthest ring of hell. And then, one morning, around three a.m., I heard Skimp whimpering from his bunk. I go over there, because he had nightmares a lot. I usually woke him up and told him a story so he could fall back to sleep. Only, Skimp was barely there. His flesh had melted like cheese on a hot plate, until it was hard to tell were the sheets left off and Skimp began. He was making a noise through his nostrils. It was like someone snoring, only he was trying to scream. Others, too, crying out, and then I felt it—like my blood was spinning around. I heard since that it was like we got stuck in a microwave. The entire place seemed to shimmer, and I knew to cover my eyes. I had learned a little about these tests, and I knew that moist parts of the body were the most vulnerable. That's why insects aren't very affected by it—they've got exoskeletons. All their soft parts are on their insides. I felt drunk and happy, too, even while my mouth opened to scream, and I went to my hiding place, covering myself with blankets. I crawled as far back into my hiding place as I could go, and then I saw some broken concrete, and started scraping at it. I managed to push my way through it, further, into darkness. But I got away from the noise and the heat. Later, I heard that it was some test that had leaked out. Some underground nuclear testing. We were all exposed, those who survived. Never saw Skimp or Ralph again, and I was told they were transferred—back in those days, no one investigated anyone or anything. I knew they'd died, and I knew how they'd died. There were times, I'd wished I'd died, too. Every day. That's when I learned about my divinity. It was like Christ climbing the cross—he may or may not have been God before he climbed onto that cross, but you know for sure he was God once he was up there. I wasn't God before that day, but afterwards, I was."

Hype was a terrific storyteller, and while I was in awe of that ability, I stared at him like he was the most insane man on the face of the earth.

"So I found a way out," he concluded.

"If that's true, how come you don't get out?"

"It's my fate. Others can go through, but I must stay. It's my duty. Trust me, you think God likes to be on earth? It's as much an asylum out there as it is in here."

I was beginning to think that all of this talk about going through and getting out was an elaborate joke for which the only punchline would be my disappointment. I decided to hell with it all: the old man could not get me out no matter how terrific his stories were. I was going to spend the rest of my life with Joe pawing me. I went to bed early, hoping to find some escape in dreams.

I awoke that night, a flashlight in my face.

Joe said, "Get up. This is what you want, right?" His voice was calm, not the usual nocturnal passionate whisper of the Joe who caressed me. He hadn't touched me at all. I was somewhat relieved.

"Huh?" I asked. "What's going on?"

"You want to get out. Let's go. You've got to take a shower first." I felt his hand tug at my wrist. "Get the hell up," he said.

The shower was cold. I spread Ivory soap across my skin, rubbing it briskly under my arms, around my healing wound, down my stomach, thighs, backs of legs, between my toes, around my crotch. Joe watched me the whole time. His expression was constant: a stone statue without emotion.

"It doesn't have to end like this," I said. "I'm going to miss you."

"Shut up," he said. "I don't like liars."

When I had toweled myself off, he led me, naked, down the dimly lit hall. The alarm was usually on at the double-doors at the end of the hall, but its light was shut off. Joe pushed the door open, drawing me along. The place seemed dead. Hearing the sound of footsteps in the next ward, he covered my mouth with his hand and drew me quickly into an inmate's room. Then, a few minutes later, we continued on to the cafeteria. He had a key to the kitchen; he unlocked its door. I followed him through the dark kitchen, careful to avoid bumping into the great metal counters and shelves. Finally, he unlocked another door at the rear of the kitchen. This led to a narrow hallway. At the end of the hallway, another door, which was open.

Hype stood there, frozen in the flashlight beam.

"Hey," I said.

Hype put a finger to his lips. He wore a bathrobe which was a shiny purple in the light.

He turned, going ahead of us, with Joe behind me. I followed the old man down the stone steps.

We were entering the old Aurora, the one that stretched for miles beneath the aboveground Aurora. We walked single file down more narrow corridors, the sound of dripping water all around. At one point, I felt something brush my feet—a large insect, perhaps, or a mouse. The place smelled of wet moss, and carried its own humidity, stronger than what existed in the upper world. For awhile it did seem that Hype had been right: this was the furthest ring of hell.

But I'm getting out, I thought. *I'll go through any sewer that man has invented to get out. To go through. To be done with all this.*

Joe rested his hand on my shoulder for a brief moment. He whispered in my ear, "You don't have to do this. I was wrong. I love you. Don't get out."

I stopped, feeling his sweet breath on my neck. Even though I had only been in Aurora a little over four months, I had begun getting used to it. If I stayed longer, I would become part of it, and the outside world would be alien and terrifying to me. I saw it in other men, including Joe. This was the only world of importance to them.

"Why the change?" I asked.

"You don't want to go through. I want you here with me."

"No thanks." I put all the venom I could into those two words. I added, "And by the way, Joe, if I had a gun I'd shoot your balls off for what you did to me."

"You don't understand," he shook his head like a hurt little boy.

Hype was already several steps ahead. I caught up with him while Joe lagged behind.

"I'm going out through that hiding place you talked about," I guessed.

"No," he said. When he got to a cell, he led me through the open doorway.

A feeble light emanated within the room—a yellowish-green light, as if glow-worms had been swiped along the walls until their phosphorescence remained. It was your basic large tank, looking as if it had been compromised by the several earthquakes of the past few years.

Joe entered behind me. "This is where Hype and his friends lived. This is where it happened." He shined the flashlight across the green light. I shivered, because for a moment I felt as if the ghosts of those men were still here, still trapped in the old Aurora. "Tell him, Hype. Tell him."

Hype wandered the room, as if measuring the paces. "Ralph had this area. He had his papers and books—he was always a big reader. Skimp was over there," he pointed to the opposite side of the cell. "His submarine deck."

"Tell him the whole thing," Joe said.

In the green light of the room, as I glanced back at Joe, I saw that he had a revolver in his right hand. "Tell him," he repeated.

"Where the hell did you get that?" I pointed to the gun.

"You can't ever go back," Hype said. "Once you're out, you can never go back. I won't let you back. Understood?"

I nodded. As if I was ever going to want to return to Aurora.

"Tell him," Joe said to Hype. This time, he pointed the gun at Hype. Then, to me, he said, "The gun was down here. I get all my weapons here. We get all kinds of things down here. Hype is God, remember? He creates all things."

"To hell with this," I said, figuring this bad make-believe had gone too far. "You can't get me out, can you?"

Hype nodded. "Yes, I can. I am God, Joe. Those underground tests, they made me God. They were my cross. I'm the only survivor. The orderlies, the doctors, the patients, I'm the only one. That's when I became God."

"You want to get out, right?" Joe snarled at me, "Right?" He waved the gun for me to move over to the far wall.

Hype turned, dropping his robe. Beneath it, he was naked, the skin of his back like a long festering sore. The imprint of hundreds of stitches all along his spine, across the back of his ribcage. To the right of this, a fist-sized cavity just above his left thigh, on his side.

"Tell him," Joe said.

The old man began speaking, as if he couldn't confess this to my face. "Inside me is the door. The tunnel, Joe. To get through, you've got to enter me."

The must vulgar aspect of this hit me, and I groaned in revulsion.

Joe laughed. "Not what you think, Doer. Not like what you like to do to me. Or vice-versa. His skin changed after the tests. Down here, it changes again. Look—it's like a river, look!"

At first, I didn't know what he was pointing at—his finger tapped against Hype's wrinkled back.

Then, before I noticed any change, I felt something deep in my gut. A tightening. A terrible physical coiling within me, as if my body knew what was happening before my brain did.

I watched in horror as the old man's skin rippled along the spine. A slit broke open from one of the ancient wounds. It widened, gaping. Joe came closer, shining his flashlight into its crimson-spattered entry. It was like a red velvet curtain, moist, undulating. A smell like a dead animal from within. The scent, too, of fresh meat.

Joe pressed the gun against my head. "Go through."

My first instinct was to resist.

Seconds later, Joe shot a bullet into the old man's wound, and it expanded further like the mouth of a baby bird as it waits for its feedings.

Joe kissed my shoulder. "Goodbye, Doer."

He pressed the gun to my head again.

The old man's back no longer seemed to be there; now it was a doorway, a tunnel towards some green light. Green light at the end of a long red road. His body had stretched its flesh out like a skinned animal, an animal hide doorway, the skin of the world . . .

With the gun against my head, Joe shoved me forward, into it. I pushed my way through the slick red mass and followed the green light of atomic waste.

Once inside, the walls of crimson pushed me with a peristaltic motion further, against my will. Tiny hooks of his bones caught the edge of my flesh, tugging backwards while I was pressed into the opening.

We are all in here, all the others who got out through him. Only "out" didn't mean out of Aurora, not officially. We're out of our skins, drawn into that infested old man. When I had rein of him for an afternoon, I got him to go down and bribe the psych tech on duty. I pulled up both of their files, Joe's and Hype's.

Joe was a murderer who had a penchant for cutting wounds in people and screwing the wounds. This was no surprise to me. Joe is a sick fuck. I know it. Everyone who's ever been with him knows it.

Hype was a guy who had been exposed to large amounts of radiation in the fifties. He had a couple of problems, one physical and one mental. The physical one I am well aware of, for the little bag rests at the base of my stomach, to the side and back. Because of health problems as a result of the radiation, he'd had a colostomy about twenty years back.

The mental problems were also apparent to me, once I got out, once I got *through*. He suffered from a growing case of multiple personality disorder.

I pulled my file up, too, and it listed: *ESCAPE*.

I had a good laugh with Joe over these files. Then, God took over, and I had to go back down into the moist tissues of heaven and wait until it was my turn again.

There are prisons within prisons, and skins within skins. You can't always see who someone is just by looking in their eyes. Sometimes, others are there.

Sometimes, God is there.

"I am infinite," the old man said, "I contain multitudes."

Christopher Jones

Coffee Jerk at the Gates of Hell

Christopher Jones is the founder of Lost Prophet Press, and publisher/editor of Thin Coyote, *a literary journal. He is the author of two collections of poetry,* I Was a Barenaked Man from Outer Space *(Pariah Press) and Kamikaze Heart (LPP). His work has appeared in anthologies and numerous magazines, including* American Literary Review, Psychopoetica *(England),* Takahe *(New Zealand),* Southerly *(Australia),* Secrets From the Orange Couch *(Canada),* Poetry Motel, Weird Poetry, *and* North Coast Review. *After a year spent traveling around the U.S. and Canada, Jones is now back in Minneapolis/St. Paul, where he works as a nightclub bouncer and studies T'ai Chi, Hsing I Chaun, and Brazilian groundfighting.*

Maybe it's just because I'm a caffeine fiend, but the following quirky poem (about the last cup of java you will ever taste) completely stole my heart. It comes from Southerly, *a small journal published in Sydney, Australia.*

—T. W.

There's a coffee shop on Hell's verge,
the Espresso Inferno.
There's nowhere to sit, and you can't use
their bathroom, but you can stop there
before the eternal flame
for a last caffeine buzz or cold soda.

The guy at the counter, let's call him Eddie,
stands there with a patient smile,

playing Tom Waits on the stereo.
He pretends not to notice the tip jar
that's empty but for a dusty obulus or two,
and asks what he can get for the damned.

Each presents the order of his moment's desire,
and Eddie goes about filling it.
He measures out beans with the skill of long practice,
produces espresso with a thick head of cream
for the gluttonous lover who never allowed himself
to find the right woman,
elicits that elusive sigh of satisfaction.

He pours Torani and tonic and ice cream
for the scrawny poet who coughed himself to death
hating everybody, watches him spoon the coolness
into his mouth, drop the lids on his bitter blue eyes
and moan.

He coaxes forth chocolate from the can
and roasted coffees from the urn, heats milk,
fountains forth whipped cream to hand a double mocha
to the average loser across the counter,
who could never find the right combination,
who spent his life grubbing for lottery money,
feeling cheated and frustrated,
only to end up dead and here, next to the guy
who did hit the numbers.

And behind the counter Eddie smiles the way he does,
with tolerance, watches the flood of idiot humanity
course by him; in come the weak, the nasty, the stupid,
everyone you know or can imagine, the people like you or I
who desired and were denied for forty, fifty, eighty years
and then died and went to Hell.

Eddie asks them what they want and then gives it to them,
doles out cappucinos and herbal teas,
javas black and French sodas made to taste,
lets each soul feel like one tiny desire
out of their whole miserable life was fulfilled,
then packs them off to Hell, always sad
but always smiling, always patient, like he's caring for children,
he keeps doing his job,
keeps doing what he can.

Charles Grant

Riding the Black

Charles Grant started out writing science fiction and has won major awards for his short stories in that genre. However, he is better known these days for his horror fiction. He is the author of many novels including The Pet, For Fear of the Night, Raven, *and the first two volumes of his quartet of novels about the coming millennium:* Symphony *and* In the Mood. *His short fiction has been published in such anthologies as* Post Mortem, Psycho-paths, Monsters in Our Midst *and reprinted in* Best New Horror *and in previous volumes of* The Year's Best Fantasy and Horror. *He is also an award-winning editor of more than twenty-five anthologies, including the critically acclaimed* Shadows *series, and* Gothic Ghosts, *co-edited with Wendy Webb.*

"Riding the Black" was originally published in Revelations, *an anthology in which each contributor wrote (alone or with a collaborator) about a specific decade during the past hundred years. Grant's story takes place at that juncture of time when "the Bomb" and its destructiveness became something to be reckoned with. It's a sharply observed tale, using the romanticized Western hero as a lens through which to view that brave new world.*

—E. D.

hen the sun rose, it was summer white, and the shadows it cast weren't shadows at all, but simply places in the air where things went to hide until the moon returned. In a small stable too weathered to be quaint, a pair of horses shifted uneasily; in a small two-room cabin too worn to be real comfort, boards creaked and a kettle whistled faintly and a curtain stirred when a breeze slipped past the cracked window and died on the bare floor.

When the kettle stopped, there was no sound at all.

In the front yard, mostly bleached dirt and sagging grass and a handful of cacti barely the height of a child, a blue-tail lizard darted from stone to rock, freezing, darting, slipping under the low porch where the sun couldn't reach and the heat was less a furnace than a sullen, crouching thing.

What horizon there was in what directions there were might have been cut from impressive mountains had the mountains had color, had the haze not smeared the slopes and softened the peaks.

A man sat on the porch, holding a tin cup of coffee between his palms. There was no chill to dispel, but he felt one just the same, and sipped the thick liquid as if winter had somehow found its way to his marrow.

When he finished, he placed the cup beside his chair and watched the black road that passed by what passed for his home these days.

The land rolled unevenly, and out there in the high desert were sage and piñon, cactus and scrub, freestanding boulders shaped by the wind, and in the distance straight ahead a line of full-crowned pale trees that marked the bend of a narrow river that teased but never came near.

Nothing moved.

An hour later he took a slow breath and pushed himself to his feet. He stretched, rubbed an eye with a knuckle, and stretched again. He was a man without height until he was angered, without much in his face until anger tightened the sun-baked creases and narrowed the midnight eyes, without much on his bones no matter how he felt.

His shirt was plaid, cuffs rolled back once, buttons open two down, collar worn and separated from what had once been a white yoke. Jeans. Scuffed boots. A leather belt scratched thin. A Stetson with front brim dipped low.

He watched the road.

Nothing moved.

He nodded once, slowly, and slowly he turned, stepping off the porch to make his way to the relative cool of the stable. There he fed and watered the skittish black, fed and saddled the placid roan, let the black make its way into the partly grassy, spring-fed corral, where it headed immediately for the false promise of shade beneath a cottonwood too old to care. The horse wasn't quite skin and bones, but to look at him would tell anyone a good run would kill him.

When it reached the tree, it turned its head.

The man nodded, a promise, and turned away, stroking the old roan's neck, whispering to her, flattering her, telling her he had a feeling they wouldn't be alone for long.

Once in the saddle, hat settled low, he let her find her own way out to the road, to the shoulder between the macadam and the wide ditch beside it. They moved easily, the man and the long-tail horse, seldom if ever in a hurry. He was late this morning. Usually, when he left, he left just after dawn, before the day had a chance to ignite the white fire. There had been a dream, though, and the shimmering faces of absent companions long awaited and long missed; they were alone as well, and, like him, they were searching.

He rode east toward a town the land's easy rise-and-fall tucked out of sight, not bothering to try to beat the sun. There was no sense moving faster; the day and the distance would have done them in. Not even when he glanced over his left shoulder and saw the dust cloud moving toward him. He didn't stop. He rode on. An engine rode the air.

Nothing moved.

Not even the roan.

Eventually, no time at all, horse and car were abreast, ignoring one another until the car sped up and drew onto the shoulder a hundred yards ahead. The roan was forced onto the road, snorting, one ear laid back.

The driver leaned out his window, shook his head, and stared at the rider through narrow sunglasses that mirrored nothing but the sky.

"You," the driver said, smiling, "are one son of a bitch to get hold of, you know that?" A round face, little tan. Shark's teeth.

The rider looked down patiently, saying nothing.

"I swear to Christ, Rob, when the hell you gonna get a telephone?" Matt Dumont rubbed his brow, and propped his arm on the opened window. "Damn, I hate coming out here. It's like driving in a goddamn furnace."

Rob Garland moved his lips, maybe a grin, maybe not. "So don't come." A voice much deeper than the engine, or the desert night.

"How the hell else am I going to get in touch?" A voice so average, most people barely heard it. "Jesus." He patted the door gently. "Like it? Roadmaster. Picked it up for a song last month, when old Davidson packed up for Los Angeles. He bought into the Frazer people, claimed he didn't want to be disloyal." He brayed. "A banker. Can you believe it? A disloyal banker?" He brayed again.

"I'm busy, Matt. What do you want?"

"You."

Rob grunted.

"I swear, Rob, that's all. I just want to talk. Is that so bad? A cuppa at Dinah's, what do you say?"

In shifting his other arm, Dumont's elbow accidentally hit the horn rim.

The swift blare was smothered under the weight of the heat.

The roan didn't move.

"You don't need me, Matt. Hell, you don't even like me."

Dumont cocked his head and grinned, a gap between his two front teeth. "So?"

"So there ain't nothing you can say I ain't already heard a hundred times before. I didn't like what I heard then, and I sure won't like it at Dinah's." He touched fingers to hat brim. "Drive slow, Matt. You hit something out here, ain't nobody gonna find you."

"You live out here, you'll find me."

Rob touched the roan's neck to get it moving. "No," he said. "I don't think so."

"Goddamnit, Garland," Dumont shouted at his back, exasperation high. "The war's over, you idiot! When are you gonna learn times change?"

A moment later the car sped past, horn shrieking, tires stirring dust into a bloated dervish as it swept over a rise and vanished.

Rob and the roan rode on, slow as the heat that rode with them.

He was annoyed that Dumont had shown up, annoyed that his peace had been disturbed by that long-front vehicle. He had nothing against cars, but they were virtually useless out here, and idiots like Dumont drove as if the Devil himself were perched on the roof. He hoped the man wouldn't be in town when he got there. He had no desire to talk. He had done his talking, and his fighting, and his running, and his bleeding.

That was then; this was now.

And now they passed a building that had once been a spur depot when the nearby mines were still working; but the mines had been hollow since FDR died, and the tracks were long gone, forged into tanks; the roof had caved in; the doors were splintered, the windows without glass; coyote tracks in the dust; tumbleweed nesting where the conductor once stood and wiped his face with a handkerchief half as long as his arm.

They passed an old buckboard collapsed in the ditch, wheels a memory, bolts rusted, the bed filled with pebbles and weeds and the bones of a hawk's meal. Planks missing; he had taken a couple himself when winter demanded a fire.

They passed a work crew planting telephone poles, stringing wires, wondering aloud who the hell in his right mind would order all this done all the way out here in the middle of nowhere, and nowhere to go.

They ignored him.

That was fine.

A hawk on the wing drifted as the sun rose.

Shadows sank into the ground.

Eventually, no time at all, he took the roan through the high open doors of the town's only remaining stable, dismounted, and told Solomon Winks to take it easy on the old gal, she was feeling the heat worse these days.

"Shouldn't ride her so hard in weather like this, Mr. Garland," the stable hand chided, shaking his head sorrowfully at the horse, clucking to it, easing off the saddle, reaching for a damp cloth to cool the beast down.

"We walked."

The black man sighed. "She walked. You rode."

Rob laughed quietly and fed the horse a sugar cube, let her nuzzle his chest.

Solomon, wearing nothing more than coveralls and a sleeveless undershirt, hosed water into a trough. "You mind me asking why you come in, Mr. Garland? I didn't think I'd see you for another couple weeks."

"Just looking around, son, just looking around."

The white-haired man squinted at him, scars across his forehead as if he'd been chewed in his sleep. "You never just look around."

Rob shrugged. "You get the urge, you got to move, that's all." He swatted the roan's rump a good-bye for now. Then he pointed at the stable hand. "Make nothing of it, Solomon, you hear me? Believe it or not, sometimes a man gets damn bored out there all alone."

Solomon nodded.

Rob knew it was a lie.

After scooping a palmful of water from the trough, wiping it over his face, he walked on through the long high building, smelling hay and sweat and cool and warm, until he reached the door that led into the back of the feed store. He walked through to the street without greeting the clerk and paused under the motionless fringed awning.

Cars at the curb, cars at the new traffic light; pedestrians in suits and jeans and dresses and work clothes handed out when the owners were discharged and came home from the ocean to the desert. He used to know them all; now he hardly knew a dozen. They moved on, the young did, to the cities on the coast across the mountains, and the cities across the plains.

The old stayed.

The young died.

The old didn't.

And the place itself had hardly changed: the long main street shimmered darkly, heat lifting ghost arms in the distance, hiding the mountains, twisting the poles that took the place of trees, wires for branches, crossbars for twigs. The buildings mostly clapboard, some stone, a few brick. The houses, the churches, the school, all on streets behind the two-story offices and shops.

A small town lying in the desert, waiting for a city to find it.

Two blocks later he slipped through the door of the area's first restaurant, now its smallest, least-used, red-check oilcloth and standing fans and a counter along the left-hand wall, booths along the right, a handful of tables down the center and in back. A translucent shade drawn halfway down the front window to keep the glare out. Three men in the first booth, hats on wall pegs; nobody at the tables.

Nobody at the counter until he took a stool nearest the register, dropped his hat on the stool beside him, and plucked a menu from between the sugar and the catsup. As he glanced down the list, not really reading since he could recite it by rote, he heard sniggering behind him, quick whispering, an outright laugh.

His eyes closed briefly.

In the old days, he thought wistfully; in the old days.

In that moment of blessed dark he heard the faint squeak of the swinging door in the back wall and the footsteps of a woman.

"Hey," one of the men said. "Hey, cowboy."

When his eyes opened, he saw her standing in front of him, arms folded under her breasts, one thick eyebrow cocked. Her fair hair was bobbed. Her uniform equal measures of pale stains and pale color too long gone to have a name.

"Hey, you, cowboy."

Her face was high angles and soft hollows, lips dark and thick, eyes dark and seldom wide. In his youth he would have done the dance, said the words, made the promises, anything at all to see what lay beneath the buttons that strained down her front. But the century turned, and in his age he only watched, and smiled, and waited for the question.

"Sixty-two?" she asked, tip of her tongue at the corner of her mouth.

"Nope."

"Damn."

"Hey! Cowboy!"

His eyes closed again, opened, and he watched her face for one sign or another. Your call, her expression answered; it's too damn hot to think.

He knew how she felt, and let the stool turn him gradually to face the booth, and the men, and their stupid grins as they saw the years on his face, and on the backs of his hands resting lightly on his thighs.

"Sorry, old man," one of them said. "We thought you were someone else."

The other two snickered.

"Maybe you'd be right, then," he answered calmly.

Waiting.

Nothing moved.

The whir and roar of the fans in the back corners.

The whicker of a horse somewhere outside, its hooves hard on the hard road.

The youngest and tallest of the three slid easily out of the booth, his tie slightly off-center, broad lapels shrinking an ordinary chest, baggy trousers giving him a giant's legs. He moved cautiously, peering at Rob through the dust hanging starlike in the air. When one of his friends hissed at him, he shook his head violently, once, and slipped his thumbs into his high waistband.

"Do you have any idea who I am?" he asked. The gap between nose and lip was filled with a moustache, Douglas Fairbanks, and his hair was slicked back, Tyrone Power.

Rob shrugged.

"Clark," the waitress said wearily, "go someplace else, okay? I don't need this."

Clark Mitchell winked at her over Rob's shoulder. "Dinah, no trouble. Just asking a question, that's all."

His companions grinned.

Rob watched.

Clark perched on the edge of a table, one foot swinging. "So. Do you have any idea who I am?"

Stagecoach rumbling down the street behind six lathered horses, a woman and child in matching bonnets, four cavalry riders, their horses prancing. A man peering through the window, a large silver star pinned to his rawhide vest. Rob glanced at him; he moved on.

"Hey," Clark said softly. Not kindly.

Rob put his back to him, tapped the menu, and cocked an eyebrow at Dinah. "Coffee, eggs, toast, bacon, ham, butter if you got it."

"Rationing's over," she said with a quick smile. "You know, you really ought to get into town more often."

He laughed without sound, but didn't miss the question in her expression.

Or the apprehension.

It had nothing to do with the three men behind him.

"Hey, cowboy, I'm talking to you."

She plucked the menu from the counter and slid it back into its place. "Do me a favor," she said, heading for the kitchen. "Don't make a mess. I'm alone today."

A hand reached under his thigh to the stool and spun it around.

Clark smiled; there was nothing there.

"You're not very polite, old man, you know that? I ask you a question, and you ignore me. How do you expect to be a star if you ignore me?"

Rob frowned.

"See?" Clark said to the others. "I told you he doesn't know me."

Without apparent motion Rob stood, grabbed the suit's lapels, and lifted, effortlessly carried the young man to the booth, and dropped him on the seat. He leaned over, one hand now at the knot of the young man's tie, the other hand on the tongue, pulling it, making a noose.

"I don't much care who you are," he said quietly, "and I definitely don't care why you're here. You touch me again, and I'll skin you. Alive."

Clark's face mottled, his eyes bulged.

His friends gaped.

The noose tightened.

"You're a television man," Rob said, leaning closer, speaking softer. "I'm not impressed."

He released the tie with a twist and snap of his wrists, and the young man gasped, sputtered, slumped forward, as his friends finally decided to come to his rescue.

Rob stared them down.

"You were right, by the way," he told them, heading back to the counter.

"Impossible," one of them sneered. "You're too damn old."

Rob sat, smiled. "Son, you don't know what old is."

Turned his back.

Waited until he heard the batwing doors stop their creaked swinging, waited until the footsteps stomped away on the wood-slat boardwalk, waited until the jingle of spurs was overlaid by the sputtering grumble of a bus, waited until the faint odor of an oiled gun was replaced by the aroma of his meal.

The three men had gone.

Dinah leaned a hip against the counter and watched him eat, saying nothing, saying it all, while he watched her watching him, and guessed her to be settling around her mid-forties about now. She had no husband—he had run off to fight in the Pacific and hadn't returned, maybe dead, maybe not; she had no children, and no family to speak of. She had the restaurant, that was all.

And a couple of times a month, she had him, on the stool at the counter, watching her watching him.

"Rob?" she said, a young woman's voice, uncertain and a little frightened.

He ate.

"Solomon just came to the back while I was cooking."

He grunted. "The man talks too much."

"He says—"

Rob looked at her, nothing more, and she turned away to pick up a clean cloth to wipe down a counter touched with nothing but Rob's plate, and a light coat of dust.

The Horseshoe Tavern, across the street from Dinah's and one block up, had been at its corner location, it seemed, since the world had formed, a gold mine for the owners who took the gold from miners fresh from their claims, took the silver from travelers on their way to California, took the dollars from soldiers who still hadn't found time to change out of their dress uniforms and find themselves work.

It was not, and never had been, a peaceful place.

Piano players and girl singers had eventually given way to flashy jukeboxes, and now, in the back under a gallery, a half dozen men stood around a dusty Panoram, shaking their heads in amazement, but not putting in another dime. They didn't stay long. The rectangular movie screen on top of the jukebox-sized cabinet was faded, and Rita Rio and her All-Female Orchestra sounded tinny and too fast, their images scratched and fluttery. It was better to sit in the Deluxe and watch the same performers on the big screen, more for the money and easier to take.

Clay Poplar had put the soundie in five years ago. When the company stopped making them because the war needed the iron and glass and copper, he hadn't the heart to take the thing out. Not even when he had to splice the short music films together himself.

"Gonna burn that son of a bitch one day," he muttered, handing a shot glass to Rob. A grizzly in a white shirt and apron, he filled the room even when it was empty.

"Times change," Rob said. Drank. Felt the fire. Tapped the glass with a finger.

Poplar looked at him sideways. "You sure? Damn early."

Rob tapped the glass again.

The bartender poured and stood back, fussed with some glasses and a towel. "I like the movie place, you know? The Deluxe?"

Rob nodded.

"They had a picture of the Bomb on the newsreel the other night."

Rob drank.

"Hell of a thing, Rob, hell of a thing." He fussed with the bottles stacked before the etched mirror. "Truman says the Russians, they ain't our friends anymore, they got that bomb stuff, I don't know what it's called." He fussed with his apron, his voice low now, much younger. "If they got it, Rob, they'll blow up the world. That NATO thing ain't gonna be worth spit."

"You don't say," he answered, letting the last drop settle on his tongue.

Poplar had the sense to sound embarrassed when he faked a laugh. "There's a guy out there these days, a preacher man. He's got Mildred talking about the goddamn end of the world. You know, the Apocalypse and all."

"You don't say."

"Not me. I got enough to handle with drunks and whores. I leave that church stuff to her and her old lady."

Rob felt as if he'd been sitting on stools all his life. He slid off this one and dropped a dollar on the bar. Hitched at his gun belt and walked out into the sun.

A small man stood on the corner beneath the full branches of one of the few trees left on Main Street. A hand-lettered poster was tacked to the bole, tent meeting tomorrow tonight, on the east end of town, the Reverend Carl Thomas. The man wore a black suit, the trousers too short, the jacket sleeves exposing bony wrists and frayed cuffs. His left hand was held at his shoulder, gripping an open Bible, whose pages were edged with gold; his right hand beseeched passersby, long fingers in constant fluid motion, languid in the tide of heat.

Rob leaned against the tavern wall and watched as the man spoke well and earnestly to a half dozen women, all of them nodding, and a half dozen men, most of them bemused.

"There is no coincidence that both the Beast and the Bomb begin with the same letter." He clutched the open Bible to his chest, lovingly, near rapture. "There is no coincidence that the color of the Enemy is as red as the color of your young babies' blood."

Rob listened as the dozen became two dozen, and a passing policeman reminded them all, officially tolerant, that the tent was someplace else, the meeting another time, it was time to move along. The preacher smiled and told him he was merely passing the Word to those who might find themselves at the theater instead, or in some unfortunate's living room where the television had taken root.

The crowd drifted away, unspoken promises of attendance the following night.

The policeman shook his head and walked away.

The preacher looked at Rob. "Will you be there, Brother?"

Rob pushed away from the wall, touched the brim of his hat, and walked away.

"He who lives by the sword, Brother!" the preacher called.

Rob turned, walking backwards, and smiled as he tipped his hat.

The preacher blinked once in astonishment, then staggered against the tree, gripping it with one hand while the other slapped the Bible again to his heart.

"Used to be," Rob said to the little girl on the swing, "there were buffalo, and you couldn't see the ground because there were so many. Millions, I expect. Millions. And when they moved, darlin' . . . oh Lord, when they moved."

Rage and thunder trapped beneath the surface, setting horses to rearing and cattle to running and walls to shaking dust from their joints; sudden geysers of earth miles away from the running herd, trees quivering and some falling; the feeling in a man's bones, as if he were listening to God, or the Devil, screaming inside.

He leaned against the schoolyard's stockade fence, one hand in a pocket, the other tucked in his waistband. His hat was low, one leg crossed over the other at the ankle. A dozen or more boys stood around him, grinning at his stories, demanding more and begging their teacher not to send him away yet, recess was still going, and this was more fun than playing catch in the sun.

The girl, her name was Jean, wanted to know if Dale Evans was really a cowgirl.

"Oh, I think so," he said, not minding the lie. The child had little else in the desert but the look to get away. "But I think you're prettier."

She blushed.

The boys hooted.

The teacher clasped her hands and shook her head. "Mr. Garland, you're incorrigible."

He grinned at her. "Best thing I've been called all day, Miss Amy."

The boys hooted again, and started shoving each other. They were being ignored; they didn't want the old man talking to a stupid girl, or their teacher. Besides, he was old enough to be her grandfather, for gosh sake, and she shouldn't be looking at him the way she was.

"Hey," one of them said. Rob knew him as Pete. "Did you see the atomic bomb, Mr. Garland?"

The children fell silent.

Jean stopped swinging.

Pete looked around, suddenly fearful he'd said something dreadfully wrong.

Amy Russell said, "I don't think Mr. Garland is really—"

"No," Rob said gently. "I didn't see it."

"I saw it on my uncle's television. It was big."

He nodded. "I'll bet it was."

"It won the war, you know."

He nodded again. "I know."

"It looked really bad."

"I've seen worse."

Amy seemed flustered, and Rob tilted his head until he could see her, sun aura behind her auburn hair, almost but not quite penetrating her dress. When she looked away and down briefly, he couldn't help but smile, although it didn't move his lips.

"The buffalo," Jean said, close to pouting. "I want to hear about the buffalo and the Indians."

He could feel the heat, the weight of the sky.

"Too late," he said. "It's too late."

A bell rang in the schoolhouse, and there was a sudden whirlwind of children running, calling, waving good-bye, laughing at Jean, who hadn't known the old man had known that recess had ended.

Amy moved closer, edging away at the same time. "Rob, I've missed you."

He wanted to reach out, to touch her arm, but a stout woman stood in the distant doorway. "I'll be back again." He grinned, and this time his lips did the work. "You know I will. Those kids can't get enough."

She didn't move. "They're scared, Rob. It's all they talk about—the Bomb. Most of their fathers were in the Pacific." She looked around the empty yard helplessly. "I don't know what to tell them."

"Nothing," he said.

Another bell rang.

"What are you doing here, Rob? What's—"

He touched his hat brim to silence her and walked through the gate and down the street. He knew she watched; he knew others watched, too, from front lawns and behind curtained windows, and he wished little Jean hadn't asked him what it had been like, out there, before it changed.

Worse; he wished he couldn't remember.

But he couldn't help it.

Campfire to electricity, Pony Express to the telephone, railroads to trucks and cars, trenches to jet fighters; it was like riding the black when the black was young. Too fast to see anything, and when they got where they were going, it wasn't the way it had been when they started. Which is why he rode and walked slow now, taking his time, taking all the time, making sure he knew what he saw before what he saw wasn't there anymore, before it was behind him and falling behind.

He had been to Los Angeles, to San Diego, had taken the train from Denver to St. Louis. He was not, as Dumont complained bitterly to anyone who listened, a man who lived in the Past, hating the Present and sabotaging the Future. He enjoyed going to the movies, the telephone fascinated him as much as it unnerved him, and he had more than once blessed the air-conditioning in Clay Poplar's bar. Not, he amended, that it always worked, especially in the high days of late July.

But times changed.

Sooner or later, he would have to tell them.

Sooner or later, his friends would arrive.

Dumont caught him coming out of the hardware store, a small bag of nails in one hand, hammer in the other. There was a round body to go with the round face, short legs and pudgy hands, and the suit he wore was too expensive and tailored to have been purchased around here.

"Talk to me," he demanded.

"I'm going home."

"I'll dog you."

Rob laughed. "You will, that's for sure."

In the distance, the lonely cry of a locomotive, its plume rising above the rooftops because there was no wind to take it.

A mongrel rooted at the base of a hitching post, snuffling loudly.

A coolie quick-walked around the corner, saw them, and bowed himself out of sight.

"Quit it," Dumont said.

Rob walked on. The man would follow or not, he didn't much give a damn.

"Listen, Rob," the man said, keeping his voice low, leaning close without touching, "there's a guy here in town, his name is Clark Mitchell. He works for the National Broadcasting Company—NBC, like on the radio—they want to expand their television network. You know what that is, a network? People in New York can watch the same programs at the same time as the people in Los Angeles? All the places in between? They're setting up relay points and local stations. Rob, you *have* seen a television set, right? Jesus, do you have any idea what I'm talking about?"

Rob walked on; the man would keep on, or he wouldn't.

"At least tell me you've heard of Ed Sullivan and Milton Berle."

Reluctantly Rob nodded.

Dumont glanced skyward. "Thank you, God, for small favors. Anyhow, this Mitchell guy, he's like a reporter. He goes on the television at night and tells the news. Pretty big man this side of the Mississippi."

"I already have a radio," Rob said, glancing in a shop window, thinking it was about time he bought himself a couple of new shirts. He had four—one had been patched too many times to be worn in polite company, and two had stained holes. The fourth he only wore once in a while.

Later, he decided; maybe tomorrow.

"We're talking the future here, Rob," Dumont insisted, grabbing his arm, letting it go as if he'd been scorched. "All I want is ten acres, man. Ten lousy acres. Christ, you've got what, five, six thousand? What the hell would ten acres of goddamn sand lose you?"

Rob looked down at him. "Ten acres of goddamn sand."

"Very funny." Dumont mopped his face with an already sweat-stained handkerchief. "We are talking rich, Rob. You sell to me, I sell to them, and we split it."

At the corner, Rob waited for a stage to rumble by, shotgun rider saluting him with a touch to his hat. Inside, a woman in a feathery hat smiled coyly.

"I could sell it to him myself," Rob said, crossing the street.

"No, you wouldn't. But you'd sell to me, right?"

They passed the feed store, and Rob paused at the building's edge. "No."

"Why, damn it?" Dumont demanded to his back.

Rob didn't answer.

"Jesus Christ, if they drop the goddamn Bomb, all you'll have left is five, six thousand acres that won't grow a goddamn weed."

Solomon was gone.

Rob saddled the roan and walked her into the open.

Dumont shied away from the animal, mopping his face again. "Rob, please, you've got to listen to me. Mitchell isn't going to be here forever. He'll move on if we don't act now, pick someplace else." He clutched at the stirrup. "Jesus, Rob, you've got to help me get out of here, man. You're the only hope I've got left."

The stirrup twitched; the hand fell away.

"God *damn* you, Garland! You come riding in like this, on that goddamn horse, you've got half the town scared to death."

Rob leaned over and tapped the man's shoulder. "Good," he said. "They have reason."

As he rode out to the road's shoulder, a trio of young boys sped by in a convertible.

They laughed and blew the horn.

The roan didn't move.

He sat on the porch and watched the mountains turn to blood, thick and dark as the sun crept behind them. And dark motion in the sagebrush as the desert returned to life and the sky filled with birds with dark arrow wings that held them against the night wind until they dropped. Like a bomb. Until the small creatures died without making a sound.

He drank from the tin cup, but it wasn't coffee this time. A bottle rested on the porch beside his chair, and as he sipped he remembered it once tasting so fine, and wondered with a shudder why it tasted now like paint.

He finished the cup and filled it again without spilling a drop, drawing his denim jacket snug across his chest as the heat finally ended and the desert chill settled. Sounds around the cabin, scuttling and scurrying, rustling, a pebble rolling. A sweet smell on the air. A soft feel to the twilight slipping swiftly to dusk.

He drank, and saw a street, not here, down near Denver, where he had ridden in one morning and had been stopped by a kid who had a large gun in his waistband. There were pox scars on the kid's cheeks, and one ear had been mangled, but he had been determined to try, and had been insulting and snide, and Rob had killed him with one shot without ever leaving the saddle.

He paid for the funeral.

He rode on, south this time, and found work on a ranch near the hills of Santa Fe. A year later the word arrived, and someone tried, and he moved on.

He spent a winter in a cave, and a summer in a prison that finally failed to hold him; he rode a barge on the Great River, hauling wood for the steamboats and cotton for the ships and women for the men who worked the docks and levees. A year later the word arrived, and someone tried, and he moved on.

He drank again and saw more clearly, and closed his eyes and saw it all.

Something screamed in the desert just before it died.

Headlights dragged a guttering roar from east to west, never slowing.

At the back of his head an ache took root; he scowled and willed it away. This wasn't the time.

There were stars, then, and a dreamlike howling that made him smile, raise his head, return the favor. He suspected they laughed at him, the coyotes and wolves, but it always made him feel better.

Amy drove out and sat on the steps at his feet, her pleated skirt hugged around her shins. They talked about the children, the ones who were her favorites and the ones who drove her crazy and the ones who burst out crying because their daddies woke at night, hearing gunfire and fighter planes, deck cannon and grenades.

Four years after, and the dying hadn't stopped.

"And now this," she said angrily.

He lit a lantern and hung it on its hook in the porch roof. The light wasn't much, but at least he wasn't listening to a ghost.

"Which this?" he said, sitting again, crossing one leg over one knee, sipping from the cup refilled again.

"You know what I mean." She reached out and touched his boot, gripped it and tugged until he scooted the chair close, and she laid her cheek against his knee. His free hand hovered above her head, feeling it without touching it, fire in the lantern mirroring the fire in the hair. "I mean, you've seen so much, Rob. Cars and planes and more wars than I think you want to admit. You're a walking history book, and you don't even know it." She shifted a little, a finger brushed her hair and snapped away. "I've been to school, and I don't know anything, and I'm supposed to tell those kids not to be afraid."

He couldn't help it; he touched the hair, molding it to her skull, following its fall to her spine.

She sighed, and hugged his leg.

The coyotes sang.

A stagecoach thundered past, horses snorting, whip cracking.

Out of the dark.

Into the dark.

"I hate you," she said dreamily.

He grunted.

She shifted, snuggled closer. "Why are they afraid of you?"

He didn't know how to answer, and so kept his silence, hoping that this time, with this woman, there would be no time but the time they had.

So young, so soon old.

"I was thinking about driving out to that tent meeting tomorrow."

"Oh?"

She laughed, just a little. "I feel sorry for that preacher, that's all. He's so little. I don't know if anyone will take him seriously."

They would; he knew they would.

They always do.

And they're always wrong.

She drew away and turned to lean back against the post, lantern light giving her face soft shadow and softer age. "I know who you are, you know."

He said nothing.

She grinned, the age vanished. "I'm a teacher, remember? I can look things up, read, write, magical things like that."

He said nothing.

"You're an outlaw."

He inhaled deeply, let it out slowly.

She shook her head in amazement. "It's practically the middle of the century, and we've got a living, breathing outlaw living right outside town." Lantern light in her eyes. "I thought they were all dead."

The coyotes sang.

"They are," he whispered.

A gust of wind, the lantern creaked and swung, her face slipping in and out of shadow.

"Is that why they're so afraid of you? Because they think you'll—"

A long-nosed automobile pulled up behind Amy's wood-sided station wagon. Headlights cut the night and died. The engine raced. A door slammed. She adjusted her skirt, scowling at the intrusion, looking to him for a clue what to do, what to say, but he only shook his head, just enough for her to notice, and sagged just a little, abruptly adding heavy decades to his frame.

She blinked, then smiled, and turned as a man crunched across the yard.

"Mr. Garland, good evening."

Rob nodded. "Mr. Mitchell."

"Ah, you know me at last. I'll take it as a compliment." Mitchell stopped at the reach of the light, put a foot on the porch, and leaned forward, resting on an arm. Tipped his hat back, touched his chin. "And you're the schoolteacher, am I right? Miss . . . ?"

"Russell," she said primly.

He nodded. "Of course." A smile at Rob, not a shark, just a wolf. "It seems to me, Miss Russell, that we have a celebrity here in our midst."

"Is that so?"

"Well, sure. Mr. Garland here is what we in the television business call a personality."

His gaze didn't move.

"Is he really?"

"Oh, come now, Miss Russell. Are you telling me you didn't know?" Wolf's teeth. "Robert Garland, birth date unknown, death date not applicable, no fancy names like Billy the Kid or Six-gun Morgan, has served time in several jails and prisons across the West. For murder. Unfortunately it seems there isn't a jail around that can hold him."

"Is that so?"

Mitchell stopped smiling. "He's a killer, Miss Russell. I'm willing to bet there are a dozen outstanding warrants for his arrest in every state east of the Rockies and west of the Mississippi. Would you say that's right, Mr. Garland?"

"Be a hell of a coup," Rob said hoarsely. "Call the Law and tell them to arrest a tired old man who can barely sit on his old horse. Hell of a coup."

"I don't want you arrested, Mr. Garland. I just want your land."

The lantern still swinging, still creaking.

Mitchell's face, in and out of shadow.

"Do you know," he said, ignoring Amy now, "that there are over a million television sets in the country already? Do you have any idea how many people see my face every week? Do you have any idea how many people would see *your* face every night if I give the word?" He ducked his head, looked up again. "There isn't a cop in this country who wouldn't know your name."

He straightened, smoothing his tie with the flat of his palm.

Amy said, "Why?" She gestured at the night. "There are a dozen towns you could go to. Scores of them. And every one of them is bigger than ours. What the hell do you want us for? Why are you picking on Rob?"

He tipped his hat and walked away, looked over his shoulder, and said, "Because I can."

She kissed him good night.

The coyotes sang.

He lay on his bed, moonlight across his chest.

He didn't think he was a stupid man; he had seen too much not to know that worlds change and worlds collide, that people like him and Solomon, Dinah and Clay, either stood aside on their own or were moved—shoved or nudged, it didn't make much difference. It was the way of it. A young wolf sooner or later took the fight out of an old one; a young buffalo sooner or later took care of a slow bull.

He reached over the side and picked up the tin cup, realized it was empty, closed one eye in thought, then tossed the cup aside. He picked up the bottle.

He drank.

He had met them all, and loved a few, and had ridden on when he could no longer watch them die, when he could no longer bear the looks in their eyes or the feeble kisses they gave him or the quivering touch of their fingers soft on his skin, when they began to wonder and began to ask questions and began, at the last, to hate the sound and sight of him, riding on.

When he saw the way of it.

The sky held stars and a moon and shadows that flew from one slope to another.

The way of it.

Until one night held a sun.

It didn't last, but it was there, and so was the wind that battered the slopes and scoured the earth, and nothing that walked there ever walked again, and nothing that flew there ever drew another breath.

He drank.

He had ridden there that night, on the night of the sun, and had felt the wind and had seen the black the sun left behind. It neither frightened nor thrilled him.

But it saddened him, just a little.

He had grown used to it, just a little: the places, the faces, the killing and the saving; the whiskey, the mead, the wine, and the water; the huts, the towers, the long roads and mountain passes.

The riding.

He drank.

. . .

Yet there had never been a time like the time he had had today, never a time when he could finally see the road's end. Dirt or macadam, concrete or cobblestone, they always took a bend, crossed a river, wound around a mountain, slipped into a valley he hadn't noticed as he traveled.

It saddened him.

Just a little.

Not for the road's end, but for them and their not knowing.

He was old.

He was slow.

He supposed, as moonlight faded, it really was getting to be time.

But it saddened him.

Just a little.

He drank the bottle dry.

He slept.

He didn't dream.

He woke near the end of the sun's slide, rolled to sit up, held his head in his hands, and stared at the floor.

because I can

He walked to the door and held on to the jamb, squinting in the dying daylight, watching the trucks and the stages, shaking his head with a soft simple smile at the slipping back and forth, then and now. When a long gray bus passed without pausing, he turned away and wondered how it was that Dumont and Amy were the only ones who saw. He hadn't thought them all that special, a con man and a teacher, but he hadn't thought that night sun had been all that special either.

It still wasn't.

Not the way they thought.

He turned back and stood on the porch, testing the air, listening, and knew that his friends wouldn't be arriving tonight. It puzzled him for a moment; he was almost sure they'd be here, until a truck guttered by with several crates in its bed. Stenciling on the side. Television sets. One of them, he was sure, would be for Clay Poplar and his wife.

No bombs in there.

The end, just the same.

"Well," he said softly. A decision finally made.

He moved around the large room, picking up things he thought he'd like to save, and putting them back when he realized what he was doing. And as he moved, raising dust, he breathed deeply and hummed tunelessly, touching, always touching, until the day had gone. Then he reached under the bed and pulled out an old steamer, leather straps brittle and brass fittings tarnished. The leather snapped when he touched it, the lid crumpled when he lifted it, and from the black inside he used both hands to lift the black onto the mattress.

"Well," he said to the clothing he hadn't worn in so long. "Well."

He stripped.

He dressed.

He picked up his hat, wide-brimmed and black, and stepped onto the porch.

The coyotes sang.

He answered.

A shower of meteors flashed and burned, flashed and died, traces of light hopeless in their wake.

He walked around the cabin to the stable, still not truly sure he had to ride tonight until he moved inside and saw that the roan was on her side in her stall.

"Oh, Lord," he whispered, as much for himself as for the horse. He knelt beside her and stroked her warm flank, suggesting with a whisper that it would be all right, old girl, you don't want to be here, not now, not this time.

When he stood, joints popping, back stiff, a soft whicker in the next stall made him turn, raise an eyebrow, say nothing as he walked the sleek black into the yard and saddled him. And as he did, he watched the sky, watched the road, thinking there were a few things he could still do before he had to do what he had to.

A step, smooth and easy, set him on the horse's back.

A cluck, a touch, and they were on the road, riding down the center, nothing behind them and nothing above.

The coyotes stopped singing.

And in no time at all he stopped at the stable doors, seeing a light inside.

The black crossed the open space loudly, nearly prancing, and Solomon came out, scowling, until he saw Rob.

"Oh, Jesus," the old man said. He looked around frantically, every jerk and gasp telling Rob he was thinking to run, wanting to hide, terrified to do anything but stand there. Then he put a hand over his face until he stopped trembling. "I was going to go to the tent meeting, but all this work . . . Damn, I should have gone." He leaned over to look behind the black, frowned again, and scanned the yard. "You alone?"

"For a while," Rob said. "You don't have to worry."

Solomon nearly sagged, so great was his relief. "You mind me asking how long?"

Rob laughed. "You're a pest, Solomon. You want to know too much."

"I got a right."

Rob considered, and smiled. "Not very long, as these things go. But too long for you. All right?"

"Hell, no. I'm living forever."

The man on the black leaned over and shook the black man's hand, long and hard, and wheeled his horse around to head for Main Street.

Riding down the center.

Streetlights and houselights and the lights in the shops dimming as he rode past, and not brightening again.

He stopped a second time when he reached the Horseshoe Tavern. He dismounted and pushed through the door, not caring about the silence that cut the piano player off in mid-note, or the looks he received from the men at the tables back near the jukebox. He went straight to the bar and took a stool beside Dumont. The bartender was a young man, who just managed not to gape when he saw Rob sit, the surprise quickly replaced by a sneer and a word to the two women who sat at the bar's end. They looked up and giggled.

"What the hell do you want?" Dumont demanded.

Rob reached into his shirt pocket and pulled out a roll of bills bound in a string. He took the man's hand and placed the money in the palm, closed the fingers around it.

"Get out, Matt," he said, lowering his voice. "Get in that fancy Roadmaster of yours and get the hell out."

Dumont stared at the bills, blinked once, and stood. "Which way?" he said, starting for the door.

"It doesn't matter," Rob told him as he tossed a bill on the bar for Dumont's drink, stood, and followed.

Outside, easy and swift, he sat on the black and watched Dumont hurry away, stop as if he'd remembered something vital, and hurry back, reaching for but not grabbing the stirrup.

"Why me?" he asked.

Rob grinned at him. "Clay's at the meeting."

"You son of a bitch."

"Maybe. Maybe not."

Dumont nodded and left, not looking back, swinging around the corner where the tree that held the poster stood alone amid the scattered litter of its leaves.

The black tossed its head and snorted.

They rode on.

Lights dimming, fading, one or two popping out in brief sparks.

Hooves, metal hooves, echoing off stone and wood long after the town was left behind.

He saw the light in the distance, a bright white made brighter because the night was so dark.

They rode on.

Turned through a gap in a makeshift rope fence, beyond which several score automobiles and a handful of wagons were parked around the bulge of a large circus tent. Torches on poles burned around the entrance just high enough for a tall man. Bunting wrapped around the guy wires. Pennants drooped around the top.

He could hear a voice inside, but he couldn't hear the words. Not that it mattered. He knew what they said: sin and corruption and salvation and damnation and ascension and descent into a black chasm ringed with fire.

He rode inside, holding the black in check when the hundred or more on hard folding chairs realized he was there.

In front, on a high stage, the little preacher in his black suit held up his Bible, stuck in the middle of a verse, mouth open, eyes wide, a finger pointing to the canvas roof.

"You!" the preacher cried. "You . . . *dare!*"

Rob ignored him.

He eased the black forward, down the center aisle, looking at the faces for the one face he needed.

"You! Dare! In the House of the Lord!"

Amy sat on the aisle.

He saw her, he smiled, he rode on.

"Begone, Satan!" the preacher commanded.

When the black reached the stage, it snorted, laid back its ears, stamped once, and wheeled.

No one spoke, no one cried, no one prayed, no one moved.

Rob rode back up the aisle, slowly, without a sound, until he saw Amy again. She had half risen from her seat, dropped back when he reached her, and leaned over, and said, "Tell Jean and Pete the buffalo are coming."

He straightened before she could speak, scanned the faces until he saw him, smug and dapper in a new pin-striped suit, hat in his lap, looking for all the world as if all the world knew his face.

"Satan!" the preacher cried, the first sound in a while.

The second was the wind that began to billow and ripple the tent's walls, and the pennants and bunting snapped, gunshots and thunder.

Rob drew his gun and aimed it at Clark Mitchell.

"With me," he said simply.

Mitchell laughed and shrugged.

The hammer was cocked.

"With me."

Mitchell smoothed his tie, unsure and wondering.

A woman whimpered, a man muttered, the wind bulged the walls and began roaring in the desert.

"I won't say it again," Rob told him.

Mitchell defied him for a single second before rising and making his way apologetically to the aisle. "I'm sorry, Reverend," he called as he put on his hat. "You won't get away with this," he said to Rob.

The black advanced.

Mitchell backed away.

"Satan, begone from these people!" the preacher cried.

Rob looked over his shoulder, lifted his head, and the preacher froze.

You know, Rob thought, as if the preacher could hear, you know, but you won't tell them.

Mitchell broke then, yelling for help as he sprinted out of the tent.

Rob followed without haste, paused once outside to let the wind tell him where the man had gone. To the road, it seemed, and the black began to trot, puffs of dust turned to sparks, steam from its nostrils, steam from its hide.

The pennants cracked; the bunting writhed; a guy wire snapped, and the roof began to sag.

Once on the road, Rob swung the black east and let the animal run. He couldn't see Mitchell, but that was all right. The man had no imagination; he would seek cover in the night, then try to double back when he was sure Rob had passed him by.

The black ran.

Fire and smoke.

And slowed when Mitchell faded in directly ahead, hat gone, jacket flapping, looking over his shoulder and trying to run faster when he saw Rob coming toward him.

The chase didn't last long.

Rob drew even, reached down, and swatted the man's shoulder. Mitchell sprawled onto the macadam and skidded, rolled over, and scrambled to his knees, hands clasped and begging, blood between his fingers, as Rob turned and waited.

The gun was still drawn.

Blood masked the right side of Mitchell's face, oozing and sliding, bits of pebble and grit embedded in his cheek and brow, a patch of his hair pulled free, the scalp raw.

"You can't do this," Mitchell said, quaking so hard he nearly toppled. "You don't know who I am."

Rob said nothing.

"They'll have your face on every newspaper, on every screen. You can't do this!"

The black lowered its head and shook it.

"They'll know who you are, you stupid son of a bitch!" He sobbed and covered his face.

Winter wind and tumbleweeds.

"No," Rob said. "They won't."

Mitchell lowered his hands, blood smeared even to his lips and teeth. He didn't understand; an outstretched hand pleaded, *What the hell did I do to you?*

The man on the black looked back toward the tent, toward the flames just beginning to crawl up the sides, erasing some of the stars, tiny figures running away from the fire.

"You showed them the Bomb," he said, slowly turning his head back. Midnight eyes.

Mitchell swallowed, gagged, and spit. "So what?"

The man on the black jerked his head toward the tent. "The preacher tells them that means Armageddon."

"Jesus Christ, so the hell what?"

"He's wrong."

Mitchell tried to stand, fell back to his hands and knees, and whimpered. "Crazy," he whispered. "Jesus God, he's crazy."

"You are," the man told him.

He pulled the trigger.

Mitchell stiffened upright, back rigid, until the wind knocked him over.

Rob waited until another gust rolled the body into the ditch, waited until he was sure Amy had escaped the burning.

Waited until the black grew tired of standing.

And then he rode on.

A short road, this time.

And it saddened him.

Just a little.

Christopher Harman

In the Fields

Christopher Harman lives in Preston, England, and has worked in Lancashire
public libraries for the past ten years. He has sold stories to All Hallows,
Doppelganger Broadsheet, *and* Ghosts and Scholars.

"In the Fields" is a classic ghost story that first appeared in All Hallows:
The Journal of the Ghost Story Society 14.

—E. D.

T he field was empty. There had been a rustling coming from inside it and
Thomas had been buoyed up, expecting to see another walker at last,
and struggling with a map by the sound of things. But there was nobody,
and trudging into the middle of the field he failed to see any other
opening in the stone walls through which to slip out. A left-over between the
other fields, he decided. It didn't even possess the dignity of a gateway; the
opening through which he'd entered was narrow and littered with stones, as if
at some time somebody had forced an entry in a hurry.

Thomas wiped his brow; his legs were about to give way. It was as if his fatigue
of the past four days of walking had finally caught up with him when he'd
descended to the fields. Lost, he'd negotiated innumerable walls, leapt clogged
ditches as battalions of flies like tiny coals had pursued him. At least they'd left
him for the time being.

Between bumps wigged with grass and pink-flowered thistles, Thomas sat and
ate his last sandwich and drained the last dregs of coffee in his flask. He yawned,
and sensed his remaining energy draining down through his legs. Rather than
confront the glare of the sky, or the glowering dark walls, gold-patched with
lichen and which offered no shade, he cast his eyes to the ground.

He felt sleepy enough to sit, or even lie, here until nightfall. Not for the first time he wondered if the trek over the North York Moors had been worth it. He'd needed time and space to be alone, but his thoughts had drifted back to his last day at Lightburne and Co., the presentation, the awkward smiles of colleagues. His tread had beat out an internal mantra—'Last one in, first one out'—then he'd seen distant fields hanging from columns of sunlight.

The rustling made him glance up again; he cringed as something shadowed him before tumbling in a flurry of white over a wall. Thomas stood and hauled up his rucksack. A bird, no doubt. He turned unsteadily, taking in the walls. The gaps between the stones were like eye sockets waiting for his next move. For a moment he was convinced the opening had gone—as if a wall might heal itself. It was there, of course, filled in with stones in the opposite wall of a neighbouring field.

Outside the field, Thomas sensed he'd left a space that remained occupied. Sweat ran into his eyes as he scanned the gently rolling landscape criss-crossed with walls. It took a moment to resolve a dark smudge that hovered in the air into the shape of a figure standing on a wall a few fields away. Intervening walls rippled; heat haze must be doing that, but the figure was undoubtedly real, and it had seen him. Thomas didn't immediately realise that the great dark sockets examining him were binoculars.

Lacking a direct route, it took Thomas ten minutes to reach the figure, by which time he felt a little more composed. As he drew closer he saw it was a man. Short and plump, he wore an unbuttoned earth-coloured mackintosh despite the heat. No wonder his face shone like an apple.

'I'm trying to find the road to Cleygate,' Thomas called, wielding his map as if to prove it. The man eyed him blankly for a moment before recalling his precarious position. Alarmed, Thomas stepped forward as the man grimaced, half-crouching like a performer on a circus horse.

'That way—half a mile,' the man said, steady enough at last to spare Thomas a quick smile and an economical gesture behind him. Thomas felt he'd intruded in some way. Perplexed, he moved on, pausing a moment later to look back at the man, still on the wall, his binoculars blunt horns trained on the sky.

The walls of the dining room were armoured with porcelain and brasses. At the next table an elderly couple watched younger versions of themselves try to settle two small girls into their places. Thomas was famished, but at least he'd recovered a little in the three hours since he'd escaped the fields. After the episode with the man on the wall he'd trudged through more fields that were like huge, overheated rooms. But he'd found the road, and half a mile along it he'd come to a cluster of sandstone cottages, the first a guest house called Edgeley's.

A print of a figure in a pale smock stooping in a high-walled field held his attention until somebody tapped him on the shoulder. The man held invisible binoculars to his eyes, as if Thomas had already forgotten him.

'You found your way then?' he said. Thomas, surprised, managed to reply that he had, and the man seemed to see this as an invitation to sit down opposite. Jabbing a hand across the table, he knocked over the cruet. 'Barry Bampton.' Before Thomas could reveal his own name, Bampton went on, 'They can be a bit confusing, those fields.' He shook his head and chuckled to himself, as if the fields were lovable but infuriating acquaintances.

'The path just stopped. I thought I was going around in circles,' Thomas found himself explaining. Bampton, amused, began dabbing at his lips with a napkin, even though he hadn't started eating yet; then he coughed self-consciously and frowned at the soup plate the landlady placed before him.

One night would definitely be enough, thought Thomas grimly. He moulded Bampton's Bunterish features into those of Alice. She'd be teaching an evening class now. He told Bampton that his destination was Robin Hood's Bay, where his wife would be waiting. Was the other man even listening? Despite his amiable behaviour, he seemed restless, preoccupied. Thomas was aware of Bampton's chewing mouth, the occasional glance as if he was about to say something before thinking better of it. He was helping himself to another Yorkshire pudding, then was shaking the pepper-pot once more. He blinked, sniffed, began digging in his jacket pocket. Glasses, polo mints in a green stub, and a battered black notebook littered the table before he produced a handkerchief in time to catch a sneeze. And something hit the window.

Bampton rose and rushed from the room. Guests looked around them as if recovering from startling news. 'A bird,' somebody suggested. For a moment the room had seemed shrouded, as if a shutter had fallen over the deep-set panes, and Thomas couldn't put away the notion that somebody had been at the window at that instant and had smiled at him.

Bampton had left his notebook; a square inch of newspaper protruded, from which a tiny, upside-down face stared. There was the smile. The tiny, pin-prick eyes of the face challenged him to open the book. Thomas resisted until he'd consumed his bread-and-butter pudding; then, picking up Bampton's notebook, he left the room.

He paused on the stairs, and looked at the notebook more closely. It was a scrapbook. Inside were photocopies taken from maps showing irregular shapes, some of them numbered. They were almost certainly fields. A copy of a letter dated 1790 was addressed to the Bishop of York. Underlined words caught his eye: 'slayings of small beasts', 'devilish cavortings'. In newspaper cuttings the name Snyles recurred. The smiling face in the photograph headed an article entitled 'History man found dead'. The smile was inappropriate; but was it a smile? A frog-like lipless slit with turned up corners was more of an affliction, Thomas decided.

Bampton's door was open. As he passed, Thomas saw that the man was gripping the window frame as if about to propel himself out.

Inside his own room, Thomas went to the window. What had Bampton seen out there? When he had returned the man's notebook his face had been vacant, his eyes seemingly focussed on something else.

The evening fields were a litter of empty pages between the mesh of walls. Mist pooled in the fields; like strands of sheeps' wool it clung to the walls. There was a corner where it frolicked as if imitating something unseen which disturbed it.

Merely the sight of open spaces was tiring him; his limbs ached, his head thudded. He turned away from the window. It was too early to retire. He took a bath, then lay on his bed. He could hear the television in the guests' lounge. What was on tonight? The unrestrained laughter he could hear certainly wasn't coming from the guests. His spirit sagged at the number of barriers of time and space, like stone walls, between himself and Alice, himself and his former colleagues. He remembered his Walkman and tuned in to sounds of violins and flutes; he let his mind drift on a raft of lilting rhythms.

On a stone wall something danced on its corners to the music.

Just before dawn, Thomas was aware of a wild flapping. His window was full of dirty light covered in faint lines that outlined a patchwork of shapes. A shape in the centre had a mouth. He was trying to recall to whom it belonged, and what it would say if it stopped smiling, when the wind plucked it away into the paling night.

He awoke to a thudding at his door. A hoover droned outside. He reached for his watch; it was eleven. God, he'd overslept. The buffeting at his door was insistent as Thomas dressed hurriedly. Mrs Trask finished her hoovering before making an appearance in the dining room with a tray of toast and coffee. As she began to furiously polish the other tables, Thomas asked meekly if there was a bus to Cleygate. He'd need to get something more to eat, for a start.

'There was one at ten—the next's at two,' she informed a table top. He digested the information, then asked if he could book another night. He wasn't yet ready to continue the trek to the coast; he might even catch a bus the rest of the way the following morning.

Thomas stood on a stile on the wall that bounded the far side of the road from the cottages. A rotted, barely readable sign said 'Cleygate'.

Climbing down from the wall, he felt the fields rise to meet him. A breeze ruffled his clothing for a moment, like a customs official, before allowing him to move on. There were a few clouds, pale and wispy as webs. He followed the path across the field to a gate. The next field was larger and the path disappeared into long couch grass. As he crossed the next few fields, Thomas sensed he was being diverted from his course to the village. He climbed a wall to get his bearings. He wished the breeze would return. There was no sound except for his irregular, slightly wheezing breath, which was checked as he glimpsed something white at the edge of his vision. Perhaps a seagull rising and falling over a morsel.

A butterfly-like course through several more fields brought him to the place, but whatever he'd seen had gone. His breath in the hot, cloying air was full of tiny cries. His limbs ached dully. How far was he from the village? Climbing part way up a wall, he could see a few grey roofs almost submerged by bushes. He was sure that was Cleygate, but it was as if the stiles and gateways implied other pathways that led anywhere but to the village. And then he glimpsed white again, nearer now, a floundering over a wall. Not a seagull, but a sheet perhaps. Close to it a head bobbed. Thomas crossed the field and saw over the far wall of the adjacent field Bampton running back and forth, flinging a white thing above his head, like somebody waving a flag.

Thomas's grin faded as he watched. Far from waving the white thing, Bampton was reaching for it in vain as the breeze lifted and dropped it teasingly. Soon it was rising higher and higher until it merged with the diffuse radiance of the sun. Thomas waited for the same breeze to brush around him at any moment, but nearby foxgloves remained as motionless as glass, dog roses failed to nod.

Had Bampton spotted him? Was he following at a distance? That might explain the sense he had of being watched. He squinted at a sky stained a faint green after the fields. It occurred to him that a hawk or similar bird was hovering up there, hidden in sunshine.

His vision retained the green, imprinted it onto the pavement, turned the stones of the cottages into mouldy loaves. The village was cowed to silence by the fields lapping at its sides. He imagined a time when grass would carpet the main street, weeds climb the walls, green flames blaze through lower floor windows. Perhaps some of the properties were holiday cottages; walking up the main street he glimpsed green framed in the back windows of empty rooms. A concealed radio voice said it was two-thirty, then another voice began to sing in duet with the squeaks of a shammy leather. A few doors ahead a thin, bespectacled man was rubbing at a window filled with envelopes, jiffy bags, jars of sweets.

After the brightness, the inside of the shop was as cool as a cave. A flustered elderly woman was pushing coins beneath a grill like tit-bits to an animal as a precise, middle-class voice tried to reassure her about her 'stamps'. Clutching bags of crisps and a postcard showing a circle of figures in a field, Thomas examined a noticeboard as he waited. Good; there would be a bus going to the coast at nine the next morning.

He was aware of somebody watching him, but it wasn't the man cleaning the windows. A face pictured on a police notice made Thomas's memory work back towards Bampton's newspaper cutting. It was the same face, but greatly enlarged. Spare, late middle-aged features, the mouth thin as a crack in plaster. Leonard Snyles.

'Police are anxious to trace Mr Snyles, who was last seen at the Spades Hotel. Please contact police with any information.'

It was dated four months ago. The old woman glared at Thomas, or perhaps at the notice, and pulled at the door. A draught slipped in and the notices lifted gracefully. Snyles's chin flattened, the mouth rose to eat the eyes, then fell as the door shut. The noticeboard resembled an aerial view of fields.

'Looks a bit fishy, doesn't he.' An overalled woman had emerged from behind the grill. She tucked a string of grey hair behind her ear and folded her arms. Thomas murmured noncommittally and picked up a can of lager furred with dust.

'People say they saw him making notes or drawing or something. We're new here, but apparently the area has a bit of a past.' She examined the can for a price tag. 'I expect things were livelier then,' she added wistfully.

'Did he turn up?' asked Thomas.

'Yes—at the Spades.' She banged the cash till shut on Thomas's money. 'But a day later he hanged himself. He was a teacher, but he was sacked for some misdemeanour. Two local lads say they saw him talking to himself in a field.'

Thomas needed a drink, but he'd save the lager for evening. As he left the shop he looked back to see the woman plucking at drawing-pins on the noticeboard. If he'd stayed a moment later he'd have ripped down the notice himself.

Past the garage with its single unattended pump Thomas came to the Spades. In the brassy interior two squat, flat-capped old men contemplated their glasses as if they were chess pieces. Thomas, who was ravenous, ate a Ploughman's Lunch, and feeling the beginnings of a headache settled for a half pint of orange and pretended it was lager.

Green pressed between cottages at the far side of the road. The track of an airplane was a single blade of grass dividing the sky into two vast plains. Thomas considered asking about Snyles, but the barman had retreated into a dark alcove behind the bar. Only the crinkling of paper betrayed his presence—a stealthy sound, like someone trying to manipulate a broadsheet newspaper as quietly as possible. Thomas gulped down the last of his orange and left.

His footsteps tapped hollowly between the stone walls of the winding lane. A few cars passed him and left him alone between fields that held their breaths. For a time a walker, folding and unfolding his map, kept pace with him on the other side of a high wall.

Reading wouldn't distract him from the fields. He found himself at his window without thinking. Looking eastwards he saw dark blue clouds advancing into the sky. In a distant field something caught the light, then was gone. The fields were emerald-bright, yet looked as yielding as an ocean. You could drown in those fields, he thought. He lay on his bed and examined his Ordnance Survey map, then let it drop onto his face.

He was over the fields. He was a bird, or something else, floating so high his wings more than spanned the earth. As the fields folded up on each side like petals closing, he awoke to a car crunching on the drive outside. Thomas got up and saw Bampton arriving just in time for the evening meal.

Bampton's sparse hair was plastered to his scalp; there was a moustache of moisture over his upper lip. He nodded to the other guests and made his way to a corner table. From his pocket he extracted a crumpled sheet of paper and frowned at it, bit his pencil, drew a line or two against a ruler. Thomas was not the only one intrigued. Bampton caught the gaze of the two beribboned small girls, who looked immediately sheepish and shy as he winked at them.

After dinner, Thomas sat in the hallway leafing through a dog-eared copy of *Yorkshire Life*. A quiz show was in progress in the TV room. He was tempted to ring Alice, but what would he say? It would be breaking a promise to himself to contact her before the time they'd arranged to meet. A drink would settle him—no, he needed to get drunk.

At least one individual seemed happy. Bampton was trotting down the stairs, tossing his car keys and whistling a tune from *Phantom of the Opera*.

'Had a good day?' he inquired, breaking off from his whistling.

'Good enough,' Thomas answered, adding in a lower voice before he could stop himself, 'It would help if this place had a bar.'

Bampton was as alert as a dog offered a bone. 'I know a little place called the Spades,' he said eagerly.

Did he always drive like this? Thomas had wondered what they'd have to talk about, but that was now the least of his concerns. He gripped his seat and prayed that the seatbelt of the elderly Morris Minor would serve its purpose if called upon. Bampton took the bends too fast; out of the darkness, walls loomed close.

At first Thomas thought it was a stray beam caught in an overhead wire. Abruptly it thickened into a square, flew forward to fill the windscreen, and was as quickly gone again. Somebody somewhere had smiled.

Bampton stamped on the brakes. Thomas was pulled forward and then the car rocked into silence. 'A piece of rubbish, that's all,' Thomas protested to the open driver's door. Bampton's mackintosh winged about him in the headlights before he disappeared through a gateway.

The breeze carried fragments of a rustling. Bampton surely wouldn't wander far. Thomas went to the gateway and called out. Inside the field intermittent moonlight illuminated a dirt track. Should he wait, or pursue Bampton? The second option might resolve the situation sooner, he decided, setting forth along the track to the opposite gateway, where he called again.

Clouds churned like smoke from a hundred chimneys. Cold emanated from the walls. Patches of moonlight made them shift, seem insubstantial. He glimpsed movement over one. Relieved and irritated, Thomas ran through the next field and the one after, determined to give Bampton, whom he could hear, a piece of his mind.

'I take it you do know the way out of this field?' he asked, telling himself it was frustration that barely let him get the words out. He tried to dismiss the notion that the map fitted a face that could not be Bampton's. Unwillingly he searched for Snyles's features beneath the map, an outline of that smile; but to his dismay he could only detect features that would barely constitute a face at all.

This was stupid; of course it was Bampton, hands still in his pockets as if he were waiting for a bus. When Bampton abruptly took another step forward so that they were face to face, Thomas's mind jabbered at him. 'For God's sake, take that thing off!' he blurted out.

As if it had heard, the figure extracted a bright hand and proceeded to do so.

Nicholas Royle

Mbo

*Nicholas Royle was born in Sale, Cheshire, England, in 1963. He is the author of three novels—*Counterparts, Saxophone Dreams, *and* The Matter of the Heart—*and more than one hundred short stories, several of which have been selected for the anthologies* The Best New Horror, The Year's Best Fantasy and Horror, *and* The Year's Best Horror Stories. *Other recent appearances have included* Dark Terrors, Dark Terrors 2, Twists of the Tale, The Mammoth Book of Zombies, *and* The Mammoth Book of Werewolves. *He has edited the award-winning anthologies* Darklands *and* Darklands 2, *in addition to several other anthologies such as* A Book of Two Halves *and* The Time Out Book of New York Short Stories. *His book reviews have appeared in* Time Out, *the* Guardian, *the* Observer, *and elsewhere. He lives in London.*

Royle is a master of story openings and a crackerjack storyteller, as is shown in this suspenseful tale of terror that brings together two legends.

—E. D.

I t was a question of arriving at the right time. You didn't necessarily, for example, turn up at the same time each evening, but juggled various considerations, such as the heat, the number of clouds in the sky, even what type they were, whether they were cumulus or stratus or cirro-stratus—stuff like that. You wanted to turn up just at the right moment, just in time to get a seat and a good view and not a moment too soon. After all, the terrace of the Africa House Hotel was not a place you wanted to spend any more time than you absolutely had to. It simply wasn't that nice.

It wasn't nice partly because you were surrounded by all those people you had gone to Zanzibar to get away from—white people, Europeans, tourists; *mzungu,* the locals called them, red bananas. White inside but red on the outside, as soon as they'd been in the sun for a couple of hours. Apparently there was a strain of red-skinned banana that grew on the island.

And partly because the place itself was grotsville. In colonial days, the Africa House Hotel was the English Club, but since the departure of the British in 1963, it had been pretty much allowed to go to seed.

But you didn't go there for the moth-eaten hunting trophies on the walls, or the charmless service at the counter, but to sit as close to the front of the terrace as you could, order a beer and have it brought to you, and watch the sun sink into the Indian Ocean. Over there, just below the horizon—the continental land mass of Africa. Amazing really that you couldn't see it, thought Craig. It didn't really matter how far away it was—twenty miles, thirty—looking at it on the map, Zanzibar Island was no more than a tick clinging to the giant African elephant.

Craig ordered a Castle lager from the waiter who slunk oilily around the tables and their scattered chairs. He was a strange, tired-looking North African with one of those elastic snake-buckle belts doing the job of keeping his brown trousers up. Similar to the one Craig had worn at school—8,000 miles away in east London.

He didn't like ordering a Castle, or being seen with one (they didn't give you a glass at the Africa House Hotel). It was South African and everyone knew it was South African. He supposed it was all right now, but still, if people saw you drinking South African beer they'd assume you were drinking it because that's what you drank back home. In South Africa. And whereas it was all right to buy South African goods, it still wasn't all right to be South African.

And Craig wasn't, and he didn't want anyone to think he was, but not so badly that he'd drink any more of the Tanzanian Safari, or the Kenyan Tusker. One was too yeasty, the other so weak it was like drinking bat's piss.

This was his third consecutive evening at the Africa House Hotel and he was by now prepared to let people think he was—or might be—South African. He wasn't staying there, no way, uh-uh—he was staying at Mazson's, a few minutes' walk away. Air-con, satellite TV, a bath as well as a shower—and a business center. The business center was what had clinched it. Plus the fact the paper was paying.

Craig slipped the elastic band off his ponytail and shook out his fair hair, brushed it back to round up any strays, and reapplied the elastic. He took off his Oakley wraparound shades and pinched the bridge of his nose between thumb and forefinger. Stuck them back on. Squinted at the sun, still a few degrees above the bank of stratus clouds which would prevent the Africa House Hotel crowd from enjoying a proper sunset for the third evening in a row.

From behind his Oakleys, Craig checked out the terrace: people watching, with a purpose for once. News of the disappearances clearly wasn't putting these tourists off coming to Zanzibar. Mainly because there wasn't any news. Not enough of a problem in any one country to create a crisis. One weeping family from Sutton Coldfield—"Sarah just wouldn't go off with anyone, she's not that kind of girl"; a red-eyed single mother from Strathclyde—"There's been no word from Louise for three weeks now." It wasn't enough to get the tabloids interested and the broadsheets wouldn't pick up on it until they were sure there was a real story. A big story. No news was no news and, by and large, didn't make the news.

Craig had latched on to Sarah's story following an impassioned letter to the editor of his paper from the missing girl's mother. He was a soft touch, he told his commissioning editor: couldn't bear to think of those good people sitting on the edge of their floral-pattern IKEA sofa, waiting for the phone to ring, weeping—especially not in Sutton Coldfield. But MacNeill, who'd been commissioning pieces from Craig for three years, knew the young man only attached himself to a story if there was a story there. And since he was between desk assignments anyway, MacNeill let him go. On the quiet, like. Neither the Tanzanian government nor the Zanzibari police would acknowledge the problem—too damaging to the developing tourism industry, ironically—so Craig needed a cover, which Craig's sister, the wildlife photographer, came up with.

The Zanzibar leopard, smaller than the mainland species, was rumored by some to be extinct and by others to be around still, though in very small numbers. One of the guide books reckoned if there were any on the islands, they had been domesticated by practitioners of herbal medicine—witch doctors to you and me. The Zanzibari driver who collected Craig from the airport laughed indulgently at the idea. And Craig read later in another guide book that witchcraft was believed to be widely practiced on Pemba Island, 85 kilometers to the north of Zanzibar though part of the same territory. Though if you tried to speak to the locals about it, they became embarrassed or politely changed the subject. But that was Pemba, and the disappearances—thirty-seven to date, according to Craig's researches—were quite specifically from Zanzibar Island.

Thirty-seven. Twenty-three women between seventeen and thirty, and fourteen men, some of them older, mid-forties. From Denmark, Germany, Austria, Britain, France, Italy, Australia and the U.S. Enough of a problem as far as Craig was concerned. He was torn now, he was ashamed to admit, between wanting the world to wake up and make a concerted effort (thereby, hopefully, securing the earlier recovery of Sarah, or Sarah's body, and thirty-six others) and hoping he would be the first to break the story.

The cover. A naturalist based at the University of Sussex, Craig's brief was to confirm whether or not leopards still lived wild on the island. They'd even put Sussex's professor of zoology in the picture, for a consideration of course which they called a consultancy fee, so that if anyone called from Zanzibar to check up on Craig, they'd find him to be bona fide.

That afternoon, Craig had visited the Natural History Museum, quite the bizarrest of its type in his experience. Glass cases full of birds, presumably stuffed birds, but not mounted—lying down, recently-dead looking, their little feet tied together with string. Tags to identify them. Their eyes dabs of chalk. In a grimy case all on its own, the bones of a dodo wired up into a standing position. A couple of stuffed bats—the American Fruit Bat and the Pemba Fruit Bat—ten times the size of the swallow-like creatures that had flitted about his head as he'd walked off his dinner the evening before. A crate with its lid ajar: when he opened it, a flurry of flies, one he couldn't prevent going up his nose. Inside, a board with three rats fixed to it—dead again, stuffed presumably, but with legs trussed at tiny rodent ankles. No effort made to have them assume lifelike poses. No bits of twig and leaf. No glass eyes. No glass case. He dropped the crate lid.

Oddest of all: row upon row of glass jars containing dead sea creatures and deformed animal foetuses, the glass furred up with dust and calcified deposits, so you had to bend down and squint to make out the bloodless remains of a stonefish, the huge crab with the image on its shell of two camels with their masters. The conjoined duiker antelopes.

And the stuffed leopard. They hadn't done a great job on it. The taxidermist's task being to stage a magic show for eternity: the illusion of life in the cock of the head, the setting of a glassy twinkle. The Natural History Museum of Zanzibar should have been asking for their money back on this one. You could still see it was a leopard though. If you didn't know, you'd look at it and you'd say leopard. Craig examined it from every angle. This was what he was here to find. Ostensibly. It couldn't do any harm to have a good idea what one looked like.

Up on the terrace, the touts were working the crowd—slowly, carefully, with a lower-key approach than they tended to use down in Stone Town. In Stone Town the same guys would shadow you on the same streets day after day.

"Jambo," they'd say.

"Jambo," you'd reply, because it would be rude not to.

"You want to go to Prison Island? You want to go to the East Coast today? Maybe you want go to Nungwi? You want taxi?"

You ran the gauntlet going up Kenyatta Street and never had a moment's peace when you were around Jamyatti Gardens, from where the boats left for Prison Island, its coral reefs and giant tortoises. He'd read the books all right.

"Jambo." The voice was close to him. Craig sneaked a look around as he necked his beer. A young Zanzibari had moved in on a blonde English girl who had been sitting alone. The girl smiled a little shyly and the youth sat down next to her. "The sun is setting," he said and the girl looked out over the ocean. The sun had started to dip behind the bank of cloud. "You want to go to Prison Island tomorrow?" he asked, pulling a pack of cigarettes from his pocket.

The girl shook her head. "No. Thanks." She was still smiling but Craig could see she was a little nervous. Doing battle with her shyness was the adventurous spirit that had brought her this far from whichever northern market town she'd left behind. She was flattered by the youth's attentions but could never quite forget the many warnings her worried parents would have given her in the weeks before she left.

The tout went through the list and still she politely declined. In the end he changed tack and offered to buy her a drink. Craig heard her say she'd have a beer. The youth caught the waiter's eye and spoke to him fast in Swahili. Next time the waiter came by he had a can of Stella for the girl and a Coke for the tout. Craig watched as the girl popped open the Stella and almost imperceptibly shifted on her seat so that her upper body was angled slightly further away from the boy in favor of the ocean. Maybe she shouldn't have accepted the beer, thought Craig. Or maybe it was old-fashioned to think like that. Perhaps these days girls had the right to accept the beer and turn the other way. He just wasn't sure the African youth would see it like that. Whether he was a practising Muslim—the abnegation of alcohol told him that—or not.

A high-pitched whine in Craig's ear. A pin-prick in the forearm. He smacked his hand down hard, lifted it slowly to peer underneath.

Craig started, then shuddered; never able to stand the sight of blood, whether his own or anybody else's, he had once run out of the cinema during an afternoon screening of *The Shining*. He had fainted at the scene of a road accident, having caught sight of a pedestrian victim's leg, her stocking sodden with her own blood. She survived unscathed; Craig's temple bore a scar to this day where he had hit his head on the pavement.

The mosquito had drunk well, and not just of Craig either. His stomach turning over, he quickly inspected the creature's dinner which was smeared across his arm, a red blotch in the shape of Madagascar, almost an inch long. Craig wondered whose blood it was, given that the mozzie had barely had enough time to sink its needle beneath his skin. Some other drinker's? Craig looked about. Not that of the Italian in the tight briefs, he hoped. Nor ideally had it come from either of the two South African rugby players sitting splayed-legged at the front by the railing.

He spat onto a paper tissue and wiped his arm vigorously without giving it another look until he was sure it had to be clear. The energy from the slap had been used up bursting the balloon of blood; the mosquito's empty body, split but relatively intact, was stuck to Craig's arm like an empty popsicle wrapper.

This bothered him less than the minutest trace of blood still inside the dead insect's glassy skin.

When he looked up, the blonde girl had joined a group of Europeans—Scandinavians or Germans by the look of them—and was eagerly working her way into their telling of travellers tales, while the young tout glared angrily at the bank of clouds obscuring the sun, his left leg vibrating like a wire. Craig hoped he wasn't angry enough to get nasty. Doubted it—after all, chances were this sort of thing happened a lot up here. The kid couldn't expect a hundred per cent strike rate.

Craig gave it five minutes, then went over and sat next to the kid. Kid turned around and Craig started talking.

Ten minutes later, Craig and the kid both left, though not together. Craig was heading for Mazson's Hotel and bed; the kid, his timetable for the following day sorted, having spoken to Craig, was heading home as well—home for him being his family's crumbling apartment in the heart of the Stone Town, among the rats and the rubbish and the running sewage. To be fair, the authorities were tackling the sewage, but they hadn't yet got as far as the kid's block.

The group that Alison, the blonde girl, had joined was approached by another tout, an older, taller fellow. More confident than the kid, not so much driven by other motivations, less distracted—he had a job to do. With her new companions, Alison was not so nervous about getting into the trips business. She wanted to go to Prison Island, they all did; they looked around to include her as the tout waited for an answer, and she nodded, smiling with relief. Turned out they were German, two of them, the two girls, but naturally they spoke perfect English; the third girl and the boy, who appeared to be an item, were Danish, but you wouldn't know it—their English, spoken with American accents, was pretty good too.

"We were just in Goa," said Kristin, one of the German girls. "It is so good. Have you been?"

"No," Alison shook her head. "But I'd like to go. I've heard about it." She'd heard about it all right. About the raves and the beach parties, the drugs and the boys—Australians, Americans, Europeans. It had been hard enough to get permission to come to Zanzibar, especially alone, but her parents had accepted her right to make a bid for independence.

"Ach!" shouted Anna, the second German girl, flailing her bare arms as she failed to make contact with a mozzie. "Scheisse!"

"Where are you staying, Alison?" asked the Danish boy, Lief, his arm around his girlfriend's shoulder.

Alison named a cheap hotel on the edge of Stone Town.

"You should move into Emerson's House," Lief's girlfriend, Karin, advised. "That's where we're all staying. It's really cool. Great chocolate cake . . ." She looked at Lief and for some reason they sniggered. Kristin and Anna joined in and soon they were all laughing, Alison included. Their combined laughter was so loud they couldn't hear anything else.

People started to look, but, leaning in towards each other, they could only hear their own laughter.

Popo—the kid—picked up Craig outside Mazson's at nine the next morning in a battered but just about roadworthy Suzuki Jeep.

"Jambo," he said as Craig climbed in beside him. "Jozani Forest."

"Jambo. Jozani Forest," Craig confirmed their destination.

They rumbled out of town, which became gradually more ramshackle as they approached the outskirts. Popo used the horn every few seconds to clear the road of cyclists, who were out in their hundreds. No one resented being ordered to make way, Craig noticed, as they would back home. Popo's deft handling took the Jeep around potholes and, where they were too big to be avoided, slowly through them. Most of the men in the streets wore long flowing white garments and skull caps; as they got further out of town, the Arabic influence became less pronounced. The women here wore brightly coloured kikois and carried unfeasibly large bags and packages on their heads. Orderly crowds of schoolgirls in white headgear and navy tunics streamed into schools that appeared to be no more than collections of outbuildings.

Between the villages, banana plantations ran right up to the edge of the road. Huge bunches of green fruit pointed up to the sky, brown raffia-like leaves crackled in the Jeep's draught.

"You look for Red Colobus monkey?" Popo asked without taking his eye off the road.

"I told you last night," Craig reminded him. "Zanzibar leopard. I'm looking for the leopard."

"No leopard here," Popo shook his head.

"I heard the witch doctors keep them."

"No leopard."

"There are witch doctors, then?"

Popo didn't say anything as they passed through another tiny village, crowds of little children too small to be in school running up to the Jeep and waving at Craig, old men sat under a shelter made out of dried palm leaves. The children shouted after them: "Jambo, jambo!" Craig waved back.

"In Jozani Forest . . ." Popo said slowly, "Red Colobus monkey. Only here on Zanzibar."

"I know," said Craig, wiping his forearm across his slippery brow. "And the leopards? The witch doctors? I have to find them."

"No leopard here."

He wasn't going to get much more out of Popo, that was clear. When the kid swung the Jeep off the road, he reacted swiftly by grabbing his arm, but they had only pulled into the carpark for the forest. He let go of the kid's arm.

"Sorry. Took me by surprise."

Popo blinked slowly.

"No leopard here," he repeated.

The noise of the boat's engine, a constant ragged chugging, made conversation impossible. There was no point trying to make yourself heard, but that didn't stop Lief from occasionally mouthing easily understood remarks about the choppiness of the water, the heat of the sun.

The others—Karin, Anna, Kristin and Alison—grinned and nodded, although Alison's grin was a little forced. Her trip to Prison Island was always going to exact a price, even though it was only supposed to be a half-hour hop: Alison could barely walk through a puddle without getting seasick. As the 25-foot wooden craft took another dive off the top of the next crest, she lurched forward and felt her stomach do the same, only, it seemed, without stopping. She retched, assumed the crash position, fully expecting to be ditched in the drink. It didn't happen. The boat lumbered up the next heavy swell, perched an instant at its arête, and plummeted into the trough. Alison groaned.

The two Danes were chattering excitedly in their own tongue, clearly having a ball. When she looked up, Alison saw Anna and Kristin smiling down at her. "Are you okay?" one of them asked and Alison just managed to shake her head. "It's not far to the island," Anna said, looking forward, but the boat pitched to port, throwing her off her feet. She tumbled into Alison's lap, Alison dry-retching once again.

"Oh God," she moaned. "I can't stand it."

"It's not far now," Lief tried to reassure her, although he was puzzled as to why they had shifted around so much that the bow was now pointing out to sea.

"Where are we going?" Anna asked, of no one in particular, once she had picked herself up off the duckboards.

Now Kristin demanded, "What's going on?" as the bow swung around several degrees further to port. Their course could no longer be even loosely interpreted as being bound for Prison Island. "Where are you taking us?" she shouted at the boat's skipper, a lad no more than eighteen sat in the stern, his hand on the outboard throttle.

They were now heading into the wind, and spray broke over the bow every seventh or eighth wave. Alison had started to cry, tears slipping noiselessly over green cheeks. Her mouth was set in a firm, down-curved bow, her brow creased in determined abstraction.

Lief rose to his feet unsteadily and asked the skipper, "What's going on?" The 18-year-old just stared at the horizon. "We want to go to Prison Island. We paid you the money. Where are you taking us?" Still the guy wouldn't look at him.

Lief leaned forward to grab his arm, but found himself jerked back from behind. The other African, who had been squatting in the bow, motioned to Lief that he should sit down. The fingers of his left hand were wrapped around the stubby handle of a fisherman's knife.

"Sit," he ordered. "Sit." He looked at the girls. "Sit." He pointed at the wooden bench seats and everyone complied. Now Anna had started to weep as well and was not so quiet about it as Alison.

"Hands," the boy barked, his jaws snapping around the rusty gutting blade and grabbing at Lief's wrists. With a length of twine he quickly tied Lief's hands behind his back before any of the girls had the presence of mind to knock him off his feet while he had his hands occupied and was temporarily unarmed. They would live to regret this missed opportunity.

Anna and Kristin were almost paralyzed with fear. Alison was within an ace of throwing herself overboard, believing that to be actually in the water could not be worse than being in a boat on it. Still the boat struck out against the direction of the incoming waves and soon they were all soaked from the spray over the bow. The boat climbed and plunged, climbed and plunged. Alison leaned over the side and was quietly sick; she hoped it would make her feel better. It was funny how not even mortal fear could distract her from her sea-sickness.

Neither, it transpired, could the act of vomiting. If anything, she felt worse, and when the boat slipped around several degrees to port and took the waves side-on, she liked it even less. Each time the narrow craft leaned to either side she thought she was going in—again she considered doing it deliberately. Anna and Kristin were both crying, staring alternately at each other and at Lief, who was ashen-faced. Alison justified her intention to jump ship by interpreting the others' introvertedness as being an atavistic retreat into their original social groupings in the face of extreme fear. They would no more try to save her life than they would that of one of the two kidnappers, she reasoned. How long had they known her? Twelve hours. What kind of bond grew in such a short time? Not a lasting one.

She remembered what her mother had once told her, when they'd taken the ferry to Calais. "Look at the horizon," she'd said. "Watch the land. Don't look at the water." Thinking of her mother only brought fresh tears and looking left at the palm-fringed shoreline of the island some half a mile away made her feel no better. There was no way she would ever be able to swim such a distance, not even if her life depended on it. And seasickness had to be better than either drowning or being eaten by hammerhead sharks—she'd done her homework and mother nature's bizarrest-looking fish was known to nest in several of the bays around Zanzibar.

She leaned forward again in order to sneak a look at the African boy who had gone back to the bow now that Lief was tied up and neither she nor any of the three other girls appeared to be capable of making a move against him and his mate. He appeared to be searching for something on land at the same time as casting quick little glances back at his captives. If she wasn't mistaken, Alison thought he was nervous. She wondered if they could turn that to their advantage. Maybe he was new to this game, whatever it entailed.

"Listen," she addressed the others, "we've got to do something."

The three girls looked up, whereas Lief retreated further inside himself. He looked as if they might have lost him. Were it not for him, they could have all jumped overboard on a given signal and helped each other to shore. But with his hands tied behind his back, Lief would be unable to swim and the logistics of trying to drag him, lifesaving-style, over half a mile even between them seemed insurmountable.

Karin and Anna were still crying; Kristin had stopped and was calmer. "What can we do?" she wondered.

"Hey!" the boy in the bow shouted at them, brandishing his knife.

"We could all go overboard and take Lief with us," Alison whispered. "See if we can make it to the shore. Or we rush one of them, try and overpower him, knock him in, whatever. We've got to do something."

"Even if we jump in, they've got the boat, they would easily catch up with us."

The boat tipped suddenly as the boy from the bow skipped over the wooden cross-seats towards them and, sweeping his right arm in a wide arc, connected with Kristin under her jaw, knocking her completely off balance. Alison watched in horror as Kristin teetered for a second close to the gunwhale, unaware of the seventh wave about to hit the boat on the starboard side. A scarlet stripe had been drawn on her cheek by the boy's knife which had been in his hand when he hit her.

The wave smacked into the side of the boat and she was gone in a flash, vanished.

"No!" Alison screamed, clambering over to that side of the boat and leaning over. Kristin had been swallowed by the waves. Shock, presumably, having rendered her incapable of reaction. She must have taken her first breath only after hitting the water.

"You murdering bastard! You fucking . . ."

Alison leapt at the youth in her fury, but he grabbed her slender wrists and held her at bay, grinning while she struggled. She tried to kick him, but he threw her down onto the bottom of the boat where she scrambled for safety as he leaned down over her threatening with the knife.

"No more," he said.

Kristin's friend Anna had clasped her arms around her knees and was rocking to and fro on her seat, moaning softly. Karin was sobbing, caught between trying to protect Alison and looking after her distracted boyfriend.

When he was satisfied the threat to his and his partner's authority had diminished, the youth returned to his post in the bows, occasionally shouting remarks back to the stern in Swahili. Alison climbed back on to a seat, unable to control a violent trembling which had seized her limbs. She kept visualizing Kristin washed up on the beach: she would appear not to be moving, then would cough up a lungful of sea water and splutter as she fought to regain control of her breathing. When the images were blacked out by another sickening swoop down the windward side of a wave, she knew that Kristin was dead. She might eventually get washed up among the mangrove swamps of south-western Zanzibar, but her bones would have been picked clean by the hammerheads.

The boat shifted around dramatically on a shout from the look-out boy. They were heading into shore. Alison doubted whether Lief would even be able to walk.

Jozani is the last vestige of the tropical forest that had at one time covered most of the island. The Red Colobus monkeys make it a tourist attraction, but the monkeys conveniently inhabit a small corner of the forest near the road, not far from one of the spice plantations. Visitors are taken out of the car park, back across the road and down a track to where the monkeys hang out.

The first monkey Craig saw was not remotely red.

"Blue monkey," the guide said. "Over there," he pointed through the trees, "is Red Colobus."

Craig saw a number of reddish-brown monkeys of various sizes playing around in the trees; leaping from one to another, they made quite a racket when they landed among the dry, leathery leaves.

"Great," Craig said. "What about the leopards?"

The guide gave him a blank look.

"You want see main forest?"

"Yes, I want see main forest." He followed the guide back to the road and into the car park. The tour around the main forest, Craig knew, would only scratch the surface of Jozani.

"My driver can guide me," Craig said, slipping a five dollar bill into the guide's palm. "You stay here. Relax. Put your feet up. Get a beer or something."

The guide looked doubtful, but Craig beckoned Popo across. He walked slowly, with a loose stride, long baggy cotton trousers and some kind of sandals. "Tell him it's okay," Craig said to Popo. "You can take me in."

After a moment's hesitation, Popo talked rapidly to the guide, who shrugged and walked back to the reception area defined by a bunch of easy chairs and some printed information and photographs pinned up on boards.

"Let's go, Popo."

Popo headed into the forest.

They followed the path until Craig sensed they were starting to double-back on themselves. He stopped, pushed his sunglasses up over his forehead and lit a cigarette.

"I think I want to head off the path a little," he said as he offered a cigarette to Popo.

The African took a cigarette, and lit it, the $100 bill folded around the pack not lost on him.

"Do you want to take the whole pack?" Craig asked. "I have to head off the path a little way. Leopards, you know?"

"No leopard here." Popo's hand hovered in mid-air.

"Witch doctors then. You interested or not?" Craig offered him the bribe again and nodded in the direction he wanted to go. Popo took the pack of Marlboro, slipping the cash out from underneath the cellophane wrapper and folding it into his back pocket. Then he led the way into the forest proper. After a few yards he knelt down at the base of a tree. Craig knelt down beside him and looked where the kid was pointing. There were dozens of tiny black frogs, each no bigger than a finger tip, congregating on some of the broader fallen leaves.

"Here water come," said Popo. "From sea."

"Floodwater?"

"Yes. No one come here. Dangerous."

"Good. Let's go on, in that case."

As soon as they hit the sandy bottom, the youth in the bow jumped out and tugged the boat up on to the beach. The kid in the stern pulled up the outboard. Three gangly, raggedy youths walked across the beach to meet them. Alison, Karin, Lief and Anna were forced out of the boat at knifepoint and the two youths exchanged a few words with the newcomers before turning their boat around and pushing off from the shore.

Alison, Karin and Anna had to walk with their hands on their heads to the treeline; Lief's hands were still tied behind his back. His face betrayed no emotion. Alison was amazed he'd been able to get up and walk. As for Alison, her legs had turned to rubber, despite her small relief at being on dry land. Their new captors were also armed and ruthless-looking.

The wind blew through the tops of the palm trees, an endless sinister rustling. But as they trooped into the forest, the palms thinned out, their place taken by sturdier vegetation. The canopy was so high it created an almost cathedral stillness. All Alison could hear now, apart from their shuffling progress through the trammelled undergrowth, were the occasional hammerings of woodpeckers and the screams of other, unknown birds. From time to time, on the forest floor she would spot sea shells glimmering through the mulch. She jumped when she almost walked into a bat, only to discover it was a broad, brown leaf waiting to drop from its tapering branch. She swiped at it and when it didn't instantly fall she went ballistic, swinging her arms at it as if it were a punchball. The party halted and two of the African youths came towards her, their knives at the ready. She peered over the edge of sanity at the possibility of panic, stood finely balanced debating her options, caught between self-preservation and loyalty to the group.

Before she knew what she was doing she had taken flight. One of the youths might have taken a swing at her, the point of his knife flashing just beneath her nose. She couldn't be sure. Something had happened to spur her into action. Action which she instantly regretted, mainly because it was irrevocable and she knew she would never outrun the local boys; also because she had deserted her companions, which according to her own code of honor was unforgivable. Yet she couldn't be sure they wouldn't have taken the same chance. Indeed, by running, she had created a diversion which, if they had any sense, they would exploit.

These thoughts flashed through her mind as she crashed through the forest, her flesh catching on twigs and bark and huge serrated leaves yet she felt no pain. Adrenaline surged through her system. She couldn't hear her pursuers but she knew that meant nothing. These boys would be able to fly. Whatever it took, to render her bid for freedom utterly futile.

As soon as they heard the drumming, Popo became jittery. Craig didn't give him more than five minutes.

"What is it, Popo?" he asked him. "What's going on?"

"Mbo," was all he would say, his eyes darting to and fro. "Mbo."

It was faint, still obviously some way off, but unmistakably the sound of someone drumming. It wasn't the surf and it wasn't coconuts dropping from the palm trees, it was someone's hand beating out a rhythm on a set of skins. A couple of tom-toms, maybe more, the kind of thing you played with your hand, sat cross-legged—whatever they were called. Craig hadn't a fucking clue. As for Popo, he was out of there. Craig didn't even watch him go, back the way they'd come. His hundred bucks had brought him this far, which was all he'd wanted the kid to do.

A mosquito whined by his ear. He brushed it away and walked on, moving slowly but carefully in the direction of the drumming.

He stopped when he heard another sound, coming from over to his right. Another, similar sound, but more ragged, less musical. The sound that would be made, he realized, by someone running. Craig's mind raced, imagining someone running into danger, and he was about to spring forward to intercept the runner, whom he still couldn't see, when he saw hovering in the space in front of him a whole cloud of mosquitoes.

They shifted about minutely, relative to each other, like vibrating molecules, seeming at one moment to dart towards him, only to feel a restraining influence and hang back. Because of the noise of the fast approaching runner he couldn't hear their dreadful whine, but he imagined it.

And the runner appeared, crashing her way through the trees, arms and legs flying—a young girl, the young girl from the Africa House terrace, Craig realized—heading straight for the source of the drumming.

"Hey! Stop!" Craig shouted as the swarm of mosquitoes swung its thousand-eyed head to follow the girl's progress. The whole cloud tilted and curved after the girl. She screamed as they crowded around her head: hardly could she have announced her arrival any more extravagantly. Not that Craig had any idea who or what was responsible for the drumming, nor whether they represented a threat. He just had his instincts.

The girl had a head start on him. He ran as fast as he could but couldn't close on her. Too many long lunches in The Eagle. Too many fast food containers in the bin under his desk. His heart beat a tattoo against his chest. He thrust his arms out in front of him to catch a tree trunk and so managed to stop short as the girl burst through into a wide clearing, the mozzies still shadowing her.

His hand-drums lying scattered at his feet, the drummer rose to his full height—six foot something of skin and bone, unfolding like some med student's life-size prop. He was a white man, although it was impossible to judge his age. His feet and lower legs were bare, but the rest of him was clothed. Craig rubbed his eyes, which had started to go funny. Perhaps the heat and the exertion. The fear, maybe, which he acknowledged for the first time, his pulse scampering. The man's coat constantly shifted in and out of focus, like an image perceived through a stereogram. Either there was something in Craig's eyes obscuring his vision, or some filmy substance, spider's web or other insectile secretion, draped across the undergrowth between him and the clearing. The tall man moved closer to Alison, who shrank away from him. He peered at her with bulging eyes that indicated thyroid disorder. His coat settled organically around his coat-hanger shoulders. Alison screamed and the coat shimmered. She lashed out with her right hand, drew a swathe through the living, clinging coat of mosquitoes. They swarmed about her head for a moment, mingling with the swarm that had aggravated her, before gravitating back to their host.

The man's movements were slow. He seemed to make them reluctantly, as if he had no choice. His face was too sunken in the cheeks and uniformly white to betray any emotion. Stepping back from the girl, he picked up a long bone-white blood-stained instrument from the floor by his drums and strapped it over his skull. The false snout, a foot long by the look of it, wobbled hideously as he approached the girl again. The base of it—the knuckle joint, let's face it, the thing had been fashioned from a human femur—rested against his mouth. He blew through it, a low burbling whistle, at which the mosquitoes became mark-edly less agitated and settled around him; Alison sank to her knees in a dead faint and he snuffled about her prone body.

Craig was furiously considering what action he could take when a further crashing through the undergrowth announced the arrival of Alison's friends from the Africa House, bound and led by three tough-looking African youths who each mumbled what appeared to be a respectful greeting to the tall man— "Mbo," they each seemed to be saying.

Lief, the Danish boy, had remained unresponsive throughout the trek from the beach. His girlfriend, Karin, was trembling with fear and continuous shock; Anna simply screamed whenever anyone came near her. Two of the youths took hold of Karin and Anna and laid them out flat on the ground. Grabbing lengths of dried palm leaves, they wound them around the girls' ankles, going around and around several times, then over the loop in the other direction between the legs until they were secure. They left the arms. The third African youth swiftly bound Lief's ankles in the same manner. Craig had to strain to see where the three were taken: beyond the lean-to on the far side of the clearing. But what lay hidden there, Craig could not see.

The tall white-skinned man was still inspecting Alison when one of the youths returned and started to bind her around the ankles as well. The man sat down once more upon the ground, his legs becoming dismantled beneath his hazy coat like a pair of fishing rods being taken apart. He picked up his hand-drums and began to play.

Craig took advantage of the noise to retreat a few yards from the edge of the clearing back into the forest. Twenty yards back, he crept around towards the back of the camp. It took him a while, because he had to move slowly to avoid alerting anyone to his presence, but he got there. Then it took him a moment before he recognized what he was seeing, even though this was what he'd been looking for. What he'd come to Africa for.

They hung from the branches of a single tree. Like bats.

Like bats, they hung upside down.

Like bats, or like the poor creatures Craig had seen in the museum in the town—bound, each one of them, at the ankles. Three dozen at least.

Most of them were completely drained of blood, desiccated, like the Bombay duck Craig would always order with his curry just to raise a laugh. Husks swinging in the breeze. Wind-dried Bombay duck. Long hair suggested which victims were female, while bigger skeletons hinted at male—but there was no way of telling with most of the poor wretches.

Nearest the ground hung the recent additions—Karin, Anna, Lief. Craig heard the tall man coming around the side of the hut, before he saw him. The wind was not strong enough to drown out the whining concert of the mosquitoes the tall man wore around himself like so many familiars. His own insectile eyes protruded as he looked at his new arrivals, all strung up and ready for him.

Behind him came two of the youths carrying Alison.

The tall man, wearing his bone nose-flute, took a tiny step towards Anna, whose screams were torn out of her throat at his approach.

I could already smell the coppery tang of blood even before the ancient ectomorph in the coat of mosquitoes prodded the young girl's throat with the sharpened femur he wore strapped to his head.

Craig was ashamed at himself, but couldn't stop the opening sentences of his eye-witness account forming in his mind.

I was smelling the blood he had already spilt. I must have smelled it on him or in the air, because the ground beneath my feet nourished no more exotic blooms than the surrounding forest, for he spilled no blood. This exiled European, this tall, spindly shadow of a man—scarcely a man at all—drank the blood, every last drop. It was what kept him alive. I sensed this as much as deduced it as my eye ranged across the bat-like corpses suspended from his tamarind tree. At the same time I felt a shadow fall across my heart, from which I knew I should never be free, even if I were somehow to effect an escape for myself and the youngsters who had joined the monster's collection.

This was Craig's problem now. The purple prose would die a death at the hands of the paper's subs—but thinking of it in terms of the news story he had come out here to investigate helped him distance himself sufficiently to keep his mind intact, to remain alert. Whatever the odds stacked against him, he still possessed the element of surprise.

While he was still thinking, racking his brains for an escape route, the tall man's head jerked forwards, driving the tip of his bone-flute into the hollow depression of Anna's throat. Blood bubbled instantly around the puncture then disappeared as it was sucked down the bone. Craig forced his eyes shut, fighting his own terror of spilt blood. But he had heard the man's first swallow, his greedy gargle as he tried to accommodate too much at once. Craig had always believed himself the hard man of investigative journalism, hard to reach emotionally— his bed back home never slept two for more than one night at a time—and impossible to shock. His fear of the sight of blood had never been a problem before; he avoided stories which trailed bloody skirts—car wrecks and shoot-outs—not his style.

As he retched and tumbled forwards out of the concealing forest, he knew this was a story to which he would never append his byline: firstly, because he wasn't going to get out alive, and secondly, even if he did, the trauma would never allow him to relive these moments.

Two youths pounced on him, jabbering excitedly in Swahili. A third youth darted into the forest in search of any accomplices.

As the youths bound his ankles, Craig watched the tall man gulp down the German girl's blood. He drank so eagerly and with such vigorous relish, it was possible to believe he completely voided her body of all nine pints. His cheeks had colored up and Craig thought he could see a change in the man's body. It had filled out, the mosquitoes that clung to him no longer covered quite so much of his grey-white nakedness.

He wondered when his own turn would come. Would the tall man save up his victims, drink them dry one a day, or would he binge? Already, he had turned to Alison, swinging from her bonds as she tried desperately to free herself. She was a fighter. Karin sobbed uncontrollably alongside, and Lief was wherever he had gone to while they were all still on the boat. As Craig was hoisted upside down and secured by one of the youths, he thought to himself it would be preferable to go first. As if sensing his silent plea, the tall man twisted around to consider the attractions of his body over the girl's.

Popo's approach was swift and silent. The first any of those present knew of it was an abrupt cacophony: the crashing of bodies through dry vegetation, the deep-throated growling of hungry beasts, the concerted yells and screeches of our rescuers. Visually I was aware of a black and gold blur, flashing ivory teeth and ropes of saliva swinging from heavy jaws as the leopards leapt.

Popo saved my life at that point—the exact moment at which the old Craig died. It was necessary, if I were to survive. The hard-nosed journalist was as dead as the corpses swinging in the breeze higher up in the tree. He would not write up this story, I would—but not for a long time, and not for the newspapers. It's history now, become legend, myth—just as it had always been to Popo and the men of Jozani.

Those who survived it—and they are few—speak of it rarely. Lief lives quietly, on his own, in a house by the sea in his native Denmark. Karin, his former girlfriend, has returned to Africa as an aid worker. Most recently she has been in eastern Zaire: I saw her interviewed on the TV news during the refugee crisis. I have no contact with either of them. Alison and I tried to remain in touch— a couple of letters exchanged and we met once, in a bar in the West End, but the lights and the noise upset us both and we soon parted. I have no idea where she is now or what she is doing.

I left my reporter's job on medical advice and spent some time fell-walking in South Wales until I felt well enough to return to work, but on the production side this time. I never have to read the copy or look at the pictures—just make sure the words are on the page and the colors are right.

I go to Regent's Park Zoo every so often to look at the leopards. Watching them prowl around their cages reminds me of the moment in my life when I was most alive—when I saw, with an almost photographic clarity, one of Popo's leopards take a swipe with its heavy paw at the bloodsucking creature's midriff. There was an explosion, a shower of blood, Anna's blood. His skin flapped uselessly, transparently, like that of the mosquito I had swatted against my arm on the terrace of the Africa House Hotel.

Popo and his men—witch doctors or Jozani Forest guides, I never found out— untied us and lowered us safely to the ground. Later that evening, after the police had been and started the clear-up operation, Popo himself took me back to Zanzibar Town in his Suzuki. On the outskirts of town he brought the vehicle to a sudden halt, flapping his hand about his head as if trying to beat off an invisible foe.

"What's up?" I asked, leaning towards him.

"Mbo," he muttered.

I heard a high-pitched whine as it passed by my ear. I too lashed out angrily.

"Mosquito?" I asked.

"Mbo," he nodded.

It turned out I had got the little sod, despite my flailing attack. Maybe it was just stunned, but it lay in the palm of my hand. I was relieved to see that its body was empty of blood.

"We call it mosquito," I said and I shivered as I wondered if we had brought it from the forest on our clothes.

For months later, I would discover mosquitoes, no more than half a dozen or so, among the clothes I had brought back from Zanzibar. So far, they have all been dead ones.

Jeffrey Shaffer

Winner Take All

Jeffrey Shaffer is a humorist from Portland, Oregon, whose work is regularly featured on Oregon Public Radio—as well as on Prairie Home Companion, *and in the pages of* The New Yorker.

"Winner Take All" is a wonderfully loopy tale from It Came with the House, *Shaffer's new collection of "conversation pieces." I recommend this delightfully eccentric little book . . . and the story that follows.*

—T. W.

Thank goodness for youth soccer. By participating in this wonderful sport, our family has been transformed.

I had misgivings about having our daughter join the local team, no doubt about that. We've always been considered outsiders. My wife and I are both quiet, introspective, thoughtful people. So is our daughter.

But now we have a more spontaneous, outgoing attitude. Last Saturday was the final game of the season, and the start of what I believe will be an exciting new chapter in our lives.

"Pearl!" the coach screamed at my girl. "Get the hell with it! Where is your brain?!"

"Calm yourself," I suggested. "She's only a second-grader." The coach, Mr. Crumley, looked at me with disdain.

"The goalie must pay attention to the action," he said, "even when the ball is at the other end of the field. Your kid is always staring up at the sky. It's a terrible habit, and she's done it for the whole blasted season!"

"Pearl has deep thoughts," I said. "Maybe she's thinking up a cure for cancer right now." It was an inspiring possibility.

"Oh yeah, that's how all the big scientific breakthroughs in history have come about," Coach Crumley said, contemptuously.

"Well, it does happen sometimes," I said. "Philo Farnsworth claimed that he invented television while working in a field as a teenager. Looking at the long rows of plowed furrows led him to believe that visual images could be transmitted across great distances by using horizontal lines of electrons."

Coach Crumley glared at me and then he shook his head. "Were you born weird, or do you work at it?" he growled.

"And not only that," interrupted Bagley Peterson, another parent who was standing nearby, "you're also dead wrong about Philo Farnsworth inventing television. It was the pioneering work of Vladimir Zworykin that really counted."

"Actually, that's the story the RCA people would like you to believe," I said. "Zworykin was their hired gun. But Farnsworth sued to protect his patents, and the courts eventually ruled in his favor. You can look it up if you want."

"I never even heard of Philo Farnsworth," snapped Carrie Stochausen, who always stayed away from me at the games. "If he was so great, how come no one's made a movie about him?"

"We're drifting off the subject," I said. "Perhaps my daughter is looking at the sky for answers to some kind of astronomical question. Just the other day, she was asking me to explain how the solar system was formed. We had a lively debate about whether or not Pluto is a true planet."

"Oh God, here it comes," chimed in Elliot Wentworth, one of the assistant coaches. "I suppose you're one of those skeptics who believe that Pluto is technically an asteroid. Well, it's not! It's round, it has an atmosphere, and it has a satellite."

"Charon," I said, nodding. Nobody responded. "Charon is the name of Pluto's satellite," I added.

"There you go again!" Carrie declared angrily. "You're always tossing out bits of arcane information with that little smug tone of superiority. And you wonder why you don't have any friends!"

"We're not stupid people," said Warren Spicak, who had wandered over as the discussion intensified. "This is a college town, with high-tech industries and a sophisticated workforce. We don't take kindly to newcomers who move in and try to undermine the intellectual self-esteem of our clannish, tightly-knit community. And it doesn't help that you're always wearing peculiar hats!"

"What's wrong with my hat?" I said, removing it from my head for a quick inspection. "It's your basic derby. Is that bad?"

"No, but it's damn strange," said Coach Crumley.

"Your wardrobe is oddly inappropriate," Elliot Wentworth said. "Green leisure suits and a brown derby. You look like Babar the elephant wandering the streets of Paris."

"We haven't done anything to warrant this overt hostility," said my wife, gripping my hand for moral support. By now, we were completely surrounded by scowling soccer moms and dads.

"Lady, you are a piece of work!" Elliot countered. "You're wearing a jeweled tiara at a kids' soccer match! Normal people don't do things like that."

"It's just a toy," my wife answered. "Pearl bought it for me at Toy Barn, and if I don't wear it she'll be disappointed."

"She's not gonna be on my team next year," Coach Crumley said. "The kid is in some other dimension most of the time. She never listens, and she gives my other players the heebie-jeebies."

"Hey," Warren said, "wasn't it sunny just a minute ago?"

I looked up and saw dark clouds boiling overhead. The kids on the field suddenly stopped chasing the ball. There was an eerie silence, and I noticed that Pearl was reaching toward the sky with both arms outstretched.

"She's a menace!" someone yelled.

And then the air seemed to explode. A roaring clap of thunder erupted over the field like a bomb, knocking everyone flat onto the brown grass.

When I sat up, Pearl was standing beside me, looking confused and embarrassed. "I'm sorry!" she said, trying not to cry. "I just wanted them to stop being mean!" Her lower lip quivered.

"I know, honey," I agreed, "I know exactly how you feel."

"And it's okay to feel that way," my wife added, pushing herself up onto her knees and staring at me with an apprehensive expression.

The others were scattered around us, all of them lying motionless where they had fallen. I reached down and picked up Carrie Stochausen. She was thirteen inches tall with cloth skin.

"Have you turned people into dolls before?" I asked.

"No," Pearl said. "Just a dog. But I'll make them go back the way they were. It's not hard. I can do it, I promise!"

"Hold on!" I said. "Just relax. Let's take a quiet break."

"This is certainly an interesting development," my wife said.

"Very much so," I agreed. "And there's no need to rush into any decision right now. Let's load everybody into the car and discuss the situation at home."

Pearl is keeping our tiny guests in her toybox for the time being. All except for Coach Crumley, who is perched on my dresser. His little scowling face is almost endearing.

"I'm thinking about how nice it will be to have people show us a little more respect," I said to my wife that night as we reclined together in bed. "What are you thinking about?"

"So many dolls for just one girl," she answered. "Sometimes I worry about her being an only child. I don't want her to get spoiled and turn into a brat."

"Well, it's not too late to have another one," I said.

"I've thought about that," she replied. "The only risky part is that we might end up with a boy."

"Good point," I agreed. "Let's not push our luck."

Gary A. Braunbeck

Safe

Gary A. Braunbeck was born in 1960 in Newark, Ohio (the town which later inspired his Cedar Hill *stories). His first story sale was to the small press magazine* Eldritch Tales *in 1980 and his first professional sale was to Twilight Zone's Night Cry in 1985. Since then he has sold more than eighty stories to various magazines such as* Cemetery Dance *and* The Magazine of Fantasy and Science Fiction, *as well as to anthologies including* Borderlands 4, Masques III, Tombs, *and* Heaven Sent. *His fiction has been reprinted in* The Year's Best Fantasy and Horror *twice before. His most recent book is the story cycle* Things Left Behind.*

"Safe" is a modified version of the novella Searching for Survivors *(the latter containing references to other parts of Braunbeck's story cycle,* Things Left Behind). *"Safe" was published in* Robert Bloch's Psychos. *Readers might find it especially disturbing. I found it that—and incredibly moving as well.*

—E. D.

1

Violence never really ends, no more than a symphony ceases to exist once the orchestra has stopped playing; bloodstains and bullet holes, fragments of shattered glass, knife wounds that never heal properly, nightmarish memories that thrash the heart . . . all fasten themselves like a leech to a person's core and suck away the spirit bit by bit until there's nothing left but a shell that looks like it might once have been a human being.

My God, what do you suppose happened to that person?

I heard it was something awful. I guess they never got over it—hell, you can just look at 'em and know that.

Drop a pebble in a pool of water, and the vibrations ripple outward in concentric circles. Some physicists claim that the ripples continue even after they can no longer be seen.

Ripples continue.

A symphony does not cease.

And violence never really ends.

It took half my life to learn that.

2

Three days ago, a man named Bruce Dyson walked into an ice cream parlor in the town of Utica, Ohio, and opened fire with a semiautomatic rifle, killing nine people and wounding seven others before shooting himself in the head.

Some cry, others rage, many turn away, and life will go on until the next Bruce Dyson walks into the next ice cream parlor, or bank, or fast-food restaurant; then we'll shake our heads, wring our hands once again, and wonder aloud how something so terrible could happen.

Newscasts were quick to mention Cedar Hill and draw tenuous parallels between what took place there and what happened in Utica. When one of my students asked me if I was "around" for the Cedar Hill murders, I laughed—not raucously, mind you, but enough to solicit some worried glances.

"Yes, I was around. Excuse my laughing, it's just that no one has ever asked me that before."

At a special teachers' meeting held the previous evening, a psychologist had suggested that we try to get our students to talk about the killings; four of the dead and three of the wounded had attended this school.

"Do any of you want to discuss what happened in Utica?"

Listen to their silence after I asked this.

"Look, I don't want to make anyone feel uncomfortable, but odds are someone in this room knew at least one of the victims. I know from experience it's not a good idea to keep something like this to yourself. You have to let someone know what's going on inside you."

Still nothing—a nervous shrug, perhaps, a lot of downcast stares, even a quiet tear from someone in the last row of desks, but no one spoke.

I rubbed my eyes and looked toward the back wall where the ghosts of the Cedar Hill dead were assembling.

Go on, they whispered. *Remember us to them.*

"Sixteen people were shot. You have to feel something about that."

A girl in one of the middle rows slowly raised her hand. "How did you . . . how'd you deal with what happened in Cedar Hill?"

"In many ways I still *am* dealing with it. I went back there a while ago to find some of the survivors and talk with them. I needed to put certain things to rest and—wait a second."

The ghosts of the four dead students joined those from Cedar Hill. All of them smiled at one another like old friends.

I wished I could have known them.

Tell them everything.

Go on.

I nodded my head, then said to the class: "Let's make a deal. I'll tell you about Cedar Hill only if you agree to talk about Utica. Maybe getting things out in the open will make it easier to live with. How's that sound?"

Another student raised a hand and asked, "Why do you suppose somebody'd do something like that?"

Tell the tale, demanded the ghosts.

Remember us to them . . .

3

I've gotten a little ahead of myself.

My name is Geoff Conover. I am thirty-six years old and have been a high school history teacher for the last seven years. I am married to a wonderful woman named Yvonne who is about to give birth to our first child, a boy. She has a six-year-old girl from her previous marriage. Her name is Patricia, and I love her very much and she loves me, and we both love her mother and are looking forward to having a new member added to our family.

This story is not about me, though I am in it briefly under a different name. It's about a family that no longer exists, a house that no longer stands, and a way of life once called Small Town America that bled to death long before I explained to my students how violence never really ends.

I did go back to Cedar Hill in hopes of answering some questions about the night of the killings. I interviewed witnesses and survivors over the telephone, at their jobs, in their houses, over lunches, and in nursing homes; I dug through dusty files buried in moldy boxes in the basements of various historical society offices; there were decades-old police reports to be found, then sorted through and deciphered; I tracked down more than two hundred hours' worth of video-tape, then subjected my family to the foul moods that resulted from my watching them; dozens of old statements had to be located and copied; and on one occasion I had to bribe my way into a storage facility in order to examine several boxes of aged evidence. There were graves to visit, names to learn, individual histories lost among bureaucratic paper trails that I had to assemble, only to find they yielded nothing of use—and I would be lying if I said that I did not feel a palpable guilt in deciding that so-and-so's life didn't merit so much as a footnote.

I do not purport to have sorted everything out. In some instances the gaps between facts were too wide and I had to fill them with conjectures and suppositions that, to the best of my knowledge and abilities, provided a *rightness* to the story that nothing else could. Yvonne says I did it to forgive myself for having survived, to be free of the shame, anger, guilt, and confusion that have for so long threatened to diminish me. She may be right. No one asked me to do it; nonetheless, certain ghosts demanded it of me—and I say this as a man who'd never thought of himself as being particularly superstitious.

I cleared my throat, smiled at the ghosts in the back of the room, and said to my students, "In order for you to understand . . ."

4

... what took place in Cedar Hill, you first have to understand the place itself, for it shares some measure of responsibility.

If it is possible to characterize this place by melting down all of its inhabitants and pouring them into a mold so as to produce one definitive citizen, then you will see a person who is, more likely than not, a laborer who never made it past the eleventh grade but who has managed through hard work and good solid horse sense to build the foundation of a decent middle-class existence; who works to keep a roof over his family's head and sets aside a little extra money each month to fix up the house, maybe repair that old back-door screen or add a workroom; who has one or two children who aren't exactly gifted but do well enough in school that their parents don't go to bed at night worrying that they've sired morons.

Perhaps this person drinks a few beers on the weekend—not as much as some of his rowdier friends but enough to be social. He's got his eye on some property out past the county line. He hopes to buy a new color television set. He usually goes to church on Sundays, not because he wants to but because, well, you never know, do you?

This is the person you would be facing.

This is the person who would smile at you, shake your hand, and behave in a neighborly fashion.

But never ask him about anything that lies beyond the next paycheck. Take care not to discuss anything more than work or favorite television shows or an article from this morning's paper. Complain about the cost of living, yes; inquire about his family, by all means; ask if he's got time to grab a quick sandwich, sure; but never delve too far beneath the surface, for if you do, the smile will fade, that handshake will loosen, and his friendliness will become tinged with caution.

Because this is a person who feels inadequate and does not want you to know it, who for a good long while now has suspected that his life will never be anything more than mediocre. He feels alone, abandoned, insufficient, foolish, and inept, and the only thing that keeps him going sometimes is a thought that makes him both smile and cringe: that maybe one of *his* children will decide, *Hey, Dad's life isn't so bad, this burg isn't such a hole in the ground, so, yeah, maybe I'll just stick around here and see what I can make of things.*

And what if they do? How long until they start to walk with a workman's stoop, until they're buying beer by the case and watching their skin turn into one big nicotine stain? How long until they start using the same excuses he's used on himself to justify a mediocre life?

Bills, you know. Not as young as I used to be. Too damn tired all the time. Work'll by God take it out of you.

Ah, well ... at least there's that property out past the county line for him to keep his eye on, and there's still that new color television set he might just up and buy ...

Then he'll blink, apologize for taking up so much of your time, wish you a good day, and head on home because the family will be waiting supper.

It was nice talking to you.

Meet Cedar Hill, Ohio.

Let us imagine that it is evening here, a little after ten P.M. on the seventh of July, and that a pair of vivid headlight beams have just drilled into the darkness on Merchant Street. The magnesium-bright strands make one silent, metronome-like sweep, then coalesce into a single lucent beacon that pulls at the vehicle trailing behind.

Imagine that although the houses along Merchant are dark, no one inside them is asleep.

The van, its white finish long faded to a dingy gray, glides toward its destination. It passes under the diffuse glow coming down from the sole streetlight, and the words "Davies' Janitorial Service" painted on its side can be easily read.

The gleam from the dashboard's gauges reveals the driver to be a tense, sinewy man whose age appears to fall somewhere between a raggedy-ass forty-five and a gee-you-don't-look-it sixty. In his deeply lined face are both resignation and dread.

He was running late, and he was not alone.

A phantom, its face obscured by alternating knife slashes of light and shadow, sat on the passenger side.

Three others rode in the back.

None of them could summon enough nerve to look beyond the night at the end of his nose.

The van came to a stop, the lights were extinguished, and with the click of a turned key, Merchant Street was again swallowed by the baleful graveyard silence that had recently taken up residence there.

The driver reached down next to his seat and grabbed a large flashlight. He turned and looked at the phantoms, who saw his eyes and understood the wordless command.

The driver climbed out as the phantoms threw open the rear double doors and began unloading the items needed for this job.

Merchant Street began to flicker as neighbors turned on their lights and lifted small corners of their curtains to peek at what was going on, even though no one really wanted to look at the Leonard house, much less live on the same street.

The driver walked up onto the front porch of the Leonard house. His name was Jackson Davies, and he owned the small janitorial company that had been hired to scour away the aftermath of four nights earlier, when this more or less peaceful industrial community of forty-two thousand had been dragged—kicking, screaming, and bleeding—into the national spotlight.

Davies turned on his flashlight, gliding its beam over the shards of broken glass that littered the front porch. As the shards caught the beam, each glared at him defiantly: *Come on, tough guy, big macho Vietnam vet with your bucket and Windex, let's see you take us on.*

He moved the beam toward a bay window on the right. Like all the first-floor windows of the house, this one was covered by a large sheet of particle board crisscrossed by two strips of yellow tape. A long, ugly stain covered most of the outside sill, dribbling over the edge in a few places down onto the porch in thin, jagged streaks. Tipping the beam, Davies followed the streaks to another stain, darker than the mess on the sill and wider by a good fifty percent. Just outside this stain was a series of receding smears that stretched across the length of the porch and disappeared in front of the railing next to the glider.

Footprints.

Davies shook his head in disgust. Someone had tried to pry loose the board and get inside the house. Judging by the prints, they'd left in one hell of a hurry, running across the porch and vaulting the rail—scared away, no doubt, by neighbors or a passing police cruiser. Probably a reporter eager to score a hefty bonus by snapping a few graphic photos of the scene.

Davies swallowed once, loud and hard, then swung the light over to the front door. Spiderwebbing the frame from every conceivable angle were more strips of yellow tape emblazoned with large, bold, black letters: "Keep Out by Order of the Cedar Hill Police Department." An intimidating, hand-sized padlock held the door securely closed.

As he looked at the padlock, a snippet of Rilke flashed across his mind: *Who dies now anywhere in the world, without cause dies in the world, looks at me—*

And Jackson Davies, dropout English Lit major, recent ex-husband, former Vietnam vet, packer of body bags into the cargo holds of planes at Tan Son Nhut, onetime cleaner-upper of the massacre at My Lai 4, hamlet of Son My, Quang Ngai Province, a man who thought there was no physical remnant of violent death he didn't have the stomach to handle, began muttering, "Goddamn, god*damn*, *goddamn*," and felt a lump dislodge from his groin and bounce up into his throat and was damned if he knew why, but suddenly the thought of going into the Leonard house scared the living shit out of him.

Unseen by Davies, the ghosts of Irv and Miriam Leonard sat on the glider a few yards away from him. Irv had his arm around his wife and was good-naturedly scolding her for slipping that bit of poetry into Davies's head.

I can't help it, Miriam said. *And even if I could, I wouldn't. Jackson read that poem when he was in Vietnam. It was in a little paperback collection his wife gave to him. He lost that book somewhere over there, you know. He's been trying to remember that poem all these years. Besides, he's lonely for his wife, and maybe that poem'll make it seem like part of her's still with him.*

Could've just gone to a library, said Irv.

He did, but he couldn't remember Rilke's name.

Think he'll remember it now?

I sure do hope so. Look at him, poor guy. He's so lonely, God love 'im.

Seems antsy, don't he?

Wouldn't you be? asked Miriam.

That was really nice of you, hon, giving that poem back to him. You always were one for taking care of your friends.

Charmer.

What can I say? Seems my disposition's improved considerably since I died.

Oh, now, don't go bringing that up. There's not much we can do about it.

How come that doesn't make me feel any better?

Maybe this'll do the trick, said Miriam. *"Who laughs now anywhere in the night, without cause laughs in the night, laughs at me."*

Don't tell me, tell the sensitive poetry soldier over there.

I just did.

They watched Davies for a few more seconds: he rubbed his face, then lit a cigarette and leaned against the porch railing and looked out into the street.

It's not right, said Irv to his wife. *What happened to us wasn't fair.*

Nothing is, dear. But we're through with all of that, remember?

If you say so.

Worrier.

Yeah, but at least I'm a charming worrier.

Shhh. Did you hear that?

Hear what?

The children are playing in the backyard. Let's go watch.

A moment later, the wind came up, and the glider swung back, then forward, once and once only, with a thin-edged screech.

Jackson Davies dropped his cigarette and decided, screw this, he was going to go wait down by the van.

He turned and ran into a phantom, then recoiled. The phantom stepped from the scar of shadow and into the flashlight's beam, becoming Pete Cooper, one of Davies's crew managers.

Davies, through clenched teeth, said, "It's not a real good idea to sneak up on me like that. I have a tendency to hurt people when that happens."

"Shakin' in my shoes," said Cooper. "You gettin' the jungle jitters again? Smell that napalm in the air?"

"Yeah, right. Whacked-out Nam vet doing the flashback boogie, that's me. Was there a reason you came up here, or did you just miss my splendid company?"

"I just . . ." Cooper looked over at the van. "Why'd you bring the Brennert kid along?"

"Because he said yes."

"C'mon, fer chrissakes! He was *here*, you know? When it happened?"

Davies sighed and fished a fresh cigarette from his shirt pocket. "First of all, he wasn't here when it happened, he was here *before* it happened. Second, of my forty-eight loyal employees, not counting you, only three said they were willing to come out here tonight, and Russ was one of them. Do you find any of this confusing so far? I could start again and talk slower."

"What're you gonna do if he gets in there and sees . . . well . . . everything and freezes up or freaks or something?"

"I talked to him about that already. He says he won't lose it, and I believe him. Besides, the plant's going to be laying his dad off in a couple of weeks and his family could use the money."

"Fine. I'll keep the other guys in line, but Brennert is *your* problem."

"Anything else? The suspense is killing me."

"Just that this seems like an odd hour to be starting."

Davies pointed at the street. "Look around. Tell me what you don't see."

"I'm too tired for your goddamn riddles."

"You never were any fun. What you don't see are any *reporters* or any trace of their nauseating three-ring circus that blew into this miserable burg a few nights back. The county is paying us, and the county decided that our chances of being accosted by reporters would be practically nil if we came out late in the evening. So here we are, and I'm no happier about it than you are. Despite what people say, I do have a life. Admittedly, it isn't much of one since my wife decided that we get along better living in separate states, but it's a life none-theless. I just thank God she left me the cats and the Mitch Miller sing-along records, or I'd be a sorry specimen right about now. To top it all off, I seem to have developed a retroactive case of the willies."

A police cruiser pulled up behind the van.

"Ah," said Davies. "That would be the keys to the kingdom of the dead."

"You plan to keep up the joking?"

Davies's face turned into a slab of granite. "Bet your ass I do. And I'm going to keep on joking until we're finished with this job and loading things up to go home. The sicker and more tasteless I can make them, the better. Don't worry if I make jokes; worry when I stop."

They went to meet the police officers, unaware that as they came down from the porch and started across the lawn, they walked right through the ghost of Andy Leonard, who stood looking at the house where he'd spent his entire, sad, brief, and ultimately tragic life.

5

On July fourth of that year, Irv Leonard and his wife were hosting a family reunion at their home at 182 Merchant Street. All fifteen members of their immediate family were present, and several neighbors stopped by to visit, watch some football, enjoy a hearty lunch from the ample buffet Miriam had prepared, and see Irv's newly acquired pearl-handled antique Colt Army .45 revolvers.

Irv, a retired steelworker and lifelong gun enthusiast, had been collecting fire-arms since his early twenties and was purported to have one of the five most valuable collections in the state.

Neighbors later remarked that the atmosphere in the house was as pleasant as you could hope for, though a few did notice that Andy—the youngest of the four Leonard children and the only one still living at home—seemed a bit "dis-tracted."

Around 8:45 that evening, Russell Brennert, a friend of Andy's from Cedar Hill High School, came by after getting off work from his part-time job. Wit-nesses described Andy as being "abrupt" with Russell, as if he didn't want him to be there. Some speculated that the two might have had an argument recently that Andy was still sore about. In any case, Andy excused himself and went upstairs to "check on something."

Russell started to leave, but Miriam insisted he fix himself a sandwich first. A few minutes later, Andy—apparently no longer upset—reappeared and asked if Russell would mind driving Mary Alice Hubert, Miriam's mother and Andy's grandmother, back to her house. The seventy-three-year-old Mrs. Hubert, a widow of ten years, was still recovering from a mild heart attack in December and had forgotten to bring her medication. Brennert offered to take Mary Alice's house key and drive over by himself for the medicine, but Andy insisted Mrs. Hubert go along.

"I thought it seemed kind of odd," said Bill Gardner, a neighbor who was present at the time, "Andy being so bound and determined to get the two of them out of there before the fireworks started. Poor Miriam didn't know what to make of it all. I mean, I didn't think it was any of my business, but somebody should've said something about it. Andy started getting outright rude. If he'd been my kid, I'd've snatched him bald-headed, acting that way. And after his mom'd gone to all that fuss to make everything so nice."

Mrs. Hubert prevented things from getting out of hand by saying it would be best if she went with Russell; after all, she was an "old broad," set in her ways, and everything in an old broad's house had to be *just so* . . . besides, there were so many medicine containers in her cabinet, Russell might just "bust his brain right open" trying to figure out which was the right one.

As the two were on their way out, Andy stopped them at the door to give Mrs. Hubert a hug.

According to her, Andy seemed "really sorry about something. He's a strong boy, an athlete, and I don't care what anyone says, he should've got that scholarship. Okay, maybe he wasn't as bright as some kids, but he was a fine athlete, and them college people should've let that count for something. It was terrible, listening to him talk about how he was maybe gonna have to go to work at the factory to earn his college money . . . everybody knows where that leads. I'm sorry, I got off the track, didn't I? You asked about him hugging me when we left that night . . . well, he was always real careful when he hugged me never to squeeze too hard—these old bones can't take it . . . but when he hugged me then, I thought he was going to break my ribs. I just figured it was on account he felt bad about the argument. I didn't mean to create such a bother, I thought I had the medicine with me, but I . . . forget things sometimes.

"He kissed me on the cheek and said ' 'Bye, Grandma. I love you.' It wasn't so much the words, he always said that same thing to me every time I left . . . it was the way he said them. I remember thinking he was going to cry, that's how those words sounded, so I said, 'Don't worry about it. Your mom knows you didn't mean to be so surly.' I told him that when I got back, we'd watch the rest of the fireworks and then make some popcorn and maybe see a movie on the TV. He used to like doing that with me when he was littler.

"He smiled and touched my cheek with two of his fingers—he'd never done that before—and he looked at Russ like maybe he wanted to give him a hug, too, but boys that age don't hug each other, they think it makes them look like queers or something, but I could see it in Andy's eyes that he *wanted* to hug Russ.

"Then he said the strangest thing. He looked at Russ and kind of . . . *slapped* the side of Russ's shoulder—friendly, you know, like men'll do with each other when they feel too silly to hug? Anyway, he, uh, did that shoulder thing, then looked at Russ and said, 'The end is courage.' I figured it was a line from some movie they'd seen together. They love their movies, those two, always quoting lines to each other like some kind of secret code—like in *Citizen Kane* with 'Rosebud.' That kind of thing.

"It wasn't until we were almost to my house that Russ asked me if I knew what the heck Andy meant when he said that.

"I knew right then that something was wrong, terribly wrong. Oh Lord, when I think of it now . . . the . . . the *pain* a soul would have to be in to do something . . . like that . . ."

Russell Brennert and Mary Alice Hubert left the Leonard house at 9:05. As soon as he saw Brennert's car turn the corner at the end of the street, Andy immediately went back upstairs and did not come down until the locally sponsored Kiwanis Club fireworks display began at 9:15.

Several factors contributed to the neighbors' initial failure to react to what happened. First, there was the thunderous noise of the fireworks themselves. Since White's Field, the site of the fireworks display, was less than one mile away, the resounding boom of the cannons was, as one person described, "damn near loud enough to rupture your eardrums."

Second, music from a pair of concert hall speakers that Bill Gardner had set up in his front yard compounded the glass-rattling noise and vibrations of the cannons. "Every Fourth of July," said Gardner, "WLCB [a local low-wattage FM radio station] plays music to go along with the fireworks. You know, 'America the Beautiful,' 'Stars and Stripes Forever,' Charlie Daniels's 'In America,' stuff like that, and every year I tune 'em in and set my speakers out and let fly. Folks on this street want me to do it, they all like it.

"How the fuck was I supposed to know Andy was gonna flip out?"

Third and last, there were innumerable firecrackers being set off by neighborhood children. This not only added to the general racket but also accounted for the neighbors' ignoring certain visual clues once Andy moved outside. "You have to understand," said one detective, "that everywhere around these people, up and down the street, kids were setting off all different kinds of things: firecrackers, sparklers, bottle rockets, M-80s, for God's sake! Is it any wonder it took them so long to tell the difference between an exploding firecracker and the muzzle flash from a gun?

"Andy Leonard had to've been planning this for a long time. He knew there'd be noise and explosions and lights and a hundred other things to distract everyone from what he was doing."

At exactly 9:15 P.M., Andy Leonard walked calmly downstairs carrying three semiautomatic pistols—a Walther P.38 9mm Perabellum, a Mauser Luger 7.65mm, and a Coonan .357 Magnum—as well as an HK53 5.56mm assault rifle, all of which he'd taken from his father's massive oak gun cabinet upstairs.

Of the thirteen other family members present at that time, five—including Irv Leonard, sixty-two, and his oldest son, Chet, twenty-five—were outside watching the fireworks. Andy's two older sisters Jessica, twenty-nine, and Elizabeth, thirty-four (both of whose husbands were also outside), were in the kitchen hurriedly helping their mother put away the buffet leftovers so they could join the men on the front lawn.

Jessica's three children—Randy, age seven; Theresa, four; and Joseph, nine and a half months—were in the living room. Randy and his sister had just finished changing their baby brother's diaper and were strapping him into his safety seat so they could hurry up and get outside. Joseph thought they were playing with him and so thrashed and giggled a lot.

They didn't notice their uncle.

Elizabeth's two children—Ian, twelve, and Lori, nine—were thought to be already outside but were upstairs in the "toy room," which contained, among other items, a pool table and a twenty-seven-inch color television for use with Andy's extensive video game collection.

By the time Andy walked downstairs at 9:15, Ian and Lori were already dead, their skulls crushed by repeated blows with, first, a gun butt, then a pool cue, and, at the last, billiard balls that were crammed into their mouths after their jaws were wrenched loose.

Laying the HK53 across the top of the dinner table, Andy stuffed the Mauser and blood-spattered Walther into the waist of his jeans, then walked into the kitchen, raised the .357, and shot his sister Jessica through the back of her head. She was standing with her back to him, in the process of putting some food into the refrigerator. The hollow-point bullet blew out most of her brain and sheared away half of her face. When she dropped, she pulled two refrigerator shelves and their contents down with her.

Andy then shot Elizabeth—once in the stomach, once in the center of her chest—then turned the gun on his mother, shooting at point-blank range through her right eye.

After that, things happened very quickly. Andy left the kitchen and collided with his niece who was running toward the front door. He caught her by the hair and swung her face-first into a fifty-inch-high cast-iron statue that sat against a wall in the foyer. The statue was a detailed reproduction of the famous photograph of the American flag being raised on Mt. Suribachi at Iwo Jima.

Theresa slammed against it with such force that her nose shattered, sending bone fragments shooting backward down her throat. Still gripping her long strawberry-blond hair in his fist, Andy lifted her off her feet and impaled her by the throat on the tip of the flagstaff. The blood patterns on the wall behind the statue indicated an erratic arterial spray, leading the on-scene medical examiner to speculate she must have struggled to get free at some point; this, along with the increase in serotonin and free histamine levels in the wound, indicated Theresa had lived at least three minutes after being impaled.

Seven-year-old Randy saw his uncle impale Theresa on the statue, then grabbed the carrying handle of Joseph's safety seat and ran toward the kitchen. Andy shot him in the back of his right leg. Randy went down, losing his grip on Joseph's safety seat, which skittered across the bloodsopped tile floor and came to a stop inches from Jessica's body. Little Joseph, frightened and helpless in the seat, began to cry.

Randy tried to stand, but his leg was useless, so he began moving toward Joseph by kicking out with his left leg and using his elbows and hands to pull himself forward.

Nine feet away, Andy stood in the kitchen entrance watching his nephew's valiant attempt to save the baby.

Then he shot Randy between the shoulders.

And the kid kept moving.

As Andy took aim to fire again, the front door swung open, and Keith Shannon, Elizabeth's husband, stuck his head in and shouted for everyone to hurry up and come on.

Keith saw Theresa's body dangling from the statue and screamed over his shoulder at the other men out on the lawn, then ran inside, calling out the names of his wife and children.

He never stopped to see if Theresa was still alive.

Andy stormed across the kitchen and through the second, smaller archway that led into the rooms on the front left side of the house. As a result of taking this shortcut, he beat Keith to the living room by a few seconds, enabling him to take his brother-in-law by surprise. Andy emptied the rest of the Magnum's rounds into Keith's head and chest. One shot went wild and shattered the large front bay window.

Andy tossed the Magnum aside and pulled both the Mauser and the Walther from his jeans, holding one pistol in each hand. He bolted from the living room, through the dining room, and rounded the corner into the foyer just as Irv hit the top step of the porch.

Andy kicked open the front door. For the next fifteen seconds, while the sky ignited and Lee Greenwood sang how God should bless this country he loved, God bless the U.S.A., the front porch of the Leonard house became a shooting gallery as each of the four remaining adult males—at least two of whom were drunk—came up onto the porch one by one and was summarily executed.

Andy fired both pistols simultaneously, killing his father, his uncle Martin, his older brother Chet, and Tom Hamilton, Jessica's husband.

A neighbor across the street, Bess Paymer, saw Irv's pulped body wallop backward onto the lawn and yelled for her husband, Francis. Francis took one look out the window and said, "Someone's gone crazy." Bess was already dialing the police.

Andy went back into the house and grabbed the rifle off the dining-room table, picked up the Magnum as he passed back through the living room, then headed for the kitchen, where Randy, still alive, was attempting to drag Joseph through the back door. When he heard his uncle come into the kitchen, Randy reached out and grabbed a carving knife from the scattered contents of the cutlery drawer, which Miriam had wrenched free on her way down, then threw himself over his infant brother.

"That was one brave kid," an investigator said later. "Here he was, in the middle of all these bodies, he had two bullets in him so we know he was in a lot of pain, and the only thing that mattered to him was protecting his baby brother. An amazing kid. If there's one bright spot in all this, it's knowing that he loved his brother enough to . . . to . . . ah, hell, I can't talk about it right now."

For some reason, Andy did not shoot his nephew a third time. He came across the kitchen floor and raised the butt of the rifle to bludgeon Randy's skull, and that's when Randy, in his last moments, pushed himself forward and jammed the knife in his uncle's calf. Then he died.

Andy dropped to the floor, screaming through clenched teeth, and pulled the knife from his leg. He grabbed his nephew's lifeless body and heaved it over onto its back, then beat its face in with his fists. After that, he loaded fresh clips into the pistols, grabbed Joseph, stumbled out the back door to the garage, and drove away in Irv's brand-new pickup.

At 9:21 P.M., the night duty dispatcher at the Cedar Hill Police Department received Bess Paymer's call. As was standard operating procedure, the dispatcher, while believing Bess had heard gunfire, asked if she were certain that someone had been shot. This dispatcher later defended this action by saying, "Every year we get yahoos all over this city who decide that the Kiwanis fireworks display is the perfect time to go out in their backyard and fire their guns off into the air— well, the Fourth and New Year's Eve, we get a lot of that. We had every unit out that night, just like every holiday, and there were drunks to deal with, bar fights, illegal fireworks being set off—M80s and such, traffic accidents . . . holidays tend to be a bit of a mess for us around here. Seems that's when everybody and their brother decides to act like a royal horse's ass.

"The point is, if we get a report of alleged gunfire during the fireworks, we're required to ask the caller if anyone's been hurt. If not, then we get to it as soon as we can. If we had to send a cruiser to check out every report of gunfire that comes in on the Fourth, we'd never get anything else done. I didn't do anything wrong. It's not my fault."

It took Bess Paymer and her husband the better part of two minutes to convince the dispatcher that someone had gone crazy over at the Leonard house and shot everyone.

Francis, furious by this point, grabbed the phone from his wife and informed the dispatcher in no uncertain terms that they'd better make it fast because he was grabbing his hunting rifle and going over there himself.

A cruiser was dispatched at 9:24 P.M.

At 9:27, a call came in from the Leonard house; by noon the next day, that phone call had been replayed on every newscast in the country:

"This is Francis Paymer. My wife and I called you a couple of minutes ago. I'm standing in the . . . the kitchen of the Leonard house . . . that's One-eighty-two Merchant Street . . . and I've got somebody's brains stuck to the bottom of my shoe.

"There's been a shooting here. A little girl's hanging in the hallway, and there's blood all over the walls and the floors, and I can't tell where one person's body ends and the next one begins because everybody's dead. I can still smell the gunpowder and smoke.

"Is that good enough for you to do something? C-could you maybe please if it's not too much trouble send someone out here NOW? It might be a good idea, because the crazy BASTARD WHO DID THIS ISN'T HERE—

"—and I think he might've took a baby with him."

By 9:30 P.M., Merchant Street was clogged with police cruisers.

And Andy Leonard was halfway to Moundbuilder's Park, where the Second Presbyterian Church was sponsoring Parish Family Night. More than one hundred people had been gathered at the park since five in the afternoon, picnicking, tossing Frisbees, playing checkers, or flying kites. A little before nine, the president of the Parish Council had arrived with a truckload of folding chairs that were set up in a clearing at the south end of the park.

By the time Francis Paymer made his famous phone call, one hundred seven parish members were seated in twelve neat little rows watching the fireworks display.

Between leaving his Merchant Street house and arriving at Moundbuilder's Park, Andy Leonard shot and killed six more people as he drove past them. Two were in a car; the other four had been sitting out on their lawns watching the fireworks. In every case, Andy simply kept one hand on the steering wheel while shooting with the other through an open window.

At 9:40 P.M., just as the fireworks kicked into high gear for the grand finale, Andy drove his father's pickup truck at eighty miles per hour through the wooden gate at the northeast side of the park, barreled across the picnic grounds, over the grassy mound that marked the south border, and went straight down into the middle of the spectators.

Three people were killed and eight others injured as the truck plowed into the back row of chairs. Then Andy threw open the door, leaped from the truck, and opened fire with the HK53. The parishioners scrambled in panic, many of them falling over chairs. Of the dead and wounded at the park, none was able to get farther than ten yards away before being shot.

Andy stopped only long enough to yank the pistols from the truck. The first barrage with the rifle was to disable; the second, with the pistols, was to finish off anyone who might still be alive.

At 9:45 P.M., Andy Leonard crawled up onto the roof of his father's pickup truck and watched the fireworks' grand finale. The truck's radio was tuned in to WLCB. The bombastic finish of *The 1812 Overture* erupted along with the fiery colors in the dark heaven above.

The music and the fireworks ended.

Whirling police lights could be seen approaching the park. The howl of sirens hung in the air like a protracted musical chord.

Andy Leonard shoved the barrel of the rifle into his mouth and blew most of his head off. His nearly decapitated body slammed backward onto the roof, then slid slowly down to the hood, smearing a long trail of gore over the center of the windshield.

Twenty minutes later, just as Russell Brennert and Mary Alice Hubert turned onto Merchant Street to find it blocked by police cars and ambulances, one of the officers on the scene at the park heard what he thought was the sound of a baby crying. Moments later, he discovered Joseph Hamilton, still alive and still in his safety seat, on the passenger-side floor of the pickup. The infant was clutching a bottle of formula that had been taken from his mother's baby bag.

6

I stopped at this point and took a deep breath, surprised to find that my hands were shaking. I looked to the ghosts, and they whispered, *Courage.*

I swallowed once, nodded my head, then said to my students, "That baby was me.

"I have no idea why Andy didn't kill me. I was taken away and placed in the care of Cedar Hill Children's Services." I opened my briefcase and removed a file filled with photo-copies of old newspaper articles and began passing them around the room. I'd brought some of my research along in case I'd needed it to prompt discussion. "The details of how I came to be adopted by the Conover family of Waynesboro, Virginia, are written in these articles. Suffice it to say that I was perhaps the most famous baby in the country for the next several weeks."

One student held up a copy of an article and said, "It says here that the Conovers took you back to Cedar Hill six months after the killings. Says you were treated like a celebrity."

I looked at the photo accompanying the article and shook my head. "I have no memory of that at all. At home, in a box I keep in my filing cabinet, are hundreds of cards I received from people who lived in Cedar Hill at that time.

Most of them are now either dead or have moved away. When I went back I could only find a few of them.

"It's odd to think that, somewhere out there, there are dozens, maybe even hundreds, of people who prayed for me when I was a baby, people I never knew and never will know. For a while I was at the center of their thoughts. I like to believe these people still think of me from time to time. I like to believe it's those thoughts and prayers that keep me safe from harm.

"But as I said in the beginning, this story isn't really about me. If there's any great truth here, I'm not the one to say what it might be. The moment that officer found that squalling baby on the floor of that truck, I ceased to be a part of the story. But it's never stopped being a part of me."

7

Details were too sketchy for the eleven P.M. news to offer anything concrete about the massacre, but by the time the local network affiliates broadcast their news-at-sunrise programs, the tally was in.

Counting himself, Andy Leonard had murdered thirty-two people and wounded thirty-six others, making his spree the largest single mass shooting to date. (Some argued that since the shootings took place in two different locations they should be treated as two separate incidents, while others insisted that since Andy had continuously fired his weapons up until the moment of his death, including the trail of shootings between his house and the park, it was all one single incident. What could not be argued was the body count, which made the rest of it more than a bit superfluous.)

Those victims were what the specter of my uncle was thinking about as Jackson Davies and Pete Cooper walked through him.

Andy's ghost hung its head and sighed, then took one half-step to the right and vanished back into the ages where it would relive its murderous rampage in perpetuity, always coming back to the moment it stood outside the house and watched as two men passed through it on their way toward a police officer.

8

Russell Brennert looked at the two other janitors who'd come along tonight and knew without asking that neither one of them wanted him to be here. Of course not, *he* had known the crazy fucker, *he* had been Andy Leonard's best friend, *his* presence made it all just a bit more real than they wanted it to be. Did they think that some part of what had driven Andy to kill all of those people had rubbed off on him as well? Probably—at least that would explain why they hadn't told him their names.

Hell with it, he thought. Call them Mutt and Jeff, and leave it at that.

He checked to make sure each plastic barrel had plenty of extra trash bags. Then Mutt came over and, fighting the smirk trying to sneak onto his face, asked, "Hey, Brennert—that's your name, right?"

"Yeah."

"We were just wonderin' if, well, it's true, y'know?"

"If *what's* true?"

Mutt gave a quick look to Jeff, who turned away and oh-so-subtly covered his mouth with his hand.

Russell dug his fingernails into his palms to keep from getting angry; these guys were going to pull something, or say something, he just knew it.

Mutt sniffed dryly as he turned back to Russell. He'd given up trying to fight back the smirk on his face.

Russell bit his lower lip. *Stay cool, you can do it, you need the money...*

"We'd just been wonderin'," said Mutt, "if it's true that you and Leonard used to... go to the movies together."

Jeff snorted a laugh and tried to cover it up by coughing.

Russell held his breath. "Sometimes, yeah."

"Just the two of you, or you guys ever take dates?"

You're doing fine, just fine, he's a mutant, just keep that in mind...

"Sometimes it was just him and me. Sometimes he'd bring Barb along."

"Yeah, yeah..." Mutt leaned in, lowering his voice to a mock-conspiratorial whisper. "The thing is, we heard that the two of you went to the drive-in together a couple of days before he shot everybody."

Fine and dandy, yessir. "That's right. Barb was going to come along, but she had to baby-sit her sister at the last minute."

Mutt chewed on his lower lip to bite back a giggle. Russell caught a peripheral glimpse of Davies and Cooper heading back up to the porch with one of the cops.

"How come you and your buddy went to the drive-in all by yourselves?"

"We wanted to see the movie." *Jesus, Jackson, get down here, will you?*

Russell didn't hear all of the next question because the pulsing of his blood sounded like a jackhammer in his ears.

"... thigh?"

Russell blinked, exhaled, and dug his nails in a little deeper. "I'm sorry, could you run that by me again?"

"I said, last week after gym when we was all in the showers, I noticed you had a sucker bite on your thigh."

"Birthmark."

"You sure about that? Seemed to me it looked like a big ol' hickey."

"Stare at my thighs a lot, do you?"

Mutt's face went blank. Jeff jumped to his feet and snarled, "Hey, watch it, motherfucker."

"Watch what?" snapped Russell. "Why don't you feebs just leave me alone? I've got better things to do than be grilled by a couple of redneck homophobes."

"Ha! *Homo*, huh?" said Mutt. "I always figured the two of you musta been butt buddies."

"Fag bags," said Jeff, then the two flaming wits high-fived each other.

Russell suddenly realized that one of his hands had reached over and gripped a mop handle. *Don't do it, Russ, don't you dare, they're not worth it.* "Think whatever you want. I don't care." He turned away from them in time to see a bright blue van pull up behind the police cruiser. A small satellite dish squatted like a gargoyle on top of the van, and Russell could see through the windshield that Ms. Tanya Claymore, Channel 9's red-hot news babe, was inside.

"Oh shit," he whispered.

One of the reasons he'd agreed to help out tonight—the money aside—was so he wouldn't have to stay at home and hear the phone ring every ten minutes and answer it to find some reporter on the other end asking for Mr. Russell Brennert, oh this is him, I'm Whatsisname from the In-Your-Face Channel, Central Ohio's News Authority, and I wanted to ask you a few questions about Andy Leonard blah-blah-blah.

It had been like that for the last three days. He'd hoped that coming out here tonight would give him a reprieve from everyone's constant questions, but it seemed—

—*put the ego in park, Russ. Yeah, maybe they called the house and Mom or Dad told them you'd be out here, but it's just possible they came out in hopes of getting inside the house for a few minutes' worth of video for tomorrow's news.*

Mutt smacked the back of his shoulder much harder than was needed just to get his attention. "Hey, yo! Brennert, I'm talking to you."

"Please leave me alone? Please?"

All along the murky death membrane that was Merchant Street, porch lights snapped on and ghostly forms shuffled out in bathrobes and housecoats, some with curlers in their hair or shoddy slippers on their feet.

Mutt and Jeff both laughed, but not too loudly.

"What's it like to cornhole a psycho, huh?"

"I—" Russell swallowed the rest of the sentence and started toward the house, but Mutt grabbed his arm, wrenching him backward and spinning him around.

One of the tattered specters grabbed her husband's arm and pointed from their porch to the three young men by the van. Did it look like there was some trouble?

The ghosts of Irv and Miriam Leonard, accompanied by their grandchildren Ian, Theresa, and Lori, stood off to the side of the house and watched as well. Irv shook his head in disgust, and Miriam wiped at her eyes and thought she felt her heart aching for Russell, such a nice boy, he was.

On the porch of the Leonard house, an impatient Jackson Davies waited while the officer ripped down the yellow tape and inserted the key into the lock.

"Jackson?" said Pete Cooper.

"What?"

Cooper cleared his throat and lowered his voice. "Do you remember what you said about no reporters being around?"

"Yeah, so wha—" Then he saw the Channel 9 news van. "Ah, fuck me with a fiddlestick! They plant a homing device on that poor kid or something?" He watched Tanya Claymore slide open the side door and lower one of her too-perfect legs toward the ground like some Hollywood starlet exiting a limo at a movie premiere.

"Dammit, I *told* you bringing Brennert along would be a mistake."

"Thank you, Mr. Hindsight. Let *me* worry about it?"

Cooper gestured toward the news van and said, "Aren't you gonna do something?"

"I don't know if I can." Davies directed this remark to the police officer unlocking the door. The officer looked over his shoulder and shrugged, then said, "If she interferes with your crew performing the job you pay them for, you've got every right to tell her to go away."

"Just make sure you get her phone number first," said Cooper.

Davies turned his back to them and stared at Tanya Claymore. If she even so much as *looked* at Russell, he'd drop on her like a curse from heaven.

Down by the trash barrels and buckets, Mutt was standing less than an inch from Russell's face and saying, "All right, bad-ass, let's get to it. People're sayin' that you maybe knew what Andy was gonna do and didn't say anything."

"I didn't," whispered Russell. "I didn't know."

Some part of him realized that Tanya's cameraman had turned on his light and was taping them, but he was backed too far into a corner to care right now.

"Yeah," said Mutt contemptuously. "I'll just bet you didn't."

"I *didn't* know, all right? He never said . . . a thing to me."

"According to the news, he was in an awful hurry to get you out before he went gonzo."

For a moment, Russell found himself back in the car with Mary Alice, turning the corner and being almost blinded by visibar lights, then that cop came over and pounded on the window and said, "This area's restricted for the moment, kid, so you're gonna have to—" and Mary Alice shouted, "Is that the Leonard house? Did something happen to my family?" And then the cop shone his flashlight in and asked, "You a relative, ma'am?" and Mary Alice was already in tears, and Russell felt something boiling up from his stomach because he saw one of the bodies being covered by a sheet, and then Mary Alice screamed and fell against him and a sick cloud of pain descended on their skulls—

"*I had no idea*, okay?" The words fell to the ground in a heap. Russell thought he could almost see them groan before the darkness put them out of their misery. "Do I have to keep on saying that, or should I just write it in braille and shove it up—"

"—you knew, you *had* to know!" The mean-spirited mockery of earlier was gone from Mutt's voice, replaced by anger with some genuine hurt wrapped around it. "He was your best friend!"

You need the money, Russell.

"Two of 'em was always together," said Jeff, just loud enough for the microphone to get every word. "Everybody figured that Brennert here was gay and was in love with Andy."

Three hundred dollars, Russell. Grocery money for a month or so. Mom and Dad will appreciate it.

It seemed that both of his hands were gripping the mop handle, and somehow that mop was no longer in the bucket.

He heard a chirpy voice go into its popular singsong mode: "This is Tanya Claymore. I'm standing outside the house of Irving and Miriam Leonard at One-eighty-two Merchant Street, where—"

"You wanna do something about it?" said Mutt, pushing Russell's shoulder. "Think you're man enough to mess with me?"

Russell was only vaguely aware of Davies coming down from the porch and shouting something at the news crew; he was only vaguely aware of the second police officer climbing from the cruiser and making a beeline to Ms. News Babe; and he was only vaguely aware of Mutt saying, "How come you came along to help with the cleanup tonight? Idea of seeing all that blood and brains get you hard, does it? You a sick fuck just like Andy?" But the one thing of which he was fully, almost gleefully aware was that the mop had become a javelin in his hands and he was going to go for the gold and hurl the thing right into Mutt's great big ugly target of a mouth—

Three hundred dollars should just about cover the emergency room bill—

Then a hand clamped down so hard on Mutt's shoulder that Russell thought he heard bones crack.

Jackson Davies's smiling face swooped in and hovered between them. "If you're finished with this nerve-tingling display of machismo, we have a house to clean, remember?" Still clutching Mutt's shoulder in a Vulcan death-grip, Davies hauled the boy around and pushed him toward one of the barrels. "Why can't you use your powers for good?"

"Hey, we were just—"

"I know what you were *just*, thank you very much. I'd appreciate it"—he gestured toward Jeff—"if you and the Boy Wonder here would get off your asses and start carrying supplies inside." Russell reached for a couple of buckets, but Davies stopped him. "Not you, Ygor. You stay here with me for a second." Mutt and Jeff stood staring as Ms. News Babe came jiggling up to Russell in all of her journalistic glory.

Davies glowered at the two boys and said, "Yes, her bazooba-wobblies are very big, and no, you can't touch them. Now get moving before I become unpleasant."

They became a blur of legs and mop buckets.

Russell said, "Mr. Davies, I'm sorry, but—"

"Hold that thought."

Tanya and her cameraman were almost on top of them; a microphone came toward their faces like a projectile.

"Russell?" said Tanya. "Russell, hi. I'm Tanya Claymore, and—"

"A friend of mine once stepped on a Claymore," said Davies. "Made his sphincter switch places with his eardrums. I was scraping his spleen off my face for a week. Please don't bother any member of my crew, Ms. Claymore."

The reporter's startling green eyes widened. She made a small, quick gesture with her free hand, and her cameraman swung around to get Davies into the frame.

"We'd like to talk to *both* of you, Mr. Davies—"

"Go away." Davies looked at Russell, and the two of them grabbed the remaining buckets and barrels and started toward the house.

Tanya Claymore sneered at Davies's back, then turned around and waved to the driver of the news van. He looked over, and she mimed talking into a telephone receiver. The driver nodded his head and picked up the cellular phone. Tanya gave her mike to the cameraman and took off after Davies.

"Mr. Davies, please, could you—dammit, I'm in heels! Would you wait a second?"

"She wants me," whispered Davies to Russell. Despite everything, Russell gave a little smile. He liked Jackson Davies a lot and was glad this man was his boss.

Tanya stumbled up the incline of the lawn and held out one of her hands for Davies to take hold of and help her.

"Are those fingernails real or press-ons?" asked Davies, not making a move.

Russell put down his supplies and gave her the help she needed. As soon as she reached level ground, she offered a sincere smile and squeezed his hand in thanks.

Davies said, "What's it going to take to make you leave us alone?"

Her eyes hardened, but the smile remained. "All I want is to talk to the both of you about what you're going to do."

"It's a little obvious, isn't it?"

"Central Ohio would like to know."

"Oh," said Davies. "I see. You're in constant touch with central Ohio? Champion of the common folk in your fake nails and designer dress and tinted contacts?"

"Does all that just come to you or do you write down ahead of time and memorize it?"

"You're not being very nice."

"Neither are you."

They both fell silent and stood staring at each other.

Finally, Davies sighed and said, "Could we at least get our stuff inside and get started first? I could come out in a half hour and talk to you then."

"What about Russell?"

Russell half raised his hand. "*Russell* is right here. Please don't talk about me in third person."

"Sorry," said Tanya with a grin. "You haven't talked to *any* reporters, Russell. I don't know if you remember, but you've hung up on me twice."

"I know. I was gonna send you a card to apologize. We always watch you at my house. My mom thinks you look like a nice girl, and my dad's always had a thing for redheads."

Tanya leaned a little closer to him and said, "What about you? Why do you like watching me?"

Russell was glad that it was so dark out, because he could feel himself blushing. "I, uh . . . I—look, Ms. Claymore, I don't know what I could say to you about what happened that you don't already know."

The radio in the police cruiser squawked loudly, and the officer down by the vans leaned through the window to grab the mike.

"All right," said Tanya, looking from Davies to Russell, then back to Davies again. "I won't lie to either of you. The news director would really, really prefer that I come back tonight with some tape either of Russell or the inside of the house. I almost had to beg him to let me do this tonight. Don't take this the wrong way—especially you, Russell—but I'm sick to death of being a talking head. Don't ever repeat that to anyone. If—"

"Oh, allow me," said Davies. "If you don't come back tonight with a really boffo piece, you'll be stuck reading TelePrompTers and covering new mall openings for the rest of your career, right?"

Tanya said nothing.

Russell looked over at his boss. "Uh, look, Mr. Davies, if this is gonna be a problem, I can—"

"She's lying, Russ. Her news director is all hot to trot for some shots of the inside of the house, and he'll do anything for the exclusive pictures, won't he? Up to and including having his most popular female anchor lay a sob story on us that sounds like it came out of some overbaked nineteen-forties melodrama.

Nice try, though. Goddammit—it wouldn't surprise me if you and your crew were the ones who tried to break in."

Tanya looked startled. "What? Someone tried to break into the house?"

"Wrong reading, sister. Don't call us, we'll call you."

The hardness in Tanya's eyes now bled down into the rest of her face. "Fine, Mr. Davies. Have it your way."

The officer in the cruiser walked up to his partner on the porch, and the two of them whispered for a moment, then came down toward Davies and Tanya.

"Mr. Davies," said the officer who'd unlocked the door, "we just received orders that Ms. Claymore and her cameraman are to be allowed to photograph the inside of the house."

Behind her back, Tanya gave a thumbs-up to the driver of the news van.

"What'd you do," asked Davies, "have your boss call in a few favors, or did you just promise to fuck the mayor?"

"*Mr. Davies,*" said one of the officers. The warning in his voice was quite clear. "Ms. Claymore can photograph only the foyer and one other room. You'll all go in at the same time. I will personally escort Ms. Claymore and her cameraman into, through, and out of the house. She can only be inside for ten minutes, no more." He turned toward Tanya. "I'm sorry, Ms. Claymore, those're our orders. If you're inside longer than ten minutes, we're to consider it to be trespassing and are to act accordingly."

"Well," she said, straightening her jacket and brushing a thick strand of hair from her eye, "it's nice to see that the First Amendment's alive and well and being slowly choked to death in Cedar Hill."

"You should attend one of our cross burnings sometime," said Davies.

"You're a jerk."

"How would you know? You never attend the meetings."

"That's enough, boys and girls," said Officer Lock and Key. "Could we move this along, please?"

"One thing," said Tanya. "Would it be all right if we got some shots of the outside of the house first?"

"You'd better make it fast," said Davies. "I feel a record-time cleaning streak coming on."

"Or I could get them later."

Russell had already walked away from the group and was setting his supplies on the porch. The front door was open and the overhead light in the foyer had been turned on, and he caught sight of a giant red-black spider clinging to the right-side wall—

He turned quickly away and took a breath, pressing one of his hands against his stomach.

Mutt and Jeff laughed at him as they walked into the house.

Pete Cooper shook his head and dismissed Russell with a wave of his hand.

The ghosts of the Leonard family surrounded Russell on the porch, Irv placing a reassuring hand on the boy's shoulder while Miriam stroked his hair and the children looked on in silence.

Tanya Claymore's cameraman caught Russell's expression on tape.

It wasn't until Jackson Davies came up and took hold of his hand that Russell snapped out of his fugue and, without saying a word, got to the job.

And all along Merchant Street, shadowy forms in their housecoats and slippers watched from the safety of front porches.

9

Even more famous than Francis Paymer's phone call is Tanya Claymore's videotape of that night. It ran four and a half minutes and was the featured story on Channel 9's six o'clock news broadcast the following evening. Viewer response was so overwhelming that the tape was broadcast again at seven and eleven P.M., then at six A.M. and noon the next day, then again, reedited to two minutes, forty-five seconds, at seven and eleven P.M.

It is an extraordinary piece of work, and I showed it to my students that day. I eventually received an official reprimand from the school board for doing it— several of the students had nightmares about it, compounding those about the Utica killings—but I thought they needed to see and hear other people, strangers, express what they themselves were feeling.

The ghosts wanted to see it again, as well.

As did I—and why not? In a way, it is not so much about the aftermath of a tragedy as it is a chronicle of my birth, a point of reference on the map of my life: *This is where I really began.*

10

The tape opens with a shot of the Leonard house, bathed in shadow. Dim figures can be seen moving around its front porch. Sounds of footsteps. A muffled voice. A door being opened. A light coming on. Then another. And another.

Silhouettes appear in an upstairs window. Unmoving.

The camera pulls back slightly. Seen from the street, the lights from the house form a pattern of sorts as they slip out from the cracks in the particleboard over the downstairs windows.

It takes a moment, but suddenly the house looks like it's smiling. And it is not a pleasant smile.

All of this takes perhaps five seconds. Then Tanya Claymore's voice chimes softly in as she introduces herself and says, "I'm standing outside the house of Irving and Miriam Leonard at One-eighty-two Merchant Street, where, as you know, four nights ago their son Andy began a rampage that would leave over thirty people dead and over thirty more wounded."

At that very moment, someone inside the house kicks against the sheet of particleboard over the front bay window and wrenches it loose while a figure on the porch uses the claw end of a hammer to pull it free. The board comes away, and a massive beam of light explodes outward, momentarily filling the screen.

The camera smoothly shifts its angle to deflect the light. As it does so, Tanya Claymore resolves into focus like a ghost on the right side of the screen. Whether it was purposefully done this way or not, the effect is an eerie one.

She says, "Just a few moments ago, accompanied by two members of the Cedar Hill Police Department, a team of janitors entered the Leonard house to begin what will most certainly be one of the grimmest and most painful cleanups in recent memory."

She begins walking up toward the front porch, and the camera follows her. "Experts tell us that violence never really ends, no more than a symphony ceases to exist once the orchestra has stopped playing."

As she gets closer to the front door, the camera moves left while she moves to the right and says, "And like the musical resonances that linger in the mind after a symphony, the ugliness of violence remains."

By now she has stepped out of camera range, and the dark, massive bloodstain on the foyer wall can be clearly seen.

At the opposite end of the foyer, a mop head drenched in foamy soap suds can be seen slapping against the floor. It makes a wet, sickening sound. The camera slowly zooms in on the mop and focuses on the blood that is mixed in with the suds.

The picture cuts to a well-framed shot of Tanya's head and shoulders. It's clear she's in a different room, but which room it might be is hard to tell. When she speaks, her voice sounds slightly hollow and her words echo.

"This is the only time that a news camera will be allowed to photograph the interior of the Leonard house. You're about to see the kitchen where Miriam Leonard and her two daughters, Jessica Hamilton and Elizabeth Shannon, spent the last few seconds of their lives, and where seven-year-old Randy Hamilton, with two bullets in his small body, fought to save the life of his infant brother, Joseph.

"The janitors have not been in here yet, so you will be seeing the kitchen just as it was when investigators finished with it."

For a moment, it looks as if she might say something else, then she lowers her gaze and steps to the left as the camera moves slightly to the right and the kitchen is revealed.

The sight is numbing.

The kitchen is a slaughterhouse. The contrast between the blood and the off-white walls lunges out at the viewer like a snarling beast escaping from its cage.

The camera pans down to the floor and follows a single splash pattern that quickly grows denser and wider. Smeary heel- and footprints can be seen. The camera moves upward: part of a handprint in the center of a lower counter door. The camera moves farther up: the mark of four bloody fingers on the edge of the sink. The camera moves over the top of the sink in a smooth, sweeping motion and stares at a thick, crusty black whirlpool twisting down into the garbage disposal drain.

The camera suddenly jerks up and whips around, blurring everything for a moment, a dizzying effect, then comes to an abrupt halt. Tanya is standing in the doorway of the kitchen with her right arm thrust forward. In her hand is a plastic pistol.

"This is a rough approximation of the last thing Elizabeth Shannon saw before her youngest brother shot her to death."

She remains still for a moment. Viewers cannot help but put themselves in Elizabeth's place.

Tanya slowly lowers the pistol and says, "The question for which there seems to be no answer is, naturally, 'Why did he do it?'

"We put that question to several of the Leonards' neighbors this evening.

Here's what some of them had to say about seventeen-year-old Andy, a young man who now holds the hideous distinction of having murdered more people in a single sweep than any killer in this nation's history."

Jump-cut to a quick, complicated series of shots.

Shot 1: An overweight man with obviously dyed hair saying, "I hear they found a tumor in his brain."

Insert shot: Merchant Street as it looked right after the shootings, clogged with police cruisers and ambulances and barricades to keep the growing crowd at bay.

Shot 2: A middle-aged woman with curlers in her hair saying, "I'll bet you anything it was his father's fault, him bein' a gun lover and all. I heard he beat on Andy a lot."

Insert shot: Lights from a police car rhythmically moving over a sheet-covered body on the front lawn.

Shot 3: An elderly gentleman in a worn and faded smoking jacket saying, "I read there were all these filthy porno magazines and videotapes stashed under his mattress, movies of women having relations with animals and pictures of babies in these leather sex getups . . ."

Insert shot: Two emergency medical technicians carrying a small black body bag down the front porch steps.

Shot 4: A thirtyish woman in an aerobics leotard saying, "I felt that he was always a little *too* nice, you know? He never got . . . angry about anything."

Insert shot: A black-and-white photograph of Andy taken from a high school yearbook. He's smiling, and his hair is neatly combed. He's wearing a tie. The voice of the woman in shot 4 can still be heard over this photo, saying, "He was always so calm. He never laughed much, but there was this . . . *smile* on his face all the time . . ."

Shot 5: A little girl of six, most of her hidden behind a parent's leg, saying, "I heard the house was haunted and that ghosts told him to do it . . ."

Insert shot: A recent color photograph of Andy and Russell Brennert at a Halloween party, both of them in costume. Russell is Frankenstein's monster, and Andy, his face painted to resemble a smiling skeleton, wears the black hooded cloak of the Grim Reaper. He's holding a plastic scythe whose tip is resting on top of Russell's head. The camera moves in on Russell's face until it fills the screen, then abruptly cuts to a shot of Russell in the foyer of the Leonard house. He's on his knees in front of the massive bloodstain on the wall. He's wearing rubber gloves and is pulling a large sponge from a bucket of soapy water. A caption at the bottom of the screen reads: "Russell Brennert, friend of the Leonard family."

He squeezes the excess water from the sponge and lifts it toward the stain, then freezes just before the sponge touches the wall.

He is trembling but trying very hard not to.

Tanya's shadow can be seen in the lower righthand corner of the frame. She asks, "How do you feel right now?"

Russell doesn't answer her, only continues to stare at the stain.

Tanya says, "Russell?"

He blinks, shudders slightly, then turns his head and says, "Wh-what? I'm sorry."

"What were you thinking just then?"

He stares in her direction, then gives a quick glance to the camera. "Does he have to point that damn thing at me like that?"

"You have to talk to a reporter eventually. You might as well do it now."

He bites his lower lip for a second, then exhales and looks back at the stain. "What're you thinking about, Russell?"

"I remember when Jessie first brought Theresa home from the hospital. Everyone came over here to see the new baby. You should've seen Andy's face."

Brennert's voice begins to quaver. The camera slowly moves in closer to his face. He is oblivious to it.

"He was so . . . *proud* of her. You'd have thought she was *his* daughter."

He reaches out with the hand not holding the sponge and presses it against the stain. "She was so tiny. But she couldn't stop giggling. I remember that she grabbed one of my fingers and started . . . chewing on it, you know, like babies will do? And Andy and I looked at each other and smiled and yelled, 'Uncle attack!' and he s-started . . . he started kissing her chubby little face, and I bent down and put my mouth against her tummy and started blowing real hard, you know, making belly-farts, and it tickled her so much because she started giggling and laughing and squealing and k-kicking her legs . . ."

The cords in his neck are straining. Tears well in his eyes, and he grits his teeth in an effort to hold them back.

"The rest of the family was enjoying the hell out of it, and Theresa kept squealing . . . that delicate little-baby laugh. Jesus Christ . . . he *loved* her. He loved her *so much*, and I thought she was the most precious thing . . . she always called me 'Uncleruss'—like it was all one word."

The tears are streaming down his cheeks now, but he doesn't seem aware of it.

"I held her against my chest. I helped give her baths in the sink. I changed her diapers—and I was a helluva lot better at it than Andy ever was . . . and now I gotta . . . I gotta scrub this off the wall."

He pulls back his hand, then touches the stain with only his index finger, tracing indiscernible patterns in the dried blood.

"This was her. This is all that's . . . that's left of the little girl she was, the baby she was . . . the woman she might have grown up to be. He loved her." His voice cracks, and he begins sobbing. "He loved all of them. And he never said anything to me. I didn't know, I swear to *Christ* I didn't know. This was her. I— oh, *goddammit!*"

He drops down onto his ass and folds his arms across his knees and lowers his head and weeps.

A few moments later, Jackson Davies comes in and sees him and kneels down and takes Russell in his arms and rocks gently back and forth, whispering, "It's all right now, it's okay, it's over, you're safe, hear me? Safe. Just . . . give it to me, kid . . . you're safe . . . that's it . . . give it to me . . ."

Davies looks up into the camera, and the expression on his face needs no explaining: *Turn that fucking thing off.*

Cut to: Tanya, outside the house again, standing next to the porch steps. On the porch, two men are removing the broken bay window. A few jagged shards of glass fall out and shatter on the porch. Another man begins sweeping up the shards and dumping them into a plastic trash barrel.

Tanya says, "Experts tell us that violence never really ends, that the healing process may never be completed, that some of the survivors will carry their pain for the rest of their lives."

A montage begins at this point, with Tanya's closing comments heard in voice-over.

The image, in slow motion, of police officers and EMTs moving sheet-covered and black-bagged bodies.

"People around here will say that the important thing is to remove as many physical traces of the violence as possible. Mop up the blood, gather the broken glass fragments into a bag and toss it in the trash, cover the scrapes, cuts, and stitches with bandages, then put your best face forward because it will make the unseen hurt easier to deal with."

The image of the sheet-covered bodies cross-fades into film of a memorial service held at Randy Hamilton's grade school. A small choir of children is gathered in front of a picture of Randy and begins to sing. Underneath Tanya's voice can now be heard a few dozen tiny voices softly singing "Let There Be Peace on Earth."

"But what of that 'unseen hurt'? A bruise will fade, a cut will get better, a scar can be taken off with surgery. Cedar Hill must now concern itself with finding a way to heal the scars that aren't so obvious."

The image of the children's choir dissolves into film of Mary Alice Hubert standing in the middle of the chaos outside the Leonard house on the night of the shootings. She is bathed in swirling lights and holds both of her hands pressed against her mouth. Her eyes seem unnaturally wide and are shimmering with tears. Police and EMTs scurry around her, but none stops to offer help. As the choir sings, "To take each moment and live each moment in peace e-ter-nal-ly," she drops slowly to her knees and lowers her head as if in prayer.

Tanya's voice-over continues: "Maybe tears will help. Maybe grieving in the open will somehow lessen the grip that the pain has on this community. Though we may never know what drove Andy Leonard to commit his horrible crime, the resonances of his slaughter remain."

Mary Alice dissolves into the image of Russell Brennert kneeling before the stain on the foyer wall. He is touching the dried blood with the index finger of his left hand.

The children's choir is building to the end of the song as Tanya says, "Perhaps Cedar Hill can find some brief comfort in these lines from a poem by German lyric poet Rainer Maria Rilke: 'Who weeps now anywhere in the world, without cause weeps in the world, weeps over me.'"

The screen fills with the image of Jackson Davies embracing Russell as sobs rack his body. Davies glares up at the camera, then closes his eyes and lowers his face, kissing the top of Russell's head. This image freezes as the children finish singing their hymn.

Tanya's voice once more, soft and low, no singsong mode this time, no inflection whatsoever: "For tonight, who weeps anywhere in the world, weeps for Cedar Hill and its wounds that may never heal.

"Tanya Claymore, Channel 9 News."

11

After the tape had finished playing and the lights in the classroom were turned back on, a student near the back of the room—so near, in fact, that Irv Leonard's ghost could have touched the boy's head, if he'd chosen to—raised his hand and asked, "What happened to all those people?"

"Tanya Claymore was offered a network job as a result of that tape. She eventually became a famous news anchor, had several public affairs with various coworkers, contracted AIDS, became a drug addict, and drove her car off a bridge one night. Jackson Davies remarried his ex-wife, and they live in Florida now. He'll turn seventy-one this year. Mary Alice Hubert died of a massive coronary six months after the killings. Most of Cedar Hill turned out for her funeral. Russell Brennert stayed in Cedar Hill and eventually bought into Jackson Davies's janitorial service. When Davies retired, Russell bought him out and now owns and operates the company. He'll turn fifty-two this year, and he looks seventy. He never married. He drinks too much and has the worst smoker's hack I've heard. He lives in a small four-room apartment with only one window—and that looks out on a parking lot. He told me he doesn't sleep well most of the time, but he has pills he can take for that. It still doesn't stop the dreams, though. He doesn't have many friends. It seems most people still believe he must have known what Andy was going to do. They've never forgiven him for that." I looked at the ghosts and smiled.

"He was so happy when I told him who I was. He hugged me like I was his long-lost son. He even wept. I invited him to come and visit me and my family this Christmas. I hope he comes. I don't think he will, but I can hope."

The room was silent for a moment, then a girl near the front, without raising her hand, said, "I knew Ted Gibson—he was the first person that Dyson shot. He . . . he always wanted me to go to Utica with him to try their ice cream. I was supposed to go with him that day. I couldn't . . . and I don't even remember why. Isn't that terrible?" Her lower lip quivered, and a tear slipped down her cheek. "Ted got killed, and all I could think of when I heard was I wonder what kind of ice cream he was eating."

That ended my story, and began theirs.

One by one, some more hesitant than others, some angrier, some more confused, my students began talking about their dead or wounded friends, and how they missed them, and how frightened they were that something so terrible could happen to someone they knew, maybe even themselves, had the circumstances been different.

The ghosts of Cedar Hill listened, and cried for my students' pain, and understood.

12

Before they left that day, someone asked me why I thought Andy had done it. I stopped myself from giving the real answer—what I perceive to be the real answer—and told them, "I think losing out on the scholarship did something to him. I think he looked at his future and saw himself being stuck in a factory job for the rest of his life and he became angry—at himself, at his family, at the town where he lived. If he had no future, then why should anyone else?"

"Then why didn't he kill his grandmother and Russell, too? Why didn't he kill you?"

Listen to my silence after he asked this.

Finally, I said, "I wish I knew."

I should have gone with my first answer.

I think it runs much deeper than mere anger. I think when loneliness and fear drive a person too deep inside himself, faith shrivels into hopelessness; I think when tenderness diminishes and bitterness intensifies, rancor becomes a very sacred thing; and I think when the need for some form of meaningful human contact becomes an affliction, a soul can be tainted with madness and allow violence to rage forth as the only means of genuine relief, a final, grotesque expression of alienation that evokes *feeling something* in the most immediate and brutal form.

The ghosts of my birth seem to agree with that.

You read the account of the Utica killings in the paper and then move quickly on to news about a train wreck in Iran or a flood in Brazil or riots in India or the NASDAQ figures for the week, and unless you are from the town of Utica or in some way knew one of the victims or the man who killed them, you forget all about it because you can't understand how a person, a *normal enough* person, a person like you and me, could do such a horrible thing. But he did, and others like him will, and all you can hope for is not to be one of the victims. You pray you will be safe. It is easier by far to understand the complicated financial maneuverings of Wall Street kingpins than an isolated burst of homicidal rage in a small Midwestern city.

They are out there, these psychos, and always will be. Another Andy Leonard could be bagging your groceries; the next Bruce Dyson might be that fellow who checks your gas meter every month. You just don't know—and there's the rub.

You *won't* know until it's too late.

I wish you well, and I wish you peace. My penance, if indeed that's what it is, must nearly be paid by now. The ghosts don't come around as much as they used to. The last time I saw them was the night my son was born; they came to the hospital to look at him, and to tell me that I was right, that those prayers spoken by strangers for the baby I once was are still protecting me, and will keep myself and my family safe from harm.

I'll pray, as well. I'll pray that the next Andy Leonard or Bruce Dyson doesn't get that last little push that topples him over the line; I'll pray that these psychos go on bagging groceries or checking gas meters or delivering pizzas and never raise a hand to kill, that the police in some other small town will be quick to stop them from getting to you if they ever do cross the line; I'll pray that no one ever picks up a paper and reads your name among the list of victims.

Because that kind of violence never really ends.

I hold my son. I kiss my wife and daughter.

The story is over.

Except for those who survived.
We continue.
Safe from harm, I pray.
Safe . . .

Howard Waldrop

El Castillo de la Perseverancia

Howard Waldrop—who hails from Mississippi and now lives in Washington State—is one of the most delightfully iconoclastic writers working today. His highly original books include Them Bones, A Dozen Tough Jobs, Howard Who?, *and* All About Strange Monsters of the Recent Past. *His most recent book is a new collection,* Going Home Again. *He has won both the Nebula and World Fantasy Awards for his unforgettable story "The Ugly Chickens."*

"El Castillo de la Perseverancia," a tale mixing Aztec myth with modern wrestling, is pure Waldrop: audacious, unpredictable, and hilariously gonzo. Originally published in the World Fantasy Convention Program Book, it is reprinted from the December issue of Asimov's SF *magazine.*

—T. W.

—For Fred Duarte and Karen Meschke, and Miguel Ramos; John D. Berry who came up with exactly the right word at exactly the right time, and Pat Cadigan who knew it had to be a junior college.—HW

1

Every day, Rhonda had passed the bright pink wall on the Avenida Guerrero opposite the Bella Vista Hotel on the way to her art classes. Today it was neither bright nor altogether pink. Someone had sprayed a dark blue cloudlike smudge across three meters of it, and in the cloud, had painted in neon green, in Spanish:

The World, which has slumbered so long, now begins to awaken . . .

A few other passersby noticed it, made *tsking* noises and continued on. One man, wearing two hats, a derby topped by a planter's hat, stopped, hands on hips, staring. He slowly shook his head.

"Next thing you know, the *alcalde* will ask for new taxes to clean such messes," he said, not to her, or to anyone.

Rhonda went on toward the Cortes Palace. She remembered how confusing the streets were to her when she had first come here six months ago. When she found that the College of Fine Arts was next to Hernan Cortes's old summer home, she realized she could find her way to classes from anywhere in the town except from across the barrancas, or from out past the Morelos State Penitentiary, places she'd only been a couple of times sketching for her classes.

She neared the old *zocalo* and tried to imagine what it had been like here five hundred years ago; probably too many guys in jaguar skins and parrot feathers running around.

There was a furniture and appliance store ahead. A man was in the front window setting up a display. She neared it. He was arranging dozens of alarm clocks—quartzes, electrics, windups—and clock radio phones on small tilted shelves, from one side of the large window to the other, reaching back behind him through a small doorway that opened back into the store. Small hands passed the timepieces out to him.

He looked up and saw Rhonda watching him, and smiled at her over his dapper mustache. He was dressed in a natty suit, *muy guapa*, the locals would say. He said something back through the small door; the thick glass muffling his words. A rectangle of cardboard came out. The man laid it down, laid his head on his steepled horizontal hands, feigning sleep. Then he picked up one of the clocks, shook it around like it was coming apart, and made big circles with his thumbs and index fingers around his eyes, mouth agape.

Then he turned the rectangle around. In Spanish, the sign said:

¡The whole world, which wants to sleep so long, can now wake itself up!

A chill went through Rhonda, a true horripilation through her whole upper body and down her right leg.

The man had a puzzled look on his face. He had placed the sign in its holder among the clocks, indicating his wares for sale with spread hands.

She slowly shook her head no.

The man looked crestfallen, then straightened himself, shot his cuffs, and crawled back through his little door.

As Rhonda turned to continue on to class, a 1965 blue and white Ford Galaxie convertible came by her, its top down.

In the car were three masked and cloaked wrestlers.

2

The three men walked into the office of the registrar in the *colegio menor*.

"¿*En que puedo servirle?*" asked the woman at the desk without looking up.

"*Sí*," said the older of the three men. "I am Señor Nadie. These are my compañeros, El Ravo Tepextehualtepec, and El Hijo de la Selva, whom I was fortunate enough to pass on the street on my way here in my car, and offered a ride, as we were all coming here to inquire about classes."

The woman had looked up. The older man was dressed in tights, boots and a black cape, but had a bare chest, with salt and pepper hair on it. His mask, which like those of the others covered his whole head, had a question mark on the face of it. The second was in a head-to-foot body suit, with red shorts and boots, a yellow cloak, and on the chest and mask was a yellow lightning bolt. The third was naked but for a loincloth and jungle boots. His mask was woodland camo.

"You have your B.U.P.'s?" asked the woman.

"Certainly," said El Ravo Tepextehualtepec, whom all his fans called El Ravo Tepe, to differentiate him from all the other El Ravos in the sport.

"Day or night classes?" she asked.

"Day, of course," said El Hijo de la Selva. "Night is when we wrestle."

3. Hecho en Mexico

Outside, near his pickup, his dog barked twice.

"Hush, Hecho," he said.

He put on the face mask and the disposable gloves over his plastic coveralls, cranked up the compressor and began spraying primer paint all over the taped and mudded drywall.

All around were the sounds of hammering and nailguns. Two weeks ago this part of Yucatán was a newly drained swamp. Now it was three rows of apartment blocks on the outskirts of a town that had not been there a year before, workers' rooms for the byproducts of the tourist trade.

At least now they gave you gloves and coveralls and masks. When he'd started as a painter's helper two years ago, at the age of seventeen, you went to work and sprayed the stuff all week and threw away your clothes on *viernes*. You got the stuff off your body with paint thinner and Go-Jo Cleaner.

He could hear Hecho begin to whine even over the *brrrupping* noise of the compressor. "Hush!" he yelled out, muffled. He turned off the compressor.

There was a long whine, and the sound of shaking in the pickup bed.

He looked out. The rope with which he tied his dog in the pickup was frayed and hung over the side. He saw his dog running, a half-meter of rope dangling from its collar. It climbed a pile of lumber scraps at the end of the site.

"Come back here!" he said. As he cupped his hands to yell, he tore the coveralls open on the latchplate on the doorjamb.

Hecho lay down on the lumber pile, head between his paws. He had never done that before. *Loco perro.*

He turned to go back to the inside room, passing the stacks of medicine-cabinet mirrors at the front door. Why they had been stacked there, when half the apartments weren't even weathered-in yet, he had no idea.

He pulled down his face mask and pulled off the gloves, which were stuck now to the torn plastic coveralls by the primer paint, so he let them dangle. He'd have to get another pair when he put on new coveralls anyway.

The dog yowled and ran away.

He stopped. In the mirror, the torn plastic flapped like another skin. The gloves hung like newly shed hands from the ends of his arms. His face mask with a big smear of grey across it looked like another loose mouth and jaw next to his own.

He was turning to admire the effect when something put him on like a cheap suit.

4

A slow Wednesday night at the Arena Tomalin:

After the prelims, El Hijo de la Selva fought Dinosaurito in a three-fall event. He won the first fall, lost the second, and won the third.

Then, to louder applause from the sparse crowd, El Ravo Tepe took on El Buitré Marvelloso. He won the first fall, lost the second, won the third and the match.

Two masked women wrestlers allowed all but the most iron-kidneyed a chance to visit the *taza de retrete.*

The main event: Señor Nadie contra La Pocilga Desordenada, a Tabascan who had failed at sumo in Japan, and who had come back and sat on a series of lesser *luchadores* until he gained the chance to go against the top-rated masked wrestler.

Señor Nadie won the first fall with a combination of wristlocks and outside-bar-stepover-toeholds. La Pocilga won the second by falling onto Señor Nadie as soon as the round started. At the end of the third fall, Señor Nadie left the ring victorious while the maintenance crew tried to get La Pocilga out of the snarled net that had been the ring ropes and turnbuckles. Two spectators had been hit by the flying ringposts and were treated for cuts and bruises.

Such was wrestling in Quanahuac.

5. Sin Horquilla

He was at the company picnic in the park outside Ciudad Juarez to which he had taken his wife and children every year for the past twelve years. Today he was playing washer toss with three other older men while all around him younger people and their families played hundred-to-a-side soccer. The park was filled with screams of joy and pain, discord and harmony, like any other Sociedad Anonima outing.

Suddenly, the El Pato® sauce he'd been sampling since nine in the morning caught up with him.

"¡Condenar!" he said. Sweat broke out on his mustached upper lip. He took off for the line of old outhouses at the far edge of the park.

"That's the fastest I've seen him move in many years," said one of his co-workers.

He slowed a little when he realized he would make it. A woman came out of the one he was headed for, slamming the heavy wooden door on its tired screen-door spring. The local priest, there to bless the chalupas at the big sit-down outdoor dinner that night, came out of another.

"Excuse me, padre," he said, crossing himself. As he reached for the worn brass doorhandle, the horseshoe nailed above the doorway fell down with a clang. He hesitated, then went in. When he was through, he would find a rock to nail the iron thing back up with. The door closed behind him.

The priest experienced a horripilation that stopped and turned him. He looked around. He fixed his collar and shook his shirt cuffs where they stuck out from his cassock.

There was a sound like giant rubbery wings behind him.

Something hit the ceiling of the third outhouse from the inside. There was a thrashing around, and a smash against the walls. Then another series of thumps up against the inside of the slanted corrugated tin roof that buckled it.

A sound of low mumbling came from the outhouse, then a third thrashing, then silence.

The priest started toward it. He wondered if the man had suffered a heart attack or a seizure of some kind.

"Are you all right?" he asked, reaching for the doorhandle, looking around to see if he could see the company doctor.

He swung the door open. The man's head lolled, the whites of his eyes showing. Then they came down and snapped into focus on the priest.

"In Christ's name . . ." said the priest.

"Fuck your God," said the man, and headed for the line of cars parked across from the soccer field.

6

Rhonda walked by the wall again on her way to meet Federico, the Italian student in her life-drawing class.

The wall had been painted over the week before—there was a pink swath, done with a roller, through most of the design. In another week the enamel would bleed through the pink latex, and the words would show again.

Federico was to meet her at the Cine, just off the Avenida Morelos. They were going to see *Las Manos de Orlak* con Peter Lorre, and *La Maldición de la Momia* con Lon Chaney menor. The Cine Morelos seemed to stay in business by showing films that had been on American television for fifty years.

She realized she'd gone one block too far on the Avenida Guerrero, and turned to her left. She saw one of the diagonal streets leading down the block behind the Bella Vista Hotel and headed toward it.

She passed an upscale cantina—one of the tourist traps, no doubt—and heard music coming out. Lounge music must sound the same in every country.

A smooth baritone came out of the speakers—she pictured the tuxedoed smoothie to whom it belonged. He did not have a mustache, and never would.

Then she heard his words:

> My world, so asleep in its bed,
> woke to the morning of your love.

She stopped, hand on the doorframe, and looked inside.

The singer was old, bleary-eyed, and looked as if he'd come out second in his youth in a clawhammer fight. He was dressed like Leo Carillo, who had played Pancho in the old *Cisco Kid* television show, hat and all, or like a Latino Andy Devine. He saw Rhonda and smiled at her over his salt-and-pepper walrus mustache.

She turned and went down the street toward the Cine Morelos.

Far off in the distance the two volcanoes loomed in the last of the blue-purple light.

7

The air was cool and smelled good outside the dressing rooms behind the Arena Tomalin.

There were already two cigarette glows in the dark against the far wall of the little courtyard reserved for the wrestlers.

The man who had just come out lit one of his own with a lighter from the left pocket of his dressing gown.

"Ay," he said, "Some night, eh?"

"We were talking of the same thing. Not at all like last week."

"During a night like this," said the man who had just come out, "I ask myself, what would Santo have done in the same situation."

"Ah, Santo," said one of the others.

"Or Blue Demon," said the other.

"They do not make them like Santo anymore. Such grace and sureness, both in the ring and out."

"Like when he fought the Frankenstein monster in the Wax Museum."

"Or the Martians, like in *Santo Contra la Invasión de los Marcianos!*"

"Or when he teamed with Blue Demon to fight the Nazis in Atlantis!"

"The Vampire Women? What about those?"

"Which Vampire Women? *The Vampire Women* was *un roncador grande*. I spent days watching it one afternoon," said one of the men who had been there first.

"No, no. Not the *Vampire Women* movie, that was bad. The *Santo en la Venganza de los Mujeres Vampiros.*"

"Oh, sí. Putting Santo in any movie improves it."

"Have you seen the Crying Woman movies? Or the *Mummies of Guanajuatos?*"

"Of course. Or the Aztec Mummy films. Ah, that Popoca. To think he was in love five hundred years with the dead princess. The pains he went through . . ."

"And *La Nave de los Monstruos!* Uk, Zak and Utir! Espectro of the Planet Death! Tor the Robot. That was a movie!"

"To think how it must be," said one of them, "to wrestle cleanly, to be famous, to play yourself in movies of your own adventures. . . ."

They all sighed.

"What Santo probably would have done on such a messed-up wrestling night as this," said the youngest, "is to have tried to forget about it, and go home and get a good night's sleep."

"As I am," said the second.

"And me," said the third.

Their three cigarettes became flying red dots in the night, bouncing sparks in the concrete courtyard.

The door to the dressing rooms opened, they went in, and it closed.

8. Soy Un Hombre Más Pobre . . .

The limo dropped him outside his Mexico City office, at the corner of Salvador and Piño Suarez.

He went inside, nodding to the guard, took his elevator to the private entry to his office, went inside and put his sharkskin attaché on the corner of his desk. There were three pieces of paper in his IN box that he had to sign sometime during the day. There was a package on the credenza all the way across the office.

A light blinked on his phone. He picked it up. "*¿Bueno, y que?*" he said. It was the president of the American company he worked for. He listened. "*En seguida. Entonces. Sí. No. Sí, sí. Buenos días.*" He hung up.

He got the package from the antique dealer and unwrapped it, using his mammoth ivory scrimshaw letter opener.

Inside was the Cantinflas chocolate mug, the carnival glass pitcher with the 1968 Olympics commemorative design etched into it, and a book, a recognition guide to European mushrooms. They were not for him, but gifts for executives of other companies who had an interest in them. He looked at them a moment, wondering at the things people spent their time acquiring. He started to call his secretary and reached for the key on his computer. He bumped the book off onto the stainproof pile carpet.

It flipped open to the chapter on morels, and an old 1000-peso note fell out. Once it had been worth $120.00 US. After the fourth devaluation, it was worthless. He bent to pick it up.

He realized it was *all* about money. Everything. Entirely. From beginning to end, every second of it, even from before till after.

There was a surflike pounding in the air. He looked up and knew what he would see, and sure enough, the four hundred billion coins, doubloons, sesterces, pieces of eight, yen, marks, francs, and pine-tree shillings washed over him in a cleansing, baptismal wave.

Now that he understood, he laughed. It was simple, so utterly simple.

9

In three different provinces that week, three new *luchadores enmascarados* appeared on Amateur King of the Hill match nights. One wore a red horned mask, one a mask that was the mask of a human head and face with a zipper through it, one wore the mask of a globe of the earth. The speed with which they dispatched all comers was the only topic of the conversation of those who saw them.

Who were those guys? Where had they come from?

10

She poured non-dairy creamer into her coffee and watched it soak up all the brown color. Nothing that dissolves instantly can be good for you, she thought. When she had started classes six months ago, there were still pots of cream or milk at the end of the student cafeteria serving line.

It was mid-afternoon, a Tuesday, so her first break for lunch, the choice being ten A.M. Or then. There were few people there, the occasional professor, a group of provincial eighteen-year-olds like a flock of birds, solitaries and couples.

She usually sat in the corner, as far away from the serving line as she could, so she wouldn't be bothered. Most local guys were pretty much jerks about women. So were most American guys; it was just that the local guys were more honest about it.

As she'd entered, she'd seen that the tables where she'd like to sit had people at them, but now as she turned away from the creamer, she saw they'd all emptied out. There were china cups and plates on the dark brown serving trays scattered around, napkins with lipstick on them, paper cups. As she neared the farthest table, she saw there was a paperback book lying, creased and dogeared, near one of the trays.

She looked up to see if anyone was moving away. No one.

She sat, took a drink of coffee, opened her microwave burrito, and looked at the book. A collection of dramas. But not, as she turned the pages, by Rudolfo Usigli or Lope de Vega, but a collection of medieval English Mystery and Morality plays, with transliterated Middle English on one page, and Spanish on the other. It was by a couple of Italians.

A double-dogear marked a play called *The Castle of Perseverance*. She turned back to the introduction, read part of it. It was evidently a play like *Everyman*, which she had seen in high school, with personified evils and goods and a (to the modern mind) yokel of a protagonist, like Goofy, only dumb. In this case he was called Mankind.

She put the book with hers, finished her burrito and the caffeined chemical drink, and headed for her three P.M. painting class.

11

He adjusted his mask and let himself into the apartment with a key.

There was no one there. He went to the music system and turned it on. A preset radio station came on, volume at six. He turned it down. The song was

? and the Mysterians' "96 Tears." When it was nearly over it faded and up came "Sleepwalk" by Santo and Johnny. It was the same all over Mexico; stations from the Estados Unidos leaked in all over the FM band. He wondered how powerful their stations were.

He loosened his shirt and found himself a Tres Equis in the refrigerator. He was halfway through it when he heard a key in the lock and the woman came in.

"Oh," she said. "You're already here. Sorry." She had a shopping bag and a grocery sack with her.

"Uf!" she said, putting the grocery sack on the counter, and opening the refrigerator. "The traffic! The crowding! I thought I would swoon!" She closed the door, the empty sack flew into the garbage. "They are tearing up Calle las Casas again." She walked into the bedroom. Through the open door he saw her pass back and forth, more or less clothing alternately covering and revealing different parts of her.

"Then I ran into the son of that French film director, the one who worked in Brazil so many years. The father, I mean. I still don't know what *el hijo* does for a living." She stayed out of sight. There was the sound of running water.

He took another swallow of beer.

She passed by naked; a second later she went by covered from neck to ankles, then came back by hopping through some garment on one foot.

"He tried to catch me up on some gossip that you would not be interested in. It made very little sense, even to me," she said.

He slowly moved the beer around in the bottom of the can with a slight swirling motion of his hand.

She stood in the bedroom doorway. She wore white silk hose and red high heels. The single other garment was a red and black lace cupless push-up bustier that ended at the navel, and from which the garter clips hung. She had on a thick woven gold-link necklace. Her glistening black hair stood out from around the Creature From the Black Lagoon mask she now wore.

"Come here, you big lug," she said, crooking her finger.

He put the beer can down beside the chair, stood as if in a dream, and began to walk.

12

—Caramba! What a fight! Now El Diablo Peligroso has Lobo Gris in the *cangrejo Monterrey*! The Grey Wolf is begging for mercy! Now the referee puts the question. ¿Que? ¡Grito Tio! Yes, yes, Señores y Señoras; El Diablo Peligroso remains undefeated since appearing on the scene less than a month ago!—

—the inside-bar-stepover-toehold. Now Vestido Zooto works on—wait! Wait! Yes. ¡Cielo! Carne Xipe has broken loose! He's under—now out! Wait. Yes, yes, now he has Vestido Zooto in the *ialacran de pecho*! Yes, yes! The pectoral scorpion has done its work. Carne Xipe wins again. They are taking Zooto out of the ring in agony. His arms hang useless at his sides—

. . .

—The crowd boos. Not much has happened. El Balón Gordo reaches out—what happened? Oh, look, look! El Mundo Grosero has El Balón in his famous hold, *el sueño de Japón*. El Balón is groggy. He's reaching for—El Mundo is using only one hand—he's, he's looking at his watch! What a gesture! Late for supper, eh, Mundo? There goes El Balón. He's on his knees, he's falling. He's down. Goodness gracious! Mundo is already leaving the ring! Now the referee is counting *him*!—he's put one foot back in the ring—he's in. *Now* he's the winner. The crowd is on its feet—listen to them. They are booing and cheering at the same time! Never have I seen this! Never—

"Your correspondent has asked himself again and again; where did these *luchadores* come from? How could they rise so fast in the world of wrestling? What are their goals? They are all three undefeated. The fans both love them and hate them; they want to see them like the fabled Juggernaut, unstoppable. And they want to see them stopped, dead cold. And there are only three who could possibly do it: the three shining companions—they know who they are—sure, professional, persevering, unpresuming. The only question is: when and where will the fight be? The whole wrestling world; no, all Mexico asks. We await our answer."

Pin-Down Martinez
Estrellas de Luchadores

13

Rhonda sat up in bed, chilled and panting. She'd had a dream that made no sense that she could remember; it had only irritated her that it was taking so long and nothing was happening. Then she'd jerked awake, thinking she was cold.

Instead the room was stifling. She found her glasses on the bedside table, went to the window of her rented room and opened it.

More hot air came in. She undid her pajama-top buttons, stood at the window. The clock said 0110.

Around the edges of the four-story building behind the rooming house she saw soft flashes. She leaned out the left window.

Lightning played off clouds above the distant twin volcanoes. She could only see the shape of Iztacchihuatl, but saw residual flashes, which must be beyond Popocatépetl, and further south. Maybe the storm was coming this way, though most of their weather came from the west, off the Pacific.

There was no thunder; the storm was thirty kilometers away. In a minute or two came the faintest stirring of a breeze, so slight she did not know from which direction. The air coming into the room was slightly cooler. She stayed there, elbows resting on the windowsill. The clock said 0211.

She turned on the light and wrote her aunt, who'd sent her a blanket two weeks before, a thank-you aerogramme. Then she turned off the light and went back to sleep.

She was surprised to find, when she left for class the next morning, that it had rained during the night, and the streets were dark and glistening under a cerulean sky with not a hint of cadmium white in it.

14

"I want flesh," said Carne Xipe, moving around the office ceaselessly. "I want them to worship flesh, the flesh, food, meat. As when the pyramids—battle, blood sacrifice! Sacrifice—" He rubbed the mask that covered his head, the mask of a head with a zipper through it.

"Of course you do," said Mundo Grosero, tapping a cigarette on the face of his watch.

"Bah!" said Diablo Peligroso. "Flesh is no good unless there is the worship of the power behind it. Inversion. Their religion turned upside down, backward. Renunciation. Flesh is just one way. No God! Evil. Ha ha. Let them know they are tempted, and there is nothing, *nothing* at the other end. Call on their God, hear an empty echo. I am the call. *I* am the empty echo. I want them to call out and only hear themselves calling out." His red horned mask, and the eyes in it, were filled with pain.

"Of course you do," said Mundo Grosero.

Carne Xipe and El Diablo Peligroso looked at him.

"And what do *you* want for them?" asked El Diablo.

"That's easy," said El Mundo Grosero, flicking out his Safari lighter so that the flame stood up to the end of his cigarette. A smile turned up through the Southern Western Hemisphere of his mask.

"I want to make them all just like *yanquis*."

15

"You have to fight them," said Señor Sanabria, the head of the wrestling *federacíon*.

"To paraphrase a boxer," said Señor Nadie, "We don't *have* to do anything but be Latino and die."

Señor Sanabria looked back and forth from El Ravo Tepe to El Hijo. "Help me," he said.

"I hate to say it," said El Ravo Tepe, "but the big question-mark guy is right. We know nothing of these gents. We don't know their aims, whether they are honorable."

"You've fought plenty of people," said Sanabria, "with, shall we say, *espiritus groseros* before. Especially you, Señor Nadie. Remember El Gorilla Acapulcano? El Gigante Gordo?"

"Those were merely dirty wrestlers," said Señor Nadie.

"Sí," said El Hijo, the youngest. "Or so I've heard."

"Then it's not the money?" asked the president.

"Of course not!" said El Hijo de la Selva. He looked at the other two. "Or do I speak out of turn?"

"I'd do it for five old centavos—" They all laughed "—actually, ten," said Señor Nadie, ". . . if I were sure of two things. Myself. And them."

"That goes for me, too," said El Ravo Tepe.

"Also," said El Hijo.

"Then," said Señor Sanabria. "I must bring up an indelicate inducement." He reached in his desk, pulled out some Xeroxed pages of typed copy.

"It's from Pin-Down Martinez, isn't it?" asked Señor Nadie. "He still uses that outmoded Underwood Standard at the wrestling magazine office."

"Only it's not for the *Estrellas*," said Sanabria. "It's a guest editorial for the Saturday morning newspaper. He sent a copy over this morning." He offered it to Señor Nadie.

"Tell me."

"He says if you three do not take the challenge, he will believe for once and for all those scurrilous rumors are true, that wrestling matches are fixed."

El Ravo was on his feet. El Hijo de la Selva was looking for something to throw, and somewhere to throw it.

Señor Nadie held up his hand.

"*¿Compañeros?*"

16

¡GIGANTIC SPECTACLE!
ARENA TOMALIN
¡BATTLE OF THE AGES!

LUCHA LIBRE

FREE-FOR-ALL WRESTLING
STYLO TEJAS DEATH-MATCH
con Barbed Wire

Los Campañeros de los Arenas:
SEÑOR NADIE
EL RAVO TEPEXTEHUALTEPEC
y
EL HIJO DE LA SELVA
contra
EL MUNDO Grosero
EL CARNE Xipe
y
EL DIABLO Peligroso

MIERCOLES 2 NOVIEMBRE en punto de 9
ARENA TOMALIN

¡Vds. Ahi o Vds un Trasnochadé!

17

Rhonda was coming down with a cold or sore throat or the flu. She ached all over, but after her last class, she took the book she had found in the cafeteria to the college Lost and Found. She had been meaning to do it for a week or two, but had remembered it that morning, before she became really miserable.

"I found this book," she said to the student behind the desk.

"*¡Ay, caramba!*" he said. "It must be made of gold." He looked it over, and at the piece of paper in his hand. "Lucky you," he said, handing it over to her.

"Reward," it said. "Lost book. Anthology of plays. *Plays of Mystery and Morality* ed. Malcondotti and Prolisse. En Español with English text on facing page. Call NAhuatl 4–1009. Reward."

She picked up the phone on the desk and called someone who wasn't the one with the offer of the reward, but said that he would be back soon. She gave him her mailing address, and told him to pick up the book at the lost and found.

She put the phone back on the cradle. "The person calling for the book is named José Humanidades," she said to the student on the desk. "He says please make a note of that and not give it to anyone else."

"*Efectamente*," he said, reaching for a pen and paper.

Two days later, she received an envelope with no return address. Inside were two tickets to a wrestling match at the Arena Tomalin, and a piece of paper that said, "Thanks for finding it."

By then, her cold had already raged and was on the ebb tide, she was miserable, and had been taking cough suppressant with codeine for eighteen hours.

18

First Federico was going with her, then he wasn't, then he was.

Rhonda started for the Arena Tomalin, which was used for every kind of sporting event in this town. As she turned the corner and saw the huge lines, she stopped. Never before in her life had she been to a wrestling match or considered going to one.

She'd had another big dose of cough medicine just before she'd left the *pension*, and had gotten a little unsteady on her feet.

She sat on the low wall across from the arena. She saw that TV trucks were parked off to one side, their satellite antennae pointed at the same spot in the sky. Why would anyone come to a wrestling match if it were on TV?

To her left, on another building, was a bright blue cloud spray, and in the middle of it, in neon green, the slogan:

> That world, which has slumbered so long,
> Now begins to awaken.

She stared at it. It was the only one she had seen besides that first one across from the Hotel Bella Vista. She got up and moved toward the long lines of people at the doors of the Arena.

"Immediate seating for blue reserved seat tickets through the blue door by the ticket booth," said an usher with a megaphone to the crowd. "Immediate reserved seating through the blue door."

She looked down. Her tickets were blue.

She left a note and a ticket for Federico at the window and followed another usher to a seat in the third row. She looked around. Television cameras were on platforms built around the domed ceiling of the sportatorium, and reporters with minicams walked back and forth in front of the ring.

There were four long aisles into the place. People rushed to and fro.

"¡Dulces de algodón!" yelled a man with a tray in front of him in which fluffy pink head-sized balls were stuck. "¡Dulces de algodón!" Rhonda noticed she was four seats over from the aisle, which probably meant she would be handing food and money back and across each way all night. Or however long it took.

In a few minutes, the announcer came out. The audience applauded and cheered. He began to speak, and they were with him until the word "preliminaries" came out.

The crowd was on its feet, booing and whistling. The booing stopped when two clowns dressed as masked wrestlers came down the eastern and western aisles. Their masks had large red noses on the front of them, their tights were baggy, and they had on boots with meter-long toes.

They went through all the motions. Just as they prepared to grapple for the first time, a huge bank of the arena lights sputtered out, then all the lights around the ceiling, except for those on the side of the ring with Rhonda.

Giant shadows of the two wrestling clowns sprang up onto the far wall of the place. They were ten meters high. Rhonda watched them, instead of the clowns, as did other spectators. The titanic figures swirled and swooped. The crowd began laughing and applauding. The clowns redoubled their efforts.

Soon both the noses were gone—one clown bounced the other one's like a jack-ball off the canvas mat. The second pulled an athletic supporter out of his shorts, put the other one's nose in it, whirled it around and around his head and let go like a slingshot, hitting the other right between the eyeslits. He fell to the canvas with a thud, stiff-legged.

The crowd roared with laughter. To Rhonda, who had been watching the big shadows, it didn't seem that funny.

They had fixed the lights.

Other people with reserved seats had begun to file in around her—she had never thought wrestling, like opera, was something you could be fashionably late to. The people had talked during the entire clown act, and now were talking through the match between the two clean-cut non-masked wrestlers in the one-fall, ten-minute time limit match.

Some people farther back were on their feet, yelling encouragement. Some people could get excited about almost anything.

She looked around. Still no Federico.

That match over, the crowd grew restless as technical people put up the two-and-a-half-meter-high cyclone fence with two strands of barbed wire on top, and two cages, at diagonal corners of the square.

Rhonda nodded in the warm air. The cough medicine was still working on her. The next thing she knew, there was a fanfare on the speakers, jolting her awake.

"Señores and Señoras," said the announcer, his voice echoing and rising, "Let's get ready to escaramuzar!" The crowd went crazy.

"The Challengers:

"From Ciudad Juarez, El Diablo Peligroso!"

The north door of the Arena flew open with Spielberg light effects, and coming down the aisle was a man in red tights with a horned, masked head.

"From Mexico City, El Mundo Grosero!"

The west door opened, the lights blinded everybody, and a wrestler with blue and green tights, and a mask of the globe of the earth came down that aisle.

"From the Yucatán, El Carne Xipe!"

From the south, amid the lights, came a man with a flesh-colored cape, flesh-colored body suit with red gashes in it and—at first Rhonda thought he had no mask on, but as he passed, she saw that his mask was the mask of a normal-looking head, with a zipper through it, all the way from the base of the neck, over the top and down to the chin.

The three wrestlers got to the ring at the same time and got into the little cage in their corner of the ring.

"Ladies and Gentlemen," yelled the announcer. "The Champions. The Compañeros of the Ring: Señor Nadie, El Ravo Tepextehualtepec and El Hijo de la Selva!!!"

The roar that went up was earsplitting. The three men bounded up the eastern aisle, waving to the crowd, and went into their cage, where the maintenance people waited.

"A Texas-style barbed-wire Death Match, no time limit, for the true championship team of all Mexico. Once the contestants are in, the match begins. It ends only when one team, or member of a team, remains conscious or in the ring. For this, there is no referee," said the announcer. "Officials of the Mexican Union of All-Professional Wrestling are explaining to each team the conditions of the match. . . ."

"What do you mean?" asked El Ravo Tepe, "no unmasking? The official said it was legal. What fun is it to fight another *enmascarado* if you can't take off his mask?"

"Would you like it done to you?" asked Señor Nadie.

"Has never happened. And never will," said El Ravo.

"I am of two minds," said El Hijo. "I would not like it done to me. In many ways it cheapens the sport. But then, there are some people who deserve unmasking. They are not worthy of the mask. Humiliation is the only thing they understand. I have done it once; the guy asked for it. But I didn't like it."

"The true *enmascarado* has no need of such displays," said Señor Nadie. "Would that we all had the spirit and wisdom of a Santo or a Demonio Azul. Then would we know when an opponent is truly defeated, rather than just unconscious. We could all, in a normal match, quit before the count, and still know we had won. Bullfighting must be a lot like that, only in the end, someone or something dies, and there must be blood on the sand."

The two others were quiet in the cage, then El Hijo spoke.

"I know one thing. Those *pavos* we fight will have no compunction about taking off our masks."

"Heads inside or not," said El Ravo Tepe.

Rhonda listened to the conversation around her.

"—*a de J.C.*" said the man in the front row to someone else.

A candy hawker came by. Rhonda passed some jujubes and money across from right to left and left to right.

"Aw, go ahead," said another man to the woman beside him. "It won't hurt." He held up a candied apple. "Caramel. Look." He bit into it. "Yummmm."

"I'm on a diet," she said. "My doctor told me not to."

The guy with the fruit for sale stood nervously licking his lips.

"No," she said, finally.

"Aw, phooey," said the man. "Give me another one, though." He took the candied fruit on the stick and bit into it, turning toward the ring. He sat with one in each hand.

"¡Dulces! ¡Dulces de algodón!" said another concessionaire, beside her on the aisle. She noticed the small badge on his hat. Hummingbird Foods, Southern Division, in the shape of a smiling cloisonné hummer.

". . . so he burned up the meat," said a man with his hat on to the priest beside him dressed in street clothes. He bit into a potato-and-egg burrito. "Look, all he did was get some of the recipe a little wrong. No reason to get upset, just get some more meat and do it right."

"¡Achicharados!" yelled another foodseller. "¡Achicharados! Hot dripping achicharados!"

"I hope we get to see some real holds," said a girl who had not yet had her quinceaños to the boy beside her as she clutched a copy of Estrellas de Luchadores to her.

"¡Bomba zumbida!" said the boy. "¡Una bomba atomica!"

"Sure, we'll give you the horse," said a man in a business suit to another dressed as a rancher, "just put up all your property as collateral."

". . . John Wayne," said a woman. "When he died, everything changed. I said, things will never ever be the same with the Duke dead, I assure you that. Why, the communists . . ."

An old man sighed a row back. "The Japanese. Los Alemanes. ¡Ay de mi!"

"¡Achicharados!" yelled the barker.

A beerseller came by. Someone past Rhonda stopped him. He passed over a bottle of beer, Rhonda passed the money back, and the change. The person next to her tapped her on the shoulder. He held up an abrebotella that was attached by an elastic cord to an Orvis pin-reel on the Hummingbird Foods man's white jacket. She pulled it over to the man with the beer bottle. He opened the cap. Foam went everywhere, and he let go of the bottle opener. It zeeted back and thumped the beerseller in the chest.

"¡Mal educado!" said the vendor, glaring and moving on.

The house lights went down. The bell rang.

The wrestlers charged from their cages into the ring. The technical people knocked the cages down in a trice, and one locked each door with a Club®.

By then, no one was watching the maintenance men.

Rhonda tried to keep up with what was going on. Everyone was screaming. The devil-suit wrestler had the Tarzan-guy in some kind of stranglehold. The guy with the globe for a head had the whole head of the guy with the question mark in one big hand. The guy with a face for a mask had both his hands into the chest of the guy with the lightning bolts.

Then it all changed, and everybody had a different hold on everybody else. Punches flew. Feet pounded. Somebody smashed against the cyclone fence. The barbed wire whined. There were screams inside and outside the ring. Sinews cracked. She heard the sound of breathing, from the crowd, the wrestlers, herself. She saw drops of sweat on the canvas, and imagined how hot it was out there.

Then the lights went out again, everywhere but her side of the arena, and the giant shadows sprang up. The three guys who'd come in together looked around a second, which gave their opponents time to jump on their heads again.

"¡Caracoles!" he said. He was an old man now, and the TV was turned up loud so he could hear it.

He watched what was happening.

"I am truly needed," he said to himself. He reached for his cane, pulled himself up, reached the balance point, went backward into the chair again.

Then he swung up and stood, pushing with his cane to keep from going too far forward.

"¡Ay de mi!" He started toward the closet in the back room.

He had not wrestled in more than thirty years. He had not even played himself in the movies for twenty-five. He had watched a series of younger, stronger men wrestle under his name, and people who could actually act play him in the films. When they'd had the huge going-away party for him when he left the sport, it was an actor up there getting all the silver watches and memberships in country clubs.

He tried to keep an eye on the TV from the back room. He opened the closet door with a key. He looked over the rows of silver masks and tights, the cloaks and capes. When he had put them aside, and moved to this retirement community, no one had known.

He reached for one of his special masks. He was more than two hundred kilometers away. He would have to call his Air Force general friend, get a jet, parachute into the Arena Tomalin through the skylight, just as he had done in the old days.

His cane caught on a pair of tights and he fell forward, smashing his head against the back of the closet. He came up bleeding, silver sequins and rhinestones stuck on his gashed forehead. He pressed a pair of tights against the cut, moved back to the living room and his chair.

"¡Uf!" he said. "¡No tengo energia como lo!"

He sat in his chair, bloody tights wadded against his balding head, tears running down his face.

On the TV, Carne Xipe had El Hijo de la Selva in the Deltoid Grinder hold.

"I don't understand," yelled El Hijo to Señor Nadie. "We keep knocking them down but they won't—Ouch! Yahh!"

There was a pop of sinews as El Diablo Peligroso grabbed him three or four places.

"We must keep on, amigos," said Señor Nadie. He grabbed El Mundo Grosero where it would do the most good, going from an inside to an outside-stepover-bar-toehold, forgetting for a second that the object was not a fall, but to remove him from the ring.

From somewhere, Carne Xipe stuck a finger in the eyeslit of his mask and poked.

Señor Nadie screamed and caught the hand as he fell. He was dragged toward the side of the ring by two pairs of hands.

Then he saw El Ravo's boots out of his good eye, and the hands let go, and Señor Nadie came up, throwing punches and kidney chops, eye watering.

The big shadow of the devil and the world crossed the lightning.

Then the forest eclipsed the world, and the question mark sailed through the air and took out the masked unmasked shadow.

With grunts from below, the shadows loomed up and up the far walls.

Somebody screamed, louder than ever, and there was the sound of breaking bone.

They stood panting, El Hijo de la Selva holding his useless left hand. Even his mask was twisted with pain.

The three challengers closed in on them, their strength seemingly renewed. Carne Xipe had his arms out to the sides, ready to reapply the Pectoral Scorpion. El Diablo Peligroso moved sideways back and forth, waiting for his chance to get into the Monterrey Crab. El Mundo Grosero had his right arm out, head high, wanting one of the champions to walk into the Japanese sleephold.

Closer and closer they came.

"We must persevere," said Señor Nadie, barely able to keep his breath going. "We must fight the best fight of our lives, cleanly and—"

A woman was screaming above all the other noise in the darkened arena.

"¡Desvestidos las máscaras!" she shrieked.

The wrestlers did not know to whom she was yelling.

Then in English: "Take off their masks!"

The noise in the sportatorium went way down.

"Rip off their masks, you namby-pamby jerks!" she yelled through the silence.

The champions looked at each other, then charged in.

Rhonda looked around her. For a second, everyone in the Arena Tomalin looked back. Then their heads turned away as the wrestlers collided.

She sat back down.

El Hijo de La Selva pulled with his good hand at the barely moving head of Carne Xipe. The mask of the mask of a face came loose, like pulling off a second skin. El Hijo jerked back—underneath was the same face as on the mask. Then he pulled the mask completely off, and the body quit struggling.

There was a river beyond the darkness, leading toward a place that was light. A dog stood on the bank of the river, barking, jumping back and forth. He stepped into the water, and the dog ran in a splashing circle around him, then began to swim, looking back over its shoulder, barking encouragement.

He swam toward the light, following the dog, familiar yet not the same as before.

Then they were on the other side in the light.

El Ravo Tepextehualtepec swung El Diablo Peligroso around and around by the horns, faster and faster, keeping a turning point on the Club® in the enemy corner. The mask began to loosen as El Diablo pulled a couple of g's. Then the mask came over the chin, ripping cartilage from his nose, blood flying, and he sailed through the air into the corner post like a sack of cement.

The nun pointed to the block of granite as big as Mount Everest. And he saw far up it the tiny hummingbird brushing the edge of the block with its wings.

A small polished groove encircled the block.

He sighed. He was at a kind of peace. He was getting exactly what he deserved.

Señor Nadie sat on the heaving chest of El Mundo Grosero. There was nothing left for El Mundo to do, and not much to do it with. Señor Nadie heard the cheering as El Ravo and El Hijo finished their work.

He leaned down very close to the Indian Ocean where the mouth was; it twisted away, revealing the Australian and Pacific ear.

Señor Nadie grabbed the whole Eastern Hemisphere with his large hand. He leaned down close to the ear and pulled.

"*Caducidad*," he said as he did.

He rushed northwest through the air, swooped over mountains, came down close to the fields, zoomed faster, went past a town out to a shack in the Salinas Valley, went down to the ground, through the door, across the room, and up between a woman's legs.

And came right back out again.

"A girl," said the midwife.

They were going to name her Elena Esperanza por América Rodriguez when it came time for the christening, and they were going to raise her to have it better than they had, and get a good education, and become a doctor or a teacher or an astronaut.

Wait, he wanted to say, there has been some mistake. I'm not a girl, I'm a grown man. I'm not being born to a poor illegal family in California, I'm a rich man living in Mexico City. I'm not even really a wrestler, I'm an arbitrageur, an executive. I have more platinum cards than other people my age have hemorrhoids. I am feared in my field. I can destroy people's lives, close down whole towns with a memo. There has been some mistake. I will make a few phone calls and clear all this up. *That* was what he meant to say.

What he said was:

"WAAAAAAAAAAHHHHHH!"

19

Rhonda went by the painted-over wall on her way to classes. She came even with the furniture and appliance store in the early morning, and saw the little dapper man was finishing a new display, this time of those tiny model beds that would be perfect in a three-year-old's palace.

He saw her, brightened, indicated his wares, reached back through the small door and took out a placard and put it on the easel:

> Now the world, awake so long,
> Can find easeful slumber.

She smiled. He smiled, then climbed through the door and was gone.

Rhonda walked on, and again the blue and white Ford Galaxie went by.

Only this time, the wrestlers had on their question mark, lightning bolt, and camouflage masks, but were wearing jeans and T-shirts, except the older one driving, who wore a bush jacket over his T-shirt. They turned out of sight down toward the colegio menor.

Señor Nadie was on his way to his woodworking class. El Ravo Tepe was taking electronics. And El Hijo de la Selva was enrolled in gardening.

Brennen Wysong

The Sin-Eater's Tale

Here's a tale of American fantasy you won't easily forget, involving an ancient Scottish rite as practiced in the American South during the Civil War. Chilling, moving, and beautifully told, Brennen Wysong's unusual story comes from the Spring/Summer issue of Black Warrior Review.

Brennen Wysong, a native of West Virginia, received an M.F.A. from Cornell University, where he is currently a lecturer, and associate editor at Epoch *magazine. His stories have appeared (or are forthcoming) in* High Plains Literary Review, Story, Alaska Quarterly Review, Glimmer Train Stories, Black Warrior Review, Indiana Review, The Massachusetts Review, *and* The Georgia Review. *He is presently working on a novel entitled* The Stonehouse Family Songbook, *which traces four generations of country musicians in West Virginia.*

—T. W.

I tell my granddaughter this story.

There was a sin-eater. Over a century ago in these parts, he came out of the hills in search of the dead. He heard rumors of a train returning from the war. With its engine still lurching along the tracks, its pistons hissing steam atop the platform, the sin-eater joined the crowd and watched a half-dozen battered veterans step down from their compartments. *Cannon-fodder,* he heard whispered. *Where's my baby?* a woman wailed. From the beast-reeking cattle cars, the coffins were hefted out through the slatted light and placed in a line reaching beyond the dry goods shop, accumulating down the rutted road toward a puddle where a boy floated a paper boat. A dampness seeped through the boxes' uncaulked seams. A chill filled the joints of the casket bearers. When they pried the nails from the swelled wood, the sin-eater saw the dead packed tight in their coffins with ice. The crowd swept the cold gruel from the faces of their loved ones. They kissed bloated cheeks, wept deep into the crooks of necks. But the warmth of their lips and the salt of their tears proved unfit for bringing the dead back from this vast and solitary tundra.

Late that night, the sin-eater entered the homes of the deceased and rested his palm upon their open coffins. Knots of small children climbed all around him, touching the casket's smooth satin lining, sitting bandy-legged atop the box as if it were a bucking bronco. The sin-eater scattered them by sounding the wood with a knock from his knuckles. *This man, this soldier, this once-child, he would say, has lived and died by the thunder of muskets and lightning-fire of cannons. He has fought for the shackling of a race and has in due turn ensured the enslavement of himself. For all are equal in the eyes of God. He Himself will girth each soul in His hands, be it more massive than the hills where you dwell, smaller than the cauldron's blackest cinder.* The sin-eater went on to tell the mourners he was the practitioner of an ancient ritual. He carried them back to a forgotten Scotland with his voice, telling them of a Highland rite once bequeathed to their kin, grown mute in their own blood with the crossing of an ocean many generations ago. By performing this ritual, he would assure the safe passage of the sinner's soul to Heaven. He snapped the buttons from the dead man's shirt and then asked the mourners to write down the misdeeds of the deceased on a piece of paper. In a pinched and eye-baffling script, a tearful mother stated, *Samuel Stackhouse was known to tar, feather, and hog-tie a soapbox abolitionist in Richmond.* One wrote an ornate pantoum telling of a soldier's numerous offenses. Another, rather vaguely, stated, *Of both the venial and the outright damnable kind were Christian Syler's sins.* When the piece of paper had made its rounds, the sin-eater drew up a list of his prices toward the bottom of the page. Nickels, dimes, quarters, all started adding up, which sent the mourners' fingers fishing deep into their pockets. Then the sin-eater scratched the sinner's name from the sheet and filled in the blank with his own signature. He placed the scrawled page upon the dead man's chest, asked that the deeds themselves enter the paper, and chewed the sheet into a pulp he could swallow. The mourners watched the paper slide behind the bulging coils of his windpipe. After he'd received his payment for the ritual, the sin-eater sought out the next soul to be pardoned. He saved many a man from damnation that night. The various statements joined in a massive tale that weaved its way through his entrails. *Silas Pinchbeck waded naked before the battle of Gettysburg with the daughter of a Union officer. One morning in Vicksburg, Silas Pinchbeck picked off a dozen song birds with a silver-plated pistol and watched their bloody feathers drift across the battlefield. Silas Pinchbeck stole a blind man's watch in Augusta, Georgia. Silas Pinchbeck drove the honed steel of his sabre between the shoulder blades of runaway slaves. Silas Pinchbeck. . . .* As the story gathered itself throughout the night, the sin-eater became a very rich man.

Children are too entirely hard to please these days. My granddaughter, who just turned fourteen in May, visits me down here in Flatrock for a couple weeks every summer. Since I seldom need to make plans at my age, I find us slipping instantly into the routine we've managed to establish over the last few years. We pull down the back-cracked board games from the hall closet and use pocket change for the missing pieces. We wade among the stones of Kitchen's Creek and she laughs at my ropy white calves as the water laps below the slacks' cuffs I grasp in my fists. We sip sodas under the town's tin awnings and blow notes across the bottles' glass mouths. When I mention catching fireflies in Mason jars, she says they have plenty enough fireflies in the Charleston suburbs. When she asks about the broken console TV, I tell her once again that it's there to hold up my begonias, whose growth I find far more fascinating to watch than any of the reruns. Her visits down here always seem to go a little something like that.

So today I thought maybe something new, a story, a tale that struck awe in my spine and brooded over me like a vast gloom when I was her age. But all she talks are these fashion magazines and missing a boy named Travis or Trevor and how she can't wait to go shopping for new school clothes that will surely impress one or the other or both of them. When I consider the huge gap between my granddaughter and me, how we will each touch a century the other troubles in even conceiving, I wonder if I should even bother continuing with the tale. I realize my granddaughter never saw those last Civil War veterans wandering our streets with all the luster crushed from their eyes. I know she doesn't think about that once-disputed border between Virginia and West Virginia, between slave and free state, that crossed through our very own back yards. And a boy named Johnny Paul, wearing knee socks and a satchel strapped across his shoulder, never snuck up behind her, grabbed a couple fingers' worth of flab at her hip, and sang into her ear,

> The sin-eater's gonna get ya',
> Flay ya', fillet ya',
> Make your soul pay.
> He'll heat ya', he'll eat ya',
> Start countin' down your days.

So should I bother showing a fourteen-year-old girl, whose idea of awe is having her pigtails pulled by a boy named Travis or Trevor, that this story has grown far beyond where I've just taken it? Maybe I could simply leave the sin-eater here as a rich man who's saved many souls. Maybe there is closure enough in the happiness such riches could bring, in the somewhat-weakly drawn-out moral of such a grand sacrifice.

"Papaw," my granddaughter says. "Is that it?"

"What more could you want?"

"That ending. Maybe if the sin-eater had done his ritual for free, then he'd have been a better man."

My granddaughter shows a sharpness I didn't expect here. Maybe I'll allow that her magnet school teaches more than just science and computers. "Okay then," I say, "he did it for free."

She gets up from her chair with a pretend huff and I recognize that sass I saw in her mother at this age. "How about lunch then?" she says. "I'll open a can of soup, let you think on it some more."

Maybe the story's like a can. Once it's open, there's no way to shut it back up. We eat the hot beef and barley, and I continue with the tale, pausing every now and then to wipe my runny nose upon my cuff.

So the six veterans who survived the war soon heard of the sin-eater and the doom booming in his voice. As their wives shaved the lice-ridden hair from their heads, they brooded upon the fate awaiting them after death. They pinned their shirt sleeves above their stumps, remembered their fingers touching the solid wood of axe handles, sinking just-honed blades into honeyed hams, running through the auburn hair of women, and believed their memories already carried a curse. Medals of honor jangled discreetly behind their breast pockets. When they turned to the Book, those bullet-stopping Bibles carried on the battlefield, the veterans found little comfort in God's Word. They imagined the shot that would have torn clean through those pages from cover to cover, collecting verses of salvation on the projectile's tip, suddenly making those words into a highly palpable thing, locking their hearts like a devout reader's soul on the final and consummate *Amen*.

Death beckoned. Death beckoned these veterans because they believed they could only be saved by passing into the hands of the sin-eater. While they were meant to die on distant battlefields, they expired in the places of their birth. The sin-eater straddled a handsome stallion, rode down from his mansion in the hills, and performed his ritual over their bodies. His fingers closed all the eyes in Flatrock that had seen battle. He headed home to his wife this one last time. Slapping his crop against the horse's rump, his gunny-sack packed with the spoils of a war waged within his own soul, the sin-eater forded runs and rode among outcroppings of granite and slid across the sun's first blaze like a silhouette cut from black paper by a shaky-handed artist. He came across a stand of apples tangled along the ridge's spine. When, suddenly, he saw a figure perched in his path, he dug the heels of his kid boots into the horse's ribs, jerked at fistfuls of its mane, twisting its wild-eyed head sideways. The morning-warmed fruit hung fragrant from the trees.

Standing there in typical cloven-hoofed and horned form, the devil touched the horse's flanks and stilled the beat of its raging blood. The sin-eater felt the slowed knock of the beast's heart, sensed a chill reaching up through its hide and into his loins. The devil smiled at the sin-eater. He liked games and he offered the man a deal to save his soul. If the sin-eater could show him the nature of human knowledge, reveal the gift God voiced into every chaotic lump, then the devil would free him of his burden. The sin-eater figured himself a fine enough stump orator. He accepted the devil's offer. He snapped an apple from its branch and told the devil that seeing the fruit was one way of knowing it. After he'd pared the fruit and sunk his teeth into its flesh, he said that eating it let his body experience its textures and flavors. The sin-eater remained silent for a moment. He then considered his own ritual, how the deeds of the sinner, though already committed, could be conjured up in the present with the words written on the page. Silas Pinchbeck, he thought, waded naked before the battle of Gettysburg with the daughter of a Union officer. He went on to tell the devil he believed a text about apples was a further way toward gaining some kind of understanding of the fruit. *And yet*, the sin-eater said, *words will always offer a shadowy veiled knowledge of the actual event. As in my ritual, the words must again become what they describe in the world. It is an alchemy of the highest order, one where the finest gold is transformed back into the most base of metals. For you can read, "When an apple seed is folded into the soil, it will grow into a tree and come to bear fruit." But a fathomless gulf will remain until those words are returned to the event where their true essence lies.* The devil nodded in approval. He then cleaved the ground with his hoof, pinched the seeds from the apple in the sin-eater's grasp, and buried them in the soil. *The proof of such knowledge,* the devil said, *will take some time. But I'm sure your soul is worth the years of wait.*

Most folks in Flatrock who tell this tale cannot recall how many winters the sin-eater warmed that apple sapling in the snow, how many summers he pruned back its blighted leaves, before it swelled with its first fruit or withered on toward a barren death.

Maybe devils just don't do it for my granddaughter. Maybe if I cast her Travis or Trevor in a role, sent him deep into the woods to keep watch over a man bearing witness to the growth of an apple tree, then she'd sit on the edge of her seat and listen up. But she seems dissatisfied at this point. The magnitude of the sin-eater's endeavor seems somewhat lost to her. When I was a child of her age, I heard a version of this tale that ended with nothing more than the devil burying the seeds and then speaking his final sentence. With the teller's last words, a vast silence sent our imaginations wandering toward a soundly-locked conclusion to the story. Johnny Paul and I had to know if the sin-eater sat and watched long enough to save his soul or if he walked away from those seeds and eternally damned himself. We waited. We sat and waited for that tree to grow in some storyteller's mind and bear fruit in his voice.

Unlike my granddaughter, we knew our Bibles backwards and forwards at her age. Even before the moss had sprouted in the depths of our armpits and between our hips, we quoted obscure laws from Exodus that pertained to the violation of virgins. We wondered at Onan's seed spilt upon the burning ground and how Samson managed to slaughter a thousand men with the jawbone of an ass. We also knew how the sin-eater's apple was drawn from the very fruit that cracked between Eve's teeth, how the devil and his temptation came from Christ wandering through the wilderness. These stories were made real to us by our own Preacher Karnes, who slapped his oily leather-backed Bible at the walnut pulpit, in the depths of a brush arbor erected beside a baptismal creek, before he told us the smoking brimstone devil himself crouched directly beneath our folding chairs. So for Johnny Paul and me, the sin-eater's tale held the immediacy and familiarity of Preacher Karnes' sermon. We couldn't stand the story ending with the uncertainty laid forth in those words spoken by the devil.

But the version I've just told my granddaughter offers yet another series of possibilities and no real conclusions. While the sin-eater may in fact have sat long enough to see the tree grow, there is no guarantee that it actually came to blossom and bore fruit. His eyes, grown dim from years of watching, may have witnessed nothing more than the withering of the bough. And furthermore, this ending seems to hold little regard for the sin-eater's free will. So suppose that he decided not to abandon the seeds that the devil planted. Then suppose he saw the tree blossom. Then where couldn't I take my granddaughter?

I tell her how Johnny Paul and I heard the tale told as such. Though frightened of how deep we'd be drawn into it, we tracked down a woman of such incredible age that only the knitting needles clicking between her fingers could possibly reveal her sex to us. Her collapsing shack rested high up in the hills. To get there, we forded creeks that left a squeak in our sneakers. We bellied storm-felled hardwoods, pinkening the skin on our chests, stoking a fire within our breasts. Once inside her dark quarters, we smelled the lazy fingers of smoke rising from the clay pipe she clutched between her jaws, and the wild herbs hanging in tight fragrant clumps along the ceiling beams. From under the folds of her knitting, she brought out a fist that seemed to have been buried within the earth for centuries. One of her knuckles unfolded and a fingernail ticked three times against the tabletop. We reached into our pockets for our money. When she tapped once more, a monstrous swell of smoke began pouring forth from her cheeks. I dug through my pockets, through those things that catch a young boy's eye in the woods and end up there, until I found my last nickel, which I laid on the wood as the white ghosts still boiled from the old woman's lungs.

The sin-eater's breath warmed the first apple blossom on a frozen morning in April. He cupped his aged fingers around the closed petals, exhaled in a low whistle across the flower's pistil. It was the first time in years he'd heard any sound break between his lips. When the sun rose over the ridge's spine and blazed across his back, he felt his skin prickle with the blood slowly thawing below his rags. He cast his shadow away from the bloom. The petals opened with the quiet of hands separating after a prayer. He slept. For he knew, come nightfall, when the last heat escaped from the earth, he would need to ring the tree with fire, building a wall of warmth against winter's last hold on these high hills, against this frost still glimmering like mica on the grass where he rested until sunset. He dreamed of the first fruit then. It held such an ideal form that his mind could conceive of little more than its plump roundness. There in the deep folds of his dream, he searched for the words to describe the fruit. But after years of not speaking, not hearing another person's voice, not reading a single word, the sin-eater feared he'd lost his language and the way in which it described and defined the world around him. He woke. He tried to interpret the labels stitched into his vest and britches, found the ornate lettering had been eaten by the moths who circled his head at night. With fingers as gnarled and toughened as the apple wood, he picked at a frayed gold thread, unraveled the few remaining letters, and obliterated them from his mind. Setting a fire against the sky, extinguishing the stars with its roils of smoke, the sin-eater stared through the flames with a great sense of loss. He shed the embers' ashy coats through the night with a stick and wondered if the unfolding blossoms would fathom the perfection his mind could barely even conjure.

June brought honey bees. Teeming among the branches and leaves, they carried pollen and dropped from bloom to bloom. The sin-eater traced their orbits and pinpointed their every dive. He watched them light on the collapsing rack of weathered bones that had been the horse he rode. Pinching one of the bees from the horse's emptied eye socket, he placed it humming on his tongue and listened to it resonate in his head like the now-lost voice that had once echoed through his skull. He tasted the pollen from the bee's wings. He tried to imagine his aged and wracked body in blossom, something coming to fruit within him. Since he neared the end of his trial, a trial lasting many falls bearing no apples, many winters carrying a promise of death, the sin-eater wondered if his burden was now slowly being exhumed from his blood. He ruminated over his feces and kept the scent of his flatulence under close scrutiny. Lifting a Mason jar of urine to the morning light, he swirled it against the sides and watched it bead across the lines of measurement raised within the glass. But he found no sign of his sins. He discovered not a single sentence, a single word, even a comma, that he'd swallowed all those years ago, which made him wonder how his release from this orchard would finally be punctuated.

One morning in August, the sin-eater looked down the bending line of a branch and saw at its farthest reach a small dot that he took for an apple. Still green, hard as any stone, the fruit brought a flood of tears to his eyes. He expected the devil to drop into his sight at any moment. He grinned through his remaining teeth, laughed as he thought of the devil brooding over the defeat dealt to him. But the sin-eater found himself alone long into that afternoon, into the next day, the next week, until the apple ripened and bent the branch under its weight. For fear that the devil had forgotten him there, he climbed to the highest branch of the tree with his knife clamped between his gums. The sin-eater began carving his story into the bark. It spiraled around the limbs, dropped down the apple tree's smooth trunk, telling of those veterans with the luster crushed from their eyes, the long journey through the woods, until he reached this very moment of his life, and wrote, *I am now writing that I am writing that I am writing that.* . . . Realizing he could go no further, the sin-eater plucked the girthy fruit from the bough and tucked it away among the folds of his rotten clothing. He returned to the tree and added, *P.S. I've taken the first fruit and gone home.*

Walking through the woods, realizing he'd already written himself into the future, the sin-eater watched the devil drop into his view and ruin his immediate plans of returning home. The devil asked him if he'd finally given up on his attempt to discover the essence behind his own statement. The sin-eater brought forth the apple and said, *The statement I've spoken, I've now experienced. Those words, as I told you when we first met, are returned to the event where their true essence lays.* The devil stroked his beard to a sharp and shiny point with his fingertips. *I believe,* he remarked, *that you said, "lies. Where their true essence lies." And to me, that seems quite the paradox, even worthy of an attempt by your God to prove. Now I must beg you, how can a word, in its true essence, lie?* The sin-eater felt both fear and anger storm through his entrails. *But even if I used the word "lies,"* he said, *I did not mean the verb to refer in any way to its definition of falsehood.* The devil smiled then. *There. Now. That is exactly the point. Because in any event you should have. For whether you mean it or not, the words you speak are boundless, open to endless meanings, harder to hold than a handful of water, harder to break than a bucking bronco. If you had stuck to your paradox just now, told me that a word's essence tells a lie through its multiple meanings, you would now be a man free of his countless sins.*

. . .

Johnny Paul and I wanted to knock the old woman from her wicker rocker. We felt cheated, hoodwinked, ready to ask for our money back, because we'd given her three weeks of Sunday offerings meant for Preacher Karnes' congregation plate. Her lips, tied tight around the stem of her pipe, which had almost gone cold by the end of her story, did not even part to exhale a last breath. Her ember cracked and glowed down into its ash. Then a thin trickle of blue smoke dribbled from her nostrils. When I heard the legs of Johnny Paul's chair scrape back across the worn floorboards, I gave the old woman one final look. "You can trust the devil," she said, "just about far as you can throw him. Try as I might for something quite different, he fooled me right into that very ending."

By telling my granddaughter what the old woman said to us, I ready her for what I must soon offer in way of a cumbersome gift. Because before we left late that afternoon, the old woman told Johnny Paul and me that the sin-eater's fate now rested in our own imaginations. She uncrossed her knitting needles in a quick swish of steel and offered me the piece of yarn pinched between her thumb and finger. "You can take this to help find your way out of the woods," she said. "If you reach the end of the line and don't know where you are, you can always track your path back here." We dropped down from the porch, a cloud of dust boiling around our shoes and across the ivy climbing along the railing. As we walked down into the hollow, the knitting unraveled from the broad folds draped across the old woman's caved-in shoulders. "And if you reach the end of the line and do in fact know where you are," she called down to us, "light the yarn on fire. This here's a quiet and little known place. At my age, I'd prefer no more visitors." Fire would crawl through the hollow that evening. We would imagine it creeping up the steps, leaving a shadow of ash scattered across the floorboards, offering the old woman's drowsing body an enormous and all-consuming warmth.

Johnny Paul, who became Jack in his teens, John later in life, then a name carved upon a gravestone overlooked by a lichen-eyed cherub, would leave me with all that we could manage to gather that day and thereafter. The devil had a certain wit and cunning, an ability to match our every move, that led our whispering in circles and down paths where walls rose before us. Our words formed labyrinths. Their meanings echoed back and forth through seemingly endless halls. When Johnny Paul received that first taste of death during his long illness, he whispered his sour reek into my ear and told me he'd figured a way to end the tale. "After I've passed on," he said, "remain silent until your own time comes. Only the final locking of our hearts and tongues can quiet down the devil."

Until today, I've continued to remain silent and merely ruminative. But as I believed the telling itself might lead me toward another conclusion, that I could at least engage my granddaughter in the tale otherwise, I once again took the sin-eater into the woods and sought a way to deliver him from the devil's grasp. This silence between us leaves me wishing for other mouths. For I am a very old man. I look at my granddaughter, hoping she'll understand the story, all that has come to surround it, all that has in the end come to surround me. Only her voice can allow me to know that I'm not alone in here.

"You told me, Papaw," she says, "that the devil thought words were all lies, right? Then what about the sin-eater's ritual? What, I mean, about the words he used there?"

"Are you referring," I ask, "to the words he eats?"

"Yeah. Are they true?" she asks. "Can they really stand for the misdeeds themselves?"

I sit back in my rocker, the tick of wicker filling the silence. "I don't know," I say. "Let's try it out."

When the devil's words finished their echoing among the hollows, the sin-eater expected an old-fashioned boiling of brimstone in his entrails and a whiff of burning sulfur in his nostrils. There was a moment where he waited, his voice poised on defeat, ready to offer his soul up to the fate he believed awaited it. But then he was struck with a strange idea that went exactly opposite to what he was about to say in his defense. *I know what you expect of me*, he began. *I need only say the sins I ate were not real sins. For if I acknowledge them as mere words, having no true essence, as you say, I would appear to be pure because the acts themselves will have remained all along with the dead who committed them. But I know I am a sinner. I am a sinner made of many mouths and the stories they tell. Those words filling many pages still weave me as I speak. While this is a precarious existence at best, there seems but one sin greater than those I already carry. And that is to clamp my remaining teeth against the words which have breathed me into being, to deny those sins I must now face to find redemption.*

"I'm sorry," I tell my granddaughter. "When I started speaking, I saw your mistake and couldn't allow the sin-eater to also be fooled into it."

"Where then," she asks, "does he go from here?"

"We," I say, "the question should now be, where do we go from here?"

When the sin-eater arrived at his home that evening, he saw a girl on the porch who appeared to be the very same child-bride he'd kissed on the cheek before departing for Flatrock all those years ago. She slapped at a dusty rug draped over the porch railing, her loose hair tossed above her shoulders against the light. The sin-eater wondered if his whole ordeal had been a dream, a sudden slumbering in the woods, a series of brutal seasons conjured up in his mind, which in fact had lasted a few short hours rather than all these years. But his fingers traced the lines of age furrowed below his eyes. His rags reeked of earth and woods. And from below the folds of his shirt, he brought forth an apple. He sounded its ripeness with a tap of his forefinger and then called out his wife's name.

A startled expression grew across the girl's face before she disappeared into the house. Climbing the porch, the sin-eater looked for something sure and familiar. His nostrils sought a gust from the honeysuckle that had once twined around the railings, a warm breath of the stew his wife had set to simmer the morning he'd left. Before the memory in his bones could ache for what was no longer there, a woman stepped into the doorway with her wet hands wringing themselves in an apron. The sin-eater now wondered if this was the woman he'd married all those years ago. He spoke her name again, asked her if she was indeed his wife. She shook her head, said, *No, Father.*

After he was guided into the parlor and sat in a chair where he once smoked deeply on his pipe, the sin-eater heard how his wife had been pregnant the day he'd left for Flatrock. During the delivery, she had died, while his daughter had lived. And this young girl, sitting here in silence, whom he'd at first mistaken for the child-bride he'd married, was in fact his granddaughter. Her large dark eyes loomed above her cheekbones. They conveyed a raw purity and a capacity for great understanding. Looking at his granddaughter, the sin-eater saw his own blood running across the generations, driven through the harsh seasons of his life without his foreknowledge, a seemingly full-fleshed precursor to his will. He knew then what he must do for his redemption.

He went to her at night. Where the moon broke upon his granddaughter's bed, the sin-eater sat and told his tale to the slumbering child wrapped within the quilts. She could not help but dream the story into being. She watched Civil War veterans pinning their shirt sleeves above their stumps, crouched with two boys as they sent a line of fire crawling through the woods, felt the warmth her grandfather breathed against the apple blossom. The sin-eater took great care with his words, for he knew not what devilish trick might descend upon his voice, trapping his granddaughter in the world he unspun from the silence. While the risks seemed great, he knew the tale must be told to save his soul. In every breath, a prayer.

His granddaughter began to speak in her sleep. I tell my granddaughter how she talked of the apple blossom and quoted obscure laws from Exodus. When the sin-eater reached the point in his story where he had to decide if there is any meaning in what we speak, his granddaughter reminded him of his own ritual of eating words. She told him they could get out of the woods by saying that those sentences never joined their deeds, which would prove that the sins had always remained with the dead who committed them. I then tell my grand-daughter how she's been fooled by the devil. By disavowing the words that have created her and the sin-eater, she has set her own tale toward a different con-clusion. I tell my granddaughter how the devil has trapped her there, how the sin-eater must walk out of the woods alone, calling back to her, trying to retrieve her from beneath the boughs of an apple tree, where she is slowly erased from his gaze.

Steven Millhauser

A Visit

It is always a pleasure to be able to include a story from Steven Millhauser in the pages of this annual—and this year he's back with another strange, enchanting, and thoroughly unclassifiable tale, reprinted from The New Yorker.

Millhauser is the author of several important and highly entertaining works of phantasmagorical modern fiction, including From the Realm of Morpheus, In the Penny Arcade, The Barnum Museum, *and* Little Kingdoms. *He won the World Fantasy Award for the first of his stories published in* The Year's Best Fantasy and Horror, *titled "The Illusionist" (1989), and last year he won the Pulitzer Prize for his novel* Martin Dressler. *Millhauser lives in upstate New York and teaches at Skidmore College.*

—T. W.

Although I had not heard from my friend in nine years, I wasn't surprised, not really, to receive a short letter from him dashed off in pencil, announcing that he had "taken a wife," and summoning me to visit him in some remote upstate town I had never heard of. "Come see me on the 16th and 17th" was what he had actually written. "Be here for lunch." The offhand peremptory tone was Albert all over. He had scribbled a map, with a little black circle marked "Village" and a little white square marked "My house." A wavy line connected the two. Under the line were the words "3½ miles, more or less." Over the line were the words "County Road 39." I knew those desolate little upstate villages, consisting of one Baptist church, three bars, and a gas station with a single pump, and I imagined Albert living at an ironic distance, with his books and his manias. What I couldn't imagine was his wife. Albert had never struck me as the marrying kind, though women had always liked him. I had plans for the weekend, but I cancelled them and headed north.

I still considered Albert my friend, in a way my best friend, even though I hadn't heard from him in nine years. He had once been my best friend and it was hard to think of him in any other way. Even in the flourishing time of our friendship, in the last two years of college and the year after, when we saw each other daily, he had been a difficult and exacting friend, scornful of convention though quiet in his own habits, subject to sudden flare-ups and silences, earnest but with an edge of mockery, intolerant of mediocrity and cursed with an unfailing scent for the faintly fraudulent in a gesture or a phrase or a face. He was handsome in a sharp-featured New England way—his family, as he put it, had lived in Connecticut since the fall of the Roman Empire—but despite the inviting smiles of girls in his classes he confined himself to brisk affairs with leather-jacketed town girls with whom he had nothing in common. After graduating, we roomed together for a year in a little college town full of cafés and bookstores, sharing the rent and drifting from one part-time job to another, as I put off the inevitable suit-and-tie life that awaited me while he mocked my conventional fear of becoming conventional, defended business as America's only source of originality, and read his Plato and his *Modern Chess Openings* and tootled his flute. One day he left, just like that, to start what he called a new life. In the next year I received postcards from small towns all over America, showing pictures of Main Streets and quaint village railroad stations. They bore messages such as "Still looking" or "Have you seen my razor? I think I left it on the bathtub." Then there was nothing for six months, and then a sudden postcard from Eugene, Oregon, on which he described in minute detail a small unknown wooden object that he had found in the top drawer of the bureau in his rented bedroom, and then nine years of silence. During that time I had settled into a job and almost married an old girlfriend. I had bought a house on a pleasant street lined with porches and maples, thought quite a bit about my old friend Albert, and wondered whether this was what I had looked forward to, this life I was now leading, in the old days, the days when I still looked forward to things.

The town was even worse than I had imagined. Slowly I passed its crumbling brick paper mill with boarded-up windows, its rows of faded and flaking two-family houses with sagging front porches where guys in black T-shirts sat drinking beer, its tattoo parlor and its sluggish stream. County Road 39 wound between fields of Queen Anne's lace and yellow ragweed, with now and then a melancholy house or a patch of sun-scorched corn. Once I passed a rotting barn with a caved-in roof. At 3.2 miles on the odometer I came to a weathered house near the edge of the road. A bicycle lay in the high grass of the front yard and an open garage was entirely filled with old furniture. Uncertainly I turned onto the unpaved drive, parked with the motor running, and walked up to the front door. There was no bell. I knocked on the wooden screen door, which banged loudly against the frame, and a tall, barefoot, and very pale woman with sleepy eyes came to the door, wearing a long rumpled black skirt and a lumberjack shirt over a T-shirt. When I asked for Albert she looked at me suspiciously, shook her head quickly twice, and slammed the inner door. As I walked back to the car I saw her pale face looking out at me past a pushed-aside pink curtain. It occurred to me that perhaps Albert had married this woman and that she was insane. It further occurred to me, as I backed out of the drive, that I really ought to turn back now, right now, away from this misguided adventure in the wilderness. After all, I hadn't seen him for nine long years; things were bound to be different. At 4.1 miles on the odometer I rounded a bend of rising road and saw a shadowy house set back in a cluster of dusty-looking trees. I turned in to the unknown dirt drive, deep-rutted and sprouting weeds, and as I stepped on the brake with a sharp sense of desolation and betrayal, for here I was, in the god-forsaken middle of nauseating nowhere, prowling around like a fool and a criminal, the front door opened and Albert came out, one hand in his pocket and one hand waving.

He looked the same, nearly the same, though browner and leatherier than I remembered, as if he had lived all those years in the sun, his face a little longer and leaner—a handsome man in jeans and a dark shirt. "I wondered if you'd show up," he said when he reached the car, and suddenly seemed to study me. "You look just the way you ought to," he then said.

I let the words settle in me. "It depends what I ought to look like," I answered, glancing at him sharply, but he only laughed.

"Isn't this a great place?" he said, throwing out one arm as he began carrying my travelling bag to carry toward the house. "Ten acres and they were practically giving it away. First day after I bought the place I go walking around and bingo! What do you think I found? Grapes. Billions of grapes. An old fallen-down grape arbor, grapes growing all over the ground. Italy in New York. Wait till you see the pond."

We stepped into the shade of the high trees, a little thicket of pines and maples, that grew close to the house. Big bushes climbed halfway up the windows. It struck me that the house was well protected from view, a private place, a shadowy isle in a sea of fields. "And yet," I said, looking around for his wife, "Somehow I never thought of you as getting married, somehow."

"Not back then," he said. "Watch that rail."

We had climbed onto the steps of the long, deep-shaded front porch, and I had grasped a wobbly iron handrail that needed to be screwed into the wood. A coil of old garden hose hung over the porch rail. A few hornets buzzed about the ceiling light. On the porch stood a sunken chaise longue, an old three-speed bicycle, a metal garbage can containing a rusty snow shovel, and a porch swing on which sat an empty flowerpot.

He opened the wooden screen door and with a little flourish urged me in. "Humble," he said, "but mine own." He looked at me with a kind of excitement, an excitement I couldn't entirely account for, but which reminded me of the old excitement, and I wondered, as I entered the house, whether that was what I had been looking for, back then. The house was cool and almost dark, the dark of deep shade lightened by streaks of sun. Under the half-drawn windowshades I saw bush-branches growing against the glass. We had entered the living room, where I noticed a rocking chair that leaned too far back and a couch with one pillow. Ancient wallpaper showed faded scenes of some kind repeating themselves all over the room. Albert, who seemed more and more excited, led me up the creaking worn-edged stairs to my room—a bed with a frilly pink spread, a lamp table on which lay a screwdriver with a transparent yellow handle—and quickly back down.

"You must be starving," he said, with that odd quiver of excitement, as he led me through an open doorway into a dining room that was almost dark. At a big round table there were three place settings, which glowed whitely in the gloom. One of the round-backed chairs appeared to be occupied. Only as I drew closer through the afternoon darkness did I see that the occupant was a large frog, perhaps two feet high, which sat with its throat resting on the table edge. "My wife," Albert said, looking at me fiercely, as if he were about to spring at my face. I felt I was being tested in some fiendish way. "Pleased to meet you," I said harshly, and sat down across from her. The table lay between us like a lake. I had thought she might be something else, maybe a stuffed toy of some sort, but even in the dark daylight I could see the large moist eyes looking here and there, I could see her rapid breathing and smell her marshy odor. I thought that Albert must be making fun of me in some fashion, trying to trick me into exposing what he took to be my hideous bourgeois soul, but whatever his game I wasn't going to give myself away.

"Help yourself," Albert said, pushing toward me a breadboard with a round loaf and a hunk of cheese on it. A big-bladed knife lay on the table and I began cutting the bread. "And if you'd cut just a little piece of cheese for Alice." I immediately cut a little piece of cheese for Alice. Albert disappeared into the kitchen and in the room's dusk I stared across the round table at Alice before looking away uncomfortably. Albert returned with a wax carton of orange juice and a small brown bottle of beer, both of which he set before me. "The choice," he said with a little bow, "is yours entirely." He picked up the piece of cheese I had cut for Alice, placed it on her plate, and broke it into smaller pieces. Alice looked at him—it seemed to me that she looked at him—with those moist and heavy-lidded eyes, and flicked up her cheese. Then she placed her throat on the table edge and sat very still.

Albert sat down and cut himself a piece of bread. "After lunch I want to show you the place. Take you down to the pond and so on." He looked at me, tilting his head in a way I suddenly remembered. "And you? It's been a while."

"Oh, still a roving bachelor," I said, and immediately disliked my fatuous tone. I had a sudden urge to talk seriously to Albert, as we'd done in the old days, watching the night turn slowly gray through our tall, arched windows. But I felt constrained. It had been too long a time, and though he had summoned me after all these years, though he had shown me his wife, it was all askew somehow, as if he hadn't shown me anything, as if he'd kept himself hidden away. And I remembered that even then, in the time of our friendship, he had seemed intimate and secretive at the same time, as if even his revelations were forms of concealment. "Not that I have any fixed plan," I continued, "I see women, but they're not the right one. You know, I was always sure I'd be the one to get married, not you."

"It wasn't something I planned. But when the moment comes, you'll know." He looked at Alice with tenderness and suddenly leaned over and touched the side of her head lightly with his fingertips.

"How did you," I began, and stopped. I felt like bursting into screams of wild laughter, or of outrage, pure outrage, but I held myself down; I pretended everything was fine. "I mean, how did you meet? You two. If I may ask."

"So formal! If you may ask! Down by the pond—if I may answer. I saw her in the reeds one day. I'd never seen her before, but she was always there, after that. I'll show you the exact place after lunch."

His little mocking rebuke irritated me, and I recalled how he had always irritated me, and made me retreat deeply into myself, because of some little reproach, some little ironic look, and it seemed strange to me that someone who irritated me and made me retreat into myself was also someone who released me into a freer version of myself, a version superior to the constricted one that had always felt like my own hand on my throat. But who was Albert, after all, that he should have the power to release me or constrict me—this man I no longer knew, with his run-down house and his ludicrous frog-wife. Then I ate for a while in sullen silence, looking only at my food, and when I glanced up I saw him looking at me kindly, almost affectionately.

"It's all right," he said quietly, as if he understood, as if he knew how difficult it was for me, this journey, this wife, this life. And I was grateful, as I had always been, for we had been close, he and I, back then.

After lunch he insisted on showing me his land—his domain, as he called it. I had hoped that Alice might stay behind, so that I could speak with him alone, but it was clear that he wanted her to come with us. So as we made our way out the back door and into his domain she followed along, taking hops about two strides in length, always a little behind us or a little before. At the back of the house a patch of overgrown lawn led to a vegetable garden on both sides of a grassy path. There were vines of green peas and stringbeans climbing tall sticks, clusters of green peppers, rows of carrots and radishes identified by seed packets on short sticks, fat heads of lettuce and flashes of yellow squash—a rich and well-tended oasis, as if the living center of the house were here, on the outside, hidden in back. At the end of the garden grew a scattering of fruit trees, pear and cherry and plum. An old wire fence with a broken wooden gate separated the garden from the land beyond.

We walked along a vague footpath through fields of high grass, passed into thickets of oak and maple, crossed a stream. Alice kept up the pace. Alice in sunlight, Alice in the open air, no longer seemed a grotesque pet, a monstrous mistake of Nature, a nightmare frog and freakish wife, but rather a companion of sorts, staying alongside us, resting when we rested—Albert's pal. And yet it was more than that. For, when she emerged from high grass or tree shade into full sunlight, I sensed for a moment, with an inner start, Alice as she was, Alice in the sheer brightness and fullness of her being, as if the dark malachite sheen of her skin, the pale shimmer of her throat, the moist warmth of her eyes, were as natural and mysterious as the flight of a bird. Then I would tumble back into myself and realize that I was walking with my old friend beside a monstrous lumbering frog who had somehow become his wife, and a howl of inward laughter and rage would erupt in me, calmed almost at once by the rolling meadows, the shady thickets, the black crow rising from a tree with slowly lifted and lowered wings, rising higher and higher into the pale blue sky touched here and there with delicate fernlike clouds.

The pond appeared suddenly, on the far side of a low rise. Reeds and cattails grew in thick clusters at the marshy edge. We sat down on flat-topped boulders and looked out at the green-brown water, where a few brown ducks floated, out past fields to a line of low hills. There was a desolate beauty about the place, as if we had come to the edge of the world. "It was over there I first saw her," Albert said, pointing to a cluster of reeds. Alice sat off to one side, low to the ground, in a clump of grass at the water's edge. She was still as a rock, except for her sides moving in and out as she breathed. I imagined her growing in the depths of the pond, under a mantle of lily pads and mottled scum, down below the rays of green sunlight, far down, at the silent bottom of the world.

Albert leaned back on both elbows, a pose I remembered well, and stared out at the water. For a long while we sat in a silence that struck me as uncomfortable, though he himself seemed at ease. It wasn't so much that I felt awkward in Alice's presence as that I didn't know what I had come all this way to say. Did I really want to speak at all? Then Albert said, "Tell me about your life." And I was grateful to him, for that was exactly what I wanted to talk about, my life. I told him about my almost-marriage, my friendships that lacked excitement, my girlfriends who lacked one thing or another, my good job that somehow wasn't exactly what I had been looking for, back then, my feeling that things were all right but not as all right as they might be, that I was not unhappy but not really happy either, but caught in some intermediate place, looking both ways. And as I spoke it seemed to me that I was looking in one direction toward a happiness that was growing vaguer, and in the other direction toward an unhappiness that was emerging more clearly, without yet revealing itself completely.

"It's hard," Albert then said, in the tone of someone who knew what I was talking about, and though I was soothed by his words, which were spoken gently, I was disappointed that he didn't say more, that he didn't show himself to me.

And I said, "Why did you write to me, after all this time?" which was only another way of saying, why didn't you write to me, in all this time.

"I waited," he said, "until I had something to show you." That was what he said: something to show me. And it seemed to me then that if all he had to show me after nine years was his run-down house and his marshy frog-wife, then I wasn't so badly off, in my own way, not really.

After that we continued walking about his domain, with Alice always at our side. He showed me things, and I looked. He showed me the old grape arbor that he had put back up; unripe green grapes, hard as nuts, hung in bunches from the decaying slats. "Try one," he said, but it was bitter as a tiny lemon. He laughed at my grimace. "We like 'em this way," he said, plucking a few into his palm, then tossing them into his mouth. He pulled off another handful and held them down to Alice, who devoured them swiftly: flick flick flick. He showed me a woodpecker's nest, and a slope of wild tiger lilies, and an old toolshed containing a rusty hoe and a rusty rake. Suddenly, from a nearby field, a big bird rose up with a loud beating of wings. "Did you see that!" cried Albert, seizing my arm. "A pheasant! Protecting her young. Over there." In the high grass six fuzzy little ducklike creatures walked in a line, their heads barely visible.

At dinner Alice sat in her chair with her throat resting on the edge of the table while Albert walked briskly in and out of the kitchen. I was pleased to see a fat bottle of red wine, which he poured into two juice glasses. The glasses had pictures of Winnie-the-Pooh and Eeyore on them. "Guy gave them to me at a gas station," Albert said. He frowned suddenly, pressed his fingertips against his forehead, looked up with a radiant smile. "I've got it. The more it *snows* tiddely-pom, the more it *goes* tiddely-pom." He poured a little wine into a cereal bowl and placed it near Alice.

Dinner was a heated-up supermarket chicken, fresh squash from his garden, and big bowls of garden salad. Albert was in high spirits, humming snatches of songs, lighting a stub of candle in a green wine bottle, filling our wineglasses and Alice's bowl again and again, urging me to drink up, crunching lustily into his salad. The cheap wine burned my tongue but I kept drinking, taken by Albert's festive spirit, eager to carry myself into his mood. Even Alice kept finishing the wine he put in her cereal bowl. The candleflame seemed to grow brighter in the darkening air of the room; through bush-branches in the window I saw streaks of sunset. A line of wax ran down the bottle and stopped. Albert brought in his breadboard, more salad, another loaf of bread. And as the meal continued I had the sense that Alice, sitting there with her throat resting on the table edge, flicking up her wine, was looking at Albert with those large eyes of hers, moist and dark in the flamelight. She was looking at him and trying to attract his attention. Albert was leaning back in his chair, laughing, throwing his arm about as he talked but it seemed to me that he was darting glances back at her. Yes, they were exchanging looks, there at the darkening dinner table, looks that struck me as amorous. And as I drank, I was filled with a warm, expansive feeling, which took in the room, the meal, the Winnie-the-Pooh glasses, the large moist eyes, the reflection of the candleflame in the window, the glances of Albert and his wife; for after all, she was the one he had chosen, up here in the wilderness, and who was I to say what was right, in such matters.

Albert leaped up and returned with a bowl of pears and cherries from his fruit trees, and filled my glass again. I was settling back with my warm, expansive feeling, looking forward to a night of talk stretching lazily before me, when Albert announced that it was getting late, and he and Alice would be retiring. I had the run of the house. Just be sure to blow out the candle. Nighty night. Through the roar of wine I was aware of my plunging disappointment. He pulled back her chair and she hopped to the floor. Together they left the dining room and disappeared into the dark living room, where he turned on a lamp so dim that it was like lighting a candle. I heard him creaking up the stairs and thought I heard a dull thumping sound, as I imagined Alice lumbering her way up beside him.

I sat listening to the thumps and creaks of the upper hall, a sudden sharp rush of water in the bathroom sink, a squeak—what was that squeak?—a door shutting. In the abrupt silence, which seemed to spread outward from the table in widening ripples, I felt abandoned, there with the wine and the candle and the glimmering dishes. Yet I saw that it was bound to be this way, and no other way, for I had watched their amorous looks; it was only to be expected. And hadn't he, back then, been in the habit of unexpected departures? Then I began to wonder whether they had ever taken place, those talks stretching into the gray light of dawn, or whether I had only desired them. Then I imagined Alice hopping onto the white sheets. And I tried to imagine frog-love, its possible pleasures, its oozy raptures, but I turned my mind violently away, for in the imagining I felt something petty and cruel, something in the nature of a violation.

I drank down the last of the wine and blew out the candle. From the dark room where I sat I could see a ghostly corner of the refrigerator in the kitchen and a dim-lit reddish couch-arm in the living room, like a moonlit dead flower. A car passed on the road. Then I became aware of the crickets, whole fields and meadows of them, the great hum that I had always heard rising from back yards and vacant lots in childhood summers, the long sound of summer's end. And yet it was only the middle of summer, was it not, just last week I had spent a day at the beach. So for a long time I sat at the dark table, in the middle of a decaying house, listening to the sound of summer's end. Then I picked up my empty glass, silently saluted Albert and his wife, and went up to bed.

But I could not sleep. Maybe it was the wine, or the mashed mattress, or the early hour, but I lay there twisting in my sheets, and as I turned restlessly, the day's adventures darkened in my mind and I saw only a crazed friend, a ruined house, an ugly and monstrous frog. And I saw myself, weak and absurd, wrenching my mind into grotesque shapes of sympathy and understanding. At some point I began to slide in and out of dreams, or perhaps it was a single long dream broken by many half-wakings. I was walking down a long hall with a forbidden door at the end. With a sense of mournful excitement I opened the door and saw Albert standing with his arms crossed, looking at me sternly. He began to shout at me, his face became very red, and bending over he bit me on the hand. Tears ran down my face. Behind him someone rose from a chair and came toward us. "Here," said the newcomer, who was somehow Albert, "use this." He held up a handkerchief draped over his fist, and when I pulled off the handkerchief a big frog rose angrily into the air with wild flapping of its wings.

I woke tense and exhausted in a sun-streaked room. Through a dusty window I saw tree branches with big three-lobed leaves and between the leaves pieces of blue sky. It was nearly nine. I had three separate headaches: one behind my left eye, one in my right temple, and one at the back of my head. I washed and dressed quickly and made my way down the darkening stairs, through a dusk that deepened as I drew toward the bottom. On the faded wallpaper I could make out two scenes repeating themselves into the distance: a faded boy in blue lying against a faded yellow haystack with a horn at his side, and a girl in white drawing water from a faded well.

The living room was empty. The whole house appeared to be deserted. On the round table in the twilight of the dining room the dishes still sat from dinner. All I wanted was a cup of coffee before leaving. In the slightly less gloomy kitchen I found an old jar of instant coffee and a chipped blue teapot decorated with a little decal picturing an orange brontosaurus. I heard sharp sounds, and through the leaves and branches in the kitchen window I saw Albert with his back to me, digging in the garden. Outside the house it was a bright, sunny day. Beside him, on the dirt, sat Alice.

I brought my cup of harsh-tasting, stale coffee into the dining room and drank it at the table while I listened to the sounds of Albert's shovel striking the soil. It was peaceful in the darkish room, at the round brown table. A thin slant of sun glittered in the open kitchen. The sun-slant mingled with the whistle of a bird, leaves in the window, the brown dusk, the sound of the shovel striking loam, turning it over. It occurred to me that I could simply pack my things now, and glide away without the awkwardness of a leave-taking.

I finished the dismal coffee and carried the cup into the kitchen, where the inner back door stood slightly open. There I paused, holding the empty cup in my hand. Obeying a sudden impulse, I opened the door a little more and slipped between it and the wooden screen door.

Through the buckled screen I could see Albert some ten feet away. His sleeves were rolled up and his foot was pressing down on the blade of the shovel. He was digging up grassy dirt at the edge of the garden, turning it over, breaking up the soil, tossing away clumps of grass roots. Nearby sat Alice, watching him. From time to time, as he moved along the edge of the garden, he would look over at her. Their looks seemed to catch for a moment, before he returned to his garden. Standing in the warm shade of the half-open door, looking through the rippling screen at the garden quivering with sunlight, I sensed a mysterious rhythm between Albert and his wife, a trembling lightness or buoyancy, a kind of quivering sunlit harmony. It was as if both of them had shed their skins and were mingling in air, or dissolving into light—and as I felt that airy mingling, that tender dissolution, as I sensed that hidden harmony, clear as the ringing of a distant bell, it came over me that what I lacked, in my life, was exactly that harmony. It was as if I were composed of some hard substance that could never dissolve in anything, whereas Albert had discovered the secret of air. But my throat was beginning to hurt, the bright light burned my eyes, and setting down my cup on the counter, which sounded like the blow of a hammer, I pushed open the door and went out.

Albert turned around in the sun. "Sleep well?" he said, running the back of his hand slowly across his dripping forehead.

"Well enough. But you know, I've got to be getting back. A million things to do! You know how it is."

"Sure," Albert said. He rested both hands on the top of the long shovel handle and placed his chin on his hands. "I know how it is." His tone struck me as brilliantly poised between understanding and mockery.

He brought my bag down from my room and loaded it in the car. Alice had hopped through the dining room and living room and had come to rest in the deep shade of the front porch. It struck me that she kept carefully out of sight of the road. Albert bent over the driver's window and crossed his arms on the door. "If you're ever up this way," he said, but who would ever be up that way, "drop in." "I'll do that," I said. Albert stood up and stretched out an elbow, rubbed his shoulder. "Take care," he said, and gave a little wave and stepped away.

As I backed up the dirt driveway and began edging onto County Road 39, I had the sense that the house was withdrawing into its trees and shadows, fading into its island of shade. Albert had already vanished. From the road I could see only a stand of high trees clustered about a dark house. A few moments later, at the bend of the road, I glanced back again. I must have waited a second too long, because the road was already dipping, the house had sunk out of sight, and in the bright sunshine I saw only a scattering of roadside trees, a cloudless sky, fields of Queen Anne's lace stretching away.

Sonia Gernes

A Globe of Glass

Sonia Gernes was born in Winona, Minnesota, and is a professor of English at Notre Dame. She has published poetry, stories, and novels including A Breeze Called the Fremantle Doctor: Poems/Tales, Women at Forty, The Mutes of Sleepy Eye, Brief Lives, and The Way to St. Ives. In 1993 she was featured on the video "North American Women Writers' Spirit and Society."

"A Globe of Glass" is a magical tale spun as delicately as the art of the Franconian glass-blower at the heart of the story. It comes from the fall issue of The Georgia Review.

—T. W.

The day that I was born—in the Old Country, in Franconia—a baby floated up to God in a canopy of red balloons. My mother saw it: a poppy of many petals blooming against the sky. She said at first it looked like the bishop's cope floating by magic over the town, then it became a flower trailing something white. As it grew closer, drifting toward the west, she could see that twenty or thirty red balloons were bearing a small oval basket.

My mother was on her way to the furnace by the river, to bring my father his midday meal. My father was a master glazier and citizen of Arnstein. He worked, as his father had, in a shop in the lower floor of our house, framing windows and cutting glass. But when the window business was slow, he turned to blowing glass containers, a skill he had learned as a journeyman. For this, he would use a fine silver sand and melt it in a special forge next to the blacksmith's by the river.

When the glazier's forge was fully fired, as it was the day that I was born, my father would not come home to eat. After all, glass that is poppy-red and ready for blowing is more important than a pork hock and spaetzle. So my mother was bringing dinner in a basket that day in late September—enough for him and the apprentice. Her belly weighed more than her basket, she says, and the steepness of the hill was knitting a stitch in her side, so she paused just below the gate in the city wall, put down her basket and rested her backside on a stone post left over from the days when the city had a drawbridge. That's when the canopy of balloons caught her eye.

Arnstein is not a very large city even now. Then it boasted about three thousand souls, mostly huddled inside the old city wall. And the Wern is not a very large river, so everything was rather close together and my mother's eyes were good. This is important, because when the falconer stepped out of the Bishop's wood on the other side of the Wern, she could see him clearly. Falconry was not much of a sport in our region, even for the well-to-do, but my mother recognized him for what he was: a man with a bird of some sort, perhaps a peregrine, on his leather-wrapped wrist; he was wearing a green vest and a green hat of a style that was not familiar.

The sight was nothing she had expected to see: a lazy red flower bobbling in the sky, a falconer shading his eyes against the glint the sun made on the water. For a moment everything was still, she says, as though a painter had posed it for his brush, and then she saw the leather wrist across the river flick, and the falcon's wings gulp the air as it rose, rose above the freckled water. The falcon seemed wary at first, or perhaps confused—after all, this prey was neither a rodent nor a feckless lark—but after some cautious reconnaissance, it flew high above the balloons, circled twice, and dropped down like a stone, talons skidding across the red rubber.

She laughed, my mother says, to see the prey turn to air. The falcon clenched itself and pulled back against expected weight, but it captured only three smart pops of sound and a shred of red rubber that dangled from its claw. That shred might have been a bit of flesh dripping blood, she says, but the falcon ignored it, gaining height for a second attack. Then it circled, dropped silent and swift. More balloons burst, and this time the falcon recovered faster, rose and fell without circling, and when about a third of the balloons had vanished into little retorts like guns from another valley, the canopy began to drift, left and downward, until it tangled about halfway up in the linden tree just beyond my father's forge. My mother does not know what happened to the falcon.

"Franz, come look! Come look!" she called, stumbling toward the door of the forge. She had forgotten the stitch in her side, the bulk of her eight-and-a-half months belly. She had grabbed her basket in one hand and her skirts in the other and ran most of the path. But when she reached the door, my father had just inserted the blowing tube into the furnace and was drawing out a fiery glob, tensing his cheeks to form a perfect glass to sell in the market in Wurzburg.

"Kurt, go look," he said to the apprentice, thinking it was nothing, for my mother was always excitable. My father continued to draw in his breath, pouching cheeks that were almost as strong as his hands, for in the glass-blowing trade, air must triumph over all the other elements. My father blew a perfect glass that day—the most beautiful he had ever produced—but only one, for in the time it took him to stretch the glob to the proper size, flatten the bottom, and open the top, Kurt was up the tree. And in the time it took to draw out another molten orb and pouch his cheeks for the first and then the second blow, my mother had the basket in her arms, and her shrieks were much louder than any furnace.

"Tell what it looked like," I sometimes say, because she is apt to forget that part and skip to the letter.

"Wax," she says, "wax made at dusk and getting darker. A boy child almost newborn, wrapped in a christening dress with lace all down the front, wearing a little knitted bonnet."

"Tell what he had in his hand," I say.

"A toy soldier, a tiny one carved out of wood and painted like those that come in sets from a campaign. It was tied to his wrist with a scrap of ribbon."

"And the other ribbons?" I prompt.

"White ribbons wrapped like swaddling clothes," she says. "They're what held him in, but a blue ribbon bound the letter to his chest . . ."

She likes to recite the letter. She remembers it by heart:

Heavenly Father:

I send my little Kilian up to You with all the balloons that I have left. The Madonna will take care of him if I am delayed. He brings the soldier to give to his father, the last that ever he made. I hid it in my bodice when the men came.

Tell Kilian to wait for me. Soon I shall float too.

Maria Sabina Knopf

Because the woman signed her name, the constable was able to trace her: a village about thirty kilometers away, a story of despair that was all too common in those years. Her husband was a toymaker, a craftsman like my father, but young and a little reckless, and heavily in debt. He got drunk the night his son was born, boasted that his best feats had been performed in the dark, and taking his hunting knife and two of his friends, went off to the woods to poach a trophy in honor of his heir. There was no moon that night, the villagers said; the stars were clouded over. So perhaps they got lost, or perhaps something frightened them. Perhaps the landowner's dogs took their scent, and as they ran they lost their sense of direction. In any event, only two of the men fell into the quarry they all knew was there, and only one of them died, but in less time than the sun takes to make its daily round, Maria Sabina was both a mother and a widow.

That in itself might have been enough to turn her brain, but grief thinned her milk, and the child wailed, and her husband had been secretive about the debts. Her own people were farm laborers, gone east toward Poland in search of better crops to pick, so she was alone in the shop, crooning to the babe, when the men came with a warrant for all her husband's chattel. She may have snapped then, separating reason from the hands that moved, the voice that spoke. Or she may have remained preternaturally calm, thrusting the balloons into her petticoat pocket while the men were examining the tools. She may have put more than the tiny soldier into her bodice. When the men left, saying they would return on the morrow for what remained—the cider casks in the base-ment, the klefters of cut firewood—she closed all the shutters behind them and lit a light in the shop and one in the kitchen. (That much was known in the village—a neighbor remembered seeing the lights.) Then Maria Sabina took a small whitewashed basket that was left to her. Whether or not she had helium, she knew how hot air ascends, and how in happier days her husband prepared balloons for the festivals.

Sometime near dawn, in a wind that rattled the windows of those who happened to be awake, she floated the child up to God. And whether he had died in the night or still breathed when she cut the basket loose—or whether she smothered him to make the journey shorter—no one would know. She kept the promise she made in the letter: she too floated soon. They found her in the river.

My mother, of course, did not know Maria Sabina's story when the apprentice reached for a basket whose contents he could not see and dropped it down to her. All she knew was that in the last month of her sixth pregnancy (she was thirty-three years old, and one child was already dead), there had been a sudden gaiety in the sky—a red bloom above the late September trees. The sight had lifted her flagging energy; and now a mysterious parcel had descended. She held out her arms to receive it, then lifted her apron for a surer catch.

She thought it was wax when she first beheld it—a little Jesus like the one in the Christmas crèche—but the color, of course, was wrong, and then she noticed a crease of dirt at the child's tiny wrist, little grains of dried-pus sand at the corners of his eyes, and she knew that this was real.

"And then?" I used to say, but at this point the story always switches to my father. He tells how he heard her screams and put down the half-blown glass to rush out to the linden tree. He remembers that she was clutching the basket with locked fingers, her arms fully extended with elbows also locked and a look he had never seen spread across her face, as though all the goblins that ride in the night had suddenly come and fetched her.

Kurt had come down from the tree, and together he and my father pried the basket loose, made her sit down, and brought her the beer from the dinner basket. People came running, of course. The blacksmith brought a bucket of river water to cool her off, and his wife, who had caught sight of the balloons just as they reached the linden tree, took the basket away in the direction of the parish church, crooning as though it really were the Baby Jesus.

My mother did not speak and did not attempt to rise, but she was breathing strangely, rolling her eyes into her head and arching her back as my father had seen her do when she was in labor before, and the pains were too swift to allow many words.

"Quick," he said to Kurt, "the midwife—the house next to the butcher's on Market."

Kurt was fleet of foot in youth, though later he was crippled, and before my mother had broken her silence, he was back again, the midwife panting behind him.

"No, no," the midwife said when my father wanted to pull his wife up the hill in a vegetable cart and put her into the big carved bed in the chamber off the dining room, "You ought not to move her at all, but you'll have to for decency's sake" (for some of the crowd was still there gawking).

That's how it happened that I was born in a glazier's forge, in the farthest corner, on a sand sack that was the cleanest thing they could find, with a furnace full of molten glass glowing to one side and sweat greasing all three of their bodies.

The birth was quick, I'm told. I lived, and my mother lived, and when she was sure I had turned properly pink and my cry was lusty as any of her others, she began to speak again. "Eva," she said. "Name her Eva, because the world stopped and now it has begun again." (That's how she tells it, anyway. My father says I was named for his sister who agreed to be godmother when they took me to the church.)

The story would seem to end there—a baby pink and howling, a woman carried up the hill, the toymaker's child gone back to God. But if you had entered the glazier's forge that day and looked around, there on the workbench, forgotten when the screams began, was the glass my father was blowing when my mother reached for the toymaker's son. He had already made one, you remember: a perfect glass, straight and true, in that greenish tint the river takes when the mist lifts on an autumn morning. The second was barely formed. It was still little more than an awkward bubble, collapsed on the side where in haste he had put it down. And the material itself—perhaps from the sudden jarring, perhaps from cooling too fast—was cracked and crazed, a jumble of lines, intact and yet internally shattered.

My father broke it off the tube and flung it back into the furnace to melt again, because at this point he did not need a reminder. He had already seen his baby's eyes when she ceased her lusty howl and opened them to take in the world of a glazier's forge. One eye was perfect, a soft gray-green that would clarify into a color like the steady pool below a spring. The other was cracked, crazed, rolling loose in the socket. Splinters of green seemed to cover the space where the pupil should have been, and the whole was made of shards that failed to form a circle.

It was not the end of things. My mother gave birth five more times in the next seven years, though always in her bed, and always without portents. Three of those five children lived, so there were eight of us in all, one son and seven daughters, and people in Arnstein said things could be worse. I grew, a thin girl with a fine, straight nose, a forehead too white and too tall, and brown hair with no hint of the red that the sun still found in my mother's. I saw whatever I could with one perfect eye, and that sight has brought me as far as America, but alone of my sisters, I am unwed. I listen again and again to the tale of my birth, each time hoping that it will come out a little differently, each time trying to find out how lives come to be.

And the falconer? Whence came the falconer?

"It's hard to know," my mother always says, leaning back as though glad this tale is done. "It's hard to know in a case like this, if he came from God or the devil."

Ellen Kushner and
Delia Sherman

The Fall of the Kings

Ellen Kushner is the author of Swordspoint: A Melodrama of Manners *and the World Fantasy Award–winning* Thomas the Rhymer. *Delia Sherman is the author of* Through a Brazen Mirror *and the Mythopoeic Award–winning* The Porcelain Dove. *"The Fall of the Kings" is the first published collaboration from this talented pair. The story is related to Kushner's* Swordspoint, *a sparkling, archly witty novel reminiscent of Dorothy Dunnett or Georgette Heyer, yet with a language all its own. Kushner and Sherman's sexy new novella comes from* Bending the Landscape, *an anthology of stories on gay and lesbian themes edited by Nicola Griffith and Stephen Pagel.*

In addition to writing, Kushner is also the host/coproducer of Sound & Spirit, *a weekly radio program featuring an engaging mix of music, myth, spirituality, and philosophical thought from around the world (broadcast nationally on PRI). Sherman is a Consulting Editor for Tor Books, as well as a book reviewer and critic. They divide their time between homes in Boston, Massachusetts, and New York City.*

—T. W.

When Basil St. Cloud arrived at the Great Hall an hour before the Master Historian's lecture, it was already aswarm with black robed scholars. The timid were lined three deep below the steps giving access to the deep horseshoe of benches. The more enterprising simply climbed the benches themselves to capture prime seats. It looked as if the

whole University had turned out to hear Master Tortua lecture on the subject
of his famous book, *Hubris and the Fall of the Kings*.

Master Tortua was the greatest living scholar on the history of the ancient
monarchy. He was also Basil's first teacher, his champion before the University
Examiners, and his friend. His illness this past year had been a source of grief
to his young protégé, and it was with a sense of the world having righted itself
at last that Basil settled in his seat opposite a stained-glass window and prepared
to be enlightened.

But he was not enlightened. Master Tortua's illness had left him the doddering
ghost of the scholar who, barely six years ago, had introduced a young country
boy to the dark glories of the city's past. Where once he had developed arguments, Tortua presented rambling anecdotes that sounded more like palace gossip than history; where once he had thundered, he mumbled while the spittle
gathered in the corners of his mouth. Some men left; some shaded their eyes;
some conferred in shocked whispers. Basil blinked and stared at the high arched
window across from him. It was ancient, a thousand years or more, and the
figures in the center panel were stiff and formal—a man robed in black and a
hart with a collar of gold around its neck. The hart was kneeling to the man,
who caressed its head with his outstretched hand. A pool of impossibly blue
water sparkled at their feet and a flat, golden sky arched over their heads.

Time passed; Master Tortua mumbled. More men left. The sun moved in the
sky and came burning through the colored glass of the window, dyeing the faces
below with green and brown and blue. Basil noticed one young man who seemed
drenched in gold, the light burnishing his long fall of bronze-dark hair and gilding his pale skin. He was slouched forward in his seat with his ankle on one
knee, his elbow on the other, and his chin in his hand, looking very interested
and somewhat puzzled. He glanced up, and Basil found himself holding his gaze
across the horseshoe. The boy smiled, parted his lips as though he would speak.
Basil hastily turned his eyes back to Master Tortua, who was talking about the
magical rituals of the ancient court wizards. Basil winced. It was lucky that no
one was likely to take him seriously. In the old days, men had been thrown in
prison for less.

When at length Master Tortua had meandered away into silence, Basil descended to the podium where the old scholar was wiping his spectacles.

"Welcome back, Master Tortua," he said gently. "How good to see you well."

Tortua blinked at him. "Roger . . . ? No, it's young St. Cloud, isn't it? How
did you enjoy the lecture?"

Basil could only say dryly, "You seem to have changed your mind about the
court wizards since *The Fall of the Kings*."

The old man drew up all his wrinkles like a pleased tortoise. "Why, yes, Basil,
I have. Been reading, you know, while I was ill, and it all started to come clear.
The power of the royal blood, the hold the wizards had over the kings—it doesn't
make sense if it wasn't founded on something real, don't you see? They must
have had true magic. Stands to reason."

"So you said," Basil murmured. "But the law says otherwise."

"The law." The old man was grandly dismissive. "Drafted by a clutch of frightened old women. The law means nothing." He fell silent, munching his jaws.
"It's a pity about *the book of the King's Wizard*. If we could find that—"

Basil sighed. "Ah, yes. The notorious book of spells, passed down from one King's Wizard to the next. I'm sure the Council of Lords tossed it immediately into the nearest fire, when they found it, and put an end to that nonsense forever."

The old man shook his head regretfully. "A waste, I call it—a waste of human knowledge."

"A waste indeed," said Basil, and let someone else elbow him out of the way to speak to the old teacher.

Basil St. Cloud lectured on the history of the monarchy five mornings a week. Despite the earliness of the hour, he had something of a following among the city's nobility. Young lords idling a few years in study liked hearing how the last kings fell from honor and strength into decadence. They liked hearing how their own ancestors had saved the country by deposing Gerard the Wicked sensibly and legally. It made them feel the weight of the centuries behind them, to hear their names invoked, their family histories analyzed. Basil, who found the modern aristocracy effete and faddish, hoped by his lectures to sow the seeds of true nobility, the nobility of the ancients, in their much-declined descendants.

The room in which he lectured was no help to him, being dank as a well and redolent of rotting straw and torch smoke. His students were little more than the tops of heads bent earnestly over tablets and a small scratching of pencils. Sometimes he thought it was like lecturing to hens in a yard. They were always attentive—sometimes excessively, when a student became confused between devotion to his subject and devotion to the handsome young master, with his firm mouth, ironic voice, and his demand for precise and well-informed argument. Basil had grown accustomed to such attentions, had even occasionally enjoyed them, when the student was bright and good to look at. He always knew when a student was interested in that particular way, for he would suddenly be overcome by an intense self-consciousness, as though he'd been stripped naked, as he did the morning after Master Tortua's lecture.

Basil stumbled over a phrase and cleared his throat firmly. "Hilary always insisted upon hunting the sacrifice himself and bringing it to the wizards to be prepared. The court wizards approved of King Hilary, even though almost no one else did."

A movement caught his eye: a head nodding slowly, as though in wry understanding; a head covered with bronze-dark hair pulled back in a ribbon. A long head, with slanting cheekbones and a long, arching nose. A familiar head, he thought as he went on, "Hilary went about the kingship with a kind of mad intensity unmatched by . . ."

Ah. He had it now. The young man from Master Tortua's lecture. The young man who had smiled at him, who was smiling at him again. Basil hurriedly lowered his eyes to his notes and kept them, and his mind, firmly on King Hilary and his peculiarities. Which, in his later years, centered increasingly on beautiful young men and women of no birth and little common sense, one of whom had cut his throat for him. Hilary had been naked save for a fine deer skin, and the young murderer had been discovered weeping over the corpse, his monarch's blood smeared over his face and chest.

"The court wizards questioned him, of course," Basil said, "but they could get nothing out of him save the babblings of madness. He died under the questioning, much irritating Hilary's heir Gerard, who had been looking forward to executing the traitor. Not to be cheated of his revenge, King Gerard commanded that the corpse be drawn, quartered, and burned just as if it had been alive. Gerard was a great believer in following the rules. As we shall see tomorrow, when I will discuss the early years of his reign."

The University bell tolled heavily over his last words, and there was a general rustle and scuffle as the students gathered up their effects. There was little talking, and more than one shocked and troubled face. They'd always known the last kings were corrupt and mad—it was one of the city's truths, like the economic usefulness of the river. But they'd never really thought what *corrupt* and *mad* meant until the story of Hilary's death brought it home to them. Basil had just been reading about it in the letters of a certain Hieronymous, Lord Tielman, uncovered in a clutch of old books and papers he'd bought from Foster Rag-and-Bone. It was a story he'd been unable to resist sharing at once with his students, clearly to good effect.

"Thank you." It was the long-haired young man, standing below the lectern. "That was interesting, about King Hilary and his lover. Can you tell me any more about it?"

Basil brought up his head sharply. "No," he said and forced a smile. "Really, how could I? It was three hundred years ago, and the records are sketchy."

"Just so," said the young man. "All those details, about the deer skin and the slit throat, they aren't in any of the standard histories. I'd be interested to know your sources."

Basil, who intended to amaze the scholarly world with his discovery at his own leisure, looked down his nose. "Quite," he said. "Will you hear some advice, Master . . . ?"

"Campion." The young man swept a courtly bow. "Theron Campion."

"Master Campion. A scholar's facts are a scholar's honor. Question them, and you question his honesty. I was not made a Master of this University for inventing colorful details."

"Of course not, Master St. Cloud." His glance flicked up mischievously. "Your youth precludes those privileges of invention granted to poor Master Tortua. But . . . how charming of you if you had been!"

His eyes were greenish. Basil found that he was looking into them. Theron Campion smiled engagingly; Basil fought down a disproportionate anger. "Dishonor is hardly a jesting matter," he said. "Good day to you."

Returning to his rooms through the crowded streets of University Town, Basil was jostled by a chattering crowd of students in black gowns, who apologized when they realized who he was. One of them wore his hair long like Theron Campion. It looked better on Campion, Basil thought, and wondered if the young man would turn up again at his lectures. Not that it mattered. Basil had more important things to think about. Like the book he was writing, the book that would make him more famous than Master Tortua; the book that, later that evening, he found himself regarding with the bitterest frustration. Hieronymous was being singularly coy and unhelpful, Basil could no longer remember his own argument, his head ached, and his mouth was as dry as the Twelve-Months' drought. A cup of wine would cure at least part of what ailed him, he thought, and might help him sort out the rest.

The Blackbird's Nest was a noisy, cheerful tavern at the river edge of University Town, popular with students and the younger masters, like Basil. When Basil came in, he saw that a hilarious group of students had colonized the fire, and was shouting and arguing over some point of philosophy. One boy had his foot up on the table, lunging like a swordsman with an accusing finger at his laughing opponent's nose. Basil sat at an empty table and watched them over the edge of his beer. It hadn't been that long since he'd been one of them—no, that wasn't strictly accurate. Basil St. Cloud had never had the time for tavern jests, nor the money for the sort of drunk these boys were on. Basil St. Cloud's assault on scholarship had been single-minded, his rise concomitantly swift. He might be near these students in age, but in rank and learning he far surpassed them, and he thought the bargain a fair one.

For a moment he considered taking part in the discussion. All he'd have to do was raise his voice, and the center would shift to him, a lodestone potent as the pole. But he was sick of company tonight, and attention and even debate. So he turned his back on the students, addressed himself to the fowl pie, which was excellent, and was contemplating another tankard when a student detached himself from the group by the fire and headed toward Basil's corner.

"Master St. Cloud," said the student. "Good evening."

This time, Basil recognized him immediately. "Master Campion, isn't it?" asked Basil. "Good evening to you."

"May I sit down?" The green eyes were a little glassy with drink, the white hand heavy on the table's edge.

"I'd just as soon you didn't."

Campion staggered, catching himself against Basil's shoulder. "Whoops," he said. "Sorry. Just sit here quietly. You won't know I'm here." He eased himself onto the bench next to Basil, thigh to thigh. Basil jumped as though the touch had burned him.

"Sorry," said Campion again, and moved over.

"Don't you think you should go home while you can still walk?" Basil asked.

"I'm not so drunk as all that," said Campion. "I can still say 'Seven seditious swordsmen sailed to exile in Sardinopolis.' Shall I buy you a drink? The wine's not so bad here, if you know what to ask for." He smiled like a cat who knows where the cream is kept. "I know what to ask for."

Basil laughed. "I'll wager you do. No, you shall not buy me wine."

"Brandy, what about brandy? Or beer. Men who drink beer are seldom beautiful, but it's the exception proves the rule, or so 'Long John' Tipton would have us believe."

" 'Long John'?" Basil said. "Is that how you refer to Master Tipton? What do you call me, then?"

The boy smiled a very creamy smile. "Now, that would be telling. But I should like to call you Basil, if you will permit it."

The question should never have been asked, but having been asked, it hung between them like a challenge. "I can't stop you," Basil said.

"Oh, yes, you can. One hard look from your eyes could turn me to stone. Everyone is afraid of you."

"You exaggerate."

"I do not, sir. I always pay ver-ry particular attention when you speak." An aristocratic drawl was beginning to bleed through his University sharpness. "Though, mostly, I watch your mouth. It is severe. Austere. It bears watching."

"I wasn't aware that you had had much opportunity to watch it before today. You are hardly a regular attendee of my lectures."

"It's a morning lecture," Campion explained apologetically. "I have come before, though. I've watched you talk about the Barley Wars and the rise of the Inner Council and the Ophidian Invasion and the court wizards. You're wrong about the wizards, you know."

He looked so earnestly owlish that Basil smiled. "No, I don't. In fact, I have very good evidence that they believed that the magic they performed was real."

"Nonsense. You have no idea what was going on in their minds; you only think you do."

From a mere student, that was a remarkable piece of rudeness, yet, "What were the court wizards?" the boy went on, cutting off any protest Basil might have made. "What was their function, after all? They were counselors to the kings. They gave advice. All this business about their seeing into men's hearts, binding the kings with chains of gold . . . it's figurative language. Any poet can tell you that. They were like you, Basil: they sifted the evidence, looking for truth. They were scholars of the heart." Pleased, he repeated it: "Scholars of the heart. And because they were good scholars, they got it right often enough to be credible and thus maintain a reputation for working magic."

The boy spoke earnestly, leaning close enough for Basil to smell the brandy on his breath. His point was sufficiently interesting to give Basil pause. Campion, taking his silence for surrender, sat back on the bench with a complacent smile. "I knew you'd agree, once I'd explained it to you," he said.

Basil recoiled. "Agree? On *that* argument? Master Campion, you astonish me. Has no one bothered to teach you the principles of debate?" And he commenced to depress the boy's pretensions in a well-reasoned and constructed exposition of Theron's rhetorical shortcomings, ending up, ". . . and furthermore, Master Campion, you yourself have no more idea of what the wizards really were than Master Tortua does. You believe what you want to believe, on no more evidence than your own inability to extrapolate beyond the known."

"Are you suggesting—*you*, Master St. Cloud—that I try believing in wizardry to expand my imaginative range? To . . . let me see now . . . *to set about inventing colorful details?*"

Basil gritted his teeth. "I am suggesting that you leave yourself open to the possibility of evidence as yet uncovered."

"Such as?"

A student reeled past them, or nearly—at the last moment he did a drunken bounce off the table and into Theron's lap. "Bugger off, Hammond." Theron dumped him on the ground. Hammond wandered off in the other direction, with people shouting after him.

"We can't talk here," Basil snapped. "I can barely hear myself think."

"It's cold out," Theron objected.

"My rooms are close by. There's something I want to show you. Will you come?"

"Certainly," said Theron. "Lead on."

The argument continued unabated all the way to Minchin Street. Basil lived up four pair of stairs in an old stone building that had originally been a royal archive. Some time shortly after the fall of the kings, it had been cut up into a warren of more or less cramped rooms for the use of masters and lecturers. It was furnished with an iron bedstead, a table and a chair, and scores of books and papers that were piled and drifted on the floor, against the walls, in the corners, and spread out on the mattress like an eager lover.

"The scholar's mistress," observed Theron, folding his body down onto the bed. He laid his hand on one closely written sheet. "Is this what you wished me to see?"

On the way from the Nest, Basil had had ample time to regret his impulsive invitation. "No," he said coldly.

"Do you have a mistress?"

Basil, who was poking up the fire, jerked upright, his lips compressed. The young man returned his look gravely, like a curious child. He'd loosed his shirt at the neck, laying open the fine linen to bare the hollow of his throat, which was also fine, and very white. Firelight polished the fold of hair over his shoulder and touched the high curves of his brow and his aquiline nose with a warm light, lending them the look of alabaster or carved ivory. His eyes, shadowed, were blank.

The room spun once around Basil and settled again, realigned around Theron, a figure descended from the marble frieze above the Council Hall and sitting on his bed, the living image of an ancient king. "Majesty," he whispered, bowing his head.

"What?" Theron moved two books on to the floor, clearing a larger space on the bed. "I can't hear you. Come and sit beside me."

The movement had broken the illusion, but not the enchantment. Basil no longer saw one of his beloved kings come again, but rather a king among men, all passion and pride. He wanted that pride, to caress it into full potency and then to break it to his will and his desire. He took one step toward the bed, and then another, holding out his hand for Theron to grasp and pull him down into a long kiss that broke only when Basil pushed Theron back onto a pile of papers.

"Watch out," Theron murmured against Basil's mouth. "She has nails."

"What?"

"Your mistress. She's scratching my back. And this can't be doing her any good. Let's get rid of her."

Basil propped himself up on his elbow and leaned over Theron to scoop papers and books off the end of the bed, lifting him to get at the papers he was lying on, pressing against his belly, working his hands under the tight waistcoat, the fine linen shirt, to the strong, smooth back beneath. The young man's flesh was warm and supple under Basil's hands; his mouth was sweet and firm under Basil's lips. Kissing him, Basil could think of nothing else, but he made no objection when Theron rolled him away, laughing, and helped him disentangle himself from his master's robe and the neat suit of clothes beneath it.

When they were both naked, Basil reached for him, and hesitated, suddenly shy. Theron put his hand to Basil's chest and ruffled the dark hair that crossed it. His fingers were cold. "I've always fancied a fur coverlet," he said. "Come and warm me."

And Basil did warm him, until they threw the blankets on the floor, and they flared and leapt and burned themselves out to lie at last in a smoldering glow of satisfaction.

Basil said sleepily, "Tell me something. Have you in fact been following me? I seemed to see you everywhere."

The young man swept a shimmer of bronze hair from his face. "I seemed to see you everywhere. But—yes, it was by design. I noticed you before you noticed me."

"I noticed you at once!"

Basil felt the smile against his skin. "No, you didn't. I attended lectures; I saw you in the Nest surrounded by your students, your particular followers—"

Basil chuckled. "I love the way you say that."

"What?"

"Par-*tic*-u-lar. You sound as though you're picking up something tiny with silver tweezers. Never mind. Go on."

The student shifted uncomfortably, as though he were thinking of protesting. "Well . . . I studied you until I knew you, or at least the parts of you that were available to me: your learning, your passion, the way your voice slows when you answer a question. I studied your hands, and wondered what they would feel like on me; the clear skin of your face with the beard just coming through. I wondered about all that, and about the rest of you I could not see, and I wanted you to know me. I wanted you to see me. I wanted you to feel my eyes on you like fingers under your robe."

"Have you gotten what you wanted?"

Theron trailed his hand down Basil's breastbone to his belly. "Yes," he said. "I have."

After Theron had gone, Basil hung over the edge of the bed and groped under it for a battered wooden trunk. He released the hasps and opened it upon bundles of yellowed paper tied neatly with tape and a package wrapped in an old linen shirt, which he picked up and settled in his lap. He eased aside the folds of cloth like petals to lay bare a small, thick book bound in brown leather sueded with age and damp. Stamped on the cover was a tall crown, its gilding all worn away save for a few flakes lingering at the tip of one of its sharp points. The leather reminded him of Theron's skin, cool and a little sticky with drying sweat; the crown reminded him of Theron's face, white as marble against his dark hair spread on the pillow. Basil felt his sex swell and press against the book in his lap. Now he owned them both, he thought; the precious book and the precious man.

"I have to go home tonight," Theron had said. "Sophia worries when I don't come home at all."

"Sophia?" A tiny serpent stirred in Basil's chest.

"Lady Campion. My mother."

The serpent quieted. "Your mother. You are certainly a dutiful son."

Theron laughed. "Not in the general way, I'm not."

Campion, Campion, Basil thought . . . he knew plenty of dead ones. An old family, but fairly minor in the great scheme of things. There was a Bertram Campion who saw King Tybalt slain at Pommerey; a Raymond Campion who was a notable cartographer. But what the Campions had done lately, he had no idea. He'd have to ask someone, but he'd better be careful about it.

The next morning, Basil lectured as always. Theron was not present, which was not really a surprise. Basil was conscious of disappointment nonetheless, and a certain sense of betrayal. By the time he got to the Nest, he'd decided that the young noble and the events of the night were best drowned in something stronger than his usual beer.

The first thing that met his eye was Leonard Rugg, Master of Metaphysics, sitting at the end of a bench, morosely staring into a bowl of snapdragon gone cold. Basil excused himself to his students and approached him. "Good day to you, Master Rugg."

"Sit down, St. Cloud," said the metaphysician. "Have you heard the latest?"

"Probably not."

"You should get out more. Youngster like you." Rugg peered at him over the rim of the bowl. "You look pale. Stir your blood. I'll pass along my mistress if you like—the bitch. Stir anyone's blood." Master Rugg looked contrite. "Begging your pardon. The bitch."

Basil snagged the potboy, ordered brandy, and settled back. "Is that the latest? It sounds old to me."

"Oh, no, no. It's Tremontaine again. Trouble all 'round. Lady Sophia's trying to endow a chair for *women,* if you please—"

"Lady Sophia?" Basil sat up sharply. "Lady Sophia *Campion?*"

"That's the one."

"I suppose young Theron is trouble, too."

"Really?" Rugg looked more cheerful. "Never saw anything wrong with him myself; harmless enough puppy—though I hear that last mistress of his did him some damage. Still, no harm in him. Been coming to classes since he was a lad. One after the other. Can't stick to a subject, loves 'em all: an academic flirt, eh? Still, he probably knows more about history than I do . . . and more about metaphysics than you do. What kind of trouble's he in?"

"Ah, disappointment to the family?" Basil hazarded.

"Ha!" Leonard Rugg roared. "It would take a lot of work for him to give Campion's family a sleepless night, after what the father put them through."

"Oh?"

Rugg said expansively, "Oh, no one can say the old man wasn't generous to the University. But one can't imagine him as a *husband,* if you catch my drift."

Basil gave up. "Leonard," he said. "Who is Theron Campion's father?"

"Oh, don't you know? He's dead. Something in your line, I'd think, St. Cloud: Tremontaine, the Mad Duke. That one."

Basil said frostily, "I don't do modern history."

His colleague took pity: "A scandal from start to finish. Attended University back before any noble would have been caught dead here. He became a swordsman's paramour. But they let him inherit Tremontaine anyhow. He filled the house with scholars, reprobates, and lovers of all, ah, shapes and sizes. He was finally driven into exile, left the duchy to his niece, and came back years later with a beautiful foreigner in tow, claiming to be his lawful wife, who conveniently produced an heir four months after the Mad Duke's death."

"And that is the Lady Sophia."

"Damned queer woman. But, odds are, the boy will still inherit on his cousin's death."

"Inherit the duchy?"

"So it really doesn't matter what he studies, does it?"

"On the contrary," said Basil shortly. "I think it matters a great deal. If there's one thing ancient history has to teach us, it's the importance of educating the ruling class in the realities of life."

Rugg laughed. "They'll hardly learn that in University, dear boy."

"Oh, I don't know," a voice above them drawled. "Unheated lecture rooms, watered beer, incomprehensible feuds, indiscriminate sex, casual violence, and a general shortage of sleep seems uncommonly like real life to me."

Basil started. He wondered how much of the conversation Theron had overheard. He wondered if Theron were sorry about what had happened the night before. He wondered whether the beating of his heart was visible through the thick stuff of his robe. He thought it might be.

Theron was speaking. "Master St. Cloud, I wonder if I might trouble you for a word in private?" His light voice sounded annoyed, but that just might have been the drawl. Basil turned to look at him. The long mouth was hard and still.

Leonard Rugg punched him on the arm. "New student, eh? Congratulations, St. Cloud. Don't take a copper less than 20 for the term. He can afford it, can't you, my lord?"

Theron smiled tightly. "Yes," he said. "I can."

"Shut up, Leonard," said Basil. "I'm not exactly new at this, you know." He rose and looked around the tavern. "There," he indicated one of the empty tables with his chin.

The walk across the room was a journey across a wasteland. Basil imagined Rugg and the students whispering and snickering. Determined to hold fast to his dignity, Basil lifted his head to see Theron convulsed with silent laughter.

"Was I perfect?" he chortled. Basil stared at him suspiciously. "Well, *Master* St. Cloud?"

"Campion, are you mad?" Basil snapped.

"I'm sorry." The student wiped tears from his eyes. "I'm ruining the effect, aren't I?" He reached across the table, touched Basil's hand lightly. The scholar's insides lit up like fireworks. "Let us discuss fees, then, so as not to disappoint Master Rugg. Tell me—" he leaned forward. Basil smelled his mouth, sweet with mint and the tang of his breath. "How much must I pay for another lesson like last night's?"

His eyes were flecked with gold. Reading nothing in them but a warm and friendly conspiracy, Basil smiled. "I wonder," he said, "if you remember your lesson."

"Perfectly," the boy smiled back. "I paid particular attention. And now I would know more."

"Would you, indeed?"

Basil realized that he was flirting—flirting *after* he'd achieved his conquest—and that it was delightful.

"You are the subject of my study, Master St.—Basil. I desire to understand you thoroughly, to uncover your mysteries, to pass examinations in your history and your tastes."

Basil laughed. "My history is not so interesting as yours, Master Campion."

"Oh?" said Theron, then, in a very different voice: "What has old Firenose been telling you? That I have a boundless appetite for men, women, and ponies? Or merely that I changed lovers as often as I change suits of clothes? Not quite true. I deny the ponies. Are you going to bar me from your classes?"

He looked at once haughty and so wounded that Basil reached out to comfort him. Theron glanced down at Basil's hand, square and dark against his own fair skin, and smiled. "A tutorial," he murmured. "I've an hour free before Thurgood's lecture."

Two hours later, they lay together in a welter of discarded garments and blankets. Theron unwound himself and poked through the tangle until he found a black scholar's robe, which he draped over his shoulders.

"My father," he said, settling back into Basil's embrace, "was a colorful character. I thought, when I was younger, that I would try to be more colorful still. Finding that to be impossible, I settle for pleasing myself. I've nothing to apologize for. A variety of lovers is a family tradition, really."

Basil touched the thin, sensitive lips. "It's an older tradition than that. There's evidence that the kings were encouraged to take many lovers of both sexes. The wizards—"

"Wizards and kings," interrupted Theron. "They're dead, Basil, and beyond all feeling. I'm not."

"That's just the point. You carry their seed—"

"Shut up, Basil." The boy stopped his mouth with lips and tongue. Basil pulled away from his kiss and pinned him flat to the bed with the weight of his body and his hands around his wrists. He gripped him hard enough to feel the long bones under the flesh.

"You don't want to hear me, do you?" hissed Basil. Theron moaned. "I know you've the blood in you, I can smell it on your skin, taste it in your mouth, hear it in your heartbeat."

Theron struggled under him, half-angry, half-laughing, wholly aroused. "You've been studying too hard, Basil," he panted. "I'll have to see to it that you get out more."

"Be silent!"

Theron opened and shut his mouth and began breathing hard through his nose. Basil lowered his head, kissed Theron on each temple, just above the hollow where the bronze-dark hair sprang back from the brow. The boy shivered from head to foot. Basil shifted his grip so that he held Theron stretched taut, and the world narrowed to the damp slide of skin over skin, the unbearable vulnerability of the secret places, the fierce, hot joy of possession, of shooting his seed, his whole being, into his lover's pliant, trembling body. Silently Theron yielded to him, and silently received him until he spent his passion in a high, clear cry like a wounded animal's. Then Basil turned his lover over and laid his head on Theron's breast.

For a time, the only sound in the room was the hushing of the fire and the lovers' slowing breaths. Then Theron said, "I love it when you lose control. It excites me. It frightens me."

"Not so much as it frightens me."

"Why?"

Basil thought of the dark and wordless place Theron's struggling had sent him. His body had been shot through with lightning, burning with infinite power. "I am not myself," he said shortly.

"You are wonderful," said Theron.

The days passed in a jumble of lectures, students, and hours in Theron's arms, interrupted by his lover's rushing off to an appointment with his cousin or the theatre with his mother or a ball or a horse-race. In Theron's spotty absences, Basil found himself studying not Hieronymous' letters, but the book stamped with the crown, the book he dared tell no one he possessed. Though the text itself was written in no language he knew, the headings were in an antique dialect, quaint but clear: "A Spelle for Forcynge of the Trutthe of Those Suspect of Treeson"; "A Spelle of Glamour and Hony-tonge." Sometimes he was near to weeping with frustration over the nonsense syllables that followed, which promised so much and delivered so little. What was the use of a piece of history that could not be read, he asked himself, and buried the book in the trunk until curiosity drove him to take it out again.

Thus caught between love and fruitless labor, Basil's teaching suffered. One morning he found himself delivering the same lecture he'd given the week before; one morning he woke to hear the University bells tolling noon and one of his students banging at his door and demanding to know whether he were well or ill.

"Ill indeed, to be awakened so rudely," Basil shouted through the door. "Go away, Justis. I'll be there tomorrow."

He slapped the lump that was Theron snickering under the blankets. When the student's footsteps were gone into the ringing of the bells, Basil pulled the boy out from under them, almost angrily unweaving the wild web of hair from his sleep-thick face, entering his mouth with kisses until he felt his body's yielding. When Theron lay, a warm and satisfied heap across him, he breathed in their mingled scent and felt perfectly happy. He could hear the smile in Theron's voice as he said, "I wish I spoke a hundred languages, to tell you how much I love you."

The pleasure of the moment snapped. Basil laid his finger across Theron's lips, sealing them shut. "Don't say that. Don't say you love me."

Theron kissed his fingertip. "Why not?"

"Because that is something that should not be said between your father's son and mine."

"My dear," Theron purred in amusement. "I've told you: my father was a notorious libertine."

"And you're doing your best to follow in his footsteps."

"God!" Theron swore, and flopped back on the pillow. "I get enough of that from the Duchess! I don't need it from you, too. My mother thinks he was a saint; my duchess cousin thinks he was a satyr. And, I might add, they both wonder what I'm doing spending all my free time down here with you. Or, rather, they do not wonder—which is almost worse. I am what I am—no more, no less—and I would very much appreciate it if you could all stop measuring me against dead dukes I've never even met!"

Basil said, "I've offended you. I'm sorry."

Theron was silent a while. Then, trying for a lighter tone, he offered: "When you ask a girl to dance three times at a single ball, it means you're serious about her. It's the same with this: you can't make love with someone three times and not fall in love."

Basil shifted uncomfortably. "You make it sound like a magic spell: three times and you're caught."

"It would depend on the timing, I suppose." Campion gave the question his full attention. "Three times in one year would be safe, but three times in one week, and you can't help falling in love."

Basil said indulgently, "You're confusing the body with the heart."

"People do, you know." Theron raised himself on one elbow. "But I'm willing to entertain the notion that you have them neatly divided. Maybe for you it takes something more direct." His fingers made an elaborate pass over Basil's face.

Before he could complete it, Basil caught his wrist and pulled him down into his arms. "Don't, Theron. It's not something to joke about."

"Are you going to cry me to the Council for practicing magic? Even though my spells never work?"

"You've no need of spells, my lord."

"It's you who are magical, Basil. Who could resist the enchantment of your eyes, your neck, your broad chest and narrow hips, your—"

"Stop!" Basil was laughing as Theron kissed each beloved feature, struggling to get away. Then the bell rang again.

Theron yelped, jumped out of bed, and began diving for his scattered clothes. "My tailor! I've stood him up twice already, and he's fitting my coat for the Montague ball next week."

Basil found Theron's stockings and his belt. "Be at my lecture tomorrow?"

"Without fail. I am particularly keen to hear your opinion of Hilary's walrus-oil treaty with Arkenvelt."

In his warm room in his mother's house, Theron Campion stood still while a servant dressed him for the Montague ball. Fine linen against his skin, followed by layers of more linen, stiff with embroidery, then brocaded silk, rounded with collar and cuffs of lace. A wide gold chain was laid across his chest. His long hair was brushed and oiled and bound with a velvet ribbon. He had eaten nothing for hours; come rushing home from Basil's just in time to change. His consequent pallor, and the unusual hair, gave him an antique air that his lover would have approved of.

The ball was already crowded when he got there; he bowed and swam his way through well-dressed women of every age and size until a hand at his elbow stopped him: "Young Campion! Pried you away from your books, have we?"

He was in a knot of men he knew. They wanted to talk about politics and the latest fashion in lovers, which did not seem to include dark and brilliant university masters. He said nothing; he couldn't bear their inevitable sly pleasantries. Of course he could not escape the usual jokes about his father, the mad, bad old duke. Theron smiled mechanically and took a glass of wine from a passing tray. He began to feel much better after he'd downed it.

A fragile-looking girl with dark hair came into view just past the swirl of pattern in the tailored shoulders around him. Her hair was severely upswept, exposing delicate ears. The few tendrils that escaped onto her neck served to enhance its frailty.

One of his companions followed Theron's look. "Ah!" he said archly. "The true purpose for our sojourn in these parts: the flowers in the garden of maidenhood, ripe for the plucking."

"Harris!" a young man expostulated. "I hope you do not mean my sister!"

"Plucking," explained Harris smoothly, "is a very considerable enterprise, involving ladders of contracts, baskets of jewels, and volumes of vows."

"*Is* it your sister?" Theron asked.

"*It's* not the cat, you rogue!"

But he achieved his introduction. Lady Genevieve Randall smiled shyly. Her skin was fine and flawless, with a ripe-peach glow; Theron had to stop himself from reaching out to touch it, just to feel it under his fingers. Even her shoulders, rising from a calyx of lace, glowed faintly golden in the flattering candlelight.

But he might take her hand if he asked her to dance, and so he did. They trod the measures of a slow *pas*, and he was careful to exert no pressure of the fingers that might alarm a young girl fresh from the schoolroom. He could not help looking, though, at the wisps of hair at the nape of her neck as the two of them moved back and forth, gravely dipping and bobbing. A sheen of moisture appeared on her upper lip; he wished he might bend down and lick it off.

Genevieve's mother met them as they came off the dance floor. Lady Randall inquired after the health of his mother, into his studies, and after his cousin the Duchess. Theron took pains not to say anything particularly original. He'd learned long ago that it put people off; they admired his intellect from a distance and tolerated his eccentricities as long as he did not ask them to participate.

He was able to dance once again with Genevieve Randall, carefully avoiding the third time by taking several other partners. While getting a cooling drink, he was cornered by a politically active noble who wanted to know where he stood on the proposed new corn levy, filling out Theron's professed indifference with a full set of opinions of his own. By the time Theron returned to the floor, the Randalls, mother, daughter, and son, had gone. No longer hungry or thirsty, Theron suddenly longed for bed, the closest bed he could find, which was in a small room on Minchin Street.

From experience, Basil knew that his lover was unlikely to come to him until well past midnight, leaving him hours to devote to scholarship. He knew he should work on his book—he'd not so much as looked at a page since the night he'd met Theron. He opened the trunk to get out Hieronymous' papers, found himself holding the book of spells instead, opened to the "Spelle for Summonynge of a Absente Mann." His eyes scanned the incomprehensible words, then he shut the book with a decided snap, folded it in its cloth, took up the letters, sat himself at his table, and began to sort through papers.

Gradually, he began to reconstruct the elements of his argument. The last time he'd looked, it had seemed impossible. Now, it was obvious that he'd gone off-track in his discussion of Petronius' *Chronicles*. He picked up a pen, uncapped the ink-well, and some hours later, was happily engaged when a perfumed gentleman appeared in the shadows at his door.

"Am I disturbing you?"

"No." Basil closed the ink-well and rubbed his cramped fingers. "No. I was just winding down. Are you cold? Come in by the fire."

"There isn't any fire. You've let it go out."

"So I have, so I have." Basil peered in the woodbasket; it was empty. "Sit down and take some brandy while I fetch up some wood. Here," snagging the quilt from the bed, "wrap this around your legs. I won't be a moment. This wizard business is fascinating, fascinating. There's a way in which it explains everything about us—the Council, the fall of the kings, even the swordsmen."

"I don't want to hear it just now," said Theron petulantly.

For the first time, Basil looked straight at him. "Oh, my dear," he said. The boy looked like a doll, white face and glittering eyes above an elaborate costume.

"I'm tired," he said. "Please let me lie down."

"Are you all right?"

"Yes—but never mind the fire. Just come and warm me."

Basil undressed him, save for his chain and rings, and covered them both with every blanket he possessed, as well as both his scholar's gowns and Theron's rich cloak. "There," he said when the boy stopped shivering. "Better?"

"Yes. I'm sorry—I should not have disturbed your work. But I'm cold and weary and my cheeks ache from smiling. All I want is to rest quiet and warm."

But Theron seemed disinclined to sleep. He responded to Basil's kisses as if he would lose himself in them; and in some measure, he did, until at last they both were lost and found again.

Basil licked sweat from his lover's throat. "Why do you go to these parties if they upset you so?"

"I must. It wouldn't do for me to disappear into University, however much I want to. Someday I must take my place among the nobles of this city. They have to know me. My mother put up with a great deal of nonsense from these people over my birth and my inheritance—I owe it to her, and to my family, to do the thing properly."

"You speak as though you were not one of 'them.'"

Theron gave an embarrassed shrug. "I am, by birth. Someday I shall take my seat in Council. . . ."

"But you don't look forward to it."

"There is so much I want to study first!"

"But, Theron . . ." Basil fingered the chain whose precious links had left its mark on both men's chests. "Theron, you are no scholar."

"*What?*"

"Not a real one," Basil went on gently. "Not by temperament. You must know that."

Theron turned away from him, but Basil kept on. "Why can't you be proud of what you are? A great noble, from the seed of kings . . ."

"*Damn* your kings! Sometimes I think you take me only because Hilary's not available!"

"Hush." Basil gave the chain a tweak. "I am trying to tell you something important. The kings no longer rule. You nobles have taken their place, and must strive to be better than they were."

Theron sighed, burying his face in Basil's chest. "I know. I do know. But it is hard, being two people all the time. I wish I could . . . hire someone else to go to parties for me—to remember people's names and families, and to be charming when I don't feel like it."

"You mean like a wife?"

Basil meant it ironically, but the young nobleman answered candidly, "Yes. I will have to marry someday, for the title and the lineage and all. Already they are circling, the mamas with eligible daughters. I don't know what I will do! Marry, I suppose, and get it over with."

"The kings didn't need wives," said Basil. "They had their wizards."

"Oh, really? How did they reproduce?"

"The wizards chose their women for them. From what I've been able to gather, the king was a stag, both monarch and prey. When he was crowned, he hunted and killed a deer, and when his end came, he took a deer's form and was killed in his turn, whether by the wizard or the next king, I don't know. What I do know is that he begot as many children as he could while he reigned."

Theron murmured, "What an extraordinary amount you do know. And in the end, did the wizards corrupt the kings, or was it the kings corrupted the wizards?"

Basil opened his mouth to give him the standard answer, and realized that he knew better now. There were things no book could teach. "Love," said Basil, "allows for no corruption. It is a fire that burns away all impurity. As I love you, mind, body, and soul."

"I know," Theron whispered. His fingers in Basil's hair were at once soothing and tantalizing. He turned Basil over, looked tenderly down into his face. The chain brushed Basil's chest. Basil felt that he might melt, whether into tears or honey he was not sure. Salt or sweet, it made no difference.

"We're even now," the nobleman said. "Love for love." And he laid the chain around the scholar's neck.

There was a pause, full of breath and waiting. Theron grinned. "Have you ever loved anyone else?"

It was not what Basil had wanted him to say. "No," he said, rather sharply. "Never."

"Never?" Theron tweaked the chain. "Not very experienced, are you?"

"I never pretended to be. I've had other lovers, of course."

"Really? How many?"

Basil tabulated his actual conquests, added the ones he might have had if he had cared to try for them, and answered, "Eight. Or so."

"Eight. Or so. And you never told one you loved him?"

"It was of the body only. You're different; the way I feel about you is like nothing I've ever known." Basil stopped and smoothed the chain, warm and heavy across his breast.

"I'm glad," said Theron. "It's always better when heart and body agree. Come kiss me, and see."

When he next encountered Genevieve Randall, Theron knew she was the answer to all his problems. They were at the theatre, he with his cousins in the Tremontaine box, and she in the Randall box, accompanied by suitable chaperones. He couldn't take his eyes off her: her slim neck, her bright eyes, the way her hand flew to her mouth at the comic bits, the careful way she always turned her head to reply to others' comments, the air of propriety that breathed from her like perfume. He quickly bought some flowers, and gained access to her box at intermission. Lady Genevieve seemed pleased; her mother, Lady Randall, seemed very pleased.

Lord Theron regretted that he couldn't offer to escort them to their carriage after the play, but, he explained, "There is a lecture I must attend." The girl's eyes widened; boldly he went on, "I am so often at University. You will think me very dull."

"Oh, no," said Lady Genevieve. "It must be very exciting."

"It is exciting," he said, and took his leave.

And there it was, a neat solution. He hoped Basil would approve, but he feared that he might misunderstand unless Theron explained it all very carefully. Basil could be a bit dense about the modern world and its demands; sometimes Theron envied him the simplicity of his concerns. Perhaps if he couched it all in terms of ancient kings, a dynastic necessity—that there would be a social fuss, a legal ceremony, and then it would be over, and everything back to where it was for them. . . . He'd just have to go carefully, that's all. And then he could have everything he desired.

The Blackbird's Nest was filled with black robes, smoke, the smell of beer, and the hard, quick rattle of scholarly debate. Basil was happily arguing the relative antiquity of the three ducal houses with two of his best students. It wasn't until the tavern emptied as students scrambled for afternoon lectures that he realized Theron was not among them. Which was odd, as Basil was sure Theron had said this morning, as they kissed and parted, that he would be. Basil waited a little longer, and was rewarded for his patience by the sight of his lover arriving, breathless, as the University bell tolled twice.

Theron flung himself onto the nearest bench. "Sorry! Beer? No, wait—it's two already—I must get to Tipton's Mathematics—"

"Theron, what is it you're wearing?" The young noble's black robe was crookedly buttoned over a pair of tight-fitting yellow striped breeches and an embroidered waistcoat.

"Sorry—had to go see the lawyer this morning, no time to change—"

"Here." Basil redid the buttons. "Cover them up, and maybe no one will laugh at you. Lawyer, eh? Nothing's wrong, I hope?"

"Oh, no. I think it will all be fine. Thanks, Basil, I'm off—"

"Wait." The black whirlwind froze. "Theron, wait. Tell me if you're coming to Minchin Street tonight."

"Will you be there?"

"Will you?"

"Yes."

"Then so will I."

But he was not there, though Basil started at every rattle of the street door, every step on the stair. Theron stuck to no fixed schedule; Theron was often late. At last Basil fell asleep in his chair with a book in his lap, and woke up, cramped and cold and miserably weary, as dawn was silvering the city.

Theron appeared at his lecture that morning, neat and well-rested and very late. Basil could say nothing, but from the low murmurs it was clear his other students were saying it for him. Basil found his place again, and went on about the ceremonial duties of the later kings, pointedly never meeting the one pair of eyes he felt burning on him. Afterward, he ignored Theron and allowed Justis Blake to monopolize him all the way back to the Blackbird's Nest. Justis was in heaven; Basil hoped Theron was in hell, but was prepared to forgive him at the slightest sign of penitence.

But Theron had disappeared as soon as he stepped through the door into a crowd of black-robed young nobles who were slapping him on the back as if he'd done something heroic. No doubt he'd hear about it later. Basil turned away, but was intercepted by a well-dressed young man who stuck out his ringed hand to shake.

"I'm Clarence Randall. I—that is, my mother—I mean, I wondered if I might attend your lectures? On the kings? If it isn't too late?"

Basil forced himself to smile. He couldn't afford to turn away paying students, not if he wanted to keep brilliant but impoverished ones, like Justis. "Well, Lord Clarence, the term is almost over and the kings totter on the brink. But if you'd rather not wait until next year, read the Tortua *Hubris*, and perhaps we can arrange a tutorial."

Lord Clarence nodded, grinning. "I'll get the book from Campion," he said, and pushed off shouting, "Campion! Hey, Campion!" Basil, following close in his wake, came up in time to hear him say, "Thank you, Theron. I'll return it, I promise. Oh, yes. You'll be at the Godwin ball tonight, won't you? My sister asked me."

Basil caught his lover's gaze past Randall's head, saw his eyes widen, shift, veil themselves under the heavy oval lids as Theron turned away to put his arm around the young nobleman's shoulders. "Not the place to be talking of balls, my dear," he said, and then they were out of Basil's hearing.

Simple bewilderment rooted Basil to the spot, followed close upon by rage. Someone, Justis, was plucking at his sleeve, repeating his name; he shook him off roughly and strode blindly through the crowd, paying no more heed to what they might be saying than the cawing of so many crows. Theron was hiding something from him. Was he ashamed of Basil after all? Did he have another lover?

Basil's antidote to everything was work. All that long afternoon and evening, he wrote and crossed out sentence after sentence, wrote and crumpled page after page, until at last he found himself sitting among a snowdrift of spoiled sheets, unable to think of anything but Theron's face turning from him. Whatever was going on, he would lie about it, try to charm or kiss his way out of a confrontation. Basil thought he could bear anything better than Theron's false protestations of love and innocence. He rose and went to the bed, and opened the wizard's book.

The text had been written by several hands. The earliest spells were all of rule and dominion, scrying and sooth-saying: practical spells to ease the difficulties of ruling. But later spells had no purpose that Basil could see but control and revenge. They had titles like "A Spelle for the Drynge of a Mann's Seede" and "A Spelle to Turne Men into Beastes." They were written in a thick, brownish ink that Basil suspected to be blood.

Basil went back a few pages, a few hundred years. He hesitated over "A Spelle for the Un-covring of Hidden Trothe," then began to read it aloud as he had read it silently a hundred times before. The nonsense syllables clashed and slid in his mouth like rough pebbles. When he came to an end, he looked around the room, half-expecting to see the candle burn black or an evil and shapeless shadow seething in the corner. But all looked as it always had, homely, cluttered, shabby, and prosaic. Basil sighed, shut the book, and was swaddling it once more in its soft cerements when the door opened behind him.

"I've been having the most excruciating evening," Theron announced. "I've been conversing with debutantes, flattering dowagers, and listening to politically minded nobles discourse upon the salt tax. Comfort me, my dear, before I explode from an excess of respectability."

He wore full ball-dress. His hair was oiled and pulled back into a glossy club held by a jeweled clip. Rings weighed down his hands and a pearl hung from the lobe of one ear. He was flushed and a little unsteady and obviously quite excited. He held out a hand to Basil, who ignored it.

"Aren't you glad to see me?" Theron asked plaintively.

Basil laid the book on the table. "I did not expect you tonight. I was working. You interrupted me."

"You've never minded being interrupted before." Theron closed the door behind him and stepped into the room, stripping off his cloak and tossing it into a corner. "And you won't mind it this time, either." He came up behind Basil and put his arms around his chest. He smelled sweet and complicated, of perfumed oil and red wine and desire. He leaned over Basil's shoulder and rubbed his face like a great cat. The pearl in his ear brushed against Basil's cheek, smooth and hard as glass.

Basil shook him off. "That earring." The pearl had seared his cheek like a torch, ice and fire at once; as he spoke, he knew his words were truth. "That earring is a woman's jewel. She gave it to you tonight, from her own ear as you begged it."

The flushed face turned pale. "Nonsense, Basil."

"Nonsense, indeed. It does not become you, my lord, to lie."

Now two spots of color, like red bites, stained Theron's cheeks. "There we have it. So if I were no lord, but just a common man, might I lie with your good will?"

"But you're not one, are you? You think you may do what you like, with whom you like, to whom you like—"

"That isn't true!"

"Isn't it?" Basil asked icily. "You say that you reject the blood of kings, yet you reveal it with your every action. Arrogant, careless . . ."

"But that's what you want from me, isn't it?" Theron drew away to lounge provokingly by the fire. "What is it that you so love in me, if not that?"

Basil clenched his hands, words flashing through his mind like shooting stars, disconnected, unrecoverable. "I thought you were of the true blood," he said at last. "I thought that you were pure."

"And now you realize your mistake." The slow voice was harsh with anger. "You wanted an ancient king, and all you got was me. Only Theron. I am so sorry that I disappoint you."

A dark joy flooded through Basil. Theron's pain called to him like desire. He had never touched his lover so deeply, even when he spoke of love. He said, "Come here, Theron. You do not disappoint me."

But Theron turned away. "I thought you knew me. I thought you loved me. But you never looked at me; you never saw me—just the image of what you wanted me to be."

"I do know you. Come here." The nobleman shrugged his brocaded shoulders. His proud head was low; the earring hung like a tag of ownership. "Come," Basil coaxed. "Let me see your new pearl. Tell me about your conquest."

"Ah," Theron rallied with mock gallantry. "The hunt is on." He turned to face his inquisitor, very pale, still holding back, as if he were afraid to let Basil touch him. "I don't know how you guessed where this came from, but it's just a flirtation." He laughed mirthlessly. "What do you think I *do* at these balls, after all? Mathematical proofs?"

Basil held out his hand. "Come tell me about it."

Theron shook his head. "No." The earring danced.

Basil smiled. "What did you have to do to get it? Did you tell her you loved her, too?"

"Stop it."

"I do know you, you see. You may not be the true scholar you'd like to be, but you are a scholar of the heart."

"Shut up!"

"I'm sorry if I offend you, my lord."

"That is enough." Theron could barely bite the words out for anger. He flung himself to the door and fumbled at the latch, which rattled with his trembling.

Basil gathered up the rich cloak, dusted it down with his hand. "Your cloak, my lord?"

"*Damn* you!" Theron snatched the cloak from him and was gone.

Basil sighed with satisfaction. Knowledge was sweet, and power was sweeter. With something approaching awe, he wrapped the book back up in its cloth. "Un-covering of Hidden Trothe" indeed.

The Blackbird's Nest was jammed with drunken boys. Someone had been liberal, and the liberality had included Master Rugg.

"Looking for your true love?" the drunken master asked as Basil surveyed the mess. "You've just missed him. He stood it as long as he could, but it seems his mind is nicer than his judgment."

"Stood what?" asked Basil.

"Listen," said Rugg.

A voice raised itself above the general roar: "I've got one, I've got one! To Campion: May his rod never falter!"

"Good one, Reynold, good. How about this? To Campion: May his bride's maidenhead prove as tight as his lover's arsehole!"

There was a brief, shocked silence. "Hammond, you fool," said someone, and "Oh, bugger," said Hammond, catching sight of Basil standing at Rugg's elbow.

Basil surveyed the crowd: flushed faces turned up to him or down to their cups and tankards, bearded, clean-shaven, round, hollow-cheeked, young as he'd never felt himself, waiting for him to react.

"Just a joke," rumbled Rugg uncomfortably. "High spirits, eh? Youth."

"It's traditional," said Basil evenly, "to toast a man on the occasion of his betrothal." He took the cup from Rugg's lax hand and lifted it to the room. "To Campion. May his dedication to his name and lineage not go unrewarded." He put the cup to his lips and drained it, unsurprised to find it an excellent red wine. Hadn't Campion said the Nest kept good wine if you knew how to ask for it?

Silent bewilderment greeted his toast, and silence followed him as he turned on his heel and strode out of the tavern into a bright, cold afternoon. Basil felt no anger as he walked through the narrow streets, just a slow bleeding away of mind and spirit that could only be stanched by the sight of Theron Campion on his knees before him, weeping.

When he reached his room on Minchin Street, Basil closed the door and locked it, sat at his table and laid his hand upon the cover of the Book of Spells.

He turned through the book, searching for the spell he needed, hesitated over "A Spelle to Entrappe the Spirrit" and "A Spelle to In-Force Love," rejected them; came to "A Spelle to Turne Men into Beastes." He read it once and then again, his mind filling with images of green leaves and still waters, of a kneeling stag and a collar of gold and a black-robed man. The third time, he read aloud.

Conversing in a gilded drawing room on the Hill, Lord Theron Campion felt the green leaves of the wood close around him. He lifted his head and gave a peculiar, belling cry.

"My dear, what is it?" Lady Randall stood over him, trying to reach beyond her corsets to help him to his feet. Theron's body felt heavy, his sex was a weight between his legs. For once, he had no words to answer. Lady Genevieve hurried to his side in a rustle of skirts.

"No!" he cried hoarsely, arm upraised to fend her off. "Don't—"

The girl's scent filled his nostrils. He stumbled to his feet while his hands still sought the floor. The scent of woman overpowered him. "I must go." He lowered his head and ran, kicking aside the presents he had brought her, moving, not to the door, but to the window, the fresh air. The glass baffled him for a moment, but it gave way to his battering and fell in a glittering rain onto the patterned carpet. Then he leapt through the window and fled through the garden, head high, nostrils flared to catch the scent of the hunt.

Basil sat with the book between his hands. Under his scholar's robe, he was naked and barefoot. The night had grown chilly, but he felt no cold, all his being concentrated on listening for the king's arrival. Knowledge burned through his palms. He was coming; he was close. There was a clattering on the stairs as of booted feet or hooves, and then the door shook under a powerful, rhythmic pounding. He was come.

Basil rose, took up his candle, and opened the door. Theron lifted his head and looked at him, wild-eyed. There was blood on his forehead; his unbound hair was spangled with blood and broken glass. His sides were heaving with the force of his panting. His fawn-colored coat was torn and streaked with mud and wet leaves.

"My lord," said Basil, and stepped back. Theron stumbled after him to the bare middle of the chamber, where he stood trembling, just beyond Basil's reach.

Basil felt in the long sleeve of his robe and drew forth the chain Theron had given him. The heavy links lay heaped in his hand, glowing in the candlelight, burning his fingers like ice.

"Come," said Basil.

Theron stood stiff-legged, his head raised unnaturally high, his fine-carved nostrils flared.

"Come," said Basil again, and held the chain out over his outstretched palms, a golden garland.

Theron swung his head and cried out, an animal's sound in a man's throat.

"Come," said Basil a third time, and Theron fell awkwardly to his hands and knees before him. Basil bent to lay the gold chain gently around his neck and caressed his head, heedless of glass. The blood from his hand ran between Theron's eyes, tinging the tears that streaked Theron's cheeks as he murmured, "My king, my lord, my love, my own."

Bill Lewis

Coyote and the White Folks

Sheela Na Gig

Bill Lewis is an acclaimed English poet, storyteller, and performance artist who often works with the magical themes of Old and New World mythology. His performance venues have included the London Institute of Contemporary Arts, the Cambridge International Poetry Festival, and the Avon Festival; he also takes his poetry into schools, hospitals, and prisons. He has performed his work across the U.S. and in South America, where his poetry has been translated into Spanish.

The following two poems are reprinted from Lewis's most recent collection, An Intellect of the Heart, *available from Lazerwolf Press (66 Glencoe Rd., Chatham, Kent, U.K.). "Coyote and the White Folks" is a wry look at Native American trickster legends; "Sheela Na Gig" is a sensuous evocation of ancient Celtic lore concerning the Green Man's female counterpart.*

—T. W.

Coyote and the White Folks

Coyote watches the pilgrims land.
He'd been getting bored anyway.

After ten thousand years the native
population was wise to his tricks.

Fact is, he'd been too good at his
profession. Done himself out of a job.

Coyote invents the stock market.
              Everyone falls for it.

Coyote teaches military tactics to Custer.
(That can be the only explanation.)

Coyote writes scripts for soap operas.
Everyone says they're like real life.

Coyote writes scripts for real life.
Everyone says it's just like soap operas.

Coyote works as a spin doctor, gets
a movie actor elected as president.

Coyote says, I think it's going to be
quite a few years until my retirement.

Sheela Na Gig

Wind kissed are my tumuli.
Wet mud sucks the iron spade.

Anoint this nub of my flesh
for it is the hub of my wheel.

It is the polar axis of the
spinning palace of the year.

Caress this crevice of clay
with agriculture and archangels.

Rub the plough with fennel and
incense, hallowed soap and salt.

Ride me with hobby horses and
dig me with the archaeology of
your rain drenched desire.

Furrow me with antler picks.
Sow me with a semen of light;

the oyster ejaculations of dawn,
              mistletoe berries
      caught in a linen apron.

I pull back the moss-moist labia
and you see the winter is pregnant

with the spring and spring has
summer curled and fetal in her womb.

And inside summer, autumn waits
dreaming in golden hibernation.

Michael Cadnum

The Flounder's Kiss

Michael Cadnum lives in northern California and is the author of thirteen novels including St. Peter's Wolf, Skyscape, The Judas Glass, Zero at the Bone, In a Dark Wood *(about Robin Hood), and* Heat. *He has also published several collections of poetry, most recently* The Cities We Will Never See *and two illustrated books for children,* The Lost and Found House *and* Ella and the Canary Prince *(based on Cinderella).*

"The Flounder's Kiss" is based on the Grimm fairy tale "The Fisherman and His Wife." Cadnum's version follows the traditional tale of greed but transforms it into something more cheeky and simultaneously more sinister than the original.

—E. D. and T. W.

My beautiful bride said if you spend all your time fishing the river, you catch nothing but monkfish and bream. You get water wens all over your feet. If you want money, she said, you go sea fishing.

So there I was, a river man all my life, marrying after I had nine gray hairs, pricing fisher's small-craft at the weekly sale. Most of those belly-up clinker-builts belong to dead fishermen, their bodies feeding crabs, and everybody knows it. It keeps the prices down, but I decided to be a beach fisher, and I had some luck. You have to take the long view. You like whelks, you eat whelks. Shellfish don't bother me. When I don't catch anything, the tide all the way to the sunken merchantman in the mouth of Zeebruge harbor, I trudge back and start clamming. Eight, nine you have supper.

Yanni, my rose-cheeked wife, would say, "All day out there, and you come home with what?" That lovely mouth of hers, working nonstop.

"I have six fine cockles," I would say. Or, if the tide had run well, two fine whiting. Or two soles, or John Dory, or a dozen pier mussels. Whatever it was, and they were always prime. I don't want to eat anything diseased or deformed or that looks peculiar. The fact is some days I can't bring myself to eat fish. It's not just that fish flop around with their mouths open. They have slits they breathe through and eyes that look up like pennies, and there's nothing you can do to tell a fish to lie still. You can use one of those mallets especially made for shutting fish up, head hammers, the dorymen around here call them in their usual jocular way, but about the only thing you can say to a fish is nothing.

Tourists love it. We put on these wooden mud-treaders, and you can hear them calling to their kids, "Look, how darling, wooden shoes." And I, for one, always wave and smile. I know they can't help it, so far from home and nothing to look at but a man going to work with about twenty ells of net on his back.

"You bother to catch one pilchard, Weebs, you might as well catch a hundred," my wife would say. Always sewing, needle winking up and down. Skirts, blouses, collars, gloves. "I might as well be a herring gull you come back with such tiny little fish."

"It takes a lot to maneuver the net with just two arms," I would answer. "You need a strong back and a feel for the current."

"You've got talent, Weebs," she would respond. "A rare genius. You ought to win a prize for being able to work for less money than anyone who ever scraped mud."

"You want me to catch flounder."

"Eels," Yanni would reply, squinting at her needle.

"Eels have two hearts," I would say. "They crawl over land. They have conventions in the ocean, they have nests in the hills. An eel is too complicated to eat. I like pilchards. You can hold a fish like that in your hand."

"Men," my wife would say.

"There's something about a herring that says I'm made for eating, it's okay to eat me, I have an eye on each side of my head, and I am going to be eaten by something I never saw coming, it might as well be you."

"Catch something worth the effort," she would reply. Bored, having given up on me. But still talking about it, one of those people who can't shut up. She would walk into a room making announcements saying she was cold, I would be late for high tide, why was it so dark, where was her darning.

It was a glorious day for watching clouds. I had caught nothing. The sea was filthy, a gale out of the northwest. All the horsefishers were in their stables. The sailorfishers were sipping juniper spirits by their fires, and there was only I myself, on the broad flat beach. I didn't want to come home wet with rain and wet with brine, blue and nothing to show for it but a pocketful of limpets.

You cast your net and it looks pretty, black lace spreading out. When it drifts down over the water there is a splash where the netting settles, and the sound of it is what satisfies. Casting the net, you feel the waves calm under the span you mended, and sometimes I could do it well into the dark, regardless whether or not I caught a fingerling.

I was almost ready to quit for the night. One more cast, I told myself. Just one more. It's a serene sight, the net sweeping up, hanging over the waves, lifting with the wind. The net drifted onto the sea. And it happened. The net tugged, tightened. And there it was as I hauled in the net, the famous fish, the size of a Michaelmas tureen, fat and silver.

I have a great aversion to flounders. I can't stand to take them by the tail, much less slit one open. They have their eyes close together on one side of their head, and they swim around blind on one side, looking up at the sky with the other. I want something simple to eat, not a living curiosity.

I realized, however, that it was worth a guilder or two, a fish like this, an armload, and while I am not the most gifted fisherman alive, I am no fool. I pulled the one-sided creature out as it flopped in the net. I dragged it onto the beach and untangled the net, and then I heard something. I looked up, looked around, my head tilting this way and that. The wind was whistling, and I was not sure what I heard.

Maybe it was a tourist talking, one of the day-trip spinsters out of Southampton; they ferry across and flirt at a distance. They say things like "what a wonderful fish you have just caught," in German, as though I would ever speak a syllable of the language. The tourists are the equivalent of herring themselves, the poor dears. It would be just like one to be chattering in a rising wind in the dusk in the middle of nowhere. Not just talking, arguing, jabbering to make a point.

I stooped to gather in enough fish to buy a silver thimble and a bolt of silk when I realized that the muttering was close to my ear. I dropped the flounder. It smacked the sand and made that shrugging flopping I hate in fish—why can't they just fall asleep and die? The fish said clearly, but in a small voice, "Wish. Go ahead wish. Just wish. Any wish. Don't wait—wish."

I seized my gutting knife and just about used it, out of horror. But instead I asked it a question. My brother shovels waffles into the oven on a paddle and has a cellar of cheese. My sister married a brewer, and has beer and fat children. My father took tolls on a bridge with carved seraphim and saints, burghers and fair ladies and military men calling him by name, wishing him well.

And I was talking to a fish.

And the fish was talking back. "Any wish. Then let me go."

It was persistent, this idiot babble. So I made a wish. I asked for a bucket full of herring, pink-gilled, enough for tonight and a few left over for the market.

By candlelight Yanni picked a spinebone from her mouth and said, her eyebrows up, not wanting to admit it, "That was most delicious, Weebs. Most tasty little fish I have ever supped upon."

"There's a story behind that fish," I said.

She gave me one of her bedroom glances, dabbed her pretty lips.

"But never mind," I said.

"Tell me," she said.

I pushed my plate away, put my elbows on my table, and took a sip of beer, dark brew, tart, almost like vinegar. I smiled. I said, "You won't believe it."

Not a quarter of an hour later I was wading into the surf. "Fish!" I called. "Big fish! Flounder!"

It was raining hard. Despite what you might have heard, there was no poem, no song. There was a lump on my head, and one eye was swelling shut. I bellowed into the wind, now straight out of the north. "One more boon," I asked.

Waves broke over me, drowning the sound of my voice. There were no fish.

The fish were vanished from the sea. I stood drenched, about to turn away, when the fish was there at my side, its eyes two peas side by side.

"One more!" I said. I was standing in a storm talking to a fish, and before shame or common sense could silence me I repeated Yanni's desire.

I hurried back, running along the dike. Cows with their big, white foreheads stared at me from within their mangers, and when I half collapsed in my cottage she seized me by my jerkin and turned me around. "Look!"

The kettle had unbent its hook, fallen into the fire, solid gold and impossible to drag out of the embers. "It's going to melt!" she cried.

"You wanted it turned to gold," I said.

"Go back and get this made into money."

I panted, dripping, catching my breath. "Money?"

"Coins! Sovereigns, ducats, dollars. We can't do anything with this."

"It's beautiful!"

"And then ask for brains, Weebs. For you. For inside your head."

"You should try to be more patient, dear Yanni," I said. I think it was the only time I had ever offered her such advice.

She put her hands on her hips. In her apron and her cap she told me what she thought of me. All this time I had thought her pensive, moody, emotional. But I thought she loved me.

I took my time. The wind was warm, out of the west now, and there were a few stars. When I was a boy I would want to stand outside in the wind and feel my sweater and my sleeves billow and flow, flying. Both feet on the ground, but flying in my heart.

"Fish! Magic flounder!"

It must have known. Once it began to trade in human desire it was finished. No net is worse. It nosed upward, out of the waves. Why it even listened I cannot guess. I thrust my hand into a gill, seized a fin, and hauled the creature with all my strength. I dragged it up where the sand was dry, black reeds, gulls stirring, croaking.

The fish was talking nonstop. I tugged my knife free of the belt and cut the flounder, gills to tail, and emptied him out on the sand.

There has been some question about my wife. Some say the fish renounced the boons, took it all back, and sent us into poverty. Some say my wife left me, taking the golden kettle with her, swinging it by one fist, strong as she was famous to be.

Proof against this is the kettle I still possess, heavy as an anvil, chipped at slowly over the years, shavings of pure gold to buy feather quilts and heifers. And this is not the only precious metal in my house. A golden pendant the shape of a woman's mouth dangles ever at my breast.

A parting gift? some ask.

Or a replacement for her, suggests the even-smarter guest with a chuckle, enjoying my roast goose.

Fish do not die quickly. They take their time. And even a magic fish is slow to understand. Give me silence, I wished, crouching over him, knife in hand. Silence, and the power to bring her back someday, should it please me, one kiss upon her golden lips.

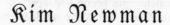

Paul J. McAuley and
Kim Newman

Residuals

Paul J. McAuley's first major success as a writer was in 1988, when he won the Philip K. Dick Award for his debut novel, Four Hundred Billion Stars. *Subsequent books include* Secret Harmonies, Eternal Light, Red Dust, *and* Pasquale's Angel *(winner of the Sidewise Award for best long-form alternate history), the short story collections* The King of the Hill *and* The Invisible Country, *and the anthology* In Dreams *(coedited with Kim Newman). He won the 1995 British Fantasy Award for his short story "The Temptation of Dr. Stein" and the 1996 Arthur C. Clarke Award and the Campbell Memorial Award for his novel* Fairyland.

Kim Newman's epic historical vampire novel, Anno Dracula, *won several genre awards, including the International Horror Critics Guild Award. His other novels include* The Bloody Red Baron *(sequel to* Anno Dracula), The Night Mayor, Bad Dreams, Jago, The Quorum, *and a series of gaming novels under the pseudonym Jack Yeovil. His short fiction is collected in* The Original Dr. Shade and Other Stories *(including the British Science Fiction Award–winning title story) and* Famous Monsters. *Some of his nonfiction titles are* Nightmare Movies, *the Bram Stoker Award–winning* Horror: 100 Best Books *(edited with Stephen Jones), and* The BFI Companion to Horror. *His most recent book, a collection of connected short stories, is a collaboration with Eugene Byrne called* Back in the USSA.

"Residuals," an eerie look at the UFO abduction phenomenon, was first published in Asimov's Science Fiction *magazine.*

—E. D.

On his way out, the motel guy switches on the TV and the AC without bothering to ask if I want either. The unit over the door rattles and starts to drip on the purple shag carpet. On a dusty screen, a cowboy hunkers down over the Sci-Fi Channel station ident, squinting from under a Stetson. It ought to be like looking at myself because the cowboy is supposed to be me. But it's not.

The Omega Encounter is always playing somewhere on a rerun channel, I guess, but here and now it's like an omen.

I'm still living off the Omega residuals because it's my version of what went down, officially adapted from the "as told to" book Jay Anson did for me. Nyquist sold Starlight, the book Tom Fuckin' Wolfe wrote with him, for twenty times as much to Universal.

There's a little skip where there used to be a shot of a fly-blown, bloodied rubber cow carcass. It could be a censor cut or a snip to reduce the running time. When E. W. Swackhamer directed Omega, there were thirteen minutes of commercials in an hour of TV; now there are eighteen, so five minutes of each hour have to be lost from everything made before the nineties.

I don't unpack, except for the bottles of Cuervo Gold Tequila I bought at the airport, and sit up on the bed, watching two days of my life processed and packaged as a sixteen-year-old movie-of-the-week.

It's gotten to the part where I find the first of the mutilated cattle. I'm showing one to Mr. Nyquist, played by Dennis Weaver the way he plays McCloud, shrewd and upright. To tell the truth, Nyquist was always half bombed even before it all started, and had a mean streak in him that was nothing to do with drink. The bastard would hit Susan when he was loaded, going off like a firecracker over the slightest thing and stomping out, banging the screen door hard, leaving her holding her cheek and me looking down at my dinner. He was crazy even then, I guess, but still able to hold it down.

The movie makes me a lot more talkative than I ever was around Nyquist. Susan is Cybill Shepherd in her post–Last Picture Show, pre-Moonlighting career slump. I am Jan-Michael Vincent in his post-birth, pre-death career trough.

I watch until I follow the slime trails in the grass and see the lights of the mothership off in the distance hovering above the slough, and then I flip channels because I can't stand to watch anymore.

They didn't have the budget to do the aliens properly on TV and only used long shots, but I still don't want to watch. I can take the expensive computer-controlled models in the movie because they're too real in the way Main Street in Disneyland is too real. So perfect a reproduction it doesn't fool anyone for a second. But show me a couple of out-of-focus midgets jumping around inside silvered plastic bags in slow motion with the setting sun behind them, and my imagination fills in the blanks. The sour reek. And the noise the things made as they hopped around, like they were filled with Jell-O and broken bones.

QVC is less of a blow to the heart. I drink tequila out of the bathroom glass and consider calling a toll-free number to order a zircon chandelier. Then I drink some more and decide against it.

Despite Steven Spielberg, Harrison Ford (as Nyquist), and five million prein-flation bucks of ILM, *Starlight: The Motion Picture* was a box-office disappoint-ment. By the time the effects were developed, *Omega* had spun off a mid-season replacement series with Sam Groom (as me) and Gretchen Corbett that got canceled after three episodes. The aliens were old news, and everybody knew how the story came out. In *Starlight*, I'm rewritten as a codger farmhand who sacrifices himself for Boss Man Ford, stealing the film with a dignified death scene. Richard Farnsworth got an Oscar nomination for Best Supporting Actor, but lost out to the gook in *The Killing Fields*.

I give up TV and call my agent, using the room phone because my mobile doesn't want to work out here in the desert, all that radar, or the microwave signals they send to the secret Moon colony (ha ha), and I tell him where I am. He says to watch my ass, and that when I get back he thinks he might have another hardware store commercial lined up ("fix your Starship, lady?"). It's just for New York cable, but it'll pay the rent a while. He doesn't think I can pull off this reunion, is what it is, and I tell him that, and then I hang up and I watch an old *Saturday Night Live* for a while.

I was on one show for about five minutes, in a Conehead episode with Dan Aykroyd and Jane Curtin. Can't hardly remember that night—I was drunk at the time—but now I guess those five minutes are always showing somewhere, just like everything else that ever went through a transmitter. If aliens out there have been monitoring our broadcasts like they did in old movies to explain why they speak perfect English, just about the first question we'd ask them was if they taped those lost episodes of *The Honeymooners*. I watch Chevy Chase do Jerry Ford falling over just about everything in the studio set, and drink some more tequila, and fall asleep a while.

It's been a long day, the flight out from New York delayed two hours, then a long drive through Los Angeles, where I've never driven because I was chauf-feured around when all the deals were in the air, and which is ten times more packed with traffic than I remember, and out into the high desert along Pear-blossom Highway with all the big trucks driving in bright sunlight and blowing dust with their headlights on.

The phone wakes me up. I use the remote to turn down Dave Letterman, and pick up. A voice I haven't heard for twenty years says, "Hello, Ray."

At first, only the *Enquirer* and the *Weekly World News* were interested. But when the reports came back and the FBI slapped a security classification on them, and Elliot Mitchell started making a fuss because he was transferred to the Texas panhandle and his field notes and his twenty rolls of film and six hours of cassette recordings were "lost," *Newsweek* and *Rolling Stone* showed up. Tom Wicker's piece in *Rolling Stone* said it was all part of a government plot stretch-ing back to Roswell, and that the U.S. Army was covering up tests with hallu-cinogenic weapons.

Then the artifacts went on view, and ten types of expert testified they were "non-terrestrial." It wasn't a government conspiracy any more, it was a goddamn alien *invasion*, just like Nyquist and me had been saying. Mitchell had rewritten his field notes from memory, and sent photocopies to *Science* and *Nature*. He even got his name as discoverer on the new hyperstable transuranic element, which along with the bodies was one of the few tangible residues of the whole thing. I wonder how he felt when Mitchellite was used in the Gulf War to add penetrative power to artillery shells?

Then the Washington *Post* got behind the story, and all the foreign press, and the shit hit the fan. For a while, it was all anybody talked about. We got to meet President Carter, who made a statement supporting our side of things, and declared he would see that no information was withheld from the public.

I was on the *Tonight Show* with Johnny Carson, back when that meant something. I did Dick Cavett, *CBS News* with Walter Cronkite, *60 Minutes* with Mike Wallace, *NBC Weekend News* with Jessica Savitch. Me and Nyquist were scurrying to get our book deals sorted out, then our screen rights. People were crawling all over, desperate to steal our lives, and we went right along with the feeding frenzy.

We wrapped each other up with restraints and gag orders, and shot off our mouths all the time. Mitchell was out of the loop: instead of deals with Hollywood producers and long lunches with New York publishers, he got tied up in a civil liberties suit because he tried to resign from the U.S. geological survey and the government wouldn't let him.

Then the Ayatollah took the hostages, and everyone had something else to worry about. Carter became a hostage in his own White House and most of the artifacts disappeared in the C-130 aircrash the conspiracy theorists said was staged. Reagan never said anything on record, but the official line changed invisibly when he became President. The reports on the reports questioned the old findings, and deposits of Mitchellite showed up on Guam and somewhere in Alaska.

I did *Geraldo* with Whitley Strieber and Carl Sagan, and came off like a hick caught between a rock and a hard place. I had started drinking by then, and tried to punch out one or the other of them after the show, and spent the night in a downtown holding tank. I faced a jury of skeptics on *Oprah* and was cut to pieces, not by reasoned scientific arguments and rationalizations but by cheapshot jokes from a studio audience of stand-up wannabes.

I told my side of it so many times that I caught myself using exactly the same words each time, and I noticed that on pre-recorded shows, the presenter's nods and winks—always shot from a reverse angle after the main interview—were always cut in at exactly the same points. An encouraging dip of the head laced with a concerned look in the eyes, made in reaction to a cameraman's thumb, not an already-forgotten line from me.

Besides *The Omega Encounter* and *Starlight*, there were dozens of books, movies, TV specials, magazine articles, a Broadway play, even a music album. Creedence Clearwater Revival's "It Came Out of the Sky" was reissued and charted strongly. Some English band did a concept album. John Sladek and Tom Disch collaborated on a novel-length debunking, *The Sentients: A Tragi-Comedy*. That's in development as a movie, maybe with Fred Ward.

Sam Shepard's *Alienation*, which Ed Harris did on Broadway and Shepard starred in and directed for HBO, looked at it all from the dirt farmer's point of view, suggesting that Nyquist and me were looking for fresh ways of being heroes since we'd lost touch with the land. The main character was a combination of the two of us, and talked in paragraphs, and the scientist—Dean Stockwell on TV—was a black-hatted villain, which displeased Mitchell no end. He sued and lost, I recall.

By then I was looking at things through the blurry dimple at the bottom of the bottle, living off the residuals from commercials and guest appearances in rock videos and schlock direct-to-video horror movies shot by postmodernist *auteurs* just out of UCLA film school, though I recall that Sam Raimi's *The Color Out of Time* was kind of not bad.

Then I read in *Variety* that Oliver Stone has a treatment in development raking the whole thing up, blaming it all on J. Edgar Hoover, Armand Hammer and Henry Kissinger. There was an article in the New York *Times* that Norman Mailer had delivered his thousand-page summation of the phenomenon, *The Visitation*. And that's where I got the idea to get in touch with Mitchell and make some cash on the back of Stone and Mailer's publicity, and maybe Mitchell had been reading the same articles, because before I can begin to think how to try and track him down, he calls me.

I drive past the place I'm to meet Mitchell and have to double back, squinting in the glare of the big rigs that roar out of the darkness, all strung up with fairylights like the spaceship in *Closer Encounters*. I do what sounds like serious damage to the underside of the rental when I finally pull off.

The ruins are close to the highway, but there's a spooky feeling that makes me leave the car's headlights on. Out across the dark desert basin, where the runways of Edwards Air Force Base are outlined in patterns of red and green lights a dozen miles long, some big engine makes a long drawn-out rumble that rises to a howl before cutting off.

I sit in the car and take a few pulls on my bottle to get some courage, or at least burn away the fluttering in my gut, looking at the arthritic shapes that Joshua trees make in the car headlights. Then I make myself get out and look around. There's not much to the ruins, just a chimney stack and a line of pillars where maybe a porch stood. People camping out have left circles of ash in the sand and dented cans scattered around; when I stumble over a can and it rattles off a stone, I realize how quiet the desert is, beyond the noise of the trucks on the highway. I get a feeling like the one I had when the three of us were waiting that last night, before we blew up the mothership, and have to take another inch off the level of the tequila to calm down.

That's when my rental car headlights go out and I almost lose it, because that's what happened when they tried to kidnap me, the lights and then the dashboard on my pickup going out and then a bright light all around, coming from above. That time, I had a pump-action shotgun on the rack in the cab, which is what saved me. Now, I have a tequila bottle with a couple of inches sloshing in it, and a rock I pick up.

A voice behind me says my name, and I spin and lose my balance and fall on my ass, the tequila bottle emptying over my pants leg. A flashlight beam pins me, and behind it, Elliot Mitchell says, "This was the last socialist republic in the USA, did you know that? They called the place Llano del Rio. This was their meeting hall. They built houses, a school, planted orchards. But the government gave their water rights to the local farmers and they had to move out. All that's left are the orchards, and those will go because they're subdividing the desert for housing tracts to take LA's overspill."

I squint into the light, but can't see anything of the man holding it.

"Never put your faith in government, Ray. Its first instinct is not to protect the people it's supposed to serve but to protect its own self. People elect politicians, not governments. Don't get up. I'm happier to see you sitting down. Do you think you were followed here?"

"Why would I be followed? No one cares about it anymore. That's why I'm here."

"You want to make another movie, Ray? Who is it with? Oliver Stone? He came out to see me. Or sent one of his researchers anyway. You know his father was in the Navy, don't you, and he's funded by the UN counterpropaganda unit, the same one that tried to assassinate Reagan. The question is, who's paying you?"

"Crazy Sam's Hardware back in Brooklyn, if I do the ad."

I have a bad feeling. Mitchell appears to have joined the right-wing nuts who believe that little black helicopters follow them everywhere, and that there are secret codes on the back of traffic signs to direct the UN invasion force when it comes.

I say, "I don't have any interest except the same one that made you want to call me. We saved the world, Elliot, and they're ripping off our story . . ."

"You let them. You and Nyquist. How *is* old Nyquist?"

"Sitting in a room with mattresses on the walls, wearing a backward jacket and eating cold creamed corn. They made him the hero, when it was *us* who blew up the mothership, it was *us* who captured that stinking silver beachball, it was *us* who worked out how to poison most of them."

I put the bottle to my lips, but there's hardly a swallow left. I toss it away. This isn't going the way I planned, but I'm caught up in my anger. It's come right back, dull and heavy. "We're the ones that saved Susan, not her lousy husband!"

"We didn't save her, Ray. That was in your TV movie, *The Omega Encounter*. We got her back, but the things they'd put inside her killed her anyway."

"Well, we got her back, and if fuckin' Doc Jensen had listened, we *would* have saved her, too!"

I sit there, looking into the flashlight beam with drunken tears running down my face.

"How much do you remember, Ray? Not the movies, but the *real thing?* Do you remember how we got Susan out of the mothership?"

"I stay away from shopping malls, because they give me flashbacks. Maybe I'm as crazy as Nyquist. Sometimes, I dream I'm in one of those old-fashioned hedge mazes, like in *The Shining*. Sometimes, I'm trying to get out of the hospital they put us in afterward. But it's always the same, you know."

Mitchell switches off the flashlight. I squint into the darkness, but all I see is swimming afterimages.

"Come tomorrow," Mitchell says, and something thumps beside me.

It is a rock, with a piece of torn paper tied to it. Under the dome light of the rental car, I smooth out the paper and try to make sense of the map Mitchell has drawn.

Two days. That's how long it took. Now, my life is split into Before and After. What no one gets is that the thing itself—the event, the encounter, the invasion, the incursion, the whatever—was over inside two days. I've had head colds and belly-aches that lasted a whole lot longer. That's what marks me out. When I die, my obits will consist of three paragraphs about those two days and two sentences about everything else. Like I said about Jan-Michael, I have a post-birth, pre-death rut for a life. Except for those two days.

After about a decade, it got real old. It was as if everyone was quizzing me about some backyard baseball game I pitched in when I was a kid, blotting out all of the rest of my life—parents, job, marriages, kid, love, despair—with a couple of hours on the mound. I even tried clamming up, refusing to go through it all again for the anniversary features. I turned my back on those two days and tried to fix on something else worth talking about. I'd come close to making it with Adrienne Barbeau, didn't I? Or was it Heather Locklear? Maybe it was just in one of the scripts and some actor played me. I was doing harder stuff than alcohol just then.

That phase lasted maybe three months. I was worn down in the end. I realized that I *needed* to tell it again. For me, as much as for everyone else. I was like those talking books in that Bradbury novel—yeah, I admit it, I read science fiction when I was a kid, and doesn't *that* blow my whole story to bits, proving that I made it all up out of half-remembered bits of pulp magazine stories—my whole life was validated by my story, and telling it was as necessary to me as breathing. Over the years, it got polished and shiny. More than a few folks told me it sounded like Bradbury.

"A million years ago, Nyquist's farm was the bottom of the ocean," I would always begin, paraphrasing the opening of my book. "Susan Nyquist collected sea-shells in the desert. Just before I looked up and saw the spinning shape in the sky, I was sifting through the soft white sand, dredging up a clam-shaped rock that might once have been alive . . ."

No, I'm not going to tell it all again here. That's not what this is about at all.

Do you know what a palimpsest is? It's old parchment that has been written on once, had the writing rubbed out, and been written on again. Sometimes several times. Only, with modern techniques, scientists can read the original writing, looking underneath the layers.

That's my story. Each time I've told it, I've whited out the version underneath. It's built up, like lime on a dripping faucet. In telling it so many times, I've buried the actual thing.

Maybe that's why I've done it.

Regardless of the movies, it wasn't a B picture, with simple characters and actions. Okay, there were aliens (everyone else calls them that except Strieber, so I guess I can too), a woman was taken, and we poisoned most of them and dug out dynamite and blew up their spaceship (I've never liked calling it that—it was more like one of Susan's shells blown up like a balloon, only with light instead of helium or air). We saved the world, right?

Or maybe we just killed a bunch of unknowable Gandhis from the Beyond. That's what some woman accused me of at a book-signing. She thought they'd come to save us, and that we'd doomed the world by scaring them off.

That gave me a shock. I tried to see the story the way she might.

It didn't play in Peoria. The woman—pink bib overalls, bird's-nest hair, Velma-from-*Scooby-Doo* glasses, a "Frodo Lives!" badge—hadn't seen the visitors, the aliens.

She hadn't seen what they'd done to Susan.

But I was up close.

The little fuckers were evil. No, make that Evil. I don't know if they were from outer space, the third circle of Hell, or the Land of Nod, but they weren't here to help anyone but themselves.

What they did to the cattle, what they did to Susan, wasn't science, wasn't curiosity. They *liked* taking things apart, the way Mikey Bignell in third grade liked setting fire to cats, and Mikey grew up to get shot dead while pistol-whipping a fifty-two-year-old married lady during a filling station hold-up. If the visitors ever grow up beyond the cat-burning phase, I figure they could do some serious damage.

I am not just trying to justify what we did to them.

Now, without trying to tell the story yet again, I'm tapping into what I really felt at the time: half-scared, half-enraged. No Spielberg sense of wonder. No TV movie courage. No Ray Bradbury wistfulness.

"Inside the Ship was all corridors and no rooms, criss-crossing tunnels through what seemed like a rocky rubber solid stuff. Mitchell went ahead, and I followed. We blundered any which way, down passages that made us bend double and kink our knees, and trusted to luck that we'd find where they'd taken Susan. I don't know whether or not we were lucky to find her or whether they intended it. I don't know if we were brave and lucky, or dumb rats in a maze.

"Mitchell claims the thing told us where to go, flashed a floor-plan into our minds, like the escape lights in an airliner. I guess that's his scientific mind talking. For me, it was different. I had a sense of being myself and being above myself, looking down. We didn't take a direct route to Susan, but spiraled around her, describing a mandala with an uneven number of planes of symmetry. It was like the New Math: finding the answer wasn't as important as knowing how to get there, and I think Mitchell and I, in our different ways, both flunked."

I didn't say so in the book, but I think that's why what happened to Susan afterward went down. When we dragged Susan, alive but unconscious, out of the hot red-black half-dark at the heart of the ship we were too exhausted to feel any sense of triumph. We went in, we found her, we got her out. But we didn't get the trick quite right.

Here's how I usually end it:

"Nyquist was shaking too bad to aim the rifle. I don't amount to much, but while I can't shoot good enough to take the eye out of the eagle if you toss a silver dollar in the air, nine times out of ten I'll at least clip the coin. Mitchell was shouting as he ran toward us with two of the things hopping after him. The reel of wire was spinning in his hands as he ran. Nyquist snapped out of it and tossed me the gun"—in his version, he gets both of the critters with two shots, bing-bang—"and I drew a bead, worried that Mitchell would zigzag into the line of fire, then put a bullet into the first alien. Pink stuff burst out of the back of it in midleap, and it tumbled over, deflating like a pricked party balloon.

"Even from where I was, I could smell the stink, and Nyquist started to throw up. The second critter was almost on Mitchell when I fired again, the hot casing stinging my cheek as I worked the bolt, and fired, and fired, and kept shooting as Mitchell threw himself down in a tangle of wire while the thing went scooting off back toward the ship. My hands shaking so bad I sliced my hand bad when I trimmed the wires back to bare copper. Mitchell snatched them from me and touched them to the terminals of the truck's battery.

"We didn't have more than a dozen sticks of low-grade dynamite for getting out tree stumps, and Mitchell hadn't had time to place them carefully when those things came scooting out like hornets out of a bottle. And Mitchell hadn't even wanted to do it, saying that the ship must be fireproofed, like the Apollo module, or it wouldn't have survived atmospheric entry. But it was our last best hope, and when the sticks blew, the ship went up like a huge magnesium flare. I put my hands over my eyes, and saw the bones of my hands against the light. The burst was etched into my eyeballs for months. It hardly left any debris, just evaporated into burning light, blasting the rock beneath to black crystal. You can still see the glassy splash where it stood if you can get the security clearance. There was a scream like a dying beast, but it was all over quickly. When we stopped blinking and the echo was dead, there was almost nothing where the ship had been. They were gone."

Is that an ending? If it is, what has the *rest* of my life been? An epilogue, like on some Quinn Martin series episode, with William Conrad reporting that I am still at large, still running off my mouth, still living it down?

Or has it just been an interlude before the sequel?

I wake up the next morning with the shakes. There's not even fumes in the tequila bottle I clutched to my chest all night, and nothing but warm cans of Dr Pepper in the motel vending machine, so I drive the mile into town and buy a twelve pack of Bud, giving thanks to California's liberal liquor-license laws. I'm coming out of the 7-Eleven when two men in sunglasses fall in step with me on either side, and I don't need to see their badges to know what they are.

They make me leave my beer in the car and take me across the dusty highway to the town's diner, an Airstream trailer with a tattered awning shading one side. The older guy orders coffee and pancakes, and grins across the table while his partner crowds me on the bench. I can't help looking through the greasy window at my car, where the beer is heating up on the front seat, and the older guy's grin gets wider. He gets out a hip flask and pours a shot into my coffee, and I can't help myself and guzzle it down, scalding coffee running down my chin.

"Jesus," the young guy, Duane Bissette, says, disgusted. He's the local field agent, blond hair slicked back from his rawboned face. He hasn't taken off his mirrorshades, and a shoulder harness makes a bulge under his tailored suit jacket.

"Judge not," the other guy says, and pours me another shot, twinkling affably. He has curly white hair and a comfortable gut, like Santa Claus's younger brother. He's hung his seersucker jacket on the back of his chair. There are half-moon sweat stains under his arms, and sweat beads under his hairline. "Ray's living out his past, and he's having a hard time with it. Am I right, or am I right?"

I ignore the rye whiskey in the coffee mug. I say, "If you want to talk to me, talk to my agent first. Murray Weiss, he's in the Manhattan Directory."

"But you're one of us," the older guy says, widening his eyes in mock innocence. "You got your badge, when? '77? '78?"

It was 1976 and I'm sure he damn well knows it, done right out on the White House lawn, with a silver band playing and the Stars and Stripes snapping in the breeze under a hot white sky. The Congressional Medal of Honor for me and Nyquist, and honorary membership in the FBI. I'd asked for that because if it was good enough for Elvis, it was good enough for me. It was the last time I saw Nyquist, and even then he was ignoring me with the same intensity with which I'm right now ignoring that rye.

I say, "Your young friend here was polite enough to show me his badge. I don't believe I know you."

"Oh, we met, very briefly. I was part of the team that helped clean up." He smiles and holds out his hand over the coffee mugs and plates of pancakes, then shrugs. "Guerdon Winter. I'll never forget that first sight of the crater, and the carcass you had."

"You were all wearing those spacesuits and helmets. 'Scuse me for not recognizing you."

The FBI agents looked more like space aliens than the things we killed. They cleared out everything, from the scanty remains of the mothership to my collection of tattered paperbacks. I still have the receipts. They took me and Nyquist and Mitchell and put us in isolation chambers somewhere in New Mexico and put us through thirty days of interrogation and medical tests. They took Susan's body and we never saw it again. I think of the C-130 crash, and I say, "You should have taken more care of what you appropriated, Agent Winter."

Guerdon Winter takes a bite of pancake.

"We could have had that alien carcass stuffed and mounted and put on display in the Smithsonian, and in five years it would have become one more exhibit worth maybe ten seconds' gawping. The public doesn't need any help in getting distracted, and everything gets old fast. You know better than me how quickly they forget. You're the one in showbiz. But we haven't forgotten, Ray."

"You want me to find out what Mitchell is doing."

"Mitchell phoned you from a pay phone right here in town ten days ago, and you wrote him at the box number he gave you, and then you came down here. You saw him last night."

Duane Bissette stirs and says, "He's been holed up for two years now. He's been carrying out illegal experiments."

"If you were following me you could have arrested him last night."

Guerdon Winter looks at Duane Bissette, then looks at me. He says, "We could arrest him each time he comes into town for supplies, but that wouldn't help us get into his place, and we know enough about his interrogation profile to know he wouldn't give it up to us. But he wants to talk to you, Ray. We just want to know what it is he's doing out there."

"He believes you have the map," Duane Bissette says.

I remember the scrap of paper Mitchell gave me last night and say, "You want the map?"

"It isn't important," Guerdon Winter says quickly. "What's important is that you're here, Ray."

I look out at my rental car again, still thinking about the beer getting warm. Just beyond it, a couple of Mexicans in wide-brimmed straw hats are offloading watermelons from a dusty Toyota pickup. One is wearing a very white T-shirt with the Green Lantern symbol. They could be agents, too; so could the old galoot at the motel.

I know Duane Bissette was in my motel room last night; I know he took Mitchell's map and photocopied it and put it back. The thing is, it doesn't seem like betrayal. It stirs something inside me, not like the old excitement of those two crystal-clear days when everything we did was a heroic gesture, nothing like so strong or vivid, but alive all the same. Like waking up to a perfect summer's day after a long uneasy sleep full of nightmares.

I push the coffee away from me and say, "What kind of illegal experiments?"

If Mitchell hadn't been a government employee, if they hadn't ridiculed and debunked his theories, and spirited him off to the ass end of nowhere—no Congressional Medal ceremony for him, he got his by registered mail—if they hadn't stolen the discovery of Mitchellite from him, then maybe he wouldn't have ended up madder than a dancing chicken on a hot plate at the state fair. Maybe he wouldn't have taken it into his head to try what he did. Or maybe he would have done it anyway. Like me, he was living in After, with those two bright days receding like a train. Like me, he wanted them back. Unlike me, he thought he had a way to do it.

Those two agents don't tell me as much as I need to know, but I suspect that they don't know what it is Mitchell is doing. I have an idea that he's building something out in the desert that'll bring those old times back again.

Driving out to Mitchell's place takes a couple of hours. The route on the map he gave me is easy enough: south along Pearblossom's two-lane blacktop, then over the concrete channel of the aqueduct that carries water taken from Washington State—did you see *Chinatown*? yeah, there—and up an unmade track that zigzags along the contours of the Piñon Hills and into a wide draw that runs back a couple of miles. The light in the draw is odd. Cold and purple, like expensive sunglasses. Either side of the road is nothing but rocks, sand, dry scrub, and scattered Joshua trees.

I start to feel a grudging sympathy for Agent Bissette. No matter how he hangs back, it's impossible to tail a car out here without your mark knowing. I have the urge to wait for a dip that puts me momentarily out of his sight and swerve off into a patch of soft sand, sinking the rental like a boat in shallows, creating another unexplained mystery.

Mitchell's place is right at the top of the draw, near the beginning of the tree line. In the high desert, trees grow only on the tops of the mountains. The FBI parks under a clump of stunted pines and lets me go on alone. I'm lucky they didn't want me to wear a wire. They'll just wait, and see if I can cope with Crazy

Elliot. For them, it'll be a boring afternoon, with maybe an exciting apprehension about nightfall.

Me, I'm going back to the Days of Sharp Focus.

The rye in the coffee has burned out and I've not touched the soup-warm beer on the passenger seat. I can feel the heat steaming the booze out of my brain. I'm going into this alone.

I get out of the rental, aware of Winter and Bissette watching me through the tinted windshield of their Lincoln Continental. Of Mitchell, there's not a trace. Not even footprints or tire marks in the sandy track. I crouch down, and run a handful of warm sand through my fingers, making like an Indian tracker in some old Western while I ponder my next move.

There are tine-trails in the sand. The whole area has been raked, like a Japanese garden. I can imagine Mitchell working by night, raking a fan-shaped wake as he backs toward the paved area I see a dozen yards away.

I walk across the sand, and reach the flagstones. This was the floor of a house that's long gone. I can see the fieldstone hearth, and the ruts where wooden walls had been.

Beyond the stone is a gentle incline, sloping down maybe twenty feet, then leveling off. Down there, protected from sight, Mitchell has been building. I look at his paper, and see what he means. The FBI think it's a circuit diagram, but it really *is* a map. Mitchell has made himself a maze, but there's nothing on his map that shows me how to get through it.

I know now where the old timbers of the house have gone. Mitchell has cannibalized everything carriable within a mile, and some things I would have sworn you'd need a bulldozer at least to shift, but he must have had a few truckloads of chickenwire, wood, and just plain junk hauled out here. The archway entrance is a Stonehenge arrangement of two 1950s junkers buried hood-first like standing stones, with their tailfins and clusters of egg-shaped rear lights projecting into the air. A crosspiece made of three supermarket shopping carts completes the arch.

There are other old cars parked and piled in a curving outer wall, built on with wire and wood. And all over the place, sticking up through the sand, are sharp spars and spines that sparkle in the sun.

I know that glittery look, a glinting like the facets of an insect's eye or 1970s eye makeup under fluorescent disco lights. It's Mitchellite.

I walk up to the gateway and stop, careful not to touch the spars. They dot everything—stone, wood, metal—like some sort of mineral mold. Crusty little alien points that seem to be growing out of the ordinary Earth stuff. About ten years ago, a couple of crazy English physicists claimed you could use Mitchellite to get unlimited energy by cold fusion and end up with more Mitchellite than you started with, but they were debunked, defrocked, and for all I know defenestrated, and that was the end of it. But maybe they were right. It looks like the Mitchellite is transmuting ordinary stuff into itself.

There's an iron crowbar, untouched by Mitchellite, propped against a stone. I pick it up, heft it in my hands. It has a good weight. I always felt better with a simple tool, something you could trust.

Planks are set between the half-buried cars, a path into the interior of the maze. They are pocked with Mitchellite spars that splinter the rotten wood from the inside. I smash down with the crowbar and split a plank, scraping away bone-dry wood fragments from the Mitchellite nerve-tangles that have been growing inside, sucking strength from the material.

It looks fragile, but it doesn't crumple under my boots.

On the other side of the arch hangs a shower curtain that leaves a three-foot gap beneath it. I push it aside with the crowbar and step into the maze.

The structure is open to the sky, mostly. The walls are of every kind of junk, wood, lines of rocks or unmortared concrete blocks, even barbed wire, grown through or studded with Mitchellite. A few yuccas rise up from the maze's low walls, their fleshy leaves sparkling as if dusted with purplish snow. The floor is made of Mitchellite-eaten planks. There are stretches of clean, unmarked sand. But by each of them is propped a rake, for obscuring footprints. By the first rake is a pane of glass in the sand, and in the hollow under the glass is a handgun wrapped in a plastic baggie, and a handwritten note. *In case of F(B)IRE smash glass.* So that's what the crowbar is for. I leave the gun where it is and turn and stare at the maze again.

After a while I fish out the map and look at it. It takes me a while even to work out where I am, but with a creepy chill I realize I'm standing on the spot where Mitchell has drawn a stick figure. In the center of the map is a white space, where there's another, bigger stick figure. Dotted throughout are smaller figures, drawn in red. I know what they're supposed to be. Some are drawn over black lines that represent walls.

I call out Mitchell's name.

The maze funnels my own voice back to me, distorted and empty.

"Ray, come on, what are you waiting for?"

It was obviously a doorway. Mitchell bent down low—the round opening was the creatures' size—and squeezed into the ship.

I hesitated, but thought of Susan, and the things that had taken her.

"I'm coming, Mitchell."

I followed the geologist. Inside, was another world.

"I'm coming, Mitchell."

I know at once what he's done. This isn't really a maze. It's a model, twice as big again as the real thing, of the aliens' ship.

My knees are weak and I'm shaking. I'm back on the mandala path. I'm above myself and in myself, and I know where to go. I know the route, just as I know the ache that sets into my knees after a minute, an ache that grows to a crippling pain. Just as I remember finding Susan. And finding out later what they'd done to her.

Mitchell took the lead, that time. I followed, forgetting Nyquist chicken-heartedly frozen at the entrance, not daring to go further.

Remembering, I follow Mitchell's lead again. Around and inward, a spiral across a DNA coil or a wiring diagram, a bee-dance through catacombs. The route is a part of me.

The deeper inside the maze I get, the more Mitchellite there is. The original wood and stone and wire and concrete has been almost completely eaten away.

Purple light glitters everywhere, dazzling even through my sunglasses. Without them, I'd be snow-blind in a minute.

When the process is finished, when there's nothing more of Earth in the maze, will this thing be able to fly? Will Mitchell carry the war to the enemy?

"Ray," someone—not Mitchell—shouts, from behind me.

It's the FBI. I thought I was supposed to haul Mitchell out on my own. Now the pros are here, I wonder why I've bothered.

I feel like a sheep driven across a minefield. A Judas goat.

I got into the maze and I'm still alive, so Guerdon Winter and Bissette know it's safe.

I turn, shading my eyes against the tinted glare that shines up from everything around me. The agents are following my footprints. Bissette doesn't duck under the crossbar of an arch nailed up of silvery grey scraps of wood, and scrapes his forehead against a Mitchellite-spackled plank.

I know what will happen.

It's like sandpaper stuck with a million tiny fishhooks and razorblades. The gentlest touch opens deep gashes. Bissette swears, not realizing how badly he's hurt, and a curtain of blood bursts from the side of his head. A flap of scalp hangs down. Red rain spatters his shades.

Bissette falls to his knees. Guerdon Winter plucks out a handkerchief from the breast pocket of his sweat-stained seersucker jacket. A bedsheet won't staunch the flow.

"You can't go on," Guerdon Winter tells the junior agent, who can't protest for the pain. "We'll come back for you."

Naturally, Guerdon Winter has his gun out. When Mitchell and I went into the mothership, we didn't even think of guns. I left my shotgun in the pickup, and Nyquist held on to his rifle like it was a comforter blanket and wouldn't give it up to us. Some heroes, huh? Every single version of the story rectifies the omission, and we go in tooled up fit to face Bonnie and Clyde.

The FBI has made a bad mistake.

They've changed the story again. By adding the guns, and maybe themselves, they've made me lose my place.

I don't know which way to go from here.

My feet and my spine and my aching knees were remembering. But the memory's been wiped.

Bissette is groaning. His wound is tearing worse—there are tiny particles of alien matter in it, ripping his skin apart as they grow—and the whole right side of his head and his suit-shoulder are deep crimson.

"Ray," prompts Guerdon Winter. There's a note of pleading in his voice.

I look at the fork ahead of us, marked with a cow's skull nodding on a pole, and suddenly have no idea which path to take. I look up at the sky. There's a canopy of polythene up there, scummy with sand-drifts in the folds. I look at the aisles of junk. They mean nothing to me. I'm as blank as the middle of the map Mitchell gave me.

Then Winter does something incredibly stupid. He offers me a hipflask and smiles and says, "Loosen up, Ray. You'll do fine."

I knock the flask away, and it hits a concrete pillar laced with Mitchellite and sticks there, leaking amber booze from a dozen puncture points. The smell does something to my hindbrain and I start to run, filled with blind panic just the way I was when I followed behind Mitchell, convinced alien blimps would start nibbling at my feet.

I run and run, turning left, turning right, deeper and deeper into the maze. The body remembers, if it's allowed. Someone shouts behind me, and then there's a shot and a bullet spangs off an engine block and whoops away into the air; another turns the windshield of a wheelless truck to lace which holds its shape for a moment before falling away. I leap over a spar of Mitchellite like an antelope and run on, feeling the years fall away. I've dropped the map, but it doesn't matter. The body remembers. Going in, and coming out. Coming out with Susan. That's the name I yell, but ahead, through a kind of hedge of twisted wire coated with a sheen of Mitchellite, through the purple glare and a singing in my ears, I see Mitchell himself, standing in the doorway of a kind of bunker.

He's older than I remember or imagined, the Boy Scout look transmuted into a scrawny geezer wearing only ragged oil-stained shorts, desert boots, and wraparound shades, his skin tanned a mahogany brown. I lean on the crowbar, taking great gulps of air as I try and get my breath back, and he looks at me calmly. There's a pump-action Mossbauer shotgun leaning on the wall beside him.

At last, I can say, "This is some place you got here, Elliot. Where did you get all the stuff?"

"It's a garden," Mitchell says, and picks up the shotgun and walks off around the bunker. He has half-healed scars on his back. Maybe he brushed a little too close to something in his maze.

I follow. The bunker is a poured concrete shell, a low round dome like a turtle shell half-buried in the dry desert dirt. There's a battered Blazer parked at the back, and a little Honda generator and a TV satellite dish. A ramp of earth leads up to the top of the bunker, and we climb up there and stand side by side, looking out over the maze. It extends all around the bunker. The sun is burning over our shoulders, and the concentric spirals of encrusted junk shimmer and glitter, taking the light and making it into something else, a purple haze that glistens in the air, obscuring more than it reveals.

"How long have you been doing this, Elliot? It looks like you've been here years."

Elliot Mitchell says, "You ever been to South America, Ray? You should have. They're very big on flying saucers in South America. Out in Peru, there are patterns of stones in the deserts that only make sense from the air. Like landing strips, parking aprons."

A chill grips me. "You're building a spaceport?"

"We never had any evidence that they came from outer space," Mitchell says.

"What are you saying, they're from *Peru?* There's some bad shit on Earth, but nothing like those things. What are you doing here, Elliot? Trying to turn yourself into one of them? Listen, if you've found anything out, it'll mean a shitload of attention. That's what I . . ."

"More talk shows, Ray? More ten-line fillers in *Time?* I had some guy from the *National Enquirer* come by a month or so ago. He tried to get in. Maybe he's still in here, somewhere."

I remember the red marks on Mitchell's map, in the otherwise blank space of the maze.

I say, "You let me in, Elliot."

"You understand, Ray. You were *there*, with me. You know what it was like. Only you and me really know what it was like."

I see why he wants me here. Mitchell has built this for a purpose, and I'm supposed to tell the world what that is. I say, "What are you planning, Elliot? What are you going to do with all this?"

Mitchell giggles. "I don't control it, Ray. Not anymore. It's more and more difficult to get out each time. When we went to get Susan, where did we go?"

He's setting me up for something. I say dumbly, "Into the ship. That's how I knew to get to you here. This is like the ship."

"It's how I started it out. But it's been *growing*. Started with a bare ounce of Mitchellite, grew this garden over the template I made. Now it grows itself. Like the ship. We went in, and we went somewhere else. Not all the way, because it hadn't finished growing, but a good way. Back toward where they came from. Wherever it was."

"You're saying the ship didn't come from Outer Space?"

"It *grew* here. Like this." Mitchell makes a sweeping gesture with the shotgun, including everything around him. He's King of the Hill. "Once a critical density had been reached, the gateway would have opened, and they would have come through."

"They *did* come through. We poisoned them, we shot them, we blew up their fucking ship—"

"Mitchellite is strange stuff, Ray. Strange matter. It shouldn't exist, not in our universe, at least. It's a mixture of elements all with atomic weights more than ten times that of uranium. It shouldn't even get together in the first place without tremendous energies forcing the quarks together, and it should fly apart in a picosecond after its creation. But it doesn't. It's metastable. It makes holes in reality, increases quantum tunneling so that things can leak through from one universe to another. That's how they probed us. Sent a probe through on the atomic scale and let it grow. Maybe they sent millions of probes, and only one hit the right configuration. Before we sent up astronauts, we sent up chimps and dogs. That's what they did. They sent through seeds of the things we saw, and they lodged and grew."

"In the cows."

Great chunks had been ripped out of the cows I found. Nyquist thought it was chainsaw butchers, until I dug around and found the blisters inside the meat. Like tapeworm cysts. And Susan, Susan, when we got her out . . .

"In the cows," Mitchell says. "That was the first stage. And then they took Susan. That was the second stage, Ray. First chimps, then the astronauts. But we stopped it."

"Yeah. We stopped it."

Mitchell doesn't hear me. He's caught up in his own story.

He says, "They gave the first *astronauts* ticker-tape parades down Wall Street, but what happened to the chimps? First time around they picked us up and husked us of our stories and forgot us. *Second* time is the ticker-tape parade."

Susan never came around. That was a blessing at least. Doc Jensen wouldn't believe me when I told him that I figured what had happened to the cattle was happening to her. Not until that night, when the things started moving under her skin. He tried to cut them out then, but they were all *through* her. So I did the right thing. Doc Jensen couldn't, even though he saw what was inside her. He'd still stuck with his oath, even though he had a bottle of whiskey inside him. So I did what had to be done, and then we went out and blew up the ship.

Mitchell tells me, "You have to believe it, Ray. *This* time they won't forget us. This time we'll control it. They tried to discredit me. They stole my records, they said I was as crazy as Nyquist and tried to section me, they made up stories about finding terrestrial deposits of Mitchellite. Well, maybe those were real. Maybe those were from previous attempts. It's a matter of configuration."

He gestures with the shotgun again, and that's when I cold-cock him.

He thought I'd be on his side. He thought I wanted nothing more than fame, than to get back the feeling we had in those two days. He was right. I did. His mistake was that he thought I'd pay *any* price. And forgetting to put on a shirt.

The crowbar bounces off his skull, and he falls like an unstrung puppet. I kick the shotgun off the domed roof and then he looks up at me and I see what he's done to himself. The sunglasses have come off, and his left eye is a purple mandala.

When I finish, there isn't much left of the top of his head. In amongst the blood and brains: glittering purple-sheened strands, like cords of fungus through rotten wood. A couple of the things inside him try to get out through the scars on his back, but I squash them back into Mitchell's flesh.

After I kill Mitchell, I take the gasoline from his generator and burn the dome without looking to see what's inside it, and smash as much of the whole center of the maze as I can. I work in a kind of cold fury, choking in the black smoke pouring out of the dome, until I can hardly stand. Then I toss the crowbar into the flames and walk out of there.

There's no sign of the FBI agents, although their car is still there when I get out. Winter and Bissette are still back there, incorporated. I hope to God they're dead, although it isn't likely. But the maze has stopped growing, I know that. The light's gone from it. There's a cell phone in the glove compartment, and I use the redial button and tell the guy on the other end that Winter and Bissette are lost, that the whole place has to be destroyed.

"Don't go in there to look for them. Burn it from the air, it would give them a kindlier death. Burn it down and blow it up. Do the right thing. I made a start. They won't come back."

When I say it, for the first time, it sounds finished.

Molly Brown

The Psychomantium

Molly Brown's first published sf story, "Bad Timing," won the British Science Fiction Award for Best Short Story of 1991. Since then, she's had about thirty short stories published. She has worked in various genres, including crime and historical, but mostly in sf and fantasy. Her books include a science fiction thriller for teenagers, Virus, Cracker: To Say I Love You, *and a humorous seventeenth-century whodunnit,* Invitation to a Funeral. *Her latest project is a multiple award–winning online tour of Restoration London, which can be found at* http://www.okima.com/.

"The Psychomantium" was originally published in Interzone 116.

—E. D.

By the time Samantha Stockard arrived in Meadow Lane the market was deserted, the traders gone, the stalls packed away, the road strewn with rubbish. She parked her car in front of the café.

She walked up to the window and looked inside. A man in a white apron was mopping down the floor. Behind him, a young woman sat alone in a plastic booth. She seemed to match the description supplied by Marcia Anson: late teens or early 20s, long yellow hair twisted into dreadlocks, jeans ripped at both knees, oversized jumper looking more than a little frayed, a rhinestone stud glinting in the flesh between her mouth and chin. A cracked mug sat on the table in front of her; she stared down at it without expression, oblivious to Samantha's presence on the other side of the glass.

Samantha stared at the young woman, transfixed. She'd seen her before, she was certain of it. But where? Perhaps it would come to her later, once they'd had a chance to speak.

She walked around to the entrance. It was locked. She knocked on the glass.

The man in the apron waved her away. She knocked again, gesturing for him to come to the door.

He finally put down his mop and opened the door a crack. "Sorry, love. We're closed."

"I don't want to order anything; I just want to talk to that girl," she said, nodding towards the booth. "It'll only take a minute."

The man narrowed his eyes, taking in Samantha's neatly groomed bob and office-style clothing. "In some kind of trouble, is she?"

"Not at all," she assured him. "I just want to talk to her."

"All right." He stepped aside to let her pass, then touched her on the arm, lowering his voice to a whisper. "You mind yourself, love. Anna's a bit . . ." He tapped the side of his head with one finger. "Know what I mean?"

On the one hand, she was relieved to hear the other woman referred to as Anna; that meant she'd definitely found the right person. On the other, she didn't like the way the man kept pointing at his head. "I'm sorry?"

"She's got something wrong upstairs, love. I let her sit in the café sometimes, so long as she don't bother me customers, 'cause she's only young and I feel sorry for her, but I wouldn't credit anything she says if I were you. And I wouldn't turn my back on her," he added darkly.

She looked over at Anna and watched her set the cracked mug upside down on the table, then lean forward to sniff the base. "I'll keep that in mind."

She walked over to the booth and introduced herself. "I understand you knew a woman named Eleanor Burdon."

Anna glanced up at Samantha then quickly looked away. "You're surrounded by flickering shadows of forgotten ghosts, shrouded by the clinging remains of the person you were and the place you came from. You don't belong here."

"Come again?"

"Eleanor Burdon," Anna muttered, gazing down at the table. "Poor old dearie. Only met her the once, you know. She was just like you. Lost and confused and frightened. Gives me a headache to look at you, you know that? You're so blurred around the edges, you keep shimmering in and out of focus like a reflection in a rippled pool."

A stream of brown liquid was dripping off the edge of the table; Anna's upside-down mug hadn't been completely empty. Samantha turned to leave; this was a waste of time.

"You don't belong here," Anna called after her. "You know that, don't you? Deep down inside, you know it. Or at least you suspect. You've started to suspect, haven't you? That's why you're here, isn't it?"

Samantha stopped and turned around. Anna was right: that was exactly why she was there. Maybe it didn't matter that the girl was obviously off her rocker; Eleanor Burdon had worried that she might be going mad, and now it was just possible that Samantha was losing her mind, too. Maybe it took someone crazy to understand what was going on; maybe that's why Eleanor had said that Anna had believed her and understood. Samantha had to take a chance; she had to tell her. "I think something terrible happened to me this morning, but I can't remember what it was."

. . . .

Samantha had tried to hide her nervousness as she followed her new boss, Janet Hale, down the dimly-lit tenth-floor corridor of the north London tower block where Eleanor Burdon had lived. The old woman's flat was all the way down at the end, then around a corner. Samantha had followed Janet's example and stepped into her hooded white coveralls in the hallway outside the flat. They had each put on rubber gloves, and then Janet had opened the door.

"Oh my God!" Samantha reeled backwards, raising a hand to her mouth.

"You're not going to throw up, are you?" Janet asked her.

Samantha shook her head.

"Just try and hold your breath a minute," Janet said, "while I get some air into the place." She disappeared into the flat.

Samantha pulled her hood up, covering her chin-length hair, then reached into her bag for a surgical mask.

She found Janet in the living room, opening every window.

Walking into the dead woman's lounge was like walking into an oven. Samantha moved around the room slowly, sweating in the street clothes beneath her coveralls and trying not to breathe too deeply; despite the open windows, the pungent odor of rotted meat was overpowering.

Yellow foam erupted through the worn upholstery of the dark green settee. A bowl on the floor held several clumps of furry green cereal. A mug sat on top of the television, sprouting something that looked like asparagus and smelled like vomit. A folding metal table was buried under a mountain of yellowing paper: old newspapers, letters, God knew what. More paper overflowed from the half-open drawers of a small wooden cabinet. The threadbare carpet was littered with balls of hair and dust and foam from the sofa.

Janet shook her head and tsk'd, pursing her lips and deepening the furrows between her eyebrows. "Look at this place." She glanced at her younger companion. "All right, Sammy?"

Samantha gritted her teeth; no one had called her "Sammy" since she was ten years old. And she'd felt ill from the moment they'd picked up the key from the caretaker. Janet had introduced him as Hughie, adding that they'd known each other more than 30 years. He looked about Janet's age—mid to late 50s— with a shiny bald pate and thick tufts of reddish hair growing from his ears.

Hughie had insisted they have a cup of tea before going upstairs. Samantha had sipped her tea in silence, trying not to stare at the caretaker's ears—until he'd started regaling them with the story of how he'd come to discover the body, which he did in graphic detail. After that, she couldn't even drink her tea. And she still couldn't stop thinking about some of the things he'd said, like how he could have sworn the old woman was moving until he realized it was only the maggots wriggling.

"I'm fine," she lied.

Janet looked dubious. "You sure? You're awfully pale."

"I'm fine." This was Samantha's first case; she didn't dare admit to feeling sick for fear she'd end up back in the housing department where she'd spent the last three years as a typist.

"If you say so." Janet opened the door to another room and vanished inside. Samantha stayed where she was, not certain if she was expected to wait for

Janet's instructions or impress her with her initiative. She was 23 years old, with an expensive haircut, a car and a mortgage, but Janet seemed to think she was some kind of naïve child. She decided to impress her with her initiative. She crossed over to the table to look through some of the dead woman's papers.

"Sammy, come here," Janet called from the other room Samantha sighed. So much for initiative.

She walked up to the open door and saw that Janet was in the kitchen. "I want you to see this," Janet said, opening each and every cupboard. Apart from a jar of tea bags and a couple of glasses and plates, the shelves were empty. She opened the refrigerator. It, too, was empty, except for one carton of something solid that used to be milk. "No food," she said, shaking her head. "Not a crumb. You often find that." She lifted the flap to the ice-making compartment and stuck her hand inside.

"What are you doing?"

"Sometimes they hide things in there."

"Hide what?"

Janet shrugged. "Money, jewelry, whatever." She reached behind the fridge and unplugged it, then walked past Samantha to open another door, this time to the bathroom. Nothing there but a tub and a sink and an old fashioned gas water-heater. A towel had been draped across the medicine cabinet. Janet lifted a corner of the towel, revealing the cabinet's mirrored front, and chuckled to herself.

"What's funny?" Samantha asked her.

"Hughie's covered all the mirrors again. He does it every time."

Janet left the room before Samantha could ask why. She shrugged and followed her back into the lounge. There was only one door left. As they approached it, Samantha thought she heard something: the whine of a distant motor, perhaps. Janet took a deep breath and reached for the handle. "This'll be it, then," she said.

"Bloody hell," she said a moment later.

The noise Samantha had heard was the buzzing of insects; the windows were covered with bluebottle flies. The moment the door opened, they swirled into the air, becoming a whirring black cloud heading straight for the two women. Samantha screamed, batting her hands wildly in front of her face. Janet calmly crossed the room to open the windows, shooing as many of them as she could outside. "Why don't you start on those papers in the lounge?" she asked, sounding tired.

Samantha didn't bother telling her that was what she'd been trying to do when Janet had called her into the kitchen. She was just grateful to get away from the flies and the sickening stench of death; the smell was even worse in the bedroom where the old woman had lain undiscovered for two weeks in the middle of a summer heatwave. She was beginning to have second thoughts about this job; maybe secretarial work wasn't so bad after all.

Janet followed her into the living room. "You know what to look for?"

"Yes."

The older woman pulled a chair up to the table and gestured for Samantha to sit down. "Insurance policy documents, a will, anything with an address . . . even just a name."

They'd been through this back at the office. "I know."

"Okay," Janet said, heading back into the bedroom. "Shout if you need me."

Samantha pulled off her gloves and started organizing the chaos in front of her into tidy stacks. There were dozens of unopened envelopes, some addressed to Mrs. E. Burdon, others addressed to Occupier. Some said things like: *You may already be a lucky winner.* Others had the words *Final Demand* printed across the top. She put them to one side, to look at later, then picked up a spiral-bound notebook. She flicked through several pages. Nothing useful, just a lot of twee little rhymes written in a precise—if slightly shaky—hand, each ending with the words: *by Eleanor Burdon.*

She could hear Janet through the wall. Rummaging through the old woman's wardrobe and chest of drawers, looking for anything of value that might be passed on to a relative—if they could find any—or sold at auction to pay for the funeral. Then she heard Janet call her name.

She put down the notebook and looked into the bedroom. The remaining flies had settled into a huddle around a light fixture in the ceiling.

Janet was on her hands and knees beside the bed. "Help me with this."

Samantha knelt down beside her and saw a large trunk pushed up against the wall. She got hold of one end while Janet grabbed the other. They pulled it out only to find it wouldn't open. "You any good at picking locks?" Janet asked.

"I've never tried," Samantha said carefully, not certain if that was meant to be a joke or not.

"Then I guess we'll have to find the key." Janet stood and walked over to an old-fashioned dressing table to look through the dead woman's jewelry box. The dressing-table mirror had been covered with a sheet.

Further along the wall behind the dresser, a floor-length black curtain hung across a narrow doorway. Samantha wondered what was behind it. Then she looked down. "Oh God," she said, leaping to her feet.

Janet turned around. "What's the matter?"

Samantha pointed to the discoloured patch of floor that marked the spot where the old woman had lain as clearly as if her body had been traced in chalk. And she'd just been kneeling on it.

Janet made a little tsk'ing noise. "Poor thing, to lie there like that for so long with no one knowing. Trouble is, it could happen to any one of us, Sammy. Any one of us. I always used to tell my children, you won't let that happen to me, will you? But my son married a woman in California and my daughter's in Australia. I'll be lucky if I see my grandchildren once a year. So who'll miss me if something happens? Who'll even know?"

Samantha shrugged, feeling uncomfortable with the way the conversation was going. "They'd miss you at work," she said.

"But I'm retiring year after next, Sammy, remember?" She shook her head and smiled. "Sorry, I don't mean to come over so morbid. It's just . . ."

She turned back to the jewel box on the dresser. "I was younger than you when I started, you know." She laughed. "My first year, I nearly got the sack for wearing my skirts too short; they told me as a representative of local government, my knees had to remain covered at all times."

Samantha walked over to the black curtain and pulled it to one side, revealing a walk-in cupboard, empty except for a wooden chair and a full-length mirror on a metal stand.

"Janet, why does Hughie always cover the mirrors?"

"It's an old superstition. When someone dies, you're supposed to cover every mirror in the house so the soul of the deceased doesn't get trapped behind the glass. And one thing you don't want is ghosts getting stuck inside a looking glass, because you know what they do when that happens? They reach out and grab any person who becomes reflected in that mirror, and they take them far away."

"Away? Away where?"

"Bournemouth," Janet said. "Where do you think?" She smiled and raised an eyebrow. "Know why it's seven years bad luck to break a mirror?"

Samantha shook her head.

"Because it takes seven years for the soul to renew itself."

"Pardon me?"

"The idea is the reflection represents your soul, so if you shatter the reflection, it stands to reason the soul will be shattered as well. Then, as if that wasn't enough, what do you think your shattered soul fragments go and do? They only get themselves imprisoned inside the shards of glass! Stupid things. No wonder it takes seven years to sort them out." She laughed. "So now you know."

Samantha giggled. "Now I know." She started to draw the curtain back across the mirror.

"Tah-dah!" Janet exclaimed triumphantly.

Samantha let go of the curtain and swung around, startled.

"Told you I'd find it," Janet said, holding up a small key.

Samantha knelt beside her boss as she turned the key in the trunk lock and suddenly everything else—the smell, the insects, even the outline of a neglected corpse only inches away from their feet—was momentarily forgotten. The trunk was full of treasures. Beautiful, sparkling treasures.

"Oh, it's gorgeous!" Janet gasped, carefully unfolding a floor-length red silk dress wrapped in tissue paper. It must have been 50 or 60 years old but it was in perfect condition. Beneath it, she found a ballgown—white, embroidered with gold—and a long jet-black sheath covered in shiny glass beads.

There were shoes and handbags, some leather, some alligator, some velvet studded with rhinestones. There were long white gloves, hats with veils, capes with fur-trimmed hoods, silk stockings with seams. In a large padded envelope at the bottom, they found a scrapbook full of press clippings and faded black and white photos of a beautiful dark-haired woman dancing in a variety of glittering costumes, sometimes with a male partner, sometimes as part of a chorus line, sometimes alone beneath a spotlight.

"So that was Eleanor Burdon," Janet said, carefully turning the brittle pages. "Sometimes I'm glad we don't know the future, Sammy. I mean, look at her, smug as the cat that got the cream, wasn't she? Would she have wanted to know how it was all going to end? And if anybody'd told her, you think she would have believed them for one moment? I doubt it. Bet she had the world at her feet in those days. Bet she thought she always would." She sighed and shook her head. "Poor thing."

"Poor thing," Samantha agreed, nodding.

Janet put the book to one side and picked up the black beaded dress. She stood, holding it in front of her; the hem dragged on the floor. "She was tall, that Eleanor. More like you."

"I'm only five seven."

"Taller than me. Taller than most of the old lady's generation." She told Samantha to stand up, then pressed the dress into her hands. "Now hold it up properly. Here, that really suits you. Have a look at yourself. Go on."

Samantha pulled down her mask and turned to face the mirror in the cupboard. She nearly laughed out loud; she looked ridiculous holding a beaded dress in front of a pair of baggy coveralls with a surgical mask hanging loose around her neck.

Then something went wrong. Everything reflected in the glass seemed to develop a kind of after-image, like a photographic double-exposure. Including her. She seemed to have two bodies, one superimposed over the other. She moved her head a few inches to one side; her duplicate head followed a fraction of a second later. She blinked several times, trying to clear her vision, but couldn't get her two sets of overlapping eyes to open and close in sync; one always seemed a millisecond behind the other.

Then everything went black. "Janet?" she said.

No reply.

"Janet, where are you?" she said, fighting back panic. "Janet, I can't see!" She heard a sound of creaking hinges, then a beam of light cut through the darkness, moving in a graceful arc as it illuminated her surroundings, section by section.

She was standing on a bare concrete floor surrounded by black walls splashed with large red letters spelling something she couldn't make out. Then she realized why she couldn't read the writing: it was backwards. She had managed to decipher the first word—*Gateway*—when she was blinded by a torch beam shining into her eyes.

She heard at least two sets of approaching footsteps, and then the beam moved on. She stood rooted to the spot, unable to believe they hadn't seen her.

"Bloody hell," a man's voice said as the light fell onto a young woman with long blonde hair, slowly swaying in mid-air, a rope around her neck.

Samantha tried to run, but she couldn't move. She tried to scream, but no sound came out.

Janet suddenly crossed in front of her, pulling the curtain across the cupboard doorway. She seemed angry. "Are you mutt and jeff or something, girl? I've been telling you the last ten minutes: stop admiring yourself and put that bloody dress away, we've got work to do!"

"Ten minutes?" Samantha repeated. It seemed like less than ten *seconds* since Janet had handed her the beaded gown. She became aware of a tingling sensation in her hands. She looked down and saw they were clenched into tight fists, the knuckles white. And they were shaking. Could she really have *lost* ten minutes? She let go of the dress, carefully uncurling her aching fingers, and saw a line of deep ridges where her nails had dug into her palm.

Nothing about the room she was in seemed right, though she had no idea exactly what was wrong. She looked up at the light fixture in the middle of the ceiling, half-expecting to see a squirming mass of flies. There weren't any, of course; the flat reeked of insecticide. The chemical smell was so strong she could taste it.

She reeled over to one of the windows and stuck her head outside, gasping for breath. "I must have blacked out from the fumes. I'm sorry, I'm really sorry."

"Come on, girl," Janet said, "let's get you out of here for a bit."

They knocked on several of the neighbors' doors before they left the building. No one they spoke to knew anything about the old woman, though one suggested they try the residents' association.

There they found a man who knew Eleanor Burdon. He said she used to be quite active in the association, serving on the pensioners' committee, though she'd resigned three or four years ago. "She was 80-odd and getting a bit frail," he explained. He also said she had a daughter somewhere: possibly Canada, though he couldn't be sure.

"Do you know the daughter's name?" Janet asked him.

He shook his head. "I only know it wasn't Burdon. Eleanor was widowed twice, and I'm sure she said the daughter was from the first marriage."

"Thanks for your help," Janet said, turning to leave.

"You know who you ought to ask about Eleanor," the man called after them. "They do a writing workshop at the community center, down the north end of the estate. Eleanor was always writing poems and things."

The sign on the padlocked front door of the community center read: *Closed as of 15 June due to lack of funding. If you are unhappy about this, write to the council.*

They put Eleanor's trunk into a storage locker, then crossed the hall to the Arts Department, which the latest round of cuts had reduced to a single desk at the back of Social Services. Of course as funeral officers their "office" wasn't any better, consisting of two desks in the Environmental Services Department, sandwiched between Refuse Collection and Vermin Control.

It only took a minute in the Arts Department files to find the name and phone number of the woman who'd run the creative-writing workshop on the Verdant Meadows Estate. Janet decided Samantha should be the one to make the phone call; the only way to learn was to do.

Samantha returned to her desk in Environmental Services, dialled the woman's number and introduced herself. The workshop leader, a Mrs. Marcia Anson, confirmed that Eleanor Burdon had once been an enthusiastic member of her writing class, but had stopped coming the previous autumn. "Do you know how she died?"

"I think she had a stroke," Samantha said. "Something to do with her brain, anyway."

"Oh, dear," Mrs Anson tutted. "When did it happen?"

"Some time during the second week of June; I don't—"

"Well, she was still alive on the twelfth," Mrs Anson interrupted. "I saw her in the café in Meadow Lane Market, sitting in a booth beside the window. I would have stopped to say hello, but she seemed to be in the middle of a rather intense conversation and I didn't like to interrupt. Of course now I wish I had."

"Who was she talking to?"

"Some young girl; I doubt she was more than 20. Looked a bit like one of those anti-road protester types, all torn clothes and messy blonde hair, with some kind of ring through her lower lip. I have no idea what she and Eleanor could have found to talk about, really. I mean, Eleanor always took such care of her appearance; what could those two possibly have had in common?"

"Ask her about Eleanor's family," Janet whispered.

"Did Mrs. Burdon ever talk about her family?"

"Not really. I think she had a daughter somewhere, but that's all I know."

"Ask about friends," Janet prompted.

"Did Mrs. Burdon have any friends that you know of?"

"I think she used to be involved in the residents' association. You might want to ask someone there."

"Well, we can strike that one of our list," Janet said as Samantha put down the receiver. She reached into one of the bulging carrier bags full of paper they'd brought back from the dead woman's flat. She pointed to another, on the floor beside Samantha's feet. "Look for anything with an address."

"I know, I know," Samantha said, emptying the sack onto her desk.

Most of the bag's contents turned out to be rubbish: junk mail, bills, old calendars, expired money-off coupons, recipe cards and so on, all of which could go straight into the bin.

A short while later, Janet stood up and put on her jacket. "It's almost five. Go home, girl, and forget about the dead until tomorrow."

Samantha yawned and rubbed her eyes. "All right." She slid her chair back from the desk and crossed over to the coat rack where she'd hung her jacket that morning. She glanced towards the doorway and saw that Janet was already gone; she hadn't waited.

Samantha sighed and shook her head. What did she expect? A slap on the back? A round of applause? After the way she'd passed out in the dead woman's flat that morning, she needed to prove herself more than ever. But how?

The only way she could think of was to keep working.

She crossed back to her desk and started sorting through another mound of paper. There were several letters from someone named Pamela—no surname— with a return address in Paris. She printed off one of their standard letters and put it in the "out" tray. Sending the letter made her feel as if she'd finally accomplished something, even though there was little hope of getting a reply— the most recent of Pamela's notes was dated 1975.

She found several black and white photographs of a man in a military uniform. She turned one over and saw the words: *Terry, home on leave, 1943.* Husband? Brother? Lover? She had no way of telling.

She put the photos into an envelope for safe keeping, then picked up the notebook she'd seen on the old woman's table that morning and started flicking through it again. Nothing but page after page of handwritten verses. Completely useless.

She was about to put it down when the neat script of the previous pages suddenly gave way to an almost illegible scrawl.

Must hurry! Memory fading. Like dream, one moment so clear, the next, gone forever. Saw a girl. Room with black walls. Something written in red paint, letters backwards. Spelling? No, too late, already forgotten. The girl: blonde hair, eyes pale blue, wide open and staring. Rope around neck. Hanging from a pipe? Not sure. So young, so sad. Wearing jeans, I think. Getting vague now.

Just looked at clock. Lost four hours! How? Seems like minutes. Something is wrong. Room seems strange, everything strange.

Feels different. Can't say how. Knew a minute ago, but it's gone now. Whatever I thought I knew, gone.

Samantha put down the notebook, shivering. Something was nagging at the back of her mind, something about footsteps and a beam of light. She shook her head and forced her attention back to the notebook.

The old woman's writing reverted to her original precise hand.

11 June.

I just re-read the above and freely admit it sounds like the ravings of a madwoman. Yet 24 hours have passed and I am still unable to shake the feeling that I am in the wrong place and I don't know how I got here.

12 June.

I now know what has happened and I think I know how to fix it. I told Anna everything . . .

Anna had to be the young woman Marcia Anson had seen with Eleanor.

She not only believed me, she understood. We talked for hours about choices and probabilities, the physical and the mental and infinite numbers of universes. Then I brought her back here to see the psychomantium . . .

"The what?" Samantha said out loud.

. . . and she confirmed that it was hers.

My only hope now is to go back the way I came.

The rest of the book was blank.

Anna nodded to the seat across from hers. "Sit down," she said quietly, "and maybe I'll tell you what you want to know."

Samantha sat. "Eleanor Burdon wrote in her notebook that she'd talked to you about your psycho . . . something."

Anna picked up a salt shaker and tossed it from one hand to the other, giggling. "Psychomantium. Never heard the word myself 'til I met the old woman."

"Well, what is it? What does it do?"

Anna emptied some salt onto her palm and licked it, glancing sideways at Samantha. "It's a mirror used for contacting the other side."

"The other side? You mean the dead? Eleanor Burdon was trying to contact the dead?"

"Well, she was that age, wasn't she? Not so long to go herself, wanting to know who or what was waiting for her. And it worked, of course. She *did* contact the dead. Only trouble was, the dead person she contacted was *me*."

Samantha threw up her hands. "Well, thank you for your time."

Anna put the salt shaker back on the table. "No, you don't understand." She pulled back one of her sleeves, revealing several scars across her wrist. "I've been out of hospital almost six months now; they closed my ward. I've got these pills I'm supposed to take, but they make my tongue swell up . . ." She shrugged and rolled the sleeve back down.

"Anyway, about three, four weeks ago, I found some rope in a rubbish bin. I imagined myself with it wrapped tight around my neck, my face bloated and purple, my lifeless body swaying in the breeze. I even imagined my soul, plummeting into hell. I saw myself writing a sign in big letters so everyone would know where I'd been all these years and where I was going. It would be so easy, I thought, so easy . . .

"But I didn't do it; I only thought about it, right? And then I guess I started walking. I don't remember where I went or what I did, but it felt like I'd been going in circles for hours. And then I get back to the place where I've been staying and it's been done over! Everything I own is gone, including this full-length mirror on a metal stand. A few days after that, some old dearie comes up to me, claiming she's seen me in this mirror she bought off a market stall. She said she'd been sitting in the dark, waiting for spirits to appear in the glass, when suddenly she sees *me*, hanging dead from a rope. I was gobsmacked. She gave me a perfect description in every detail of something I had *considered* doing but hadn't actually done.

"It was then I started to notice the way the old woman kept shifting in and out of focus, and I soon found that if I stared at her hard enough, she became almost transparent." Anna raised her pale blue eyes to meet Samantha's. "Just like you."

Samantha looked down at her arms and saw they were covered in goosebumps. Somewhere in the distance, she imagined she could hear the sound of buzzing insects.

Samantha sat on a folded blanket in the middle of a bare concrete floor. The room was dark and almost bare of furniture. A large pipe ran from one corner of the floor, up a wall and across the ceiling.

Anna lit a kerosene lamp and placed it on the floor before her. "Welcome to my place."

"I've been here before, haven't I? In a dream. I remember it from a dream."

Anna didn't answer.

"But the room was different then. The walls were painted black—there was something written on them, but I couldn't make out the words. I heard a window being forced open and then I heard footsteps. It was a dream, wasn't it? Or am I dreaming now?"

"Does it matter?"

"It matters to me. I don't understand where I am. I don't understand what's happening. The last thing I remember is looking in a mirror . . ."

Anna sat on a wooden crate, her face hidden in shadow. "How much do you want to bet there's at least one universe where *you're* the one who's dead, not me? Must be at least one, don't you think?"

"Universe?" Samantha repeated. "What do you mean—a parallel universe?"

"It's all about possibility, isn't it? I saw something about it on TV while I was in hospital. Every possibility has to happen somewhere. So sometimes I'm dead, sometimes you are, sometimes neither of us, sometimes both of us. And sometimes one of us is a ghost, trapped inside a mirror."

Samantha thought back to what Janet had said: that trapped spirits reached out to grab the living. "Are you saying I'm stuck inside a mirror?"

"I'm saying you're stuck inside a universe. Where that universe is, I don't know."

Samantha thought back to the last line in Eleanor Burdon's notebook: *My only hope now is to go back the way I came.*

She must have tried to go back through the mirror.

And it had killed her.

The sign outside the local library said that they were open until eight o'clock on Mondays and Tuesdays. Samantha glanced at her watch—nearly a quarter past seven—and hurried up the stairs to the reference section.

She found what she was looking for in a book on folklore and superstition: *The reflection in the mirror mirrors the soul. If the glass holding your reflection should ever be broken, expect seven years' despair and misfortune, for seven years be required for the renewal of the soul.*

To break the cycle and release the soul, the broken pieces must be collected together and buried in the earth.

It was after midnight when Samantha opened the door to Eleanor Burdon's flat and walked through to the bedroom, carrying a hammer and a sheet.

She wrapped the sheet around the mirror, laid it down on the floor and attacked it with the hammer, shattering the glass. She put on a pair of gloves before she picked up the sheet full of jagged splinters and carried it downstairs, placing it in the boot of her car.

Then she drove to the nearest park and buried all the pieces.

Samantha went into the office early the next morning. She picked up the dead woman's notebook and started going through it page by page. Nothing but twee little rhymes.

"Hello, Sammy," Janet said brightly when she came in half an hour later. "Quite the early bird, aren't you?"

Samantha sighed. "I'm still trying to find an address for Mrs Burdon's daughter, but so far, nothing. Not even a clue."

"What are you talking about, you silly thing? We wrote to her yesterday; don't you—" She was interrupted by a ringing telephone. "Janet Hale," she said, lifting the receiver. She listened a moment, then reached across her desk for a notepad.

They went out on a new case later that morning: a former psychiatric patient who'd hung herself three weeks earlier.

Samantha followed Janet into a dark ground-floor room with a bare concrete floor. The walls were painted black with the words: *Gateway to Hell* splashed across them in huge red letters. The room was empty of furniture.

Janet shook her head. "Can you credit it? They reckon somebody burgled the place with the poor girl's body still hanging from that pipe. I sometimes wonder what kind of world it is we're living in, Sammy, what kind of world."

"I wonder," Samantha agreed, nodding.

Michael Chabon

In the Black Mill

Michael Chabon is the author of the novels The Mysteries of Pittsburgh *and* Wonder Boys *and the collection* A Model World and Other Stories.

Chabon is not a horror writer nor even generally a fantasist. "In the Black Mill," originally published in the June 1997 issue of Playboy, *is an exception, a story in the Lovecraftian tradition. Its author is meant to be August Van Zorn, the writer whose Arkham House collection* The Abominations of Plunkettsburg and Other Tales *inspires the narrator of* Wonder Boys.

—E. D.

In the fall of 1948, when I arrived in Plunkettsburg to begin the fieldwork I hoped would lead to a doctorate in archaeology, there were still a good number of townspeople living there whose memories stretched back to the time, in the final decade of the previous century, when the soot-blackened hills that encircle the town fairly swarmed with savants and mad diggers. In 1892 the discovery, on a hilltop overlooking the Miskahannock River, of the burial complex of a hitherto-unknown tribe of Mound Builders had set off a frenzy of excavation and scholarly poking around that made several careers, among them that of the aged hero of my profession who was chairman of my dissertation committee. It was under his redoubtable influence that I had taken up the study of the awful, illustrious Miskahannocks, with their tombs and bone pits, a course that led me at last, one gray November afternoon, to turn my overladen fourth-hand Nash off the highway from Pittsburgh to Morgantown, and to navigate, tightly gripping the wheel, the pitted ghost of a roadbed that winds up through the Yuggogheny Hills, then down into the broad and gloomy valley of the Miskahannock.

As I negotiated that endless series of hairpin and blind curves, I was afforded an equally endless series of dispiriting partial views of the place where I would spend the next ten months of my life. Like many of its neighbors in that iron-veined country, Plunkettsburg was at first glance unprepossessing—a low, rusting little city, with tarnished onion domes and huddled houses, drab as an armful of dead leaves strewn along the ground. But as I left the last hill behind me and got my first unobstructed look, I immediately noted the one structure that, while it did nothing to elevate my opinion of my new home, altered the humdrum aspect of Plunkettsburg sufficiently to make it remarkable, and also sinister. It stood off to the east of town, in a zone of weeds and rust-colored earth, a vast, black box, bristling with spiky chimneys, extending over some five acres or more, dwarfing everything around it. This was, I knew at once, the famous Plunketts-burg Mill. Evening was coming on, and in the half-light its windows winked and flickered with inner fire, and its towering stacks vomited smoke into the autumn twilight. I shuddered, and then cried out. So intent had I been on the ghastly black apparition of the mill that I had nearly run my car off the road.

" 'Here in this mighty fortress of industry,' " I quoted aloud in the tone of a newsreel narrator, reassuring myself with the ironic reverberation of my voice, " 'turn the great cogs and thrust the relentless pistons that forge the pins and trusses of the American dream.' " I was recalling the words of a chamber of commerce brochure I had received last week from my hosts, the antiquities department of Plunkettsburg College, along with particulars of my lodging and library privileges. They were anxious to have me; it had been many years since the publication of my chairman's *Miskahannock Surveys* had effectively settled all answerable questions—save, I hoped, one—about the vanished tribe and con-signed Plunkettsburg once again to the mists of academic oblivion and the thick black effluvia of its satanic mill.

"So, what is there left to say about that pointy-toothed crowd?" said Carlotta Brown-Jenkin, draining her glass of brandy. The chancellor of Plunkettsburg Col-lege and chairwoman of the antiquities department had offered to stand me to dinner on my first night in town. We were sitting in the Hawaiian-style dining room of a Chinese restaurant downtown. Brown-Jenkin was herself appropriately antique, a gaunt old girl in her late 70s, her nearly hairless scalp worn and yellowed, the glint of her eyes, deep within their cavernous sockets, like that of ancient coins discovered by torchlight. "I quite thought that your distinguished mentor had revealed all their bloody mysteries."

"Only the women filed their teeth," I reminded her, taking another swallow of Indian Ring beer, the local brew, which I found to possess a dark, not entirely pleasant savor of autumn leaves or damp earth. I gazed around the low room with its ersatz palm thatching and garlands of wax orchids. The only other people in the place were a man on wooden crutches with a pinned-up trouser leg and a man with a wooden hand, both of them drinking Indian Ring, and the bar-tender, an extremely fat woman in a thematically correct but hideous red muu-muu. My hostess had assured me, without a great deal of enthusiasm, that we were about to eat the best-cooked meal in town.

"Yes, yes," she recalled, smiling tolerantly. Her particular field of study was great Carthage, and no doubt, I thought, she looked down on my unlettered band of savages. "They considered pointed teeth to be the essence of female beauty."

"That is, of course, the theory of my distinguished mentor," I said, studying the label on my beer bottle, on which there was printed Thelder's 1894 engraving of the Plunkettsburg Ring, which was also reproduced on the cover of *Miskahannock Surveys*.

"You do not concur?" said Brown-Jenkin.

"I think that there may in fact be other possibilities."

"Such as?"

At this moment the waiter arrived, bearing a tray laden with plates of unidentifiable meats and vegetables that glistened in garish sauces the colors of women's lipstick. The steaming dishes emitted an overpowering blast of vinegar, as if to cover some underlying stench. Feeling ill, I averted my eyes from the food and saw that the waiter, a thickset, powerful man with bland Slavic features, was missing two of the fingers on his left hand. My stomach revolted. I excused myself from the table and ran directly to the bathroom.

"Nerves," I explained to Brown-Jenkin when I returned, blushing, to the table. "I'm excited about starting my research."

"Of course," she said, examining me critically. With her napkin she wiped a thin red dribble of sauce from her chin. "I quite understand."

"There seem to be an awful lot of missing limbs in this room," I said, trying to lighten my mood. "Hope none of them ended up in the food."

The chancellor stared at me, aghast.

"A very bad joke," I said. "My apologies. My sense of humor was not, I'm afraid, widely admired back in Boston, either."

"No," she agreed, with a small, unamused smile. "Well." She patted the long, thin strands of yellow hair atop her head. "It's the *mill*, of course."

"Of course," I said, feeling a bit dense for not having puzzled this out myself. "Dangerous work they do there, I take it."

"The mill has taken a piece of half the men in Plunkettsburg," Brown-Jenkin said, sounding almost proud. "Yes, it's terribly dangerous work." There had crept into her voice a boosterish tone of admiration that could not fail to remind me of the chamber of commerce brochure. "*Important* work."

"Vitally important," I agreed, and to placate her I heaped my plate with colorful, luminous, indeterminate meat, a gesture for which I paid dearly through all the long night that followed.

I took up residence in Murrough House, just off the campus of Plunkettsburg College. It was a large, rambling structure, filled with hidden passages, queerly shaped rooms and staircases leading nowhere, built by the notorious lady magnate, "the Robber Baroness," Philippa Howard Murrough, founder of the college, noted spiritualist and author and dark genius of the Plunkettsburg Mill. She had spent the last four decades of her life, and a considerable part of her manufacturing fortune, adding to, demolishing and rebuilding her home. On her death the resultant warren, a chimera of brooding Second Empire gables, peaked Victorian turrets and baroque porticoes with a coat of glossy black ivy, passed into the hands of the private girls' college she had endowed, which converted it to a faculty club and lodgings for visiting scholars. I had a round turret room on the fourth and uppermost floor. There were no other visiting scholars in the house and, according to the porter, this had been the case for several years.

Old Halicek, the porter, was a bent, slow-moving fellow who lived with his daughter and grandson in a suite of rooms somewhere in the unreachable lower regions of the house. He too had lost a part of his body to the great mill in his youth—his left ear. It had been reduced, by a device that Halicek called a Dodson line extractor, to a small pink ridge nestled in the lee of his bushy white sideburns. His daughter, Mrs. Eibonas, oversaw a small staff of two maids and a waiter and did the cooking for the dozen or so faculty members who took their lunches at Murrough House every day. The waiter was Halicek's grandson, Dexter Eibonas, an earnest, good-looking, affable redhead of 17 who was a favorite among the college faculty. He was intelligent, curious, widely if erratically read. He was always pestering me to take him out to dig in the mounds, and while I would not have been averse to his pleasant company, the terms of my agreement with the board of the college, who were the trustees of the site, expressly forbade the recruiting of local workmen. Nevertheless I gave him books on archaeology and kept him abreast of my discoveries, such as they were. Several of the Plunkettsburg professors, I learned, had also taken an interest in the development of his mind.

"They sent me up to Pittsburgh last winter," he told me one evening about a month into my sojourn, as he brought me a bottle of Ring and a plate of Mrs. Eibonas' famous kielbasa with sauerkraut. Professor Brown-Jenkin had been much mistaken, in my opinion, about the best-laid table in town. During the most tedious, chilly and profitless stretches of my scratchings-about in the bleak, flinty Yuggoghenies, I was often sustained solely by thoughts of Mrs. Eibonas' homemade sausages and cakes. "I had an interview with the dean of engineering at Tech. Professor Collier even paid for a hotel for Mother and me."

"And how did it go?"

"Oh, it went fine, I guess," said Dexter. "I was accepted."

"Oh," I said, confused. The autumn semester at Carnegie Tech, I imagined, would have been ending that very week.

"Have you—have you deferred your admission?"

"Deferred it indefinitely, I guess. I told them no thanks." Dexter had, in an excess of nervous energy, been snapping a tea towel back and forth. He stopped. His normally bright eyes took on a glazed, I would almost have said a dreamy, expression. "I'm going to work in the mill."

"The *mill*?" I said, incredulous. I looked at him to see if he was teasing me, but at that moment he seemed to be entertaining only the pleasantest imaginings of his labors in that fiery black castle. I had a sudden vision of his pleasant face rendered earless, and looked away. "Forgive my asking, but why would you want to do that?"

"My father did it," said Dexter, his voice dull. "His father, too. I'm on the hiring list." The light came back into his eyes, and he resumed snapping the towel. "Soon as a place opens up, I'm going in."

He left me and went back into the kitchen, and I sat there shuddering. *I'm going in.* The phrase had a heroic, doomed ring to it, like the pronouncement of a fireman about to enter his last burning house. Over the course of the previous month I'd had ample opportunity to observe the mill and its effect on the male population of Plunkettsburg. Casual observation, in local markets and bars, in the lobby of the Orpheum on State Street, on the sidewalks, in Birch's general store out on Gray Road where I stopped for coffee and cigarettes every morning on my way up to the mound complex, had led me to estimate that in truth, fully half of the townsmen had lost some visible portion of their anatomies to Murrough Manufacturing, Inc. And yet all my attempts to ascertain how these often horribly grave accidents had befallen their bent, maimed or limping victims were met, invariably, with an explanation at once so detailed and so vague, so rich in mechanical jargon and yet so free of actual information, that I had never yet succeeded in producing in my mind an adequate picture of the incident in question, or, for that matter, of what kind of deadly labor was performed in the black mill.

What, precisely, was manufactured in that bastion of industrial democracy and fount of the Murrough millions? I heard the trains come sighing and moaning into town in the middle of the night, clanging as they were shunted into the mill sidings. I saw the black diesel trucks, emblazoned with the crimson initial M, lumbering through the streets of Plunkettsburg on their way to and from the loading docks. I had two dozen conversations, over endless mugs of Indian Ring, about shift schedules and union activities (invariably quashed) and company picnics, about ore and furnaces, metallurgy and turbines. I heard the resigned, good-natured explanations of men sliced open by Rawlings divagators, ground up by spline presses, mangled by steam sorters, half-decapitated by rolling Hurley plates. And yet after four months in Plunkettsburg I was no closer to understanding the terrible work to which the people of that town sacrificed, with such apparent goodwill, the bodies of their men.

I took to haunting the precincts of the mill in the early morning as the six o'clock shift was coming on and late at night as the graveyard men streamed through the iron gates, carrying their black lunch pails. The fence, an elaborate Victorian confection of wickedly tipped, thick iron pikes trailed with iron ivy, enclosed the mill yard at such a distance from the mountainous factory itself that it was impossible for me to get near enough to see anything but the glow of huge fires through the begrimed mesh windows. I applied at the company offices in town for admission, as a visitor, to the plant but was told by the receptionist, rather rudely, that the Plunkettsburg Mill was not a tourist facility. My fascination with the place grew so intense and distracting that I neglected my work; my wanderings through the abandoned purlieus of the savage Miskahannocks grew desultory and ruminative, my discoveries of artifacts, never frequent, dwindled to almost nothing, and I made fewer and fewer entries in my journal. Finally, one exhausted morning, after an entire night spent lying in my bed at Murrough House staring out the leaded window at a sky that was bright orange with the reflected fire of the mill, I decided I had had enough.

I dressed quickly, in plain tan trousers and a flannel work shirt. I went down to the closet in the front hall, where I found a drab old woolen coat and a watch cap that I pulled down over my head. Then I stepped outside. The terrible orange flashes had subsided and the sky was filled with stars. I hurried across town to the east side, to Stan's Diner on Mill Street, where I knew I would find the day shift wolfing down ham and eggs and pancakes. I slipped between two large men at the long counter and ordered coffee. When one of my neighbors got up to go to the toilet, I grabbed his lunch pail, threw down a handful of coins and hurried over to the gates of the mill, where I joined the crowd of men. They looked at me oddly, not recognizing me, and I could see them murmuring to one another in puzzlement. But the earliness of the morning or an inherent reserve kept them from saying anything. They figured, I suppose, that whoever I was, I was somebody else's problem. Only one man, tall, with thinning yellow hair, kept his gaze on me for more than a moment. His eyes, I was surprised to see, looked very sad.

"You shouldn't be here, buddy," he said, not unkindly.

I felt myself go numb. I had been caught.

"What? Oh, no, I—I——"

The whistle blew. The crowd of men, swelled now to more than a hundred, jerked to life and waited, nervous, on the balls of their feet, for the gates to open. The man with the yellow hair seemed to forget me. In the distance an equally large crowd of men emerged from the belly of the mill and headed toward us. There was a grinding of old machinery, the creak of stressed iron, and then the ornamental gates rolled away. The next instant I was caught up in the tide of men streaming toward the mill, borne along like a cork. Halfway there our group intersected with the graveyard shift and in the ensuing chaos of bodies and hellos I was sure my plan was going to work. I was going to see, at last, the inside of the mill.

I felt something, someone's fingers, brush the back of my neck, and then I was yanked backward by the collar of my coat. I lost my footing and fell to the ground. As the changing shifts of workers flowed around me I looked up and saw a huge man standing over me, his arms folded across his chest. He was wearing a black jacket emblazoned on the breast with a large M. I tried to stand, but he pushed me back down.

"You can just stay right there until the police come," he said.

"Listen," I said. My research, clearly, was at an end. My scholarly privileges would be revoked. I would creep back to Boston, where, of course, my committee and, above all, my chair would recommend that I quit the department. "You don't have to do that."

Once more I tried to stand, and this time the company guard threw me back to the ground so hard and so quickly that I couldn't break my fall with my hands. The back of my head slammed against the pavement. A passing worker stepped on my outstretched hand. I cried out.

"Hey," said a voice. "Come on, Moe. You don't need to treat him that way."

It was the sad-eyed man with the yellow hair. He interposed himself between me and my attacker.

"Don't do this, Ed," said the guard. "I'll have to write you up."

I rose shakily to my feet and started to stumble away, back toward the gates. The guard tried to reach around Ed, to grab hold of me. As he lunged forward, Ed stuck out his foot, and the guard went sprawling.

"Come on, professor," said Ed, putting his arm around me. "You better get out of here."

"Do I know you?" I said, leaning gratefully on him.

"No, but you know my nephew, Dexter. He pointed you out to me at the pictures one night."

"Thank you," I said, when we reached the gate. He brushed some dust from the back of my coat, handed me the knit stocking cap, then took a black bandanna from the pocket of his dungarees. He touched a corner of it to my mouth, and it came away marked with a dark stain.

"Only a little blood," he said. "You'll be all right. You just make sure to stay clear of this place from now on." He brought his face close to mine, filling my nostrils with the sharp medicinal tang of his aftershave. He lowered his voice to a whisper. "And stay off the beer."

"What?"

"Just stay off it." He stood up straight and returned the bandanna to his back pocket. "I haven't taken a sip in two weeks." I nodded, confused. I had been drinking two, three, sometimes four bottles of Indian Ring every night, finding that it carried me effortlessly into profound and dreamless sleep.

"Just tell me one thing," I said.

"I can't say nothing else, professor."

"It's just—what is it you do, in there?"

"Me?" he said, pointing to his chest. "I operate a sprue extruder."

"Yes, yes," I said, "but what does a sprue extruder *do*? What is it *for*?"

He looked at me patiently but a little remotely, a distracted parent with an inquisitive child.

"It's for extruding sprues," he said. "What else?"

Thus repulsed, humiliated and given good reason to fear that my research was in imminent jeopardy of being brought to an end, I resolved to put the mystery of the mill out of my mind once and for all and get on with my real business in Plunkettsburg. I went out to the site of the mound complex and worked with my brush and little hand spade all through that day, until the light failed. When I got home, exhausted, Mrs. Eibonas brought me a bottle of Indian Ring and I gratefully drained it before I remembered Ed's strange warning. I handed the sweating bottle back to Mrs. Eibonas. She smiled.

"Can I bring you another, professor?" she said.

"No, thank you," I said. Her smile collapsed. She looked very disappointed. "All right," she said. For some reason the thought of disappointing her bothered me greatly, so I told her, "Maybe one more."

I retired early and dreamed dreams that were troubled by the scratching of iron on earth and by a clamoring tumult of men. The next morning I got up and went straight out to the site again.

For it was going to take work, a lot of work, if my theory was ever going to bear fruit. During much of my first several months in Plunkettsburg I had been hampered by snow and by the degree to which the site of the Plunkettsburg Mounds—a broad plateau on the eastern slope of Mount Orrert, on which there had been excavated, in the 1890s, 36 huge molars of packed earth, each the size of a two-story house—had been picked over and disturbed by that early generation of archaeologists. Their methods had not in every case been as fastidious as one could have hoped. There were numerous areas of old digging where the historical record had, through carelessness, been rendered illegible. Then again,

I considered, as I gazed up at the ivy-covered flank of the ancient, artificial hillock my mentor had designated B-3, there was always the possibility that my theory was wrong.

Like all the productions of academe, I suppose, my theory was composed of equal parts of indebtedness and spite. I had formulated it in a kind of rebellion against that grand old man of the field, my chairman, the very person who had inculcated me with a respect for the deep, subtle savagery of the Miskahannock Indians. His view—the standard one—was that the culture of the builders of the Plunkettsburg Mounds, at its zenith, had expressed, to a degree unequaled in the Western hemisphere up to that time, the aestheticizing of the nihilist impulse. They had evolved all the elaborate social structures—texts, rituals, decorative arts, architecture—of any of the world's great religions: dazzling feats of abstract design represented by the thousands of baskets, jars, bowls, spears, tablets, knives, flails, axes, codices, robes and so on that were housed and displayed with such pride in the museum of my university, back in Boston. But the Miskahannocks, insofar as anyone had ever been able to determine (and many had tried), worshiped nothing, or, as my teacher would have it, Nothing. They acknowledged neither gods nor goddesses, conversed with no spirits or familiars. Their only purpose, the focus and the pinnacle of their artistic genius, was the killing of men. Nobody knew how many of the unfortunate males of the neighboring tribes had fallen victim to the Miskahannocks' delicate artistry of torture and dismemberment. In 1903 Professor William Waterman of Yale discovered 14 separate ossuary pits along the banks of the river, not far from the present site of the mill. These had contained enough bones to frame the bodies of 7000 men and boys. And nobody knew why they had died. The few tattered, fragmentary blood-on-tanbark texts so far discovered concerned themselves chiefly with the recurring famines that plagued Miskahannock civilization and, it was generally theorized, had been responsible for its ultimate collapse. The texts said nothing about the sacred arts of killing and torture. There was, my teacher had persuasively argued, one reason for this. The deaths had been purposeless; their justification, the cosmic purposelessness of life itself.

Now, once I had settled myself on spiteful rebellion, as every good pupil eventually must, there were two possible paths available to me. The first would have been to attempt to prove beyond a doubt that the Miskahannocks had, in fact, worshiped some kind of god, some positive, purposive entity, however bloodthirsty. I chose the second path. I accepted the godlessness of the Miskahannocks. I rejected the refined, reasoning nihilism my mentor had postulated (and to which, as I among very few others knew, he himself privately subscribed). The Miskahannocks, I hoped to prove, had had another motive for their killing: They were hungry; according to the tattered scraps of the Plunkettsburg Codex, very hungry indeed. The filed teeth my professor subsumed to the larger aesthetic principles he elucidated thus had, in my view, a far simpler and more utilititarian purpose. Unfortunately, the widespread incidence of cannibalism among the women of a people vanished 4000 years since was proving rather difficult to establish. So far, in fact, I had found no evidence of it at all.

I knelt to untie the canvas tarp I had stretched across my digging of the previous day. I was endeavoring to take an inclined section of B-3, cutting a passage five feet high and two feet wide at a 30 degree angle to the horizontal.

This endeavor in itself was a kind of admission of defeat, since B-3 was one of two mounds, the other being its neighbor B-5, designated a "null mound" by those who had studied the site. It had been thoroughly pierced and penetrated and found to be utterly empty; reserved, it was felt, for the mortal remains of a dynasty that failed. But I had already made careful searches of the 34 other tombs of the Miskahannock queens. The null mounds were the only ones remaining. If, as I anticipated, I found no evidence of anthropophagy, I would have to give up on the mounds entirely and start looking elsewhere. There were persistent stories of other bone pits in the pleats and hollows of the Yuggoghenies. Perhaps I could find one, a fresh one, one not trampled and corrupted by the primitive methods of my professional forebears.

I peeled back the sheet of oiled canvas I had spread across my handiwork and received a shock. The passage, which over the course of the previous day I had managed to extend a full four feet into the side of the mound, had been completely filled in. Not merely filled in; the thick black soil had been tamped down and a makeshift screen of ivy had been drawn across it. I took a step back and looked around the site, certain all at once that I was being observed. There were only the crows in the treetops. In the distance I could hear the Murrough trucks on the tortuous highway, grinding gears as they climbed up out of the valley. I looked down at the ground by my feet and saw the faint imprint of a foot smaller than my own. A few feet from this, I found another. That was all.

I ought to have been afraid, I suppose, or at the least concerned, but at this point, I confess, I was only angry. The site was heavily fenced and posted with NO TRESPASSING signs, but apparently some local hoodlums had come up in the night and wasted all of the previous day's hard work. The motive for this vandalism eluded me, but I supposed that a lack of any discernible motive was in the nature of vandalism itself. I picked up my hand shovel and started in again on my doorway into the mound. The fifth bite I took with the little iron tooth brought out something strange. It was a black bandanna, twisted and soiled. I spread it out across my thigh and found the small, round trace of my own blood on one corner. I was bewildered, and again I looked around to see if someone were watching me. There were only the laughter and ragged fingers of the crows. What was Ed up to? Why would my rescuer want to come up onto the mountain and ruin my work? Did he think he was protecting me? I shrugged, stuffed the bandanna into a pocket and went back to my careful digging. I worked steadily throughout the day, extending the tunnel six inches nearer than I had come yesterday to the heart of the mound, then drove home to Murrough House, my shoulders aching, my fingers stiff. I had a long, hot soak in the big bathtub down the hall from my room, smoked a pipe and read, for the 15th time at least, the section in *Miskahannock Surveys* dealing with B-3. Then at 6:30 I went downstairs to find Dexter Eibonas waiting to serve my dinner, his expression blank, his eyes bloodshot. I remember being surprised that he didn't immediately demand details of my day on the dig. He just nodded, retreated into the kitchen and returned with a heated can of soup, half a loaf of white bread and a bottle of Ring. Naturally after my hard day I was disappointed by this fare, and I inquired as to the whereabouts of Mrs. Eibonas.

"She had some family business, professor," Dexter said, rolling up his hands in his tea towel, then unrolling them again. "Sad business."

"Did somebody—die?"

"My uncle Ed," said the boy, collapsing in a chair beside me and covering his twisted features with his hands. "He had an accident down at the mill, I guess. Fell headfirst into the impact mold."

"What?" I said, feeling my throat constrict. "My God, Dexter! Something has to be done! That mill ought to be shut down!"

Dexter took a step back, startled by my vehemence. I had thought at once, of course, of the black bandanna, and now I wondered if I were not somehow responsible for Ed Eibonas' death. Perhaps the incident in the mill yard the day before, his late-night digging in the dirt of B-3 in some kind of misguided effort to help me, had left him rattled, unable to concentrate on his work, prey to accidents.

"You just don't understand," said Dexter. "It's our way of life here. There isn't anything for us but the mill." He pushed the bottle of Indian Ring toward me. "Drink your beer, professor."

I reached for the glass and brought it to my lips but was swept by a sudden wave of revulsion like that which had overtaken me at the Chinese restaurant on my first night in town. I pushed back from the table and stood up, my violent start upsetting a pewter candelabra in which four tapers burned. Dexter lunged to keep it from falling over, then looked at me, surprised. I stared back, chest heaving, feeling defiant without being sure of what exactly I was defying.

"I am not going to touch another drop of that beer!" I said, the words sounding petulant and absurd as they emerged from my mouth.

Dexter nodded. He looked worried.

"All right, professor," he said, obligingly, as if he thought I might have become unbalanced. "You just go on up to your room and lie down. I'll bring you your food a little later. How about that?"

The next day I lay in bed, aching, sore and suffering from that peculiar brand of spiritual depression born largely of suppressed fear. On the following morning I roused myself, shaved, dressed in my best clothes and went to the Church of St. Stephen, on Nolt Street, the heart of Plunkettsburg's Estonian neighborhood, for the funeral of Ed Eibonas. There was a sizable turnout, as was always the case, I was told, when there had been a death at the mill. Such deaths were reportedly uncommon; the mill was a cruel and dangerous but rarely fatal place. At Dexter's invitation I went to the dead man's house to pay my respects to the widow, and two hours later I found myself, along with most of the other male mourners, roaring drunk on some kind of fruit brandy brought out on special occasions. It may have been that the brandy burned away the jitters and anxiety of the past two days; in any case the next morning I went out to the mounds again, with a tent and a cookstove and several bags of groceries. I didn't leave for the next five days.

My hole had been filled in again, and this time there was no clue to the identity of the filler, but I was determined not to let this spook me, as the saying goes. I simply dug. Ordinarily I would have proceeded cautiously, carrying the dirt out by thimblefuls and sifting each one, but I felt my time on the site growing short. I often saw cars on the access road by day, and headlight beams by night, slowing down as if to observe me. Twice a day a couple of sheriff's deputies would pull up to the Ring and sit in their car, watching. At first whenever they appeared, I stopped working, lit a cigarette and waited for them to arrest me. But when after the first few times nothing of the sort occurred, I relaxed a little and kept on with my digging for the duration of their visit. I was resigned to being prevented from completing my research, but before this happened I wanted to get to the heart of B-3.

On the fourth day, when I was halfway to my goal, George Birch drove out from his general store, as I had requested, with cans of stew, bottles of soda pop and cigarettes. He was normally a dour man, but on this morning his face seemed longer than ever. I inquired if there were anything bothering him.

"Carlotta Brown-Jenkin died last night," he said. "Friend of my mother's. Tough old lady." He shook his head. "Influenza. Shame."

I remembered that awful, Technicolored meal so many months before, the steely glint of her eyes in their cavernous sockets. I did my best to look properly sympathetic.

"That is a shame," I said.

He set down the box of food and looked past me at the entrance to my tunnel. The sight of it seemed to disturb him.

"You sure you know what you're doing?" he said.

I assured him that I did, but he continued to look skeptical.

"I remember the last time you archaeologist fellows came to town, you know," he said. As a matter of fact I did know this, since he told me almost every time I saw him. "I was a boy. We had just got electricity in our house."

"Things must have changed a great deal since then," I said.

"Things haven't changed at all," he snapped. He was never a cheerful man, George Birch. He turned, hitching up his trousers, and limped on his wooden foot back to his truck.

That night I lay in my bedroll under the canvas roof of my tent, watching the tormented sky. The lantern hissed softly beside my head; I kept it burning low, all night long, advertising my presence to any who might seek to come and undo my work. It had been a warm, springlike afternoon, but now a cool breeze was blowing in from the north, stirring the branches of the trees over my head. After a while I drowsed a little; I fancied I could hear the distant fluting of the Miskahannock flowing over its rocky bed and, still more distant, the low, insistent drumming of the machine heart in the black mill. Suddenly I sat up: The music I had been hearing, of breeze and river and far-off machinery, seemed at once very close and not at all metaphoric. I scrambled out of my bedroll and tent and stood, taut, listening, at the edge of Plunkettsburg Ring. It *was* music I heard, strange music, and it seemed to be issuing, impossibly, from the other end of the tunnel I had been digging and redigging over the past two weeks—from within mound B-3, the null mound!

I have never, generally, been plagued by bouts of great courage, but I do suffer from another vice whose outward appearance is often indistinguishable from that of bravery: I am pathologically curious. I was not brave enough, in that eldritch moment, actually to approach B-3, to investigate the source of the music I was hearing; but though every primitive impulse urged me to flee, I stood there, listening, until the music stopped, an hour before dawn. I heard sorrow in the music, and mourning, and the beating of many small drums.

And then in the full light of the last day of April, emboldened by bright sunshine and a cup of instant coffee, I made my way gingerly toward the mound. I picked up my shovel, lowered my foolish head into the tunnel and crept carefully into the bowels of the now-silent mound. Seven hours later I felt the shovel strike something hard, like stone or brick. Then the hardness gave way, and the shovel flew abruptly out of my hands. I had reached, at last, the heart of mound B-3.

And it was not empty; oh no, not at all. There were seven sealed tombs lining the domed walls, carved stone chambers of the usual Miskahannock type, and another ten that were empty, and one, as yet unsealed, that held the unmistakable, though withered, yellow, naked and eternally slumbering form of Carlotta Brown-Jenkin. And crouched on her motionless chest, as though prepared to devour her throat, sat a tiny stone idol, hideous, black, brandishing a set of wicked ivory fangs.

Now I gave in to those primitive impulses; I panicked. I tore out of the burial chamber as quickly as I could and ran for my car, not bothering to collect my gear. In 20 minutes I was back at Murrough House. I hurried up the front steps, intending only to go to my room, retrieve my clothes and books and papers and leave behind Plunkettsburg forever. But when I came into the foyer I found Dexter, carrying a tray of eaten lunches back from the dining room to the kitchen. He was whistling lightheartedly and when he saw me he grinned. Then his expression changed.

"What is it?" he said, reaching out to me. "Has something happened?"

"Nothing," I said, stepping around him, avoiding his grasp. The streets of Plunkettsburg had been built on evil ground, and now I could only assume that every one of its citizens, even cheerful Dexter, had been altered by the years and centuries of habitation. "Everything's fine. I just have to leave town."

I started up the wide, carpeted steps as quickly as I could, mentally packing my bags and boxes with essentials, loading the car, twisting and backtracking up the steep road out of this cursed valley.

"My name came up," Dexter said. "I start tomorrow at the mill."

Why did I turn? Why did I not keep going down the long, crooked hallway and carry out my sensible, cowardly plan?

"You can't do that," I said. He started to smile, but there must have been something in my face. The smile fizzled out. "You'll be killed. You'll be mangled. That good-looking mug of yours will be hideously deformed."

"Maybe," he said, trying to sound calm, but I could see that my own agitation was infecting him. "Maybe not."

"It's the women. The queens. They're alive."

"The queens are alive? What are you talking about, professor? I think you've been out on the mountain too long."

"I have to go, Dexter," I said. "I'm sorry. I can't stay here anymore. But if you have any sense at all, you'll come with me. I'll drive you to Pittsburgh. You can start at Tech. They'll help you. They'll give you a job. . . ." I could feel myself starting to babble.

Dexter shook his head. "Can't," he said. "My name came up! Shoot, I've been waiting for this all my life."

"Look," I said. "All right. Just come with me, out to the Ring." I looked at my watch. "We've got an hour until dark. Just let me show you something I found out there, and then if you still want to go to work in that infernal factory, I'll shake your hand and bid you farewell."

"You'll really take me out to the site?"

I nodded. He set the tray on a deal table and untied his apron.

"Let me get my jacket," he said.

I packed my things and we drove in silence to the necropolis. I was filled with regret for this course of action, with intimations of disaster. But I felt I couldn't simply leave town and let Dexter Eibonas walk willingly into that fiery eructation of the evil genius, the immemorial accursedness, of his drab Pennsylvania home-town. I couldn't leave that young, unmarked body to be broken and split on the horrid machines of the mill. As for why Dexter wasn't talking, I don't know; perhaps he sensed my mounting despair, or perhaps he was simply lost in youthful speculation on the unknown vistas that lay before him, subterranean sights forbidden and half-legendary to him since he had first come to consciousness of the world. As we turned off Gray Road onto the access road that led up to the site, he sat up straight and looked at me, his face grave with the consummate adolescent pleasure of violating rules.

"There," I said. I pointed out the window as we crested the rise. The Plunkettsburg Ring lay spread out before us, filled with jagged shadows, in the slanting, rust-red light of the setting sun. From this angle the dual circular plan of the site was not apparent, and the 36 mounds appeared to stretch from one end of the plateau to the other, like a line of uneven teeth studding an immense, devouring jawbone.

"Let's make this quick," I said, shuddering. I handed him a spare lantern from the trunk of the Nash, and then we walked to the edge of the aboriginal forest that ran upslope from the plateau to the wind-shattered precincts of Mount Orrert's sharp peak. It was here, in the lee of a large maple tree, that I had set up my makeshift camp. At the time the shelter of that homely tree had seemed quite inviting, but now it appeared to me that the forest was the source of all the lean shadows reaching their ravening fingers across the plateau. I ducked quickly into my tent to retrieve my lantern and then hurried back to rejoin Dexter. I thought he was looking a little uneasy now. His gait slowed as we approached B-3. When we trudged around to confront the raw earthen mouth of the passage I had dug, he came to a complete stop.

"We're not going inside there," he said in a monotone. I saw come into his eyes the dull, dreamy look that was there whenever he talked about going to work in the mill. "It isn't allowed."

"It's just for a minute, Dexter. That's all you'll need."

I put my hands on his shoulders and gave him a push, and we stumbled through the dank, close passage, the light from our lanterns veering wildly around us. Then we were in the crypt.

"No," Dexter said. The effect on him of the sight of the time-ravaged naked body of Carlotta Brown-Jenkin, of the empty tombs, the hideous idol, the outlandish ideograms that covered the walls, was everything I could have hoped for. His jaw dropped, his hands clenched and unclenched, he took a step backward. "She just died!"

"Yesterday," I agreed, trying to allay my own anxiety with a show of ironic detachment.

"But what . . . what's she doing out here?" He shook his head quickly, as though trying to clear it of smoke or spiderwebs.

"Don't you know?" I asked him, for I still was not completely certain of his or any townsman's uninvolvement in the evil, at once ancient and machine-age, that was evidently the chief business of Plunkettsburg.

"No! God, no!" He pointed to the queer, fanged idol that crouched with a hungry leer on the late chancellor's hollow bosom. "God, what is that thing?"

I went over to the tomb and cautiously, as if the figure with its enormous, obscene tusks might come to life and rip off a mouthful of my hand, picked up the idol. It was as black and cold as space, and so heavy that it bent my hand back at the wrist as I hefted it. With both hands I got a firm grip on it and turned it over. On its pedestal were incised three symbols in the spiky, complex script of the Miskahannocks, unrelated to any other known human language or alphabet. As with all of the tribe's inscriptions, the characters had both a phonetic and a symbolic sense. Often these were quite independent of one another.

"Yu . . . yug . . . gog," I read, sounding it out carefully. "Yuggog."

"What does that mean?"

"It doesn't mean anything, as far as I know. But it can be read another way. It's trickier. Here's tooth . . . gut—that's hunger—and this one——" I held up the idol toward him. He shied away. His face had gone completely pale, and there was a look of fear in his eyes, of awareness of evil, that I found, God forgive me, strangely gratifying. "This is a kind of general intensive, I believe. Making this read, loosely rendered, hunger . . . itself. How odd."

"Yuggog," Dexter said softly, a thin strand of spittle joining his lips.

"Here," I said cruelly, tossing the heavy thing toward him. Let him go into the black mill now, I thought, after he's seen *this*. Dexter batted at the thing, knocking it to the ground. There was a sharp, tearing sound like matchwood splitting. For an instant Dexter looked utterly, cosmically startled. Then he, and the idol of Yuggog, disappeared. There was a loud thud, and a clatter, and I heard him groan. I picked up the splintered halves of the carved wooden trapdoor Dexter had fallen through and gazed down into a fairly deep, smooth-sided hole. He lay crumpled at the bottom, about eight feet beneath me, in the light of his overturned lantern.

"My God! I'm sorry! Are you all right?"

"I think I sprained my ankle," he said. He sat up and raised his lantern. His eyes got very wide. "Professor, you have to see this."

I lowered myself carefully into the hole and stared with Dexter into a great round tunnel, taller than either of us, paved with crazed human bones, stretching far beyond the pale of our lanterns.

"A tunnel," he said. "I wonder where it goes."

"I can only guess," I said. "And that's never good enough for me."

"Professor! You aren't——"

But I had already started into the tunnel, a decision that I attributed not to courage, of course, but to my far greater vice. I did not see that as I took those first steps into the tunnel I was in fact being bitten off, chewed and swallowed, as it were, by the very mouth of the Plunkettsburg evil. I took small, queasy

steps along the horrible floor, avoiding insofar as I could stepping on the out-
raged miens of human skulls, searching the smoothed, plastered walls of the
tunnel for ideograms or other hints of the builders of this amazing structure.
The tunnel, or at least this version of it, was well built, buttressed regularly by
sturdy iron piers and lintels, and of chillingly recent vintage. Only great wealth,
I thought, could have managed such a feat of engineering. A few minutes later
I heard a tread behind me and saw the faint glow of a lantern. Dexter joined
me, favoring his right ankle, his lantern swinging as he walked.

"We're headed northwest," I said. "We must be under the river by now."

"Under the river?" he said. "Could Indians have built a tunnel like this?"

"No, Dexter, they could not."

He didn't say anything for a moment as he took this information in.

"Professor, we're headed for the mill, aren't we?"

"I'm afraid we must be," I said.

We walked for three quarters of an hour, until the sound of pounding machinery became audible, grew gradually unbearable and finally exploded directly
over our heads. The tunnel had run out. I looked up at the trapdoor above us.
Then I heard a muffled scream. To this day I don't know if the screamer was
one of the men up on the floor of the factory, or Dexter Eibonas, a massive
hand clapped brutally over his mouth, because the next instant, at the back of
my head, a supernova bloomed and flared brightly.

I wake in an immense room, to the idiot pounding of a machine. The walls are
sheets of fire flowing upward like inverted cataracts; the ceiling is lost in shadow
from which, when the flames flare brightly, there emerges the vague impression
of a steely web of girders among which dark things ceaselessly creep. Thick coils of
rope bind my arms to my sides, and my legs are lashed at the ankles to those of the
plain pine chair in which I have been propped.

It is one of two dozen chairs in a row that is one of a hundred, in a row filled
with men, the slumped, crew-cut, big-shouldered ordinary men of Plunkettsburg
and its neighboring towns. We are all waiting, and watching, as the women of
Plunkettsburg, the servants of Yuggog, pass noiselessly among us in their soft,
horrible cloaks stitched from the hides of dead men, tapping on the shoulder of
now one fellow, now another. None of my neighbors, however, appears to have
required the use of strong rope to conjoin him to his fate. Without a word the
designated men, their blood thick with the dark earthen brew of the Ring
witches, rise and follow the skins of miscreant fathers and grandfathers down to
the ceremonial altar at the heart of the mill, where the priestesses of Yuggog
throw oracular bones and, given the result, take hold of the man's ear, his foot,
his fingers. A yellow snake, its venom presumably anesthetic, is applied to the
fated extremity. Then the long knife is brought to bear, and the vast, immemorial hunger of the god of the Miskahannocks is assuaged for another brief
instant. In the past three hours on this Walpurgis Night, nine men have been
so treated; tomorrow, people in this bewitched town, that in a reasonable age,
has learned to eat its men a little at a time, will speak, I am sure, of a series of
horrible accidents at the mill. The women came to take away Dexter Eibonas
an hour ago. I looked away as he went under the knife, but I believe he lost the
better part of his left arm to the god. I can only assume that very soon now I

will feel the tap on my left shoulder of the fingers of the town librarian, the grocer's wife, of Mrs. Eibonas herself. I am guiltier by far of trespass than Ed Eibonas and do not suppose I will survive the procedure.

Strange how calm I feel in the face of all this; perhaps there remain traces of the beer in my veins, or perhaps in this hellish place there are other enchantments at work. In any case, I will at least have the satisfaction of seeing my theory confirmed, or partly confirmed, before I die, and the concomitant satisfaction, so integral to my profession, of seeing my teacher's theory cast in the dustbin. For, as I held, the Miskahannocks hungered; and hunger, black, primordial, unstaunchable hunger itself, was their god. It was indeed the misguided scrambling and digging of my teacher and his colleagues, I imagine, that awakened great Yuggog from its 4000-year slumber. As for the black mill that fascinated me for so many months, it is a sham. The single great machine to my left takes in no raw materials and emits no ingots or sheets. It is simply an immense piston, endlessly screaming and pounding like the skin of an immense drum the ground that since the days of the Miskahannocks has been the sacred precinct of the god. The flames that flash through the windows and the smoke that proceeds from the chimneys are bits of trickery, mechanical contrivances devised, I suppose, by Philippa Howard Murrough herself, in the days when the revived spirit of Yuggog first whispered to her of its awful, eternal appetite for the flesh of men. The sole industry of Plunkettsburg is carnage, scarred and mangled bodies the only product.

One thought disturbs the perfect, poison calm with which I am suffused—the trucks that grind their way in and out of the valley, the freight trains that come clanging in the night. What cargo, I wonder, is unloaded every morning at the docks of the Plunkettsburg Mill? What burden do those trains bear away?

P. D. Cacek

Dust Motes

P. D. Cacek's *fiction has been published in a number of anthologies, among them* David Copperfield's Tales of the Impossible, *Peter S. Beagle's* The Immortal Unicorn, *and the* Hot Blood *series from which came "Metalica," winner of the Bram Stoker Award for Superior Achievement in Short Story for 1996. Her short fiction is collected in* Leavings. *She recently made her novel debut with* Night Prayers.

Cacek is one of the few writers who has made her reputation solely on her short fiction. "Dust Motes," originally published in Gothic Ghosts, *shows why.*

—E. D. and T. W.

W hy is it that all the architecturally overdone, Neo-Greco-inspired, Carnegie-endowed libraries look alike?

The same towering canyons of words and ideas that press down on the back of your neck even if you keep your eyes lowered to the scuffed parquet beneath your feet . . . the same milk-glass lights, cool green shades to minimize the glare, suspended over the banquet-size tables on thin cords from a ceiling so high it could be mistaken for the sky at twilight . . . the same windows, set high so as to be unobtrusive, so the outside world might be forgotten by those cloistered within . . .

. . . and the same shafts of dust-choked golden light that always seem to spill into the otherwise dark caverns despite the time of day. Or the month of year.

When I was younger I used to love the shafts of light—tiptapping on Buster Brown shoes from one radiant beam to the next until either my mother or the librarian would tell me to stop . . . or find the one I thought the brightest and twirl in it, my skirt lifting unladylike, until the dust swirled around me like a golden cloud.

When I was younger.

Now I only noticed the dust.

Why the hell did I think coming here would be a good idea? I could have just stayed home and drugged myself into mental oblivion with pain medication and the midday soaps.

Except I had already done that for the last eight months, ever since the tiny, hard pebble in my right breast turned out to be a monster I had never even dreamt of back when I could still see the golden light and make the dust dance.

Besides, home meant waiting for calls that had been well-rehearsed beforehand to cheer me up, with pity so thick it would sound like static on the line. Or worse yet, it meant waiting for the calls that never came from those who thought that by acknowledging me the cancer would somehow seek them out.

Either way it meant waiting for someone to remember I was, at least for the present, still alive. And I was tired of it.

Just as I was tired of *people* who still had the luxury of having time to wait.

When an old man in a pale gray suit brushed against my arm and looked as if he were about to say something, I moved out of the relatively bright foyer and into the book-lined twilight. The library was more crowded than I'd expected (or hoped) it would be on an early spring afternoon.

A covey of teenage girls in Catholic school uniforms whispered to one another at a small table near the Information/Check Out counter. Middle-age women in housedresses and older men (although none as nicely dressed as my would-be friend from the foyer) moved idly through columns of bookshelves or sat at the row of tables . . . some reading bound volumes, some newspapers; some hunched over yellow, legal-size notebooks furiously scribbling away, some gossiping while others listened; some (those dressed in layers of mismatched clothes) sleeping, heads on folded arms.

An Hispanic boy of about twelve, obviously truant, slumped against the paneled wall near the history section and glared . . . at nothing in particular. Two women about my own age, one pushing a sleeping baby in a stroller with a squeaky wheel past the romance aisle, laughed.

Why not? *They* had their whole lives in front of them.

I could feel the sudden anger compete with the Valium I'd had for breakfast and self-conciously lifted my hand to brush the hair off my forehead. It was an old habit and one that hadn't died simply because I no longer had hair to push aside.

My fingers touched the padded crown on the custom-made bandanna that one of the "Cancer Specialists" had handed to me while a student nurse (young, bright, *alive*) shaved off the few wisps of auburn still rooted to my scalp.

"It will grow back," the specialist informed me, smiling while she checked off her good deed on the clipboard she carried, "once the treatments are over."

I remembered that smile—forced, pitying, and more than just a little grateful that she wasn't the one being turned into a human cue ball. Or having to wear the god-awful flowered bandanna in public.

Or dying.

When I lowered my hand I noticed my fingers were trembling even though I couldn't feel it.

I tried not to listen to the sounds of my footsteps as I walked. They sounded hollower here than they did at home (or at the clinic) . . . less substantial.

A little girl wearing a starched white party dress was standing in the pool of dusty sunlight in front of the children's section; turning slowly, arms outstretched . . . the same way I used to.

Back when I still believed in the possibilities of "happily ever afters."

When her slow dance finally turned her toward me our eyes met . . .

. . . for only an instant . . .

. . . and then I moved on—quickly—ignoring the sorrow and pain I'd seen in her round green eyes the same way strangers (and friends) pretend to ignore the bandanna covering my head and the reason behind it.

Whatever problem the child was having, it was nothing compared to mine.

I got as far as the periodicals before stumbling and banging my right hip into a ladder-backed chair. The resulting sound, unlike my footsteps, wasn't hollow *or* insubstantial . . . it bounced off the high ceiling and echoed through the darkened corridors like a thunderclap. Three women at the far end of the table looked up from the magazine recipes they were copying and glared at me.

How dare I disturb them.

Breathing as slowly as I could so I wouldn't attract any *more* attention by panting, I pulled out the chair I'd bumped and let my body collapse into it. The seat had the same hard polished, butt-numbing shape I remembered so well.

Oh yeah, this was a *lot* better than curling up on the sofa in front of the tube.

The women were still watching me. I could feel their eyes, like cobwebs against my skin, as I reached into the pile of magazines the librarian hadn't had a chance to put away, and instantly found myself leafing through articles and ads geared toward surviving the first "traumatic weeks" of motherhood.

Right.

I forced myself—face relaxed, hands trembling only slightly, fingers itching to claw out the photogenically enhanced smiles—to keep turning the pages. Pretending

. . . that somewhere in the future I really might consider having children . . .

. . . and that I really *had* a future . . .

. . . and the bandanna was only a fashion statement . . .

. . . and everything really would turn out "happily ever after" if I just wished upon a star or found the end of the rainbow or could be awakened from this dream by a handsome prince on a white horse—as long as the prince didn't mind bald princesses with one breast who might never be able to produce heirs to the throne, that is.

I got as far as a full-page ad showing a leggy "mother" in swirling gauze standing in a field of daisies smiling down at a nude baby in her arms while Disneyesque bluebirds and butterflies fluttered through a cerulean sky dotted with golden-edge rose-colored clouds. A white unicorn mare and her foal grazed in the cool blue mist just out of focal depth.

The ad was for a diaper-rash medication.

"A blatant attempt to capture the style of Maxfield Parish, don't you think?" a low voice suddenly rumbled from over my right shoulder. "Although I can't remember if he ever painted unicorns. I know he did angels, of course, but . . ."

The legs of my chair scraped against the floor (*again*) as I jumped and I could feel a newer, more improved glare-fest coming from the far end of the table as I turned.

Oh, God.

It was the old man in gray.

I frowned and honed the edges of my glare to the razor's sharpness that had served me so well in late-night bar encounters and drunken office Christmas parties. Once upon a time . . .

Go away. Leave me alone!

So naturally he came around to the opposite side of the table and sat down across from me. His chair didn't scrape.

"I am sorry to disturb you, but . . ." He had a clipped somewhere-back-East-with-money accent, but his voice modulated more for the daylight world outside the library than inside it. God, the women at the end of the table must really be having a hissy fit.

". . . you can see me, can't you?"

I *think* I nodded. Or maybe I just asked him what the hell he was talking about. Loudly. Either way he clapped his long-fingered hands and one of the women got up and stormed away.

"You can . . . dear Lord, you really *can* see me. I told the others someone would come . . . someday, but . . . You don't know what this will mean to them. You *still* can see me, can't you?"

He stopped talking and smiled at me, slowly lowering his hands to the table top. The polished wood showed a reverse image of the old man—deepening the gray silk of the jacket and the pink (*Jesus, he was wearing rouge!*) on his cheeks; and exaggerating the line of his square chin while making his pale blue eyes seem smaller and closer set than they naturally were. I found myself staring at the image instead of the man and slowly sliding my chair away from the table.

Crazy people have always frightened me.

And it was obvious that this old man, for all his East Coast polish and implied wealth, was a well bred loon. Asking me if I could *see* him . . . unless . . . Christ, I bet he was exposing himself under the table.

This time I didn't care if my chair scraped or not. I stood up quickly and took a step toward the exit. The two other women had already fled in the direction their companion had taken, when *he* stood up.

Right through the table top and its scattered display of magazines.

My back teeth clinked together when I sat down again.

I had seen stage magicians slice women in half, both horizontally and vertically, and one had even beheaded a woman and carried her head out into the audience where it winked and flirted silently on cue . . . but this didn't appear to be any kind of "illusion." The old man in gray silk and rouged cheeks had simply stood up *into* the table.

Only no one had said "Abracadabra."

And I was beyond applauding.

He finally noticed me staring and sat down quickly—his jacket front and tie disappearing into the wood, then coming out whole when he sat back in the chair.

"I am sorry," he said, straightening the line of his tie. "Please excuse me, it was just that I was so excited about finding you . . ."

"Me?" I heard myself ask.

"Well," he said, still loud enough to attract the attention of every librarian in the place, "someone *like* you . . . who is caught between life and death. Straddling the cosmic fence, so to speak. What is it? Cancer?"

"Who *are* you?"

The old man nodded as if I'd just confirmed what he suspected and laced his fingertips together beneath his chin, sighing softly like a college professor confronting a student on a less-than-brilliant term project.

"And it must be in remission or else you wouldn't feel well enough to be here. Yes, of course, that probably explains why we don't see many of the dying here. . . . But, then again, why would somebody teetering on the edge of life want to visit a library? I would think it'd be torture, to see all the books you might never have a chance to read. Augh, horrible thought.

"May I ask why you came? Not that we're not grateful that you—"

This time I didn't mince words. And I didn't whisper. "Who the *hell* are you?"

He looked up and blinked. "Oh, my . . . I do get carried away sometimes, don't I. Think I'd learn after all this time." Squaring his shoulders, he leaned forward (shirt-front and tie sliding effortlessly into the table) and extended his right hand. "My name is Howard Roth and I've been dead seven years. High blood pressure, not enough exercise . . . you know the sort of thing."

He paused and cocked his head to one side, pale blue eyes blinking.

"Is there some—"

"—thing I can do for you, ma'am?"

The new voice took me by surprise and I yelped. Loudly. My voice rising to the shadowed ceiling and swirling through the dusty, golden light. When the echoes finally died, I heard chairs scraping and the sound of more than one pair of leather soled shoes heading toward the entrance.

Quickly.

I guess I'm not the only one who feels uncomfortable in the near vicinity of "crazies."

Part of me wanted to find the people scurrying away and tell them that I was perfectly sane . . . *dying*, but sane; but it was all I could do to swivel toward the woman in the matching vest and chino short set standing next to me. And convince *her*.

"Is there a problem?" she asked again when my eyes finally made the long journey from cinched-in waist to name tag (MS. MESSIE/ASSISTANT LIBRARIAN) to golden chain to golden hair and amber eyes.

My first impression was that she should have been draped over some tropical sea-drenched rock, modeling the latest in should-not-appear-in-public-without-liposuction swimsuit. God only knows what her first impression of me was. . . .

. . . no, the tight almost-wrinkles around her peach-color lips told me that much.

"Yes," I said, pointing across to the old man despite the muttered instructions not to, "he's bothering me. Would you please tell him to leave me alone?"

"I really wish you hadn't done that." Howard Roth sighed. "They might ask you to leave."

"Me?" I turned and glared at him. "Why would they ask *me* to leave?"

But instead of answering, he shook his head and pointed to the assistant librarian.

The amber eyes had darkened and the lines had deepened by the time I turned around. I must have looked the same when I first thought Howard Roth was simply a crazy old man and not a—

"I told you," he said softly—but still loud enough for Ms. Messie to hear. But there was no indication that she could. Or did. "The *untouched* living can't see us. Please, we desperately need to speak to you. Tell her it was a mistake or a side-effect of your medication. Please."

"Um, ma'am," Ms. Messie said after another quick glance to what appeared to her to be an empty chair, "I really think I'm going to have to ask you to leave unless . . ."

"You mean you didn't *see* him?" I said quickly, ignoring Howard Roth's hollow (*ghostly*) groan. "The . . . man over by the newspaper rack. Oh, he's gone. But . . . he was *exposing* himself . . . I think . . . I think he might have gone into the *children's* section."

I'm not sure what it was—either the thought that a man would have to be a pervert to expose himself to a bald, *dying* woman or a quick mathematical rundown of the lawsuits that would occur if such a man displayed the "family jewels" to a minor—but the blond-haired, amber-eyed *living* woman actually mumbled an apology and hurried away.

The sound of applause made me turn around. Howard Roth was beaming like a proud father. A *dead* proud father.

"I am impressed, Miss . . ." The beam faded only slightly as he extended his hand the way he had earlier. "Dear me, in all the confusion I seem to have failed to ask your name."

This time I reached out to take his hand. And watched my fingers pass through his as easily as he had passed through the top of the table. Only the tiniest chill lingered against the palm of my hand. I don't know why this bothered me, all things considered, but for a moment I forgot how to breathe. When I finally remembered the air trapped in my lungs came out as a rush of words.

"Leslie Carr and oh, God, you really are a ghost, aren't you?"

Howard Roth, *ghost*, chuckled. "Yes, I am, my dear Leslie. Ah, Leslie . . . one of my favorite names. 'A queen, too, is my Lesley,/And gracious, though blood-royal,/ My heart her throne, her kingdom,/And I a subject loyal.' James Whitcomb Riley. Do you know his work? No? Ah, I am sorry to hear that. Marvelous poet . . . I can hardly wait to meet him.

"Shall we go?"

The chill that had touched my hand traveled up my arm and into the hollow left by my metastasized breast.

"Go?" I asked. "Go where?"

Howard Roth stood up and walked through the table instead of going around it. My, the things I have to look forward to.

"To meet the others," he said, stopping at the junction where periodicals met current events and holding out his hand.

The little girl in white came slowly around the corner and took his hand. No wonder she looked so out of place in the library. She'd been dressed for a funeral.

Hers.

If I had tried to stand at that moment I would have passed out.

"It's all right, Minka," Howard Roth said to the dead child, "the lady can see you."

A shy smile appeared at the corners of her mouth as she looked up. It was only when I saw her away from the dusty golden beam of light that I realized her cheeks had been rouged a shade lighter than the old man's.

Maybe her family had used the same mortician that worked on Howard.

I closed my eyes and covered them with a trembling hand. "Oh, God."

"Yes, it is sad when someone is so young. Minka was only four." He clicked his tongue and I felt the chill against the scar tissue on my chest burrow beneath the smooth, taut skin. "A horrible accident, her mother had left her alone only for a moment in the tub . . . her baby sister had started crying . . . ah, well. She's been here fifty-three years—forty-nine years longer than she'd been alive."

My hand dropped to my lap with an audible thump. *Fifty-three years!* Here . . . haunting this place.

"What am I supposed to do?" I asked, leveling myself unsteadily to my feet. The chill, like the cancer that had invaded my body, had finally worked its way into my heart. I couldn't feel it beating.

Howard Roth patted the little girl's pale hand and smiled when he looked at me. They both seemed so real. So—how did he phrase it?—*untouched.*

Alive.

"Just listen," he said, then smiled at the little girl who had died decades before I was even born. "All of us here left life . . . unexpectedly; either by accident or violence or by simply ignoring their doctor's advice. My dear Leslie, we died unprepared and so missed the opportunity to relate that one incident which made our existence on this plane worthwhile."

Jesus, why hadn't my Sunday school teachers told me you had to pass a test to get into heaven?

"And . . . you want *me* to listen to these . . . stories?"

The ghost of Howard Roth winked at me. "Precisely."

I took a step forward and felt the chill race into my legs. "But why here? And why me?"

"I have already told you, my dear Leslie, why it is that you can see and hear us. And as to this place?" Another wink and he tucked the little girl's hand beneath his arm and began to walk them both toward the library's main room. "What better place to find someone to listen to stories?"

So I followed them, the ghostly old man and child as they moved through the living as silent and invisible as the specks of dust dancing in the fading light, to a small alcove set far back along a section of shelved stacks labeled HISTORY/ANCIENT.

Where the rest were waiting.

My shoulder brushed against a thick volume covered in cracked red leather and toppled it from the shelf; but here, in this particular section, there was no one to notice.

No one alive, that is.

There must have been over two hundred of them in the alcove—standing ramrod straight or slumping comfortably against the shelves, a few even "sitting" at a small rectangular table near the back wall; talking quietly among themselves in voices hushed and calm . . . suitable for a library.

I leaned against my own section of books, listening to them . . . catching the occasional word or phrase (dull, mundane stuff actually—more concerned about the chances of a certain baseball team making it to the World Series and how much gas prices had gone up since that particular speaker's death than in questioning the cosmic joke that had *trapped* them here) . . . until, one by one, they noticed me.

"My dear friends," Howard Roth said, shooing the little girl toward a strikingly beautiful black woman in red serge, "this is Leslie Carr who, out of the kindness of her soul and despite great personal suffering, has come to listen."

I have to admit that getting a standing ovation from ghosts was something I had never thought to achieve. Or even hoped for.

When the summer storm of applause trickled down to a few perfunctory claps, Howard Roth stepped forward and offered me his arm. Winking as I tried to balance my living flesh against his . . . and winking again at the little girl in white when she giggled at my obvious lack of skill.

"Who would you like to hear first?" he asked after I'd taken a seat at the table.

They huddled before me—silent, smiling; some with hands clasped in what looked like prayer, others sullen as if this was too easy a solution. I was like a queen, surveying her loyal subjects . . . like that woman in the poem Howard Roth had quoted earlier. And then I saw the Hispanic boy who had glared at me when I first entered the library. He was slumped against a row of fat volumes he probably wouldn't have read even if he'd lived . . . the angry look making him look older than he was.

Than he *had* been.

When he died.

Yeah . . . I was queen all right. Leslie the First, Queen of the Dead.

Huzzah.

Without thinking, I brushed my fingers against the lock of hair that should have been there. But wasn't. At least *my* leaving wouldn't be unexpected.

Tugging the front of the bandanna lower on my forehead, I took a deep breath and jerked my chin toward the angry boy I had originally thought was only truant from school.

"Him," I told Howard in case there was any doubt, "the boy over there."

Howard nodded his agreement. "Berto, Leslie has chosen you first."

It was obvious by his reaction that the boy had seldom been chosen first for anything . . . except, perhaps, death. He suddenly stood taller, his backbone unkinking itself almost audibly as the angry mask slipped from his face. Beneath it lay the features of a frightened child—eyes wide, mouth partially opened, cheeks pale and sunken in, with no trace of rouge or mortician's craft. How long had making-up a corpse been standard practice? Since the '30s? The '20s?

Jesus, how long had he been here . . . waiting for someone to listen?

"Come along, Berto," Howard said, no trace of impatience in his voice—but why should there be, he had all the time in the world. "Tell Leslie what made you special."

Berto came forward, the cuffs of his trousers hanging over the tops of ratty-looking sneakers, his hands all but lost in the unhemmed coat sleeves. His death must have been unexpected . . . his family hadn't even had time to tailor a hand-me-down.

"I . . ." He stopped and cleared his voice like a child forced to recite at a school Founder's Day program. A breeze, possibly from some recessed air-conditioner vent I couldn't feel, began ruffling his oversized suit. "I . . . I saved a dog from gettin' drown."

That was it?

I don't know what I expected to hear—maybe something along the lines of his being a musical prodigy or being the sole support for his family or even having died while rescuing blind orphans from a burning building.

Just something . . . a little more *spectacular* than saving a dog from drowning, for God's sake.

But Berto didn't seem to notice my obvious lack of enthusiasm. He was smiling now, his face glowing. Christ, it really was *glowing!* And it wasn't just his face.

Dusty gold light, as if a window had suddenly been opened in the row of books, poured down over Berto—blurring the fine edges of his body as the breeze rippled and tugged at him.

"It was just a puppy," Berto continued, and I found myself leaning forward, straining to hear. It was almost as if the light, which was now so bright that it softened the lines of his body into a fuzzy blur, was doing the same thing to his voice.

Squinting against the glare, I pushed the bandanna away from my ears and held my breath.

"This man he was really mean n' he'd got this puppy n' was gonna drown it 'cause he didn't want no more dogs . . ."

The light became an incandescent flame with Berto as its white-hot core.

". . . so he puts it in this flour sack n' . . . throws it in the river back of his house only . . . I see it . . . n' go in t' get it. It . . . was a real . . . little puppy . . . but . . . I . . . saved . . . its

". . . life . . ."

The light blinked out taking Berto, whose one glorious moment of life had been to save a mongrel puppy, with it.

I felt the tears strike the back of my hands before realizing I was crying. It'd been so long—eight months exactly—that I thought I'd forgotten how.

"Thank you for Berto," Howard Roth said softly. "Who would you like to hear next?"

I didn't have to think. Swallowing hard, I pointed to the little girl in white who'd been waiting fifty years.

"A loving choice, dearest Leslie. Minka, you're next."

She was already glowing even before she stopped before me.

"I scare rat away from bebe sister." She giggled and was gone.

That fast. No muss, no fuss. As if the light was as eager for her as she for it.

Good-bye, Minka, I whispered silently to the empty air in front of me. *God bless.*

"Next," I said out loud, and smiled at an old black man in a shiny blue suit.

· · · ·

I went back to the library every day for a month—greeting Ms. Messie at the doors when they opened and bidding her a polite farewell when she finally made her way back to the HISTORY/ANCIENT section to kick me out each night. I know she thought I was crazy, but now it didn't matter . . . nothing mattered but the ghosts' stories.

Not that listening didn't take something out of me, it did. Sometimes I was so numbed by what they felt was the greatest moment of their lives ("Ah returned dis twenty dollah bill ah found on da floor o'da market, ad did." "I shared the last piece of birthday cake with my brother." "I lit a candle in church for the homeless." "I got an A-plus on my last spelling test and a gold star and the teacher put it up on the wall.") that I could barely stumble home.

But sometimes . . . no, every time, in that last moment before the light blinked out, I was able to feel some of their joy . . . their peace.

I don't know when I stopped being afraid to die, but I think it was about a week or two before I noticed that Howie (as he preferred to be called, probably because it made me laugh) and the remaining ghosts were becoming transparent.

"What's happening?" I hissed, dropping my Thermos of juice and sack lunch to the table before nearly collapsing into a chair. "Why do you *look* like that?"

Howie lifted his hands and looked at them, turning them palms up, then palms down.

"What's different from the way I look?" he finally asked.

"You're—" Christ, how do you say this delicately to a ghost? "—a little, um . . . glassy."

"Glassy?"

I didn't think it was going to be that easy.

"You know . . . diaphanous, sheer, translucent . . . dammit, Howie, you're all fading."

He looked back at his hands. The others just looked worried.

"Are you sure, Leslie?"

I nodded. "Forgive the comparison, but all of you are starting to look like overlays in a B-rated horror movie."

Howie clasped his transparent hands together and brought them to his chin. "I'm so happy for you, Leslie," he said.

I shook my head. "What do you mean?"

"Don't you understand, my dearest Leslie? We're fading because you're slipping from the shadows back into the light. You're going to *live*, Leslie . . . and the living can't see us."

"Oh, God."

I leaned forward in my chair, my fingers wringing creases into the flowing skirt of the sundress I had chosen on a whim that morning. I *had* felt better in the last few weeks—stronger . . . Jesus, alive.

"Howie? Oh, God, Howie, I can barely see you."

"It's all right," he whispered back, "we can wait."

"NO!" Now I *know* Ms. Messie must have heard that, hell, the whole damned library probably did, but I didn't care. All they could do was throw me out. Or try to. "Look, there still may be enough time. I can still see you . . . a little. It's like you're blending into the background. Quick, tell me your story, Howie."

"No." His voice was even softer than a whisper. "Miriam . . . first."

Miriam Horowitz, of the Bronx Horowitzes, glided forward and lowered her blue-tinted head toward mine.

"I . . . let . . . my . . . sister . . . marry . . . the . . . man . . . I . . . loved . . . according . . . to . . . our . . . father's . . . wis—"

And she was gone. But this time there was no heavenly luminescence. At least none that I could see.

"Hurry," I told the others, squinting as their outlines became more diffused. "I don't know how much longer I'll be able to hear you."

Their voices were barely audible, competing suddenly with other muted sounds I hadn't noticed before: the hum of traffic in the street outside, the rattle of book carts, the fluttering swish of pages being turned.

"Hurry."

". . . gold medal . . . in junior . . . Olympics . . ."

". . . read to . . . my son . . . every . . . night . . ."

". . . let my mother . . . pick out my . . . wedding dress . . ."

And on. And on. Their voices so soft I could hardly hear them over the beating of my own heart. But I listened. And nodded. And smiled when they ceased to be. And prayed that the light I could no longer see had finally come for them.

"Howie?"

The alcove looked empty. Emptier than I'd ever seen it.

"Oh, Jesus—Howie? Howie, where are you?"

There! A faint ripple in the air just to my left . . . like a heat mirage . . . no, like the swirling clouds of dust I used to dance with as a child.

"Howie, is that you?"

The faintest hint of a pale gray suit and bright blue eyes hovered in the air before me. He was smiling.

"You look like the Cheshire cat," I told him, "but I can still see you. Quick, Howie, tell me the one thing in your life that made you special."

His lips moved silently. God, no . . . not yet. Please, not yet.

"Say it again, Howie," I said, raising my own voice as if it were some sympathetic volume control. "Slower."

". . . — . . . said . . . my—Leslie . . . that . . . *this*—the . . . —proud of . . ."

"What . . . this?"

Very slowly, the ghost of Howard Roth lifted his hand and touched my cheek. The chill lingered for only a second but it was enough.

". . . this . . ." he whispered, and disappeared.

I don't know how long I sat there, listening to the hushed mutterings and shoe-clacks and fluttering of pages, but it seemed like a long time. Not as long as Howie and the others had waited, but long enough to accept the fact that I was going to live.

For a while yet, anyway.

And maybe . . . just maybe when my time did come, if I was caught unaware, someone would come to listen to me.

I left the library in slow, even steps . . . pausing only long enough in a beam of golden light to twirl the dust motes—and whoever might be standing there unnoticed—into a dance.

Of life.

Pat Mora

La Muerte

Pat Mora is an award-winning Chicana poet, novelist, and children's book writer who currently divides her time between Santa Fe and Cincinnati. Her books include House of Houses, Agua Santa: Holy Water, Chants, *and* Nepanthla: Essays from the Land in the Middle. *The following poem marks Mora's second appearance in* The Year's Best Fantasy and Horror, *and it's a privilege to welcome her back.*

"La Muerte" comes from Mora's beautiful (and beautifully illustrated) new collection, Aunt Carmen's Book of Practical Saints. *These interconnected poems are based on Catholic faith and legendry as seen through the eyes of eighty-year-old "Aunt Carmen"—in particular, the stories of the* santos *(carved wooden saints) of northern New Mexico. La Muerte (death), says Mora, "also known as Doña Sebastiana, is depicted as a skeletal woman, not a saint but a stark reminder of the horror of 'bad' death."*

—T. W.

You don't belong, fea Doña Sebastiana.

Some pull you in a rock-filled cart,
a penance they impose
when the priest's not looking.
They fear his frowns.
He fears mine and well he should.

I've cleaned this church
for over forty years, swept,
mopped, dusted, sewed for my saints,
kept them company, my chatter

like butterflies around
the flowers and candles I refresh.
"Shhhh. It's not your house,"
my husband whispers, as if I don't know
it's the holy home of mi Diosito,
home of Divine Order.
¡Ay! What must He think,
this modern religion with no backbone,
no Latin, no chanting, no confession,
no fiery scolding, just priests frowning
and electric candles. A church that fears
fire—and women. The same world inside
and out. No transformation. No mystery.

Instead of organ music and a hidden
choir, voices drifting down,
soft as white feathers,
some churches are a circus, tambourines
and snare drums. Next they'll want
clowns to make the children laugh.
If they want entertainment,
tell them to stay home
or at the malls, their other homes.
Over my dead body, tambourines
and snare drums. They tried,
remember? I grabbed this broom
and swept them out the door,
smacked their ankles hard as I could.

The priest is scared
of me, and that's how I want it.
I've earned my space.
I know about scaring men.
Haven't I been married for sixty years?
Marriage works best
when men think we're volcanoes,
¿verdad, Comadre? Los hombres
walk more carefully around us then.

Over my dead body.

You don't scare me, Doña Sebastiana.
I see people walk around you,
their mouth open like yours.
May your unblinking eyes remind them
of the horror: an unholy death.
Let me bless myself to scare away
the thought. Not like my parents' death.
Their glowing souls slipped right into
the waiting hands of Jesus, Mary, and Joseph,

their two souls, fighters, yes, but moral.
When I use the word, my children
and grandchildren frown.
Truth makes them squirm
which shows their goodness.

Ash Wednesday. "Thou art dust
and unto dust though shalt return,"
the priest said today. He frowns
when I drag you from this closet at Lent.
You don't belong,
but I save what can be useful.
You're not official, yet you're persistent,
¿verdad, Comadre? You and I
can be informal. Dos viejitas.
You don't scare me.
I'll look you eye to eye.

Shoot, Doña Sebastiana. Go ahead.
Slipping out of this crumpled body
will probably feel good, like slipping off
my winter coat in spring. I'll feel
lighter, more my true self,
ready to visit with mis santos,
have a real conversation, revel
in their words, shining, like candles.

Christopher Fowler

Spanky's Back in Town

Christopher Fowler lives and works in central London, where he runs The Creative Partnership, producing TV and radio scripts, documentaries, trailers, and promotional shorts. He has published seven novels including Roofworld, Rune, Red Bride, Darkest Day, Spanky, Psychoville, *and* Disturbia. *He is also the author of six story collections, the two most recent being* Flesh Wounds *and* Personal Demons, *and of the graphic novel from DC Comics* Menz Insanza. *His story "The Master Builder" was filmed by CBS-TV as* Through the Eyes of a Killer *(1992) starring Tippi Hedren. "Left Hand Drive," based on his first short story, won Best British Short Film in 1993.*

"Spanky's Back in Town" brings back Fowler's memorably mischievous character from the eponymous novel. The story is reprinted from Dark Terrors 3: The Gollancz Book of Horror *edited by Stephen Jones and David Sutton.*

—E. D.

1. The History of Rasputin's Casket

Can't we go any faster?' Dmitry turned around in the seat, punching at the driver's fur-clad back. Behind him one of the wolves had almost caught up with the rear-runners of the sleigh and was snapping at the end of his flapping scarf.

'This is new snow over old,' the driver shouted. 'The tracks have hardened and will turn us over.'

The horses were terrified, their heads twisting, their eyes rolling back in fear of the baying creatures behind the sleigh. Scarcely daring to look, Dmitry counted seven—now eight—of the wolves, swarming so close that he could feel their hot breath on the icy rushing air. He glanced down at the terrified child in his arms and pulled the bearskin more tightly around her deathly pale face.

'We'll never make it in time,' cried Yusupov, 'it will be dark before we reach Pokrovskoye.'

They could see the black outline of the town on the horizon, but already the sun was dropping below the tops of the trees. The sleigh clattered and crunched its way across deep-frozen cart tracks, swaying perilously, the wolves howling close behind, falling over each other in their efforts to keep up. One of the largest, a fearsome yellow-eyed beast the size of a Great Dane, suddenly threw itself forward and seized Dmitry's scarf-end in its jaws. The wool pulled tight, choking him as he clawed at his throat. Yusupov yanked it away from his brother's neck and pulled hard, feeling the weight of the animal on the other end. 'See, Dmitry,' he cried, 'look in the eyes of our pursuer now!'

He released the scarf sharply and the creature fell back, tumbling over itself. But it had his scent, and would follow the sleigh into the darkness until its jaws were filled. Dmitry cradled the infant in his arms, protecting her from buffets as the sleigh hammered over a ridge of ice. They had taken her hostage to effect their escape from the private apartments of Rasputin himself, but now they no longer had need of her. After all, the casket was now in their possession, and its value was beyond calculation. He knew that Yusupov was thinking the same thing. Behind them, the wolves were becoming braver, jumping at the rear of the sledge, trying to gain a hold with their forepaws. Thick ribbons of spittle fell along the crimson velvet plush of the seat-back as the animals yelped and barked in frustrated relay.

'They will not stop until they feed,' he shouted. 'We must use the child. She slows us down.'

'But she is innocent!'

'If we fail in our mission, many thousands of innocents will perish.'

'Then do it and be damned!'

Dmitry slipped the wild-eyed girl from the bear-fur. In one scooping motion he raised her above his head, then threw her over the end of the sleigh. She had only just begun to scream as the wolves imploded over her, seizing her limbs in their muscular jaws. The two young Bolsheviks watched for a moment as the animals swarmed around their meal, the sleigh briefly forgotten. The child's cries were quickly lost beneath the angry snarling of the feed. A sudden splash of blood darkened the evening snow. The driver huddled tighter over his reins, determined not to bear witness to such events. The next time he dared to look back, all he could see was a distant dark stain against the endless whiteness, and the sated wolves slinking away with their heads bowed between their shoulders, ashamed of their own appetites.

Yusupov studied the horizon once more, trying to discern the lights of the approaching town. He was twenty-three, and had already felt the hand of death close over him. He prayed that Casparov would be waiting at the bridge, that he had found a way of evading their pursuer. It was essential for them to find a hiding place for the casket in Pokrovskoye.

'Perhaps we are safe now,' said Dmitry as the sleigh turned towards the smoking chimneys of the town. 'May we have the strength to do what must be done.'

· · ·

'Our story begins in the reign of Tsar Nicholas II, in the year 1908,' said Dr Harold Masters, studying his uninterested students as they lolled in their seats. 'Starving Bolsheviks fled across Russia with a precious cargo; a jewelled casket fashioned by Karl Fabergé and stolen from Rasputin himself, its contents un-known—and yet the men in the sleigh were willing to die to preserve it. Their flight from Rasputin's secret shrine at St Petersburg was doomed, but before they were brutally murdered in mysterious circumstances, we know that the casket was passed on, to make its way in time to New York.

'In the late 1920s a family of wealthy Franco-Russian emigrants who had escaped to America on the eve of the October revolution sailed on the SS *Britannique* to Liverpool. The ship's passenger inventory tells us that the jewel-box was in their possession then, listed as inherited family property. But following the tragedy on board their ship . . .'

The sun had set an hour ago, but the sea was still blacker than the sky. Alexandrovich Novikov stood watching the churning wake of the ship, his gloved left hand clasping the wooden railing. Powerful turbines throbbed far beneath his feet, and he rode the waves, balancing as the liner crested the rolling swell of the sea. Back in the state room his wife, his brother and his children chattered excitedly about their new life in England, trying to imagine what, for them, was quite unimaginable. They would have new names, he had decided, European names that others would be able to pronounce without difficulty. They were being given a second chance, and this time the family would prosper and grow. There remained but one task for him to accomplish; the removal of the final obstacle to their safety. He reached inside his coat and withdrew the Fabergé casket. The value of the jewelled casing meant nothing to him, for its loss was but a small price to pay for the safekeeping of his family.

He weighed it in his hand, worried that the rising wind might catch and smash it against the side of the ship. He had drawn back his arm, ready to hurl it into the tumbling foam below, when someone snatched at his coattail, spinning him around and causing him to lose balance on the tilting wet deck. Before he could draw breath, the stars filled his vision and he saw the railing pass beneath his legs, then the great black steel side of the ship, as the sound of the monstrous churning propellors pounded up around him.

Sinking into the ocean, Alexandrovich Novikov was dragged under by the great spinning blades and cleft in two, the pieces of his body lost for ever in the frothing white foam. On the deck he had left, the unthrown casket slid beneath a stairwell with the rolling of the ship and was retrieved by a passing steward, whereupon the alarm was raised and a frantic search begun for its missing owner.

'And so we arrive in London,' continued Dr Masters. 'The bereaved Franco-Russian family who moved there from Liverpool in 1928 planned to build property in the city—but their assets were badly damaged in the financial crash of the following year. The headquarters of their empire, a magnificent building on the north bank of the Thames designed by the great Lubetkin, went unfinished. Here, the trail of Rasputin's jewelled box finally goes cold. We have to presume that it was sold off to the owner of a private collection as the family fought debts and a series of appalling personal tragedies . . .'

The building beside the old Billingsgate Market had never been properly finished, and now its poorly-set foundations had been pulled up to clear the site and make way for a new Japanese banking syndicate. It was during the third month of digging, just prior to the new concrete foundations being poured into their moulds, that the little casket, wrapped in an oilskin cloth and several layers of mildewed woven straw, was unearthed. The find was briefly mentioned on the six o'clock news that night, and excited speculation from experts about what might be discovered inside.

Before the box could be opened, however, it was sent to the British Museum to be cleaned and X-rayed. From the ornamentation of an exposed corner section of the casing it was already assumed to have been manufactured by a Russian jeweller, possibly the great Fabergé himself, which made it extremely valuable and placed it in the ownership of the royal court of Tsar Nicholas. It was, perhaps, too early to hope that the box might contain documents pertaining to that fascinating, tragic family.

The casket was entrusted to an unlikely recipient, a twenty-seven-year-old woman named Amy Dale who worked at the museum. In usual circumstances such a high-profile find would have been offered for examination to one of the more experienced senior staff, but Amy was having an affair with a hypertense married man named Miles Bernardier who functioned as the present director of the excavation, and Miles was able to take a procedural shortcut that allowed him to assign the find himself. This was not as dishonest as it sounds, for Amy was fast becoming recognized as a luminary in her field, and as her own department head was overseas for two months advising an excavation in Saudi Arabia, the pleasurable task of uncovering the casket's secrets fell to her.

The night before Amy was due to have the casket X-rayed, a supposedly psychic friend from the Mediterranean ceramics department seized her hands in the Museum Tavern and warned her that something strange was about to happen in her life. She pushed a hand through her frizzy blonde hair, laughing off his prediction, and ordered up another round of drinks. While they drank and chatted, the mud-encrusted casket, sealed in a large Ziploc bag, sat in a basement vault of the British Museum waiting for its secrets to be exposed to the light.

2. The Appearance of the Daemon

The sun was scorching down in a sapphire sky the morning Spanky came back to town. The wind had changed direction, from the faintest breeze drifting down across the south to a fierce fresh blast that stippled the surface of the Thames and brushed against pedestrians in the Strand, ruffling them like hair being combed the wrong way.

Balancing delicately as he placed one patent black Church's Oxford-toecapped shoe after the other, Spanky walked along the electrified third rail of the London, Chatham & Dover Railway, crossed the bridge over the river into Cannon Street station and carefully sniffed the air. Beneath the fumes of the choked city, behind the oil of machinery and ozone crackle of electricity, beyond the perfumes and deodorants and the smell of warm working flesh, he caught the faintest tang of enamel and oilskin, wolf urine and sea-brine and city soil. It was quite enough to tell him that the object of his search was within a five-mile radius.

On the station platform he almost melted into the crowd, just another devilishly handsome young man arriving in the teeming city with an unrevealed agenda. Spanky's purpose, though, was single and specific; to locate the casket currently residing in the vault at Amy Dale's department.

A smile teased those who caught his eye; he permitted himself that. He could afford to be happy, for the battle was already half-won. He had seen the girl on television, speaking nervously into a microphone, pointing back at a great hole in the ground. The network had even taken the trouble to label her for him, displaying her name and place of employment. It only remained for him to meet with the girl and explain, in calm and rational tones, that he needed her to give back what was rightfully his.

Nah, he thought, I'll just take the casket and rip her guts into bloody shreds—to teach her a lesson.

Spanky was weary of walking the earth. He loathed gravity. If only he could shed his cloak of skin, free himself of his fleshy shackles and return to the skies. It was not possible yet; he could only operate in corporeal form. And he had been here too long, so long he had almost forgotten his true purpose, shifting from one body to the next, growing careless, even being cheated and forced to flee by an idiot mortal—the shame of it! How the mighty had fallen! He had hidden in two further bodies since that humiliating day. A balding, overweight ambulance attendant had provided him with a temporary home until he found someone more appropriate. This new body had belonged to one Chad Morrison, a none-too-bright twenty-seven-year-old male model with wavy black hair, shocking blue eyes and a jawline as sleek as the contours of a classic coupé. It would certainly last him until he had reclaimed the contents of the casket. After that, he would have no further reason to return to earth and live among these miserable mortals, not when Paradise beckoned . . .

Out in the street, he listened to the sounds that lay hidden beneath the belching traffic and chattering offices. Spanky's senses were attenuated far beyond mortal range. He had heard the girl speak on television. In the maelstrom of humanity he could find her voice again, as easily as plucking a single yellow flower in a forest of bluebells. Satisfied that his instincts were correct, he set off along the pavement at a brisk clip, a jaunty swagger in his step and a cheery whistle on his lips. This time he would cover his tracks as he went. A trip to the excavation was called for. Then on to the girl and the treasure.

From the Thames, the gap between the buildings was like a missing tooth. Square off-white office blocks rose on either side. Thundering drills and a pair of slender yellow cranes picked at the site like dentists' utensils.

Miles Bernardier stood at the edge of the great earth-encrusted hole and peered down on the vast rusted mesh of iron rods that were about to be buried in concrete. Time had run out. He had requested a larger excavation window, and the request had been denied. Six lousy days, was that too much to ask? The wheels of commerce would not be halted, however. The DTI was worried that a historically significant find would be announced. Building would have to be stopped while the site was evaluated, and the Japanese might get cold feet. But who knew what else lay buried in the clay? The site had been repeatedly built upon for well over a thousand years. The casket had been discovered in a pocket of air created by some broken planks just eleven feet down. Beneath the rotted wood lay a brick lining from what appeared to be a far older building, but now, with the pouring of several thousand tons of concrete, it would remain undiscovered for yet another century.

Ahead of him, a piledriver was rising slowly in the air to drop its weight on one of the upright iron posts marking out the building perimeter. Bernardier adjusted his yellow hard hat against the buffeting wind from the river, and carefully skirted the edge of the pit. He wanted to call Amy, to see if she had started work on the casket, but the noise was too great here. He was walking back to one of the foremen's cabins when something pushed at the backs of his legs, and he slipped over on to the wet clay soil.

'Damn!' He rose awkwardly, inspected the damage, then looked about for someone to blame. There was no one within five hundred yards, and no sound but the rising wind and the dull thud of the piledriver. Bernardier was due to have lunch in the city today, and the knees of his suit were smeared with gobbets of mud. He wondered if there was time to go home and change. For a moment nothing moved on the construction site, save for a few scraps of birds fighting the thermals above the river. Earlier the area had been filled with workmen. Where was everyone now?

The second blow caught him hard in the small of the back, and sent him sprawling on to his face. Frightened now, he pulled himself free of the sucking mire and searched about wildly. Impossibly, the area was deserted. Clouds had momentarily darkened the sun and the site had taken on an eerie dimness, as if history had returned to an earlier time. He tried to rise from his knees, but his shoes would not grip on the slippery clay. An odd smell hung in the air, something ancient and musky. Something bad.

The third blow was to his face, and shattered both the lenses of his glasses. This time he slid straight over the edge of the hole, landing on his back at the bottom, in time to see the downward arc of the piledriver descending over him. It was too late to stop the fall of the massive steel rod, which was powered by an explosion of compressed air. The shaft slammed down, bursting his skull like a rock dropped on an Easter egg. By the time the accident siren sounded, Bernardier's twitching body had settled so deeply into the sludge that it could have been mistaken for another historical find.

'Very innocent,' Gillian was saying, 'but then you always were.' Amy held the receiver away from her ear and waved a hand at her assistant. 'The heat's too high, turn it down, it'll boil over,' and into the receiver, 'Yes, mother, I know.'

'And now this man you're seeing, do you really think it's such a good idea? I mean, he's not only married, he's your boss. Is he worth jeopardizing your career for?'

'I think I have to be the best judge of that, mother.' In truth Miles's continual philandering had almost persuaded her to end the affair, but she refused to launch on to this conversational track as it would mean hearing a new triumphant tone in her mother's voice.

'But I didn't call for this, to criticize. Who am I, just a woman who spent eight agonizing hours in labour with you. I called to say how wonderful you looked on the television. I was so proud.'

Someone had entered the room and was standing before her. Someone from outside—he didn't smell of chemicals. There was something nice in the air, old-fashioned and comforting, from her childhood. Lavender-water?

'Mother, I have to go now.' She lowered the twittering receiver back to its cradle and raised her eyes to the visitor.

'Can I help you?'

Her pulse stuttered. The man was a living angel. His pupils peered from beneath dark-knitted eyebrows like twin cobalt lasers. He had a jawline you could design a car around. Navy jacket, grey T-shirt, faded blue jeans cut tight around the crotch, brown work-boots. Behind him, two secretaries were peering around the door in unembarrassed awe.

'Yes, you can,' said the vision. 'I'm looking for Amy Dale.'

'That's me,' she laughed, feeling as if she had won a prize. Her assistants melted away, afraid of interrupting something private.

It was here. He could smell it in the air, its history of viscera and madness. He could taste it on the tip of his tongue, the cupreous tang of blood and death and misery. So close, after all this time.

'Excuse me, I was expecting someone far less attractive.' He smiled and the heavens opened.

'Now why would you expect that?' she asked, flattered.

'The way Miles Bernardier described you—' he trailed off. 'Not like this.'

The bastard, she thought. How typical of him to denigrate her to a stranger, as though he had to frighten off potential rivals.

'Chad Morrison.' He proffered his manicured hand and she shook it.

'So, Mr Morrison,' she smiled back, puzzled by his relaxed attitude—a rare thing in a world of obsessive academics, 'what are you here for?'

'The casket,' he genially replied.

'Oh?' Her brow furrowed. Territories were jealously guarded at the museum. 'What field are you in?'

'Forgive me,' he gave his head a little shake, 'I thought Mr Bernardier had already spoken to you about this.'

'No, he's out at the excavation today.' She unbuttoned her lab coat and pointed to a glass partitioned office. 'We can talk in there.'

Seated before her, he explained, 'I'm not attached to the museum, Miss Dale. I'm mainly an advisor to auction houses in my capacity as an authority on the works of Karl Fabergé. Your director called me in to help you verify the origin of your find.'

Miles had entrusted her with the investigation. Why did he have to interfere by sending her experts? Of course, she would have had to pull in her own independent specialists, which could be a time-consuming process, so perhaps he was trying to make her job easier. The museum staff comprised many brilliant, dedicated professionals, but she was not aware of anyone with expertise in this field. Better to accept the offer. He was awfully pretty.

'Thank you, Mr Morrison. I'd be interested in your impressions of what you've heard so far, sight unseen.'

'Well.' He leaned forward a little and the scent he exuded changed. His aftershave was something spicy and musky, not at all what she expected. He looked the citrus type. 'I can forgive the Russian revolution many things, Miss Dale, but not the destruction of Fabergé. He died in exile, you know, a broken man, his art reviled by men unable to tolerate luxury of any kind. But this find is fascinating. Its placement is correct. Fabergé knew England, and was partly educated here. Such a creation would date from the time he switched from producing jewellery and cigarette boxes to more fantastical items, say the early 1880s, before he began to produce the celebrated eggs.

'A number of objects we know he personally produced have never been traced. There are catalogue numbers and full descriptions of the missing items, and one of them fits the casket's specifications. Fabergé's sons assisted him, and there was a workshop here in London, facts which would provide circumstantial evidence for the find. Of course, there were also many forgeries produced. I would have to see the piece to be more exact.'

'I'll have to verify your appointment with Mr Bernardier. Just a formality.' She smiled and raised the telephone receiver.

He loved this part. Taking a chance. Out at the edge. He could not afford to let her find out about Bernardier, not at this stage of the game. He had no supernatural powers here, only natural ones in this earthbound body, but those would be enough. Enough to fog her senses and divert the call in her brain, to make her hear another voice.

Watching him, she mechanically punched out random digits and listened. Her mouth opened, but she did not speak. He concentrated harder. Searching her for details he found the usual human pain—aching loneliness and lack of fulfilment, but also—what was this?—Miles, not just a work colleague but a lover. Miles was sleeping with her. He probed deeper into her mind. She was not happy with the arrangement, not happy at all. He was married. Not much of a lover, either. She hadn't lost very much, then. He released her. She swayed back a little, looked flustered, lowered the receiver, aware of a vague conversation in her head, unaware of the dead line. She smiled to cover her confusion.

'That all seems to be in order, Mr Morrison. When would you like to examine the casket?'

'How about right now?' he suggested.

3. The Unveiling of the Secret

'I'm sure you understand the need for strict security in this matter,' she said, allowing a total stranger to follow her into the maze of basement corridors.

'But of course,' he agreed, sniffing the air and scenting the proximity of the treasure, barely able to contain his excitement, 'we wouldn't want just anyone walking in here.'

Amy led the way to a further green-walled passage separated from the main building by two sets of steel doors and an electronic swipe-code. 'We have to bring items from this section up personally,' she explained. 'They can't be trusted to assistants, and they're not allowed to leave our sight until they're returned.'

Beyond the doors, a series of white-walled rooms housed large square drawers with brass handles, like a morgue. Amy checked the reference number on her requisition sheet and searched the containers.

'It's over here,' he said, lifting the index number from her mind and matching it to a nearby drawer.

Amy looked at him oddly. 'How do you know?' she asked, moving past him to check. It was the right drawer. She took a key from her pocket and slipped it into the lock. The moisture-pocked bag inside gave no clue to its contents. 'You're never sure what's best with a find like this,' she said, carefully removing the bag. 'This plastic is supposed to "breathe" and sustain a natural moisture equilibrium. We could have placed it in a dry environment, but if the casket contains paper materials they could be ruined.'

He was barely listening to her. The presence of the casket had enveloped and overwhelmed his senses. It was less than three feet from him, but he could not take it from her here. There were other technicians in the secure area. He could hear their bodyweight shifting past him in the nearby rooms. Back in the corridor he had an insane thought, that he could snatch the thing from her and escape from the building with it beneath his arm. He would have to wait until he was beyond the secure area. Another problem; in this body, he could not run. Morrison had sustained a football injury that had left him with damaged tendons in his left leg. Besides, mere escape lacked dignity. He wanted them to see what they had found. Better to wait until he was alone with Amy in the lab, after the other assistants had gone for the night. It would be foolish to screw up now, for the sake of a few hours.

'It'll be some time before we reach the interior of the package,' said Amy. 'It might be rather boring for you, but you can stay and help me if you want.'

'Just tell me what to do,' smiled Spanky, removing his jacket.

By six o'clock they had succeeded in removing the outer straw wrappers and had sectioned them for dating. The oilskin, too, had been photographed at every stage, and the whole process documented. It was laborious, but necessary if mistakes were to be prevented. Amy's chaotic blonde hair had fallen into her eyes so often that she had bunched it back with a rubber band. She was hunched so far over the brilliantly illuminated desktop that she had developed a crick in her neck. A hot wire of pain scratched across the top of her shoulderblades as she sat up.

'Here, let me give you a massage. Tip your chair back.' Spanky lowered broad hands to her neck and pressed his thumbs down in a smooth circular motion.

'You read my mind. Thanks, that feels good.' She sat further back and closed her eyes. Another assistant scuttled from the room. 'At least we've only one layer to go, some kind of tissue.'

'Cloth-papers from Rasputin's apartment,' he said absently. 'He kept the casket out of the light and bound in calico.'

'You must be a really big authority on this,' she murmured, succumbing to the motion of his hands.

'Oh, you have no idea how big.'

'Pieces of hidden history . . .'

'Crossing-points of the past. Everything holds something different within. The truth becomes fabulous, and fables hold truth.' His voice had dropped to a sea-murmur. Fingers slipping over her throat.

'You soon start to see the attraction . . .'

'Attraction?' His hands smoothed and smoothed. The nape of her neck tingled, a warm glow spreading to the top of her breasts. She forced herself to concentrate.

'Of—archaeology.'

'Ah, of course.'

They were alone in the laboratory. The last assistant had quietly closed the door behind her.

'Right.' He swiftly removed his hands and shifted her chair-back to an upright position once more. 'Let's do it.'

She looked wide-eyed at him. 'Here?'

He gestured at the table-top. 'The last layer. Come on.'

Even with tweezers and generous smears of lubricant, the greased wrapping proved difficult to remove, and flapped back on to the casket lid. Amy peered through the illuminated magnifier. 'I think I've got it this time.' She gripped the tweezers more tightly.

Twined ribbons of inlaid gold surrounded an intricate frieze of dancing mythological figures. You could see no detail from studying the russet splodges on the lid, but Spanky knew that the ancient gods lay beneath a layer of grime, longing for the chance to shine again. There had been many containers across the centuries for the treasure held inside, but this was the best casket so far. Ten inches by six, and six deep, it sat on the Formica-topped desk awaiting inspection, a spectacular relic from a forgotten world. They had removed soil from a tiny gold-rimmed keyhole with a Water Pik. The rest of the wrapping was easier to remove. As it slid away, Amy cautiously wiped a finger across the lid, and the precious figures revealed themselves.

'It's beautiful,' she whispered.

'And we can open it.' Spanky opened the top button of his shirt and removed a slender gold key from around his neck. He could feel his fingers trembling in anticipation. She stared at him, then at the filigreed key. What did he mean?

'I can unlock the casket, Amy.' He could not resist sounding boastful.

'Where did you get that?' She reached up to touch the key, then withdrew her hand, as if wary of being scalded.

'It's been in my possession for many, many years.'

The casket was behind her. She positioned herself before it protectively. 'I don't understand.'

'You don't have to.'

'I can't let you open it.'

'Why not?'

'This is of historical importance. A senior member of staff must be present.'

'Then let's send for Mr Bernardier.' If you don't mind summoning a mud-caked headless corpse, he thought, smiling grimly. The director had never known what hit him. A pity, that. Spanky enjoyed taking credit for his work.

'You know exactly what's inside the box, don't you?'

'Of course I do,' he answered. She was a smart girl. There was no more need for subterfuge now that he was so close to his goal. 'I've always known.'

'Perhaps you'd like to tell me.' She could feel her unease growing by the second. The museum was closed for the night. Only a few of the research departments scattered in the building's cul-de-sac corridors would still be inhabited by lingering personnel.

'All right. Have a seat.' Outside, the warm weather had finally broken and it was starting to rain. 'Listen carefully, and don't question anything I have to say.'

Sensing the danger she was in, Amy dropped to the chair.

'I am not like you. Not—human. I am *Spancialosophus Lacrimosa*. If you find it easier, you can call me Spanky. God had seven fallen angels. Seven daemons. Seven rogue creatures of inspiration and vengeance, banned from Heaven for refusing to worship Man. Damned to a watery limbo existence between Earth and Paradise. Only allowed to visit Earth in the encumbrance of a mortal shell, to be entered upon the invitation of the owner. But I am not like my fellow daemons. I have little of their boundless patience. I am not content to wait for ever, until God, in his infinite wisdom and mercy, sees fit to readmit us to his Kingdom. And now there is a chance to do more than just return to grace. There is a chance to rule for all eternity. It's all to do with the box.'

Amy snapped around to check that the casket was still there beside her in its nest of wet straw. What if this lunatic tried to snatch it? How would she ever stop him?

'You want to see inside? Take a look.' He unlooped the key from his neck and handed it to her, savouring the moment. 'Do it,' he commanded.

The key was so worn and delicate that she was frightened of breaking it in the lock. To her surprise it turned easily. The lubricant and the Water Pik must have loosened the mechanism. And of course, it had been built by Fabergé. With trembling fingers, she raised the lid. The interior was completely dry. Beneath several layers of fine grey silk were—

'Iron rings. Seven of them. One for each of us. The rings of Cain. Forged by Adam's first son. How is your knowledge of the Bible?' He grinned at her, inching closer to the opened casket, holding out his hand for the return of the golden key.

'Let me refresh your memory. Cain was a tiller of the ground, driven from the Earth by God for slaying his brother Abel. Doomed to become a fugitive and a vagabond. Cain tried to atone for his sin by appealing to us, God's other fallen children. He brought us gifts, the rings he forged from the ore beneath his feet. But just as we despised Adam, so we despised his offspring. We refused his offer, and Cain threw the rings back into the earth.

'It took many centuries for us to truly understand the power of the rings. You see, if we had accepted them, we would have been restored to Paradise. That was Cain's gift to us, and we turned it down. It was only by accident that I discovered the truth. But by then, the rings were lost. I've tracked them through time and across the world. Now I've been here too damned long. I can't get back to my home without them. The others won't let me in empty-handed.'

Obviously the man was crazy. Amy knew that the safest solution to her dilemma was to play along until she could find a way to summon help. 'Is that what you want, to be restored to Paradise?' she asked.

'Of course. Wouldn't you?' Spanky drew a step nearer.

'Only this time, we'll have the element of surprise on our side.'

'What do you mean?'

'Well, we wish to rule, obviously. God has had everything his way for *far* too long. You have no idea how boring he has made the celestial heavens. We'll change all that. You wait, you'll feel the effects all the way down here. It'll be like having the worst neighbours in the universe living right overhead.'

'You're mad.' She hadn't meant to say it. The words had just slipped out. He laughed at her.

'If you think what I want is so very illogical, good luck with the rest of the world. A little respect is all anyone wants.'

Amy made a grab for the casket, and was surprised when he made no attempt to stop her. Instead, he watched as she took it from the desk and clutched it protectively across her breasts, smearing mud and pieces of straw on her lab jacket.

'We'd better get going,' he said, checking his watch. 'The others are expecting us.'

'What do you mean?' She looked frantically about for someone to help her. Why was it that the one time she would welcome an interruption, none came?

'Cain protected the rings. They can only be returned to us by a mortal. Lucky you.' He grinned mischievously as he grabbed her hand and pulled her towards the door. 'You get to see where we live. You'll be the first human being ever to meet my brothers and sisters. I'm sure *Spancialosophus Dolorosa* will take a shine to you.'

4. The Denial of Icarus

She pulled back from him. 'Wait, I have to set the alarm system. I'm the last one out.'

'You're lying to me, Amy.' He bared his teeth and yanked her arm hard. 'Don't try to trick me. I can see inside your head.'

They passed from the lab along a corridor, and on to a broad staircase. Miles should have come for her by now, but they passed no one, not even Dr Harold Masters, who was usually making tea in the cubby-hole beside the staircase at this time of the evening.

Spanky's gripping hand felt as though it was burning into her wrist. At the main entrance, the two security guards barely looked up from their desks to wish her goodnight. Couldn't they see that she was in trouble?

The rain sizzled against Spanky's back as he strode across the museum forecourt with her. Amy maintained her grip on the casket, frightened that she would be punished if she tried to fling it away. 'Where are we going?' she gasped, frantically trying to keep up with him.

'To the departure point,' he snapped, barely bothering with her. He crossed Museum Road, half-dragging her upright as she slipped on the wet tarmac. He moved so quickly that she found herself being bodily lifted by him at moments when the traffic seemed about to crash into them. Onwards they moved, through Holborn and down towards the Embankment.

They were standing in the centre of Waterloo Bridge with the great rain-swollen river sweeping beneath them, broadening out on its way to the sea. 'Why here?' she shouted, the roar of wind and traffic filling her ears.

'I need a good run-up,' he replied. 'Got a tight grip on the casket?'

He checked the box pressed against her sodden breast, then produced an old-fashioned cut-throat razor from his coat and passed it to her with his free hand. 'Hold this. I'm letting go of you for a moment. If you try to escape I will kill you, Amy, I think you know that.' Spanky tore off his jacket and shirt, throwing them out into the Thames.

'I want you to take the razor and run it along my spine.' He pointed to his broad rain-spattered back. 'Do it quickly.' He snapped open the blade for her.

Shaking with cold and fear, she suppressed a shudder of horror as she touched the blade to the point he indicated between his shoulderblades.

'You'll have to push harder than that. Pull it straight down. As deep as you can.'

Wincing, she did as she was told, pushing on the blade and dragging it down. The edge sliced smoothly and cleanly as the skin of his back opened in a widening crimson slit. Spanky was drawing breath in low, guttural gasps, part in pain, part in the pleasure of release from his confinement. As the blade reached his trouser-belt he slapped it from her hand. The razor skittered across the pavement and slid into the gutter. Swathes of blood washed across his back, diluting in the downpour.

Spanky bent forward with an agonised shout and the epidermis split further apart across his back. From within the carapace of skin, two enormous black wings unfolded like opening umbrellas. As the joints clicked and cracked, the membranes between them flexed and stretched and grew. At first she thought they were made of black leather, but now she saw that they were composed of thousands of tiny interlocking black feathers. He seized her hand and climbed on to the balustrade of the bridge, dragging her up on the ledge with him. The fully opened wings spanned a distance of eighteen feet above them.

'Hold on to your hat. Here we go.'

As they launched from the bridge, Amy screamed and howled into the racing clouds above. They swooped down to the scudding grey water, then up and along the path of the river, moving so fast that they outdistanced the falling rain. The pain in her clutched wrist was excruciating. He turned and brought his face close to hers, shouting as the great black wings beat powerfully above them.

'You have the casket.'

'Yes,' she shouted back as they started to climb, 'I have the casket.'

'Then we can make the crossing.' He pumped his membraneous wings faster, ever faster, so that they flexed and shook from humerus to metacarpal, and it seemed that they were moving beyond the speed of earth and weather and light and time.

Something bright shone in her eyes. She forced herself to look up. Ahead in the clouds, a dazzling area of light had cleared the grey rain to send a Mandelbrot set of fractal colours spiralling down towards them, like pieces of rainbow glass from an exploded kaleidoscope.

'You see it?' he bellowed, 'you see it? That's where we're going. Inside there.'

'No!' she screamed, knowing instinctively that the experience would kill her instantly. This was not a sight for mortal eyes. But they were racing forward at such a velocity that nothing could stop them from reaching the area now. Piercing shards of diamond brilliance enveloped them as they left the Earth behind forever.

And just as they reached it—it was gone. Slammed shut, vanished, the colours all disappeared, nothing ahead except endless cold grey sky.

Spanky's face was contorted in fury and terror.

'The rings of Cain!' he yelled at the heavens. 'I am returning with the rings!' Already his wings were parting with the impossible velocity, flesh and feathers tearing off in strips, revealing birdlike bloody bones beneath.

With nothing to propel them, their speed slowed. For a moment, it seemed that they were hanging in the air. 'You have the rings,' he screamed at her.

'No, I told you—I have the casket.' The box was still unlocked. She had emptied the rings out as they flew. He had not noticed. With all his energy and concentration centred elsewhere, he had not seen the seven iron bands scatter in the wind and fall back towards the river, and now the doorway home was closed once more.

A sharp crack resounded above them as the great wings bloodily shattered and folded, and with a sickening lurch they dropped back towards the Earth. Spanky's anguished howling filled her tortured ears every metre of the way.

Down and down.

The glutinous silt of the river formed undulations across the expanding estuary at Dartford. It trapped all manner of debris swept out with the heavy ebb tide. It cradled Amy's unconscious body, rolling her gently against the shore until some kind old souls spotted her, and dragged her out to warmth and safety. Inside Amy's jacket they found an old casket, gripped so tightly that the corners had bruised her flesh.

Spanky's broken form had fallen more heavily and plunged much deeper, to be snagged by the twisted metal on the riverbed. Held firmly in place, Chad Morrison's body undulated against the current. His earthly form was dead, from the fall, from the loss of blood, but the daemon was still alive and imprisoned within. There was nothing Spanky could do but stare out from his blanched shell in endless horror, gripped by his prison of bloating dead flesh, held in turn by the detritus of the river, beneath that great protector of the city.

He was aware of everything, and unable to do anything. He even thought he saw one of the precious rings float by, inches from his eyes. Eventually he allowed his senses to dull and close, lulled to a dreamless sleep by the lunar tides.

Somewhere inside the wide pulsing currents of the sea, the seven rings of Cain tumbled and drifted, lost to man and lost to angels.

'And that is how Karl Fabergé's most magnificent casket, so beautifully restored by Amy Dale, came to be exhibited here at the British Museum,' said Dr Harold Masters, eyeing his bored students as they sprawled and drifted in various states of semi-consciousness about the lecture room like dumped shop mannequins. Honestly, he thought, you try to bring history alive for the young, but you might as well not bloody bother.

Denise Duhamel

Marriage

Denise Duhamel, one of America's most interesting young poets, is the author of Girl Soldier, The Woman with Two Vaginas, *and* Smile! *Her work has been widely published in the* Chicago Review, The White Wall Review, El- lipses, Poet Lore, *and other journals, as well as in the books* Mondo Barbie *and* Between the Cracks: the Daedalus Anthology of Kinky Verse.

"Marriage" appeared in The National Poetry Magazine of the Lower East Side, *and in* Kinky, *Duhamel's most recent publication, which is a fabulous collection of poems about . . . well, about Barbie dolls. In gems such as "Barbie in Therapy," "Apocalyptic Barbie," and "Why Barbie and Ken Don't Dress in Underwear," Duhamel neatly skewers any number of gender issues with the sharp point of her pen. Most women who grew up in the last thirty years will relate to Duhamel's hilarious fantasies about Barbie, Midge, Skipper, and Ken. And probably a lot of men will, too.*

—T. W.

Barbie wonders if it's cheating
when she dreams of fashion doll boyfriends
Mattel never made for her to play with.
One with rastafarian dreadlocks—
spun with fuzz, not stiff
like the arcs of a plastic Jello mold.
Another chubby and balding
with John Lennon glasses.
And a third with a big sexy nose
like Gerard Depardieu.
Still, she supposes, Ken is harmless enough.

His pecs kept at bay by her stiff unyielding breasts.
And there's nothing he can force on her
when she's not in the mood.
She remembers discontinued Midge's last words:
"Hey, Barbie, it's a marriage, don't knock it."
From the stack of boys' toys across the aisle,
GI Joe occasionally gives Barbie the eye,
though he's not exactly what she has in mind.
In her box, elastic bands hold back her arms
and the plastic overlay she peers through
distorts her view of the world.
It's not only a romantic fling she desires:
there are hot air balloon rides,
night school classes, charity work.
Barbie comforts herself
knowing she's not much different
from the rest of us, juggling gratitude,
ambition, passivity, and guilt.

Nicholas Royle

Kingyo no fun

Although "Kingyo no fun" is as contemporary as "Mbo," the scene is exotic in a completely different way: It takes place in the art and gay club scene of Amsterdam. The reader will either take the narrator at his word and empathize with him utterly—or not. The story will chill, whichever way it is read. It was first published in Love in Vein 2.

—E. D.

Everybody knows one. You've either met one or you know one by reputation. Not everybody suffers, however, to the extent that James has suffered. And while that's partly circumstance, it's also partly James's own fault, through his innocence—which has a lot to do with why I love him. This one's name was Simon but it could have been anything. It could have been William or Terry, or Carolyn or Suzi. They're all the same. They're all *kingyo no fun*. I've known them, you've known them. And James has known them. Only James doesn't know how to shake them off like most people do.

We were in Amsterdam for the weekend. A long weekend. It was late spring sometime in the mid-1990s. I think it was late May. That summer would break all records for mean temperatures and hours of sunshine and already by the end of April it was beginning to get seriously hot. James was doing publicity for his new book and I was hanging around with him. He likes me being around when he's doing this stuff. It's not that we make a big show of it, but I'm always there, if anybody wants to know. If anybody's wondering. About James, you know. There's a light. Okay? And it's a red kind of a light.

He's not a gay writer, he's fond of saying. He's just a writer who happens to be gay. You come on as a gay writer and you get asked to do all the representative stuff. ACT UP and Outrage and fundraising for AIDS charities. James says he's got nothing against doing some of that stuff—and he works hard for a good cause—but he doesn't want to get labeled. And I think that's cool. He doesn't want to cut his sales by half in order to please a minority. So I hang around and meet people but I don't, you know, stick my tongue down his throat and my hand down his pants while he's schmoozing some new agent or flirting with pretty-boy publishers. I do have a sense of restraint. I can be diplomatic. It's not half as much fun but I can do it.

The gig was some weird conjunction of writing and visual art in a small gallery off the Herengracht—*gracht* being the Dutch word for canal. The place was crawling with conceptual artists being studiedly unkempt and unshaven—boys *and* girls, this being the year Della Grace famously "stopped plucking"—and, frankly, a little bit dirty. I longed to take one of them aside and ask why they thought it necessary to go around looking like extras out of some Eastern Bloc movie of the 1970s. In whose eyes could it possibly make them look like better artists?

But I didn't, because I had to think of James.

The artists were all meant to be exhibiting new stuff and the writers reading from recently published work. One video artist showed his new "piece," which consisted of him wearing a gorilla suit and jumping up and down—quite strenuously for a self-proclaimed slacker. Over the course of twelve minutes—the overgenerous running time of this video—the gorilla suit gradually falls apart, leaving the artist naked and generally looking a bit of an asshole. Wouldn't have been half as bad if he'd had a decent body, I said later to James. Another artist showed a glass case full of miniature houses pinned down like dead butterflies. The work was entitled, *Househunting 1995*.

There was worse, believe me, but hey, you know, life's too short.

James was doing his thing. There was a microphone but James never uses them because he's blessed with a mellifluous, sonorous voice—he can project to the end of next week. And if he's reading from a book or script he prefers to keep one hand free. He ranges to and fro in order to include the entire audience, trying to give good value. He's a real pro. There was a photographer guy climbing all over the seats and crates that were stacked up at the side of the gallery, taking shot after shot after shot, and sometimes getting right in close, but James just carried on, totally unfazed. When he cracked jokes people laughed. His timing was good and I noticed he'd give them a look as he delivered a new gag. He knew that even given the language barrier he could make them laugh if (a) they liked him and (b) they realized *when* they were supposed to laugh.

When he'd done I noticed this guy go up to talk to him. Nothing unusual in that. People are always going up to get books signed or just to say hi, so they can say to their friends they met a famous author. This guy looked about thirty-six or thirty-seven, unruly hair and a thrift-store jacket, but perfectly normal compared to some of the freaks James occasionally attracts. I watched James politely listen to the guy and respond with some larger-than-life gesture—not to impress, that's just the way he is—and then, because someone else was waiting to say something, the guy stepped back and kind of melted into the crowd.

"Because that was the extent of it," James was to tell me much later, "I thought he was okay. But when he came up to me again at the end of the evening, when we'd all hung around with whoever we were hanging around with for just about long enough, and were all about ready to go and move on, he came up to me again and I don't know what he said but he started talking and straightaway I knew—I knew this guy was bad news. I don't know how I missed it earlier. I guess because he wasn't talking to me for long enough and didn't have a chance to show what a complete asshole he was. But as soon as he started, when he came up to me again later, as soon as he started I knew I was in big trouble."

"That look?"

"That look."

Kingyo no fun always have the look. Always. But you can't always tell on the look alone because other people can have the same look and be okay. It's a kind of a crazed look in the eyes. Hell, who am I telling this shit! You know this. You've seen the look. You do sometimes get normal people who have the look, or who appear to have it—the lights are on and there *is* somebody at home. With *kingyo no fun*, the lights are burning for sure, every goddamn fucking window, but there ain't *nobody* sitting in that house. And that's the whole problem in, like, a real small pecan shell. Never occurred to me before. You got the whole problem right there.

So when I ambled over to join James because it looked like people might be about to make a move, this guy—Simon—was hanging around like a bad smell. He appeared quite impervious to hints. No amount of subtle body language seemed able to shift him.

"So we going, James, or what?" I said with a trace of impatience.

James was turned the other way. "I think a couple of the guys are joining us for a drink." He turned to face me. Simon was side on to the two of us; he didn't turn away, just watched, this little smile like a worm making its way slowly across the lower half of his face. "You wanna go for a drink?" James said, sort of to both of us. Jeez, that stung. "Coupla English guys. Writers. They seem pretty cool. Tall guy suggested we go get a beer."

"A drink's a good idea," said Simon, the *kingyo no fun*.

"Why don't you go fuck yourself? You're not invited, pal," I wanted to say, but I heard James falling over himself to be nice to the guy.

"Wanna go get a beer, Simon? Whaddya say, huh?"

Jesus, James. Didn't God give you eyes? Don't you ever fucking use them? You wanna fucking use them, man.

"Yeah, that'd be cool," said the *kingyo no fun*.

Cool. Yeah, it'd be *fucking* cool. Mr. Kingyo No Fucking Asshole.

Calm, calm, some shrink was going inside my head. *Yeah, calm, you don't know what it's like, guy.*

So we headed out of the art gallery, James shaking hands with the gallery owner on the way, in pursuit of the two English writers, and with Simon, naturally, bringing up the rear.

"Where would you like to go?" I heard the shorter of the two English guys ask James.

"Wherever," James replied, looking around to include me.

The *kingyo no fun* said: "There's a nice place just up here. Shouldn't be too busy."

The tall English guy, whose name turned out to be Ben, acquiesced quite happily; his shorter companion, Matthew, fell uncomplainingly into line; and James, easygoing as ever, nodded brightly. I looked across the canal at a crowd spilling out of a bar, wondered what was wrong with that place, but Ben and Matthew had already struck off in the direction indicated by Simon, who had fallen in next to James and was animatedly talking *art* with him. Because of some major construction work that ran alongside the canal, I couldn't squeeze alongside them and had to follow on behind. This, you will appreciate, pissed me off.

Kingyo no fun operate differently in different countries when it comes to bar etiquette. The goal is always the same: to avoid paying. Okay, okay, I know some of you will have come across people you *think* are *kingyo no fun* who *do* buy drinks in order to ingratiate themselves with the people they're leeching off of. But hey, get this, they're not real *kingyo no fun* because the *kingyo no fun* conforms to a rigid set of regs.

James and I, although we were both born and raised in New York City, live in London, England, and have done for about ten years. James likes the scene— by which I mean the literary scene, not the gay scene. He likes that too. A little too well. But that's another story. We met in Heaven about three years ago. We had both been in London seven years already, having come from pretty much the same neighborhood in New York originally, and not having met previously in London. "Kinda weird, huh?" James would say to me later.

"What's weird?" I asked him.

"Well, you know. It's kind of a coincidence you turning up like that and, you know, we're both from New York, both in Heaven that night, both been on the scene some time and never met up before."

"Coincidence? There's no such thing," I said.

When we met, James was with a group of leathermen. I'd been following them with my eyes for about ten minutes when one of them approached me and asked if I wanted a drink. Sure, I said. Why not? And rather than let this guy take me off to some dark corner, which was what he appeared to have on his mind, I used him to help me enter the group. It was the tallest guy I had my eye on. The one with long sculpted sideburns and a Nick Cave T-shirt. The one with big eyes. The one called James.

So that was the night we met and from then on we stuck together—James slightly less convincingly than me from time to time, but he always came back, always apologized and I always forgave him.

Living in England you have to get used to pubs. A pub is like a bar without the sense of being in a bar. You can get a beer and all, but it's like getting a beer in a mall—it's kind of like Bar-Lite, you know, or Diet-Bar. I'm talking about the pubs in London. I can't tell you about the quaint little old country pubs because we haven't gone out to the country. We did go to High Wycombe once to score some powder, but I don't think that counts. Jesus, I sure hope it don't count. And one of the things about pubs is that groups go there together, or they meet up there, and they kind of take it in turns to go get the drinks. Only there's no bar tab, so by the end of the evening everybody has bought everybody else a drink. Or that's how it's supposed to work. The *kingyo no fun* in any group sits right back in his or her seat whenever the glasses start to look empty. He is not going to buy anybody else a drink if he can help it. Because he's a fuckin' freeloader, man. That's his entire philosophy. He's gonna sit right back and let everybody else get on with it. Of course, he'll still accept his beer every time some other poor sucker goes up to the bar to get it. And somehow, don't ask me how, he gets away with it.

If you're in a group—jeez, even if that group is only two people and one of them is *kingyo no fun*—and you're walking toward the pub, the *kingyo no fun* starts to hang back, real subtle-like so nobody knows what's going on, but he hangs back and puts an arm around the last person to enter the pub ahead of him, just to make sure. This way he'll be the last person to reach the bar and there's no way he'll have to buy a drink if they're only staying for one or two.

In Amsterdam, Simon, *kingyo no fun*, led us into the crowded bar. *Jesus, what's this guy doing?* I thought. Could I have been mistaken? But once I, and the others, had fought our way through the throng and caught up with Simon, I realized he knew exactly what he was doing. He'd found the only free table in the place. And he'd sat down already. He was guarding our seats. We could hardly expect him to get up and go to the bar now because he was keeping our table for us. That was his job and boy didn't he do it well. So, Ben and Matthew went off to the bar and James and I sat down with Simon. I had this sneaking suspicion that the two English guys would take the opportunity to slip away, unable to take any more of Simon's company, but when I craned my neck I could just make out Ben standing at the bar talking to one of the bartenders— nice looking guy, about twenty, twenty-one, very tall, blond, healthy tan. Yeah, right—look but don't touch.

James had gone and sat right next to Simon. There was no need for that, I thought. We could have both sat right over the other side of the table—it was quite a wide table—in order to make sure we kept all the seats necessary. But James is like that. He doesn't think. Sometimes I have to think for him. Ben and Matthew reappeared, Ben carrying a tray with five opened bottles of Beck's on it. Matthew helped by distributing the beers and then we were all clinking bottles and saying stuff. Simon was grinning all over his face. Yeah, of course he was. He was doing okay.

No one was saying anything so I thought I'd start the ball rolling. "So what about all that art shit?"

"Oh, I know some of those guys," Simon said.

Yeah, he would.

"I think some of their stuff's fascinating, don't you?" He directed his question at James, who raised his bottle to his lips and nodded.

Simon was English and, unlike his two compatriots, talked like he had a ten-pound salmon up his ass. Like someone out of a 1960s movie. Someone who lives in a little mews flat off the King's Road in Chelsea. I looked at him looking at James. His skin was a little too white, like thin dough, and his eyes were punched into it like raisins. The left eye bore a slight imperfection on the iris. A little yellow fleck, like a tendril of broken egg yolk.

"Do you live in Amsterdam?" Ben asked him.

"Yes. I have a rather sweet little place not far from here," he said, looking around for a glass. "On Laurierstraat."

"What do you do?" Matthew this time.

"Oh, you know, I write. Not like you guys." The word "guys" sounded forced in his mouth. "I write about shows and films and art. I suppose I'm a critic."

"Who do you write for?"

"Oh, there's an English-language magazine, *Time Out Amsterdam*. I do some stuff for them. I speak Dutch so I can write for the local press as well. It's really rather a good setup."

Although it was Matthew who'd asked the question, Simon looked at James most of the time while he was answering. And then he went too far. The guy crossed the line. James wore a ring on the second finger of his left hand. It was an impressive ring, a beautiful ring with a serpent design and a polished piece of jet set into it. I'd chosen it and I'd bought it and James wore it always. It occasionally won admiring glances, but people didn't normally go so far as to do what Simon did.

He reached across and touched the ring with his own second finger and his other fingers touched James's. I saw them alight on James's hand, as carefully and gently as Apollo 11 touching down on the moon, while he made pathetic little noises, practically cooing over the ring.

I exploded. I stood up abruptly, jarring the table across the floor and upsetting two bottles of Beck's, and I roared: "Get your fucking hands off of him! Right now!" I sprawled across the table in an attempt to grab at him. I saw my fingers curl like talons, my nails itching to sink into him. His face went completely pale as he staggered back, murmuring something unintelligible. James looked shocked. Ben was hunched over his Beck's snuffling and spluttering, lost somewhere between hysteria and bafflement. And Matthew had thrust an arm across my chest to restrain me. Still I struggled to reach him. People all over the bar had turned to watch. Wide eyes and open mouths were everywhere like a barload of Munch screamers.

I backed off and glowered at Simon for the last time before turning and stalking out of the bar, knocking the elbow of some guy near the door as I left. He sent me out into the night with a volley of abuse—in Dutch, fortunately, so that I didn't have a clue what he was saying. I was churning up inside, had to get out. It was either that or start a fight. With Simon; with the guy near the door; Jesus, even with James. Or with Ben for finding the whole humiliating episode so goddamn funny. Or Matthew for egging Simon on, asking his questions, instead of icing him out right from the start.

I barely slowed down for a couple of blocks, then I became aware how my heart was racing and I stopped. I leaned against a handrail on a bridge over one of the city's eighteen million canals. I felt some of the anger pass out of me and float away on the oily wake of a pleasure boat. Only some of it, though. I was still cursing Simon when I noticed a tall figure loping down the street from the direction of the bar. At first I thought it was Ben, come to snuffle at me, but then I recognized James's slight stoop, the rounded shoulders, the victim look. His long legs covered acres of cobbled street with each stride. He came alongside me and leaned on the parapet, looking out at the lights on the water.

"Don't," I said, expecting a lecture. "Just . . . don't."

I could hear his breathing, slightly faster than normal.

"Let's go back," he said softly. "To the apartment."

Back on Utrechtsedwarsstraat, where we were staying in a cute little apartment loaned by a former girlfriend of James's, we chilled out. ("Girlfriend," I'd said, my eyes popping out on stalks. Jesus, you just never knew. "Oh Christ, just a friend. I couldn't fuck a girl," he said, grabbing my hand. "I love them too much. I've got too much respect for them to do *that*." He pronounced "that" with genuine distaste.) We drank a couple of beers in the backyard, where we sat naked, because it was warm enough. And because we wanted to. There was a party going on two or three houses farther down and the frantic, hectic techno beats started to open me up a little. I apologized to James for the outburst in the bar and James asked me if I wanted to take an E. I didn't know if I did, so I said no, and I knew James wouldn't take one without me. We do everything together.

"Fuck it, why not?" I said after all.

So James broke out the little wooden pillbox I bought for him in Paris and produced a couple of white doves. I checked we had plenty water in the refrigerator and we took one each and sat around in the yard listening to the whooping and screaming taking place a couple of doors down. A Marc Almond single that I liked at the time came on and I started singing along. "I wanna be adored," I fluted. "And explored." I was dancing around the yard. James was watching me, still drinking steadily. Then I came on, with a real big whoosh. I just took off like a goddamn rocket. I'd come on so quickly because I'd had nothing to eat and because, in any case, they were real good doves. James was a little slower to get it, but pretty soon we were lying on the floor of the yard, the sounds of the party washing over us, staring up at the sky. James liked to watch the stars fade in and out. I looked for faces and stuff in the clouds. I ran my hands over his chest. James has a chest covered with thick, dark hair and on E it felt completely different—very, very soft. It seemed as if I could feel every single strand of hair as it passed beneath my hand and each one was indescribably soft. His skin became sort of rubbery. I leaned over him. His pupils were enormous. I told him. "Your pupils are totally immense," I said, and he put his hand around the back of my neck, pulling me down onto him, his tongue sinking into my mouth and his lips closing around mine. His free hand sought out my dick and played with it. It was pretty soft but James is an expert. There's never been anybody better. As we kissed he worked at my dick until it had become curiously big and long but still not very hard. This was pretty typical in our experience of E. I broke off the kiss and looked at his dick. It was like mine, lying flopped over his thigh, so I took it in my right hand and moved his foreskin up and down, over the glans. My jaw was clenching because of the E and I didn't have any spit to spare. I stood up. "Hang on," I said, my head spinning because I got up too fast. I went into the apartment and fetched a bottle of water from the kitchen. Standing over James I tipped the bottle back and chugged almost half a pint. I felt it trickle down my chin and knew James would be watching it run down my white body. "Wow," I said, my head back, staring at the sky. It was so big. The things you think! The things you say! I lay back down next to James, only the other way this time, and held his dick for a moment, feeling the soft downy hairs at its base before slipping it into my mouth and pulling back his foreskin. It felt and tasted beautiful, rolling around inside my mouth, but my jaw kept clenching. James was moaning softly. I knew what he'd be doing: staring at the stars, thinking weird thoughts. He was still stroking my dick as I sucked his and it was real nice but at some point you gotta face up to the facts: we weren't going to get hard enough to do it. Maybe we didn't even wanna fuck. I didn't wanna do it to James. The thought of him doing it to me was kinda nice but I could live without it and after a while we found we were both just lying there again, staring up at the sky, our blood ebbing.

Later, I don't know when, much later, we got cold and made it in to the bedroom, where we crashed out. If I dreamt, I didn't remember anything.

When I woke, James was not around.

Ten minutes later, having checked the backyard, the bathroom, under the bed, and inside one or two cupboards, I established that he had gone. This was strange. James isn't that kind of a person. He never just goes out. He needs a reason. He needs a good reason.

It was twenty before eleven. We'd slept late because of the E. Or I had, at least. I had no way of knowing how long James had been asleep. I felt pretty rough, my jaw still clenching and my limbs aching, although we'd neither of us been very energetic while we'd been up. Outside it was another hot day. When I stepped out the front door there was a hooting of klaxons from the Prinsengracht and a clatter of bicycles heading down Amstel. From a pay phone I called the hotel where Ben and Matthew were staying. They hadn't seen James but Ben was able to give me Simon's address. Apparently he'd been handing out his business card after I'd stormed out of the bar the night before. I thanked Ben, who merely sniggered in reply, and I left the kiosk. Simon's street was close by the gallery and the bar, as he had said. I rang his bell, then stepped back to look up at the front of the building. The windows were all closed and there was no clear sign of life. A cloud shaped like a snowman drifted over the top of the building. My neck began to ache from leaning back and looking up. I cursed Simon. And James—he'd fallen for a routine.

Just across the street from the apartment house was a coffeeshop. The sweet, sickly miasma of dope overpowered even the smell of freshly ground beans. I got a large cappuccino and sat by the window, where I could watch the street door to Simon's building. I ordered a second cappuccino. A couple of tables away a woman wearing Oakley wraps sat reading a Dutch newspaper. There was a little direct light in the coffeeshop but not too much. I guess she could have gotten along okay without the shades. I looked back across the street. *Kingyo no fun* is a Japanese expression meaning goldfish shit. The first time I heard it, the significance was not entirely clear to me. Matter of fact, it didn't mean a damn thing.

The Oakley woman's partner came back from the bathroom. He was wearing a slithery, artificial snakeskin shirt in some shiny yellow and green fabric, tight black jeans, and beat-up Nike Airs a couple of years out of date. On anybody else the combination would have looked awful, but this guy wore it well. Real well. He had a kind of glamour. He almost shone. I figured he was a rock star on vacation or someone off of the TV. He was casually toking on a spliff the size of a California redwood, which again would have looked like an affectation if he'd been anybody else. But this guy was genuine. Just like James is genuine.

Something somewhere clicked. Not just somewhere. In my head somewhere.

I dropped a couple of crumpled colorful bills on the counter and left the coffeeshop. So urgent was it that I reach Simon's door—I'd seen a guy go to enter it while I was reaching for my stash of guilders—I didn't look, but just dashed across the street.

It was real close. I heard a jangling bell, a woman's voice, and I escaped with a knock on the back of my left heel. *Uh-huh, pretty fortunate*, I thought in a daze as faces stared down at me from the windows of the tram which groaned slowly by. Cyclists weaved lenticular patterns around me as I gawped open-mouthed in the middle of the street, bells ringing, horns hooting, whistles blowing. The guy who'd been about to enter Simon's building was poised on the threshold, the door held open by his hand. Maybe, if I hadn't nearly been knocked down by the tram, he wouldn't have still been there and I would have been unable to enter. Everything happens for a reason.

I snapped back, dodging more bicycles as I hurried to catch the big blond-wood door. A blur of bell pushes told me Simon's apartment number. The guy stood and watched as I mounted the stairs three at a time. I guess I didn't much care what he thought.

I stood outside the door to Simon's apartment. A big brass number seven on the door. I got my breath back. If I was right, though, there was no need to compose myself. I pushed the door with a finger and it swung open, creaking just a little for good measure. I went in.

I knew instantly that the place was not empty. At least not quite. Sure there was no sign of James, but then I hadn't expected there to be. Simon was good, real good. He was good *kingyo no fun*. There's good and bad, by which I mean how successful he got to be rather than what a good guy he was. Clearly, he was not a good guy. But then who is? Simon was a master of his craft. I knew that within moments of entering his place, because I could sense that part of him was still there. I scouted round to look for it. I have experience. I knew what I was looking for. The traces take different forms. Sometimes you see stuff lying right there in the middle of the floor, like fresh slough, picking up the light and handing it straight back to you—like the shirt the rock-star guy in the coffeeshop was wearing. It's like an old snakeskin or wings that an insect has no more use for.

There was nothing like that in Simon's apartment. He was more highly evolved.

I didn't want to waste valuable time looking for traces of Simon when I knew I should be out there hunting down . . . "James." But you can't help it. And I guess I still had a little bit of my mind that needed convincing. I stared hard at the surfaces in the apartment, the things he had lying around like props. The magazines and newspapers, the novels in English and Dutch with realistically broken spines, a word processor with the cursor blinking. An ashtray full of dead cigarettes—not Simon's—a stack of bland CDs: Prince, George Michael, Jesus Christ even the Gypsy Kings. Hal Hartley videos, some French shit: Eric Rohmer, Robert Bresson, Maurice Pialat. I wasn't getting anything except further evidence that he was good at what he did. This cultural vacuum—it was no coincidence, no coincidence at all.

I stared harder and tried first to shorten my focus, then to extend it, to focus beyond the walls. It's like goofing around with a stereogram: it can take time, but if you get a glimpse, the rest comes easy. And there on the wall, or through the wall, between the poster for the Van Gogh Museum and the Arnolfini print, I got it. I managed to lose the basic building blocks of the poster, the frame, the bare wall, the print, and in the interstices I saw him, a trace of him. The sneer, the twisted lip, even the fleck in the eye. His signature on the wall. Like the shadow of the Hiroshima victim or the casts at Pompeii. I looked away, then looked back and it was still there. He was still inhabiting this place, even in his absence. And *by* his absence I now knew that he was inhabiting James.

Trashing the place would do no good. Some things are eternal. And I had to find "James." It was an outside chance but worth a few minutes of my time to continue searching the apartment for any detail that might, in spite of his efforts, give me a real clue to the nature of him. Something that might tell me where to start looking. I swept the set dressings aside now—the CDs, the videos and the books, the cheap point-and-shoot camera, the bottles of liquor, and the unwrapped packs of Camel Lites. Most of the cigarette butts in the ashtray were rouged with lipstick, but in a city like Amsterdam you couldn't take that as proof they had been smoked by women. Or by transvestites, or transsexuals—you could take nothing for granted here. It was one reason why James and I liked coming here and why we'd leapt eagerly on the gallery invitation when it arrived at the end of a dull month-long trail of book launches in private Soho drinking clubs, the Museum of the Moving Image, and subterranean fetish joints in Spitalfields. Amsterdam was special, it was different. But I knew it could make finding "James" even harder.

The quotes. You want me to explain the quotes? Like I said, Simon is good *kingyo no fun*. He gets right inside, like all *kingyo no fun*, but then he stays there. He doesn't get shut out in a couple of days like the amateurs. He's there for keeps, or for as long as he wants to be.

Kingyo no fun try to get up their host's ass. They're shit trying to get back up the asses of bright shiny charismatic people—the goldfish of the world. Not the perch, the gudgeon, or the minnows. The goldfish. They hang around, the *kingyo no fun*, just like goldfish shit—you ever sat and watched a fish tank, seen a goldfish take a crap, and noticed the long string of crap that trails after it for as long as it takes to work loose? It can take minutes, hours, days. Some goldfish are never seen without *kingyo no fun*.

The world is divided into two groups of people: those who are not *kingyo no fun* and those who are. Not all goldfish shine as brightly, however. James shone brightly. The guy in the coffeeshop shone brightly, and the woman with him kept her shades on pretty much the whole time, you can be sure of that; he shone so brightly, she'd have had to.

At first they're just easing in, laying the groundwork. Later they'll strip naked, lose their clothes, their skin, their patina of ordinariness—leave it lying on the floor or fused into the fabric of the walls—and slowly, messily work their way in. Once inside, the less successful *kingyo no fun* stay there an hour or two. To the rest of the world they've just disappeared. But that's all the goldfish can bear, and the goldfish outgrows them, rejects them, and the *kingyo no fun* are back to being themselves again, but strengthened, nourished.

Those are the amateurs, the part-timers.

The business—and Simon was the business, that was clear—stays up there.

It's not a gay thing, wanting to get up somebody's ass in this way. It's a people thing. A weak-people thing. I know, I've seen it.

Further proof of that was to be found in Simon's bedroom. After his thoroughness in other respects I was astonished to find, nestling within the pages of a Jeffrey Archer novel—so far so good—a photograph. Just a little six-by-four glossy print, not very well taken, of a black hooker standing in a doorway in the Red Light District. It was the one thing in the whole apartment—with the exception of the stereogrammatical trace of the *kingyo no fun* himself, and the clothes I'd seen him wearing the night before dumped in the otherwise empty laundry basket—that was not entirely *faux*.

Apart from the girl herself, there was a clue in the picture. The rows and rows of doors in Amsterdam's Red Light District are pretty much homogeneous. Narrow doors that are almost entirely glass, with a brown or a red curtain on the inside that can be drawn across. Beyond the door a foreshortened passageway and another doorway, into the hooker's room. The girl stands in the street doorway, or sits on an elevated stool either in the doorway or in the room's picture window, which can also be curtained off. It all looks so artificial—a hurried though professional-looking construction of glass and alloy—and tacked on to whatever real buildings lie at the rear, that you wonder if behind the shallow little rooms with their air freshener and single washbasin lurk a league of unscrupulous gentlemen who sneak in from the back when the curtains are drawn to help themselves to your billfold and plastic.

Bounded by Zeedijk to the north, Kloveniersburgwal to the east, Oude Hoogstraat, Oude Doelenstraat and Damstraat to the south, and Warmoesstraat to the west, the Red Light District is roughly heart-shaped—a real, messy, asymmetrical human heart rather than its cartoon symbol. It rests, snug and reliable, in the oldest part of Amsterdam, functioning twenty-four hours a day on some streets. Men—and a steady stream of sightseers of both sexes—are drawn through its venous streets and capillary alleyways, past yards and yards of flesh that is stretched and pressed, twisted and uplifted.

James and I had spent an hour on our first day wandering round the district. We might not have wanted to buy, but that didn't mean we weren't interested in taking a look—it's something different, something you don't see in London, or New York for that matter.

Of course, most of the doorways face onto canals and the majority of those that don't are squeezed into narrow alleyways. The doorway in Simon's picture fell into neither of these two groups. His black hooker worked a street broader than the alleyways that connected Oudezijds Voorburgwal to Oudezijds Achterburgwal and the angle of his shot revealed that a stone building rather than a canal was on the other side of it. When I applied my recollection of the area to close study of the map I found I was able to narrow down the possible locations. The girls worked in six-hour shifts, so I wouldn't necessarily see the black girl even if I found her street, but it was all I had to go on.

I needed James back, if only for confirmation. And he needed me. Now more than ever.

If I knew Simon half as well as I thought I did, I was on the right track.

. . .

There were fewer streets that fitted the bill than I had thought. In fact, I only had to tour the area once more before I was able to pin down the location. The strongest clue was the fraction of stonework visible on the far right of the picture, which formed part of whatever building faced the hooker's doorway. I soon realized, as I walked around the outside of the massive structure for the second time, that this was the Oude Kerk—the Old Church.

The street was in back of the Oude Kerk, little more than an alleyway connecting one of the canals, the Oudezijds Achterburgwal, to Warmoesstraat, and along it, opposite the church, a row of hookers' windows and doorways. I walked by once, then twice, trying to identify the doorway, but they all looked pretty much the same. The hookers themselves were more varied. There were a few Africans, a handful of Thai or Filipino girls, and one or two Europeans. Several talked directly to me as I walked by; one black girl caught my hand and tried to drag me into her doorway. "Fuckee, suckee," she said, her painted lips and pneumatic breasts trembling. I held my ground and withdrew the photograph from the back pocket of my Levi's.

"Do you know this girl?" I asked her. She took hold of the picture with long-nailed glittery fingers and called out to a colleague two doors down. They spoke in French, which I did not understand, the second hooker looking at me appraisingly as I switched my gaze from one to the other. The first girl answered me. "She is not there," she said in halting but charming English.

"Where is she?"

"She is . . . later. *Plus tard. Plus tard elle sera là.*"

I understood that much.

"Where? Here?" I pointed to the doorway behind the girl who was talking to me.

"She is there," the other girl said, pointing at a closed door twenty-five yards farther along toward the canal. "Not now. Later."

"Yeah, later," I said. "Like, when later?"

The girls both shrugged.

There was a beat. The three of us stood there in a triangle of silence broken only by the clicking of the first girl's nails on a long string of beads she wore around her neck.

"Fuckee, suckee?" she said hopefully.

I went back later and recognized her instantly. The slightly haughty angle she held her head at. The red earrings. And, frankly, the enormous breasts, thrust upward and outward in apparent defiance of the laws of nature. I hesitated a moment before approaching her. In that moment, I knew, everything could still change. I could leave undone what I was about to do. I could walk away and never see "James" or Simon ever again.

But then neither would I ever be able to look myself in the eye again.

I took a different photograph from the pocket of my shirt and walked across the street to where she stood. As I accelerated so did everything else. A train of events had been set in motion, even before I spoke to her, simply by my deciding to speak to her.

She told me her name was Stephanie and that she was from the Cameroon. I said that was cool but had she seen this guy. She told me she saw many, many guys. This one was special, I told her. Had she seen him? I slipped a twenty from my pocket. Yeah, she'd seen him. Did she expect to see him again?

Yeah, she nodded.

"What about you?" she suggested. "You are a nice man."

I warned her not to get her hopes up, then took out my billfold and said we had business to discuss. As I watched her eyes greedily counting the notes, I knew she'd go for the deal. She sold her own body for hard cash, why not others' as well?

Crouching in a space no bigger than a closet, my breathing becoming wheezy, my knee joints seizing up, I plugged my eye to the tear in the curtain and watched and waited. Stephanie stood outside and touted for business. I had said that for the money I was giving her she should simply wait for "James" to show up, but she wouldn't buy that.

I said, "What if he comes and you're busy and he goes with someone else?"

She told me he'd wait. He didn't just want to fuck. He wanted to fuck her. I winced. He'd paid already, she explained. Paid up front.

I wondered whose money it was. I wouldn't put it past the little bastard.

When she led her first john into the little room and drew the curtains at the front, I asked myself again if I couldn't have waited in the street for "James" to show up and tackled him there. But I knew I couldn't. I had to be 100 percent sure before I did anything, and for that I needed a close-up view. I fastened my eyes shut as Stephanie unclipped her sturdy brassiere and the john—a nervous-looking Scandinavian type—put a hand to his belt buckle. It seemed to go on forever but could only have lasted five or ten miserable minutes.

Stephanie saw two more clients. I merely checked them out quickly, then tried to switch off while she got on with it. I began to experience the absolute vertiginous depression that naturally accompanies the destruction—or imminent destruction—of everything you live for. At the same time I was tortured by flashes of hope. Even when fully convinced that you face total disaster, your mind is a wellspring of mad optimism. You never know . . . even when you do.

I didn't even know what I would do when the time came. By not properly arming myself did I somehow think I was molding the future, fixing the right conditions for a better outcome? I was a fool, had always been a fool. I should never have trusted James. With him it wasn't a matter of choice—he trusted everyone. And got fucked as a result.

Maybe I was a fool to think it had been a matter of choice in my case. I was, after all, no more a free agent than Simon was. Only he was better at it than me.

I heard conversation, half-recognized voices out on the street. I stuck my eye to the hole. There it was, he was, they were—James's tall, stooping figure was twisted into a gangling, distressing compromise. Standing by the doorway leering at Stephanie as if she were a glossy six-by-four in a skin mag rather than a human being. I hunched up a fraction, tried to flex my muscles, oil my joints. I heard a sound behind me but guessed it was an acoustical trick and dismissed it.

"James" was inside the air-freshened chamber now, his spine bent unnecessarily beneath the artificial ceiling, his body contorted, limbs abruptly snaking this way and that like power cables brought down in a storm. His face writhed with tics and spasms as two souls fought for its control. Stephanie rounded him neatly, interposing herself between him and me so that I was spared the worst as he unbuckled his black Levi's, but I could still see his face—that once proud countenance become this battered canvas for a wrestling bout of light and shade. His eyes flashed once like a horse's—suffering but devoid of ordered intelligence. That look strengthened my resolve, but I found myself rooted to the spot, watching in horrified fascination as he started to thrust in and out of the still-standing Stephanie. His movements were ungainly but full of physical power, truly a case of mind over matter as Simon turned James's flesh into his servant. James's comments about fucking women came back to me and I don't think I imagined that lost, hurt look in his creased brow. If I squinted I could just make out in his left eye a small but distinct fleck of yellow.

This time behind me I did hear a noise, but I was too late to do much about it. There was a rush of air and a scuffling noise, then a sudden cold sensation in the small of my back. I twisted round and felt something scrape against my vertebrae. Something inside my body. The wiry African who had stabbed me then tried to bundle me over, but I thumped him hard and low, dug the knife out of my back with one twist, and, when the man started to uncurl his winded body, opened him with it swiftly from groin to throat. I stepped right back to avoid the hot, slippery tumble of his intestines, and with a crash I brought down the curtain, rail and all.

"James" stumbled back, total confusion writ large across his crumpled face, and Stephanie spun round to face me. I quickly considered dispatching her for the double cross but in a split-second decision—I am at least conversant with humanity—chose not to. She couldn't be blamed for not trusting me.

I looked at "James," who tottered backward unsteadily, and had a brief true vision of his liver and lights slipping quietly from a sewage outfall into the Herengracht and the soupy green water closing implacably over the still, small muscle of his heart. I knew that Simon's viscera were packed into the much-loved body of the man in front of me, just as his sick thoughts and wicked desires coiled in the scoured cranium I had for ten years stroked and kissed each night in our bed. In my hand was clutched the means to guarantee James's release into oblivion from this squalid and barbaric tenancy.

Proficient, cunning, and ultimately successful, Simon would have believed himself eternal, but I was holding the gutting knife and he was in poor shape to resist. Some *kingyo no fun*, after all, are more eternal than others.

Norman Partridge

Bucket of Blood

Norman Partridge's short fiction has been published regularly in suspense, mystery, and horror magazines and in anthologies. His first collection, Mr. Fox and Other Feral Tales, *won the Bram Stoker Award, and his second collection,* Bad Intentions, *was a World Fantasy Award nominee. He is the author of three novels,* Slippin' into Darkness, Saguaro Riptide, *and* The Ten Ounce Siesta. *He coedited (with Martin H. Greenberg) the anthology* It Came from the Drive-In. *Partridge has worked in libraries and steel mills. He loves fifties rock 'n' roll, drive-in movies, and old paperbacks where the bad guys get away with murder.*

Partridge's best short horror fiction is strongly rooted in reality, as was the last story we took from him for this series, "The Cut Man," about the world of boxing. Here is another story that packs a wallop, "Bucket of Blood," originally published in Cemetery Dance.

—E. D.

ighway 50 cuts a ragged wound across the belly of California, finally ripping across the border into Nevada. A little slice north and you're in Virginia City. And when you're done there—and if you're lucky—it's east on 50 until 95 slashes south.

Tonopah... Scotty's Junction... Beatty and Amargosa Valley and Indian Springs.

And straight on into Vegas.

According to the AAA California/Nevada TourBook, *the trip should take nine hours.*

We say fuck the AAA California/Nevada TourBook.

Me and Mitch, that is. We've got us a Mustang convertible, and it's tanked to

the gills with Chevron Premium. Two sixes of iced Pacifico in the trunk, bricks of
every kind of cheese known to man because Mitch can't control himself in a grocery
store, an old Hamm's Beer display sign that lights up and an authentic Jayne
Mansfield hot water bottle and a dozen matchbooks from various incarnations of
the Mustang Ranch (because Mitch can't control himself in an antique shop,
either), T-shirts from every tourist trap along the way, and a couple of pairs of
swimming trunks.

No swimming tonight, though. The cold desert air bites like a pissed-off rattle-
snake tossed onto smoldering campfire coals, but we've got the top down anyway.

Even though we've got the heater cranked full blast, I'm shivering behind the
wheel—leather coat zipped up tight, face numb as the hide of a zombie that
stumbled off a midnight movie screen. Mitch is a hardcase, of course. No coat for
this boy—he's wearing that T-shirt. The one he got up the street from the Bucket
of Blood Saloon while I bided my time, stretching the last sip of a three buck beer
that I couldn't afford.

It's an eye catcher, the shirt is. Bullet holes cratering high on the chest, bright
red blood drizzling over the legend:

SLOWEST GUN
IN
VIRGINIA CITY, NEVADA

The sign over the batwing doors said Bucket of Blood Saloon. Inside, Big John
Dingo stood straight and tall, black eyes shining like fresh tarantula blood, lips
twisted into a snarl.

"Fill yer hand, ya sorry sonofabitch!"

"Hold on," Mitch began. "I'm not ready—"

"Not with yer pecker, idiot!" the gunfighter growled. "Fill yer hairy palm with
a six-gun, 'cause I'm about to blow yer pimply ass south of eternity!"

The batwing doors swung open. Big John clutched a fistful of Colt .45 while
Mitch made a grab for his pistol.

Mitch missed the holster entirely. He was laughing way too hard—one hand
searching for his pistol, the other wrapped around a beer.

The gunfighter's pistol sparked. "HAHAHAHAHA!" he screeched. "Another
pencil-dicked pilgrim eats it! No one outdraws Big John Dingo! I can fuck longer
and draw faster than any man alive! I never come up for air! I live on pussy and
hot lead! Drop a quarter, ya redneck peckerwood! Try your luck! HAHAHA-
HAHA!"

Mitch swigged beer and turned away from the mechanical gunman.

"More quarters?" the bartender asked.

"No." Mitch laughed at the mannequin as the batwing doors closed on the
tiny booth. "Where the hell did you get this thing?"

"Used to be in a drug store over in Carson City. A kid's game, right along
with the gum machines and the fiberglass pony ride. Of course, the gunfighter
didn't talk like that when he was outdrawing six-year-olds. My boss hired a fellow
who did a little work on him. He juiced the gunfighter's speed a little, recorded
a new tape and—"

"You think your boss would sell it?" Mitch interrupted.

"Well, I don't know . . ."

Mitch drained his beer. "What do you think, Kurt? Would the crowd down at the bar love this thing, or what?"

I nodded. "Sure they would. But what about you? I mean, can you imagine listening to Big John Dingo all night long, every night?"

The mechanical gunfighter kicked into gear as if on cue. "C'mon ya candy-assed cocksuckers! Yer dicks are wrapped in Tom Jones' old socks! Ya got cojones the size of goober peas! Ain't a one of you man enough to take on Big John Dingo!"

Mitch set his empty beer on the counter. "I guess it would get old pretty fast."

"Good Tom Jones line, though," I said.

Mitch did some business with the bartender, stocking up on Bucket of Blood Saloon souvenirs. A T-shirt, a coffee cup, even a cassette tape featuring Big John Dingo's witty repartee. In just under three minutes, Mitch dropped thirty bucks and change.

And he wasn't done yet. "Want another round?" he asked, his wallet still open.

I shook my head.

"C'mon. I'm buyin'."

"No. I'm okay."

"C'mon." Mitch sidled up on the barstool next to me. "Ease off a little. Stop worrying. I thought you were going to leave all that money shit behind for the weekend. Sure you're hurting now, but what was it you said?"

"This too will pass."

"Yeah. It fuckin' will. Things will come around for you, same way they came around for me. Right now you're hurting, and I'm not. It's as simple as that. So let me buy you a—"

Mitch left it there. Suddenly, he was staring over my shoulder, transfixed, and I knew that look.

I knew what I'd see before I even turned. She'd be tall and dark. Thin. That was a given. When it came to women, Mitch definitely favored a certain type. Genus Gen X, species Morticia Adamsette.

But this one wasn't dressed in black, which was kind of a surprise. She wore a white T-shirt with faux bullet holes that streamed equally faux blood.

"Hey," Mitch said. "Where'd you get that shirt?"

"That's not the question," she said.

Mitch raised his eyebrows. "What is?"

"The question is what you'll give me for it."

They laughed. Mitch bought her a drink. Her name was Doreen. Past the expected pleasantries, I kept my mouth shut and didn't get in the way. Hell, I could barely afford my own drink, let alone someone else's.

Mitch and Doreen talked about T-shirts until that went dead, and then they found something else to talk about, and pretty soon I noticed that Doreen's hand was on Mitch's thigh.

Doreen made the inevitable trip to the Ladies', and Mitch got down to business.

"You mind?" Mitch asked.

"No, man," I said. "Go for it."

"You okay? I mean, you've got enough money, right?"

"Yeah," I said. "Go on. Have fun. If I'm not here, I'll be in the car."

Mitch and Doreen left together, heading for the shop that sold the SLOWEST GUN IN VIRGINIA CITY T-shirts, which was where Doreen worked. She said that she lived in a little apartment above the place, and there was only one reason I could think of for her to impart that particular information.

The bartender and I traded grins as Mitch and Doreen crossed the plank sidewalk outside the saloon. The old guy was all ruined around the eyes and someone had stove in his nose a long time ago. Even though he worked in a saloon, he looked like he managed to spend a lot of the time in the sun. According to his nameplate, his name was Roy and he hailed from Albuquerque, New Mexico.

That info didn't do me any good—I'd never been to Albuquerque. But Roy knew how to keep a conversation moving without any help. Just as smooth as Johnny Carson, he asked, " 'Nother round?"

I thought about my wallet first.

Then I thought about Mitch . . . and Doreen.

"Why not," I said. "Maybe I'll be here awhile."

"Knowing Doreen, I can practically guarantee it, amigo."

Roy grinned and opened a bottle. I had four bucks in my pocket, the last of the money I'd brought on our trip. A weekend getaway—some gambling, a few thrift shops, a few tourist traps. We were heading home tomorrow, anyway. If Mitch got lucky with Doreen and I ended up spending the night in Mitch's Mustang, eating crackers and cheese and drinking Pacifico, that would suit me just fine. Most nights I didn't do that good at home.

Feeling fuck-it-all magnanimous, I peeled off three bucks for the beer, and tipped Roy my last dollar, and raised my bottle.

"Here's to true love," I said.

"Yeah," Roy said, soaping Doreen's lipstick off her empty glass. "Right."

My hands are angel white in the moonlight. Mitch—head back, eyes closed—wears the beatific expression of a saintly corpse. Trapped between his Converse All-Stars is a change bucket, the kind slot players use to collect their winnings. This one's from the Bucket of Blood Saloon. A first class souvenir. It's half full, brimming, contents gleaming in the moonlight.

Get me to Vegas, one of those five star casinos with five buck slots, and I'm putting that bucket to work for me.

Maybe it's the bucket that's lucky. Maybe the shiny contents. Or maybe it's me.

One thing's for certain—I can't lose.

Not tonight, anyway.

I've got to get to Vegas.

Before my luck runs out.

Mitch owned a couple of clubs in San Francisco, hole-in-the-wall joints in the Mission District. He started out on the cheap, backed only with a little bit of an inheritance from his dad, and there wasn't anything fancy about either place. Just a come-one-come-all attitude, a half-dozen beers on tap, clean glasses, and live music a couple nights a week. Mitch said that the secret to his success was throwing a good party every night. He definitely knew how to do that.

We'd been friends for a long time—since high school—and I was real happy for him. But mostly I wished I could be real happy for me, too. I'd been making my living as a writer for the last five years, but mine was a strictly hanging-on-by-the-skin-of-my-teeth kind of existence. I was more than a little tired of worrying about the rent, and the credit card bill, and the beater of a car that had been rolling atop four balding tires for the last five thousand miles. And I was sure enough sick of eating bologna sandwiches for dinner.

I knew that in a lot of ways I was luckier than most. I sold everything I wrote. Four published novels under my belt, and a fifth on the way. Every one of them had garnered good reviews, and I had a drawerful of laudatory quotes from writers I admired.

But I'd never come close to making the kind of score I wanted to make. No publisher had ever shot the big advance my way, or offered to send me on tour, or put a single penny into publicizing my books. No Hollywood bigwigs had optioned any of my novels for the movies. People I respected told me that I had a bright future and that financial success was just around the corner. But I'd been hearing that for so long it annoyed me more than anything else.

People told me other things, too. Like *money isn't everything*. Of course, it was my considered opinion that people who spoke about money in those terms slapped filet mignon on the barbecue grill whenever the mood struck them and fed the scraps to the dog. To put it plainly, they hadn't eaten a bologna sandwich in many many moons.

My stomach growled. There was a popcorn machine at the end of the bar. Popcorn was free if you were buying a beer. I helped myself to a bowl.

I glanced at my watch. It was a little past eight o'clock. Mitch must have gotten lucky. The tourist crowd at the saloon was starting to thin out. Plenty of barstools stood vacant, and the clatter of the slot machines was practically nonexistent. Roy was chatting with a few local alcoholics who appeared glued to their stools, but his heart sure didn't seem to be in it.

No such problem with Big John Dingo. He waited behind the barroom doors, the cassette tape rolling endlessly, spewing his rattler-rough come-on for just one more quarter.

A guy wandered up to the mechanical gunslinger. He sure didn't seem like the type. He looked as trail worn as Big John himself, and he wore a T-shirt that proclaimed: TOP HAND AT THE MUSTANG RANCH.

The T-shirt was black, but the material was so faded that it couldn't disguise several angry smears of machine oil. I wondered if the guy was a biker. He looked the part. I was just about to congratulate myself for my keen observational skill when he produced a key from a ring chained to his belt, unlocked Big John Dingo's change box, and pawed a mound of quarters into his hand.

The take wasn't much more than what Mitch fed the machine a couple hours earlier. The greaseball wandered over to Roy and stacked quarters carefully on the bar. He slid two stacks to Roy and kept the other for himself.

"Fucked up way to make a living," the guy said.

Roy stared at the greaseball. Or maybe he was staring at the greaseball's T-shirt. Because what Roy said was, "There's worse ways."

316 -- Norman Partridge

The words sent an uncomfortable shiver up my spine. For a second I thought there might be trouble, but the greaseball only shrugged and pocketed his quarters. He wandered over to one of the slot machines and fed the one-armed bandit until his money was gone. Then he glanced around the room, like he was waiting for someone.

I knew how that felt, the same way I knew that this guy had made a *mucho grande* mistake—he'd shot his pathetic little wad and come up short one beer in his hand, so he didn't have an excuse to hang around.

"I'll be back," he said, and his shadow followed him outside like a thirty-weight stain.

"Wonderful," Roy said.

I finished my popcorn and wandered around the saloon. The slots were old, not the electronic gizmos you find in Reno, Tahoe, and Vegas. Some of 'em, I could imagine dusty miners pulling the handles. After all, the Bucket of Blood Saloon had been open since 1876.

My boots made muffled thuds against the weathered floorboards. A silver-haired lady smiled at me from behind the cashier's cage. "Try your luck?" she asked. "How about a roll of quarters?"

I shrugged and looked down, embarrassed by my empty pockets. Then I spotted it, on the floor in front of a quarter slot machine. A single quarter, gleaming in a pool of soft yellow light.

I looked around. The greaseball was long gone. I sure wasn't going to chase after him. Maybe he'd dropped the quarter. But maybe he hadn't. I'd watched several people play the slots in the last few hours. Any one of them might have dropped that quarter.

I picked it up and slipped it into the slot machine.

I pulled the handle.

Three plums spun into place.

The one on the right shuddered a little.

Then a buzzer sounded, because the plum held firm.

"I'm thinking maybe another bar is the way to go," I say. "If my luck holds in Vegas, I'll go in on it with you as a partner. Of course, it would be your show . . ."

I glance over at Mitch, but he doesn't say a word. His head hangs low. He's staring into the brimming slot bucket between his feet.

"Yeah," I say, backtracking in case I made a mistake. "Maybe that's a bad idea. You've already got two bars. That's nothing new for you. What we need is a challenge."

I drive on, through Tonopah. I'm not stopping. Not for anything. All I want is Vegas, another casino, a big one with acres of slots.

Dollar machines. Five dollar machines. Ten dollar machines.

"Movies," I say. "We take one of my short stories. Do the damn thing ourselves. I write it. You produce it. We find a director who'll get the motherfucker right."

I slap the steering wheel with my hand. Yeah. That's a hell of a good idea. Mitch has the connections, too. There's a pack of young gun movie guys who hang out at one of his clubs.

Man, I'm not even cold anymore. I honk the horn, long and loud.

I step on the gas.

. . .

I played the quarter slots for an hour. And then the dollar slots for two. Finally I ended up at a big monster of a dollar machine called THE BUCKET OF BLOOD.

God knows how many pulls on that sucker.

Fifteen of them hit jackpots.

Two hundred silver dollars. Five hundred silver dollars. Seven-fifty. A piddly seventy-five. And on like that. Enough to fill up three Bucket of Blood Saloon slot buckets.

But those jackpots were just small change. The last one was the big one. Three black buckets tripped into view, each one dripping blood.

Ten thousand dollars.

The machine didn't pay that one, of course. Roy handed me the check. I stared at it hard.

One of the barflies laughed. "I guess you're buying!"

"I guess I am!" I said, not taking my eyes off the check.

The barfly stared over my shoulder at all those zeros. I could smell rum on his breath, but I didn't spare him a glance. Not when I had the check to look at.

"You won ten thousand bucks off a *quarter?*" The barfly's voice trembled with awe. "You gotta be the luckiest man alive!"

I started to tell the story again. I couldn't help myself. How I was broke . . . flat . . . busted. How I found the quarter on the floor. How I figured what the hell and dropped it into the closest one-armed bandit—

A hand dropped on my shoulder and just about spun me out of my boots.

"That was my goddamn quarter."

Surprisingly, I recognized the voice. The words were spoken by Big John Dingo, but it was the greaseball who had hold of my shoulder. They were one in the same. It shouldn't have surprised me. After all, the greaseball had fixed the old arcade machine. He'd obviously supplied the gunfighter's voice, too.

His eyes seared me like a hunk of dead steak. "I want my money."

"Fuck that." I shook him off and stood my ground. "I won that money. It's mine."

"You won it with my fuckin' quarter, dickhead. Give it up or there's gonna be trouble."

"No way—"

A crashing blow from a big right hand and I felt like I was headed for the promised land. My knees banged hard against the weathered floorboards and a loud creak tore the air. For a second I couldn't decide if the sound came from the floorboards buckling or my own tired bones—

"That's enough, Big John."

It was Roy's voice. I couldn't see him. I was on my knees, looking at Big John's belt buckle. It was probably the only thing on him that was clean. Polished silver, and I could see my reflection in it, funhouse mirror-style.

I looked more than a little perplexed. And that's the way I felt. The greaseball's name was Big John, same as the gunslinging dummy. It was crazy. *Twilight Zone* stuff. I halfway expected to look over at the slot machine and see Rod Serling standing there—

But there was only Big John. He grabbed a handful of my hair and tilted my head until my eyes found his. He drew back that right hand again and I cringed.

"You give me that money—"

Roy's voice again, accompanied by a sharp clicking sound. "I mean it, Johnny boy. Don't give me a reason."

The greaseball let me go. A couple of the barflies helped me to my feet. I turned to the bar and saw Roy standing there, a pistol in his hand.

"I want that money, pilgrim," Big John said. "I've a right to it. It's mine. If you think you're leavin' Virginia City without givin' it to me, you'd better think again, you pencil-dicked motherfucker."

I could barely whisper. "Not one dime," I said.

"That's enough." Roy cut me off with a sharp glance. "Say another word, and I'll throw the both of you out."

Big John headed for the door. "I got a gun of my own," he said. "I'll be back."

"Wonderful," Roy said.

A second later the bartender slammed a shot of whiskey onto the bar.

I drank it straight down.

"I've got to get out of here," I said. "I've got to find my buddy. That girl . . . Doreen . . . you know where she lives?"

Roy nodded. "Apartment above a T-shirt shop. Across the street, about a half a block up."

Jesus. That wasn't much help. Every other store on the street was a T-shirt shop. "What's the name of the place?" I asked.

Roy looked me dead in the eye.

"Big John's," Roy said, and then he sighed.

Happiness. Yeah. I know the definition of that.

Scotty's Junction in your rearview mirror and Vegas comin' up.

"Let that motherfucker try to mess with us!" I yell. "His ass didn't know what he was in for!"

Mitch doesn't say a word. I wonder if I've gone too far. I'm damn happy about the money. I'm happy about Big John, too. But Mitch isn't.

Maybe it's Doreen . . . Maybe that's it . . . Maybe he's worried about her.

Hell. He doesn't have to worry. Big John isn't going to lay a hand on Doreen. Not anymore.

I glance over at Mitch, at his T-shirt. At those bullet holes. I want him to be happy. I want us to be like Yul Brynner and Steve McQueen, headed for boot hill in The Magnificent Seven.

What was it Steve asked when those lousy sidewinders took a shot at Yul?

"You get elected?" Yeah. That was it.

I ask Mitch, "You get elected?"

He doesn't say a word. So I say them for him.

"No, but I got nominated real good."

"You don't want to mess with him," Roy said. "Big John Dingo's a real asshole. He's been around town for a few years now. Blew in with a string of schemes that were gonna make him rich. He thought so, anyway. First it was the Big

John Dingo Gunslinger machine. He fixed that old relic up for us, got the idea that he was gonna sell them things to every bar in the nation. Of course, reality sort of disabused him of that notion. Then it was the T-shirt shop. Then . . . well, poor Doreen . . . Shit, she ain't the homecoming queen, but ain't no girl deserves to have her man turnin' her out."

I heard what Roy said, but I was about three steps past him. "Let me borrow your gun."

"Let me call the sheriff."

"No," I said. "We don't have time for that. Dingo's crazy. He said he was going after his own gun. And if he finds Doreen with my buddy—"

"He don't know the fella's your friend. Hell, Doreen with another man . . . that's just business as usual, as far as Big John's concerned."

"Oh, yeah. He won't mind finding another man banging his girl after some lucky son of a bitch made a fortune off a quarter that he dropped on a barroom floor."

"Don't forget him gettin' run off by a geriatric bartender with a gun," one of the barflies put in.

"Yeah." Roy sighed. "You boys maybe have a couple of good points there."

"You bet your ass we do," I said. "Let me borrow your gun."

Roy stared down at the pistol. Then he glanced at the three buckets of dollar coins resting on the bar.

He squinted at me. "Can't loan you my gun," he said. "But might be you could get me to sell it, if the price was right."

I pushed one of the buckets his way.

"I don't know . . ." Roy said.

I pushed another bucket across the bar.

Roy smiled. "That'll about do her."

If Mitch doesn't want to talk, that's fine with me.

Maybe he wants to pout. Maybe he wishes he would have hung around, tried his luck on the slots instead of chasing after Doreen.

He's used to bailing me out. He's used to it.

But that's not what happened tonight.

Tonight the shoe was on the other foot.

Tonight it was my turn.

Maybe Mitch can't handle that. I don't care. I stare down at the bucket between his feet.

I don't care at all.

Let him pout.

I shove a tape into the cassette deck.

I pump up the volume and punch the gas.

The not-so-bright lights of Beatty, comin' right up.

I stepped onto the plank sidewalk—the gun clutched in one sweaty hand, the bucket of dollar coins cradled under my other arm—and I almost bumped into him.

Mitch, all bright-eyed and bushy-tailed, wearing a SLOWEST GUN IN VIR-GINA CITY T-shirt and carrying a bag of high-priced souvenirs.

"Shit," he said, spotting the gun in my hand. "What the hell are you doing, Kurt?"

I'm holding onto this damn bucket of dollars, I thought. *That's what I'm doing. You damn near made me spill my money all over this fucking sidewalk—*

"Kurt," Mitch said. "Hey, Kurt. What's up with the gun?"

"Did you see him?" I asked, glancing over Mitch's shoulder at the empty street.

"Who?"

"Dingo." I shook my head, trying to clear it, but shaking my head only made me feel the punch I'd taken, and my ears started to ringing again.

"Who are you talking about?"

"John," I shouted, barely able to hear myself. "John Dingo. Did you see him?"

"*Big* John Dingo?" Mitch laughed. "Sure I saw him. He walked straight out of the Bucket of Blood on those mechanical legs of his, and we had us a shootout on Main Street. I sent him to that big toy store in the sky."

"No," I said. "John Dingo is *real,* Mitch. He's *Doreen's* guy. And if he sees us, he's going to gun us down."

Mitch swore and started in with a barrage of questions. Most of them were about Doreen. I didn't have a clue to the answers he was after. They weren't important, anyway. But if I could get Mitch out of town faster by implying that a jealous boyfriend was after his hide, that was all right with me. I didn't have time to explain about the money, and how I'd gotten it.

I started talking. I held tight to the bucket of dollars. Dingo wanted that money. My money. He wanted to take it from me.

Maybe it *was* his quarter that I found on the floor. But even if it was Dingo's, that didn't mean that the money I'd won belonged to him, too.

I won that money. Dingo didn't. It was mine. The bucket of dollar coins. And the ten thousand dollar check.

Mine. And I was damn sure going to keep it.

The most I owed Big John Dingo was a quarter.

But the son of a bitch wasn't going to get that much out of me.

Not one thin dime.

Not one plug nickel.

Not one red fucking cent.

I turned and started down the street. The gun felt good in my hand.

"Hey," Mitch said. "Hey! Where the hell do you think you're going! Wait up!"

Just past Beatty, Mitch starts talking.

"Miserable sidewinder shuffled off his mortal coil in the streets of Virginia City," he says. *"That boy pissed on the wrong sombrero, and that's for damn sure!"*

"Yeah," I say. "Yeah!"

Mitch has a head of steam up now. The sleep did him good. He's talking and talking . . .

And then we're laughing and laughing . . .

Screeching laughter in the dry desert night.

It was way past time to kiss Virginia City goodbye. I pressed the gas pedal and the Mustang pulled away from the curb.

"Jesus!" Mitch said. "Is that him?"

It was. Big John Dingo, top hand at the Mustang Ranch, striding down the street with a gun in his hand.

His back was to us.

"Turn around," Mitch said. "Before he sees us! Flip a U-turn, and let's get the hell out of here!"

I watched Dingo walk. Oh, he had some strut in him. Like fucking John Wayne. Like he was a real big man with that gun in his hand. Like his pockets were jinglin' with silver dollars, and his belly was full of filet mignon and the best whiskey in the house.

Big John Dingo wasn't walking like a man who repaired arcade games and sold T-shirts. He wasn't walking like a man who ate bologna sandwiches for dinner while million-dollar schemes percolated in his brain. And he damn sure wasn't walking like a man who turned out his own woman.

No. He was strutting like a gunslinger with notches on his gun.

Like the top hand at the fucking Mustang Ranch.

I put the car in neutral.

I gunned the motor.

"Kurt!" Mitch yelled. "What the fuck are you *DOING!*"

Big John turned. I flicked the headlights on bright, and I saw it in his eyes. All the hate. All the self-loathing. All the lust for a buck. All those things that he bottled up day in and day out. All the misery that had tunneled up from the dark pit of his soul because he might have dropped a quarter on the floor of the Bucket of Blood Saloon.

It was a lot to take in all at once, but I knew the look in those eyes all too well.

I saw it every time I stared into a mirror.

I glanced down at the bucket of dollars between Mitch's feet. At the same time I tapped my shirt pocket, heard the ten thousand dollar check crinkle within.

I glanced at my reflection in the rearview mirror.

My eyes were different now.

"Kurt!" Mitch said. "Jesus Christ! Turn the car around!"

I slammed the Mustang into gear just as Big John fired his pistol, and I ran over the bastard a couple of seconds after the bullets pitted the windshield, and I heard him scream as the Mustang dragged him a half-mile down the road.

When the Mustang spit out his miserable carcass and the back wheels kicked him loose, Big John was all done screaming.

Mitch is telling it again as we drive down the Strip.

"Last fool I shot was slower than Columbus comin' to America," he says. "Miserable sidewinder shuffled off his mortal coil in the streets of Virginia City. That boy pissed on the wrong sombrero, and that's for damn sure!"

I'm not listening. My senses are alive. I can smell the money here. Just like I can see the neon.

It shines through the bullet holes in the windshield. It bathes Mitch in an otherworldly glow. It spills over the slot bucket between his feet, pooling with the coins and Mitch's blood.

But he's okay. Mitch is okay.

He's talking.

Even though he's got a couple bullet holes in his chest, he's talking.

I want everyone to hear what he has to say.

Gunslinger quick, I reach for the cassette deck and turn up the volume.

"HAHAHAHAHA!" Mitch screeches. "Another pencil-dicked pilgrim eats it! No one outdraws Big John Dingo! I can fuck longer and draw faster than any man alive! I never come up for air! I live on pussy and hot lead! Drop a quarter, ya redneck peckerwood! Try your luck! HAHAHAHAHA!"

A. Alvarez

Mermaid

A. Alvarez is a poet, novelist, literary critic, and author of many highly praised nonfiction books on topics ranging from suicide and divorce to poker, North Sea oil, and mountaineering. His most recent book is Night: An Exploration of Night Life, Night-Language, Sleep and Dreams. He lives in London and is a frequent contributor to The New Yorker and The New York Review of Books.

The enchanted siren's song that follows comes from the July 28, 1997 issue of The New Yorker.

—T. W.

Supple and slippery above and below,
Sliding wide-eyed under my hands
With a smile like daybreak,

You swim into my life only at night,
Bringing the shush of waves and shingle,
The smell of salt and distance,
The gull cries, the moan of seamarks,
And the broken sweep of light,
From shrouded promontories.

You ride the storms and calms,
You plunge and surf,
Cruise the depths with sharks and stingrays,
And flicker through the feet of children
Paddling in the shallows,

To end up here in the dark between the sheets,
In the gap between dreaming and waking,
Coming ashore with your smile,
Your sea scent and thrashing tail,
Still slippery from the creation.

Caitlín R. Kiernan

Estate

Caitlín R. Kiernan was born near Dublin, Ireland, but has lived most of her life in the southeastern U.S. Her short fiction has appeared in a number of anthologies, including Love in Vein 2, Darkside: Horror For the Next Millennium, High Fantastic, Dark Terrors 2, Lethal Kisses, *and* Sandman: Book of Dreams. *Her first novel,* Silk, *was recently published and she writes for DC Comics'* The Dreaming. *Kiernan currently lives in a renovated overalls factory in Birmingham, Alabama.*

"Estate," according to Kiernan, was inspired in part by a drive along the Hudson River Valley on a misty, cold afternoon in February 1996. She reports that she was reading a lot of Charles Fort and Edward Gorey, and suffered a recent obsession with the Great American industrialists.

"Estate" was first published in Dark Terrors 3: The Gollancz Book of Horror, *edited by Stephen Jones and David Sutton.*

—E. D.

Rough and hungry boy, barely nineteen, that first time Silas Desvernine saw the Storm King, laid bright young eyes to raw granite and green rash rising up and up above the river and then lost again in the Hudson morning mist. The craggy skull of the world, he thought, scalped by some Red Indian god and left to bleed, grain by mica grain, and he leaned out past the uncertain rails of the ferryboat's stern, frothy wakeslash on the dark water and no reflection there. He squinted and there was the railroad's iron scar winding around its base, cross-tie stitches and already the fog was swallowing the mountain, the *A. F. Beach's* restless sidewheel carrying him away, upriver, deeper into the Highlands, towards Newburgh and work in Albany and he opens his leathery old eyelids and it's deadest winter 1941, not that wet May morning in 1889. Old, old man, parchment and twigs, instead of that boy and he's been nodding off again, drifted away and her voice has brought him back. Her voice across the decades, and he wipes away a stringy bit of drool at the corner of his mouth.

"Were you dreaming again?" she asks, soft, velvet tongue from her corner and he blinks, stares up into the emptycold light spilling down through the high windows, stingy, narrow slits in the stone of the long mansard roof. And "No," he mumbles, No, knows damn well there's no point to the lie, no hiding himself from her, but at least he's made the effort.

"Yes. You were," she says, Jesus that voice that's never a moment older than the first time and the words squeeze his tired heart. "You were dreaming about Storm King, the first time you saw the mountain, the first morning . . ."

"Please," no strength in him, begging and she stops, all he knows of mercy. He wishes the sun were warm on his face, warm where it falls in weaktea pools across the clutter of his gallery. Most of his collection here, the better part, gathered around him like the years and the creases in his stubbled face. Dying man's pride, dead-man-to-be obsession, *possessions*, these things he spent a life gathering, stolen or secreted but made his own so they could be no one else's. The things sentenced to float out his little forever in murky formalin tombs, specimen jars and stoppered bottles, a thousand milky eyes staring nowhere. Glass eyes in taxidermied skulls, bodies stuffed with sawdust; wings and legs spread wide and pinned inside museum cases. Old bones yellowed and wired together in shabby mockeries of life, older bones gone to silica and varnished, shellacked, fossilized. Plaster and imagination where something might have been lost. Here, the teeth of leviathans, there, the claws of a behemoth; a piece of something fleshy that once fell from the sky over Missouri and kept inside a bell jar. Toads from stones found a mile underground. Sarcophagi and defiled Egyptian nobility ravelling inside, crumbling like him, and a chunk of amber as big as an orange and the carbonized hummingbird trapped inside fifty million years.

A narwhal's ivory tooth bought for half a fortune and he once believed with the unflinching faith of martyrs that it was a unicorn's horn. Precious bit of scaly hide from the Great Sea Serpent, harpooned off Malta in 1807, they said and never mind that he knew it was never anything but the peeling belly of a crocodile.

"There's not much more," she says, "A day, perhaps," and even her urgency, her fear, is patient, wetnurse gentle, but Silas Desvernine closes his eyes again, prays he can slip back, fifty-two trips wrong way round the sun and when he opens them he'll be standing on the deck of the ferry, the damp and chill no match for his young wonder, his anticipation and a strong body and the river rolling slow and deep underneath his feet.

"No," she says, "I'm still here, Silas."

"I know that," he says and the December wind makes a hard sound around the edges of this rich man's house.

After the War, his father had run, run from defeat and reprisal and grief, from a wasted Confederacy. World broken and there would be no resurrection, no reconstruction. Captain Eustace Desvernine, who'd marched home in '65 to the shallow graves of wife and child, graves scooped from the red Georgia clay with free black hands. And so he faded into the arms of the enemy, trailing behind him the shreds of a life gone to ash and smoke, gone to lead and worms, hiding himself in the gaslight squalor and cobbled industrial sprawl of Manhattan; the first skyscrapers rose around him, and the Union licked its wounds and forgot its dead.

Another marriage, strong Galway girl who gave him another son, Silas Josiah; the last dregs of his fortune into a ferry, the *Alexander Hamilton*, sturdy name that meant nothing to him but he'd seen it painted on the side of a tall building. So, the Captain (as Silas would always remember him, the Captain in shoddy cap and shoddier coat on wide shoulders) carried men and freight from Wee-hawken to the foot of West 42nd Street. Later, another boat, whitewashed side-wheeler, double-ender he'd named the *A. F. Beach* and the year that Robert E. Lee died, the Captain began running the long route between New York and Albany.

And one night, when Silas was still eighteen years old, almost a man himself and strong, he stood beside his father in the wheelhouse of the *A. F. Beach*. The Captain's face older by the unsteady lamp as they slipped past the lights of West Point on their way downriver. The Captain taking out his old revolving pistol, Confederate-issue Colt, dullshine tarnish and his callused thumb cocking the hammer back while Silas watched, watched the big muzzle pressed against the Captain's left temple. Woman's name across his father's lips then, unfamiliar "Carrie" burned forever into Silas' brain like the flash, the echo of the gunshot trapped between the high cliffs, slipping away into the river night and pressed forever behind his eyes.

"Are you sure that's the way it happened?" she asked him once, when he told her. Years and years ago, not so long after he brought her to his castle on Pollepel Island and she still wore the wings, then, and her eyes still shone new dollar silver from between the narrow bars of her cage.

"I was young," he said, "Very young," and she sighed, short and matter-of-fact sigh that said something but he wasn't certain what.

Whole minutes later, "Who was she?" and him already turned away, unpacking a crate just arrived from Kathmandu; "What?" he asked, but already remembering, the meaning of her question and the answer, absently picking a stray bit of excelsior from in his beard and watching those eyes watching him.

"Carrie," she said. "Who was Carrie?"

"Oh," and "I never found out," he lied, "I never tried," no reason, but already he felt the need to guard those odd details of his confessions, scraps of truth, trifling charms. Hoarding an empty purse, when all the coins have gone to beg-gars' hands.

"Ah," she said and Silas looked too quickly back to the things in the crate, pilfered treasures come halfway around the world to him, and it was a long time before he felt her eyes leave him.

Pollepel Island: uneven jut of rock above water where the Hudson gets wide past the Northern Gate, Wey-Gat, the long stony throat of Martyr's Reach, greenscab at the foot of Newburgh Bay; white oak and briar tangle, birch skin over bones of gneiss and granite. Bones of the world laid down a billion years ago and raised again in the splitting of continents, divorce of lands; birth of the Highlands in the time of terrible lizards, then scraped and sculpted raw, made this scape of bald rock and gorge during the chill and fever of ice ages. And Pollepel Island like a footnote to so much time, little scar in this big wound of a place.

Silas Desvernine already a rich man when he first came here. Already a man who had traded the Captain's ragtag ferries for a clattering empire of steel and sweat, Desvernine Consolidated Shipyard, turning out ironclad steamers, modern ships to carry modern men across the ocean, to carry men to modern war. And Pollepel chosen for his retreat from industry, the sprawling, ordered chaos of the yard, the noise and careless humanity of Manhattan. First glimpse, an engraving, frontispiece by Mr. N. P. Willis for *American Scenery*: tall sails and rowboat serenity, Storm King rising in the misty distance. The island recalled from his trips up and down the river and the Captain had shown him where George Washington's soldiers sank their *chevaux-de-frises*, sixty-foot logs carved to spikes and tipped with iron, set into stone caissons and dropped into the river off Pollepel to pierce the hulls of British warships.

And this valley already a valley of castles, self-conscious stately, Millionaire's Row decades before Silas' architects began, before his masons laid the first stones, since the coming of the men of new money, the men who nailed shining locomotive track across the nation or milled steel or dug ore and with their fortunes built fashionable hiding places in the wilderness; cultivated, delusory romance of gentleman farmers in brick and marble, iron spires and garden pools. But Silas Desvernine was never a man of society or fashion, and his reasons for coming to Pollepel Island were his own.

Modest monstrosity, second-hand Gothic borrowed from his memory of something glimpsed on a business trip to Scotland, augmented with the architect's taste for English Tudor, and the pale woman he married, Angeline, his wife, never liked the great and empty halls, the cold and damp that never deserted the rooms. The always-sound of the river and the wind, restless in the too-close trees, the boats passing in the night.

If he'd permitted it, Angeline Desvernine would have named the awful house, given a name to tame it, to bind it, make it her home, maybe, instead of whatever else it was. But *No*, Silas said, stern and husbandly refusal, and so no poet ostentation, no Tioranda or Oulagisket or Glenclyffe on his island, just Silas' castle, Silas' Castle.

His dream, and the long night on the Storm King is never precisely the same twice and never precisely the way things happened. And never anything but the truth. The dream and the truth worn thin, as vellum-soft, streampebble-smooth, these moments pressed between the weight of now and then and everything before, and still as terrible.

Younger but not young, reaching back and she takes his hand, or Angeline takes his hand, neither of them, but an encouraging squeeze for this precarious slow climb up and up, above the river, while Prof. Henry Osborn talks, lectures like the man never has to catch his breath, "Watch your step there. A lot of loose stone about," and Silas feels sixty instead of forty-five.

Somewhere near the summit, he lingers, gasping, tearing water eyes and looks down and back, towards his island; a storm coming, on its way up the valley and so twilight settling in early, the day driven like dirty sheep before the thunder-heads, bruisebelly shepherds and the muddy stink of the river on the wind.

"A shame about this weather, though, really," Osborn sighs. "On a clear day, you can see the Catskills and the Shawangunks."

Of course, Osborn wasn't with him that day, this day, and he knows that dimly, dim dream recollection of another history; another climb mixed in with this, the day that Osborn showed him a place where there were broken Iroquois pottery and arrowheads. Osborn, man whose father made a fortune on the Illinois Central and he's never known anything but privilege. The rain begins, then, wet and frying noise, and Henry Osborn squints at the sky, watches it fall as the drops melt his skin away, sugar from skeleton of wrought iron and seam welds; "On a clear day," he whispers from dissolving lips, before his jaw falls, clank and coppertooth scatter, and Silas goes on up the mountain alone.

No one ever asked him the *why* of the collecting, except her. Enough whats and wheres and hows, from the very few who came to the island. The short years when Angeline was alive and she held her big, noisy parties, her balls for the rich from other castles down the valley, for gaudy bits of society and celebrity up from New York City or Philadelphia or Boston. Minor royalty once or twice. The curious who came for a peek inside the silent fortress on Pollepel. Long nights when she pretended this house wasn't different, and he let her play the game, to dull the edge of an isolation already eating her alive.

Later, new visitors, after The Great War that left him more than wealthy, no counting anymore, and Angeline in her lonely grave on the western edge of the island, their son gone to Manhattan, the yard run by so many others that Silas rarely left the island. Let whatever of the world he had need of come to him, and never more than one or two at a time, men and women who came to walk his still halls and wonder at this or that oddity. All of them filled with questions, each their own cyclopedia of esoteric interrogations, lean and shadowy catechists, a hundred investigators of the past and future, the hidden corners of this life and the next. Occultists, spiritualists, those whose askings and experiments left them on the bastard edges of science or religion. They came and he traded them glimpses of half-truths for the small and inconsequential things they'd learned elsewhere. All of them single-minded and they knew, or mostly thought they knew, the why, so no point to ever asking.

That was for her, this one thing he'd brought back to Pollepel that he was afraid of and this one thing he loved beyond words or sanity. The conscious acquisition that could question the collection, the collector.

"I have too much money,' he said once, after the purchase of a plaster replica of Carnegie's *Diplodocus* skeleton to be mounted for the foyer and she asked the sense of it and "It's a way of getting rid of some of the goddamned money," he said.

She blinked her owlslow, owlwise blink at him, her gold and crimson eyes scoffing sadly.

"You know the emptiness inside you, Silas. These things are a poor substitute for the things you're missing." So he'd drawn the draperies on her cage and left them drawn for a week, as long as he could stand to be without the sight of her.

. . .

Nineteen eighteen, so almost three years after his son was pulled screaming from his wife's swollen body, pulled wet and blind into the waiting, dogjawed world; helpless thing the raw colour of a burn. His heir and Silas Desvernine could hardly bear the sight of it, the squalling sound of it. Angeline almost dying in the delivery nightmare of blood and sweat, immeasurable hours of breathless pain and there would be no others, the doctor said. Named for father and grand-father's ghost, Eustace Silas, sickly infant that grew stronger slowly, even as its mother's health began to falter, the raising of her child left to indifferent servants; Silas seeing her less and less often, until, finally, she rarely left her room in the east wing.

And one night, late October and the first winter storm rolling down on Pollepel from the mountains, arctic Catskill breath and Silas away in the city. Intending to be back before dark, but the weather so bad and him exhausted after hours with thickheaded engineers, no patience for the train, so the night spent in the warmth and convenience of his apartment near Central Park.

Some dream or night terror and Angeline left her rooms, wandered half-awake, confused, through the sleeping house, no slippers or stockings, bare feet sneak-thief soft over Turkish carpets and cold stone, looking for something or someone real. Someone to touch or talk to, someone to bring her back to this world from her clinging nightmares. Something against the storm rubbing itself across the walls and windows, savage snowpelt, wild and wanting in and her alone on the second story: the servants down below, her child and his nurse far away in an-other part of the house that, at that derelict hour, seemed to weave endlessly back upon itself. Halls as unfamiliar as if she'd never walked them, doors that opened on rooms she couldn't recall. Strange paintings to watch over her, stranger sights whenever she came to a window to stand staring into the swirling silver night, bare trees and unremembered statuary or hedges. Alien gardens, and all of it so much like the dream, as empty, as hungry; lost in her husband's house and inside herself, Angeline came at last to the mahogany doors to Silas' gallery, wood like old blood and his cabinet beyond, and how many years since she'd come that way? But *this* she recognized, hingecreak and woodsqueal as she stepped across the threshold, the crude design traced into the floor there, design within designs that made her dizzy to look directly at.

"Silas?" and no answer but the storm outside, smothering a dead world. Her so small, so alone at the mouth of this long and cluttered room of glass and dust and careful labels, his grotesquerie, cache of hideous treasures. Everything he loved instead of her; the grey years of hating herself flashing to anger like steam, then, flashing to scalding revelation. Something in her hands, aboriginal weapon or talisman pulled from its bracket on the wall and she swung it in long and ruthless arcs, smashing, breaking, shadow become destroyer. Glass like rain, shatter puddles that sliced at the soles of her feet, splinter and crash and the sicksweet stench of formaldehyde. Angeline imagining gratitude in the blank, green eyes of a two-headed bobcat that tumbled off its pedestal and lay fiercely still, stuffed, mothgnawed, in her path.

And the wail rising up from the depths of her, soul's waters stagnant so long become a tempest to rival the fury and thundervoice of the blizzard. Become a war-cry, dragging her in its red undertow, and when she reached the far side, the high, velvet drapes hiding some final rivalry: tearing at the cloth with her hands, pulling so hard the drapes ripped free of brass rings and slipped like shedding skin to the floor.

Iron bars and at first nothing else, gloom thick as the fog in her head, thick as jam, but nothing more. One step backwards, panting, feeling the damage to her feet, and the subtle shift of light or dark, then, all the nothing coalescing, made solid and beautiful and hateful, hurting eyes that she understood the way she understood her own captivity, her own loneliness.

And the woman with wings and shining bird eyes said her name, *Angeline*, said her name so it meant things she'd never suspected, some way the name held everything she was in three syllables. One long arm out to her, arm too long and thin to believe, skin like moonlight or afterbirth, fingers longer still and pointing to the door of the cage. Padlocked steel and the interlace design from the threshold again, engraved there like a warning; "Please," the woman in the cage said, "Please, Angeline."

Angeline Desvernine ran, then, ran from even the possibility of this pleading thing, door slammed shut behind her, closing it away and closing away the fading illusion of her victory. Almost an hour before she found her way back to her own room, trailing pools and crusting smears of blood from her ruined feet; crawling, hands and knees, at the end. She locked her door, and by then the sound of servants awake, distant commotion, her name called again and again, but there was no comfort left after those eyes, the ragged holes they'd put in her. No way not to see them or hear that silk and thorny voice.

Most of the storm's fury spent by dawn, by the time the maids and cooks and various manservants gave up and called for someone from the stables to take the door off its hinges.

First leadflat light in the empty room, the balcony doors standing open wide and tiny drifts of snow reaching almost to the bed. They found her hanging from the balustrade, noose from curtain cord tiebacks, snow in her tangled black hair, crimson icicles from the sliced flesh of her toes and heels. And her eyes open wide and staring sightless toward the Storm King.

"They're my dreams," he says, whispers loud, and she says "They're lies," and he keeps his eyes on the last colourless smudges of afternoon and says low, mumbled so she won't hear. "Then they're my lies."

This time, this dog-eared incarnation of the climb up Storm King and he's alone, except for the thunder and lightning and rain like wet needles against exposed skin, wind that would take him in its cold fist and fling him, broken, back down to the rocks below, to the impatient, waiting river. No sign anymore of the trail he's followed from the road, faintest path for deer or whatever else might come this way and now even that's gone. He can see in the white spaces after the thunder, flashpowder snapshots of the mountain, trees bending and the hulk of Breakneck across the river, Storm King's twin. Jealous Siamese thing severed by the acid Hudson, and he thinks *No, somewhere deep they're still connected*, still bound safe by their granite vinculum below the water's slash and silt.

Thunder that sounds like angels burning and he slips, catches himself, numb hands into the roots of something small that writhes, woodsy revulsion at his touch, and he's shivering now, the mud and wet straight through his clothes. He lies so still, waiting, to fall, to drown in the gurgling runoff, until the thunder says it's time to get moving again and he opens his eyes. And he's standing at the summit, little clearing and the tall stone at its heart like a stake to hold the world in place. Grey megalith like things he's seen in England or Denmark or France and in the crackling brief electric flash he can see the marks made in the stone, marks smoothed almost away by time and frost and a hundred thousand storms before. Forgotten characters traced in clean rivulets like emphasis. He would turn and run from the place and the moment, *If you had it to do over again, If you could take it back,* but the roots have twisted about his wrists, greensftick pythons and for all his clever, distracting variations, there's only this one way it can go.

She steps out of the place where the stone is, brilliant moment, thinnest sliver of an instant caught and held in forked lightning teeth; the rain that beads, rolls off her feathers, each exquisite, roughgem drop and the strange angles of her arms and legs, too many joints. The head that turns on its elegant neck and the eyes that find him, sharp face and molten eyes that will never let him go.

"Nothing from the Pterodactyle, I shouldn't think," says Professor Osborn, standing somewhere behind him, "though the cranium is oddly reminiscent of the *Dimorphodon,* isn't it?" and Silas Desvernine bows his head, stares down at the soggy darkness where his feet must be and waits for the leather and satin rustle of her wings, gentle loversound through the storm. The rain catches his tears and washes them away with everything else.

The funeral over and the servants busy downstairs when Silas opened the doors of his gallery; viewed the damage she'd done for the first time, knew it was mostly broken glass and little that couldn't be put right again, but the sight hurt his chest, hurt his eyes. Heart already so broken and eyes already so raw but new pain anyway. No bottom to this pain, and he bent over and picked up his dodo, retrieved it from a bed of diamond shards and Silas brushed the glass from its dusty beak and rump feathers. Set it back on the high shelf between passenger pigeons and three Carolina parakeets. Another step closer to her cage, the drapes still pulled open, and his shoes crunched. Her, crouched in the shadows, wings wrapped tight about her like a cocoon, living shield against him, and he said, "What did you do to her, Tisiphone?" And surprised at how calm his voice could be, how empty of everything locked inside him and clawing to get out.

The wings shivered, cringed and folded back; "That's not my name," she said.

"What did you do to her, Megaera?"

"Shut up," words spit at the wall where her face was still hidden, at him, "You know that I'm not one of the three, you've known that all along."

"She couldn't have hurt you, even if she'd wanted to," he said, hearing her words but as close as he would ever come to being able to ignore them: her weak, and his grief too wide to cross even for her voice. "Did you think she could hurt you?" he said.

"No," and shaking her head now, forehead bang and smack against brick and he could see the sticky, black smear she left on the wall.

"Then you did it to get back at me. Is that it? You thought to hurt me by hurting her."

"No," she said and that was the only time he ever saw her cry, if it was crying, the dim phosphorescence leaking from the corners of her eyes. "No, *no* . . ."

"But you know she's dead, don't you?" and "Yes," she said, small yes too quick and it made him want to wring her white throat, lock his strong hands around her neck and twist until he was rewarded with the pop and cartilage grind of ruined vertebrae. Squeeze until her tongue hung useless from her lipless mouth.

"She never hurt anyone, Alecto," he hissed and she turned around, snake-sudden movement and he took a step away from the bars despite himself.

"I asked her to *help* me," and she was screaming now, perfect, crystal teeth bared. "I asked her to free me," and her hurt and fury swept over him, blast furnace heat rushing away from her, and faint smell of nutmeg and decay left in the air around his head.

"I *asked* her to unlock the fucking cage, Silas!" and the wings slipped from off her back and lay bloody and very still on the unclean metal and hay-strewn floor of the cage.

In the simplest sense, these things, at least, are true: that during the last week of June 1916, Silas Desvernine hired workmen from Haverstraw to excavate a large stone from a spot near the summit of Storm King, and that during this excavation several men died or fell seriously ill, each under circumstances that only seemed unusual if considered in connection with one another. When the foreman resigned (mink-eyed little Scotsman with a face like ripe cranberries), Silas hired a second crew and in July the stone was carried down and away from the mountain, ingenious block-and-tackle of his own design, then horse and wagon, and finally, barge, the short distance upriver to Pollepel Island. Moneys were paid to a Mr. Harriman of the Palisades Interstate Park Commission, well enough known for his discretion in such matters, and no questions were asked.

And also, that archaeologists and anthropologists, linguists and cryptographers were allowed brief viewings of the artifact over the next year and only the sketchiest, conflicting conclusions regarding the glyphs on the stone were drawn: that they might have been made by Vikings, or Phoenicians, or Minoans, or Atlanteans; that they might be something like Sanskrit, or perhaps the tracks of prehistoric sea worms, or have been etched by Silas Desvernine himself. The suggestion by a geologist of no particular note, that the stone itself, oily black shale with cream flecks of calcite, was not even native to the region, was summarily ignored by everyone but Silas. Who ignored nothing.

One passing footnote mention of "the Butterhill Stone" in a monograph on Mahican pottery and by 1918 it was forgotten by the busy, forgetful world of men and words beyond the safeguarding walls of Silas' Castle.

"Wake up," she says. "You must wake up," and he does, gummy blink, unfocused, and the room's dark except for the light of brass lamps with stained glass shades like willows and dragonflies and drooping, purple wisteria.

"You're dying, Silas," and he squints towards the great cage, cage that could hold lions or leopards and she looks so terribly small in there. Deceptive contrast of iron and white, white skin, and she says, "Before the sun rises again . . ."

Big sigh rattle from his bony chest and "No," looking about the desk for his spectacles. "No, not yet," but she says "You're an old man, Silas, and old men die, eventually. All of them."

"Not yet," and there they are, his bifocals perched on a thick book about African beetles, "there's a new war, new ships that have to be built," and he slips them on, frame wire bent and straightened and bent again so they won't sit quite right on his face any longer. Walking cane within reach, but he doesn't stand, waits for the murky room to become solid again.

"Let me go now," she says, as if she hasn't said it a thousand thousand times before, as if it were a new idea, never occurred to her before and he laughs. Froggy little strangled sound more like a burp. "You're trying to trick me," he says, grins his false-toothed grin at her and one crooked finger pointed so there can be no doubt. "You're not a sibyl," and it takes him five minutes to remember where he's put his pocket watch.

"I can hear your tired old heart and it's winding down, like your watch," and there it is, in his vest pocket; 4:19, but the hour hand and minute hand and splinter second hand still as ice. He forgets to wind it a lot these days, and how much time has he lost, dozing at his desk? Stiff neck crane and he can see stars through the high windows.

"You can't leave me here, Silas."

"Haven't I *told* you that I won't?" still watching the stars, dim glimpse of Canes Venatici or part of the Little Bear, and the anger in his voice surprising him. "Haven't I said that? That I'll let you go before I die?"

"You're a liar, Silas Desvernine. You'll leave me here with all these other things that you've stolen," and he notices that her eyes have settled on the tall glass case near her cage, four tall panes and the supporting metal rods inside, the shrivelled, leathery things wired there. The dead feathers that have come loose and lie scattered like October leaves at the bottom of the case.

"You would have destroyed them if I hadn't put them there," he mumbles, "Don't tell me that's not the truth," turning away, anything now to occupy his attention, and it was true, that part. That she'd tried to eat them after they'd fallen off, *Jesus Christ*, tried to *eat* them, before he took them away from her, still warm and oozing blood from their ragged stumps.

"*Please*," she whispers, softest, snowflake excuse for sound, and "Please, Silas," as he opens a book, yellowbrown paper to crackle loud between his fingers, and adjusts his bent spectacles.

"I keep my promises," grumbled, and he turns a dry page.

Steve Stern

The Sin of Elijah

Steve Stern is a magic realist of a unique stripe. His writing tends to involve imagery and icons from Jewish lore and culture. His works include The Moon and Ruben Shein, Lazar Malkin Enters Heaven, *and* A Plague of Dreamers.

"The Sin of Elijah" is a wildly original, hilarious, and ultimately disturbing work of fantasy about a voyeuristic, sex-obsessed angel and the innocent souls whose lives he overturns. It comes from Prairie Schooner's *special issue of Jewish-American writers, Spring 1997.*

—T. W.

S omewhere during the couple of millennia that I'd been commuting between heaven and earth, I, Elijah the Tishbite—former prophet of the Northern Kingdom of Israel, translated to Paradise in a chariot of flame while yet alive—became a voyeur. Call me weak, but after you've attended no end of circumcisions, when you've performed an untold number of virtuous deeds and righteous meddlings in a multitude of bewildering disguises, your piety can begin to wear a little thin. Besides, good works had ceased to generate the kind of respect they'd once commanded in the world, a situation that took its toll on one's self-esteem; so that even I, old as I was, had become susceptible from time to time to the *yetser horah*, the evil impulse.

That's how I came to spy on the Fefers, Feyvush and Gitl, in their love nest on the Lower East Side of New York. You might say that observing the passions of mortals, often with stern disapproval, had always been a hobby of mine; but of late it was their more intimate pursuits that took my fancy. Still, I had standards. As a whiff of sanctity always clung to my person from my sojourns in the Upper Eden, I lost interest where the dalliance of mortals was undiluted by some measure of earnest affection. And the young Fefer couple, they adored each other with a love that surpassed their own understanding. Indeed, so fervent was the heat of their voluptuous intercourse that they sometimes feared it might consume them and they would perish of sheer ecstasy.

I happened upon them one miserable midsummer evening when I was making my rounds of the East Side ghetto, which in those years was much in need of my benevolent visitations. I did a lot of good, believe me, spreading banquets on the tables of the desolate families in their coal cellars, exposing the villains posing as suitors to young girls fresh off the boat. I even engaged in spirited disputes with the *apikorsin*, the unbelievers, in an effort to vindicate God's justice to man—a thankless task, to say the least, in that swarming, heretical, typhus-infested neighborhood. So was it any wonder that with the volume of dirty work that fell to my hands, I should occasionally seek some momentary diversion?

You might call it a waste that one with my gift for camouflage, who could have gained clandestine admittance backstage at the Ziegfeld Follies when Anna Held climbed out of her milk bath, or, slipped unnoticed into the green room at the People's Theater where Tomashevsky romped au naturel with his zaftig harem, that I should return time and again to the tenement flat of Feyvush and Gitl Fefer. But then you never saw the Fefers at their amorous business.

To be sure, they weren't what you'd call prepossessing. Feyvush, a cobbler by profession, was stoop-shouldered and hollow-breasted, nose like a parrot's beak, hair a wreath of swiftly evaporating black foam. His bride was a green-eyed, pear-shaped little hausfrau, freckles stippling her cheeks as if dripped from the brush that daubed her rust-red pompadour. Had you seen them in the streets—Feyvush with nostrils flaring from the stench, his arm hooked through Gitl's from whose free hand dangled the carcass of an unflicked chicken—you would have deemed them in no way remarkable. But at night when they turned down the gas lamp in their stuffy bedroom, its window giving on to the fire escape (where I stooped to watch), they were the Irene and Vernon Castle of the clammy sheets.

At first they might betray a charming awkwardness. Feyvush would fumble with the buttons of Gitl's shirtwaist, tugging a little frantically at corset laces, hooks and eyes. He might haul without ceremony the shapeless muslin shift over her head, shove the itchy cotton drawers below her knees. Just as impatiently Gitl would yank down the straps of her spouse's suspenders, pluck the studs from his shirt, the rivets from his fly; she would thrust chubby fingers between the seams of his union suit with the same impulsiveness that she plunged her hand in a barrel to snatch a herring. Then they would tumble onto the sagging iron bed, its rusty springs complaining like a startled henhouse. At the initial shock of flesh pressing flesh, they would clip, squeeze, and fondle whatever was most convenient, as if each sought a desperate assurance that the other was real. But once they'd determined as much, they slowed the pace; they lulled their frenzy to a rhythmic investigation of secret contours, like a getting acquainted of the blind.

They postponed the moment of their union for as long as they could stand to. While Feyvush sucked on her nipples till they stood up like gumdrops, Gitl gaily pulled out clumps of her husband's hair; while he traced with his nose the line of ginger fur below her navel the way a flame follows a fuse, she held his hips like a rampant divining rod over the wellspring of her womb. When their loins were finally locked together, it jarred them so that they froze for an instant, each seeming to ask the other in tender astonishment: "What did we do?" Then the bed would gallop from wardrobe to washstand, the neighbors pounding on their ceilings with brooms, until Feyvush and Gitl spent themselves, I swear it, in a shower of sparks. It was an eruption that in others might have catapulted their spirits clear out of their bodies—but not the Fefers, who clung tenaciously to one another rather than suffer even a momentary separation from their better half.

Afterwards, as they lay in a tangle, hiding their faces in mutual embarrassment over such a bounty of delight, I would slope off. My prurient interests satisfied, I was released from impure thoughts; I was free, a stickiness in the pants not-withstanding, to carry on with cleansing lepers and catering the weddings of the honest poor. So as you see, my spying on the Fefers was a tonic, a clear case of the ends justifying the means.

How was it I contrived to stumble upon such a talented pair in the first place? Suffice it that, when you've been around for nearly three thousand years, you develop antennae. It's a sensitivity that, in my case, was partial compensation for the loss of my oracular faculty, an exchange of roles from clairvoyant to voyeur. While I might not be able to predict the future with certainty anymore, I could intuit where and when someone was getting a heartfelt shtupping.

But like I say, I didn't let my fascination with the Fefers interfere with the performance of good works; the tally of my *mitzvot* was as great as ever. Greater perhaps, since my broader interests kept me closer than usual to earth, some-times neglecting the tasks that involved a return to Kingdom Come. (Sometimes I put off escorting souls back to the afterlife, a job I'd never relished, involving as it did what amounted to cleaning up after the Angel of Death.) Whenever the opportunity arose, my preoccupation with Feyvush and Gitl might move me to play the detective. While traveling in their native Galicia, for instance, I would stop by the study house, the only light on an otherwise deserted street in the abandoned village of Krok. This was the Fefers' home village, a place existing just this side of memory, reduced by pogrom and expulsions to broken chimneys, a haunted bathhouse, scattered pages of the synagogue register among the dead leaves. The only survivors being a dropsical rabbi and his skeleton crew of dis-ciples, it was to them I appealed for specifics.

"Who could forget?" replied the old rabbi stroking a snuff yellow beard, the wen on his brow like a sightless third eye. "After their wedding he comes to me, this Feyvush: 'Rabbi,' he says guiltily, 'is not such unspeakable pleasure a sin?' I tell him: 'In the view of Yohanan ben Dabai, a man may do what he will with his wife; within the zone of the marriage bed all is permitted.' He thanks me and runs off before I can give him the opinion of Rabbi Eliezer, who suggests that, while having intercourse, one should think on arcane points of law. . . ."

I liked to imagine their wedding night. Hadn't I witnessed enough of them in my time?—burlesque affairs wherein the child bride and groom, martyrs to arranged marriages, had never set eyes on one another before. They were usually frightened to near paralysis, their only preparation a lecture from some doting melamed or a long-suffering mother's manual of medieval advice. "What's God been doing since He created the world?" goes the old question. Answer: "He's been busy making matches." But the demoralized condition of the children to whose nuptials I was assigned smacked more of the intervention of pushy families than the hand of God.

No wonder I was so often called on to give a timid bridegroom a nudge. Employing my protean powers—now regrettably obsolete, though I still regard myself a master of stealth—I might take the form of a bat or the shimmying flame of a hurricane lamp to scare the couple into each other's arms. (Why I never lost patience and stood in for the fainthearted husband myself, I can't say.) Certainly there's no reason to suppose that Dvora Malkeh's Feyvush, the cobbler's apprentice, was any braver when it came to bedding his own stranger bride—his Gitl, who at fifteen was two years his junior, the only daughter of Chaim Rupture the porter, her dowry a hobbled goat and a dented tin kiddush cup. It was not what you'd have called a brilliant match.

Still, I liked to picture the moment when they're alone for the first time in their bridal chamber, probably some shelf above a stove encircled by horse blankets. In the dark Feyvush has summoned the courage to strip to his talis koton, its ritual fringes dangling a flimsy curtain over his knocking knees. Gitl has peeled in one anxious motion to her starchless shift and slid gingerly beneath the thistledown, where she's joined after a small eternity by the tremulous groom. They lie there without speaking, without touching, having forgotten (respectively) the rabbi's sage instruction and the diagrams in *The Saffron Sacrament*. They only know that the warm (albeit shuddering) flesh beside them has a magnetism as strong as gravity, so that each feels they've been falling their whole lives into the other's embrace. And afterwards there's nothing on earth—neither goat's teat nor cobbler's last, pickle jar, poppy seed, Cossack's knout, or holy scroll— that doesn't echo their common devotion.

Or so I imagined. I also guessed that their tiny hamlet must have begun to seem too cramped to contain such an abundance of mutual affection. It needed a shtetl, say, the size of Tarnopol, or a teeming city as large as Lodz to accommodate them; or better: for a love that defied possibility, a land where the impossible (as was popularly bruited) was the order of the day. America was hardly an original idea—I never said the Fefers were original, only unique—but emboldened by the way that wedded bliss had transformed their ramshackle birthplace, they must have been curious to see how love traveled.

You might have thought the long ocean passage, at the end of which waited only a dingy dumbbell tenement on Orchard Street, would have cooled their ardor. Were their New World circumstances any friendlier to romance than the Old? Feyvush worked twelve-hour days in a bootmaking loft above the butcher's shambles in Gouverneur Slip, while Gitl haggled with fishmongers and supplemented her husband's mean wages stitching artificial flowers for ladies' hats. The streets swarmed with hucksters, ganefs, and handkerchief girls who solicited in the shadows of buildings draped in black bunting. Every day the funeral trains of cholera victims plied the market crush, displacing vendors crying spoiled meat above the locust-hum of the sewing machines. The summers brought a heat that made ovens of the tenements, sending the occupants to their roofs where they inhaled a cloud of blue flies; and in winter the ice hung in tusks from the common faucets, the truck horses froze upright in their tracks beside the curb.

But if the ills of the ghetto were any impediment to their ongoing conjugal fervor, you couldn't have proved it by the Feyvush and Gitl I knew.

They were after all no strangers to squalor, and the corruptions of the East Side had a vitality not incompatible with the Fefers' own sweet delirium. Certainly there was a stench, but there was also an exhilaration: there were passions on display in the music halls and the Yiddish theaters, where Jacob Adler or Bertha Kalish could be counted on nightly to tear their emotions to shreds. You had the dancing academies where the greenhorns groped one another in a macabre approximation of the turkey trot, the Canal Street cafes where the poets and revolutionaries fought pitched battles with an arsenal of words; you had the shrill and insomniac streets. Content as they were to keep to themselves, the Fefers were not above rubbernecking. They liked to browse the Tenth Ward's gallery of passions, comparing them—with some measure of pride—unfavorably to their own.

Sometimes I thought the Fefers nurtured their desire for each other as if it were an altogether separate entity, a member of the family if you will. Of course the mystery remained that such heroic lovemaking as theirs had yet to produce any offspring, which was certainly not for want of trying. Indeed, they'd never lost sight of the sacramental aspect of their intimacy, or the taboos against sharing a bed for purposes other than procreation. They had regularly consulted with local midwives, purchasing an assortment of bendls, simples, and fertility charms to no avail. (Gitl had even gone so far as to flush her system with mandrake enemas against a possible evil eye.) But once, as I knelt outside their window during a smallpox-ridden summer (when caskets the size of bread pans were carried from the tenements night and day), I heard Feyvush suggest:

"Maybe no babies is for such a plenty of pleasure the price we got to pay?"

You didn't have to be a prophet to see it coming. What could you expect when a pair of mortals routinely achieved orgasms like Krakatoa, their loins shooting sparks like the uncorking of a bottle of pyrotechnical champagne? Something had to give, and with hindsight I can see that it had to happen on Shabbos, when married folk are enjoined to go at their copulation as if ridden by demons. Their fervent cleaving to one another (*dveykuss* the kabbalists call it) is supposed to hasten the advent of Messiah, or some such poppycock. Anyway, the Fefers had gathered momentum over the years, enduring climaxes of such convulsive magnitude that their frames could scarcely contain the exaltation. And since they clung to each other with a ferocity that refused to release spirit from flesh, it was only a matter of time until their transports carried them bodily aloft.

I was in Paradise when it happened, doing clerical work. Certain bookkeeping tasks were entrusted to me, such as totting up the debits and credits of incoming souls—tedious work that I alternated with the more restful occupation of weaving garlands of prayers; but even this had become somewhat monotonous, a mindless therapy befitting the sanatorium-like atmosphere of Kingdom Come. For such employment I chose a quiet stone bench (what bench wasn't quiet?) along a garden path near the bandstand. (Paradise back then resembled those sepia views of Baden-Baden or Saratoga Springs in their heyday; though of late the place, fallen into neglect, has more in common with the seedier precincts of Miami Beach.) At dusk I closed the ledger and tossed the garlands into the boughs of the Tree of Life, already so festooned with ribbons of prayer that the dead, in their wistfulness, compared it to a live oak hung with Spanish moss. Myself, I thought of a peddler of suspenders on the Lower East Side.

I was making my way along a petal-strewn walk toward the gates in my honorary angel getup—quilted smoking jacket, tasseled fez, a pair of rigid, lint-white wings. Constructed of chicken wire and papier-mâché, they were just for show, the wings, about as useful as an ostrich's. I confess this was a source of some resentment, since why shouldn't I merit the genuine article? As for the outfit, having selected it myself I couldn't complain; certainly it was smart, though the truth was I preferred my terrestrial shmattes. But in my empyrean role as Sandolphon the Psychopomp, whose responsibilities included the orientation of lost souls, I was expected to keep up appearances.

So I'm headed toward the park gates when I notice this hubbub around a turreted gazebo. Maybe I should qualify "hubbub," since the dead, taking the air in their lightweight golfing costumes and garden party gowns, were seldom moved to curiosity. Nevertheless, a number had paused in their twilight stroll to inspect some new development under the pavilion on the lawn. Approaching, I charged the spectators to make way. Then I ascended the short flight of steps to see an uninvited iron bed supplanting the tasteful wicker furniture; and on that rumpled, bow-footed bed lay the Fefers, man and wife, in flagrant delicto. Feyvush, with his pants still down around his hairy ankles, and Gitl, her shift rucked to the neck, were holding on to each other for dear life.

As you may know, it wasn't without precedent for unlicensed mortals to enter the Garden alive. Through the ages you'd had a smattering of overzealous mystics who'd arrived by dint of pious contemplation, only to expire outright from the exertion. But to my knowledge Feyvush and Gitl were the first to have made the trip via the agency of ecstatic intercourse. They had, in effect, shtupped their way to heaven.

I moved forward to cover their nakedness with the quilt, though there was really no need for modesty in the Upper Eden, where unlike in the fallen one innocence still obtained.

"I bet you're wondering where it is that you are," was all I could think to say.

They nodded in saucer-eyed unison. When I told them Paradise, their eyes flicked left and right like synchronized wipers on a pair of stalled locomobiles. Then just as I'd begun to introduce myself ("the mock-angel Sandolphon here, though you might know me better as . . ."), an imperious voice cut me off.

"I'll take care of this—that is of course if *you* don't mind . . ."

It was the archangel Metatron, né Enoch ben Seth, celestial magistrate, commissary, archivist, and scribe. Sometimes called Prince of the Face (his was a chiseled death mask with one severely arched brow), he stood with his hands clasped before him, a thin gray eminence rocking on his heels. He was dressed like an undertaker, the nudnik, in a sable homburg and frock coat, its seams neatly split at the shoulders to make room for an impressive set of ivory wings. Unlike my own pantomime pair, Enoch's worked. While much too dignified to actually use them, he was not above preening them in my presence, flaunting the wings as an emblem of a higher status that he seldom let me forget. He had it in for me because I served as a reminder that he too had once been a human being. Like me he'd been translated in the prime of life in an apotheosis of flames to Kingdom Come. Never mind that his assumption had included the further awards of functional feathers and an investiture as full seraph; he still couldn't forgive me for recalling his humble origins, the humanity he'd never entirely outgrown.

"Welcome to the Upper Eden," the archangel greeted the bedridden couple, "the bottommost borough of Olam ha-Ba, the World to Come." And on a cautionary note, "You realize of course that your arrival here is somewhat, how shall we say, premature?"

With the quilt hoisted to their chins, the Fefers nodded in concert—as what else should they do?

"However," continued Enoch, whose flashier handle I'd never gotten used to, which insubordination he duly noted, "accidents will happen, eh? and we must make the best of an irregular state of affairs. So," he gave a dispassionate sniff, brushing stardust or dandruff from an otherwise immaculate sleeve, "if you'll be so good as to follow me, I'll show you to your quarters." He turned abruptly and for a moment we were nose to nose (my potato to Enoch's flutey yam), until I was forced to step aside.

Feyvush and Gitl exchanged bewildered glances, then shrugged. Clutching the quilt about their shoulders, they climbed out of bed—Feyvush stumbling over his trousers as Gitl stifled a nervous laugh—and scrambled to catch up with the peremptory angel. They trailed him down the steps of the gazebo under the boughs of the Tree of Life, in which the firefly lanterns had just become visible in the gloaming. Behind them the little knot of immortals drifted off in their interminable promenade.

"What's the hurry?" I wanted to call out to the Fefers; I wanted a chance to give them the benefit of my experience to help them get their bearings. Wasn't that the least I could do for the pair who'd provided me with such a spicy pastime over the years? Outranked, however, I had no alternative but to tag along unobtrusively after.

Enoch led them down the hedge-bordered broadwalk between wrought iron gates, their arch bearing the designation GANEYDN in gilded Hebrew characters. They crossed a cobbled avenue and ascended some steps onto a veranda where a thousand cypress rockers ticked like a chorus of pendulums. (Understand that Paradise never went in for the showier effects: none of your sardonyx portals and myriads of ministering angels wrapped in clouds of glory, no rivers of balsam, honey, and wine. There, in deference to the sensibilities of the deceased, earthly standards abide; the splendor remains human-scale, though odd details from the loftier regions sometimes trickle down.)

Through mahogany doors thrown open to the balmy air, they entered the lobby of the grand hotel that serves as dormitory for the dead. Arrested by their admiration for the acres of carpets and carved furniture, the formal portraits of archons in their cedar of Lebanon frames, the chandeliers, Feyvush and Gitl lagged behind. They craned their necks to watch phoenixes smoldering like smudge pots gliding beneath the arcaded ceiling, while Enoch herded them into the elevator's brass cage. Banking on the honeymoon suite, I took the stairs and, preternaturally spry for my years, slipped in after them as Enoch showed the couple their rooms. Here again the Fefers were stunned by the sumptuous appointments: the marble-topped whatnot, the divan stuffed with angel's hair, the Brussels lace draperies framing balustraded windows open to a view of the park. From its bandstand you could hear the silvery yodel of a famous dead cantor chanting the evening prayers.

Inconspicuous behind the open door, my head wreathed in a Tiffany lampshade, I watched the liveried cherubs parade into the bedroom, dumping their burdens of fresh apparel on the canopied bed.

"I trust you'll find these accommodations satisfactory," Enoch was saying in all insincerity, "and that your stay here will be a pleasant one." Rubbing the hands he was doubtless eager to wash of this business, he began to mince backward toward the door.

Under the quilt that mantled the Fefers, Feyvush started as from a poke in the ribs. He looked askance at his wife who gave him a nod of encouragement, then ventured a timid, "Um, if it please your honor," another nudge, "for how long do we supposed to stay here?"

Replied Enoch: "Why, forever of course."

Another dig with her elbow failed to move her tongue-tied husband, and Gitl spoke up herself. "You mean we ain't got to die?"

"God forbid," exhaled Enoch a touch sarcastically, his patience with their naiveté at an end: it was a scandal how the living lacked even the minimal sophistication of the dead. "Now, if there are no further questions . . . ?" Already backed into the corridor, he reminded them that room service was only a bell pull away, and was gone.

Closing the door (behind which my camouflaged presence made no impression at all), Feyvush turned to Gitl and asked, "Should we have gave him a tip?"

Gitl practically choked in her attempt to suppress a titter whose contagion spread to Feyvush. A toothy grin making fish-shaped crescents of his goggle eyes, he proceeded to pinch her all over, and together they dissolved in a fit of hysterics that buckled their knees. They rolled about on the emerald carpet, then picked themselves up in breathless dishevelment, abandoning their quilt to make a beeline for the bedroom.

Oh boy, I thought, God forgive me; now they'll have it off in heaven and their aphrodisiac whoops will drive the neutered seraphim to acts of depravity. But instead of flinging themselves headlong onto the satin counterpane, they paused to inspect their laidout wardrobe—or "trousseau" as Gitl insisted on calling it.

Donning a wing collar shirt with boiled bosom, creased flannel trousers, and a yachting blazer with a yellow Shield of David crest, Feyvush struck rakish poses for his bride. Gitl wriggled into a silk corset cover, over which she pulled an Empire tea gown, over which an ungirded floral kimono. At the smoky-mirrored dressing table she daubed her round face with scented powders; she made raccoon's eyes of her own with an excess of shadow, scattered a shpritz of sparkles over the bonfire of her hair. Between her blown breasts she hung a sapphire the size of a gasolier.

While she carried on playing dress-up, Feyvush tugged experimentally on the bell-pull, which was answered by an almost instantaneous knock at the door. Feyvush opened it to admit a tea trolley wheeled by a silent creature (pillbox hat and rudimentary wings) who'd no sooner appeared than bowed himself out. Relaxing the hand that held the waived gratuity, Feyvush fell to contemplating the covered dish and pitcher on the trolley. Pleased with her primping, Gitl rose to take the initiative. The truth was, the young Mrs. Fefer was no great shakes in the kitchen, the couple having always done their "cooking" (as Talmud puts it) in bed. Nevertheless, with a marked efficiency, she lifted the silver lid from the dish, faltering at the sight of the medicinal blue bottle underneath. Undiscouraged, however, she tipped a bit of liver brown powder from the bottle onto the plate, then mixed in a few drops of water from the crystal pitcher. There was a foaming after which the powder assumed the consistency of clotted tapioca. Gitl dipped in a finger, gave it a tentative lick, smacked her lips, and sighed. Then she dipped the finger again, placing it this time on her husband's extended tongue. Feyvush too closed his eyes and sighed, which was the signal for them both to tuck in with silver spoons. Cheeks bulging, they exulted over the succulent feast of milchik and fleishik flavors that only manna can evoke.

Having placated their bellies, you might have expected them to turn to the satisfaction of other appetites. But instead of going back to the bedroom, they went to the open windows and again looked out over the Garden. Listening to the still warbling cantor (to be followed in that evening's program by a concert of Victor Herbert standards—though not before at least half a century'd passed on earth), they were so enraptured they forgot to embrace. Up here where perfection was the sine qua non, they required no language or gesture to improve on what was already ideal.

Heartsick, I replaced the lampshade and slunk out. I know it was unbecoming my rank and position to be disappointed on account of mere mortals; after all, if the Fefers had finally arrived at the logical destination of their transports, then good on them! What affair was it of mine? But now that it was time I mounted another expedition to the fallen world—babies, paupers, and skeptics were proliferating like mad—I found I lacked the necessary incentive. This is not to say I was content to stay on in Paradise, where I was quite frankly bored, but neither did a world without the Fefers have much appeal.

It didn't help that I ran into them everywhere, tipping my fez somewhat coolly whenever we crossed paths—which was often, since Feyvush and Gitl, holding hands out of habit, never tired of exploring the afterlife. At first I tried to ignore them, but idle myself, I fell into an old habit of my own. I tailed them as they joined the ranks of the perpetual strollers meandering among the topiary hedges, loitering along the gravel walks and bridle paths. I suppose that for a tourist the Garden did have its attractions: you've got your quaint scale reproductions of the industries of the upper heavens, such as a mill for grinding manna, a quarry of souls. There's a zoo that houses some of the beasts that run wild in the more ethereal realms: a three-legged "man of the mountain," a sullen behemoth with a barnacled hide, a petting zoo containing a salamander hatched from a myrtle flame. But having readjusted my metabolism to conform to the hours of earth, I wondered when the Fefers would wake up. When would they notice, say, that the fragrant purple dusk advanced at only a glacial pace toward dawn; that the dead, however well-dressed and courteous, were rather, well, stiff and cold?

In the end, though, my vigilance paid off. After what you would call about a week (though the Shabbos eve candles still burned in the celestial yeshivas), I was fortunate enough to be on hand when the couple sounded their first note of discontent. Hidden in plain sight in their suite (in the pendulum cabinet of a grandfather clock), I overheard Feyvush broach a troubling subject with his wife. Having sampled some of the outdoor prayer minyans that clustered about the velvet lawns, he complained, "It ain't true, Gitteleh, the stories that they're telling about the world." Because in their discourses on the supernatural aspects of history, the dead, due to a faulty collective memory, tended to overlook the essential part of being alive: that it was natural.

Seated at her dressing table, languidly unscrolling the bobbin of her pompadour, letting it fall like carrot shavings over her forehead, Gitl ventured a complaint of her own. He should know that in the palatial bathhouse she attended—it was no longer unusual for the couple to spend time apart—the ladies snubbed her. "For them, to be flesh and blood is a sin."

She was wearing a glove-silk chemise that might have formerly inspired her husband to feats of erotic derring-do. Stepping closer, Feyvush tried to reassure her, "I think they're jealous."

Gitl gave a careless shrug.

At her shoulder Feyvush continued cautiously, "Gitl, remember how," pausing to gather courage, "remember how on the Day of Atonement we played 'blowing the shofar'?"

Gitl stopped fussing with her hair, nodded reflexively.

"Do you remember how on Purim I would part like the pages of Megillah . . ." here an intake of air in the lungs of both parties ". . . your legs?"

Again an almost mechanical nod.

"Gitl," submitted Feyvush just above a whisper, "do you miss it that I don't touch you that way no more?"

She put down the tortoiseshell hairbrush, cocked her head thoughtfully, then released an arpeggio of racking sobs. "Like the breath of life I miss it!" she wailed, as Feyvush, his own frustrations confirmed, fell to his knees and echoed her lament.

"Gitteleh," he bawled, burying his face in her lap, "ain't nobody fency yentzing in Kingdom Come!" Then lifting his head to blow his nose on a brocaded shirtsleeve, drying his eyes with same, he hesitantly offered, "Maybe we could try to go home . . ."

"Hallelujah!"

This was me bursting forth from the clock to congratulate them on a bold resolution. "Now you're talking!" I assured them. "Of course it won't be easy; into the Garden you got without a dispensation but without a dispensation they won't never let you leave . . ." Then I observed how the Fefers, not yet sufficiently jaded from their stay in heaven, were taken aback. Having leapt to their feet, they'd begun to slide away from me along the paneled walls, which was understandable: for despite my natty attire, my features had become somewhat crepe-hung over the ages, my rheumy eyes tending toward the hyacinth red.

Recalling the introduction I never completed upon their arrival, I started over. "Allow me to present myself: the prophet Elijah, at your service. You would recognize me better in the rags I wear in the world." And as they still appeared dubious, Gitl smearing her already runny mascara as if in an effort to wipe me from her eye, I entreated them to relax: "You can trust me." I explained that I wanted to help them get back to where they belonged.

This at least had the effect of halting their retreat, which in turn called my bluff.

"You should understand," I began to equivocate, "there ain't much I can do personally. Sure, I'm licensed to usher souls from downstairs to up, but regarding vicey-versey I got no jurisdiction, my hands are tied. And from here to there you don't measure the distance in miles but dozens of years, so don't even think about starting the journey on your own . . ."

At that point Gitl, making chins (their ambrosial diet had endowed her with several extra), planted an elbow in Feyvush's ribs. He coughed once before speaking. "If it please your honor," his listless tone not half so respectful as he'd been with Enoch, "what is it exactly you meaning to do?"

I felt a foolish grin spreading like eczema across my face. "What I have in mind . . . ," I announced on a note of confidence that instantly fell flat, because I didn't really have a clue. Rallying nonetheless, I voiced my determination to intercede with the archangel Metatron on the couple's behalf.

Who was I kidding? That stickler for the letter of the Law, he wouldn't have done me a favor if his immortality depended on it. Still, a promise was a promise, so I sought out his high-and-mightiness in his apartments in the dignitaries' wing of the hotel. (My own were among the cottages of the superannuated cherubim.)

Addressing him by his given name, I'm straightaway off on the wrong foot.

"Sorry . . . I mean Metatron, Prince of the Face (such a face!), Lesser Lord of the Seventy Names, and so forth," I said, attempting to smooth his ruffled pride. It seemed that Enoch had never gotten over the treatment attending his translation, when the hosts mockingly claimed they could smell one of woman born from a myriad of parasangs away. "Anyhow," putting my foot in it deeper, "they had a nice holiday, the Fefers, but they would like already to go back where they came."

Seated behind the captain's desk in his office sipping a demitasse with uplifted pinky, his back to a wall of framed citations and awards, the archangel assumed an expression of puzzled innocence. Did I have to spell it out?

"You know, like home."

"Home?" inquired Enoch, as if butter wouldn't melt on his unctuous tongue. "Why, this is their home for all eternity."

Apparently I wasn't going to be invited to sit down. "But they ain't happy here," I persisted.

"Not happy in Paradise?" Plunking down his cup and saucer as if the concept was unheard of.

"It's possible," I allowed a bit too emphatically. Enoch clucked his tongue, which provoked me to state the obvious. "Lookit, they ain't dead yet."

"A mere technicality," pooh-poohed the archangel. "Besides, for those who've dwelt in Abraham's Bosom, the earth should no longer hold any real attraction."

Though I was more or less living proof to the contrary, rather than risk antagonizing him again, I kept mum on that subject. Instead: "Have a heart," I appealed to him. "You were alive when you came here . . ." Which didn't sound the way I meant it. "Didn't you ever want to go back?"

"Back?" Enoch was incredulous. "Back to what, making shoes?"

That he'd lowered his guard enough to mention his mortal profession made me think I saw an angle. "Feyvush is a cobbler," I humbly submitted.

"Then he's well out of it." The seraph stressed the point by raising his arched brow even higher, creating ripples that spoiled the symmetry of his widow's peak. "Besides, when I stitched leather, it was as if I fastened the world above to the world below."

"But don't you see," I pleaded, the tassle of my fez dancing like a spider in front of my eyes till I slapped it away, "that's what it was like when Feyvush would yentz with his bride . . ." This was definitely not the tack to have taken.

"Like I said, he's better off," snapped Enoch, rising abruptly from his swivel chair to spread his magnificent wings. "And since when is any of this *your* business?"

Conversation closed, I turned to go, muttering something about how I guessed I was just a sentimental fool.

"Elijah . . . ," the angel called my name after a fashion guaranteed to inspire maximum guilt.

"Sandolphon," I corrected him under my breath.

". . . I think it's time you tended to your terrestrial errands."

"Funny," I replied in an insipid singsong, "I was thinking the same thing."

You'll say I should have left well enough alone, and maybe you're right. After all, without my meddling the Fefers would still be in heaven and I pursuing my charitable rounds on earth—instead of sentenced for my delinquency to stand here at this crossroads directing traffic, pointing the pious toward the gates, the wicked in the other direction, not unlike (to my everlasting shame) that nazi doctor on the railroad platform during the last apocalypse. But who'd have thought that, with my commendable record of good works, I wasn't entitled to a single trespass?

When I offered the Fefers my plan, Gitl elbowed Feyvush, then interrupted his diffident "If it please your honor—" to challenge me herself: "What for do you want to help us?"

"Because," since my audience with the archangel I'd developed a ready answer, "I can't stand to see nobody downhearted in Paradise. This is my curse, that such *rachmones*, such compassion I got, I can't stand it to see nobody downhearted anywhere." Which was true enough. It was an attitude that kept me constantly at odds with the angelic orders, with Enoch and Raziel and Death (between whom and myself there was a history of feuding) and the rest of that coldblooded crew. It was my age-old humanitarian impulse that compelled me to come to the aid of the Fefers, right? and not just a selfish desire to see them at their shtupping again.

Departing the hotel, we moved through whatever pockets of darkness the unending dusk provided—hard to find in a park whose every corner was illumined by menorahs and fairy lights. Dressed for traveling (Feyvush in an ulster and fore-and-aft cap, Gitl in automobile cape and sensible shoes), they were irked with me, my charges, for making them leave behind a pair of overstuffed Gladstone bags. Their aggravation signified an ambivalence which, in my haste to get started, I chose to ignore, and looking back I confess I might have been a little pushy. Anyway, in order not to call attention to ourselves (small danger among the indifferent immortals), I pretended I was conducting yet another couple of greenhorns on a sightseeing tour of the Garden.

"Here you got your rose trellis made out of what's left of Jacob's Ladder, and over there, that scrawny thing propped on a crutch, that's the *etz ha-daat*, the Tree of Knowledge . . ."

When I was sure no one was looking, I hauled the Fefers behind me into the shadows beneath the bloated roots of the Tree of Life. From a hanger in their midst I removed my universal luftmensch outfit—watch cap, galoshes, and patched overcoat—which I quick-changed into after discarding my Sandolphon duds. Then I led the fugitives into a narrow cavern that snaked its way under the Tree trunk, fetching up at the rust-cankered door of a dumbwaiter.

I'd discovered it some time ago while looking for an easier passage to earth. My ordination as honorary angel, while retarding the aging process, had not, as you know, halted it entirely, so I was in need of a less strenuous means of descent than was afforded by the branches of the Tree of Life. An antique device left over from the days when the Lord would frequent the Garden to send the odd miracle below, the dumbwaiter was just the thing. It was a sturdy enough contraption that, notwithstanding the sponginess of its wooden cabinet and the agonizing groans of its cables, had endured the test of time.

The problem was that the dumbwaiter's compactness was not intended to accommodate three people. A meager, collapsible old man, I'd always found it sufficiently roomy; but while the Fefers were not large, Gitl had never been exactly svelte, and both of them had put on weight during their "honeymoon." Nevertheless, making a virtue of necessity, they folded themselves into a tandem pair of S's and allowed me to stuff them into the tight compartment. This must have been awkward for them at first, since they hadn't held each other in a while, but as I wedged myself into the box behind them and started to lower us down the long shaft, Feyvush and Gitl began to generate a sultry heat.

They ceased their griping about cramped quarters and began to make purring noises of a type that brought tears to my eyes. I felt an excitement beyond that which accrued from our gathering speed, as the tug of gravity accelerated the dumbwaiter's downward progress. The cable sang as it slipped through my blistering fingers; then came the part where our stomachs were in our throats and we seemed to be in a bottomless free-fall, which was the dizzy, protracted prelude to the earth-shaking clatter of our landing. The crash must have alerted the cooks in the basement kitchen of Ratner's Dairy Restaurant to our arrival; because, when I slid open the door, there they were: a surly lot in soiled aprons and mushroom hats, looking scornfully at the pretzel the Fefers had made of themselves. I appeased them as always with a jar of fresh manna, an ingredient (scarce in latter-day New York) they'd come to regard as indispensable for their heavenly blintzes.

If the plummeting claustrophobia of the dumbwaiter, to say nothing of its bumpy landing, hadn't sufficiently disoriented my charges, then the shrill Sunday brunch crowd I steered them through would have finished the job. I hustled them without fanfare out the revolving door into a bitter blast of winter barreling up Delancey Street from the river.

"Welcome home!" I piped, though the neighborhood bore small resemblance to the one they'd left better than three-quarters of a century ago. The truck horses and trolleys had been replaced by a metallic current of low-slung vehicles squealing and farting in sluggish procession; the pushcarts and garment emporia had given way to discount houses full of coruscating gadgetry, percussive music shuddering their plate-glass windows. Old buildings, if they weren't boarded up or reduced altogether to rubble, had new facades, as tacky as hoop skirts on dowagers. In the distance there were towers, their tops obscured by clouds like tentpoles under snow-heavy canvas.

Myself, I'd grown accustomed to dramatic changes during my travels back and forth. Besides, I made a point of keeping abreast of things, pumping the recently departed for news of the earth, lest returning be too great a jolt to my system. But the Fefers, though they'd demonstrated a tolerance for shock in the past, seemed beyond perplexity now, having entered a condition of outright fear.

Gitl was in back of her husband, trying to straighten his crimped spine with her knee, so that he seemed to speak with her voice when she asked, "What happened to the Jews?" Because it was true that, while the complexions of the passers-by ran the spectrum from olive to saffron to lobster pink, there were few you could've identified as distinctly yid.

I shrugged. "Westchester, New Rochelle, Englewood, the Five Towns they went, but for delicatessen they come back to Delancey on Sundays." Then I grinned through my remaining teeth and made a show of protesting, "No need to thank me," though who had bothered? I shook their hands, which were as limp as fins. "Well, goodbye and good luck, I got things to do . . ."

I had urgent business to attend to, didn't I?—brisses, famines, false prophets in need of comeuppance. All right, so "urgent" was an exaggeration. Also, I was aware that the ills of the century had multiplied beyond anything my penny ante philanthropies could hope to fix. But I couldn't stand being a party to Feyvush and Gitl's five-alarm disappointment. This wasn't the world they knew; tahkeh, it wasn't even the half of what they didn't know, and I preferred not to stick around for the heartache of their getting acquainted. I didn't want to be there when they learned, for instance, that Jews had vanished in prodigious numbers from more places on the face of the planet than the Lower East Side. I didn't want to be there when they discovered what else had gone out of the world in their absence, and I didn't want to admit I made a mistake in bringing them back.

Still, I wouldn't send them away empty-handed. I gave them a pocket full of heaven gelt—that is, leaves from the *Etz ha-Chaim*, the Tree of Life, which passed for currency in certain neighborhood pawnshops; I told them the shops where you got the best rate of exchange. The most they could muster by way of gratitude, however, was a perfunctory nod. When they slouched off toward the Bowery, drawing stares in their period gear, I thought of Adam and Eve leaving the Garden at the behest of the angel with the flaming sword.

I aimed my own steps in the direction of the good deeds whose abandonment could throw the whole cosmic scheme out of joint. Then conceding there was no need to kid myself, it was already out of joint, I turned around. Virtually invisible in my guise as one more homeless old crock among a multitude of others, I followed the Fefers. I entered the shop behind them, where a pawnbroker in a crumpled skullcap greeted them satirically: "The Reb Ben Vinkl, I presume!" (This in reference to Feyvush's outdated apparel and the beard that had grown rank on his reentering the earth's atmosphere.) But when he saw the color of the couple's scrip, he became more respectful, even kicking in some coats of recent vintage to reduce the Fefers' anachronistic mien.

There was no law that said Feyvush and Gitl had to remain in the old ghetto neighborhood. Owing to my foresight they now had a nest egg; they could move to, say, the Upper West Side, someplace where Jews were thicker on the ground. So why did they insist on beating a path through shrieking winds back to Orchard Street via a scenic route that took them past gutted synagogues, shtiblekh with their phantom congregants sandwiched between the bodegas and Chinese take-outs, the talis shops manned by ancients looking out as from an abyss of years? Answer: having found the familiar strange enough, thank you, they might go farther and fare even worse.

As luck (if that's the right word) would have it, there was a flat available in the very same building they'd vacated a decades-long week ago. For all they knew it was the same paltry top floor apartment with the same sticks of furniture: the sofa with its cushions like sinkholes, the crippled wing chair, the kitchen table, the iron bed; not that the decor would have meant much to Feyvush and Gitl, who didn't look to be in a nostalgic mood. Hugging myself against the cold on the fire escape, I watched them wander from room to room until the windows fogged. Then someone rubbed a circle in a cloudy pane and I ducked out of sight below the ledge. But I could see them nonetheless, it was a talent I had: I could see them as clearly in my mind as with my eyes, peering into a street beyond which there was no manicured pleasure garden, no Tree.

They went out only once. Despite having paid a deposit and the first month's rent, they still had ample funds; they might have celebrated. But instead they returned with only the barest essentials—some black bread and farfel, a shank of gristly soup meat, a greasy sack of knishes from the quarter's one surviving knisherie. Confounded by the gas range that had replaced her old coal-burning cookstove, Gitl threw up her hands; Feyvush hunched his shoulders: Who had any appetite? Then they stared out the window again, past icicles like a dropped portcullis of fangs, toward a billboard atop the adjacent building. The billboard, which featured a man and woman lounging nearly naked on a beach, advertised an airline that offered to fly you nonstop to paradise.

Hunkered below the window ledge, I heard what I couldn't hear just like I saw what I couldn't see—Feyvush saying as if to himself, "Was it a dream?" Gitl replying with rancor: "Dreams are for goyim."

At some point one of them—I don't remember which—went into the bedroom and sat on the bed. He or she was followed soon after by the other, though neither appeared conscious of occupying the same space; neither thought to remove their heavy coats. The sag of the mattress, however, caused them to slide into contact with one another, and at first touch the Fefers combusted like dry kindling. They flared into a desperate embrace, shucking garments, Gitl tugging at her husband's suspenders as if drawing a bowstring. Feyvush ripped Gitl's blouse the way a Cossack parts a curtain to catch a Jew; he spread her thighs as if wrenching open the jaws of a trap. Having torn away their clothes, it seemed they intended to peel back each other's flesh. They marked cheeks and throats with bared talons, twisting themselves into tortured positions as if each were attempting to put on the other's skin—as if the husband must climb through the body of his wife, and vice-versa, in order to get back to what they'd lost.

That's how they did it, fastened to each other in what looked like a mutual punishment—hips battering hips, mouths spewing words refined of all affection. When they were done, they fell apart, sweating and bruised. They took in the stark furnishings of their cold-water flat: the table barren of the fabric flowers that once filled the place with perpetual spring, the window overlooking a street of strangers and dirty snow. Then they went at it again hammer and tongs.

I couldn't watch anymore; then God help me, I couldn't keep from watching. When the windows were steamed, I took the stairs to the roof, rime clinging to my lashes and beard, and squinted through a murky skylight like a sheet of green ice. When they were unobservable from any vantage, I saw them with an inner eye far clearer than my watery tom-peepers could focus. I let my good works slide, because who needed second sight to know that the world had gone already to hell in a phylactery bag? While my bones became brittle with winter and the bread and knishes went stale, and the soup meat grew mold and was nibbled at by mice, I kept on watching the Fefers.

Sometimes I saw them observing each other, with undisguised contempt. They had both shed the souvenir pounds they'd brought back from eternity. Gone was Gitl's generous figure, her unkempt hair veiling her tallowy face like a bloody rag. Her ribs showed beneath breasts as baggy as punctured meal sacks, and her freckles were indistinguishable from the pimples populating her brow. Feyvush, always slight, was nine-tenths a cadaver, his eyes in their hunger fairly drooling onto his hollow cheeks. His sunken chest, where it wasn't obscured by matted fur, revealed a frieze of scarlet hieroglyphics etched by his wife's fingernails. So wasted were they now that, when they coupled, their fevered bones chuckled like matches in a box. Between bouts they covered their nakedness with overcoats and went to the window, though not necessarily together. They rubbed circles, looked at the billboard with its vibrant twosome disporting under a tropical sun; then satisfied they were no nearer the place where they hoped to arrive, Feyvush or Gitl returned to bed.

Nu, so what would you have had me to do? Sure, I was the great kibbitzer in the affairs of others, but having already violated divine law by helping them escape from *der emeser velt*, the so-called true world, was I now to add insult to injury by delivering them from the false? Can truth and deception be swapped as easily as shmattes for fancy dress? Give me a break, the damage was done: human beings were not anyway intended to rise above their stations. The Fefers would never get out of this life again, at least not alive.

So I remained a captive witness to their savage heat. I watched them doing with an unholy vengeance what I never found the time for in my own sanctimonious youth—when I was too busy serving as mighty mouthpiece for a still small voice that had since become all but inaudible. I watched the mortals in their heedless ride toward an elusive glory, and aroused by the driven cruelty of their passion, achieved an erection: my first full engorgement since the days before the destruction of the Temple, when a maiden once lifted her tunic and I turned away. At the peak of my excitement I tore open the crotch of my trousers, releasing myself from a choked confinement, and spat my seed in a peashooter trajectory over Orchard Street. When I was finished, I allowed my wilted member to rest on the frigid railing of the fire escape, to which it stuck. Endeavoring to pull it free, I let loose a pitiable howl: I howled for the exquisite pain that mocked my terminal inability to die, and I howled for my loneliness. Then I stuffed my bloody putz back in my pants and looked toward the window, afraid I'd alerted the Fefers to my spying. But the Fefers, as it turned out, were well beyond earshot.

I raised the window and climbed over the sill, muffling my nose with a fingerless mitten against the smell, and shuffled forward to inspect their remains. So hopelessly entangled were the pair of them, however, that it was hard at first to distinguish husband from wife. Of course, there was no mistaking Feyvush's crown of tufted wool for Gitl's tattered red standard, his beak for her button nose, but so twined were their gory limbs that they defied a precise designation of what belonged to whom. Nor did their fused loins admit to which particular set of bones belonged the organ that united them both.

My task was as always to separate spirit from flesh, to extricate their immortal souls, which after a quick purge in the fires of Gehenna (no more than a millennia or two) would be as good as new. The problem was that, given the intricate knot they'd made of themselves, what was true of their bodies was true as well of their souls: I couldn't tell where Gitl's left off and her husband's began. It took me a while to figure it out, but ultimately I located the trouble; then the solution went some distance toward explaining their lifelong predicament. For the Fefers had been one of those rare cases where a couple shares two halves of a solitary soul. Theirs had indeed been a marriage made in heaven such as you don't see much anymore, the kind of match that might lead you to believe God Himself had a hand in it—that is, if you didn't already know He'd gotten out of the matchmaking racket long ago.

Ray Bradbury

Driving Blind

Ray Bradbury is widely acknowledged to be one of the masters of American fantasy fiction—and has won both the World Fantasy and Nebula Awards for Life Achievement.

He is the author of more than thirty books of fantasy and science fiction, including such classics as The Martian Chronicles, Fahrenheit 451, Something Wicked This Way Comes, *and* Dandelion Wine. *As a writer for theater and television, Bradbury has been nominated for an Academy Award and has won an Emmy. He lives with his wife in Los Angeles, California.*

In 1997, Bradbury's most recent short stories were gathered together in Driving Blind. *The title story of the collection is a gentle yet incisive work of contempory fantasy, set (like so much of this author's best fiction) in small-town America.*

—*T. W.*

"D id you see that?"

"See what?"

"Why, hell, look *there!*"

But the big six-passenger 1929 Studebaker was already gone.

One of the men standing in front of Fremley's Hardware had stepped down off the curb to stare after the vehicle.

"That guy was driving with a hood over his head. Like a hangman's hood, black, over his head, driving blind!"

"I saw it, I saw it!" said a boy standing, similarly riven, nearby. The boy was me, Thomas Quincy Riley, better known as Tom or Quint and mighty curious. I ran. "Hey, wait up! Gosh! Driving *blind!*"

I almost caught up with the blind driver at Main and Elm where the Studebaker turned off down Elm followed by a siren. A town policeman on his motorcycle, stunned with the traveling vision, was giving pursuit.

When I reached the car it was double-parked with the officer's boot up on the running board and Willy Crenshaw, the officer, scowling in at the black Hood and someone under the Hood.

"Would you mind taking that thing off?" he said.

"No, but here's my driver's license," said a muffled voice. A hand with the license sailed out the window.

"I want to see your face," said Willy Crenshaw.

"It's right there on the license."

"I want to check and see if the two compare," said Willy Crenshaw.

"The name is Phil Dunlop," said the Hooded voice. "121 Desplaines Street, Gurney. Own the Studebaker Sales at 16 Gurney Avenue. It's all there if you can read."

Willy Crenshaw creased his forehead and inched his eyesight along the words.

"Hey, mister," I said. "This is real neat!"

"Shut up, son." The policeman ground his boot on the running board. "What you *up* to?"

I stood arching my feet, peering over the officer's shoulder as he hesitated to write up a ticket or jail a crook.

"What you *up* to?" Willy Crenshaw repeated.

"Right now," said the Hooded voice, "I'd like a place to stay overnight so I can prowl your town a few days."

Willy Crenshaw leaned forward. "What kind of prowling?"

"In this car, as you see, making people sit up and notice."

"They done that," the policeman admitted, looking at the crowd that had accumulated behind Thomas Quincy Riley, me.

"Is it a big crowd, boy?" said the man under the Hood.

I didn't realize he was addressing me, then I quickened up. "Sockdolager!" I said.

"You think if I drove around town twenty-four hours dressed like this, people might listen for one minute and hear what I *say?*"

"All ears," I said.

"There you have it, Officer," said the Hood, staring straight ahead, or what seemed like. "I'll stay on, 'cause the boy says. Boy," said the voice, "you know a good place for me to shave my unseen face and rest my feet?"

"My grandma, she—"

"Sounds good. Boy—"

"Name's Thomas Quincy Riley."

"Call you Quint?"

"How'd you guess?"

"Quint, jump in, show the way. But don't try to peek under my cover-up."

"No, *sir!*"

And I was around the car and in the front seat, my heart pure jackrabbit.

"Excuse us, Officer. Any questions, I'll be sequestered at this child's place."

"Six one nine Washington Street—" I began.

"I know, I know!" cried the officer. "Damnation."

"You'll let me go in this boy's custody?"

"Hell!" The policeman jerked his boot off the running board which let the car bang away.

"Quint?" said the voice under the dark Hood, steering. "What's *my* name?"

"You said—"

"No, no. What do *you* want to call me?"

"Hmm. Mr. Mysterious?"

"Bull's-eye. Where do I turn left, right, right, left, and right again?"

"Well," I said.

And we motored off, me terrified of collisions and Mr. Mysterious, real nice and calm, made a perfect left.

Some people knit because their fingers need preoccupations for their nerves.

Grandma didn't knit, but plucked peas from the pod. We had peas just about most nights in my life. Other nights she plucked lima beans. String beans? She harped on those, too, but they didn't pluck as easy or as neat as peas. Peas were it. As we came up the porch steps, Grandma eyed our arrival and shelled the little greens.

"Grandma," I said. "This is Mr. Mysterious."

"I could *see* that." Grandma nodded and smiled at she knew not what.

"He's wearing a Hood," I said.

"I noticed." Grandma was still unaffected and amiable.

"He needs a room."

"To need, the Bible says, is to have. Can he find his way up? Excuse the question."

"And *board*," I added.

"Beg pardon, how's he going to eat through that *thing?*"

"Hood," I said.

"*Hood?*"

"I can manage," Mr. Mysterious murmured.

"He can manage," I translated.

"That'll be worth watching." Grandma stitched out more green peas. "Sir, do you have a name?"

"I just *told* you," I said.

"So you did." Grandma nodded. "Dinner's at six," she said, "sharp."

The supper table, promptly at six, was loud with roomers and boarders. Grandpa having come home from Goldfield and Silver Creek, Nevada, with neither gold nor silver, and hiding out in the library parlor behind his books, allowed Grandma to room three bachelors and two bachelor ladies upstairs, while three boarders came in from various neighborhoods a few blocks away. It made for a lively breakfast, lunch, and dinner and Grandma made enough from this to keep our ark from sinking. Tonight there was five minutes of uproar concerning politics, three minutes on religion, and then the best talk about the food set before them, just as Mr. Mysterious arrived and everyone shut up. He glided among them, nodding his Hood right and left, and as he sat I yelled:

"Ladies and gentlemen, meet Mr.—"

"Just call me Phil," murmured Mr. Mysterious.

I sat back, somewhat aggrieved.

"Phil," said everyone.

They all stared at him and couldn't tell if he saw their stares through the black velvet. How's he going to eat, hid like that, they thought. Mr. Mysterious picked up a big soup spoon.

"Pass the gravy, please," he whispered.

"Pass the mashed potatoes," he added quietly.

"Pass the peas," he finished.

"Also, Mrs. Grandma . . ." he said. Grandma, in the doorway, smiled. It seemed a nice touch: "Mrs." He said, ". . . please bring me my blue-plate special."

Grandma placed what was indeed a Chinese garden done in blue ceramics but containing what looked to be a dog's dinner. Mr. Mysterious ladled the gravy, the mashed potatoes, and the peas on and mashed and crushed it shapeless as we watched, trying not to bug our eyes.

There was a moment of silence as the voice under the dark Hood said, "Anyone mind if I say grace?"

Nobody would mind.

"O Lord," said the hidden voice, "let us receive those gifts of love that shape and change and move our lives to perfection. May others see in us only what we see in them, perfection and beauty beyond telling. Amen."

"Amen," said all as Mr. M. snuck from his coat a thing to astonish the boarders and amaze the rest.

"That," someone said (me), "is the biggest darn soda fountain straw I ever seen!"

"Quint!" said Grandma.

"Well, it *is!*"

And it was. A soda fountain straw two or three times larger than ordinary which vanished up under the Hood and probed down through the mashed potatoes, peas, and gravy dog's dinner which silently ascended the straw to vanish in an unseen mouth, silent and soundless as cats at mealtime.

Which made the rest of us fall to, self-consciously cutting, chewing, and swallowing so loud we all blushed.

While Mr. Mysterious sucked his liquid victuals up out of sight with not even so much as a purr. From the corners of our eyes we watched the victuals slide silently and invisibly under the Hood until the plate was hound's-tooth clean. And all this done with Mr. M.'s fingers and hands fixed to his knees.

"I—" said Grandma, her gaze on that straw, "hope you liked your dinner, sir."

"Sockdolager," said Mr. Mysterious.

"Ice cream's for dessert," said Grandma. "Mostly melted."

"Melted!" Mr. M. laughed.

It was a fine summer night with three cigars, one cigarette, and assorted knitting on the front porch and enough rocking chairs going somewhere-in-place to make dogs nervous and cats leave.

In the clouds of cigar smoke and a pause in the knitting, Grandpa, who always came out after dark, said:

"If you don't mind my infernal nerve, now that you're settled in, what's *next?*"

Mr. Mysterious, leaning on the front porch rail, looking, we supposed, out at his shiny Studebaker, put a cigarette to his Hood and drew some smoke in, then out without coughing. I stood watching, proudly.

"Well," said Mr. M., "I got several roads to take. See that car out there?"

"It's large and obvious," said Grandpa.

"That is a brand-new class-A Studebaker Eight, got thirty miles on it, which is as far from Gurney to here and a few runaround blocks. My car salesroom is just about big enough to hold three Studebakers and four customers at once. Mostly dairy farmers pass my windows but don't come in. I figured it was time to come to a live-wire place, where if I shouted 'Leap' you might at least hop."

"We're waiting," said Grandpa.

"Would you like a small demonstration of what I pray for and *will* realize?" said the cigarette smoke wafting out through the fabric in syllables. "Someone say 'Go.' "

Lots of cigar smoke came out in an explosion.

"Go!"

"Jump, Quint!"

I reached the Studebaker before him and Mr. Mysterious was no sooner in the front seat than we took off.

"Right and then left and then right, correct, Quint?"

And right, left, right it was to Main Street and us banging away fast.

"Don't laugh so loud, Quint."

"Can't help it! This is *peacherino!*"

"Stop swearing. Anyone following?"

"Three young guys on the sidewalk here. Three old gents off the curb there!"

He slowed. The six following us soon became eight.

"Are we almost at the cigar-store corner where the loudmouths hang out, Quint?"

"You *know* we are."

"Watch this!"

As we passed the cigar store he slowed and choked the gas. The most terrific Fourth of July BANG fired out the exhaust. The cigar-store loudmouths jumped a foot and grabbed their straw hats. Mr. M. gave them another BANG, accelerated, and the eight following soon was a dozen.

"Hot diggity!" cried Mr. Mysterious. "Feel their love, Quint? Feel their *need?* Nothing like a brand-new eight-cylinder super prime A-1 Studebaker to make a man feel like Helen just passed through Troy! I'll stop now that there's folks enough for arguments to possess and fights to keep. *So!*"

We stopped dead-center on Main and Arbogast as the moths collected to our flame.

"Is that a brand-new just-out-of-the-showroom Studebaker?" said our town barber. The fuzz behind my ears knew him well.

"Absolutely spanking brand-new," said Mr. M.

"I was here first, I get to ask!" cried the mayor's assistant, Mr. Bagadosian.

"Yeah, but I got the money!" A third man stepped into the dashboard light. Mr. Bengstrom, the man who owned the graveyard and everyone in it.

"Got only *one* Studebaker now," said the sheepish voice under the Hood. "Wish I had more."

That set off a frenzy of remorse and tumult.

"The entire price," said Mr. M. in the midst of the turmoil, "is eight hundred and fifty dollars. The first among you who slaps a fifty-dollar bill or its equivalent in singles, fives, and tens in my hand gets to pink-slip this mythological warship home."

No sooner was Mr. Mysterious' palm out the window than it was plastered with fives, tens, and twenties.

"Quint?"

"Sir?"

"Reach in that cubby and drag out my order forms."

"Yes, *sir!*"

"Bengstrom! Cyril A. Bengstrom!" the undertaker cried so he could be heard. "Be calm, Mr. Bengstrom. The car is yours. Sign *here.*"

Moments later, Mr. Bengstrom, laughing hysterically, drove off from a sullen mob at Main and Arbogast. He circled us twice to make the abandoned crowd even more depressed then roared off to find a highway and test his craze.

"Don't fret," said the voice under the dark Hood. "I got one last Studebaker prime A-1 vehicle, or maybe two, waiting back in Gurney. Someone drop me there?"

"*Me!*" said everyone.

"So *that's* the way you function," said Grandpa. "*That's* why you're here."

It was later in the evening with more mosquitoes and fewer knitters and smokers. Another Studebaker, bright red, stood out at the curb. "Wait till they see the sun shine on *this* one," said Mr. Mysterious, laughing gently.

"I have a feeling you'll sell your entire line this week," said Grandpa, "and leave us wanting."

"I'd rather not talk futures and sound uppity, but so it seems."

"Sly fox." Grandpa tamped philosophy in his pipe and puffed it out. "Wearing that sack over your head to focus need and provoke talk."

"It's more than that." Mr. M. sucked, tucking a cigarette through the dark material over his mouth. "More than a trick. More than a come-on. More than a passing fancy."

"What?" said Grandpa.

"What?" I said.

It was midnight and I couldn't sleep.

Neither could Mr. Mysterious. I crept downstairs and found him in the backyard in a wooden summer recliner perhaps studying the fireflies and beyond them the stars, some holding still, others not.

"Hello, Quint!" he said.

"Mr. Mysterious?" I said.

"Ask me."

"You wear that Hood even when you *sleep?*"

"All night long every night."

"For most of your life?"

"Almost most."

"Last night you said it's more than a trick, showing off. What *else?*"

"If I didn't tell the roomers and your grandpa, why should I tell you, Quint?" said the Hood with no features resting there in the night.

"'Cause I want to know."

"That's about the best reason in the world. Sit down, Quint. Aren't the fireflies nice?"

I sat on the wet grass. "Yeah."

"Okay," said Mr. Mysterious, and turned his head under his Hood as if he were staring at me. "Here goes. Ever wonder what's under this Hood, Quint? Ever have the itch to yank it off and see?"

"Nope."

"Why not?"

"That lady in *The Phantom of the Opera* did. Look where it got *her*."

"Then shall I *tell* you what's hidden, son?"

"Only if you want to, sir."

"Funny thing is, I do. This Hood goes back a long way."

"From when you were a kid?"

"Almost. I can't recall if I was born this way or something happened. Car accident. Fire. Or some woman laughing at me which burned just as bad, scarred just as terrible. One way or another we fall off buildings or fall out of bed. When we hit the floor it might as well have been off the roof. It takes a long time healing. Maybe never."

"You mean you don't remember when you put that thing on?"

"Things fade, Quint. I have lived in confusion a long while. This dark stuff has been such a part of me it might just be my living flesh."

"Do—"

"Do what, Quint?"

"Do you sometimes *shave*?"

"No, it's all smooth. You can imagine me two ways, I suppose. It's all nightmare under here, all graveyards, terrible teeth, skulls and wounds that won't heal. Or—"

"Or?"

"Nothing at all. Absolutely nothing. No beard for shaving. No eyebrows. Mostly no nose. Hardly any eyelids, just eyes. Hardly any mouth; a scar. The rest a vacancy, a snowfield, a blank, as if someone had erased me to start over. There. Two ways of guessing. Which do you pick?"

"I can't."

"No."

Mr. Mysterious arose now and stood barefooted on the grass, his Hood pointed at some star constellation.

"You," I said, at last. "You still haven't told what you started tonight to tell Grandpa. You came here not just to sell brand-new Studebakers—but for something else?"

"Ah." He nodded. "Well. I been alone a lot of years. It's no fun over in Gurney, just selling cars and hiding under this velvet sack. So I decided to come out in the open at last and mix with honest-to-goodness people, make friends, maybe get someone to like me or at least put up with me. You understand, Quint?"

"I'm trying."

"What good will all this do, living in Green Town and thriving at your supper table and viewing the tree-tops in my cupola tower room? *Ask.*"

"What good?" I asked.

"What I'm hoping for, Quint, what I'm praying for, son, is that if I delve in the river again, wade in the stream, become part of the flow of folks, people, strangers even, some sort of kind attention, friendship, some sort of half-love will begin to melt and change my face. Over six or eight months or a year, to let life shift my mask without lifting it, so that the wax beneath moves and becomes something more than a nightmare at three a.m. or just nothing at dawn. Any of this make sense, Quint?"

"Yeah. I guess."

"For people *do* change us, don't they? I mean you run in and out of this house and your grandpa changes you and your grandpa shapes you with words or a hug or your hair tousled or maybe once a year, a slap where it hurts."

"*Twice.*"

"Twice, then. And the boarders and roomers talk and you listen and that goes in your ears and out your fingers and that's change, too. We're all in the wash, all in the creeks, all in the streams, taking in every morsel of gab, every push from a teacher, every shove from a bully, every look and touch from those strange creatures, for *you* called women. Sustenance. It's all breakfast tea and midnight snacks and you grow on it or you don't grow, laugh or scowl or don't have any features one way or the other, but *you're* out there, melting and freezing, running or holding still. I haven't done that in years. So just this week I got up my courage—knew how to sell cars but didn't know how to put *me* on sale. I'm taking a chance, Quint, that by next year, this face under the Hood will make itself over, shift at noon or twilight, and I'll feel it changing because I'm out wading in the stream again and breathing the fresh air and letting people get at me, taking a chance, not hiding behind the windshield of this or that Studebaker. And at the end of that next year, Quint, I'll take off my Hood forever."

At which point, turned away from me, he made a gesture. I saw the dark velvet in his hand as he dropped it in the grass.

"Do you want to see what's here, Quint?" he asked, quietly.

"No, sir, if you don't mind."

"Why not?"

"I'm scared," I said, and shivered.

"That figures," he said, at last. "I'll just stand here a moment and then hide again."

He took three deep breaths, his back to me, head high, face toward the fireflies and a few constellations. Then the Hood was back in place.

I'm glad, I thought, there's no moon tonight.

Five days and five Studebakers later (one blue, one black, two tans, and one sunset-red) Mr. Mysterious was sitting out in what he said was his final car, a sun-yellow open roadster, so bright it was a canary with its own cage, when I came strolling out, hands in overall pockets, watching the sidewalk for ants or old unused firecrackers. When Mr. M. saw me he moved over and said, "Try the driver's seat."

"Boy! *Can* I?"

I did, and twirled the wheel and honked the horn, just once, so as not to wake any late-sleepers.

" 'Fess up, Quint," said Mr. Mysterious, his Hood pointed out through the windshield.

"Do I look like I need 'fessing'?"

"You're ripe-plumful. Begin."

"I been thinking," I said.

"I could tell by the wrinkles in your face," said Mr. M., gently.

"I been thinking about a year from now, and you."

"That's mighty nice, son. Continue."

"I thought, well, maybe next year if you felt you were cured, under that Hood, that your nose was okay and your eyebrows neat, and your mouth good and your complexion—"

I hesitated. The Hood nodded me on.

"Well, I was thinking if you got up one morning and without even putting your hands up to feel underneath you knew the long waiting was over and you were changed, people and things had changed you, the town, everything, and you were great, just great, no way of *ever* going back to nothing."

"Go on, Quint."

"Well, if that happened, Mr. Mysterious, and you just knew you were really great to see forever, why then, Mr. M., you wouldn't *have* to take off your Hood, *would* you?"

"What'd you *say*, son?"

"I said, you wouldn't have to ta—"

"I heard you, Quint, I heard," gasped Mr. M.

There was a long silence. He made some strange sounds, almost like choking, and then he whispered hoarsely, "No, I wouldn't need to take off my Hood."

" 'Cause it wouldn't matter, would it? If you really knew that underneath, everything was okay. Sure?"

"Oh, Lord yes, sure."

"And you could wear the Hood for the next hundred years and only you and me would know what's underneath. And we wouldn't tell or care."

"Just you and me. And what would I look like under the Hood, Quint? Sockdolager?"

"Yes, sir."

There was a long silence and Mr. Mysterious' shoulders shook a few times and he made a quiet choking sound and all of a sudden some water dripped off the bottom of his Hood.

I stared at it. "Oh," I said.

"It's all right, Quint," he said, quietly. "It's just tears."

"Gosh."

"It's all right. Happy tears."

Mr. Mysterious got out of the last Studebaker then and touched at his invisible nose and dabbed at the cloth in front of his unseen eyes.

"Quintessential Quint," he said. "No one else like you in the whole world."

"Heck, that goes for *everyone*, don't it?"

"If you say so, Quint."

Then he added:

"Got any last things to upchuck or confess, son?"

"Some silly stuff. What if—?"

I paused and swallowed and could only look ahead through the steering wheel spokes at the naked silver lady on the hood.

"What if, a long time ago, you never *needed* the Hood?"

"You mean never? Never *ever?*"

"Yes, sir. What if a long time ago you only *thought* you needed to hide and put on that stuff with no eye-holes even. What if there was never any accident, or fire, or you weren't born that way, or no lady ever laughed at you, what *then?*"

"You mean I only imagined I had to put on this sackcloth and ashes? And all these years I been walking around thinking there *was* something awful or just nothing, a blank underneath?"

"It just came to me."

There was a long silence.

"And all these years I been walking around not knowing or pretending I had something to hide, for no reason, because my face was there all the time, mouth, cheeks, eyebrows, nose, and didn't need melting down to be fixed?"

"I didn't mean—"

"You *did*." A final tear fell off the bottom rim of his Hood. "How old are you, Quint?"

"Going on thirteen."

"No. Methuselah."

"He was *real* old. But did he have any jellybeans in his *head?*"

"Like you, Quincy. A marvel of jellybeans."

There was a long silence, then he said:

"Walk around town? Need to flex my legs. Walk?"

We turned right at Central, left at Grand, right again at Genesee, and stopped in front of the Karcher Hotel, twelve stories, the highest building in Green County or beyond.

"Quint?"

His Hood pointed up along the building while his voice under observed. "Thomas Quincy Riley, you got that *one last thing* look. Spit it out."

I hesitated and said, "Well. Up inside that Hood, is it *really* dark? I mean, there's no radio gadgets or see-back-oscopes or secret holes?"

"Thomas Quincy Riley, you been reading the Johnson Smith & Co. Tricks, Toys, Games and Halloween Catalogue from Racine, Wisconsin."

"Can't help it."

"Well, when I die you'll inherit this sack, wear it, and know darkness."

The head turned and I could almost feel his eyes burn the dark material.

"Right now, I can look through your ribs and see your heart like a flower or a fist, opening, closing, open, shut. You believe that?"

I put my fist on my chest.

"Yes, sir," I said.

"Now."

He turned to point his Hood up along the hotel for twelve stories.

"Know what I been thinking?"

"Sir?"

"Stop calling myself Mr. Mysterious."

"Oh, *no!*"

"Hold on! I've done what I came for. Car sales are runaway. Hallelujah. But look, Quint. Look up and touch. What if I became the Human Fly?"

I gasped. "You mean—"

"Yessireebob. Can't you just see me up six stories and eight and twelve at the top, with my Hood still on, waving down at the crowd?"

"Gee!"

"Glad for your approval." Mr. M. stepped forward and started to climb, reaching for holds, finding, and climbing more. When he was three feet up he said, "What's a good *tall* name for a Human Fly?"

I shut my eyes, then said:

"*High*tower!"

"Hightower, by God! Do we go home to breakfast?"

"Yes, *sir.*"

"Mashed bananas, mashed cornflakes, mashed oatmeal—"

"Ice cream!" I added.

"Melted," said the Human Fly and climbed back down.

Joyce Carol Oates

The Sky-Blue Ball

In addition to being a respected novelist and story writer, playwright, and essayist, Joyce Carol Oates is the Roger S. Berlind Distinguished Professor in the Humanities at Princeton University. She has won the National Book Award and was the 1994 recipient of the Bram Stoker Award for Life Achievement in Horror Fiction. Oates is the author, most recently, of Zombie, *winner of the the Bram Stoker Award for Superior Achievement in Novel;* What I Live For; First Love: A Gothic Tale; We Were the Mulvaneys; *and* Man Crazy. *She has published three collections of her darker fiction:* Night-Side, Haunted: Tales of the Grotesque, *and* Demon and Other Tales. *Her short stories have appeared in* Omni, Playboy, The New Yorker, Harper's, *and* The Atlantic Monthly, *as well as in literary magazines, and in anthologies such as* Architecture of Fear, Dark Forces, Metahorror, Little Deaths, Ruby Slippers, Golden Tears, Off Limits, Twists of the Tale, *and* Lethal Kisses. *She has also had stories reprinted in* Prize Stories: The O. Henry Awards *and* The Year's Best Fantasy and Horror. *She recently edited the anthology* American Gothic Tales *and has been honored with the Life Achievement Award given by the Horror Writers' Association.*

Oates is prolific and fearless in her writing, crossing genres with ease. "The Sky-Blue Ball" was first published in Ellery Queen's Mystery Magazine.

—E. D.

In a long-ago time when I didn't know *Yes I was happy, I was myself and I was happy.* In a long-ago time when I wasn't a child any longer yet wasn't entirely not-a-child. In a long-ago time when I seemed often to be alone, and imagined myself lonely. *Yet this is your truest self: alone, lonely.*

One day I found myself walking beside a high brick wall the color of dried blood, the aged bricks loose and moldering, and over the wall came flying a spherical object so brightly blue I thought it was a bird!—until it dropped a few yards in front of me, bouncing at a crooked angle off the broken sidewalk, and I saw that it was a rubber ball. A child had thrown a rubber ball over the wall, and I was expected to throw it back.

Hurriedly I let my things fall into the weeds, ran to snatch up the ball, which looked new, smelled new, spongy and resilient in my hand like a rubber ball I'd played with years before as a little girl; a ball I'd loved and had long ago misplaced; a ball I'd loved and had forgotten. "Here it comes!" I called, and tossed the ball back over the wall; I would have walked on except, a few seconds later, there came the ball again, flying back.

A *game*, I thought. *You can't quit a game.*

So I ran after the ball as it rolled in the road, in the gravelly dirt, and again snatched it up, squeezing it with pleasure, how spongy, how resilient a rubber ball, and again I tossed it over the wall; feeling happiness in swinging my arm as I hadn't done for years since I'd lost interest in such childish games. And this time I waited expectantly, and again it came!—the most beautiful sky-blue rubber ball rising high, high into the air above my head and pausing for a heartbeat before it began to fall, to sink, like an object possessed of its own willful volition; so there was plenty of time for me to position myself beneath it and catch it firmly with both hands.

"Got it!"

I was fourteen years old and did not live in this neighborhood, nor anywhere in the town of Strykersville, New York (population 5,600). I lived on a small farm eleven miles to the north and I was brought to Strykersville by school bus, and consequently I was often alone; for this year, ninth grade, was my first at the school and I hadn't made many friends. And though I had relatives in Strykersville these were not relatives close to my family; they were not relatives eager to acknowledge me; for we who still lived in the country, hadn't yet made the inevitable move into town, were perceived inferior to those who lived in town. And, in fact, my family was poorer than our relatives who lived in Strykersville.

At our school teachers referred to the nine farm children bussed there as "North Country children." We were allowed to understand that "North Country children" differed significantly from Strykersville children.

I was not thinking of such things now, I was smiling thinking it must be a particularly playful child on the other side of the wall, a little girl like me; like the little girl I'd been; though the wall was ugly and forbidding with rusted signs EMPIRE MACHINE PARTS and PRIVATE PROPERTY NO TRESPASSING. On the other side of the Chautauqua & Buffalo railroad yard was a street of small, wood-frame houses; it must have been in one of these that the little girl, my invisible playmate, lived. She must be much younger than I was; for fourteen-year-old girls didn't play such heedless games with strangers, we grew up swiftly if our families were not well-to-do.

I threw the ball back over the wall, calling, "Hi! Hi, there!" But there was no reply. I waited; I was standing in broken concrete, amid a scrubby patch of weeds. Insects buzzed and droned around me as if in curiosity, yellow butterflies no larger than my smallest fingernail fluttered and caught in my hair, tickling me. The sun was bright as a nova in a pebbled-white soiled sky that was like a thin chamois cloth about to be lifted away and I thought, *This is the surprise I've been waiting for.* For somehow I had acquired the belief that a surprise, a nice surprise, was waiting for me. I had only to merit it, and it would happen. (And if I did not merit it, it would not happen.) Such a surprise could not come from God but only from strangers, by chance.

Another time the sky-blue ball sailed over the wall, after a longer interval of perhaps thirty seconds; and at an unexpected angle as if it had been thrown away from me, from my voice, purposefully. Yet there it came, as if it could not not come: My invisible playmate was obliged to continue the game. I had no hope of catching it but ran blindly into the road (which was partly asphalt and partly gravel and not much traveled except by trucks) and there came a dump truck headed at me, I heard the ugly shriek of brakes and a deafening angry horn and I'd fallen onto my knees, I'd cut my knees that were bare, probably I'd torn my skirt, scrambling quickly to my feet, my cheeks smarting with shame, for wasn't I too grown a girl for such behavior? "Get the hell out of the road!" a man's voice was furious in rectitude, the voice of so many adult men of my acquaintance, you did not question such voices, you did not doubt them, you ran quickly to get out of their way; already I'd snatched up the ball, panting like a dog, trying to hide the ball in my skirt as I turned, shrinking and ducking so the truck driver couldn't see my face, for what if he was someone who knew my father, what if he recognized me, knew my name. But already the truck was thundering past, already I'd been forgotten.

Back then I ran to the wall, though both my knees throbbed with pain, and I was shaking as if shivering, the air had grown cold, a shaft of cloud had pierced the sun. I threw the ball back over the wall again, underhand, so that it rose high, high—so that my invisible playmate would have plenty of time to run and catch it. And so it disappeared behind the wall and I waited, I was breathing hard and did not investigate my bleeding knees, my torn skirt. More clouds pierced the sun and shadows moved swift and certain across the earth like predator fish. After a while I called out hesitantly, "Hi? Hello?" It was like a ringing telephone you answer but no one is there. You wait, you inquire again, shyly, "Hello?" A vein throbbed in my forehead, a tinge of pain glimmered behind my eyes, that warning of pain, of punishment, following excitement. The child had drifted away, I supposed; she'd lost interest in our game, if it was a game. And suddenly it seemed silly and contemptible to me, and sad: There I stood, fourteen years old, a long-limbed weed of a girl, no longer a child yet panting and bleeding from the knees, the palms of my hands, too, chafed and scraped and dirty; there I stood alone in front of a moldering brick wall waiting for—what?

It was my school notebook, my several textbooks I'd let fall into the grass and I would afterward discover that my math textbook was muddy, many pages damp and torn; my spiral notebook in which I kept careful notes of the intransigent rules of English grammar and sample sentences diagrammed was soaked in a virulent-smelling chemical and my teacher's laudatory comments in red and my grades of A (for all my grades at Strykersville Junior High were A, of that I was obsessively proud) had become illegible as if they were grades of C, D, F. I should have taken up my books and walked hurriedly away and put the sky-blue ball out of my mind entirely but I was not so free, through my life I've been made to realize that I am not free, as others appear to be free, at all. For the "nice" surprise carries with it the "bad" surprise and the two are so intricately entwined they cannot be separated, nor even defined as separate. So though my head pounded I felt obliged to look for a way over the wall. Though my knees were scraped and bleeding I located a filthy oil drum and shoved it against the wall and climbed shakily up on it, dirtying my hands and arms, my legs, my clothes, even more. And I hauled myself over the wall, and jumped down, a drop of about ten feet, the breath knocked out of me as I landed, the shock of the impact reverberating through me, along my spine, as if I'd been struck a sledge-hammer blow to the soles of my feet. At once I saw that there could be no little girl here, the factory yard was surely deserted, about the size of a baseball diamond totally walled in and overgrown with weeds pushing through cracked asphalt, thistles, stunted trees, and clouds of tiny yellow butterflies clustered here in such profusion I was made to see that they were not beautiful creatures, but mere insects, horrible. And rushing at me as if my very breath sucked them at me, sticking against my sweaty face, and in my snarled hair.

Yet stubbornly I searched for the ball. I would not leave without the ball. I seemed to know that the ball must be there, somewhere on the other side of the wall, though the wall would have been insurmountable for a little girl. And at last, after long minutes of searching, in a heat of indignation I discovered the ball in a patch of chicory. It was no longer sky blue but faded and cracked; its dun-colored rubber showed through the venous-cracked surface, like my own ball, years ago. Yet I snatched it up in triumph, and squeezed it, and smelled it—it smelled of nothing: of the earth: of the sweating palm of my own hand.

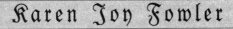

Karen Joy Fowler

The Black Fairy's Curse

Karen Joy Fowler is recognized by genre readers as one of the most thoughtful writers working in the fields of science fiction (Artificial Things) and fantasy (Sarah Canary). With her latest novel, The Sweetheart Season, a magic realist story set in small-town America, Fowler's distinctive work has gained acclaim among mainstream readers as well. She is also the author of a new collection, Black Glass.

The following story, "The Black Fairy's Curse," is a departure for this author in terms of subject matter, yet retains the elegant use of language that has become her trademark. Written for the 1997 fairy tale anthology Black Swan, White Raven, it falls neatly into the modern renaissance of literary fairy tales for adult readers—a stylistic trend set into motion by writers like Angela Carter and Robert Coover in the literary mainstream, and Tanith Lee and Robin McKinley in the fantasy field.

—T. W.

She was being chased. She kicked off her shoes, which were slowing her down. At the same time her heavy skirts vanished and she found herself in her usual work clothes. Relieved of the weight and constriction, she was able to run faster. She looked back. She was much faster than he was. Her heart was strong. Her strides were long and easy. He was never going to catch her now.

She was riding the huntsman's horse and she couldn't remember why. It was an autumn red with a tangled mane. She was riding fast. A deer leapt in the meadow ahead of her. She saw the white blink of its tail.

She'd never ridden well, never had the insane fearlessness it took, but now she was able to enjoy the easiness of the horse's motion. She encouraged it to run faster.

It was night. The countryside was softened with patches of moonlight. She could go anywhere she liked, ride to the end of the world and back again. What she would find there was a castle with a toothed tower. Around the castle was a girdle of trees, too narrow to be called a forest, and yet so thick they admitted no light at all. She knew this. Even farther away were the stars. She looked up and saw three of them fall, one right after the other. She made a wish to ride until she reached them.

She herself was in farmland. She crossed a field and jumped a low, stone fence. She avoided the cottages, homey though they seemed, with smoke rising from the roofs, and a glow the color of butter pats at the windows. The horse ran and did not seem to tire.

She wore a cloak which, when she wrapped it tightly around her, rode up and left her legs bare. Her feet were cold. She turned around to look. No one was coming after her.

She reached a river. Its edges were green with algae and furry with silt. Toward the middle she could see the darkness of deep water. The horse made its own decisions. It ran along the shallow edge, but didn't cross. Many yards later it ducked back away from the water and into a grove of trees. She lay along its neck and the silver-backed leaves of aspens brushed over her hair.

She climbed into one of the trees. She regretted every tree she had never climbed. The only hard part was the first branch. After that it was easy, or else she was stronger than she'd ever been. Stronger than she needed to be. This excess of strength gave her a moment of joy as pure as any she could remember. The climbing seemed quite as natural as stair steps, and she went as high as she could, standing finally on a limb so thin it dipped under her weight, like a boat. She retreated downward, sat with her back against the trunk and one leg dangling. No one would ever think to look for her here.

Her hair had come loose and she let it all down. It was warm on her shoulders. "Mother," she said, softly enough to blend with the wind in the leaves. "Help me."

She meant her real mother. Her real mother was not there, had not been there since she was a little girl. It didn't mean there would be no help.

Above her were the stars. Below her, looking up, was a man. He was no one to be afraid of. Her dangling foot was bare. She did not cover it. Maybe she didn't need help. That would be the biggest help of all.

"Did you want me?" he said. She might have known him from somewhere. They might have been children together. "Or did you want me to go away?"

"Go away. Find your own tree."

They went swimming together, and she swam better than he did. She watched his arms, his shoulders rising darkly from the green water. He turned and saw that she was watching. "Do you know my name?" he asked her.

"Yes," she said, although she couldn't remember it. She knew she was supposed to know it, although she could also see that he didn't expect her to. But she did feel that she knew who he was—his name was such a small part of that. "Does it start with a W?" she asked.

The sun was out. The surface of the water was a rough gold.

"What will you give me if I guess it?"

"What do you want?"

She looked past him. On the bank was a group of smiling women, her grandmother, her mother, and her stepmother, too, her sisters and stepsisters, all of them smiling at her. They waved. No one said, "Put your clothes on." No one said, "Don't go in too deep now, dear." She was a good swimmer, and there was no reason to be afraid. She couldn't think of a single thing she wanted. She flipped away, breaking the skin of the water with her legs.

She surfaced in a place where the lake held still to mirror the sky. When it settled, she looked down into it. She expected to see that she was beautiful, but she was not. A mirror only answers one question, and it can't lie. She had completely lost her looks. She wondered what she had gotten in return.

There was a mirror in the bedroom. It was dusty, so her reflection was vague. But she was not beautiful. She wasn't upset about this, and she noticed the fact, a little wonderingly. It didn't matter at all to her. Most people were taken in by appearances, but others weren't. She was healthy; she was strong. If she could manage to be kind and patient and witty and brave, then there would be men who loved her for it. There would be men who found it exciting.

He lay among the blankets, looking up at her. "Your eyes," he said. "Your incredible eyes."

His own face was in shadow, but there was no reason to be afraid. She removed her dress. It was red. She laid it over the back of a chair. "Move over."

She had never been in bed with this man before, but she wanted to be. It was late, and no one knew where she was. In fact, her mother had told her explicitly not to come here, but there was no reason to be afraid. "I'll tell you what to do," she said. "You must use your hand and your mouth. The other—it doesn't work for me. And I want to be first. You'll have to wait."

"I'll love waiting," he said. He covered her breast with his mouth, his hand moved between her legs. He knew how to touch her already. He kissed her other breast.

"Like that," she said. "Just like that." Her body began to tighten in anticipation.

He kissed her mouth. He kissed her mouth.

He kissed her mouth. It was not a hard kiss, but it opened her eyes. This was not the right face. She had never seen this man before, and the look he gave her—she wasn't sure she liked it. Why was he kissing her, when she was asleep and had never seen him before? What was he doing in her bedroom? She was so frightened, she stopped breathing for a moment. She closed her eyes and wished him away.

He was still there. And there was pain. Her finger dripped with blood, and when she tried to sit up, she was weak and encumbered by a heavy dress, a heavy coil of her own hair, a corset, tight and pointed shoes.

"Oh," she said. "Oh." She was about to cry, and she didn't know this man to cry before him. Her tone was accusing. She pushed him and his face showed the surprise of this. He allowed himself to be pushed. If he hadn't, she was not strong enough to force it.

He was probably a very nice man. He was giving her a concerned look. She could see that he was tired. His clothes were ripped; his own hands were scratched. He had just done something hard, maybe dangerous. So maybe that was why he hadn't stopped to think how it might frighten her to wake up with a stranger kissing her as she lay on her back. Maybe that was why he hadn't noticed how her finger was bleeding. Because he hadn't, no matter how much she came to love him, there would always be a part of her afraid of him.

"I was having the most lovely dream," she said. She was careful not to make her tone as angry as she felt.

Peter S. Beagle

The Last Song
of Sirit Byar

Peter S. Beagle published his charming first novel, A Fine and Private Place, before he was twenty-one. In the three decades since, his output has not been prodigious, but each new work from Beagle is so well-crafted and enchanting that his reputation as one of the twentieth-century masters of fantasy fiction is well deserved. His books include The Last Unicorn (made into an animated film), The Unicorn Sonata, and The Innkeeper's Song; his short fiction includes "Come, Lady Death," "Lila the Werewolf," and other modern classics of our field.

Beagle is one of those rare writers who can take the standard tropes of Tolkienesque "high fantasy" and fashion them into tales both traditional and utterly fresh. "The Last Song of Sirit Byar" is such a tale—set in the far corners of the imaginary land first explored in The Innkeeper's Song. The story was first published in the anthology Space Opera—a book which fell between the 1996 and 1997 publication years; it was also featured in Beagle's 1997 collection Giant Bones. "It is worth mentioning," the author writes, "that the central character of 'The Last Song of Sirit Byar' is based, freely and with old love, on a great French singer-songwriter named Georges Brassens."

Beagle (a singer-songwriter himself) lives in Davis, California, with his wife, the Indian writer-photographer Padma Hejmadi.

—T. W.

H ow much? *How* much to set down one miserable tale that will cost your chicken wrist an hour's effort at very most? Well, by the stinking armpits of all the gods, if I'd known there was that much profit in sitting in the marketplace scribbling other people's lives and feelings on bits of hide, I'd have spent some rainy afternoon learning to read and write myself. Twelve copper, we'll call it. *Twelve*, and I'll throw in a sweetener, because I'm a civilized woman under the grease and the hair. I promise not to break your nose, though it's a great temptation to teach you not to take advantage of strangers, even when they look like what I look like and speak your crackjaw tongue so outlandishly that you'd mimic me to my hog face if you dared. But no, no, sit back down, fair's fair, a bargain's a bargain. No broken nose. *Sit.*

Now. I want you to write this story, not for my benefit—am I likely to forget the only bloody man who ever meant more than a curse and a fart to me?—but for your own, and for those who yet sing the songs of Sirit Byar. Ah, *that* caught your ear, didn't it? Yes, yes, Sirit Byar, that one, the same who sang a king to ruin with a single mocking tune, and then charmed his way out of prison by singing ballads of brave lovers to the hangman's deaf-mute daughter. Sirit Byar, "the white *sheknath*," as they called him out of his hearing—the big, limping, white-haired man who could get four voices going on that antiquated eighteen-course *kiit* other men could hardly lift, let alone get so much as a jangle out of it. Sirit Byar. Sirit Byar, who could turn arrows with his music, call rock-*targs* to carry him over mountain rivers, make whiskery old generals dance like children. All trash, that, all marsh-goat shit, like every single other story they tell about him. Write this down. Are you writing?

Thirty years, more, he's been gone, and you'd think it a hundred listening to the shit wits who get his songs all wrong and pass them on to fools who never heard the man play. The *tales*, the things he's supposed to have said, the gods and heroes they tell you he sang for—believe it, he'd piss himself with laughing to hear such solemn dribble. And then he'd look at me and maybe I'd just catch the twitch at the right corner of his mouth, under the wine-stained white mustache, and he'd say in that barbarous south-coast accent he never lost, "What am I always telling you, big girl? Never bet on anything except human stupidity." And he'd have limped on.

I knew Sirit Byar from when I was eleven years old to his death, when I was just past seventeen. No, he didn't die in my arms—what are you, a bloody bard as well as a mincing scribbler? Yes, I *know* no one ever learned what became of him—I'll get to that part when I bloody well get to it. Don't gape at me like that or I'll pull your poxy ears off and send them to your mother, whatever kennel she's in. *Write*— we'll be all day at this if you keep on stopping to gape. Gods, what a town—back-country cousin-marriers, the lot of them. Just like home.

My name is Mircha Del. I was born around Davlo, that's maybe a hundred miles southwest of Fors na'Shachim. My father was a mountain farmer, clawing a little life from stone and sand, like everybody in this midden-heap. My mother had the good sense to run off as soon as she could after I was born. Never met her, don't even know if she's alive or dead. My father used to say she was beautiful, but all you have to do is look at me for the facts of that. Probably the only woman he could get to live with him up there in those starvation hills, and even she couldn't stand it for long. No need to put all that in—this isn't about her, or about him either. Now he *did* die in my arms, by the way, if that interests you. Only time I can remember holding him.

At the age of eleven, I had my full growth, and I looked just as hulking as I do now. My father once said I was meant for a man, which may be so, though I'd not have been any less ugly with balls and a beard. That's as may be, leave that out too. What matters is that I already had a man's strength, or near enough—enough anyway to get a crop in our scabby ground and to break a team of Karakosk horses—you know, those big ones? The ones they raise on meat broth?—to do our ploughing. And when our neighbor's idiot son—yes, a real idiot, who else would have been my playmate even when I was little?—got himself pinned under a fallen tree, they sent for me to lift it off him. He died anyway, mind you, but people took to calling me "the Davlo *sheknath*" for a while. I told Sirit Byar about that once, the likeness in our nicknames, and he just snorted. He said, "You hated it." I nodded. Sirit Byar said, "Me, too, always have," so maybe there was our real likeness. It made me feel better, anyway.

Well, so. There used to be a tavern just outside Davlo, called the Miller's Joy. It's long gone now, but back then it was as lively a pothouse as you could find, with gaming most nights, and usually a proper brawl after, and every kind of entertainment from gamecocks to *shukri*-fighting, to real Leishai dancers, and sometimes even one of those rock-munching strongmen from down south. My father spent most of his evenings there, and many of his mornings as he got older, so I grew in the habit of walking down to Davlo to fetch him home— carry him, more times than not. And all that's the long way of telling you how I met Sirit Byar.

It happened that I tramped into the Miller's Joy one night to find my father— purely raging I was, too, because our lone miserable *rishu* was due to calve, and he'd sworn to be home this one night anyway. I delivered the calf myself, no trouble, but there could have been, and now I meant to scorch him for it before all his tavern mates. I could hear their racket a street away, and him bellowing and laughing in the middle of it. Wouldn't have been the first time I snatched him off a table and out the door for the cold walk home. Grateful he was for it most times, I think—it told him that someone yet cared where he was, and maybe it passed for love, how should I know? He was lonely with my mother gone, and too poor for drink and the whores both, so he made do with me yelling at him.

But that night there was another sound coming from the old den, and it stopped me in the street. First the fierce thump of a *kiit* strung with more and heavier courses than the usual, and then the voice, that voice—that harsh, hoarse, tender southern voice, always a breath behind the beat, that voice singing that first song, the first one I ever heard:

> "Face it,
> if you'd known what you know today,
> you'd have done the same stupid fucking thing
> anyway...."

Yes, you know it, don't you, even in my croak? Me, I didn't even know what I was hearing—I'd never heard anything like that music before, never heard a bard in my life. Bards don't come to Davlo. There's nothing for even a carnival jingler in Davlo, never mind someone like Sirit Byar. But there he was.

He looked up when I pushed the door open. There was a whole sprawl of drunken dirt farmers between us—a few listening to him where he sat crosslegged on a table with the *kiit* in his lap; most guzzling red ale and bawling their own personal songs—but Sirit Byar saw me. He looked straight across them to where I stood in the doorway: eleven years old, the size of a haywagon and twice as ugly, and mucky as the floor of that taproom besides. He didn't smile or nod or anything, but just for a moment, playing a quick twirl on the *kiit* between verses, he said through the noise, "There you are, big girl." As though he'd been waiting. And then he went back to his song.

> "Face it,
> if she'd been fool enough to stay,
> you'd be the same mean, stupid bastard
> anyway. . . ."

There was one man crying, doubled over his table, thumping his head on it and wailing louder than Sirit Byar was singing. And there was a miner from Grebak, just sitting silent, hands clasped together, pulling and squeezing at the big scabby knuckles. As for my father and the rest, it was drinking and fighting and puking all over their friends, like any other night at the Miller's Joy. The landlord was half-drunk himself, and he kept trying to throw out little Desh Jakani, the farrier, only he wouldn't go. The three barmaids were all making their own arrangements with anyone who could still stand up and looked likely to have two coppers left in his purse at closing time. But Sirit Byar kept looking at me through the noise and the stink and the flickering haze, and he sang:

> "Face it,
> if we all woke up gods one day,
> we'd still treat each other like garbage
> anyway. . . ."

What did he look like? Well, the size of him was what I mostly saw that first night. Really big men are rare still in those Davlo hills—the diet doesn't breed them, not enough meat, and the country just hammers them low—and Sirit Byar was the biggest man I'd seen in my life. But I'm not talking about high or wide—get *this* down now—I'm talking about size. There was a color to him, even with his white hair and faded fisherman's tunic and trews; there was a purpose about him as he sat there singing that made everything and everyone in that roaring tavern small and dim and faraway, that's what I remember. And all he was, really, was a shaggy, rough-voiced old man—fifty anyway, surely—who sang dirty songs and called me "big girl." In a way, that's all he ever was.

The songs weren't *all* dirty, and they weren't all sad and mean, like that "Face It" one. That first night he sang "Grandmother's Ghost," which is just silly and funny, and he sang "The Sand Castles"—you know it?—and "The Ballad of Sailor Lal," which got even those drunken farmers thumping the tables and yelling out the chorus. And there was a song about a man who married the Fox in the Moon—that's still my favorite, though he never sang it much. I forgot about my father, I even forgot to sit down. I just stood in the doorway with my mouth hanging open while Sirit Byar sang to me.

He really could set four voices against each other on that battered old *kiit*, that's no legend. Mostly for show, that was, for a finish—what I liked best was when he'd sing a line in one rhythm and the *kiit* would answer him back in another, and you couldn't believe they'd come out together at the end, even when you knew they would. Six years traveling with him, and I never got tired of hearing him do that thing with the rhythms.

The trouble started with "The Good Folk." It always did, I learned that in a hurry. That bloody song can stir things up even today, insulting everybody from great lords to shopkeepers, priests to bailiffs to the Queen's police; but back then, when it was new, back then you couldn't get halfway through it without starting a riot. I don't *think* Sirit Byar yet understood that, all those years ago in the Miller's Joy. Maybe he did. It'd have been just like him.

Anyway, he didn't get anything like halfway through "The Good Folk," not that night. As I recall it, he'd just sailed into the third stanza—no, no, it would have been the second, the one about the priests and what they do on the altars when everyone's gone home—when the man who'd been crying so loudly stood up, wiped his eyes, and knocked Sirit Byar clean off the table. Never saw the blow coming, no chance to ward it off—even so, he curled himself around the *kiit* as he fell, to keep it safe. The crying man went right at him, fists and feet, and he couldn't do much fighting back, not and protect the *kiit*. Then Kluj what's-his-name got into it—he'd jump anybody when he was down, that one— and then my bloody father, if you'll believe it, too blind drunk to know what was going on, just that it looked like fun. He and the crying man tripped each other up and rolled over Sirit Byar and right into the legs of the big miner's table, brought the whole thing down on themselves. Well, the miner, he started kicking at them with his lumpy boots, and *that* got Mouli Dja, my father's old drinking partner, "Drooly Mouli," people used to call him—anyway, that got *him* jumping in, yelling and swearing and chewing on the miner's knees. After that, it's not worth talking about, take my word for it. A little bleeding, a lot of snot, the rest plain mess. Tavern fights.

I told you I had near to my grown strength at eleven. I walked forward and yanked my father away from the crying man with one hand, while I peeled Mouli Dja off the miner with the other. Today I'd crack their idiot heads together and not think twice about it, but I was just a girl then, so I only dropped them in a corner on top of each other. Then I went back and started pulling people off Sirit Byar and stacking them somewhere else. Once I got them so they'd stay put, it went easier.

He wasn't much hurt. He'd been here before; he knew how to guard his head and his balls as well as the *kiit*. Anyway, that many people piling on, nothing serious ever gets done. Some blood in the white mustache, one eye closing and blackening. He looked up at me with the other one and said for the second time, "There you are, big girl." I held out my hand, but he got up without taking it.

Close to, he had a wild smell—furry, but like live fur, while it's still on the *shukri* or the *jarilao*. He was built straight up and down: wide shoulders, thick waist, thick short legs and neck. A heavy face, but not soft, not sagging—cheekbones you could have built a fence, a house with. Big eyes, set wide apart, half-hidden in the shadows of those cheekbones. Very quiet eyes, almost black, looking black because of the white hair. He never smiled much, but he usually looked about to.

"Time to go," he said, calm as you please, standing there in the ruins of a table and paying no mind to the people yelling and bleeding and falling over each other all around us. Sirit Byar said, "I was going to spend the night here, but it's too noisy. We'll find a shed or a fold somewhere."

And me? I just said, "I have to get my father home. You go on down the Fors road until you come to the little Azdak shrine, it'll be on the right. I'll meet you there." Sirit Byar nodded and turned away to dig his one sea-bag out from under Dordun the horse-coper, who was being strangled by some total stranger in a yellow hat. Funny, the things you remember. I can still see that hat, and it's been thirty years, more.

I did carry my father back to our farm—nothing out of the way in that, as I said. But then I had to sit him down on a barrel, bracing him so he wouldn't go all the way over, and tell him that I was leaving with Sirit Byar. And that was hard—first, because he was too drunk and knocked about to remember who any of us were; and second, because I couldn't have given him any sort of decent reason for becoming the second woman to leave him. He'd never been cruel to me, never used me the way half the farmers we knew used their daughters and laughed about it in the Miller's Joy. He'd never done me any harm except to sire me in that high, cold, lonely, miserable end of the world. And here I was, running away to follow a bard four, five times my age, a man I'd never seen or even heard of before that night. Oh, they'd be baiting him about it forever, Mouli Dja and the rest of his friends.

I don't think I tried to explain anything, finally. I just told him I'd not be helping him with the farming anymore, but that he wouldn't need to worry about feeding me either. He said nothing at all, but only kept blinking and blinking, trying to make his eyes focus on me. I never knew if he understood a word. I never knew what he felt when he woke up the next day and found me gone.

There wasn't much worth taking along. My knife, my tinder box, my good cloak. I had to go back for my lucky foreign coin—see here, this one that's never yet bought me a drink anywhere I've ever been. My father was already asleep, slumped on the barrel with his head against the wall. I put a blanket over him—he could have them both now—and I left a second time.

The Fors na'Shachim road runs straight the last mile or so to the Azdak shrine, and I could see Sirit Byar in the moonlight from a long way off. He wasn't looking around impatiently for me, but was kneeling before that ugly little heap of stones with the snaggletoothed Azdak face scratched into the top one. "Azdak" just means *stranger* in the tongue I grew up speaking. None of us ever knew the god's real name, or what he was good for, or who set up that shrine when my father was a boy. But we left it where it was, because it's bad luck not to, and some of us even worshipped it, because why not? Our own hill gods weren't worth shit, that was obvious, or they wouldn't have been scrabbling to survive in those hills like the rest of us. There was always the chance that a god who had journeyed this far might actually know something.

But Sirit Byar wasn't merely offering Azdak a quick nod and a marketing list.

He was on his knees, as I said, with his big white head on a level with the god's, looking him in the eyes. His lips were moving, though I couldn't make out any words. As I reached him, he rose silently, picked up the *kiit* and his sea-bag, and started off on down the Fors road. I ran after him, calling, "My name is Mircha. Where are we going?"

Sirit Byar didn't even look at me. I asked him, "Why were you praying like that to Azdak? Is he your people's god?"

We tramped on a long way before Sirit Byar answered me. He said, "We know each other. His name is not Azdak, and I was not praying. We were talking."

"It'll rain before morning," I said. "I can smell it. Where are we going?"

He just grunted, "Lesser Tichni or a hayloft, whichever comes first," and that was all he said until we were bedded down between two old donkeys in an old shed on very old straw. I was burrowing up to one of the beasts, trying to get warm, when Sirit Byar suddenly turned toward me and said, "You will carry the *kiit*. You can do that." And he was sound asleep, that fast. Me, I lay awake the rest of that night, partly because of the cold, but mostly because what I'd done was finally—*finally*, mind you—beginning to sink in. Here I was, already farther from home than ever I'd been, lying in moldy straw, listening to a strange man snoring beside me. Tell you how ignorant a lump I was back then, I thought snoring was just something my father did, nobody else. I wasn't frightened— I've never been frightened in my life, which is a great pity, by the way—but I was certainly confused, I'll say that. Nothing for it but to lie there and wait for morning, wondering how heavy the *kiit* would be to shoulder all day. It never once occurred to me that I could go home.

The *kiit* turned out to be bloody heavy, strong as I was, and bulky as a plough, which was worse. Those eighteen double courses made it impossible to get a proper grip on the thing—there was no comfortable way to handle it, except to keep shifting it around: now on my back, now hugged into my chest with both arms, now swinging loose in my hand, banging against everything it could reach. I was limping like Sirit Byar himself at the end of our first full day on the road.

So it began. We stopped at the first inn after sunset, and Sirit Byar played and sang for men dirtier and even more ugly-drunk than ever I'd seen in the Miller's Joy. That was a lesson to me, for that lot paid no attention at all to "The Ballad of Sailor Lal," but whooped and cheered wildly for "The Good Folk," and made him sing it twice over so they could learn it themselves. You never know what they'll like or what they'll do, that's the only lesson there is.

Two nights and a ride on a tinker's cart later, we dined and slept in Fors na'Shachim—yes, at the black castle itself, with the Queen's ladies pouring our tea, and the chamber that Sirit Byar always slept in already made up for him. Four of the ladies were ordered to bathe me and find me something suitable to wear while the Queen had to look at me. I put up with the bath, but when they wanted to burn my clothes on the spot I threw one of the ladies across the room, so that took care of that. It quieted the giggling, besides. So I've had royalty concerning itself with what nightgown I should wear to bed, which is more than *you've* ever known, for all your reading and writing. They'd probably have bathed you, too.

And two days after that, we were on our way again, me back in the rags I'd practically been born in (they probably burned that borrowed dress and the nightgown), and Sirit Byar wearing what he always wore—they didn't sweeten *him* up to sing for the Queen, I can tell you. But he had gold coins in his pocket, thirty-six new strings on the *kiit,* a silk kerchief Herself had tied around his neck with her own fair hands, and he was limping off to sing his songs in every crossroads town between Fors and Chun for no more than our wretched meals and *dai*-beetle-ridden lodging. I was a silent creature myself in those days, but I had to ask him about that. I said, "She wanted you to stay. They did."

Sirit Byar just grunted. I went on, "You'd be a royal bard—you could have that palace room forever, the rest of your life. All you'd ever have to do is make up songs and sing them for the Queen now and then."

"I do that," Sirit Byar said. "Now and then. Don't dangle the *kiit* that way, it's scraping the road." He watched me as I struggled to balance the filthy thing on my shoulder, and for the first time since we'd met I saw him smile a very little.

"The singing is what matters, big girl," he said. "Not for whom." We walked a way without speaking, and then he continued. "To do what I do, I have to walk the roads. I can't ride. If I ride, the songs don't come. That's the way it is."

"And if you sleep in a bed?" I asked him. "And if you sing for people who aren't drunk and stupid and miserable?" I was eleven, and my feet hurt, and I could surely have done with a few more days in that black castle.

Sirit Byar said, "Give me that," and I handed him the *kiit,* glad to have it off my shoulder for a few minutes. I thought he was going to show me a better way of carrying it, but instead he retuned a few of the new strings—they won't hold their pitch the first day or two, drive you mad—and began to play as we walked. He played a song called "The Juggler."

No, you don't know that one. I've never yet met anyone who did. He hardly ever played it—maybe three times in the six years we were together, but I had it by heart the first time, as I always did with his songs. It's about a boy from a place about as wretched as Davlo, who teaches himself to juggle just because he's bored and lonely. And it turns out that he's good at it, a natural. He juggles everything around him—stones, food, tools, bottles, furniture, whatever's handy. People love him; they come miles to see him juggle, and by and by the King hears about it and wants him to live at the palace and be his personal juggler. But in the song the boy turns him down. He tells the King that once he starts juggling crowns and golden dishes and princesses, he'll never be able to juggle anything else again. He'll forget how it's done, he'll forget why he ever wanted to do it in the first place. So thank you, most honored, most grateful, but no. And it has the same last line at the end of every verse: "*Kings need jugglers, jugglers don't need kings. . . .*" I can't sing it right, but that's how it went.

He sang it to me, right there, just the two of us walking along the road, and it's likely the most I ever learned about him at one time. Never any need to explain himself, not to me or anyone. I asked him that day if it bothered him when people didn't like his songs. Sirit Byar just shrugged his shoulders as though my question were a fly and he a horse trying to get rid of it. He said, "That's not my business. The Queen likes them; your father didn't. No business of mine either way."

He really didn't care. Set this down plain, if you botch all the rest, because it's what matters about him. As long as he could make his songs and get along singing them, he simply did not care where he slept, or what he ate, or whom he sang to. I can't tell you how much didn't matter to that man. When he had money he bought our meals with it, or more strings—that old *kiit* went through them like my father through red ale and black wine—or once in a while a night at an inn, for us to clean ourselves up a bit. When there was no money, there'd be food and lodging just the same, most often no worse. For a man who could go all day saying no more than half a dozen words, he had friends in places where I'd not have thought you could even find an enemy. The beggar woman in Rivni: we always stayed with her, just as regular as we stayed at the black castle, in the abandoned henroost that was her home. The wind-witch in Leishai, where it's a respectable profession, because of the sailors. The two weavers near Sarn—brothers, they were, and part-time body-snatchers besides. That bloody bandit in Cheth na'Deka—though that one always kept him up singing most of the night, demanding first this song, then that. The shipchandler's wife of Arakli.

I'll always wonder about her, the chandler's wife. Her husband had a warehouse down near the river, and she used to let us sleep in it as long as we were careful to leave no least sign that we'd ever been there. She was a plain woman—dark, small, a bit plump, that's all I remember. Nice voice. And what there was between her and Sirit Byar I never knew, except that I got up to piss the one night and heard them outside. *Talking* they were, fool—talking they were, too softly for me to make out a word, sitting by the water, not even touching, with the moon's reflection flowing over their faces and the moon in Sirit Byar's white hair. And I pissed behind the warehouse, and I went back to sleep, and that's all.

We had a sort of regular route, if you want to call it that. Say Fors na'Shachim as a starting point—from there we'd work toward the coast through the Dungaurie Pass, strike Grannach Harbor and begin working north, with Sirit Byar singing in taverns, kitchens, great halls, and marketplaces in all the port towns as far as Leishai. Ah, the ports—the smell, salt and spice and tar, miles before you could even see the towns. The food waiting for us there in the stalls, on the barrows—fresh, fresh *courel*, *jeniak*, *boreen* soup with lots of catwort. Strings of little crackly *jai*-fish, two to a mouthful. And the light on the water, and children splashing in the shadows of the rotting pilings, and folk yelling welcome to their "white *sheknath*" in half a dozen tongues. The feeling that everything was possible, that you could go anywhere in the world from here, except back to Davlo. That was the best, better than the food, better than the smells. That feeling.

No, you'd think so, but he hardly ever sang sea-songs in the port towns. One, two, maybe, like "Captain Shallop and the Merrow" or "Dark Water Down"—otherwise he saved those for inland, where folk dream of far white isles and don't know what a merrow can do to you. In the ports he sang—oh, "Tarquentil's Hat," "The Old Priest and the Old God," "My One Sorrow," "The Ballad of the Captain's Mercy." "The Good Folk." Now *they* always loved "The Good Folk," the ports did, so there you are.

From Bitava we usually headed inland, still angling north, but no farther than Karakosk, ever. I've been told that he sang often in Corcorua; maybe, but not while I was with him. He'd no mind at all to limp across the Barrens, and he disliked most of the high northland anyway for its thin wine and its fat, stingy burghers. So I never saw anything loftier than the Durli Hills in those days, which suited me well enough—I've never been homesick for mountains a day in my life. We'd skirt the Durlis, begin bearing back south around Suk'kai, and fetch up in Fors again by Thieves' Day. A bath and a warm bed then—a few days of singing for the Queen and being made over by her ladies—and start all over again. So it was we lived for six years.

Duties? What were my *duties*? How daintily you do put it, to be sure, chicken-wrist. Well, I carried the *kiit*, and I brewed the tea and cooked our meals, when we had something to cook. A few times, mostly in Leishai, I ran off pick-pockets he hadn't seen sliding alongside, and one night I broke the shoulder of a hatchet-swinging Bitava barber who'd taken a real dislike to "The Sand Castles." For the rest, I kept him mostly silent company, talked when he wanted talk, went round with the hat after he sang, and kept an eye out at all times for that wicked west-country liqueur they call Blue Death. Terrible shit, peel your gums right back, but he loved it, and it's hard to find much east of Fors. He drank it like water, whenever he could get it, but I can't remember seeing him drunk. Or maybe I did, maybe I saw him drunk a lot and didn't know it. There were things you never could tell about with Sirit Byar.

Once I asked him, "What would you do if you weren't a bard? If you just suddenly couldn't make up songs anymore?"

I thought I knew him well enough to ask, but he stopped in the road and gaped at me as though he'd never seen me before. That was the only time I ever saw him looking amazed, startled about anything. He mumbled, "You don't know."

I stared right back at him. I said, "Well, of course I don't know. I didn't know a bloody thing about being a bard, not how it is, you won't ever talk about that. All I know is what you like to eat, where you like to sit when you sing. Maybe you think that's all a hill girl from Davlo can understand. Maybe it is. You'll never know that either."

Sirit Byar smiled a real smile then, not the almost-smile he wore for everyone always. "Listen to the songs, big girl. It's all in the songs, everything I could tell you." We walked along a way after that, and by and by he said, "A bard always hoards one last song against the day when all the others go. It happens to every one of us, sooner or later—you wake up one morning and it's over, they've left you, they don't need you anymore. No warning. No warning when they flew into you, no warning when they fly away. That's why you always save that last song."

He cleared his throat, spat into the road, rubbed his nose, looked sideways at me. "But you have to be very careful, because a bard's last song has power. You never tell that song; you never sing it anywhere; you keep it for that day when it's the only song left to you. Because a last song is always *answered*." And after that he hardly talked at all for the rest of the day.

He taught me a little about playing the *kiit*, you know. I'm sure he did it just because he'd never found anyone besides him who could even handle the thing. I'm no musician—I can't do what he could do, but I know how he did it. Someday I'd like to show someone how he played, just so it won't die with me. Not that he'd have given one tiny damn, but I do.

Every so often we'd strike a song competition, a battle of bards, especially in the southwest—it's a tradition in that country to set poets a subject and start them outrhyming one another. Sirit Byar hated those things. He'd avoid even a town where we usually did well if he heard there was a contest going on there. Because once he was recognized, he never had a choice—they'd cancel the whole event if he didn't enter. He always won, but he was always cranky for days afterward. Me, I liked the song tourneys—we ate well those days, and drank better, and some of the townsfolk's celebration of Sirit Byar was for me, too, or anyway it felt so. I was proud as any of the Queen's ladies to walk beside him in the street, holding the *kiit* so people could see the flowers woven in and out between its strings. And whenever Sirit Byar looked down through all the fuss and winked at me, bard to bard almost—well, you imagine how it was, chicken-wrist. You imagine this big freak's insides then.

No. Oh, no. Get *that* out of your head before it ever gets in, if you know what's good for you. I was eleven, lugging that *kiit*, for Sirit Byar, and then twelve and thirteen and fourteen, sleeping close for warmth in fields, barns, sheds, whores' cribs, and never in all that time. *Never.* Not once. It wouldn't have occurred to him.

It occurred to me, I'll tell you that. Yes, you can gape now, that's right, I'd be disappointed if you didn't. Listen to me now—I've had three, four times as many men as you've had women, for what that's worth. You think men care about soft skin, perfect teeth, adorable little noses? Not where I've been—not in the mines, not on the flatboats, the canal scows, not in the traders' caravans slinking through the Northern Barrens. Out there, I even get to say, "no, not now, piss off"—can you imagine *that* at least, chicken-wrist? Try.

I had my first while I was yet on the road with Sirit Byar. Not yet fourteen, me, and sneaking up on myself in every stockpond, every shiny pot, just on the off-hope that something might have changed since the last time. If I'd had a mother . . . aye, well, and what could the most loving mother have told me that the bottom of any kettle couldn't? What could Sirit Byar have said, who never looked in a glass from year's-end to year's-end? I truly doubt he remembered the color of his own eyes. Now me, I couldn't remember not knowing I was ugly enough to turn milk, curdle beer, and mark babies, but it hadn't mattered much at all until that boy at Limsatty Fair.

Ah, gods, that boy at the fair. I can still see him, thirty years gone, when I can't remember who pleased me last week. Pretty as you like, with lavender eyes, skin like brown cambric, bones in his face like kite-ribs. He was selling salt meat, if you'll believe it, and when Sirit Byar and I wandered by he looked at me for a moment, and looked politely away, so as not to stare. That's when I learned that I had a heart, chicken-wrist, because I felt such a pain in it that I couldn't believe I was still walking along and not falling dead on the spot. We were to make our camp in a field a mile from the fair, and I think I walked backward all the way. Sirit Byar had to grip me by the back of my smock and tow me like a bloody barge.

There was a little creek, and I was supposed to scoop some fish out of it for our dinner. Any hill child can do that, but instead I lay there on my stomach and cried as I've never cried in my life, before or since. I didn't think it was ever going to stop. Leave that out. No. No, keep it in. What do I care?

Sirit Byar had probably been sitting by me for a long time before I felt his hand on my neck. He never touched me, you know, except to help me on the road, or to remind me about holding the damn *kiit* just so. Once, when I was sick with the white-mouth fever, he carried me and the *kiit* both for miles until we found a mad old woman who knew what to do. This was different, this was— I don't know, leave it, just leave it. He said, "Here."

He took off the Queen's silken kerchief he always wore around his neck and handed it to me so I could dry my eyes. Then he said, "Give me the *kiit*." I just stared at him, and he had to tell me again. "Give it to me, big girl."

He tuned it so carefully, you'd have thought he was getting ready to play at the black palace once again. Then he set his back against a tree, and began to sing. It wasn't a song I'd ever heard, and it didn't sound like one of his. The rhythm wasn't any I knew, the music was jags and slides and tangles, the words didn't make any sense. I told you, I had all his songs by heart the moment I heard them, but not that song. I do have a bit of it, like this:

> "If you hear not, hear me never—
> if you burn not, freeze forever—
> if you hunger not, starve in hell—
> if you will not, then you never shall. . . ."

That line kept coming round and round again—*"If you will not, then you never shall."* It was a long song, and there was a thing about it made my skin fit all wrong on me. I lay where I was, sniffling away, while Sirit Byar kept singing, and the sun wandered down into twilight, slow as that song. At last I sat up and wiped my face with the Queen's kerchief, and remembered about our fish. I was moving myself back over to the creek when the music stopped, sudden as a doorslam, and I turned and saw the salt-meat boy from the fair.

He was still so beautiful that it hurt to look at him, but something in his face was changed. Some kind of vague, puzzled anger, like someone who hasn't been blind long enough to get used to it. But he walked straight to me, and he took my hands and drew me to my feet, and we stood staring at each other for however long. When he began to lead me away, I turned to look back, but Sirit Byar was gone. I don't know what he had for dinner that night, nor where he slept.

Me, I slept warm on a cold hillside, as they say in the old ballads, and I woke just a minute or two before I should have. The salt-meat boy was up and scurrying into his clothes, and looking down at me with such bewilderment and such contempt—not for me, but for himself—as even I haven't seen again in my life. Then he fled, carrying his boots, and I lay there for a while longer, to give him time. I didn't cry.

Sirit Byar was at the creek, breakfasting on dry bread and cheese and the last of our sour Cape Dylee wine. There was enough laid out for two. Neither of us spoke a word until we were on our way again, bound for Derridow, I think. Finally I said, "The song brought him."

Sirit Byar grunted, looked away, mumbled something. I stopped right there on the road—he actually walked along a few steps before he realized I wasn't with him. I said, "Tell me why you sang that song. Tell me now."

He was a long time answering. We stood there and looked at each other almost the way I'd stood with that salt-meat boy, years and years ago it seemed. Finally

Sirit Byar rubbed his hand across his mouth and muttered, "You're my big girl, and you were so sad."

And that was how I knew he liked me, you see. Two, almost three full years carrying his instrument, cooking his meals, grubbing up coins from tavern floors, and he'd never said. He turned right around then and started walking on, as fast as his limp would let him, and I hurried after him with the *kiit* banging the side of my knee. He wouldn't talk for a long time, not until a rainshower came up and we were huddled in the lee of a hayrick, waiting it out. I asked him, "How does it happen? The song making someone come to you."

Sirit Byar said, "Where I come from, there are songs for bringing game to the hunter—fish, birds. I just changed one a little for you."

I started to say, "Please, don't ever do that anymore," but I changed my mind halfway through. Whatever came of it, he gave me what I'd wanted most in all my life till then, and no blame to him if I woke from the dream too soon. So instead I asked, "Can you make other things happen with your songs?"

"Little things," Sirit Byar said. "The great ones who walked the roads before me—Sarani Elsu, K'lanikh-yara"—no, I never heard of them either, chicken-wrist—"*they* could sing changes, they could call rivers to them, *they* could call gods, lightning, the dead, not silly lovers." He patted my shoulder clumsily, I remember. He said, "All songs are magic, big girl. Some are more powerful than others, but all songs are always magic, always. You've seen me start our cooking fires in the rain—you remember the time I cured the farmer's dog that had eaten poison. My songs make little magics, that's all. They'll do for me."

Write that down, remember that he said just that. Remember it the next time you hear someone jabbering about Sirit Byar's great powers. *Little magics.* He never claimed anything more than that for himself. He never needed to.

Where was I? The rain let up, and we set out again, and presently Sirit Byar began singing a new song, one he hadn't yet finished, scrawling it in the air with one huge hand as we walked, the way he did. It ran so:

> "Long ago,
> before there were landlords—
> long ago,
> before there were kings,
> there lived a lady
> made all out of flowers,
> made of honey and sunlight
> and such sweet things. . . ."

Yes, of course you know it, that one got around everywhere—I've heard it as far north as Trodai, just last year. He sang it through for me the first time, the two of us shivering there in the rain, and when the sun came out, we walked on. Neither of us ever said another word about the salt-meat boy, as often as we came again to Limsatty Fair.

After that, something was a bit different between us. Closer, I don't know—maybe just easier. We talked more, anyway. I told Sirit Byar about the little scrap of a farm where I'd lived, and about how I'd chanced into the Miller's Joy that night, and that I was worried about my father—we hadn't been back to

Davlo in three years. I asked after him whenever we met someone who'd passed through there, but for all I knew he might have died the day I left. I'd go days at a time without thinking of him at all, but I dreamed about him more and more.

Sirit Byar spoke sometimes of his south-coast town—not much bigger than Davlo, it sounded—and of his older sister, who raised him after their parents' deaths. Even now I can't imagine Sirit Byar having a family, having a sister. She set his leg herself when it got crushed between two skiffs and there wasn't even a witchwife for miles. She married there, and was killed in the Fishermen's Rebellion, and he never went back. Did you ever hear anyone sing that song of his, "Thou"? Most people think that song's about one god or another, but it's not; it's for his sister. He told me that.

Bedded down one night in the straw of a byre, with an old *rishu* and her calf for company, I asked him why he'd said that in the Miller's Joy when he first saw me—*"There you are, big girl."* How he knew that I was supposed to go with him and help him and do what he told me—how I knew. Sirit Byar was sitting up across from me, fussing over a harmony on the *kiit* that never did satisfy him. He answered without looking up, "He told me. The one your folk call Azdak." I didn't understand him. Sirit Byar said, "When I came to Davlo. I saw him by the road, and we talked. He told me to watch for you."

"Azdak," I said. "Azdak. What would Azdak care about me?"

"He is the god of wanderers," Sirit Byar said. "He knows his own." The *kiit* wouldn't do a thing he wanted that evening, and he finally set it down gently in an empty manger. He went on, "Your Azdak told me you and I had a journey to make together. I didn't know what he meant then."

"Aye, and so we had, sure enough," I said. "Where was the mystery in that?"

Sirit Byar laughed. He said, "I don't think Azdak was talking about walking the roads, big girl. Gods likely don't bother much with such things."

"Well, they bloody should," I said, for he'd been limping worse than usual lately, and I'd had a stone bruise on my heel days on end. "He's no more use than our regular gods, if that's all he could tell you."

Sirit Byar shrugged. "I know only what he didn't mean, not what he did. That's how it is with gods." He stretched out on the far side of the *rishu*, wriggling himself down into the straw till all you could see of him was a big nose and a white mustache. He said, "Our real journey is yet to come," and was asleep.

Now whether it was the words or the way he said them that took hold of me, I couldn't tell you, but it was nightmare on nightmare after that—every time the damn *rishu* snuffled in her sleep, another monster turned up in mine. The last one must have been a pure beauty, because I woke up on Sirit Byar's chest, holding him tighter than ever I had the salt-meat boy. That wild, deep-woods smell of his was the most comforting thing in the wide world just then.

Well, there's comfort and comfort. I'll get this part over with quickly—no need to embarrass us both for twelve coppers. He held me for a while, petting my hair as though it might turn in his hand and bite him any minute. Then he started to put me by, gently as he could, but I wouldn't let him. I was saying, "It's dark, it's dark, you won't even see me, just this one time. Please." Like that.

Poor Sirit Byar, hey? The poor man, trying to get this whimpering hulk off him without hurting her brutish feelings. Ah, *that* one you can imagine, I can see it in your little pink eyes. Yes, well, I pushed him back down every time he sat up, and when he said, "Big girl, don't, no, you're too young," I kept on kissing him, saying, "I don't care, I won't tell anybody, please, I won't ever tell." Ah, poor, poor Sirit Byar.

He did the only thing he could do. He shoved me away, hard—big as he was, I was the stronger, but it's amazing what you can do when you're desperate, isn't it?—and jumped to his feet, panting as though we really had been doing it. For a moment he couldn't speak. He was backed into a far corner of the stall; he'd have to bolt past me to get out. I wasn't crying or laughing, or coming at him or anything, just standing there.

"Mircha," he said, and that was the only time but one he ever called me by my name. "Mircha, I can't. There's a lady."

A lady, mind you. Not a plain woman, a lady. "The bloody *hell* there is," I said. I don't think I screamed it, but who remembers? "Three years, almost, never out of each other's sight for ten minutes together, what bloody *lady?*"

"A long time," Sirit Byar said very softly. "A long, long time, big girl." The words were coming out of him one by one, two by two. He said, "I've not seen her since before you were born."

Never mind what I said to him then. If there's little enough in my life that warms me to remember, there's less that truly shames me, except for what I said to Sirit Byar in the next few moments. Just set it down that I asked him what he thought his great love was doing while he was wandering the land being forever faithful to her. Just set that much down—so—and let it alone.

Sirit Byar bore it all, big hands hanging open at his sides, and waited for me to run out of words and wind. Then he said, sounding very tired, "Her name is Jailly Doura. She is mad."

I sat down in the straw. Sirit Byar said, "Jailly Doura. There was a child. Her family married her to a man who took the child gladly, but it died." He swung his head left and right, the way he did sometimes, like an animal that can't find its old way out of a place. "It died," he said, "our child. She has been mad ever since, fifteen years it is. Jailly Doura."

Two *ls* in the name, are you getting it? I said, "Credevek. That place where the rich people live. We always walk wide of Credevek—you won't pass the city gates, let alone sing there."

"Once," Sirit Byar whispered. Slumped against the wall, gray as our old stone Azdak under the road-brown weathering, he looked like no one I'd ever seen. He said, "I sang once for her in Credevek."

"Once in fifteen years," I said. "We do better than that in Davlo. Well, maybe faithfulness is easier if you don't have to see the person. I wouldn't know." There was a calmness on me, just as new and strange as all those tears I'd shed over the salt-meat boy. I felt very old. I patted the straw beside me and said, "Come and sit. I won't attack you, I promise. Come *on*, then."

Fourteen, and ordering Sirit Byar about like a plough horse. But he came, and we sat close against each other, because the night had turned wickedly cold. Sirit Byar even laid his arm across my shoulders, and it was all right. Whatever happened, whatever it was took me for a little time, it never happened again. Not with him, not with anybody. I asked, "Did you know there was a baby?"

Sirit Byar nodded. After a while he said, "What could I have done? Her parents would have locked her away forever, rather than have her walking the roads with a moneyless, mannerless south-coast street singer. And here's a wealthy man waiting to marry her and take her to live in Credevek, and what's a street singer to do for a gently bred girl and a child?" He shivered suddenly, hard, I could feel it. He said, "I went away."

"What became of her?" He blinked at me. "I mean, after—afterward? Where is she now, who takes care of her?" In Davlo we had Mother Choy. She took in all our strays—animals, children, and the moontouched alike—and if the lot of them lived in rags, on scraps, and under rotting thatch, well, they were glad enough to get it. Sirit Byar said, "Jailly Doura's husband is a good man. Another would have sent her away, but she lives with him still, in a house just north of Credevek, and he looks after her himself. I have been to that house."

"Once," I said. Sirit Byar's hand tightened on my shoulder, hard, and his face clenched in the same way. I couldn't tell you which hurt me more. He said, "She would not come into the room. I sang all night for a dark doorway, and I could smell her, feel the air move against me when she moved, but she would not let me see her. I could not bear that. I could not bear to come back again."

I knew there was more. I knew him that well, anyway. Nothing to do but sit there in the stall, with the *rishu* snoring and her calf looking sleepily at us, and the air growing lighter and colder, both. And sure enough, in a year or two, Sirit Byar said, "I thought I could make her well. I was so sure."

He wasn't talking to me. I said, "All songs are magic, always. You told me that."

"So they are," Sirit Byar answered. "But my songs are for farmers' dogs, I told you that also. I learned that before you were born, in that house in Credevek." He turned to look at me, and his eyes were as old and weary as any I ever saw. He said, "The great ones, they could have healed her. Sarani Elsu could have brought her back. I—" and he just stopped, and his head went down.

I knew there wouldn't be another word this time, no matter how long I waited for it. So after a while I said, "So you tried to sing her madness away, and it didn't work. And you never tried again. Fifteen years."

"Her husband told me not to come back," Sirit Byar mumbled. "I left her worse off than before, what could I say to him? He is a good man, what could I say?" He looked at me for an answer, but I didn't have one. In a bit his head sagged forward again. I wriggled around until I could get comfortable with his head resting on my arm, and then I just sat like that until long into morning, while the old man slept and slept, and I just sat.

And the next day, and the days after that, you'd think none of it had ever happened. We walked the roads as usual, talking a bit more, as I've said, but we never once talked about our night in the byre, and there was never another bloody word about his Jailly Doura. Oh, I might have asked, and he might have answered, but I didn't think I wanted to know a thing more about her and him and their child than I already knew, thank you very much. No, I wasn't *jealous*— please, do me a favor—but I was fourteen and he was mine, that's all, whatever that means when you're fourteen. He wasn't my father or my lover, he was just mine. And if I *was* jealous, I had a bloody right to be, only I wasn't. Just big and ugly, the same as always.

One thing different, though. At night, usually when he thought I was asleep, he practiced a new song over and over. Or maybe it was an old one, for all I could tell—he kept his voice so low and his south-coast accent would get so thick that I couldn't make out one word in ten. Even when I really was asleep, the slidey, whispery music always filled my dreams full of faces I'd never seen, animals I didn't recognize. It sounded like a lullaby people might sing in some other country; like my lucky coin that's worth something somewhere, I've no doubt. Never had dreams like that again.

We did get to Davlo that spring—Sirit Byar went out of his usual way to make sure of it. There was nothing for him there—he didn't bother with even a single night at the Miller's Joy, but stayed with a farmer while I went on alone. I found Desh Jakani at his smithy, and he told me that my father hadn't been into the Miller's Joy for more than a month now, and that he'd been thinking seriously of going by our farm any day to look in on him. "Never the same man after you ran away," he told me. "The spirit just went out of him, everybody says so." My father hadn't had much spirit in him to begin with, and Desh Jakani was a liar born, but all the same I scrambled up that mountain track as though a rock-*targ* were after me, really thankful that I'd come home when I had, and wishing with all my heart that I were anywhere, anywhere else in the world.

The way had disappeared completely. I'd always kept things cut back at least a little, but everything—the path, the pasture, our few poor fields—everything was smothered in foxweed, ice-berry brambles and *drumak*. I looked for our *rishu* and the two Karakosk horses, but they were gone. The door of the house hung on one hinge. My father squatted naked in the doorway.

He wasn't mad, like Sirit Byar's Jailly Doura, or even very drunk. He knew me right away, but he didn't care. I picked him up—all cold bones, he was—and carried him into the house. No point in going into what it looked like; it was just the house of a man who'd given up long ago. When I left? Like enough. Likely Desh Jakani was right about that, after all.

My father never spoke a single word during the two days I stayed with him. I put him to bed, and I made soup for him—I'm no cook, and proud of it, but I can make decent soup—and managed to get some of it down his throat, while I told him all about my travels with Sirit Byar, the things I'd seen with him, the people I'd met, the songs I'd learned. I think I sang him every song I knew of Sirit Byar's during those two days, including "The Good Folk," the one that started the brawl in the Miller's Joy so long ago. He listened. I don't know what he heard, because his eyes never changed, but he was listening, I know that much. I swear he was listening.

I even told him about the salt-meat boy. That was on the morning of the third day, when I was holding him steady on the chamber pot. That's when he died, trust my father. Not a sound, not a whimper, not the tiniest fart—he was just dead in my arms, just like that. I buried him at the doorstep, because that's the way we do in Davlo, and left the door open for the animals and the creeping vines, and walked down into town one last time to join Sirit Byar.

What? What? You should see the look on your little face—you can't wait to know if we ever went to Credevek together, ever tried a second time to sing Jailly Doura back from wherever her poor ragged mind had been roaming all this long time. Well, let me tell you, for the next two years, Sirit Byar saw to it that we didn't go anywhere near Suk'hai, let alone Credevek. He'd have us veering back south as early as Chun, never mind who expected him where, or what bounty he might be passing up. When I asked, he only grunted that he was getting too old to trudge that far uphill, and anyway, those folk were all too tightfisted to make the extra miles worthwhile. Wasn't my place to argue with him, even if I'd been of a mind to. I wasn't.

Those were good years, those last two we had together. My strength had caught up with my size, and I could have carried the *kiit* all day by a couple of fingers. We tramped every road between Cape Dylee and Karakosk, between Grannach Harbor and Derridow, him writing his new songs in the air as we went, and me eyeing every pretty boy in every town square as boldly as though I were some great wild beauty who'd been the one to do the choosing all her life. There wasn't one of them as beautiful as my salt-meat boy, and they didn't all come bleating after me by night—no fear about that—but I'll tell you one thing, Sirit Byar never had to sing anybody to my bed again, no bloody fear about *that*, either. You're almost sweet when you blush, chicken-wrist, do you know that? Almost.

Yes. Yes, yes, we did go to Credevek together.

It was my doing, if you want to know. I won't say he'd never have gone without me; all I *will* say is that he hadn't been back there for—what's that make it?—seventeen years, so you figure it out. What put it into my head, that's another story. I wanted to see her, I know that. It started as a notion, just a casual wondering what she looked like, but then I couldn't get it out of my head; it kept growing stronger and stronger. And maybe I wanted to see him, too, see him with her, just to know. Just to find out what it was I wanted to know. Maybe that was it, who remembers?

So that last morning, after we'd been to Chun—I remember it was Chun, because that was one place where Sirit Byar did sing "The Juggler" in public— and came once more to the Fors na'Shachim crossroads, I said to him, as casually as I could, "That peddler yesterday, the man we traded with for the new kettle? He spoke of trouble on the Fors road. I meant to tell you."

Sirit Byar shrugged. "Bandits." One fairy tale's true, anyway—there wasn't a high-toby in the country would have laid a hand on Sirit Byar or lifted a single copper from him. They used to come out of the woods sometimes, bashful as marsh-goats, and travel along with us a little way, hanging back to encourage him to try over a new song as though they weren't there. They couldn't make him out, you see. I think they felt he was somehow one of them, but they couldn't have said why. That's what I think.

"Plague," I told him. "Fire-plague, broken out all down the Fors road between here and Dushant. He said the only safe route south was the Snowhawk's Highway. It's a good road—we can follow it as far as Cheth na'Vaudry and then cut west to Fors. We could do that."

Sirit Byar looked at me for a long time. Did he know I was lying? I've no more idea than you have. What *I* knew was that fire-plague hits the south coast, his country, at least once every ten years; people die in hundreds, thousands sometimes. He said at last, "We would have to pass through Credevek."

I didn't answer him. We stood silent at the crossroads, listening to insects, birds, the wind in the dry leaves. Then Sirit Byar said, "Azdak." Not another word. He took the *kiit* from my hand and set off toward Credevek without looking back. Limp or no limp, I had to trot to catch up with him.

So there's how we came to Credevek, which is a strange place, all grand lawns, high stone houses, cobblestone streets, servants coming and going on their masters' errands. No beggars. No tinkers, no peddlers. A few farm carts, a few children. *Quiet*. The quiet sticks to your skin in that town.

Sirit Byar marched straight down the main street of Credevek, with me trailing after him, not knowing what to do or even how to walk if I wasn't carrying the *kiit*. People came to their windows to stare at us, but no one recognized Sirit Byar, and he never looked this way or that. Straight through the town until the paved streets and the stone houses fell away, nothing much after but meadowland gone to seed, a few pastures, and the brown Durli Hills in the distance. And one big wooden house snugged down into the shadows between two foothills—you could miss it if you didn't look sharp. Sirit Byar said, "If we travel by night, we will reach the Snowhawk's Highway before noon tomorrow."

I said, "That's where they live, isn't it? That's where Jailly Doura lives."

Sirit Byar nodded. "If she lives still." He turned to look at me, and suddenly he reached out to put his hand on the side of my neck, right here. My hair, the roots of my hair, just went cold with it. He said, "Between that house and where we stand, there's our journey. That's what the god of wanderers was saying to me. Whatever happens in that house, this is why we met, you and I. I would never be here, but for you. Thank you, Mircha."

I didn't know what to say. I just said, "Well, I wanted to get out of Davlo, that's all." I tried to take the *kiit* back—I mean, it was my *job*, carrying it, from the first day—but he wouldn't let me. He swung it to his shoulder and we started on our journey.

And it was a longer journey than it looked, I can tell you. By noon, which is when we should have reached the house in the foothills, it hardly seemed any closer than when we'd first seen it. Barely this side of sunset, it was, before we'd done with trudging through empty, stony defiles and turned up a last steep road that ran between two huge boulders. There was a man waiting there. He was short and old, and the little that was left of his hair was as white as Sirit Byar's, and if he wasn't exactly fat, he looked soft as porridge, and about that color. But he faced us proudly, blocking our way like one of those boulders himself. He said, "Sirit Byar. I thought it would be today."

Now. I have to tell the rest slowly. I have to be careful, remember it right, so you can set it down exactly the way it was. Sirit Byar said, "Aung Jatt," and nothing more. He just stood looking down at the other man, the way the high, shadowed house looked down on us three. Aung Jatt didn't take any notice of me, which is difficult. He said to Sirit Byar, "You cannot see her. I will not allow it."

"It has been fifteen years," Sirit Byar began, but Aung Jatt interrupted him. "And if it had been fifty, she'd still not be healed of you, healed of your music. I told you never to return here, Sirit Byar." You know how, when you grip something too tightly, it starts shivering and slipping in your hand? Aung Jatt's voice was like that.

Sirit Byar said only, "I must sing for her once more."

"Oh, aye, once more," the old man answered him. "And when you have sung your songs of love and ghosts, dragons and sailors, and gone your way again, who will stay behind to piece what's left of her into some kind of human shape *once more*?" He mimicked Sirit Byar's deep, hoarse voice so bitterly that I giggled. I couldn't help it. Aung Jatt never took his eyes off Sirit Byar.

"She did not know me for three years after you were here," he whispered. "Three years. What possessed me to let her listen to you? What made me imagine that the music of the father might keep her from trying to follow the child? For three years, she wept in the dark and ate what I pushed under her door—for two years more, she said no word but the child's name, over and over and over. For five years after that—" He made himself stop; you could hear his throat clicking and grinding. Sirit Byar waited, blinking in the setting sun.

"Fifteen years," Aung Jatt said presently. "There are times even now when she takes me for you, do you know that?" He grinned like a dead man. "You might think that would hurt me, and in a way it does, because then she sometimes tries to kill me. I must always be watchful."

Sirit Byar closed his eyes, shook his head, and started to move around Aung Jatt, up the road toward the house beyond. Aung Jatt stopped him with a palm gently against his chest. He said, "But she has stopped calling for the child. Most often she sleeps through the night, and it has been some while since I had to feed her. And she hates you far more than I do, Sirit Byar."

You couldn't be sure, because the sunlight was slanting off the windows, but I thought I saw someone moving in the house, just for a moment, the way you can see a feeling flicker across someone's eyes and gone again. Aung Jatt went on, "She hates you because she knows—she *knows*—that the child would still be alive if you had defied her parents and stayed with her. I know better, but there." He chuckled and patted Sirit Byar's chest with his fingertips. He said, "Did I tell you when you were here before that it was a boy? I'm growing old, I forget things."

Sirit Byar said, without looking at me, "Come on, big girl," and put Aung Jatt out of his way with one arm. Aung Jatt made no protest this time. He was still smiling a little as he watched us step past him—I say *us*, but he never saw me, not for a minute. He didn't follow, and he didn't speak again until we were on the stone steps that led to the front door. Then he called after us, "Beware, Sirit Byar! The second floor is her domain—when you are there with her, you are in the moon. The servants will not ever climb the stair, and should she come down, they scuttle away into corners like beetles until she passes. Beware of her, Sirit Byar!"

I heard Sirit Byar's scornful grunt next to me—after six years, there wasn't a grunt or a snort of his I couldn't translate. But I wasn't scornful, I'll tell you that much. I said I've never been frightened, and it's true, but madmen—madwomen—make me uneasy, if you like. Madwomen in the dark make me very uneasy. Sirit Byar pushed the door open. Just before we went inside, I looked back at Aung Jatt. He was standing exactly where we had left him, and he was laughing without making a sound.

It was a fine, proud house, certainly—and remember, I've slept in a palace. Felt bigger inside than outside somehow, and it felt *soft*, too—lots of thick Tahi'rak rugs and drapes and those buttery cushions they sew in Fors out of traders' old saddle-blankets. Hardly an inch of floor or wall showing: the whole place was made like a cradle, like a special box you keep something precious and breakable in. Servants slipped past us without a word, or anyway their shadows did, for I couldn't hear their footsteps, nor our own, come to that. I couldn't hear the front door swing shut, or any sound from the outside once it had. What I did hear was someone breathing. It wasn't Sirit Byar, and it wasn't me—I don't think either of us had breathed since we came through that door. Sirit Byar touched my shoulder and nodded me left, toward the stair. You'd expect a house like this to have a grand spiral stairway, but this was just a narrow little one, not room enough for the two of us to go abreast. Sirit Byar had to hold the *kiit* tight against his side to keep it from hitting the railing. I followed him, not thinking too much, not feeling anything, because why not? Where else was I to go right then?

It was different on the second floor. Deepsea cold, it was, and thick with twilight, old stale, mushy twilight filling our eyes and ears and nostrils, like when you get smothered in the bedding when you're asleep, and then that's all you can dream. The breathing was all around us now, no louder, but quickening, eager. There wasn't another sound anywhere in the world. Sirit Byar stopped on the landing. Clearly, loudly even, he said, "Jailly Doura."

The breathing never faltered. Sirit Byar said again, "Jailly Doura. I am here."

No answer. Where we stood, I could make out a chair, a wall, another chair, a gray face floating in the air, the gray mouth of a corridor. Sirit Byar looked left and right, trying to guess where the breathing might be coming from. My eyes were growing used to the dimness now—I saw that the floating face was a painting hanging on the wall, and I saw other paintings, and lamps and braziers as tall as me, taller, all unlit, and a great dark chandelier swinging overhead. The corridor lay straight ahead of us, with high double doors on either hand. Sirit Byar said, "This way," and went forward like a man moving in his own house in full day. I hurried after him. I didn't want to be left behind, left alone in the moon.

He never looked at any of the doors, only strode along until the corridor bent right and opened out into a kind of—what?—well, like an indoor courtyard, I suppose. There must have been an opening to the sky somewhere, because the twilight was more watery here, but I still couldn't see as far as the walls of the place, and the little warm night wind I felt on my face now and then made me wonder if it *had* any walls. There were a couple of benches, and there were pale statues in alcoves—and, of all the bloody things, a tree, set right into the floor, right in the middle of the room. A *sesao*, I think, or it might have been a red *mouri*, what do I know about trees? I certainly don't know how Aung Jatt ever watered and nourished the thing, but its trunk disappeared in darkness, and its branches reached out almost as far as the bench where Sirit Byar had calmly sat down and begun tuning the *kiit*. I stood. I wanted my feet under me in that house, I knew that much.

The breathing still sounded so close I thought I could feel it sometimes, and yet I couldn't even be sure where it was coming from. Sirit Byar looked up into the tree branches and said, "Do you remember this song, Jailly Doura?" He touched the *kiit* with the heel of his hand, to get a sort of deep sigh out of all the strings, and began to sing.

I knew the song. So do you—if there's one song of Sirit Byar's that the wind carried everywhere, and that clung where it landed like a cocklebur, it was "Where's My Shoe?" Right, that funny, ridiculous song about a man who keeps losing things—his shoe, his wig, his spectacles, his false teeth, his balls, his wife—and that's the way people sing it in the taverns. But the melody's a sad one, if you whistle it over slowly, and people don't always sing the very last verses, because those are about misplacing your faith, your heart. Nobody ever sang it the way Sirit Byar sang it that night, quiet and gentle, with the *kiit* bouncing happily along, running circles all around the words. I can't listen to it now, never, not since that time.

He spoke to the tree again, saying, "Do you remember? You always liked that song—listen to this now." And his voice, that damn fisherman's growl of his, sounded like a boy's voice, and you'd have thought he'd never trusted anyone with his songs before.

He sang "The Woodcutter's Wife" next, that odd thing about an old woman who doesn't want to die without hearing someone, anyone, say, "You're my dear friend, and I love you." Anyway, she goes from her husband to her children, then to her brothers and sisters, and finally hears the words from a tired village whore, who'll say anything for money. And yet, when she does say it for money, somehow it comes out true, and the old woman dies happy. Not a song I'd choose, was it me trying to woo a madwoman out of her tree, but he knew what he was doing. About songs, he always knew what he was doing.

I think it was "The Good Folk" next, and then "The Old Priest and the Old God." By then it had gotten so dark in that strange courtyard that I couldn't see the tree, let alone Sirit Byar. He took flint and steel out of one pocket, a candle end from the other, and made a little sputtering light that he stood up on the bench beside him. He sang the song about the lady made out of flowers, and he sang "Thou," the one he wrote for his sister, and even my favorite, the one about the man and the Fox in the Moon. Never moved from where he sat in his tatter of candlelight, no more than I did. I just stood very still and listened to him singing, old song on new, one after another. I could hear Jailly Doura's heart beating somewhere near, as well as her breathing, both quick as a bird's— or a *shukri*'s—and one time I was sure I could smell her, like faraway water. Twice Sirit Byar asked, "Will you show yourself, Jailly Doura?" but no chance of that. So he just sang on to someone he couldn't see, making his magic, drawing her in through the dark, so slowly, the way you can sometimes charm a dream into letting you remember it. That's magic, too.

Then he sang the lullaby. The one he'd been practicing every night for two years. I remember a bit of it, just a little.

> "Don't fall asleep,
> don't close your eyes—
> everything happens at night.
> don't you sleep—
> as soon as you slumber,
> the sun starts to ripen,
> the flowers tell stories. . . ."

She made a sound. Not a moan, not a cry, not anything with a name or a shape. Just put down that she tried very hard not to make it. It came out of her anyway.

When she hit him, she knocked the *kiit* out of his hands. That time he couldn't save it—rugs or no rugs, I heard it crack and split, heard eighteen double courses yowl against stone. I just caught a lightning flash of her in the candlelight: matted gray hair flying, eyes like gashes in dead flesh, gaunt arms flailing out of control, beating her own head as much as Sirit Byar's. Something bright flickered in her hands against his throat. The candle fell over and went out.

The darkness was so heavy, I felt myself bending under it. I said, "Jailly Doura, don't hurt him. Please, don't hurt him." I could hear the *kiit* strings still thrashing and jangling faintly, but nothing more, not even the dreadful *breathing*. Nothing more until Sirit Byar began to sing again.

> "Don't you sleep—
> the marsh-goats are singing,
> the fish are all dancing,
> the river asks riddles. . . ."

You couldn't have told that he was singing past a dagger, or a broken piece of glass, or whatever she had been saving for him all this long while. He sounded the way he always did—gruff and south coast, and a little slower than the beat, and not caring about anything in the world but the song. He might have been back in the Miller's Joy, sitting on a table, singing it to fighting, bawling sots; he might have been trying it over to himself as we trudged down some evening road looking for a place to sleep. He sounded like Sirit Byar.

He sang it through to the end, the lullaby, so I knew she hadn't killed him yet, but that was all I did know. I couldn't see anything, I couldn't hear anything, except the footsteps beginning to shuffle slowly toward me. They dragged a little, as though she'd somehow taken on Sirit Byar's limp. I'd have run—all bloody *right*, of course I'd have run, that's just good sense, that's different from fear— but in that crushing dark the steps were coming from everywhere, the way the breathing had been at first. My knees wouldn't hold me up. I sat down and waited.

Close to, she didn't smell like a distant river at all, but like any old hill woman, like my father. She smelled lifelong tired, lifelong dirty, she smelled of clothes sweated in and slept in until they've just *died*, you understand me? I know that smell; I was born and raised to it, and I'd smell just like that now if I hadn't run off with Sirit Byar. What chilled my bowels was the notion that a wealthy madwoman, prowling a grand house among terrified servants, should smell like home.

When I felt her standing over me, with the stiff, cold ends of that hair trailing across the back of my neck, I said loudly, "I am Mircha Del, of Davlo. You should know that if you're going to kill me." Then I just sat there, feeling out with my skin for whatever she had in her hand.

Her breath on my cheek was raw and old and stagnant, a sick animal's breath. I closed my eyes, even in the darkness, the way you do when you're hoping the *sheknath* or the rock-*targ* will think you're dead. I was ready for her teeth, for her long, jagged nails, but the next thing I felt was her arms around me.

She rocked me, chicken-wrist. Jailly Doura held me in her sad, skinny arms and bumped me back and forth against her breast, pushing and tugging on me as though she were trying to loosen a tree stump in the ground. Likely she didn't remember at all how you rock somebody, but then I don't remember anybody ever rocking me in my life, except her, so I wouldn't ever have known the right way. I did have an idea that it was supposed to be more comfortable, but it wasn't bad. And the breath wasn't so awful, either, when you got used to it, nor that hair all down my face. What was bad was the little whimpering sound, so soft that I didn't truly hear it but felt it in my body, the broken crooning that never quite became tears but just shivered and shivered on the edge. That was bad, but I kept my eyes closed tight and helped her rock me, and Sirit Byar began to sing again.

It doesn't matter what he sang. I know some of the songs in my bones to this day—bloody well *should*, after all—and there were others I'd never heard before and never will again, no matter. What matters is that he sang all night long, sitting by his shattered *kiit*, with a madwoman's grieving for his only applause. Jailly Doura went on rocking me in her arms, and Sirit Byar sang about merrows and farmwives and wandering Narsai tinkers, and I'll be damned if I didn't fall off to sleep—only a little, only for a moment now and then—as though they were really my parents putting me to bed, just the way they did every night. And stone Azdak only knows what Aung Jatt thought was going on upstairs.

Dawn came suddenly, or maybe I'd been dozing again. It was like staring through rain, but I could see the courtyard around us—there were walls, of course, and a few narrow windows, and the tree wasn't *that* big—and I could see Sirit Byar, looking a bit smaller than usual himself, and white as his own hair in that rainy light. Jailly Doura was still holding me, but not rocking anymore, and sometime in the night she'd stopped making that terrible silent sound. If I turned my head very slowly and carefully, I could see most of one side of her face—a thin, lined, worn face it was, but the nose was strong and the mouth wasn't a dead slash at all, but full and tender. Her hair was a forsaken birds' nest, thick with mess—well, about like mine, as you can see. Her eyes were closed.

Sirit Byar stood up. His voice was a rag of itself, but he spoke out loudly, not to Jailly Doura this time, nor to me, but to *someone*. I couldn't tell where he was looking, what he was seeing. He said, "This is my last song. Take it. I make this bargain of my own will. I, Sirit Byar." He stood silent for a moment, and then he nodded once, slowly, as though he'd had his reply. Oh, chicken-wrist, I can still see him.

I'm not going to sing you the whole song, that last one. I could, but I'm not going to. This one dies with me, it's supposed to. But this is the ending:

> "Merchant, street girl, beggar, yeoman,
> king or common, man or woman,
> only two things make us human—
> sorrow and love, sorrow and love. . . .

> Songs and fame are vain endeavor—
> only two things fail us never.
> only two things last forever—
> sorrow and love, sorrow and love. . . ."

By the time he finished, it was light enough that I could see Aung Jatt standing in the courtyard entrance. Behind me Jailly Doura stirred and sighed, and as I turned my head she opened her eyes again. But they weren't the same eyes. They were gray and wide and full of surprise, curiosity, whatever you want—they were a young woman's eyes in a tired grown face. Maybe I had eyes like that when I was first traveling with Sirit Byar, but I doubt it. She said softly, just the way he'd said it to me, "There you are." And Sirit Byar answered her, "Here I am."

Careful now, both of us, chicken-wrist, you and me. Jailly Doura looked down at me in her arms and said—said *what*? She said, "Are you my daughter, little one?"

"No," I said. "No, no, I'm not. I wish I were." Then I was horribly afraid that I might have lost her again, saying that, driven her right back to where she'd been, but she only smiled and touched my lips and whispered, "Ah, I know. I was just hoping for a moment, one last, last time. Never mind. You have a sweet face."

I do not have a sweet face. There are ugly people who have sweet faces, much good may it do them in this world. I have the face I want, a dirty, mean wild animal's face that makes people leave me alone. Fine. Fine, I wouldn't have it different. But if ever I wanted in my life to have sweetness that somebody could see, it would have been then. I stood up, cramped and cranky, and helped Jailly Doura to rise.

She was small, really, a tiny gray barefoot person in a mucky ruin of a gown that must have cost someone a few gold *lotis* a long time ago, and that a beggar wouldn't have wiped his nose on now. She was as shaky on her feet as a newborn marsh-goat, but she wasn't mad. I looked over toward Aung Jatt, trying to beckon him over to her, but he was staring at Sirit Byar, who had stumbled down to one knee. Jailly Doura was by him before I was. She knelt before him and took his face between her hands. "Not so soon," she said. I remember that. She said, "Not so soon, I'll not have it. I will not, my dear, no. Do you hear me, Sirit Byar?"

You see, she knew better than I what he'd done. He had given up his last song to the gods, the Other Folk, whatever you people call them. And a bard's last song has power, a last song is always answered, as this one was—but what becomes of the bard when the song is over? Sirit Byar's face was a shrunken white mask, but his eyes were open and steady. He said, "Forgive me, Jailly Doura."

"Not if you leave us," she answered him. "Not if you dare leave now." But there was no anger in her voice, and no hope either. Sirit Byar made that half-grunt, half-snort sound that he always made when people were being a little too much for him. He said, "Well, forgive me or no, you are well, and I've done what was for me to do. Now I'm weary."

I wanted to touch him. I wanted to hold him the way Jailly Doura had held me all night, but I just stood with my fingers in my mouth, like a scared baby.

Sirit Byar smiled his almost-smile at me and whispered, "I'm sorry the *kiit* broke, big girl. I wanted you to have it. Good-bye." And he was gone, so. Aung Jatt closed his eyes himself, and began to weep. I remember. Jailly Doura didn't, and I didn't, but old Aung Jatt cried and cried.

I buried him myself, and the shards of the *kiit* with him, under the threshold of the house, as I'd done with my father. The others wanted to help me, but I wouldn't let them. When I was finished, I scratched a picture of Azdak, god of wanderers, on the stone stair, and I walked away. So now you know where Sirit Byar lies.

There's no more worth the telling. Aung Jatt and Jailly Doura, wanted me to stay with them as long as I liked, forever, but I only passed a few days at the house with them. What I mostly remember is washing and washing Jailly Doura's long gray-black hair in her bath, as the Queen's ladies used to do with me, four of them at a time to hold me in the tub. I always hated it, and I've not put up with it since, but it's different when you're doing it for someone else. You don't wash fifteen, sixteen years of lunatic despair away in three days, but by the time I left, Jailly Doura could anyway peep in a mirror and start to recognize the handsome, dignified mistress of a great house, with servants underfoot like *dai*-beetles and a husband who looked at her like sunrise. I don't begrudge it—whatever was hers she'd paid double-dear price for it, and double again. But I'd have liked Sirit Byar to see her this way, even once.

When I left, she walked with me down to the two great stones where we'd first met Aung Jatt, a hundred years ago. She didn't bother with saying, "Come back and visit us," and I didn't bother promising. Instead she took both my hands and swung them, the way children do, and she just said, "I would have been proud if you had been my daughter."

I didn't know how to answer. I kissed her hands, which I've never done with anybody except the Queen, and you have to do that. Then I swung Sirit Byar's old sea-bag to my shoulder, and I started off alone. I didn't look back, but Jailly Doura called after me, "So would *he* have been proud. Remember, Mircha Del!"

And I have remembered, and that's why the fit took me to have someone set it all down, the only true tale of Sirit Byar you're ever likely to hear. No, I told you I don't want it; what good's your scribble to me? I can't read it—and besides, I was there. Keep it for yourself, keep it for anyone who wants to know a little of what he was. Bad enough they mess up his songs, let them get *something* the right way round, anyway. Farewell, my chicken-wrist—here's your twelve coppers, and another for the sweet way you blush. There's an ore barge tied up at Grebak, waiting for a good woman to handle the sweep, if I'm there by tomorrow eve.

Mayra Santos-Febres

Marina's Fragrance

The lusciously erotic, surrealistic fiction has earned Mayra Santos-Febres an international reputation as one of the most interesting young Caribbean writers working today. She has won numerous awards, including the Letras de Oro and the Sarandi Juan Rulfo Prize (from French Radio). Her work was recently featured at the 1997 Afro-Hispanic Conference.

Nathan Budoff and Lydia Platon Lazaro have translated Santos-Febres's short fiction from the Spanish in Urban Oracles, *available from Brookline Books (a small press in Cambridge, Massachusetts). "Marina's Fragrance," reprinted from that volume, is a highly sensual work of magic realism, and one of the most memorable stories I've read all year.*

—T. W.

Doña Marina Paris was a woman of many charms. At forty-nine her skin still breathed those fragrances which when she was young had left the men of her town captivated and searching for ways to lick her flanks to see if they tasted as good as they smelled. And every day they smelled of something different. At times, a delicate aroma of witch's oregano would drift out of the folds of her thighs; other days, she perfumed the air with masculine mahogany or with small wild lemons. But most of the time she exuded pure satisfaction.

From the time she was very little, Doña Marina had worked in the Pinchimoja take-out restaurant, an establishment opened in the growing town of Carolina by her father Esteban Paris. Previously, Esteban had been a virtuoso clarinetist, a road builder and a molasses sampler for the Victoria Sugarcane Plantation. His common-law wife, Edovina Vera, was the granddaughter of one Pancracia Hernandez, a Spanish shopkeeper fallen on hard times, for whom time had set a trap in the form of a black man from Canovanas. He showed her what it meant to really enjoy a man's company, after she had lost faith in almost everything, including God.

Marina grew up in the Pinchimoja. Mama Edovina, who gave birth to another sister every year, entrusted Marina with the restaurant and made her responsible for watching Maria, the half-crazy woman who helped Mama move the giant pots of rice and beans, the pots of *tinapa* in sauce, of chicken soup, roasted sweet potato, and salt cod with raisins, the specialty of the house. Her special task was to make sure that Maria didn't cook with coconut oil. Someone had to protect the restaurant's reputation and keep people from thinking that the owners were a crowd of sneaky blacks from Loiza.

From eight to thirteen years of age, Marina exuded spicy, salty, and sweet odors from all the hinges of her flesh. And since she was always enveloped in her fragrances, she didn't even notice that they were bewitching every man who passed close to her. Her pompous smile, her kinky curls hidden in braids or kerchiefs, her high cheekbones, and the scent of the day drew happiness from even the most decrepit sugarcane-cutter, from the skinniest road-worker burnt by the sun, from her father, the frustrated clarinetist, who rose from his stupor of alcohol and daydreams to stand near his Marina just to smell her as she passed by.

Eventually, the effect Marina had on men began to preoccupy Edovina. She was especially worried by the way she was able to stir Esteban from his alcoholic's chair. The rest of the time he sat prostrate from five o'clock every morning, after he finished buying sacks of rice and plantains from the supplier who drove by in his cart on the way down to the Nueva Esperanza market. Marina was thirteen, a dangerous age. So one day Edovina opened a bottle of Cristobal Colon Rum from Mayaguez, set it next to her partner's chair, and went to look for Marina in the kitchen, where she was peeling sweet potatoes and plantains.

"Today you begin working for the Velazquezes. They'll give you food, new clothes, and Doña Georgina's house is near the school." Edovina took Marina out the back of the Pinchimoja over towards Jose de Diego Street. They crossed behind Alberti's pharmacy to the house of Doña Georgina, a rich and pious white woman, whose passion for cassava stewed with shrimp was known throughout the town.

It was at about this time that Marina began to smell like the ocean. She would visit her parents every weekend. Esteban, a bit more pickled each time, reached the point where he no longer recognized her, for he became confused thinking that she would smell like the daily specials. When Marina arrived perfumed with the red snapper or shrimp that they ate regularly in the elegant mansion, her father took another drag from the bottle which rested by his chair and lost himself in memories of his passion for the clarinet. The Pinchimoja no longer attracted the people that it used to. It had lapsed into the category of breakfast joint; you could eat *funche* there, or corn fritters with white cheese, coffee and stew. The office workers and road-builders had moved to a different take-out restaurant with a new attraction that could replace the dark body of the thirteen-year-old redolent with flavorful odors—a jukebox which at lunch time played Felipe Rodriguez, Perez Prado, and Benny More's Big Band.

It was in the Velazquez house that Marina became aware of her remarkable capacity to harbor fragrances in her flesh. She had to get up before five every morning so she could prepare the rice and beans and their accompaniments; this was the condition that the Velazquezes imposed in exchange for allowing her to attend the public school. One day, while she was thinking about the food that she had to prepare the next morning, she caught her body smelling like the menu. Her elbows smelled like fresh *recaillo*; her armpits smelled like garlic, onions and red pepper; her forearms like roasted sweet potato with butter; the space between her flowering breasts like pork loin fried in onions; and further down like grainy white rice, just the way her rice always came out.

From then on she imposed a regimen of drawing remembered scents from her body. The aromas of herbs came easily. Marjoram, pennyroyal and mint were her favorites. Once she felt satisfied with the results of these experiments, Marina began to experiment with emotional scents. One day she tried to imagine the fragrance of sadness. She thought long and hard of the day Mama Edovina sent her to live in the Velazquez household. She thought of Esteban, her father, sitting in his chair imagining what could have been his life as a clarinetist in the mambo bands or in Cesar Concepcion's combo. Immediately an odor of mangrove swamps and sweaty sheets, a smell somewhere between rancid and sweet, began to waft from her body. Then she worked on the smells of solitude and desire. Although she could draw those aromas from her own flesh, the exercise left her exhausted; it was too much work. Instead, she began to collect odors from her masters, from the neighbors near the Velazquez house, from the servants who lived in the little rooms off the courtyard of hens, and from the clothesline where Doña Georgina's son hung his underwear.

Marina didn't like Hipolito Velazquez, junior, at all. She had surprised him once in the bathroom pulling on his penis, which gave off an odor of oatmeal and sweet rust. This was the same smell (a bit more acid) which his underpants dispelled just before being washed. He was six years older than she, sickly and yellow, with emaciated legs and without even an ounce of a bottom. "Esculapio" she called him quietly when she saw him passing, smiling as always with those high cheekbones of a presumptuous Negress. The gossips around town recounted that the boy spent almost every night in the Tumbabrazos neighborhood, looking for mulatta girls upon whom he could "do the damage." He was enchanted by dark flesh. At times, he looked at her with a certain eagerness. Once he even insinuated that they should make love, but Marina turned him down. He looked so ugly to her, so weak and foolish, that just imagining Hipolito laying a finger upon her made her whole body begin to smell like rotten fish and she felt sick.

After a year and a half of living with the Velazquezes, Marina began to take note of the men around town. At Carolina's annual town fair that year, she met Eladio Salaman, who with one long smell left her madly in love. He had a lazy gaze and his body was tight and fibrous as the sweet heart of a sugarcane. His reddish skin reminded her of the tops of the mahogany tables in the Velazquez house. When Eladio Salaman drew close to Marina that night, he arrived with a tidal wave of new fragrances that left her enraptured for hours, while he led her by the arm all around the town square.

The ground of the rain forest, mint leaves sprinkled with dew, a brand-new washbasin, morning ocean spray . . . Marina began to practice the most difficult odors to see if she could invoke Eladio Salaman's. This effort drew her attention away from all her other duties, and at times she inadvertently served her masters dishes that had the wrong fragrances. One afternoon the shrimp and cassava came out smelling like pork chops with vegetables. Another day, the rice with pigeon peas perfumed the air with the aroma of greens and salt cod. The crisis reached such extremes that a potato casserole came out of the oven smelling exactly like the Velazquez boy's underpants. They had to call a doctor, for everyone in the house who ate that day vomited until they coughed up nothing but bile. They believed they had suffered severe food poisoning.

Marina realized that the only way to control her fascination with that man was to see him again. Secretly she searched for him on all the town's corners, using her sense of smell, until two days later she found him sitting in front of the Serceda Theater drinking a soda. That afternoon, Marina invented an excuse, and did not return to the house in time to prepare lunch. Later she ran home in time to cook dinner, which was the most flavorful meal that was ever eaten in the Velazquez dining room throughout the whole history of the town, for it smelled of love and of Eladio Salaman's sweet body.

One afternoon, while strolling through the neighborhood, Hipolito saw the two of them, Marina and Eladio, hand in hand, smiling and entwined in each other's aromas. He remembered how the dark woman had rejected him and now he found her lost in the caresses of that black sugarcane cutter. He waited for the appropriate moment and went to speak with his esteemed mother. Who knows what Hipolito told her—but when Marina arrived back at the house, Doña Georgina was furious.

"Indecent, evil, stinking black woman."

And Mama Edovina was forced to intervene to convince the mistress not to throw her daughter out of her house. Doña Georgina agreed, but only on the condition that Marina take a cut in her wages and an increase in her supervision. Marina couldn't go to the market unaccompanied, she couldn't stroll on the town square during the week, and she could only communicate with Eladio through messages.

Those were terrible days. Marina couldn't sleep; she couldn't work. Her vast memory of smells disappeared in one fell swoop. The food she prepared came out insipid—all of it smelled like an empty chest of drawers. This caused Doña Georgina to redouble her insults. "Conniving little thing, Jezebel, polecat."

One afternoon Marina decided she wouldn't take any more. She decided to summon Eladio through her scent, one that she had made in a measured and defined way and shown to him one day of kisses in the untilled back lots of the sugar plantation. "This is my fragrance," Marina had told him. "Remember it well." And Eladio, fascinated, drank it in so completely that Marina's fragrance would be absorbed into his skin like a tattoo.

Marina studied the direction of the wind carefully. She opened the windows of the mansion and prepared to perfume the whole town with herself. Immediately the stray dogs began to howl and the citizens rushed hurriedly through the streets, for they thought they were producing that smell of frightened bromeliads and burning saliva. Two blocks down the street, Eladio, who was talking to some friends, recognized the aroma; he excused himself and ran to see Marina. But as they kissed, the Velazquez boy broke in on them and, insulting him all the way, threw Eladio out of the house.

As soon as the door was closed, Hipolito proposed to Marina that if she let him suck her little titties he would maintain their secret and not say anything to his mother. "You can keep your job and escape Mama's insults, too," he told her, approaching her.

Marina became so infuriated that she couldn't control her body. From all of her pores wafted a scaly odor mixed with the stench of burned oil and acid used for cleaning engines. The odor was so intense that Hipolito had to lean on the living room's big colonial sofa with the medallions, overwhelmed by a wave of dizziness. He felt as if they had pulled the floor out from under him, and he fell squarely down on the freshly mopped tiles.

Marina sketched a victorious smile. With a firm tread she strode into Doña Georgina's bedroom. She filled the room with an aroma of desperate melancholy (she had drawn it from her father's body) that trampled the sheets and dressers. She was going to kill that old woman with pure frustration. Calmly she went to her room, bundled her things together, and gazed around the mansion. That pest, the Velazquez boy, lay on the floor in a state from which he would never fully recover. The master bedroom smelled of stale dreams that accelerated the palpitations of the heart. The whole house gave off disconnected, nonsensical aromas, so that nobody in town ever wanted to visit the Velazquez house again.

Marina smiled. Now she would go see Eladio. She would go resuscitate the Pinchimoja. She would leave that house forever. But before exiting through the front door a few filthy words—which surprised even her—escaped from her mouth. Walking down the balcony stairs, she was heard to say with determination,

"Let them say *now* that blacks stink!"

Emily Warn

Setting Celestial Signs
on Terrestrial Beings

All right, we've been inundated with a flood of angel material in the last few years. Nonetheless, Warn's lovely poem takes this tired theme and makes it soar. It comes from the summer issue of Bridges, *a small journal published in Eugene, Oregon.*

—T. W.

Creation is an emanation from the divine light; its secret is not the coming into existence of something new but the transmutation of the divine reality into something defined and limited—into a world.

—Adin Steinsaltz

1

The angels laugh at Esther's folded wings.
Too much dust on the pocked earth,
they say. So much chaos of dried leaves
and newspapers piled in innumerable languages
always blowing away. No headlines
on our wrangling behind the scenes.

Esther laughs back, My kingdom opens on pines
and mourning doves singing on red slate tiles,
on jays squabbling, acorns in their beaks.

Ach, *the angels say,* too many potatoes,
the ants falling into your tea just
as the chanting begins. We offer you
an archangel position. No more sweeping up bugs.
You can be one of the flaming *minyan,*
spinning the planet on its greased spheres.

Esther says, No thanks, I like how sparrows
and two-year-olds can't stop babbling,
how they out-trill an avalanche of cars.
Most people can't hear you. Besides,
those who do are marked by distractedness.

2

Esther opens her doors to bored angels,
tired of their one essence, of reflecting an above
and a below who want to learn the meaning of lost.

Earthbound, they remember the gate in the clouds
through which stars, moon, sun, wings,
clouds, leaves, rain, and snow hurtle.
They want to slip through trees like flocks
of sparrows. Esther teaches them to accept
what expands and contracts, as when rain stops
and collects in creeks. Muddy brown torrents
sweep away the slow gathering of dust after years
of drought. Clarity returns, rainwashed, windstripped.

3

Esther welcomes exiles and prophets, grunge bands
and migrants, madwomen, merlins and psychics,
palm readers and punks, theologians who stare
into their tea cups, their intuitions crippled.

They give her their unfinished prayers:
boxes of notebooks, paper scraps with God's
hyphenated names, an open book next to a potato grater.

Some need rungs, commas, and spikes,
need ladders, poles, cranes, and bricks, need sling shots,
rockets and wings. Some need silence. Others food.

Doubt assails Esther. Are broken prayers signs
of unmendable gods? With what chutzpah
does she think to finish them? No, not to finish,
to find and to listen, and in listening,
let them flow through her to their own unattainable ends.

minyan: (Hebrew) ten people required for the proper recitation of some Jewish prayers.

Jane Yolen

Rabbit Hole

Jane Yolen is no stranger to the pages of The Year's Best Fantasy and Horror. *Not only is this author recognized as one of the finest storytellers in America today, but she is also astonishingly prolific. Confronted each year with stories and poems published in a wide variety of venues (from children's books to mainstream anthologies to genre magazines), I always find it a difficult task to choose just one of her pieces to reprint.*

This year being no exception, it is a pleasure to include Yolen's work in the anthology once again. I selected the following story, "Rabbit Hole" (a wry look at a famous Victorian heroine), not only because the tale is delightful but also because it comes from a source many readers are likely to have missed: Wild Women, *a quirky anthology edited by Melissa Mia Hall. I could just as easily have chosen "Lost Girls" (from Yolen's new children's book,* Twelve Impossible Things Before Breakfast), *or the gorgeous dark fairy tale "Godmother Death" (from* Black Swan, White Raven). *All three are typical Yolen fantasies: written with a lyrical elegance, and packing more punch in a few brief pages than many writers achieve at far greater length.*

Dr. Yolen is the author of more than one hundred books for children, teenagers, and adults. Among the latter are Briar Rose, Cards of Grief, *and* Sister Light, Sister Dark.

She is also a folklore scholar, and teaches children's literature at Smith College. She and her husband divide their time between homes in western Massachusetts and St. Andrews, Scotland.

—T. W

The rabbit hole had been there from the first, though everything else had changed.

"Especially me," thought Alice, smoothing down her skirt and tucking the shirtwaist back in. She straightened the diamond ring on her left hand, which had a tendency to slip around now that she had lost so much weight. It was certainly going to be more difficult falling down the hole at eighty than it had been at eight. For one thing, the speed would no longer be exhilarating. She knew better now. For another, she feared her legs might not be up to the landing, especially after the operation on her hip.

Still, she wanted a bit of magic back in her life before she died and the doctor, bless him, thought she might go at any time. "Consider that you have had more than your share of years already," he had said. He'd never been a tactful man, though she appreciated his bluntness in this particular instance.

So she had sneaked away from her grandniece, set as a keeper over her, and still a bit unsteady with the cane, had come back to the meadow where it had all begun.

The tree her sister Edith and she had been reading under when that first adventure started had long been felled after a lightning strike. Council houses now took up most of the open space: tan-faced two-story buildings alike as cereal boxes. But the rabbit hole was still there, as she had known it would be, in the middle of the little green park set aside for pensioners. She opened the gate and checked around. No one else was in the park, which pleased her. It would have been difficult explaining just exactly what it was she planned to do.

Closing the gate behind her, she went over to the hole and sat down beside it. It was a smallish hole, ringed round with spikey brown grass. The grass was wet with dew but she didn't mind. If the trip down the hole didn't kill her outright, magic would dry off her skirts. *Either way . . .* she thought . . . *either way . . .*

She wondered if she should wait for the rabbit, but he was at least as old as she. If rabbits even lived that long. She should have looked that up before coming. Her late husband, Reggie, had been a biologist manqué and she knew for certain that several volumes on rabbits could be found in his vast library, a great many of them, she was sure, in French. He loved reading French. It was his only odd habit. But the white rabbit might just be late; it had always been late before. As a child she had thought that both an annoying and an endearing quality. Now she simply suspected the rabbit had had a mistress somewhere for, as she recalled, he always had a disheveled and uncomfortable look whenever they met, as if just rumpling out of bed and embarrassed lest anyone know. Especially a child. She'd certainly seen that look on any number of faces at the endless house parties she and Reggie had gone to when they were first married.

She didn't think she had time enough now to waste waiting for the rabbit to show up, though as a child she'd a necessary long patience. Those had been the days of posing endlessly for artists and amateur photographers, which took a great deal of time. She'd learned to play games in her head, cruel games some of them had been. And silly. As often as not the men she posed for were the main characters in the games, but in such odd and often bestial incarnations: griffins, mock turtles, great fuzzy-footed caterpillars. And rabbits. What *hadn't* she imagined! Mr. Dodgson hadn't been the only one who wanted her for a model, though she never understood why. She'd been quite plain as a child, with a straight-haired simplicity her mother insisted upon. That awful fringe across her forehead; those eyebrows, pronounced and arched. A good characteristic in a woman but awful, she thought consideringly, in a child. In all the photographs she seemed to be staring out insolently, as if daring the photographer to take a good picture. *What could Mr. Dodgson have been thinking?*

And then there'd been that terrible painter, Sir William Blake Richmond, for whom she'd spent hours kneeling by Lorina's side in the Llandudno sands for a portrait Father never even hung in the house. Though years later, she recalled suddenly, Lorina—who'd really never had very much art sense—displayed it without apology in her sunny apartment. *The Ghastlies*, Father had called that painting, remarking how awful his beautiful girls looked in it. And they really had: stiff and uncharming. Like old ladies, really, not young girls. The sand had hurt her knee, the sun had been too hot, and Sir William an utter fool. They'd nicknamed him "Poormond" as a joke. It was her art tutor's idea, actually—Mr. Ruskin. *A poor nickname and a poor joke as well*, she thought.

Leaning over, she peered down into the hole and thought she saw the beginnings of the shelving that lined the sides, though the first time she'd dropped down the hole it had gone—she seemed to remember dimly—straight like a tunnel for some time. *Marmalade*, she thought suddenly. That had been on the shelves. The good old-fashioned hand-made orange stuff that her governess, Miss Prickett, had insisted on, not the manufactured kind you get in the stores today. She could almost taste it, the wonderful bits of candied rind that stuck between your teeth. *Of course, that was when I had all my own.*

She sat a bit longer remembering the maps and pictures hung upon pegs that had been scattered between the shelves; and the books—had there been books or was she misremembering? And then, when she was almost afraid of actually doing it, she lowered herself feet first into the suddenly expanding hole.

And fell.

Down, down, down.

As if accommodating to her age, the hole let her fall slowly, majestically, turning over only once or twice on the way. *A queen*, she thought, *would fall this way*. Though she had no title, much as Reggie had longed to be on the Honors List. And then she remembered that in Wonderland she *was* a queen. With that thought there was a sudden deliberate heaviness atop her head. It took all the strength she could muster to reach up as she fell, but she just managed. Sure enough, a crown, bulky and solid, was sitting upon her head.

She fell slowly enough that she could adjust her glasses to see onto the shelves, and so that her skirts never ruffled more than a quarter inch above her knees. They were good knees, or at least handsome knees, still. She'd many compliments on them over the years. Reggie, of course, had adored them. She often wondered if that was why she had married him, all those compliments. He'd stopped them once they were safely wed. The crown prince himself—and Dickie Mountbatten, too—had remarked on her knees and her ankles, too. Of course that was when knees and ankles had been in fashion. It was all breast and thigh now. *Like*, she thought, *grocery chickens*. She giggled, thinking of herself on a store shelf, in among the poultry. As if responding to her giddy mood, the crown sat more heavily on her head.

"Oh, dear," she said aloud. "We are *not* to be amused." The giggles stopped.

As she continued falling, she named the things on the shelves to herself: several marmalade jars; a picnic basket from Fortnum and Mason; a tartan lap robe like the one her nanny used to wrap around her on country weekends; a set of ivory fish tile counters; a velvet box with a mourning brooch in which a lock of hair as pale as that of her own dear dead boys' was twisted under glass; a miniature portrait of the late queen she was sure she'd last seen at a house party at Scone, back in the days before it had become a tourist attraction.

She had not finished with the namings, when she landed, softly, upon a mound of dry leaves and found herself in a lovely garden full of flowers: both a cultivated rose bed and arbor, and an herb garden in the shape of a Celtic knot. It reminded her of her own lovely garden at Cuffnells, the small one that was hers, not the larger-than-life arboretum that Reggie had planted, with its Orientals, redwoods, and Douglas pine. Poor lost Cuffnells. Poor dead Reggie. Poor gone everybody. She shook her head vigorously. She would *not* let herself get lost in the past, making it somehow better and lovelier than it was. She'd never liked that in old people when she was young, and she wasn't about to countenance it in herself now. The past was a lot like Wonderland: treacherous and marvelous and dull in equal measure. Survival was all that mattered—and she was a survivor. *Of course, in the end*, she thought, *there is no such thing as survival. And just as well. What a clutter the world would be if none of us ever died.*

She took a deep breath and looked around the garden. Once, the flowers had spoken to her but they were silent now. She stood up slowly, the hip giving her trouble again, and waved her cane at them, expecting no answer and receiving none. Then she walked through the garden gate and into Wonderland proper.

"Proper!" she said aloud and gave a small laugh. Proper was one thing Wonderland had never been. Nor was she, though from the outside it must have looked it. But she could still play all those games in her head. Griffins and mock turtles and caterpillars. And rabbits. Men all seemed to fall so easily into those categories. She brushed off her skirt, which was suddenly short and green, like her old school uniform.

"Curioser and curioser," she remarked to no one in particular. She liked the feel of the words in her mouth. They were comfortable, easy.

There was a path that almost seemed to unroll before her. *A bit*, she thought, *like the new path to the Isis from Tom Quad, which Father had had dug.* She was not at all surprised when she spied a young man coming toward her in white flannel trousers, striped jacket, a straw hat, and a pair of ghastly black shoes, the kind men had worn before tennis shoes had been invented. She thought tennis shoes were aces. The young man glanced at his pocket watch, then up at her, looking terribly familiar.

"No time," he said. "No time." He stuttered slightly on the *n*.

"Why, Mr. Dodgson," she said, looking up at him through a fringe of dark hair and holding out a ringless hand. "Why, of course there's plenty of time."

And there was.

Charles de Lint

Wild Horses

Charles de Lint is a Celtic folk musician, folklore scholar, and visual artist—but in the fantasy field he is best known as a captivating storyteller specializing in bringing folkloric themes into modern urban life. His novels in this vein include Moonheart, Spiritwalk, Memory and Dream, Trader, *and* Someplace to Be Flying. *He is one of a growing number of contemporary authors whose works defy categorization, dancing on that shifting borderline between genre fantasy and mainstream magic realism.*

Much of de Lint's current fiction takes place in an imaginary city called Newford, which exists somewhere (we never know quite where) in Canada or the northern United States. The following story, part of the Newford cycle, comes from the pages of Tarot Fantastic, *a collection of stories based on tarot card themes edited by Martin H. Greenberg and Lawrence Schimel.*

De Lint and his wife, musician and artist MaryAnn Harris, live in Ottawa, Ontario.

—T. W.

Chance is always powerful. Let your hook be always cast; in the pool where you least expect it, there will be a fish.

—Ovid

1

The horses run the empty length of the lakeshore, strung out like a long ragged necklace, perfect in their beauty. They run wild. They run like whitecaps in choppy water, their unshod hooves kicking up sand and spray. The muffled sound of their galloping is a rough music, pure rhythm. Palominos. Six, seven . . . maybe a dozen of them. Their white manes and tails flash, golden coats catch the sunlight and hold it under the skin the way mine holds a drug.

The city is gone. Except for me, transfixed by the sight of them, gaze snared by the powerful motion of their muscles propelling them forward, the city is gone, skyline and dirty streets and dealers and the horse that comes in a needle instead of running free along a beach. All gone.

And for a moment, I'm free, too.

I run after them, but they're too fast for me, these wild horses, can't be tamed, can't be caught. I run until I'm out of breath and stumble and fall and when I come to, I'm lying under the overpass where the freeway cuts through Squatland, my works lying on my coat beside me, empty now. I look out across a landscape of sad tenements and long-abandoned factories and the only thing I can think is, I need another hit to take me back. Another hit, and this time I'll catch up to them.

I know I will. I have to.

There's nothing for me here.

But the drugs don't take me anywhere.

2

Cassie watched the young woman approach. She was something, sleek and pretty, newly shed of her baby-fat. Nineteen, maybe; twenty-one, twenty-two, tops. Wearing an old sweater, raggedy jeans and sneakers—nothing fancy, but she looked like a million dollars. Bottle that up, Cassie thought, along with the long spill of her dark curly hair, the fresh-faced, perfect complexion, and you'd be on easy street. Only the eyes hinted at what must have brought her here, the lost, hopeful look in their dark depths. Something haunted her. You didn't need the cards to tell you that.

She was out of place—not a tourist, not part of the Bohemian coterie of fortunetellers, buskers, and craftspeople who were set up along this section of the Pier either. Cassie tracked her gaze as it went from one card table to the next, past the palmist, the other card readers, the Gypsy, the lovely Scottish boy with his Weirdin disks, watched until that gaze met her own and the woman started to walk across the boards, aimed straight for her.

Somebody was playing a harp, over by one of the weavers' tables. A sweet melody, like a lullaby, rose above the conversation around the tables and the sound of the water lapping against the wooden footings below. It made no obvious impression on the approaching woman, but Cassie took the music in, letting it swell inside her, a piece of beauty stolen from the heart of commerce. The open-air market and sideshow that sprawled along this section of the Pier might look alternative, but it was still about money. The harper was out to make a buck and so was Cassie.

She had her small collapsible table set up with a stool for her on one side, its twin directly across the table for a customer. A tablecloth was spread over the table, hand-embroidered with ornate hermetic designs. On top of the cloth, a small brass change bowl and her cards, wrapped in silk and boxed in teak.

The woman stood behind the vacant stool, hesitating before she finally sat down. She pulled her knapsack from her back and held it on her lap, arms hugging it close to her chest. The smile she gave Cassie was uncertain.

Cassie gave her a friendly smile back. "No reason to be nervous, girl. We're all friends here. What's your name?"

"Laura."

"And I'm Cassandra. Now what sort of a reading were you looking for?"

Laura reached out her hand, not quite touching the box with its cards. "Are they real?" she asked.

"How do you mean, real?"

"Magic. Can you work magic with them?"

"Well, now . . ."

Cassie didn't like to lie, but there was magic and there was magic. One lay in the heart of the world and was as much a natural part of how things were as it was deep mystery. The other was the thing people were looking for to solve their problems with and it never quite worked the way they felt it should.

"Magic's all about perception," she said. "Do you know what I mean?"

Laura shook her head. She'd drawn her hand back from the cards and was hugging her knapsack again. Cassie picked up the wooden box and put it to one side. From the inside pocket of her matador's jacket, she pulled out another set of cards. These were tattered around the edges, held together by an elastic band. When she placed them on the tablecloth, the woman's gaze went to the top card and was immediately caught by the curious image on it. The card showed the same open-air market they were sitting in, the crowds of tourists and vendors, the Pier, the lake behind.

"Those . . . are those regular cards?" Laura asked.

"Do I look like a regular reader?"

The question was academic. Cassie didn't look like a regular anything, not even on the Pier. She was in her early thirties, a dark-eyed woman with coffee-colored skin and hair that hung in a hundred tiny beaded braids. Today she wore tight purple jeans and yellow combat boots; under her black matador's jacket was a white T-shirt with the words "Don't! Buy! Thai!" emblazoned on it. Her ears were festooned with studs, dangling earrings, and simple hoops. On each wrist she had a dozen or so plastic bracelets in a rainbow palette of day-glo colors.

"I guess not," the woman said. She leaned a little closer. "What does your T-shirt mean? I've seen that slogan all over town, on T-shirts, spray-painted on walls, but I don't know what it means."

"It's a boycott to try to stop the child-sex industry in Thailand."

"Are you collecting signatures for a petition or something?"

Cassie shook her head. "You just do like the words say. Check out what you're buying and if it's made in Thailand, don't buy it and explain why."

"Do you really think it'll help?"

"Well, it's like magic," Cassie said, bringing the conversation back to what she knew Laura really wanted to talk about. "And like I said, magic's about perception, that's all. It means anything is possible. It means taking the way we usually look at a thing and making people see it differently. Or, depending on your viewpoint, making them see it properly for the first time."

"But—"

"For instance, I could be a crow, sitting on this stool talking to you, but I've convinced everybody here that I'm Cassandra Washington, card reader, so that's what you all see."

Laura gave her an uneasy look that Cassie had no trouble reading: pretty sure she was being put on, but not entirely sure.

Cassie smiled. "The operative word here is *could*. But that's how magic works. It's all about how we perceive things to be. A good magician can make anything seem possible and pretty soon you've got seven-league boots and people turning invisible or changing into wolves or flying—all sorts of fun stuff."

"You're serious, aren't you?"

"Oh, yeah. Now fortunetelling—that's all about perception, too, except it's looking inside yourself. It works best with a ritual because that allows you to concentrate better—same reason religion and church work so well for some people. Makes them all pay attention and focus, and the next thing you know they're either looking inside themselves and working out their problems, or making a piece of magic."

She picked up the cards and removed the elastic band. Shuffled them. "Think of these as a mirror. Pay enough attention to them, and they'll lay out a pattern that'll take you deep inside yourself."

Laura appeared disappointed. But they always did, when it was put out in front of them like this. They thought you'd pulled back the curtain and shown the Wizard of Oz, working all the levers of his machine, not realizing that you'd let them into a deeper piece of magic than something they might buy for a few dollars in a place like the Pier.

"I . . . I thought it might be different," Laura said.

"You wanted it all laid out for you, simple, right? Do this, and this'll happen. Do this, and it'll go like this. Like reading the sun signs in the newspaper, except personal."

Laura shook her head. "It wasn't about me. It was about my brother."

"Your brother?"

"I was hoping you could, you know, use your cards to tell me where he is."

Cassie stopped shuffling her pack and laid it facedown on the table.

"Your brother's missing?" she said.

Laura nodded. "It's been two years now."

Cassie was willing to give people a show, willing to give them more than what they were asking for, sometimes, or rather what they were really asking for but weren't articulating, but she wasn't in the business of selling false hopes or pretenses. Some people could do it, but not her. Not and sleep at night.

"Laura," she said. "Girl. You've come to the wrong place. You want to talk to the police. They're the ones who deal with missing persons."

And you'll have wanted to talk to them a lot sooner than now, she thought, but she left that unsaid.

"I did," Laura told her.

Cassie waited. "And what?" she asked finally. "They told you to come here?"

"No. Of course not. They—a Sergeant Riley. He's been really nice, but I guess there's not much they can do. They say it's been so long and the city's so big and Dan could have moved away months ago. . . ."

Her eyes filled with tears, and her voice trailed off. She swallowed, tried again.

412 -* Charles de Lint

"I brought everything I could think of," she said, holding up her knapsack for a moment before clutching it tightly to her chest again. "Pictures. His dental records. The last couple of postcards I got from him. I . . ." She had to swallow again. "They have all these pictures of . . . of unidentified bodies and I . . . I had to look at them all. And they sent off copies of the stuff I brought—sent it off all over the country. But it's been over a month, and I know Dan's not dead. . . ."

She looked up, her eyes still shiny with unshed tears. Cassie nodded sympathetically.

"Can I see one of the pictures?" she said.

A college-aged boy looked back at her from the small snapshot Laura took out of her knapsack. Not handsome, but there was a lot of character in his features. Short brown hair, high cheekbones, strong jawline. Something in his eyes reflected the same mix of loss and hopefulness that was now in his sister's. What had *he* been looking for?

"You say he's been missing for two years?" Cassie asked.

Laura nodded. Showing the picture seemed to have helped steady her.

"Your parents didn't try to find him?"

"They never really got along. It's—I don't know why. They were always fighting, arguing. He left the house when he was sixteen—as soon as he could get out. We live—we *lived* just outside of Boston. He moved into Cambridge, then maybe four years ago, he moved out here. When I was in college, he'd call me sometimes and always send me postcards."

Cassie waited. "And then he stopped?" she said finally.

"Two years ago. That's when I got the last card. I saw him a couple of months before that."

"Do you get along with your parents?"

"They've always treated me just the opposite from how they treated him. Dan couldn't do anything right, and I can't do anything wrong."

"Why did you wait so long?"

"I . . ." Her features fell. "I just kept expecting to hear from him. I was finishing up my Masters and working part-time at a restaurant and . . . I don't know. I was just so busy, and I didn't realize how long it had really been until all of a sudden two years have gone by since he wrote."

She kept looking at the table as she spoke, glancing up as though to make sure Cassie was still listening, then back down again. When she looked up now, she straightened her back.

"I guess it was pretty crazy of me to think you could help," she said.

No, Cassie thought. *More like a little sad.* But she understood need and how it could make you consider avenues you'd never normally take a walk down.

"Didn't say I wouldn't try," she told Laura. "What do you know about what he was doing here?"

"The last time I saw him, all he could talk about were these horses, wild horses running along the shore of the lake."

Cassie nodded encouragingly when Laura's voice trailed off once more.

"But there aren't any, are there?" Laura said. "It's all . . ." She waved her hand, encompassing the Pier, the big hotels, the Williamson Street Mall farther up the beach. "It's all like this."

"Pretty much. A little farther west there's the Beaches, but that's all private waterfront and pretty upscale. And even if someone would let him onto their land, I've never heard of any wild horses out there."

Laura nodded. "I showed his picture around at the racetrack and every riding stable I could find listed in the phone book, but no one recognized him."

"Anything else?" Cassie asked.

She hesitated for a long moment before replying. "I think he was getting into drugs again." Her gaze lifted from the card table to meet Cassie's. "He was pretty bad off for a few years, right after he got out of the house, but he'd cleaned up his act before he moved out here."

"What makes you think he got back into them?"

"I don't know. Just a feeling—the last time I saw him. The way he was all fidgety again, something in his eyes . . ."

Maybe that was what she'd seen in his picture, Cassie thought. That need in his eyes.

"What kind of drugs?" she asked.

"Heroin."

"A different kind of horse."

Laura sighed. "That's what Sergeant Riley said."

Cassie tapped a fingernail, painted the same purple as her jeans, on the pack of cards that lay between them.

"Where are you staying?" she asked.

"The Y. It's all I can afford. I'm getting kind of low on money, and I haven't had much luck getting a job."

Cassie nodded. "Leave me that picture," she said. "I'll ask around for you, see what I can find out."

"But . . ."

She was looking at the cards. Cassie laid her hand over them and shook her head.

"Let me do this my way," Cassie said. "You know the pay phone by the front desk? I'll give you a call there tomorrow, around three, say, and then we can talk some more."

She put out her hand and Laura looked confused.

"Um," she began. "How much do you want?"

Cassie smiled. "The picture, girl. I'll do the looking as a favor."

"But I'm putting you to so much trouble—"

"I've been where you are," Cassie said. "If you want to pay me back, do a good turn for someone else."

"Oh."

She didn't seem either confident or happy with the arrangement, but she left the picture and stood up. Cassie watched her make her way back through the other vendors, then slowly turned over three cards from the top of the deck. The first showed a set of works lying on worn blue denim. A jacket, Cassie decided. The second had a picture of an overpass in the Tombs. The last showed a long length of beach, empty except for a small herd of palominos cantering down the wet sand. In the background, out in the water, was the familiar shape of Wolf Island, outlined against the horizon.

Cassie lifted her head and turned to look at the lake. Beyond the end of the Pier she could see Wolf Island, the ferry on a return trip, halfway between the island and the mainland. The image on her card didn't show the city, didn't show docking facilities on the island, the museum and gift shop that used to be somebody's summer place. The image on her card was of another time, before the city got here. Or of another place that you could only reach with your imagination.

Or with magic.

3

Cassie and Joe had made arrangements to meet at The Rusty Lion that night. He'd been sitting outside on the patio waiting for her when she arrived, a handsome Native man in jeans and a plain white T-shirt, long black braid hanging down his back, a look in his dark eyes that was usually half solemn, half tomfool Trickster. Right now it was concerned.

"You don't look so good," he said as she sat down.

She tried to make a joke of it. "People ask me why I stay with you," she said, "and I always tell them, you just know how to make a girl feel special."

But Joe would have none of it.

"You've got trouble," he told her, "and that means we have trouble. Tell me about it."

So she did.

Joe knew why she was helping this woman she'd never seen before. That was one of the reasons it was so good between them: Lots of things didn't need to be explained, they were simply understood.

" 'Cause you found Angie too late," he said.

He reached across the table and took her hand, wanting to ease the sting of his words. She nodded and took what comfort she could from the touch of his rough palm and fingers. There was never any comfort in thinking about Angie.

"It might be too late for Laura's brother, too," she said.

Joe shrugged. "Depends. The cops could be right. He could be long gone from here, headed off to some junkie heaven like Seattle. I hear they've got one of the best needle exchange programs in the country and you know the dope's cheap. Twenty bucks'll buy you a thirty piece."

Cassie nodded. "Except the cards . . ."

"Oh, yeah. The cards."

The three cards lay on the table between them, still holding the images she'd found in them after Laura walked away. Joe had recognized the place where the horses were running the same as she had.

"Except I never heard of dope taking someone into the spiritworld before," he said.

"So what does it mean?" Cassie asked.

He put into words what she'd only been thinking. "Either he's clean, or he's dead."

She nodded. "And if he's clean, then why hasn't he called her, or sent another postcard? They were close."

"She says."

"You don't think so?"

Joe shrugged. "I wasn't the one who met her. But she waited two years."

"I waited longer to go looking for Angie."

There was nothing Joe could say to that.

4

It was a long time ago now.

Cassie shows them all, the white kids who wouldn't give her the time of day and the kids from the projects that she grew up with. She makes top of her graduating class, valedictorian, stands there at the commencement exercises, out in front of everybody, speech in hand. But when she looks out across the sea of mostly-white faces, she realizes they still don't respect her and there's nobody she cares about sitting out there. The one person who ever meant something to her is noticeably absent.

Angie dropped out in grade nine and they really haven't seen each other since. Somewhere between Angie dropping out and Cassie resolving to prove herself, she and her childhood best friend have become more than strangers. They might as well never have known each other, they're so different.

So Cassie's looking out at the crowd. She wants to blow them off, but that's like giving in, so she follows through, reads her speech, pretends she's a part of the celebration. She skips the bullshit parties that follow, doesn't listen to the phony praise for her speech, and won't talk to her teachers who want to know what she plans to do next. She goes home and takes off that pretty new dress that cost her two months' pay working after school and weekends at McDonald's. Puts on sweats and hightops. Washes the makeup from her face and looks in the mirror. The face that looks back at her is soft, that of a little girl. The only steel is in the eyes.

Then she goes out looking for Angie, but Angie's not around anymore. Word on the street is she went the junkie route, mixing crack and horse, selling herself to pay for her jones, long gone now or dead, and why would Cassie care anyway? It's like school, only in reverse. She's got no street smarts, no one takes her seriously, no one respects her.

She finds herself walking out of the projects, still looking for Angie, but keeping to herself now, walking all over the city, looking into faces but finding only strangers. Her need to find Angie is maybe as strong as Angie's was for the drugs, everything's focused on it, looking not only for Angie but for herself—the girl she was before she let other people's opinions become more important than her best friend. She's not ready to say that her turning her back on Angie pushed her friend toward the street life, but it couldn't have helped either. But she does know that Angie had a need that Cassie filled, and the drugs took its place. Now Cassie has a need, and she doesn't know what's going to fill it, but something has to, or she feels like she's just going to dry up and blow away.

She keeps walking farther and farther until one day that jones of hers takes her to an old white clapboard house just north of the city, front yard's got a bottle tree growing in the weeds and dirt, an old juju woman sitting on the porch looking at her with dark eyes, skin so black Cassie feels white. Cassie doesn't know which is scarier, the old woman or her saying, " 'Bout time you showed up, girl. I'd just about given up on you."

All Cassie can do is stand there, can't walk away, snared by the old woman's gaze. A breeze comes up and those bottles hanging in the tree clink against each other. The old woman beckons to her with a crooked finger, and the next thing Cassie knows she's walking up to the porch, climbing the rickety stairs, standing right in front of the woman.

"I've been keeping these for someone like you," she says and pulls a pack of tattered cards out of the pocket of her black dress.

Cassie doesn't want to take them, but she reaches for them all the same. They're held together with an elastic band. When the old woman puts them in her hand, something like a static charge jumps between them. She gets a dizzy feeling that makes her sway, almost lose her balance. She closes her hand, fingers tight around the cards, and the feeling goes away.

The old woman's grinning. "You felt that, didn't you, girl?"

"I . . . I felt something."

"Aren't you a caution."

None of this feels real, none of it makes sense. The old woman, the house, the bottle tree. Cassie tries to remember how she got here, when the strip malls and fast food outlets suddenly gave way to a dirt road and this place. Is this how it happened to Angie? All of a sudden she looks at herself one day and she's a junkie?

Cassie's gaze goes down to the cards the old woman gave her. She removes the elastic and fans a few of them out. They have a design on one side; the other side is blank. She lifts her head to find the old woman still grinning at her.

"What are these?" she asks.

"What do they look like, girl? They're cards. Older than Egypt, older than China, older than when the first mama woke up in Africa and got to making babies so that we could all be here."

"But . . ." It's hard to think straight. "What are they for?"

"Fortunes, girl. Help you find yourself. Let you help other people find themselves."

"But . . ."

She was valedictorian, she thinks. She has more of a vocabulary than her whole family put together, and all she can say is, "But."

"But there's nothing on them."

She doesn't know much about white people's magic, but she's heard of telling fortunes with cards—playing cards, tarot cards. She doesn't know much about her own people's magic either.

The old juju woman laughs. "Oh, girl. 'Course there isn't. There won't be nothing on them until you need something to be there."

None of this is making sense. It's only making her dizzy again. There's a stool beside the woman's chair and she sits on it, closes her eyes, still holding the cards. She takes a few deep breaths, steadies herself. But when she opens her eyes again, she's sitting on a concrete block in the middle of a traffic median. There's no house, no bottle tree. No old woman. Only the traffic going by on either side of her. A discount clothing store across the street. A factory outlet selling stereos and computers on the other side.

There's only the cards in her hands and at her feet, lying on the pavement of the median, an elastic band.

She's scared. But she bends down, picks up the elastic. She turns over the top card, looks at it. There's a picture now, where before it was blank. It shows an abandoned tenement in the Tombs, one of the places where the homeless people squat. She's never been in it, but she recognizes the building. She's passed it a hundred times on the bus, going from school to the McDonald's where she worked. She turns another card and now she's looking at a picture of the inside of a building—probably the same one. The windows are broken, there's garbage all over, a heap of rags in one corner. A third card takes her closer to the rags. Now she can see there's somebody lying under those rags, somebody so thin and wasted there's only bone covered with skin.

She doesn't turn a fourth card.

She returns the cards to the pack, puts the elastic around them, sticks the pack in her pocket. Her mouth feels baked and dry. She waits for a break in the traffic and goes across to the discount clothing store to ask for a drink of water, but they tell her the restroom is only for staff. She has to walk four blocks before a man at a service station gives a sympathetic look when she repeats her request and hands her the key to the women's room.

She drinks long and deep, then feels sick and has to throw up. When she returns to the sink, she rinses her mouth, washes her face. The man's busy with a customer, so she hangs the key on the appropriate hook by the door in the office and thanks him as she goes by, walking back toward downtown.

Normal people don't walk through the Tombs, not even along well-trafficked streets like Williamson or Flood. It's too dangerous, a no-man's-land of deserted tenements and abandoned factories. But she doesn't see she has a choice. She walks until she sees the tenement that was on the card, swallows hard, then crosses an empty lot overgrown with weeds and refuse until she's standing in front of it. It takes her a while to work up her nerve, but finally she steps into its foyer.

It smells of urine and garbage. Something stirs in a corner, sits up. Her pulse jumps into overtime, even when she sees it's only a raggedy boy, skinny, hollow-eyed.

"Gimme something," he says. "I don't need to get high, man. I just need to feel well again."

"I . . . I don't have anything."

She's surprised she can find her voice. She's surprised that he only nods and lies back down in his nest of newspapers and rags.

It doesn't take her long to find the room she saw on the second card. Something pulls her down a long hall. The doors are all broken down. Things stir in some of the rooms. People. Rats. Roaches. She doesn't know and doesn't investigate. She just keeps walking until she's in the room, steps around the garbage littering the floor to the heap of rags in the corner.

A half hour later she's at a pay phone on Gracie Street, phoning the police, telling them about the dead body she found in the tenement.

"Her name's Angie," she says. "Angie Moore."

She hangs up and starts to walk again, not looking for anything now, hardly able to see because of the tears that swell in her eyes.

She doesn't go home again. She can't exactly explain why. Meeting the old woman, the cards she carries, finding Angie, it all gets mixed up in her head with how hard she tried to do well and still nobody really cared about her except for the friend she turned her back on. Her parents were happy to brag about her marks, but there was no warmth there. She's eighteen and can't remember ever being embraced. Her brothers and sisters were like the other kids in the projects, ragging on her for trying to do well. The white kids didn't care about anything except for the color of her skin.

It all came down to no one respecting her except for Angie, and she'd turned her back on Angie because Angie couldn't keep up.

But the cards mean something. She knows that.

She's still working at the McDonald's, only now she saves her money and lives in a squat in the Tombs. Nobody comes to find out why she hasn't returned home. Not her family, not her teachers. Some of the kids from school stop by, filling up on Big Macs and fries and soft drinks, and she can hear them snickering at their tables, studiously not looking at her.

She takes to going to the library and reading about cards and fortunetelling, gets to be a bit of an expert. She buys a set of tarot cards in The Occult Shop and sometimes talks to the people who work there, some of the customers. She never reads or hears anything about the kind of cards the old woman gave her.

Then one day she meets Joseph Crazy Dog in the Tombs, just down from the Kickaha res, wild and reckless and a little scary, but kind, too, if you took the time to get to know him. Some people say he's not all there, supposed to be on medication, but won't take it. Others say he's got his feet in two worlds, this one and another place where people have animal faces and only spirits can stay for more than a few days, the kind of place you come back from either a poet or mad. First thing he tells her is he can't rhyme worth a damn.

Everybody calls him Bones because of how he tells fortunes with a handful of small animal and bird bones, reading auguries in the way they fall upon the buckskin when he throws them. But she calls him Joe, and something good happens between them because he respects her, right away he respects her. He's the first person she tells about the old juju woman, and she knows she was right to wait because straight away he can tell her where she went that day and what it means.

5

It was almost dark by the time Cassie and Joe reached the overpass in the Tombs that was pictured on the card. At one time it had been a hobo camp, but now it was one more junkie landmark, a place where you could score and shoot without being hassled. The cops didn't bother coming by much. They had bigger fish to fry.

"A lot of hard times bundled up in a place like this," Joe said.

Cassie nodded.

Some of the kids they walked by were so young. Most of them were already high. Those that weren't, were looking to score. It wasn't the sort of place you could ask questions, but neither Cassie nor Joe were strangers to the Tombs. They still squatted themselves and most people knew of them, if they'd never actually met. They could get away with showing around a picture, asking questions.

"When did heroin get so popular again?" Cassie said.

Joe shrugged. "Never got unpopular—not when it's so easy to score. You know the drill. The only reason solvents and alcohol are so popular up on the res is no one's bringing in this kind of shit. That's the way it works everywhere—supply and demand. Here the supply's good."

And nobody believed it could hurt them, Cassie thought. Because it wouldn't happen to them and sure people got addicted, but everybody knew somebody who'd used and hadn't got strung out on it. Nobody set out to become an addict. Like most bad things, it just snuck up on you when you weren't paying attention. But the biggest problem was that kids got lied to about so much, it was hard for them to accept this warning as a truth.

They made a slow pass of the three or four blocks where most of the users congregated, showing the photo of Laura's brother when it seemed appropriate, but without much luck. From there they headed back downtown, following Williamson Street down Gracie. It was on the gay bar strip on Gracie Street that they finally found someone who could help.

"I like the hair, Tommy," Cassie said.

It was like a close-cut Afro, the corkscrew curls so purple they had to come from a bottle. Tommy grinned, but his good humor vanished when Joe showed him the picture.

"Yeah, I know him," Tommy said. "Danny Packer, right? Though he sure doesn't look like that now. How come you're looking for him?"

"We're not. His sister is and we're just helping her out. Any idea where we could find him?"

"Ask at the clinic."

Cassie and Joe exchanged glances.

"He's working there?" Cassie asked.

Tommy shook his head.

6

"What is this place?" Laura asked.

They were standing in front of an old yellow brick house on McKennitt Street in Lower Crowsea. Cassie had picked her up outside the Y a little after four and Joe drove them across town in a cab he'd borrowed from a friend.

"It's a hospice," Cassie said. "It was founded by a writer who died of AIDS a few years ago—Ennis Thompson."

"I've read him. He was a wonderful writer."

Cassie nodded. "His royalties are what keeps it running."

The house was on a quiet stretch of McKennitt, shaded by a pair of the tall, stately oaks that flourished in Crowsea. There wasn't much lawn. Geraniums grew in terra cotta planters going up the steps to the front door, adding a splash of color and filling the air with their distinctive scent. They didn't seem to make much of an impression on Laura. She was too busy studying the three-storied building, a small frown furrowing the skin between her eyebrows.

"Why did Dan want me to meet him here?" she asked.

Cassie hesitated. When they'd come to see him last night, Laura's brother had asked them to let him break the news to her. She understood, but it left her in the awkward position of having to be far too enigmatic in response to Laura's delight that her brother had been found. She'd been fending off Laura's questions ever since they'd spoken on the phone earlier and arranged to drive out here.

"Why don't we let him tell you himself," Cassie said.

Joe held the door for them. He nodded a greeting to the young woman stationed at a reception desk in what would once have been a front parlor.

"Go ahead," she told them. "He's expecting you."

"Thanks," Joe said.

He led the way down the hall to Dan's room. Rapping softly on the door, he opened it when a weak voice called out, "It's open."

Laura stopped and wouldn't go on.

"Come on," Cassie said, her voice gentle.

But Laura could only shake her head. "Oh, God, how could I have been so stupid? He's a patient here, isn't he?"

Cassie put a hand on her arm and found it trembling. "He's still your brother."

"I know. It's not that. It's just—"

"Laura?"

The voice pulled her to the door and through it, into the room. Cassie had been planning to allow them some privacy for this meeting, but now she followed in after Laura to lend her moral support in case it was needed.

Dan was in bad shape. She only knew him from the picture that Laura had lent her yesterday, but he bore no resemblance to the young man in that photograph. Not anymore. No doubt he had already changed somewhat in the years since the picture had been taken, but now he was skeletal, the skin hanging from his bones, features hollow and sunken. Sores discolored his skin in great blotches and his hair was wispy and thin.

But Laura knew him.

Whatever had stopped her outside the room was gone. She crossed the room quickly now, sat down on the edge of the bed, carefully took his scrawny hands in her own, leaned forward and kissed his brow.

"Oh, Danny. What have you done to yourself?"

He gave her a weak smile. "Screwed things up as usual."

"But this . . ."

"I want you to know—it wasn't from a needle."

Laura threw a glance over her shoulder at Cassie, then returned her attention to her brother.

"I always knew," she said.

"You never said anything."

"I was waiting for you to tell me."

He shook his head slowly. "I could never put one past you."

"When were you going to tell me?" Laura asked.

"That's why I came back the last time. But I lost my nerve. And then when I got back to the city, I wasn't just HIV-positive anymore. I had full-blown AIDS and . . ."

His voice, already weak, trailed off.

"Oh, Danny, why? What did you think—that I wouldn't love you anymore?"

"I didn't know what to think. I just didn't want to be a bother."

"That's the last thing you are," Laura assured him. "I know . . ." She had to swallow and start again. "I know you won't be getting better, but you've got to at least have your family with you. Come home with me."

"No."

"Why not? Mom and Dad will want to—"

Dan cut her off, anger giving his voice some strength. "They won't want anything to do with me."

"But—"

"You never understood, did you? We lived in the same house, but it was two different worlds. I lived in one, and the rest of you lived in the other. I don't know why things worked out that way, but you've got to accept that it's never going to change. That not even something like this could change it."

Laura didn't say anything for a long moment. She simply sat there, holding his hands, looking at him.

"It was so awful for you," she said finally. "Wasn't it?"

He nodded. "Everything, except for you."

That seemed to be too much for her, knowing that on top of his dying, how hard his life had been, right from when he was a child. She bowed down over him, holding him, shoulders shaking as she wept.

Cassie backed out of the room to join Joe where he was waiting in the hall.

"It's got to be tough," he said.

Cassie nodded, not trusting her voice. Her own gaze was blurry with tears.

7

"You never told her how you found me," Dan said later.

When Laura had gone to get tea, Cassie and Joe came back into the room, sitting on hardbacked chairs beside the bed. It was still hours until dusk, but an overcast sky cast a gloomy light into the room.

"And you won't, will you?" he added.

Cassie shook her head.

"Why not?"

"It's hard to explain," she said. "I guess I just don't want her to get the wrong idea about the cards. You don't use them or any oracular device to find answers; you use them to ask questions. Some people don't get that."

He nodded slowly. "Laura wouldn't. She was always looking for miracles to solve everything. Like the way it was for me back home."

"Her heart was in the right place," Joe said.

Dan glanced at him. "Still is." He returned his attention to Cassie. "But those cards aren't normal tarot cards."

Cassie had shown him the cards the night before, the three images that had taken her and Joe up into the Tombs and eventually to Dan's room here in the hospice.

"No," she said. "They're real magic."

"Where did you get them? I mean, can I ask you that?"

Cassie smiled. "Of course you can. They come from the same place where your wild horses are running."

"They . . . they're real?"

"Depends on how you translate real," Joe said.

Cassie gave him a light tap on his shoulder with a closed fist. "Don't start with that."

"What place are you talking about?" Dan asked.

For once, Joe was more forthcoming than he usually was with a stranger.

"The spiritworld," he said. "It's a lot closer than most people think. Open yourself up to it and it comes in close, so close it's like it's right at hand, no farther away than what's out there on the other side of that window." He paused a moment, then added, "Dangerous place to visit, outside of a dream."

"It wasn't a dream that took me there," Dan said.

"Wasn't the drugs either," Joe told him.

"But—"

"Listen to me, what took you there is the same thing that called Cassie to the old juju woman who gave her those cards. You had a need. Doesn't happen often, but sometimes that's enough to take you across."

"I still have that need."

Joe nodded. "But first the drugs you kept taking got in the way. And now you're dying and your body knows better than to let your spirit go visiting. It wants to hang on and the only thing that's keeping you going is spirit."

"What about Laura's need when she was looking for me?" Dan asked. "Why didn't the spiritworld touch her?"

"It brought her to me, didn't it?" Cassie said.

"That's true."

Dan looked away, out the window. The view he had through it was filled with the boughs of one of those big oak trees. Cassie didn't think he was seeing them.

"You know," he said after a moment, not looking away from the window. "Before all of this, I wouldn't have believed you for a moment. Wouldn't have even listened to you. But you start thinking about spiritual things at a time like this. When you *know* you're going to die, it's hard not to." His gaze returned to them, moving slowly from one to the other. "I'd like to see them again . . . those horses."

Cassie glanced at Joe and he nodded.

"When you're ready to leave," he said, "give me a call."

"You mean that? You can do that?"

"Sure."

Dan started to reach for the pen and paper that was on the table beside his bed. "What's your number?"

"We don't have a phone," Joe said. "You just think about me and those horses hard enough and I'll come take you to them."

"But—"

"He can do it," Cassie said. "Even at the best of times, he's walking with one foot in either world. He'll know when you're ready, and he'll take you there."

Dan studied Joe for a moment, and Cassie knew what he was seeing—the dark Coyote eyes, the crow's head sitting just under his human skin. There was something solemn and laughing wild about him, all at once, as though he knew a joke no one else did that wrapped him in a feral kind of wisdom that could scare you silly. But Dan was past fear.

"That's something else you discover when you're this close to the edge," he said. "You get this ability to cut away the bullshit and look right into a person, see them exactly as they are."

"So what are you seeing?" Joe asked.

Dan smiled. "Damned if I know. But I know I can trust you."

Cassie knew exactly what he meant.

8

Summer gave way to fall. On a cold October night, Cassie woke near dawn to find Joe sitting on the edge of the bed, pulling on his boots. He came over to the bed and kissed her cheek.

"Go to sleep," he said. "I might be a while."

They'd been up late that night, and she fell back asleep before she could think to ask where he was going.

9

Dan's funeral was two days later. It was a small service with few in attendance. Laura. Cassie. A few of the caregivers from the hospice. After the service, Cassie took Laura down to the lakefront. They sat on a bench at the end of the Pier where they'd first met, looking out at Wolf Island. A cold wind blew in off the lake and they sat close to each other for warmth.

"Where's Joe?" Laura asked.

"He had to go out of town."

Laura looked different to Cassie, more sure of herself, less haunted for all her sadness. She'd been working as a bartender for the past few months—"See, I knew that MA would be useful for something," she'd joked—spending her afternoons with Dan.

"It's been really hard," she said. "Especially the last couple of weeks."

Cassie put her arm around Laura's shoulders. "Probably the hardest thing you'll ever do."

"But I wouldn't give up any of it. What Dan had to go through, yes, but not my being with him."

"He was lucky you found him in time."

"It wasn't luck," Laura said.

Cassie raised her eyebrows.

"He told me about the cards." She shook her head before Cassie could say anything. "No, it's okay. I understand. I know it would be so tempting to use something like that to make all your decisions for you. I'm not asking for that." She hesitated a moment, then added, "But I was wondering . . . can they show me Dan one last time? Just so I can know if he finally caught up with those horses? Just so I can know he's okay?"

"I don't know," Cassie said. "I think the only way we ever find out where we go in the end, is when we make the journey ourselves."

Laura gave a slow nod, unable to hide her disappointment. "I . . . I guess I understand."

"But that doesn't mean we can't look."

She took her arm away from Laura's shoulders and brought out the set of cards the old juju woman had given her, sitting there on her porch with the bottle tree clinking on the lawn. Removing the elastic, she gave the cards a shuffle, then offered the pack to Laura.

"Pick one," she said.

"Don't you have to lay them out in some kind of pattern?"

"Ordinary tarot cards, yes. But you're looking to see into some place they can't take you now."

Laura placed her fingers on the top of the deck. She held off for a long moment, then finally took the card and turned it over. There were horses running along the lakeshore on it, golden horses with white manes and tails. The image was too small to make out details, but they could see a figure on the back of one of them, head thrown back. Laughing, perhaps. Finally free.

Smiling, Laura returned the card to the pack.

"Where he goes," she said, "I hope he'll always be that happy."

Cassie wound the elastic back around the cards and returned them to her pocket.

"Maybe if we believe it strongly enough, it'll be true," she said.

Laura turned to look at her. Her eyes were shiny with tears, but that lost, haunted look Cassie had seen in them that first time they met was gone.

"Then I'll believe it," Laura said.

They leaned back against the bench, looking out across the water. The sound of the ferry's horn echoed faintly across the water, signaling its return from the island.

Matthew Sweeney

Princess

Matthew Sweeney was born in Donegal, Ireland, in 1952 and has lived in London for some years. He has published five collections of poetry for adults and four books for children. He is the editor, with Jo Shapcott, of an anthology called Emergency Kit. He has won several prizes for his poetry and was recently Writer in Residence at London's South Bank Centre.

Based on a fairy tale, "Princess" is a short, bittersweet shock.

—E. D.

The boy who lives in the wrecked bus
down on the rocks, near the point
knows every yard of the long beach
that curves to the ruined castle
where the girl's skeleton lies
behind a wall—a false wall
that only the boy's discovered,
and only he knows the loose stones
that lift out to let him in,
so he can comb the long red hair
that's still attached to the skull,
and he brings her what he's found
that day on the beach, and calls her
what she was, Princess, even when
they walled her up in her room
and left her to die, alone
until the boy found her, and now
she's visited every day, and lies

surrounded by buoys, lifejackets,
lobster-floats, two odd shoes
(one with a bony foot still in it),
half of an oar, a rubber dinghy
and a driftwood sculpture the boy made
on the day he guessed was her birthday
because of the rainbow he saw
ending at the castle, as he left the bus
and ran the three miles to her,
and the rainbow went as he got there.

Jack Womack

Audience

Jack Womack hails from Kentucky and now lives in New York City. He is the author of several intelligent, iconoclastic works of science fiction, including Ambient, Random Acts of Senseless Violence, *and* Elvissey *(winner of the 1994 Philp K. Dick Award). This is not the first time Womack's stylish short fiction has graced the pages of this anthology series, but it is the first time he has appeared in the fantasy half of the book. "Audience," a rare excursion from the fields of science fiction and horror, proves Womack to be equally adept working with a magical realist setting. If this haunting story is any indication of what he can do with the fantasy form, we can only hope Womack chooses to stray in this direction again.*

"Audience" comes from The Horns of Elfland, *an anthology of music-inspired tales edited by* Sound and Spirit *radio host Ellen Kushner, along with Donald G. Keller and Delia Sherman.*

—*T. W.*

For Jane Johnson and Mike Harrison

S mall museums in large cities inevitably attract me whenever I travel. Their haphazard assemblages—randomly displayed in no evident pattern, fitfully identified by yellowing cards—on occasion contain items so memorably unsettling as to thereafter blot from the mind the holdings of the Smithsonian, or Hermitage, or Louvre. I happened upon such a place one afternoon while strolling in the Low City, near the Margarethestrasse, down an alley branching off St. Jermyn's Close. The surrounding rows of soot-shrouded houses leaned into their dank passageway; their roofs caressed rather than touched, and their shadows shut away their inhabitants from notions of time or season. Overlooking all was the Close's six-spired cathedral, which itself served, until the recent political upheavals, as the Museum of Atheistic Belief. The cathedral's carillons proclaimed the fifteenth hour as I knocked at the door of the Hall of Lost Sounds, and for a moment I feared that, in their din, my own would go unheard.

"Thank you for seeing me," the curator said as I entered. I would have guessed him to be no older than seventy. His voice held the measured resonance of a cello, and he declaimed his notes almost in the manner of a *Sprechstimmer*.

"How much?" I asked. He shook his head. "You don't charge admission?"

"Who would come?"

A wholly unrecognizable accent misted his words. Much about his place appeared medieval, but then, so did its district—while wandering its byways, I'd thought I could as well have come armed with halberd rather than backpack, ducking the splash of chamber pots and not the offers of touts. The curator lingered in his museum's antechamber as if awaiting some necessary cue before our tour could begin, and we listened to the cathedral bells clanging out their last.

"It must hearten," I offered, "hearing them again after so long."

"No other noise assaults my walls," he said. "Lost sounds are sometimes better left lost. I keep only those which tickle your ear like a lover's tongue."

The curator gestured that we should begin, and we entered the museum proper. Wooden planks attached at floor and ceiling, aligned along the left wall, partitioned half of the first room into alcoves. "Each space possesses its own eigentone," he said.

"Pardon?" I said.

"Excuse me. The reflections within are accurate, and in accordance with acoustic principles. If the audience can be satisfied, it will be."

An iron bouquet was affixed to the door frame. The curator tugged at one of its sprigs, and fire leapt hissing from the cardinal blossom. The creamy light revealed a coiled, valveless horn resembling a golden snake. Retrieving it from its cubicle, he cradled the instrument in his arms as if it were his sister's baby.

"A posthorn," he said. "The mail came four times daily, the nature of each delivery denoted by unvarying leitmotifs." Pressing its mouthpiece against his lips, the curator blew three clear, ascending notes, each possessing an oddly pitched, yet not unattractive tone. "Such music, heard across miles, foretold of letters from your lover." Lifting the horn again, he played another short series, in a sharper key. "That prepared you to receive unforeseen gifts." He coughed until his lungs rattled; then replaced the horn within its enclosure. "Every signal, continually heard from childhood into age, was as familiar as a mother's voice. Once the deliveries ended, it was decreed that the posthorn should never again be played by anyone."

"You just played it," I said.

He nodded. "In a different country. Let us go on." The next cubicle held a black telephone, its sleek skin unblemished by touchpads, screen, or dial. Two short, tintinnabulate bursts shattered the moment's stillness as unexpectedly as a mandrake's cry. "It's for you," the curator said.

When I lifted the receiver to my ear I heard a woman, speaking with a voice infused with a semblance of life. "Rhinelander Exchange," she said, pronouncing each syllable with equal emphasis. "Number, please."

"Cities were divided into Exchanges," the curator said as I hung up. "While the operator made your connection, you'd hear a musical passage chosen to best represent the Exchange dialed. My wife lived in Endicott before we married, and whenever I'd call, I'd hear passages from Messiaen, awaiting her hello."

"That's remarkable."

He smiled. "After we married we lived in Hansa, and friends listened to Webern until we answered. I should now make a point concerning historical accuracy. Your immediate experience notwithstanding, the telephone would of course have rung only if someone called you. My exhibits merely approximate a sound's original context."

"The operator's accent was the same as yours," I said. "What is your native language?"

"Lost," he said. "I should say, it's been years since I've had need to speak it."

"I've never heard such an accent before."

"And now you have," said the curator, passing through a doorway into another dim room. I followed. Though I didn't see precisely where tile supplanted the flooring's wood, I felt, before I heard, the transformation underfoot. In the center of the room was a small round table; on the table's marble top, an antique coffee grinder and porcelain candelabra holding a single, slender candle. He pulled one of two wrought-iron chairs away from the table, scraping the legs across the tile with the sound of many fingernails drawn along a blackboard.

"Sit," he said, lighting the candle; its wax crackled and snapped as the wick caught fire. As I sat, raking the other chair's iron over that ceramic floor, the curator shut his eyes, sealing himself against all distractions, and listened as if to a wombed heartbeat, his look assuring that, by dint of concentration, he would suck the sound dry of vibration before it could decay.

"Before they closed them all, my wife and I went to the cafés every evening, along with everyone else. We were quite social, once," he said, spinning the grinder's crank. "The waiter ground the beans at your table before preparing your coffee. We sat for hours, eating and talking and listening to music. Most establishments employed musicians, that their harmonics might lend melody to the crowd's drone. None of the songs were ever recorded. Transcriptions were on occasion made, but afterward, all were effaced."

"Why?"

"Because we loved them," he said. "As the evening drew on, the older patrons went along their way, leaving behind only younger couples still uncertain whether each best suited the other. At midnight, at the hour conversation settles into the whispers of those making love with words, the oublovium player came forward to take her solo."

From a bag hidden beneath the table, the curator withdrew a wooden cylinder, turned with the symmetries of an hourglass. Leaning the blunt upper end of the instrument against his collarbone, crooking one arm around its midsection, he placed the lower, open end in his lap. Then he lifted from his bag the oublovium's apparent bow, a thin rod no longer than the oublovium itself, its form reminiscent of a dandelion, tipped not with seeds but with a ball of fine wire. Inserting its tuft into the opening, the curator slid the pole along unseen strings within the instrument, rolling the rod's length between his fingers as he drew it in and out. The notes produced bore the closest affinity to those of a harp, played at impossible tempo with a multitude of hands.

"I could as well sit at a piano and strike at the keyboard with my elbows," he said. "Anyone could make such trifling motions as these, but there were few virtuosi. Women, solely, mastered the oublovium. No one plays it today. I doubt that anyone would recognize it if they saw one."

"But who closed the cafés?"

If the curator knew, perhaps he no longer had reason to tell. He shook his head, and returned his instrument to his bag. "One day they were there, and the next, they weren't."

He redirected his attentions, undoubtedly anticipating that he would be aware of the subsequent attraction before I would. The room in which we sat seemed smaller than it was, and felt ever more so the longer we sat there, but before my vague discomfort hardened into claustrophobia, I took notice of a bright, pellucid sound overhead; a faint tinkling, a clatter of miniature cymbals. Staring up I saw a mobile attached to the ceiling, made up of shiny glass shards hanging by threads, clinking together as they twirled in the candle-warmed air.

"Trams ran throughout the cities," he continued. "A staff protruded from the prow of each car, above the engine driver's window. Chimes such as those were tied to the end of each staff, and as the cars raced down the tracks, the wind signaled to those waiting at the next stop ahead, promising that their patience would be shortly rewarded. On maps, the tramlines were identified by the spectral colors, and each car's hue matched its line.

"Upon boarding, you dropped your gold token into a black fare box. When it issued your receipt, the box thanked you, not in words but with a sound truly lost. All I can offer is a description, bearing less relation to its actuality than a dead lover's lock of hair bears to the head from which it grew." The curator stood, motioning that I should do the same. "The mechanism's three notes comprised an ascending diatonic triad, impressing itself into the ear as a chirp rather than a chord, in intonation closer to a cricket's than to a bird's, yet louder, as if the insect nestled unseen within your clothing while it sang." He paused. "Can you hear it?" Before I might answer, he went on. "I've saved what could be saved, but so much was lost. If no one knows a tree falls in the forest, the question shouldn't be did it fall? but, was it there before it fell?"

We moved into another room as he spoke. There were three tiny windows on our right, admitting no purer light than might have eked through at sunset, in winter, on a cloudy day. Once more my shoes slid across a surface of altered texture; the clack of my heels reverberated against the walls with hollow echoes, and when I glanced down I saw what appeared, in the gloom, as bleached cobblestones, or the small skulls of babies.

"We rode the Blue Line, going to the seashore. At the beachfront was the spa, which was built of plum-colored bricks and had nine hundred rooms. People came from all around to enjoy the waters. A promenade encircled the spa, and ran as well down to the dockside. Seashells were used to pave their walkways, and those of the quays. Travelers inevitably remarked on our city's soundless sea, thinking the breakers pounded silently against the sand. Throughout the day and into the night the surf went unheard beneath the footsteps of thousands strolling over the shells. It's curious to realize that the only one of our sounds visitors recalled, afterward, was one they never heard.

"Every summer night when the Guildhall's clock struck ten, the Ensemble Pyrotechnique undertook their most elaborate works on the strand. We'd sit on the public terraces overlooking the ocean and watch them fire their flowers into heaven. It was on one such night I proposed to my wife. Each year, on our anniversary, we'd ride the Blue Line to the seashore, each time remembering where we'd been, each time giving thanks for where we had come, blessing that moment from that time on until there was no time left."

I'd only imagined the cry of the fare box; now, enveloping myself within the curator's descriptions, feeling seashells beneath my feet, allowing his recollections to mingle with my own, I heard the fireworks bursting with the wet pop of flashbulbs exploding in the lamps of old cameras. That a memory of sound could so intrude into the physical world wasn't surprising in itself; who hasn't heard a fragment of a hated song and, hours later, still found it there, as impacted as a bean in the ear of a child? What was not so much unexpected as unnatural was the perceived immediacy of fireworks; of the bitter tang of gunpowder, of peripheral flashes glimpsed between my horizon and the beamed ceiling's azimuth. Shutting my eyes, I heard an unseen sea's unheard heartbeat.

"The shells were removed concurrently with the tramlines," the curator said, tapping the floor with the toe of his shoe. "The Guildhall was demolished. The spa was burned to the ground."

"Why?" I asked. "What happened?" As my words bounced from the walls back into my ears, I discerned an unaccountable lowering of the timbre of my voice, and a seeming dislocation of the direction from which it came. Some acoustic anomaly, or eigentonic flaw—perhaps accidental, perhaps not—was likely responsible; yet the unsettling impression that my voice no longer came from within me, but from somewhere without, heightened my awareness of how it might feel to have my own sound taken away. I hadn't experience enough then, nor do I now, to estimate how much I would thereafter miss it. "I don't understand."

"Nor did we," he said. "Unfortunately, but unavoidably, the remainder of the museum is quite dark. Take care, hereout."

"Where is your country?" I asked; receiving no reply, I rephrased my question. "Where was it?"

He answered only by guiding me toward another room. Stepping into its twilight, I heard our shoes crunching against the floor as if, having drifted without warning into another world's stronger gravity, our bodies increased in mass, compressing all underfoot. The resulting sound was identical to one included in my own collection, but I knew of no method by which the curator could have carpeted this chamber with snow.

"In this country, the image of winter bears faint relation to its verity," he said. "In the country I knew, each season was distinguished as much by its sounds as by its climate. Most of those were not so much lost as misplaced, and so I leave their acquisition to others. In my country, the seasons so differed from one to the next that, in some years, we might have been living successively on four dissimilar planets."

The curator stopped, and together we stood in the dark. At first I thought the continuing sound of our footsteps to be nothing more than sustained echoes. "Our weather changed before we did. One year snow fell in September. We foresaw a hard winter ahead. It was, but not because of the weather, for it never snowed again."

The rhythm of the ongoing footsteps quickened, increasing in volume as well as number until it seemed we were encroached upon by multitudes. If their stamp was but a recorded beat, as I thought it must be, its verisimilitude was nonetheless so perfect that only a single taping could have separated sound from source. The curator's face was obscured by shadow, and I was unable to gather from his reaction how I should respond to the perfection of his masters.

"Our national bird flocked in such numbers as to block out the afternoon sun."

An abrupt fluttering rose and roared around us. I instinctively braced myself, to keep from being blown over by that avian hurricane, but then realized that this room's sonic properties misled me once again; even my hair remained un-ruffled in the feathery gale. The swift bombardment from above served as an appropriate counterpoint to the unremitting ground attack.

"Their popular name was the pococurante," said the curator. "The populace favored Voltaire. The birds nested in our birch forests every spring, arriving in clouds, snapping off tree limbs beneath their cumulative weight. Pococurantes were grayish-blue, and the males had yellow heads and scarlet bellies. Their mottled eggs had a fishy flavor, though the birds themselves tasted something like chicken. The call of the pococurante was inoffensive, and familiar to all."

He mimed its song, whistling two notes; the first higher, and allegro, the second lower, and largo, an onomatopoeic *uh-oh* in the key of E flat.

"Pococurantes coupled for life. If one died, the survivor mourned its mate, refusing to fly away until it, too, was killed. Their numbers declined rapidly after the trees were chopped down. When the remaining birds set off upon their last migration, they were blasted from the sky until their blood fell like rain. The last time I heard a pococurante, I was half the age I am now." Though his face remained cloaked, through the darkness I perceived his smile, and its ambiguity. "That was also the first time I heard one."

"Would you repeat their call for me?" I asked.

"Certainly."

Attuning my ear to the chords of extinction, I knew an illuminatory moment. An unlikely admixture of sorrow, fear, and nostalgia for another's memories ir-rupted through my spirit, and as I considered the criteria by which donations might be judged worthy of a Hall of Lost Sounds, I pictured seventeenth-century explorers lying sleepless during their first night on Mauritius, kept awake by the squawk of dodos; imagined Manhattanites, in the Thirties, grabbing instinctively for their glassware as the El rumbled up Sixth Avenue; tried to recall the into-nation of my prepubescent voice. Some sounds one surely expected always to hear, and so never listened at the time they were made; perhaps inevitably those noises thought most unendurable when initially heard only later proved the most precious, and most irrecoverable.

"You like that one?" Before I could state my affirmation, his thoughts wan-dered elsewhere; I doubt that he cared. "I hear it now as you hear me."

The curator led me to the far side of the room. Cries of pococurante and drum of quickstep waned, overwhelmed by a thunderous fusillade, so loud that I guessed the rest of the tour would be delivered with gestures. Still, over sharp reports of creaking wood, against an unceasing advance of caissons bumping across stone, I heard him plainly, as if he stood in a lecture hall, addressing an audience of one.

"Long before the disruptions began, delivery carts were used in our cities to conserve fuel," the curator said. "They were pressed into general service to speed our own migration. Much of what a house contained that was important could be hauled by the largest carriages. Whatever their size, the wagons never held enough. When I left, I carried my belongings with me."

However chimerical its nature, the crash of a thousand inessential wagons hurtling toward us so unnerved me that with each pass I flinched, attempting to avoid an onslaught I knew was evanescent. Without benefit of imagination, I heard horses neighing when whips cracked against their withers; drivers shouting out curses over the groan of their loads. I pretend no understanding of sonology, but I thought it impossible that any phonographic agency could so truly reproduce such pandemonium; I felt that through some subtle technique, I heard those sounds exactly as he did when they ricocheted off the walls of his skull. Possibly that was his trick, or what he wished me to believe was his trick, that he drew from his mind at command recollections so assiduously cherished as to have developed an alternate existence, nearly independent of his own. A suitable audience could be therefore gratified, assured that not only had there been a tree which fell, but that the sound it made upon falling would echo through its forest unto eternity.

"Why did you have to leave your country?" I asked.

"She left me," he said. "I should have preferred to stay. Come along, now."

Grateful to be removed from the earsplitting tumult, I followed the curator and we entered a brighter, quieter hall. In the ceiling's elliptical dome was an oculus, threaded with a strand of light. Two doors faced us, one open, one closed. Gazing into the visible threshold's abyss, I saw neither exhibits nor even room beyond. The curator stopped, and we went no farther.

"My wife and I were awakened one night by sirens," he said. "We opened our windows and watched the spa burn down. In keeping with the season we tried to reimagine what we saw as a Halloween spectacle, and shuddered at the vision of black skeletons silhouetted against an orange field. But sorrow overwhelmed our disregard of what we knew to be real, and we returned to bed, unsuccessful in our attempts to transform a funeral into a holiday. It was only the week before that we'd sat on the beachfront terraces, enjoying the fireworks, leaving before we'd intended with every expectation of returning when we wished.

"The next morning we rode our bicycles to the beach, anxious to look at ruins other than our own. On the way we passed the avenue's empty shops, where haberdashers and tobacconists, watchmakers and smiths, joiners and cobblers and ostlers plied their trades long before our grandparents were born. The cafés were shuttered. Gilt and neon signs were covered over by billboards telling of unfamiliar people and places. So crowded with those departing was the Central Station that the passengers' clamor muted that of their trains. We reached the seashore. The ashes had mixed with the sand, and as we walked over them we listened to the ocean, hearing it anew, if not for the first time. Its swell terrified my wife, and we walked our cycles home, bereft of emotion, feeling too drained to race back uphill. That morning, all anyone knew was rumors and lies, and what wasn't said didn't matter as much as what wasn't done. My country was taken from us, though if not with our wishes, then undoubtedly with dutiful acquiescence.

"Couples living in such circumstances so often find their challenges insurmountable. We talked of what we might do. All we could do was talk, and try to make the other listen. We drifted apart, all the while wanting to stay together. One day, sooner than expected, I came home to find her gone."

His expression remained unchanged as he weaved his words around me. A softer sound, its origin as enigmatic as the rest, insinuated itself into my ears, a steady uninflected jingling, heard as if it came from far beneath the floor.

"You can always speak to one who isn't there, of course, as long as you don't expect answers," the curator said. "We planted pinwheels in our gardens in memory of the dead. Miniature sleigh bells were attached to their vanes, so that when the wind spun the wheels around, the souls they honored would ascend with a soothing accompaniment."

Though his face evinced no untoward emotion—nor, in fact, any emotion at all—I perceived that he felt he should cry, even if he no longer could. The sound of his sorrow was evidently one he had been unable, or unwilling, to preserve. "Though the past survives only through its artifacts," he said, "every museum must limit its acquisitions."

"Your country," I said. "Your wife. Where are they?" Taking my arm, he walked the short distance across the hall with me, and pointed to the open door. "Listen."

Craning my head toward its darkness, I heard not silence, but the absence of sound. Staring into that void, straining to catch noises that simply weren't there, I better comprehended the true worth of his collection and how irreplaceable it would be, once it was lost. He'd deliberately left vague the magnitude of his tragedy; what else of his world was he unable to save? Did he miss what he had retained all the more? Could any public loss be greater than any private one, or did one inescapably serve as no more than grace note to the other, if they happened to coincide?

The curator began singing a tune of unsettling pitch, his notes wobbling in and out of key. The words were, I suppose, in his original tongue, a speech engorged with glottal phrasings, surprising syllabic leaps and discordant cadences, bearing no relation to any language I've heard before, or since. After a single verse and chorus, he stopped. "Our song," he told me. "The last exhibit of my museum."

As he concluded his sentence, the cathedral bells rang out the sixteenth hour, shaking the walls with sonorous peals. The curator grimaced, showing even less appreciation of their auditory terrorism. Once the toll concluded he directed me to the other door. "Now I hear my wife's voice," he said, unlatching the lock, easing me forward. "Thank you for hearing mine."

Before I could reply, he closed the door behind me. I found myself in afternoon sunlight, some distance from the alley, deafened by Gaon Prospect's cacophony—the roars of its buses and taxis and trucks, the chants of its hawkers.

Children screamed at one another, police blew whistles, car alarms blared, and a thousand radios bleated across the encompassing dissonance of Montrouge.

There were numerous cafés on the Prospect and, selecting one of more subdued ambience than the rest, I took a seat and ordered currant genever. Late into the evening I rifled the accessions of my own museum, replaying sounds as I came upon them. Too many of its holdings were unavailable, however diligent the search, but the sole surprise was that they'd been stolen with such ease; if I hadn't looked, I'd have never missed them. A friend of mine, a composer, once spoke to me of Webern: how in his music the rests contribute as much, if not more, as the notes; that having a sense of what was missing made all the clearer what remained. Until that afternoon I'd preferred tunes more easily mastered. The curator's songs stuck closer to me than I thought desirable, and only with some effort did I erase them from my mind.

Robert Clinton

Merlin

*Robert Clinton was born in 1946, raised in upstate New York, and now lives
in Boston, where he works as a designer for a custom cabinet shop. His poetry
has appeared in* Ploughshares, The Atlantic, Hanging Loose, *and other periodicals. Sarabande Books recently published his first collection,* Taking Eden;
he is currently working on his second book, Surviving Myself.

*The brevity of the following Arthurian tale belies its power, for Clinton
conjures pure magic with language as enchanted as Merlin's spells. This exquisite little piece comes from the Spring issue of* The New England Review.

—T. W.

So Ulfius departed and by adventure he met Merlin in a beggar's array, and
there Merlin asked Ulfius whom he sought, and he said he had little ado'
to tell him. "Well," said Merlin, "I know whom thou seekest, for thou
seekest Merlin; therefore seek no farther, for I am he." The moon behind
him fell in a pot. "Now what do you want with me?" said Merlin. Sir Ulfius
pretended to study his harness braid. "I will tell you this also," said Merlin.
"There is a black breeze on your king that he cannot have the woman named
Igraine. You think my dog and monkey could help you."

Ulfius said nothing until they had gotten back to the hills where Uther Pendragon kept his battle out of the weather. There he remained silent a while
longer, letting every man around him know nothing. Merlin too was silent. Then
Merlin said, "Which man here is King?" No one would answer him at once.
Then Merlin said, "By inquiring of numbered rocks I have discovered that this
man"—here he pointed vaguely at the largest tent where a morning cook-fire
was going out—"is the sorrowful king. Make him come out here." It was not

possible for knight or archer to do this. Eight sparrows rustled hard corn on the ground in front of the tent flap. "Since he won't come out to me I'll find him at home," said Merlin, unwearied.

He pulled himself into the tent and was at once looking at the king asleep with the dented crown hung on a peg overhead. There were twelve knights so equally asleep in the tent that Merlin couldn't hear himself. He put his head outside of the tent and said to those assembled men and knights, "I have what this lord wants. I can make him look as much like Igraine's duke as makes no difference." That was enough to set everyone there to staring, but no one said a word. "If one thing is promised me I will do it to him," said Merlin, but they waited for him to mention what he needed.

This time Merlin sat down in the yard in front of the King's own tent and silently sat for someone to say to him, "What, Merlin?" The sun was able to go over the sky half-way, the morning birds flew off and the birds of early afternoon arrived (there weren't any); an emissary from the besieged castle several hills distant came into camp and left immediately with no verbal response to a very gracious invitation; the fog in the little valleys below them eased and deer rose to their elbows, to their knees, and still Merlin sat and his speechless blackbirds sat around him and the badgers of the cavalry sat pouting.

"Very well," said Merlin, "I'll tell you what it is you must give me—I will take—I want the boy. The child." No one in the curved panels of steel armor and embroidered satin cloth said a single English word, although Merlin seemed to some of them to have become a flock of blackbirds in a tall ash tree, seemed to some of them to have changed into a ball of ants wrapped around a honey jar. No one spoke. Again, and for certain, no one spoke.

"Very well," said Merlin, "this is the year that will not come again. But I'll be here in ten months with a contract and the hard nurse." A few of the men got onto their feet and felt for the pommels of their iron swords, and Merlin looked eagerly there among them for what would surely next be an angry word, a plain expression of principle, a harsh challenge in the common tongue. But they were silent! They stood turning and turning in the windy field and they moved back against the trees and disappeared. "One sorrow," said Merlin, "is the bell of song remembered; but a greater one comes with the noise of writing: do any of you know why this is?"

He looked around at them with his smile, which they could not take off their steel face-plates with spatulas. But there was nothing they could say. After a very long pause Merlin decided he would answer himself at once: "You don't know why this is." Behind him even the King was awake, and many tents in the fields let heads into the late afternoon sunlight to watch what was so quiet and inwinding. The beginning of history ends the other, *unremembered* past: one man or boy, his hand held over his mouth, might just have said aloud. But that is not recorded.

Stephen Laws

The Crawl

Stephen Laws became a full-time writer in 1992, after working for the government in England. He is the author of ten horror novels including Ghost Train, Spectre, Daemonic, Somewhere South of Midnight, *and the soon-to-be-released* Chasm. *His short stories have appeared in various anthologies, magazines, and newspapers. According to Laws, the idea for this story came to him as he and his wife were driving home from Easter dinner with her parents. Just as they were passing the road sign* BOROUGHBRIDGE: HALF-MILE *he had a "most alarming and intense image . . ."*

"The Crawl" was originally published in Dark of the Night.

—E. D.

The days are bad, but the nights are always worse.

Since it all happened and I lost my job, it seems as if the front door is always the focus of my attention, no matter what I'm doing. I try to keep myself occupied, try to read, try to listen to music. But all of these things make it much worse. You see, if I really *do* become preoccupied in what I'm doing, then I might not hear it if . . .

If he . . . if it . . . comes.

I've recently had all my mail redirected to a post office box where I can go and collect it, since the clatter of the letterbox in the morning and afternoon became just too much to bear. I had to nail it up against junk mail and free newspapers. The house has become a terrible, terrible place since I lost Gill. God, how I miss her.

And in the nights, I lie awake and listen.

The sound of a car passing on the sidestreet is probably the worst.

I hear it coming in my sleep. It wakes me instantly, and I'm never sure whether

I've screamed or not, but I lie there praying first that the car will pass quickly and that the engine won't cough and falter. Then, in the first seconds after it's moved on I pray again that I won't hear those familiar, staggering footsteps on the gravel path outside; that I won't hear that hellish hammering on the front door. I listen for the sounds of that hideous, hoarse breathing. Most nights I'm soaked in sweat waiting for the sound of the door panels splintering apart. Sometimes I dream that I'm down there in the hall, with my hands braced against the wood of that front door, screaming for help as the pounding comes from the other side.

Sometimes I dream that I'm in bed, that he's got in and he's coming up the stairs.

That same slow, methodical tread.

I run to the door, trying to slam it shut as he reaches the landing. In slow motion, I turn and scream at Gill to get out quickly through the bedroom window as I heave the bedside cabinet across the floor to the door. But as I turn, Gill isn't there. She's in the bathroom at the top of the landing, so now I'm frantically tearing the cabinet away from the door as he ascends, but Gill doesn't hear him because the shower's running and I slowly pull open the door screaming her name just as the shadow reaches the landing and Gill turns from the wash basin and . . .

If I started by telling you that the whole thing began on the A1 just a half-mile from Boroughbridge, you might suppose that it has some kind of relevance for the horror that came afterwards. If it does, then that relevance has eluded me. Believe me, I've been over the whole thing many times in my mind, trying to make sense of it all. No, like all bad nightmares, it defied any logic. It seemed that we were just in the wrong place at the wrong time; like a traffic accident. Thirty seconds earlier or thirty seconds later, and maybe I'd be able to sleep at night a little better than I do these days. But since all stories start somewhere, the A1 turn-off half-a-mile from Boroughbridge was our somewhere.

The day had started badly.

We had spent Easter weekend with my wife's parents, and on the trip home Gill and I weren't speaking. There had been a party at her folks' house on the Sunday evening (we'd been there since Thursday), and that bloody personnel manager friend of theirs had been invited. I'd been made redundant from an engineering firm three years previously, and it was two years before I found another job. Not easy, but things were going fine again at last. Nevertheless, the use of my previous firm's psychometric testing to "reduce staffing levels" was a bug-bear of mine. ("What is the capital of Upper Twatland? You don't know? Then sorry, you're sacked.")

We were driving home on Easter Monday, and I had promised not to drink during the evening so that we could take turns behind the wheel. But this bastard personnel man (who I'd never met before, but whose profession didn't endear himself to me) was standing there all night, spouting off his in-house philosophy about big fish eating little fish, and only-the-strongest-will-prevail. My anger had begun as a slow-burn, and I'd had a drink to dampen the fuse. But then a second had begun to light it again. And by the third, I was just about ready for an intervention. By my fourth, I'd burned it out of my system, was having a chat with Stuart and Ann and their light-hearted banter was making everything okay again. Then, the personnel man was left on his own and, having bored his companion to tears, decided to move over to us. If he'd kept off the subject, everything would have been okay. (But then again, if we hadn't been on the A1 half-a-mile out of Boroughbridge, none of this would have happened either.)

Disregarding anything we were talking about, he started again where he'd left off.

And I'm afraid that was it. All bets off. Fuse not only rekindled, but powder-keg ignited. I could probably go on for three pages about our conversation, but since this tale is about the worst thing that ever happened to me, and not one of the best, it seems a little pointless if I do. Just let's say that without giving in to the urge for actual bodily harm, I kept a cold fury inside. I dispensed with any social airs and graces or the rules of polite party-conversation, and kept at his throat while he tried to impress us with his superior "if-they-can't-hack-it, out-they-go" credo. Like a terrier, I kept hanging at his wattles, shaking him down and finishing with a "who-lives-by-the-sword-dies-by-the-sword." Sounds obvious, but believe me; as a put-down it wasn't half bad. Maybe you had to be there to appreciate it. He left our company, and kept to other less-impolite partygoers. Stuart and Ann were pleased too, and that made me feel good.

However, I could tell by Gill's face that I wasn't going to get any good conduct medals. At first, I thought that maybe I'd overstepped the mark; been too loud, let the booze kid me that I was being subtle when in fact I was acting like Attila the Hun. But no, her tight-lips and cold demeanor were related to more practical matters than that. I'd seen off at least a half-bottle of scotch, and we had that long drive tomorrow. Remember? Well, no I hadn't. My anger had seen to that.

So by next morning we were in a non-speaking to each other situation.

I tried to hide the hang-over, but when you've been living with someone for ten years it's a little difficult to hide the signs. The two fizzing Solpadeine in the glass were the final insult. I stressed that I would take care of the second-half of the journey, but this didn't seem to hold water. Did I mention that she'd lost a baby, was still getting over it physically and psychologically, that she was feeling very tired all the time? No? Well, just sign out the Bastard Club form and I would willingly have signed.

Tight-lipped farewells to the In-laws.

And a wife's face that says she's just waiting for the open road before she lets rip.

Well, she let rip. But I probably don't have to draw you a map.

I let it go, knowing that I'd been a little selfish. But Gill always did have a habit of taking things a little too far. My temper snapped, and seconds later it had developed into the knock-down, drag-out verbal fight that I'd been trying to avoid.

BOROUGHBRIDGE, said the motorway sign. HALF MILE.

"That's the last time we spend any time together down here at Easter," said Gill.

"Fine by me. I've got more important things I could be doing."

"Let's not stop at Easter. How about spending our Christmases and Bank Holidays apart, too?"

"Great. I might be able to enjoy myself for a change."

"Maybe we should make it more permanent? Why stop at holidays? Let's just . . ."

". . . spend all of our time apart? That suits me fine."

There was a man up ahead, standing beside the barrier on the central reservation. Just a shadow, looking as if he was waiting for a break in the traffic so that he could make a dangerous run across the two lanes to the other side.

"God, you can be such a bastard!"

"You're forgetting an important point, Gill. It was people like that personnel bastard who got me the sack. You should be sticking up for me, not . . ."

"So what makes you think we need your money? Are you trying to say that what I earn isn't enough to . . ."

"For Christ's sake, Gill!"

The shadow stepped out from the roadway barrier, directly in front of us.

Gill had turned to look at me, her face a mask of anger.

"For Christ's *sake!*" I yelled, and it must have seemed to her then that I'd lost my mind when I suddenly lunged for the steering wheel. She yelled in anger and shock, swatted at me but held fast.

And in the next minute, something exploded through the windscreen.

Gill's instincts were superb. Despite the fact that the car was suddenly filled with an exploding, hissing shrapnel of fine glass, she didn't lose control. She braked firmly, hanging onto the wheel while I threw my hands instinctively up to protect my face. The car slewed and hit the barrier, and I could feel the front of the car on Gill's side crumple. The impact was horrifying and shocking. In that split-second I expected the body of that idiot to come hurtling through into our laps, smashing us back against our seats. But nothing came through the windscreen as the car slewed to a halt on the hard-shoulder, right next to the metal barrier, and with its nose pointed out into the nearside lane.

There were fine tracings of red-spiderweb blood all over my hands as I reached instinctively for Gill. Her hands were clenched tight to the wheel, her head was down and her long dark hair full of fine glass shards. I could see that her hands were also flayed by the glass and with a sickening roll in the stomach I thought she might be blinded.

"God, Gill! Are you alright?"

I pulled up her face with both hands so that she was staring directly ahead through the shattered windscreen. Her eyes were wide and glassy, she was breathing heavily. Obviously in shock, and hanging onto that wheel as if she was hanging onto her self-control.

"Are you alright?"

She nodded, a slight gesture which seemed to take great effort.

Twisting in my seat, making the imploded glass all around me crackle and grind, I looked back.

We hadn't hit the stupid bastard.

He was still standing, about thirty or forty feet behind us on the hard-shoulder. Standing there, unconcerned, watching us.

I kicked open the passenger door and climbed out. Slamming it, I leaned on the roof to get my breath and then looked back at him. He was a big man, but in the dusk it was impossible to see any real details other than he seemed to be shabbily dressed and unsteady on his feet. The sleeves of his jacket seemed torn, his hair awry. A tramp, perhaps. He was just standing there, with his hands hanging limply at his sides, staring in our direction.

"You *stupid* bastard!" I yelled back at him when my breath returned. "You could have killed my wife."

The man said nothing. He just stood and looked. His head was slightly down, as if he was looking at us from under his brows. There was something strange about his face, but I couldn't make it out.

"You stupid *fuck!*"

Then I saw that he was holding something in one hand, something long and curved in a half-moon shape. I squinted, rubbing my shredded hands over my face and seeing that there was also blood on the palms, too. The sight of more blood enraged me. Fists bunched at my side, I began striding back along the hard shoulder towards the silently waiting figure.

After ten or fifteen feet, I stopped.

There *was* something wrong with this character's face. The eyes were too dark, too large. The mouth was fixed in a permanent grin. I couldn't see a nose.

And then I realized what it was.

The man was wearing a mask.

A stupid, scarecrow mask.

It was made from sacking of some sort, tied around the neck with string. From where I was standing, I couldn't tell whether he'd drawn big, round black eyes with peep holes in the center, or whether they were simply ragged holes in the sacking. I could see no eyes in there, only darkness. Ragged stitchwork from ear to ear gave the mask its permanent grin. Bunches of straw hair poked from under the brim of the ragged fishing hat which had been jammed down hard on the head. That same straw was also poking out between the buttons of the ragged jacket. More string served as a belt holding up equally ragged trousers. The sole had come away from the upper on each boot.

As I stood frozen, taking in this ridiculous sight and perhaps looking just as stupid, the figure raised the long curved thing in its hand.

It was a hand scythe.

This one was black and rusted, but when the scarecrow raised it before its mask-face it seemed as if the edge of that blade had been honed and sharpened. Then I realized that it was this that had smashed our car windscreen. The bastard had waited for us to pass, had stepped out and slammed the damned thing across the glass like an axe.

And then the man began to stride towards me.

There was nothing hurried in his approach. It was a steady methodical pace, holding that scythe casually down at his side. His idiot, grinning scarecrow's face was fixed on me as he moved. There was no doubt in my mind as he came on.

He meant to kill me.

He meant to knock me down and pin me to the ground with one foot, while he raised that hook, and brought it straight down through the top of my skull. Then he would kick me to one side, walk up to the car and drag Gill out of the driving seat . . .

I turned and ran back to the car. As I wrenched open the passenger door, I glanced back to see that the figure hadn't hurried his pace to catch up. He was coming at the same remorseless pace; a brisk, but unhurried walk. Inside the car, Gill was still hunched in the driving seat, clutching the wheel.

"Drive, Gill!" I yelled. "For God's sake, *drive!*"

"What . . . ?"

I tried to shove her out of the driving seat then, away from the wheel and into the passenger seat. Still in shock, she couldn't understand what the hell was wrong with me. She clung tight to that wheel with one hand and started clawing at my face with the other. I looked back as we struggled. In seconds, that maniac would reach the car. He was already hefting that hook in his hand, ready to use it.

"Look!" I practically screamed in Gill's face, and dragged her head around to see.

At the same moment, the rear windscreen imploded with shocking impact.

Everything happened so fast after that, I can't really put it together in my head. I suppose that the scarecrow-man had shattered the glass with the hand scythe. There was a blurred jumble of movement in the ragged gap through the rear windscreen. And I suppose that Gill must have realized what was happening then, because the next thing I heard was the engine roaring into life.

"*Go!*" someone yelled, and I suppose it must have been me. Because the next thing I remember after that was me sitting in the back of the car, swatting powdered glass off the seat. Then I heard another impact, and looked up to see that the scarecrow was scrabbling on the boot of the car. The scythe was embedded in the metalwork, and the scarecrow was clinging on tight to it. I thrust out through the broken window and tore at the man's ragged gloves, pounding with my fists. The car bounced and jolted, something seemed to screech under the chassis, and I prayed to God that it was the madman's legs being crushed. We were moving again, but Gill was yelling and cursing, slamming her hands on the wheel. The engine sounded tortured; the car was juddering and shaking, as if Gill was missing the clutch bite-point and "donkeying" all the time.

The scythe came free from its ragged hole and the madman fell back from the boot. There was a scraping, rending sound as the hook screeched over the bodywork. To my horror, I saw that he had managed to snag the damned thing in the fender and now we were pulling him along the hard-shoulder as he clung to its handle. With his free hand, he clawed at the fender; trying to get a proper grip and pull himself upright again. His legs thrashed and raised dust clouds as we moved. Somehow, I couldn't move as I watched him being dragged along behind us. The car juddered again and I almost fell between the seats. Lunging up, I seemed to get a grip on myself.

The madman had lost his hold on the fender. We were pulling away from where he lay. I saw one arm flop through the air as he tried to turn over. Perhaps he was badly hurt? Good.

We were still on the hard shoulder, near to the barrier, as traffic flashed past us. But something had happened to the car when it hit that roadside barrier. Something had torn beneath the chassis, and Gill was yanking hard at the gear lever.

"It's stuck!" she shouted, nearly hysterically. "I can't get it out of first gear."

"Let me try . . ." I tried to climb over into the passenger seat, but in that moment I caught sight of what was happening in the rearview mirror. The scare-crow was rising to his knees, perhaps fifty feet behind us now. I lost sight of him in the bouncing mirror, twisted around to look out of the window again, just in time to see him stand. There was something slow and measured in that move-ment, as if he hadn't been hurt at all. He had retrieved the scythe.

And he was coming after us again.

Not running, just the same methodical stride. As if he had all the time in the world to catch up with us.

I faced front again. Gill was still struggling with the gears, and the speed-ometer was wavering at five miles an hour. As we juddered along on the hard shoulder, it seemed as if we were travelling at exactly the same pace as the man behind us.

"Hit the clutch!" I yelled, lunging forward again as Gill depressed the pedal. I yanked at the gearstick, trying to drag it back into second gear. The best I could do was get it into the neutral position, and that meant we were coasting to a halt. Behind us, the man started to gain. Gill could see him now, slapped my hand away and shoved the gearstick into first again.

"Who *is* he?" she sobbed. "What does he want?"

I thought about jumping out of the car and taking over from Gill in the driving seat. But by the time we did that, the madman would be on us again, and anyway, Gill was a damn sight better driver than me. There seemed only one thing we could do.

"Steer out onto the motorway," I hissed.

"We're travelling too slowly. There's too much traffic. We'll be hit."

"Maybe he'll get hit first."

"Oh *Christ* . . ."

Gill yanked hard on the wheel and the car slewed out across the motorway.

A traffic horn screamed at us and a car passed so close that we heard the screech of its tires and felt the blast of air through the shattered windscreen as it swerved to avoid us. I looked at the speedo again. We were still crawling.

I moved back to the rear window.

The radiator grille of a lorry filled my line of vision. The damned thing was less than six feet from us, just about to ram into our rear; crushing the boot right through the car. I yelled something, I don't know what; convinced that the lorry was going to smash into us, ram us both up into the engine block in a mangled, bloody mess. Perhaps it was the shock of my yell, but Gill suddenly yanked hard at the steering wheel again and we swerved to the left. I could feel the car rocking on its suspension as the lorry passed within inches, the blaring of its horn ringing in our ears. But we weren't out of danger yet. I reared towards the dash as another car swerved from behind us, around to the right, tyres screeching.

"You were travelling too *fast*, you bastard!" I yelled after it. "Too bloody *fast*!"

More horns were blaring and when I flashed a glance back at Gill I could see that she was hunched forward over the wheel. Her face was too white, like a dead person. There were beaded droplets of sweat on her forehead. In the next moment, she had swung the wheel hard over to the left again. Off balance, I fell across my seat, my head bouncing from her shoulder. I clawed at the seat rest, trying to sit up straight again. Suddenly, Gill began clawing at me with one hand. I realize now that my attempts to sit were hampering her ability to pull the wheel hard over. To my shame, I began clawing back at her; not understanding and in a total funk. She yelled that I was a stupid bastard. I yelled that she was a mad bitch. And then I was up in my seat again as Gill began spinning the wheel furiously back, hand over hand. Glancing out of the window, I could see that she had taken us right across the motorway and was taking a sliproad. The sign said: BOROUGHBRIDGE.

She had done it. She had taken us right across without hitting another vehicle. We were still crawling along, but at least we had got away from the madman behind us. I knew then that everything was okay. When we found the first emergency telephone, we would stop and ring for the police.

"Okay," I breathed. "It's okay . . . you've done it, Gill . . . we're okay now."

Until I turned in my seat and looked back to see that everything was far from okay.

The man in the fancy-dress costume was walking across the highway towards us, perhaps fifty yards back. His steps were measured, still as if he had all the time in the world, the scythe hanging from one hand. Grinning face fixed on us. Even as I looked, and felt the sickening nausea of fear again, a car swerved around him, tires screeching. Its passage made his ragged clothes whip and ruffle. Straw flew from his shoulders and his ragged trousers. By rights, it should have rammed right into him, throwing him up and over its roof. But just as luck had been with us, crossing that busy motorway, it was also with him.

Our car began its ascent of the sliproad, engine coughing and straining. Gill fumbled with the gears, trying without success to wrench them into second. The engine began to race and complain.

"He's there . . ." I began.

"I *know* he's fucking *there*!" yelled Gill, eyes still fixed ahead. "But we can't go any faster!"

The speedo was wobbling around fifteen miles an hour; even now as we ascended the sliproad, the gradual slope was having an affect on our progress. The needle began to drop . . . to fourteen . . . to thirteen.

When I looked back, I could see that nevertheless, we were putting a little distance between us and the madman. When a car flashed past, between the scarecrow and the entrance to the sliproad, I could see that fate wasn't completely on his side, after all. He wasn't invulnerable. He had waited while the car had crossed his path, and that slight wait had given us a little time. Not to mention a certain relief. The man might be mad, but he was human and not some supernatural creature out of a bad horror movie. As the car passed, he came on, the scythe swinging in his hand as he moved.

It came to me then.

There was a tool kit in the boot. If Gill pulled over, I could jump out and yank the boot open, grab a screwdriver or something. Threaten him, scare him away. Show him that I meant business.

"Pull over," I said.

"Are you joking, or what?" asked Gill.

When I looked at her again, something happened to me. It had to do with everything that had occurred over the last forty-eight hours. It had to do with the stupid fights, with my stupid behavior. But more than anything, it had to do with the expression on Gill's face. This was the woman I loved. She was, quite literally, in shock. And I'd just lashed out at her when she'd been acting on my instruction and taken us across the motorway, away from the maniac and—against all the odds—avoided colliding with another vehicle. I'd let her down badly. It was time to sort this thing out.

"Pull over!" I snapped again.

"He's still coming," she said. Her voice was too calm. Too matter of fact.

Then I realized. At this speed, I could open the door and just hop out.

Angrily, that's what I did.

I slammed the door hard as I turned to face our pursuer; just the way that people do when there's been a minor traffic "shunt" and both parties try to faze out the other by a show of aggression, using body language to establish guilt before any heated conversation begins. Inside the car, I heard Gill give a startled cry as the car shuddered to a halt.

The scarecrow was still approaching up the ramp.

I stood for a moment, praying that he might at least pause in his stride.

He didn't.

I lunged at the boot, slamming my hand on it and pointing hard at him; as if some zig-zag lightning bolt of pure anger would zap out of my finger and fry him on the spot.

"You're fucking mad and I'm fucking telling you! You want some aggro, *eh*? You want some fucking *aggro*? I'll show *you* what fucking *aggro* is all *about!*" If the 'fuck' word could kill, he should be dead already.

But he was still coming.

I swept the remaining frosting of broken glass from the boot and snapped it open. There was a tire-wrench in there. I leaned in for it, without taking my eyes off the scarecrow, and my hand bumped against the suitcase. In that moment, I knew that the wrench must be at the bottom of the boot and that all our weekend luggage was on top of it. I whirled around, clawing at the suitcase, trying to yank it aside. But I'd packed that boot as tight as it's possible to get. The only way I was going to get that wrench was by yanking everything out of there on to the tarmac.

And the scarecrow was only fifty feet from us.

I looked back to see that he was smacking the scythe in the palm of one hand, eager to use it.

"*Shit!*" I slammed the boot again and hurried back around the car.

The scarecrow remained implacable. From this distance, I could see how tall he was. Perhaps six feet-seven. Broad-shouldered. Completely uncaring of my show of bravado. And, Good Christ, I could hear him now.

He was *giggling*.

It was a forced, manic sound. Without a trace of humor. It was an insane sound of anticipation. He was looking forward to what he was going to do when he reached us. As I dragged open the passenger door, I had no illusions then. If I engaged in a hand-to-hand physical confrontation with this lunatic, he would kill me. There was no doubt about it. Not only that, but he would tear me limb from limb, before he turned his attentions to Gill. I stooped to yell at her, but she was already yanking at the gear-stick and the car was moving again; the engine making grinding, gasping sounds.

The scarecrow's pace remained unaltered.

There was a car coming up the sliproad behind him.

Some mad and overwhelming darkness inside myself made me will that car to swerve as it came up behind the scarecrow. I wanted to see it ram him up on the hood and toss him over the fence into the high grass. But then I knew what I had to do. I skipped around the front of our own car and into the road as the car swerved around the scarecrow and came up the sliproad towards us. I ran in front of it, waving my arms, flagging it down. I can still hardly believe what happened next.

The driver—male, female, it was impossible to tell—jammed their hand on the horn as the car roared straight at me. I just managed to get out of the way, felt the front fender snag and tear my trouser leg as it passed. I whirled in the middle of the road, unbelieving. The car vanished over the rise and was gone from sight. I turned back.

The scarecrow was still coming.

"For Christ's sake!" snapped Gill. "Get in."

I stumbled back into the car and we began our juddering crawl again. I wasn't in a sane world anymore. This couldn't possibly be happening to us. Where was everyone? Why wouldn't anyone help as we crawled on and on with that madman behind us? I turned to say something to Gill, studied her marble-white face, eyes staring dead ahead; but I couldn't find a thing to say. The scarecrow behind us was still coming at his even stride. If he wanted to, he could move faster, and then he'd overtake us. But he seemed content to match his speed with our own. At the moment, he was keeping an even distance between us. If our car failed or slowed, he would catch up. It was as simple as that.

We reached the rise. Down below, we could see that the road led deep into countryside. I'd lost all track of where the hell Boroughbridge might be, if it had ever existed at all. On either side of the road were fields of bright yellow wheat.

At last, God seemed to have remembered we were here and wasn't so pissed off with us, after all. As our car crested the ridge and began to move down towards the fields, it began to pick up speed.

"Oh thank God . . ." Gill began to weep then. The car's gearbox was still straining and grinding, but we *were* gathering speed. Leaning back over the seat I watched as the lip of the hill receded behind us. When the scarecrow suddenly reappeared on the top of the rise, silhouetted against the skyline, he must surely see that we were picking up speed. But he didn't suddenly alter his pace, didn't begin to run down after us. He kept at his even march, right in the middle of the road, straight down in our direction. Following the Fucking Yellow Brick Road. Soon, we'd leave him far behind.

I swung around to the front again, to see that we were doing thirty, the engine straining and gasping. I gritted my teeth, praying that it wouldn't cut out altogether. But it was still keeping us moving. When I looked back again, the silhouette of our attacker was a small blur. Another vehicle was cresting the rise behind him. I heard its own horn blare at the strange figure in the middle of the road, watched the small truck swerve around him. It seemed to me that someone was leaning out of the truck window, and the driver was giving the idiot a piece of his mind. The vehicle came on towards us, picking up speed.

Should I chance our luck again? Slow the car, jump out and try to flag down help?

"No you're not," said Gill, without taking her eyes from the road. She had been reading my mind. "I'm not slowing this car down again. I'm keeping my foot down and we're getting out of here . . ."

When I looked at the speedo, I felt as if I was going to throw up; there-and-then.

". . . and we're never, *ever* coming back to this bloody hellhole of a place," continued Gill, her voice cracking and tears streaming down her face, "As long as I ever live. Do you hear me, Paul? Not never, *ever!*"

"I've got to stop that truck before it passes us."

"You're not listening! I'm not stopping. Not for anything!"

"We are stopping, Gill! Look at the speedo! We got extra speed on the incline, that's all. Now we're slowing down on the straight. Look."

Gill shook her head, refusing to look.

The needle had fallen from thirty to twenty and was still descending.

"Will you just *look!*"

"*No!*"

I lunged around. The truck was less than two hundred yards behind us, and soon to overtake.

"Gill, look! It's a tow-truck! From a breakdown service. It's stencilled on the side. Look!"

"*No!*"

With the needle wavering at ten miles an hour, I did what I had to do. I kicked open the passenger door. Gill refused to take her eyes from the road, but clawed at my hair with one hand, screaming and trying to drag me back into the car. I batted her off and hopped out into the middle of the sun-baked dirt road. A cloud of dust enveloped me. I just made it in time. Five seconds later, and the tow truck would have overtaken us and been gone. But now the driver could see my intent. He slowed, and then as I walked back towards him, the truck trundled on up behind us, matching an even time at ten miles an hour as I hopped up onto the running-board.

The man inside had a big grin. He was about sixty, maybe even ready for retirement. Something about my action seemed to amuse him.

"Don't tell me," he said, without me having to make any opening conversation. "You're in trouble?"

Something about his manner, his friendliness, made that fear begin to melt inside me. Now it seemed that the world wasn't such a hostile and alien place as I thought it had suddenly become. I was grinning now too, like a great big kid.

"How could you tell?"

"My line of business. Been doing this for thirty-five years. People always come to me. I never go looking for them. How can I help you?"

Suddenly, looking back at the scarecrow, now perhaps two or three hundred yards away and still coming down that dirt road towards us, I didn't know what to say.

"Well . . . the car. We had a bash and . . . and it's stuck in first gear. Can't get it any faster than five, six miles an hour. Got some speed on the incline there, but it won't last."

"Okay," said the old man with the lined face and the rolled up sleeves. "Just pull her over and I'll take a look."

If my smile faltered, the old man either didn't notice or failed to make anything of it. I hopped down from the board and, realizing that I was trying to move too nonchalantly, moved quickly back to the car. Running around the front, I leaned on the window-edge, jogging alongside where Gill was still hunched over the driving wheel, still staring ahead with glassy eyes.

"We're in luck. It *is* a tow-truck. He says he'll help us."

Gill said nothing. The car trundled along at seven miles an hour.

"Gill, I said he'll help us."

Somewhere, a crow squawked, as if to remind us that the scarecrow was still there and was still coming.

"Come on, stop the car."

Gill wiped tears from her eyes, and returned her white-knuckled, two handed grip on the steering wheel.

"Stop the car!"

This time, I reached in and tried to take the keys.

Gill clawed at me, her fingernails raking my forehead. I recoiled in shock.

"I . . . am . . . not . . . stopping the car. Not for you. Not for anybody. He's still coming. If we stop, he'll come. And he'll kill us."

I thought about making another grab, then saw that the old man was leaning out of his window behind us, watching. He wasn't smiling that big smile anymore. I made a helpless, "everything's fine" gesture and stood back to let our car pass and the tow truck catch up. Then I jumped up on the running-board again as we trundled along. Behind us, I could see that the scarecrow had gained on us. The silhouette was bigger than before. Had he suddenly decided to change the rules of the game and put on a burst of speed to overtake us? The possibility made me break out into another sweat. The old man seemed to see the change in me.

"Got a problem?" His voice was much warier this time.

"Well, my wife. She . . . she won't . . . that is, she won't stop the car."

"Why not?"

"She's frightened."

"Of you?"

"Me? God, no!" I wiped a hand across my forehead, thinking I was wiping away sweat, only to see that it was covered in blood. Gill's nails had gouged me. The old man was only too aware of that blood.

"Well if she won't stop the car I can't inspect it, can I? What's she want me to do? Run alongside with the hood opened?"

"No, of course not. It's just that . . . "

"So what's she frightened of?"

"Look, there's a man. Can you see him? Back there, behind us?"

The old man leaned forward reluctantly, now suddenly wary of taking his eyes off me, and adjusted his rearview mirror so that he could see the ragged figure approaching fast from behind.

"Yeah, what about him?"

"He . . ." My throat was full of dust then. My heart was beating too fast. "He's trying to kill us."

"To *kill* you?"

"That's right. That's why the car's damaged. And he just keeps coming and won't stop and . . ." I was going to lose it, I knew. I was babbling. The old man's eyes had clouded; the sparkle and the welcoming smile were gone.

In a flat and measured voice, he said: "I don't want any trouble, mister."

"Trouble? No, no. Look, we need your help. If you just . . . well, just stop the truck here. And stand in the road with me. Maybe when he sees that there're two of us, he'll back off. Maybe we can scare him away. Then you can give us a tow. We'll pay. Double your usual rate. How's that sound?"

"Look, I just wanted to help out. I could see your car was in trouble from way off. Steam coming out from under the hood. Oil all the way back down the road. But I don't want to get involved in no domestic dispute."

"*Domestic* dispute?"

"Anything that's happening between you and the lady in the car and the fella behind has nothing to do with me. So why don't you hop down and sort your differences out like civilized people?"

"Please, you've got it all wrong. It's not like that, at all. Look, have you got a portable telephone?"

"Get off my truck."

"Please, the man's *mad*! He's going to kill us. At least telephone for the police, tell them what's happening here . . ."

"I said, get *off*!"

The flat of the old man's calloused hand came down heavy where I was gripping the window-edge, breaking my grip. In the next moment, he lunged sideways and jabbed a skinny elbow into my chest. The pain was sharp, knocking the breath out of my lungs; the impact hurling me from the running-board and into the road. I lay there, engulfed in a cloud of choking dust, coughing my guts out and unable to see anything. All I could hear was the sound of the truck overtaking our car as it roared on ahead down the country road, leaving us far behind. When I tried to rise, pain stabbed in my hip where I had fallen. I staggered and flailed, yelling obscenities after the old man.

The dust cloud swirled and cleared.

The tow-truck was gone from sight.

Behind me, the scarecrow was alarmingly close; now perhaps only a hundred yards away and still coming with that measured tread. Despite my fears, he didn't seem to have put on that burst of speed. Relentless, he came on.

Gill hadn't stopped for me. The car had moved on ahead, itself about fifty yards further down the road. Perhaps she hadn't seen what had happened between the old man and myself, didn't realize my plight. So it was hardly fair of me to react the way that I did. But I reacted anyway. I screamed at her, just as I'd screamed at the departing old man. I screeched my rage and blundered after the car, the pain in my hip stabbing like fire. Even with my staggering gait, it didn't take long to catch up with the car, making the evil mockery of the scarecrow's relentless approach all the more horrifying. If he just put on that extra spurt of speed, he could catch up with us whenever he liked. I threw open the back door of the car and all but fell inside. I tried to yell my rage, but the dust and the exhaustion and the pain all took their toll on my throat and lungs. When I stopped hacking and spitting, I tried to keep my voice calm but it came out icy cold.

"You didn't stop, Gill. You didn't stop the car for me. You were going to leave me there."

Gill was a white-faced automaton behind the wheel. She neither looked at me nor acknowledged my presence. In her shock I had no way now of knowing whether she could even hear what I was saying. I wiped more blood from my forehead, and struggled to contain the crazy feeling that I knew was an over-reaction to outright fear.

There was someone up ahead on our side of the road, walking away from us. He was a young man, his body stooped as if he had been walking a long while; with some kind of holdall over his shoulder. He didn't seem to hear us at first; his gaze concentrated downwards, putting one foot in front of the other. I moved towards Gill but before I could say anything, she said:

"Don't!"

"But we should . . ."

"No, Paul. We're not stopping."

I had no energy. Fear and that fall from the tow-truck had robbed me of strength. But as I leaned back, I saw the young man ahead suddenly turn and look at us. Quickly, he dropped his holdall to the ground and fumbled for some-thing inside his jacket. We were close enough to see the hope in his eyes when he pulled out a battered cardboard sign and held it up for us to read: HEADING WEST.

I looked at the back of Gill's head. She never moved as the car drew level and began to pass the young man. The hope in his eyes began to fade as we trundled past. Did he think we were travelling at that speed just to taunt him? I looked back over my shoulder to see that the scarecrow was still closing the gap, still coming. The fact that I was looking back seemed to give the young man some encouragement. Grabbing his holdall, he sprinted after us. I wound down the side window as he drew level.

"Come on, man." His voice was thin and reedy. He jogged steadily at the side of the car as we moved. "Give me a lift. I've been walking for hours."

"That man . . . back there . . ."

The young man looked, but didn't see anything worth following up in con-versation.

"I'm heading for Slaly, but if you're going anywhere West that's good enough for me. How about it?"

"That man . . . he's mad. Do you hear me? He tried to kill us."

Now, it seemed that he was seeing all the evidence that there was something wrong about this situation. The quiet woman with the white face and the staring eyes. The broken windows and the sugar-frosted glass all over the seats. The dents and scratches on the car as it lurched and trembled along the road, engine rumbling. And me, lying in the back as if I'd been beaten up and thrown in there, blood all over my forehead.

"You and me. If we square up to him, we can frighten him off. I'll pay you. Anything you want. And then we'll drive you where you want to go."

"I don't think so," said the young man. He stopped and let us pass him by. I struggled to the window and leaned out to look back at him. He waved his hand in a "Not for me" gesture.

"Yeah?" I shouted. "Well, thanks for fucking nothing. But I'm not joking. That guy back there is a *psycho*. So before he catches up, I'd head off over those fields or something. Keep out of his way. When he gets to you, you're in big trouble."

The young man was looking away, hands on hips as if deciding on a new direction.

"I'm telling you, you stupid idiot! Get out of here before he catches up!"

I fell back into the car, needing a drink more than I've ever done in my life. Up in front, Gill might have been a shop mannequin, propped in the driving seat. She was utterly alien to me now, hardly human at all.

"You've killed him," I said at last. Perhaps my voice was too low to be heard. "You know that, don't you? The guy back there is as good as dead."

When I turned to look back again, I could see that the young man was still walking in our direction. The scarecrow was close behind him. But still in the middle of the road. Perhaps something in the tone of my voice had registered with him, because he kept looking over his shoulder as he moved and the scarecrow got closer and closer. I couldn't take my eyes away from the rear window. There was a horrifying sense of inevitability. When it seemed that the scarecrow was almost level with him, I saw the young man pause. He seemed to speak to the scarecrow. Then he stopped, just staring. Perhaps he had seen the scarecrow's face properly for the first time.

I gritted my teeth.

The young man shrank back on the grass verge.

I could see it all in my mind's eye. The sudden lunge of the scarecrow, wielding that scythe high above his head. The young man would shriek, hold up his hands to ward off the blow. But then the scarecrow would knock him on his back, grab him by the throat and bring the scythe down into his chest. The young man would writhe and thrash and twist as the scarecrow ripped that scythe down, gutting him. Then it would begin ripping his insides out while he was still alive, the man's arms and legs twitching feebly, and then he would lie still forever as the scarecrow scattered what it found into the surrounding fields.

Except that it wasn't happening like that at all.

The man was shrinking back on the verge, but the scarecrow was still walking.

And now the scarecrow had walked straight past the young man without so much as a sideways glance. He was coming on, after us, at the same relentless pace. Now, the young man was hurrying back in the opposite direction; stumbling and fumbling at first, as if he didn't want to take his eyes off this figure in case it suddenly changed its mind and came lunging back at him. The man began to run, then was heading full pelt back in the opposite direction.

The scarecrow was coming on.

It only wanted *us*.

"You bastard!" I yelled through the shattered windscreen. "You fucking, fucking *bastard*! What was the matter with *him*, then? What do you want from us? What the hell do you *want* us for?" I think I began to weep then. Maybe I just went over the edge and became insane. But I seemed to lose some time. And I only came out of it when I realized that I could still hear weeping, and realized that it wasn't mine. When my vision focused, it was on the back of Gill's head again. She was sobbing. I could see the rise and fall of her shoulders. Looking back through the rear window, I could see that the man had continued to gain on us. He was less than fifty yards behind, and the engine was making a different sound. I pulled myself forward, and it was as if the tow-truck driver was whispering in my ear at the same time that my gaze fell on the petrol gauge.

I could see you were in trouble. Oil all the way back down the road.

The gauge was at 'empty'. We'd been leaking petrol all the way back to the motorway. Soon we'd be empty and the car would roll to a stop.

Fear and rage again. Both erupting inside to overcome the inertia and engulfing me in an insane, animal outburst. I kicked open the door, snarling. My hip hurt like hell as I staggered into the middle of the road. I tried to find something else to yell back at the approaching figure. Something that could encompass all that rage and fear. But even though I raised my fists to the sky and shook like I was having a fit, I couldn't find any way of letting it out. I collapsed to my knees, shuddering and growling like an animal.

And then, crystal clear, something came to me.

I don't know how or where. It was as if the damned idea was planted by someone else, it felt so utterly *outside*. Maybe even in that moment of pure animal hate, a cold reasoning part of me was still able to reach inside and come up with a plan. Had I had time to think about it, I would have found dozens of reasons not to do what I did. But instead, I acted. I clambered to my feet again. The scarecrow was thirty yards away; close enough for me to see that idiot, grinning face and the black-hollowed eyes. I hobbled after the car, braced my hands on the metalwork as I felt my way along it to the driver's door. I knew what would happen if I spoke to Gill, knew what she would do if I tried to stop her.

So instead, I pulled open the door, lunged in and yanked both her hands off the steering wheel. She screamed. High-pitched and completely out of control. The violent act had broken her out of that rigid stance. She began to scream and twist and thrash like a wild animal as I dragged her bodily out of the car, hanging onto her wrists. When she hit the rough road, she tried to get purchase, tried to kick at me. She was yelling mindless obscenities when I threw her at the verge. She fell badly and cried out. Twisting around, she saw the scarecrow— and could no longer move. In that split-second as I dived into the car, already slewing towards the verge and a dead-stop, I didn't recognize her face. The eyes belonged to someone else. They were made of glass.

I jammed on the brakes, felt so weak that I was afraid I couldn't do what I was going to do. My hand trembled on the gearstick.

Yelling, I rammed the gear into reverse. It went in smooth. I revved up the engine and knew that if it coughed and died from lack of petrol I'd go quite mad.

Then I let up the clutch, and this time the car shot backwards. Maybe it was twenty, thirty miles an hour. Not so fast maybe, but three or four times faster than we'd been travelling on this Crawl. And it felt like the vehicle was moving like a fucking bullet. I was still yelling as I leaned back over the seat, twisting with the wheel to get my bearings right—and the scarecrow began to loom large in my sight-line, right smack center in the rear window. Dust and gravel spurted and hissed around me.

The scarecrow just came on.

Filling the ragged frame of that rear window.

I just kept yelling and yelling as the scarecrow vanished in the dust cloud the car was making. It gushed into the car, making me choke and gag.

And then there was a heavy *crunching* thud, jarring the frame of the car. It snapped me back and then sharp-forward in the seat. The engine coughed and died. The car slewed to a stop.

I had hit the bastard—and I had hit him hard.

The car was filled with dust. I couldn't see a thing. I threw the door open and leapt out, feeling that stab of pain in my hip but not giving one flying fart about it. I dodged and weaved in the cloud, crouching and peering to see where he had been thrown. I wanted to see blood in that dry dust. I wanted to see brains and shit. I wanted to see that he'd coughed up part of his intestine on impact and that he was lying there in utter agony. I wanted to see his legs crushed; his head split apart, his scythe shattered into hundreds of little bits.

The dust cloud settled.

I warily walked around the side of the car, looking for the first sign of a boot or an outstretched hand. I strained hard to listen in the silence for any kind of sound. I wanted to hear him moaning or weeping with pain.

But there was no sound.

Because there was no one lying behind the car.

I hobbled to the grass verge. The car was still in the center of the road, so there was a chance that it had thrown him clear into one of the fields at either side. But there was no one in the grass at the left side, and when I skipped across the road to the other field, there was no sign of a body there either. I knew I had hit that bastard with killing force. But at that speed, surely he couldn't have been thrown the two hundred feet or so into the stalks of wheat out there. It couldn't be possible, unless . . . unless . . .

Unless he wasn't very heavy.

Unless he hardly weighed anything at all.

Like, maybe, he weighed no more than your average scarecrow.

The thought was more than unnerving. I cursed myself aloud. He'd had real hands, hadn't he? I'd seen them up close. But then a little voice inside was asking me: *Are you sure you saw them properly? Wasn't he wearing gloves?*

On a sudden impulse, I ducked down and looked under the car.

There was nothing there.

When I straightened up, I could see that Gill was staggering down the road towards me. She looked drunk as she weaved her way towards the car. I leaned against the dented framework, holding my arms wide, imploring.

"I know I hit him," I said. "I *know* I did. I felt the car hit him. He must be dead, Gill. I didn't want to do it, but it was the only way. Wasn't it? I'm sorry for what I did to you, just then. I shouldn't have. But I had to at least try and . . ."

She was almost at the car now; face blank, rubbing her eyes as if she might just have woken up. I felt the temptation to retreat into that safe fantasy. To pretend that none of this had happened. Lost for words, I shook my head.

I was just about to take Gill into my arms when she screamed, right into my face.

I don't know whether the shock made me react instinctively. But suddenly, I was facing in the opposite direction, looking back to the rear of the car.

And the scarecrow was right there.

Standing on the same side of the car, right in front of me, about six feet away. Grinning his stitched and ragged grin. Straw flying around his head. That head was cocked to one side again, in that half-bemused expression that was at the same time so horribly malevolent. Something moved in one of the ragged eye sockets of his "mask", but I don't think it was the winking of an eye. I think it was something alive in there; something that was using the warm straw for a nest.

The scythe jerked up alongside my face.

I felt no pain. But I heard the *crack*! when the handle connected with my jaw.

In the next moment, I was pinned back against the car. Instinctively, I'd seized the scarecrow's wrist as it bent me backwards. My shoulders and head were on the roof, my feet kicking in space as I tried to keep that scythe out of my face. He was incredibly strong, and I tried to scream when I saw that scythe turn in and down towards my right eye. But no sound would come, and I couldn't move. Somewhere behind, I could hear Gill screaming. Then I saw her behind the scarecrow, tearing at its jacket and yanking handfuls of straw away.

I slid, the impetus yanking me from the thing's grip as I fell to the road. Stunned, dazed, I saw one of the car wheels looming large; then turned awkwardly on one elbow as the scarecrow stepped into vision again. The sun was behind him, making him into a gigantic silhouette as he lifted the scythe just the way I'd envisaged he'd do it for the hitchhiker. This wasn't real anymore. I couldn't react. I couldn't move. It wasn't happening. Somewhere, a long way away, Gill was screaming over and over again; as if someone was bearing her away across the fields.

Then the car horn rang, loud and shocking.

It snapped me out of that inertia, and everything was real again.

Somehow, the scarecrow's arm was stayed.

It just stood there, a black shape against the sun, the weapon raised high.

And then the horn rang again. This time, a gruff man's voice demanded: "You put that down, *now*!"

Someone had grabbed my arm and was tugging hard. I grabbed back, and allowed myself to be pulled out of the way and around to the rear of the car. Everything focused again, out of the sun's brilliance.

Gill had pulled me to my feet, and clung tight to me as we both leaned against the battered bodywork. Neither of us seemed able to breathe now.

A car had pulled up on the other side of the road. Only fifteen or twenty feet separating the vehicles. A man was climbing out, maybe in his forties. Thick, curly grey hair. Good looking. Checked shirt and short sleeves. Perhaps he was a farmer. He looked as if he could handle himself. His attention remained fixed on what stood by the side of our own car as he slammed the door with careful force.

"I don't know what's happening here. But I know you're going to drop that."

The scarecrow had its back to us now. Its head was lowered, the scythe still raised; as if I was still lying down there on the ground, about to be impaled.

"You alright, back there?" asked the farmer.

All we could do was nod.

"Drop the scythe, or whatever it is," continued the farmer slowly. "And everything will be okay. Okay?" He moved towards our car, one hand held out gentle and soothing, the other balled into a fist just out of sight behind his back. "And you take off the fright mask, alright? Then we'll calm down and sort everything out."

The scarecrow looked up at him as he approached.

The man halted.

"Take it . . ." he began.

The scarecrow turned around to face him.

". . . easy," finished the farmer. Suddenly, his expression didn't seem as confident as it had before. He strained forward, as if studying the "mask."

The scarecrow stepped towards him.

"Oh Christ Jesus," he said, and now he didn't sound at all like the commanding presence he'd been a moment before. He backed off to his own car, groping for the door handle without wanting to turn his back on what stood before him. He looked wildly at us. "Look, mister," the farmer said to me. "If we both rush him. Maybe we can take him. Come on, that's all it needs . . ."

I moved forward, but Gill held me tight and pinned me back against the car.

The scarecrow took another step towards the farmer.

"Come *on!*" implored the farmer, fumbling with the handle.

I tried to say something. But what would happen if I opened my mouth, and the scarecrow should turn away from him and look back at *me* again?

"Please," said the man. "Help . . . help . . . me . . ."

The scarecrow held out the scythe to the farmer, a hideous invitation.

I wasn't going to speak, but Gill put a hand over my mouth anyway.

The man yelped and dodged aside as the scarecrow lunged forward, sweeping the scythe in a wide circle. The tip shrieked across the bodywork of the car, where the farmer had been standing a moment before. Flakes of paint glittered in the air. The man edged to the rear of his car as the scarecrow jammed the scythe down hard onto the roof of the vehicle. With a slow and horrible malice, the scarecrow walked towards him. As it moved, it dragged the screeching scythe over the roof with it.

"Please help me!" shouted the man. "Please!"

The scarecrow walked steadily towards him.

We saw the man run around the back of his car.

We saw him look up and down the road, trying to decide which direction. He held both arms wide to us in a further appeal.

"For God's sake, please help!"

We clutched each other, trembling.

And then the man ran off into the nearest field of wheat. He was soon swallowed by the high stalks. We watched them wave and thrash as he ran.

The scarecrow followed at its steady pace.

It descended into the high stalks, but didn't pause. It did not, thank God, turn to look back at us. It just kept on walking, straight into where the farmer had vanished, cutting a swathe ahead with its scythe. Soon, it too was swallowed up in the wheat. We watched the grass weave and sway where it followed.

Soon, the wheat was still.

There were no more sounds.

After a while, we took his car. The keys were in the dash. I drove us back to the nearest town and we rang for the police. We told the voice on the other end that we'd been attacked, and that our attacker had subsequently gone after the man who had ultimately been our rescuer. We were both given hospital treatment, endured the rigorous police investigations and gave an identical description of the man who had pursued us in his Hallowe'en costume. The police did not like the story. It didn't have, as one of the plain-clothes men had it, the "ring of truth." The fella in the tow-truck was never traced, neither was the hitchhiker. They could have given the same description, if nothing else.

But the man who stopped to help us—Walter Scharf, a local farmer, well liked—was never seen again. And he's still missing, to this day. Despite every avenue of enquiry, the police still couldn't link us to anything. That's what they began to think at the end, you see? That Scharf was somehow the attacker (maybe some sort of love-triangle gone wrong), that he was responsible for the damage to the car and/or us. And that we had killed him, and hidden him. I got a lot of hate mail from his wife. But they couldn't link us to anything.

So we got out of it alive, Gill and I.

But there was something neither of us told the police.

Something that neither of us discussed afterwards.

We never talked about the fact that when the first person to stop and volunteer to help, asked us . . . *begged* us . . . to help him: we kept quiet. We said nothing, and did nothing. And because of it, the thing went after him instead of us.

And we were *glad*.

But the darkness of that gladness brought something else into our lives.

Shame. Deep and utter shame. So deep, so profound and so soul-rotting that we couldn't live with ourselves anymore. Gill and I split up. We couldn't talk about it. We live in different cities, and neither of us drives a car anymore.

I know that she'll be having the same nights as me.

The days are bad, but the nights are always worse.

The front door is always the focus of attention, no matter what I'm doing. I'll try to keep myself occupied, try to read, try to listen to music. But all of these things make it much worse. You see, if I really *do* become preoccupied in what I'm doing, then I might not hear it if . . .

If he . . . it . . . comes.

And in the nights, I'll lie awake and listen.

The sound of a car passing on the sidestreet is probably the worst.

I'll hear it coming in my sleep. It wakes me instantly, and I'm never sure whether I've screamed or not, but I lie there praying first that the car will pass quickly and that the engine won't cough and falter. Then, in the first seconds after it's moved on I'll pray again that I won't hear those familiar, staggering footsteps on the gravel coming up the path; that I won't hear that hellish hammering on the front door. I listen for the sounds of that hideous, hoarse breathing.

Sometimes, I'll wonder if I can hear Walter Scharf distantly screaming as he runs through the dark fields of our dreams, the scarecrow close behind. Perhaps those screams aren't his, they're the screams of the next person who crossed its path. They'll fade and die . . . and the quiet of those dreams is sometimes more horrible than the noise.

And to this day, there are two things that terrify me even more than the sounds of a car, or someone walking up the drive, or the noise of that letterbox before I nailed it down.

The first is the sight and the sound of children playing "tag."

The second is a noise that keeps me out of the countryside, away from fields and wooded areas. A simple, everyday sound.

It's the sound of crows, cawing and squawking.

Perhaps frightened from their roosts by something down below and unseen, thrashing through the long grass.

Now, this crow stays home.

And waits.

And listens.

And crawls from one room to the next, making as little noise as possible.

The days are bad, but the nights are always worse . . .

Katherine Vaz

The Remains of Princess Kaiulani's Garden

Katherine Vaz won the Drue Heinz Literature Prize in 1997, and one look at Fado & Other Stories will show you why. This Portuguese-American writer draws upon her rich cultural heritage in a stunning collection of short fiction ranging from realist to magical realist works, moving skillfully between the Old World and the New. If you love fine storytelling and prose, go find this book immediately.

Vaz is the author of the novels Saudade and Mariana (published in six languages). Her short stories have appeared in numerous literary magazines, including TriQuarterly, Nimrod and The American Voice. "The Remains of Princess Kaiulani's Garden," a quietly magical tale set in Hawaii, is reprinted from Fado and Other Stories. About this story, the author notes: "Though it is true that the Portuguese brought the braguinha to Hawaii and it became known as the ukulele, and the members of the Hawaiian royal family who are mentioned did exist and the related historical events and legends occurred, the Portuguese characters are fictional, as is the story itself."

Katherine Vaz lives in Davis, California, where she is an associate professor of English at the University of California.

—T. W.

M y stomach is singing!" said King Kalakaua.

The children lined up along the wooden wall sensed their stomachs singing also—they always did, when Frank Vasconcellos played his musical instruments, especially his *braguinha*—but they were afraid to move. For one thing, their mothers had warned them that not so long ago, if the shadow of a commoner fell across the path of a king, the offender would be killed. Times were changing in Hawaii, but it was still a good idea not to make Kalakaua wrathful. Elena, Frank Vasconcellos's daughter, tried to catch the eye of her mother, Amelia, but she was sitting up very straight. A royal retinue was in their house, visitors were in attendance, and she could not allow herself to uncoil toward the music. It was a shame. Her mother wanted so absolutely to do the right things that would allow her to belong to Hawaii before she died, without stopping to think that such a rigidness ensured that she never would. Pinned to Amelia's dress was a camellia as white as her hair, and it did not flutter to the music; she would not allow it.

Elena did not think the king looked prone to wrath. He was wearing gold medals on a white suit that people said he had bought in London on a triumphal sweep across the world. They said that the cloth had been woven by naked women who had shaved their heads and bodies so as not to get a single stray hair on the material. Kalakaua looked like a messenger from the sun. Everyone was both afraid to look away from the king and afraid to look directly at him. Just the way they behaved toward the sun out in the sugarcane fields. Only her father, filling the room with the high sweet sounds that made it possible to think of motion in this heat, was in his work pants, the denims that someone far away in San Francisco had invented for the gold miners. Friends thought he was arrogant to wear something associated with gold. Even Elena's mother thought so.

The king had heard about the marvelous new instrument that the Portuguese had brought to his country and wanted to hear it for himself. He was tired of the instruments made of gourds and pebbles. Frank had completed his sugar contract the previous year and decided he wanted to make more than ten dollars a month, and was now one of Oahu's best *braguinha* makers and players. He also made the rajão, the fiddle that the workers in the taro patches liked. After arrangements were made for a concert, Kalakaua and his attendants had arrived in a lacquered carriage at the house of Frank, Amelia, and Elena Vasconcellos on the slopes of the Punchbowl.

A sharp point stabbed the back of her neck. She had ironed her dress so well that the loose threads were sticking her. Her high-buttoned shoes were pinching, and she was sorry that she had brought them all the way from the Azores. She had had three months on the *Priscilla* to fling them overboard. They were useless in Hawaii. Besides, it took a long time to button them, because her hands were too large for the rest of her. They were the result, everyone said, of having parents who married old. It was as if her mother and father had had many large dreams at their wedding but not enough strength to do more than give them to a single part of their offspring. Elena's hands hung down like huge pincers attached to a tiny lobster. In a strange way, she missed the old days when she had to fight all the time, her hands in enormous hard fists, to stop her friends from laughing at her. Now they ignored her because she and her parents were not coming back to sugar.

... Giroflé, giroflá,
Giroflé, giroflá!
Flé, flé, flé!
Flá, flá, flá! ...

Frank was singing nonsense as his fingers plucked the *braguinha*. The king loved the music with its meaningless words. He leapt to his feet and danced around the room, a strange cross between a waltz and something like a hula. Elena caught her mother looking aside, embarrassed. It was rumored that the king had had over one hundred hulas composed at his birth in honor of his penis. Elena had overheard some old women gossiping about it one day, and they scolded her for listening in. But how was having ears her fault?

Her father's music filled Elena with such wonderful sorrow.

"Flay, flay, flay!" shouted Kalakaua.

Frank, too, was jumping around the room, with the instrument cradled in his arms.

The listeners tensed. Kalakaua kept coming close to crashing into the buffet table lit with kukui nut-oil lamps, and covered with an offering of sweets, doves made of pulled sugar, tarts, pumpkin jellies, banana pies, the orange-flavored strips of fried dough called coscarões, candied papaya, and flans. Elena thought her mother was going to collapse. She had gotten up at midnight to begin the final round of baking, saying that since the hour hurt, the food would taste better. Elena dug her fingernails into her palms, the size of grapefruits, to stop from giggling. She looked over at her best friend, Madelena, whom she had met on the *Priscilla* when it was dawning on them that they were leaving the Azores forever. Madelena smiled back. Elena hoped this meant they would visit later. Sometimes she was not sure about Madelena. Ever since her father had decided that the Portuguese should follow the example of the Asians who were pushing their children out of the fields toward the trade life in Honolulu, Madelena had not been coming around as much. No one had, until the arrival of the king today.

"*Auwe!* Bloody hell!" he shouted. He bumped into the table, and two of the attendants carrying the huge feather standards, the *kahilis*, rushed over to grab the dishes falling off the edge. They caught them without dipping the *kahilis*. Elena was the only one to applaud their skill. Kalakaua turned to grin at her. Frank kept playing. She felt everyone staring, and after holding her head up and smiling a moment, then seeing that Madelena was frowning and so was Amelia, she looked at the floor, and at her uncomfortable shoes, and at her hands that were too awkward to fold neatly in her lap.

Her stomach would not sing again until later, when everyone was huddling near one end of the buffet table, holding a treat on a crisply ironed serviette but feeling too nervous to eat anything, and she abandoned her friends to walk over to Kalakaua. His presence was so immense that she was not afraid of him; her hands had taught her how to be fearless about dimensions in flesh. He was descended from the Polynesian gods and wanted to be the emperor of what the natives were beginning to call Oceania. He was eating a coconut tart. A strand was trapped in his black beard. Her stomach began a mild melody that picked up in tempo as the king took the tissue paper from beneath the tart, its edges cut in a fringe by Amelia at dawn that morning, and held it out toward the attendant.

"You look like my little niece, Kaiulani," said Kalakaua.

The attendant, reading the king's mind, pinned the square of fringed tissue paper onto Elena's dress, so that it looked like a funny paper medal.

I'm not Portuguese, she thought, not any more. I'm Hawaiian.

She reached over to the buffet table and pulled a square out from under another one of the tarts. It looked very small in the center of her palm. An attendant took it from her and hesitated. Kalakaua nodded, and the attendant pinned it onto him, next to his gold medals. Elena and the king laughed, and her stomach sang, "Enjoy your moment with the king! You have lost Madelena!"

It was true. Not long after the party, Kalakaua ordered three dozen *braguinhas* from Frank, asking him to bring them to the Iolani Palace.

When he returned home, he threw his moldy cap in the air. "I'm rich! I'm rich!" he shouted.

Amelia looked up from her darning. "What does that make me?"

"The wife of a rich man!" Frank shouted. "What you've always wanted! You may applaud!"

Elena disliked how her mother bit threads off with her teeth. Everything, it seemed, connected to her claimed that it was all well and good for her husband to be able to race about, forgetting to act his age; she had been pregnant at age forty-three, when her husband had been forty-nine, and now she was physically a mess, it was too much to stand and walk the ten paces to get the scissors when she did the mending. Better to use her teeth, before she no longer owned them.

Elena sometimes cringed in her clothes, from imagining her mother's spittle dried into the cloth. That was why she ironed everything so firmly.

"They loved me!" said her father, taking gold coins out of his pocket.

Elena put two of the coins over her eyes, to feel how round and cold they were, until her mother snatched them off and said that was a bad omen; that was how the dead had their eyes closed.

Often after that the king requested that Frank come play at royal parties, and because he was small and vigorous, the Hawaiians called him the Jumping Flea, or *ukulele*. It then turned into the name of the *braguinha*.

"Well, if it isn't the princess!" Madelena yelled one morning at Elena.

The tissue medal was starting to melt off Elena's dress. She had hoped to wear it every day for the rest of her life.

"Princess! Princess!" shouted some of the old women, when they passed her on the slopes of the Punchbowl that led to the road into town.

"Princess? Not with those hands! She should be a handmaiden!"

Elena could not fight old women. Like her mother, they were too mysterious. A certain class of them—not many, but enough to constitute a minor phenomenon—possessed a knowledge that made them quite starched: They were the ones who had married when young and suddenly, without explanation, returned to their childhood homes during the week after their wedding, to live alone past the deaths of their parents and into old age. It was understood that this was not to be commented upon. Two of these women lived here on the hillsides, and though Elena had left the Azores when she was nine, she remembered a few of them there, too. What a shame, to have elegant weddings, and then to pretend that the whole event had never occurred. Elena truly did not understand people. Why couldn't anyone say what had happened to these women? Why couldn't they be friendly to a king? What good did it do to be lunas, standing in the field ordering other people around and ending up being hated as much as if they had quit the fields entirely?

"Princess!"

"No! The handmaiden!"

"She looks like little Kaiulani, the little niece!"

The taunts, and the boys saying endless crude things, made Elena's hands swell up, until they were half again as big.

When Frank had first started making *braguinhas*, Elena and Amelia did the cooking and running of errands, to give him the time he needed. But now, with people from the court and elsewhere wanting ukuleles, new work needed to be done. Elena liked the idea of her family being ukulele people. She would be content never again to go out under the sun where any other human beings were.

She discovered, to her shock, that her hands were incapable of plucking the strings. She had no talent for it. When she begged her father to make her an apprentice, she found that she had no skill with building ukuleles either. He and her mother said it was not something for a girl to bother about, anyway. But it did bother her. She lacked the thing inside, whatever it was, that gave life to music, and she could not teach herself how to fit the frets and strings together. What was she to do with herself? Boys only noticed her to ridicule her hands. She had a long nose and small eyes. She was too short and had no breasts to speak of, even though she was fifteen. The theory that her father's earning some money might make her more attractive did not appear to be working; those hideous hands stayed in the way. And Frank was spending his new income on Honolulu's society parties as fast as he made it.

On one of the rare nights he was home for dinner, he asked Elena, "What're you good at?" They were eating poi and grilled pork.

"She doesn't need to be good at anything," said Amelia.

"Let me hear that from her," said Frank, drinking his champagne. Sometimes he let Elena pour a tablespoon into her glass of water. Amelia was starting to listen to the missionaries and thought champagne was the worst kind of devilry, being light-colored and pretty. She was mad that money was being spent on things that did not last. Elena knew that her father let her drink his champagne because he loved her, but he was too old to do more than look forward to an unrigorous ending to his own life. That included situating these women in his house somewhere amenable to them, leaving him to float away on the strains of the string music that had completed his reasons for being.

"Excuse me, your highness," said Amelia.

Frank laughed. His refusal to jump into a fight with her was going to exasperate his wife into an early grave.

"I don't know," said Elena. The poi was what the Hawaiians called two-finger, because its thickness required that many fingers to scoop it up. She watched it solidifying.

"Think," he said. "Everyone I talk to about marrying you off says you have crazy ideas."

"It's you. You're the one with the crazy ideas,' said Amelia, not looking at her daughter. "Elena is neat and clean. Boys nowadays have these absurd glamorous ideas. She does the best with what she has."

"They're those hands she's got on her."

"Shh."

It seemed to Elena that her mother was quieting him more from her own wretchedness about having a daughter with bloated hands, and not because Elena might be upset.

"Everyone is good at something. Can she bake? What's she good at?" said Frank.

Elena was accustomed to them speaking as if she were invisible, and did not blush. They were only saying what everyone knew. "Why are you asking me this? I can dance," she said.

They turned to look at her.

"No daughter of mine is going to learn the dances they do around here. They won't let you, anyhow," said Frank.

"Amen," said Amelia.

"Think again," said Frank.

"Well," said Elena, sensing that she had to answer quickly, but that her reply would haunt her. It was a shame that some gift out of the ukulele would not fit into her grasp. "Well, I like to iron. Yes. I'm good at ironing."

"Ironing is a very fine thing for a girl to know," said Amelia, clearing the plates as a signal that Frank should not open another bottle.

Even Amelia agreed that opening a laundry on Beef Street was a fair venture. It was not far from the dry goods store owned by Archibald Cleghorn, the father of Princess Kaiulani, who was in line for the throne. It was also a means of channeling some of the ukulele money before Frank spent it. Elena forgot about her vow never to yearn for places where there were other people. She often lingered on the sidewalk, hoping to glimpse Cleghorn, who had built the Ainahau estate with three lily ponds for his daughter, the future queen. Eight kinds of mango trees, and teak, cinnamon, and soap trees were on the grounds, where peacocks wandered and shook their heads with their antherlike crowns when twelve-year-old Kaiulani called to them. Fourteen varieties of hibiscus and a huge banyan grew on Ainahau. But Mr. Cleghorn did not show up at his dry goods place, any more than Elena's father came by the laundry. It was what he had built for his wife and daughter, and he was elsewhere with his ukulele.

Not far off from the laundry was the ocean, the color of limes. Elena had no time to go there, and was content to come off the hillside in the morning, alongside her mother, and head into the flat part of town, where the carriages went by with a clattering that set off the other music stored tightly in her head. Her mother never said much to her. Her mother would be sixty in two years, and she walked and talked slowly, as if expecting Elena to use her hands to lift off the burden weighing on her shoulders. When Elena did try to talk to her, it was plain that nothing delighted Amelia. To be in Hawaii, to have traveled to a new life, to have work in town, and yet to be so sour!

Elena was determined to be everything her mother was not. Washing clothing invigorated Elena; she got to hide her hands in the tanks of water when she chatted with customers. She had no trouble lifting the heavy baskets, and hardly needed the scrub brushes of torn coconut leaves that hung near the tanks. Her fingers knew how to manipulate the material. She tried to move the clothes through the water in a rhythm that suggested the sounds of a stream, in case Archibald Cleghorn, or his wife Likelike, or his daughter Kaiulani might be strolling past. But despite being the daughter of Ukulele, she could not force the water into a rhythm.

"Stop splashing," her mother would say.

"I'm not."

"Have you finished the order for the Andersons?"

"I just have to tie up the package, Mama."

"Then do it. You don't have time to splash." She would open the spigots on the wall that directed steam onto white sheets.

Elena would move her hands through the water a beat more. "Is Daddy having dinner with us tonight?"

"How should I know? When you finish with the package, here's a dress to iron." Her mother would throw something at her.

One thing Elena adored, utterly, was ironing, which she did very seriously, using the tip of the iron to trace every embroidered edge or seam, following the curve of every stitched border. The size of her hands made it easy to hold the iron upright, a metal ballerina on point. Not even her mother ironed as thoughtfully. Elena went so far as to iron the internal patterns in lace and the monograms on handkerchiefs, almost thread by thread, and she tended to the inner seams of jackets, if they could be reached by lifting the lining. She could not say what was so compelling about ironing. It was a metallic strength that made something clean and new. It was soothing, how easily power or hidden beauty could be stamped somewhere, into cloth, into a person.

That was the reason she loved the story her father once told her about Likelike, Kaiulani's mother, who hid flowers inside her piled-up hair so that everyone would think the scent was issuing directly from her. Elena tried to arrange a gardenia in her own hair in the Likelike style, but her knuckles kept knocking into each other. She came out of the storeroom, where she had been attempting to fix her hair according to her reflection made by a sheet of metal, and asked her mother for help.

"You want me to what?" her mother said, suds from the brown soap coating her arms. She pushed up her glasses and left suds on her cheek.

Elena squirmed. "You heard me."

"We have sixteen orders to finish, and you want me to play with your hair?"

"The orders will still be here. In the time we're taking to talk about it, we could have finished, Mama. I have the gardenia. We can tear it in half, and you can have part of it."

Her mother leaned over the wash tank and roared with laughter. "Where do you get your ideas? A gardenia in your hair! Ooo, you *are* a princess."

"I guess I get my good ideas from Daddy. I sure don't get them from you."

Elena did not back away as her mother came over and slapped her. The stinging on her face remained as she picked up a washboard and slopped a man's shirt over it, moving the shirt hard, as if trying to grate it. She did not glance up at her mother, who was moving on to the next task. The floor where her mother stood was spotless. What a shabby way to live! With little jobs lined up like shells that a person had to shatter with gunfire, one by one! Elena closed her eyes. Her skin throbbed. Her hands were pale from being so much in water, but they were not shrinking. They were puffing up, like dead creatures.

She heard a ukulele playing out on Beef Street.

Come in here, she ordered the sounds. Come in here, and wrap yourself around my hands. My fat dead hands. I'm Ukulele's daughter. I deserve some of what that instrument can do and some of its good fortune.

She waited, scrubbing the shirt.

"Help me pour this out, Elena," said her mother, holding up a pail of dirty water, and another task interceded.

But the next day, she recognized the shirt she had been scrubbing. A man came into the laundry wearing it and said, "Did you wash and iron this?"

Elena nodded.

"Thank you! Thank you! You know, I've had a chest cold for a week, and the moment I put this shirt on, I was cured!" he said.

Amelia looked up from her ironing board. "That's nice," she said curtly.

"Yes, it is!" he said. He grasped Elena's hands, and though she tried to pull them away, he would not let go. He did not seem to notice how huge they were.

"Thank you," she said, as the man backed out of the laundry, so that he could gaze at her the entire time he retreated.

"Well, what was that about?" asked her mother.

"I'm not sure," said Elena, but within a week, the people in Honolulu, and out on the sugar and pineapple fields, and encircling the Punchbowl's slopes, were comparing stories about the Vasconcellos Laundry. One old lady put on a skirt ironed by Elena, and could do cartwheels. She did them down the center of Emma Street. A man claimed that when he unwrapped his shirts and inhaled their fragrance, his sinuses cleared and were lined with what he swore was a scent of gardenias. When people wiped their foreheads with a Vasconcellos-ironed handkerchief, their headaches left them. A priest who had sent in his collars to be starched preached the best sermon of his life. People heading for the beaches and sharing their talk-stories would suddenly burst into song and execute some dance steps, which startled them, until they remembered that they were carrying towels that had been sent to the Vasconcellos Laundry.

Throughout the air, excitement was stretched like a string.

Elena kept her hands in the water, and neither she nor her mother knew that the one incident with the shirt had grown into a commotion until the morning that a servant from Ainahau came in and said that her mistress, Kaiulani, had heard about the laundress who made the cloth she touched more lively, the cloth that was causing all this singing and dancing in Honolulu, and she wanted to try it. The servant explained that Kaiulani was a sickly young girl, and any service rendered on her behalf would be appreciated. She spent much of her time out in her garden, hoping the air and her flowers would give her strength, but she needed some extra help.

The servant looked first at Elena and then at Amelia, and said, "Which of you has the touch?"

"What insanity—" Amelia began, but paused. The woman did seem to be from the royal family. An impressive carriage waited on Beef Street.

Elena paused, and glanced at her mother.

"It's my mother," said Elena. Giving her mother the credit was unrehearsed, and as startling to her as it was to Amelia. Elena was gratified to see that in some far recess of her heart, when called upon, she wanted her mother to shine. A momentary pleasure crossed Amelia's face.

"Yes," she said.

The servant handed over some cotton dresses with elaborate trims, and a velvet one with bows.

"They'll be ready tomorrow," said Amelia.

The servant said she looked forward to Kaiulani's dancing in her garden.

Amelia, not speaking to Elena, washed the dresses with the fine white powdered soap that they saved for undergarments. Elena could feel how carefully her mother was going over every button shank, every eyelet. She used a horsehair brush against the grain of the velvet. Elena was waiting to be called over, for her mother at least to say thank you or let her touch the princess's clothing. Only the sound of Amelia's anxious motions filled the laundry. Elena comforted herself. She was the one with ukulele powers inside her hands, a containment of the titanic sweeping event enacted by her father when he brought a new kind of music to a new country—it was under her fingers, within her, by surprise.

When she offered to iron Kaiulani's dresses and her mother declined, Elena was annoyed. Did her mother expect ukulele strains to get into the clothes without Elena's hands on them?

The servant pulled up in the carriage the next day, and Amelia gave her the dresses in packages tied up with white ribbons. Elena stayed in the back room, putting cream on her hands to soften them.

After she and her mother began their walk home that evening, they passed several young women forming a human pyramid, teasing one another as they tumbled over, and an old Hawaiian was doing a can-can number. He might have gone to the Barbary Coast and come scurrying home. The birds-of-paradise along the roadway pointed their beaks skyward, laughing.

"Mama," said Elena. "What's going in Hawaii?"

Her mother looked at her, then away. Elena knew why. It was too much to think that lone acts of ironing, as innocent as playing a ukulele, could bring a giddiness to strangers.

But once she had allowed her ukulele powers to go into the world at large, that world began to report back to her what it was doing and seeing. She heard that the Portuguese were not alone in grumbling about Kalakaua being in the pocket of Claus Spreckels, the German sugar man, who was providing the king with huge personal loans and convincing him to arrange for more low-paid Japanese workers.

There was a rumor about the whites, some of them *haoles* and some the native-born sons of the missionaries, pressuring the king into redrafting the constitution, so that only property owners could vote. That would prevent many native Hawaiians from having a say in the government. The whites wanted America to annex the islands.

Her father came home at hours when neither she nor her mother were conscious, to sleep on the couch. Right under their noses, right under their eyes, he was turning into a memory.

Kaiulani's servant returned to the laundry one morning, and both Elena and her mother looked up eagerly. The royal account was going to be theirs!

"I am to deliver a message," said the servant.

Elena turned off her iron, and Amelia dried her hands on her apron. "Yes!" said Amelia. "I know the princess has many dresses, but we're never too overworked to—"

"I am to say," said the servant, "that Princess Kaiulani is having nervous fits. She is so anxious that she went into her garden and uprooted some of the prettiest hibiscus plants, rare ones, before her father could stop her. I don't know why you would bring gladness to everyone else, and destruction to her."

"I don't think—" began Amelia.

"I've heard that her governess is leaving her to get married," interrupted Elena. "That would explain the trouble."

"No matter what is going on in the life of the princess," said the servant, "your laundry was supposed to aid her. It did not. It has had the opposite effect. I fear the happiness in the streets must be short-lived. Likelike, the mother of the princess, is recommending that no one visit your store. I'm sorry." She lowered her voice. "I truly am sorry. I never believed the stories I was hearing. They seemed out of some fantasy."

"Which is what my daughter lives in," said Amelia, her hands shaking. "Just like her father. She's the one who should have done the work, and she didn't."

The servant and her mother were looking at Elena, who stared at her mother in helpless fury.

"Weren't you the one with the touch?" asked the servant.

"My daughter said that because she gets lazy about doing her work. Look at the pile of things behind her."

The servant peered at Elena. "You didn't want to help the princess?" she asked.

"You said you didn't believe what you were hearing," said Elena, her voice controlled.

"I'm here to deliver a message. I've done that. Now, if you'll excuse me." The servant headed back to the waiting carriage, but she turned at the door and said, "I do wish you well, myself. I wanted it to be true."

"Mother," said Elena, and was speechless. Her mother had returned to her ironing. For fear of bursting out screeching, Elena hid in the storeroom, and stared at the piles of unwashed clothes with loathing. There did not seem to be much of a point in cleaning them, not if business was going to fall off and die. She did not know why it had not occurred to her that her mother was jealous. The ukulele had given Frank a place at court, and it had bestowed wonder upon Elena, but it had granted nothing to Amelia. Nothing except grief that her husband was never around—or was that its gift to her? Nothing more than she deserved!

And yet, Elena remembered being a child and her mother teaching her how to make strudel: How to use the backs of one's hands to stretch the dough that they draped over the table. This was to teach Elena patience. Whenever she tore the dough, her mother would tell her to slow down—and she did, her hands like large turtles under the thin pale yellow sheets.

Hesitating to curse her own mother, no matter what she had done, Elena prayed silently that Likelike and Kaiulani should have music enter their hearts and beat so fast that their bodies exploded. How dare they complain about their laundry! How dare they insist upon magic, and condemn her for not providing it! Once made, her prayer could not be taken back. She prayed it again to prevent herself from directing anything against her mother.

During the failing days of the laundry, Frank brought his daughter to a party at the garden of Ainahau. He wore a linen suit, and was so formal with her that she did not recognize him.

"How is your mother, Elena?" he asked as they stood in a corner of the lawn, watching the people dressed in silks and the women in feather headdresses. There were many white men with white beards, like Archibald Cleghorn.

She was wearing the boots that pinched more than ever, now that she was doing the last of her growing. She wanted her father to introduce her to his new friends and not keep her off to the side. "You could find out for yourself, Daddy."

"I come home."

"When we're asleep."

He picked up his ukulele and tested the strings. Elena saw King Kalakaua and ran toward him. He might lift the ban on bringing clothes to the Vasconcellos Laundry! After all, he was the one in charge, not Likelike. When she got close enough to him to speak, though, she stared at him in dismay. He was drunk and very old, with gray in his beard.

"Your Highness?" she said, hating how timid she sounded. "Remember me? Ukulele's daughter?"

He was in red and gold, the royal colors, and was drinking from a tumbler. He splashed a little on her as he said, "Who? Whose daughter?" He stared over her head at the groups of men scattered throughout the garden. The breeze was light, but carrying muffled sounds.

Elena looked from him to her father, who was strolling through the gardens, playing his ukulele. But the music had become common enough to linger in the background and remain there, and no one was turning to applaud. Her father had made himself a jester, a minstrel; but better that than a luna in a cane field, better to be in a place where the trees and flowers had been brought in for their calming influence on a daughter. Before she ran out, Elena saw Kaiulani wearing a European-style dress with a sailor's collar and thick black stockings. Her black hair curled down to her shoulders, and she had on a white ginger lei, the kind worn by brides. She stood with some friends, but like the king, her Papa Moi, she seemed to be barely listening to them. She had a very old spirit.

Kaiulani spotted Elena and waved. Elena, thunderstruck, waved back. *Hello, my friend, we're these children with old spirits and long histories and new music springing around us, and no idea of what to do with any of it.*

I take back the curse I put on her, I take it back, I take it back, thought Elena as she ran from the party, not telling her father good-bye. If only she could have a second chance to iron Kaiulani's dress. She would have the ukulele powers make Kaiulani do handsprings.

Surely her prayer against the princess and Likelike, since it had been silent and haphazard, would not count.

Likelike died first. Not many servants knocked out their teeth in mourning, since Likelike had been so ill-tempered with many of them. The rumor arrived, while Elena and her mother sat in the laundry waiting for the occasional person to drift in, that the king had prayed her to death. Kalakaua himself, using his powers to kill someone in his own family! His own sister! The white people were not going to help him stay on the throne, and the sugar magnates were angling to control the constitution, and the king, so the story went, had to turn to the gods. They were demanding a sacrifice from the royal family, and he chose to doom his sister.

Likelike went sad but resigned to her bed, and caught a fever. Before dying, she blurted at Kaiulani that she would never be queen.

Elena fell sick herself. The king had not been acting alone with his bad prayers. No one knew that but her. She had cursed Likelike, and Kaiulani as well! That in one angry moment something could glide across her thoughts and assist in pulling down a family was awful beyond anything she had done.

I take it back, she prayed, I take it back. Every morning for two years when she awoke, she called back the powers of what she had wished.

When Kaiulani was sent off to school in England, Elena thought of warm things, so that the princess would not be chilled. She pictured Kaiulani in wool coats and mufflers, and the fervor of these prayers made Elena's body grow and her hands shrink to meet it. They were normal. As uneventfully as that. Now that they were in proportion to the rest of her, now that people seldom brought in anything for her or her mother to iron, her hands were so ordinary as to be repellent to her.

One night when she and Amelia were alone at home, her mother said, while washing the dishes and handing them to Elena to dry, "How nice to see your problem is gone, darling."

"Gone?" said Elena. Her mother had never called her darling before. How distasteful, to be loved because she was no longer a freak. "I'll tell you what's gone, Mama," she said, continuing to dry her mother's dinner plate, "and that's Daddy. Don't you care?"

Her mother did not pause in scrubbing another plate. "No, I don't," she said. "If I care, he wins."

"He wins what?"

"I don't expect you to understand."

"I might surprise you. Maybe I'll surprise you the way I did our old customers."

"Don't start with that nonsense." She slammed a plate hard onto Elena's hand.

"Ouch. I don't know why you have to be so mean, Mama."

"You don't have to worry about us getting divorced. I'll never give him a divorce! Never! You understand me?" She was facing her daughter, and shouting. "All I wanted was not to be one of those old spinsters! Those awful women! You want to be one of them? Do you?" She shattered a dish on the floor, and Elena understood that her mother was doing it to cover the crashing sound of the thought in her head: Elena was nothing but the thing had and done, so that her mother would not be one of those pathetic ladies who married, and discovered what love involved, and returned home to die. Elena was her mother's proof that she was not a lonely woman, that she had signed herself out of that grim club.

The king went for his first sleigh ride at the insistence of the mayor of Omaha, and caught a cold that lasted for the duration of his train trip across America.

Late into the rule of Kalakaua, Elena and her mother opened a new laundry and did moderately well. No wonderful stories, however, were reported about what they washed and ironed. Frank came by occasionally to give them money for their rent, and a divorce was never mentioned.

The king died in 1891, at the Palace Hotel in San Francisco, forced out by whites who made him sign the Bayonet Constitution, which gave them the upper hand in the rules of state.

In 1897, Kaiulani took to her bed with a headache in Paris, electing not to attend a bazaar. That afternoon, a booth at the bazaar caught fire, a ceiling collapsed, and 117 people died. Her chronic illness had spared her.

She was coming home to Hawaii. Though a provisional government led by missionaries' children and sugar plantation owners had kicked out the royal family, Kaiulani would return to her garden and either rule from there or wait until this latest uproar dissipated. With her aunt, Queen Liliuokalani, deposed and out of the way, Kaiulani was first in line for the throne.

Elena thought this over with profound relief while leaning on the counter of the laundry and pictured Kaiulani lying wan in bed but smiling at the manner fate had chosen to spare her. Her hair would blow in the breeze as she rolled through the streets of Honolulu in her phaeton, to the welcoming cries of the crowd.

Elena would go to her, wave at a respectful distance, and say, Your eyes met mine, do you remember, in your garden, when neither of us understood what the adults were doing. Let me help you continue the ways of your father. Let my hands wash music into whatever wraps around you.

This did not happen for the princess, nor for Elena.

Kaiulani returned to Hawaii and was forced to while away her time at Ainahau. History could permeate the air as soundly as music. The Americans were moving in, and the kingdom seemed permanently pried away from the royal inheritors. Elena thought of Kaiulani and her retinue of peacocks watching the gardeners tending her trees, hoping that some upset would clear the path to the throne for her.

Frank continued to play at society parties, and Elena and her mother saw him infrequently. On one occasion they spotted him through the open doorway of a bar, surrounded by women. One had her arm draped over him. The others were clapping as he strummed a ukulele. Amelia stared toward him. He did not see her or Elena out on the sidewalk.

"Mama, let's go," said Elena, tugging her mother's arm.

Her mother's face went soft and white as cotton.

"Mama."

Her mother ran, her head down, pushing through the crowd. She bumped into people, who shoved her back.

"Mama!" called Elena.

Her mother was wearing a loose Mother Hubbard, and as she ran she stumbled forward, her toe hitting a tuft of grass thrusting itself through the sidewalk, and she fell and hit her head on the pavement.

"Mama, Jesus, Mama," said Elena, turning her mother over and seeing blood seep from her crown. She cradled her mother's head and screamed for help. That fast it had come, this accident so long in the making.

She prayed that her hands would grow hideously large again. If they had at one time made cloth breathe life into strangers, then it was reasonable to expect that large hands, if pressed against her mother's head, would cause life to flow into it. That was what took place, as Elena wished it. Her hands grew, she held her mother's head with them, and Amelia stayed alive. She brought tea to her mother, and ran the laundry by herself, and when her father brought flowers, Elena asked him to leave and take his useless flowers with him. She lay the big palms of both hands onto her mother's head when she had headaches, and they left her quickly, although she had become odd and daft and so relaxed that she scarcely knew who she was.

When Amelia was better and able to walk by herself, Elena wished her big hands gone, but they would not go. She soaked them for hours in the hottest water she could stand, but they stayed with her, even when she cried and pleaded for them to vanish.

Please, please, she prayed every night. They'll make me an old maid. If they don't shrink, I will never be able to be Hawaiian and step out naked to greet the dawn after my wedding night.

Tragedy struck during Elena's pleadings with her hands. Kaiulani, at the age of twenty-three, caught cold during a rainstorm and died. Something as dull as being rained upon! For lack of a warm garment, a line had ended. There were no more heirs to the throne. Elena grieved that her curse should be summoned up, but she was also afraid to cry out that it had actually been intended for her mother. That curse had been so offhanded, during a small, private moment—and for it to come to this!

It chilled her that there was no act, no matter how furtive, that did not impose itself upon the enormous backdrop of events. If anyone attempted to hide, then history would come in and envelop the smallest person in the smallest corner.

While feeding her mother her cereal, Elena realized that the curse had been much smarter than she could imagine. It knew that she had not meant to bring harm to Kaiulani or Likelike, but to her mother. Therefore here her mother was, alive but disabled by a fall. She was as easily enamored as a child. She drummed her hands on the tabletop when Elena cut up a banana. Amelia never had to comb her hair or sweep floors or worry. She did not have to feel like a woman petrified of the future.

Caring for her elderly mother was a full-time job, and even if Elena had normal hands, it was unlikely that she would find a husband. She would be her mother—or rather her mother as her mother would have continued—growing old in a panic.

Elena hung a portrait of Kaiulani in the halls.

"Pretty girl! Pretty girl!" sang Amelia. "Amen!"

"That's Kaiulani, Mama," she said.

"O! O!"

Elena would keep Kaiulani nearby, as a reminder that one could have a whole life planned out, a job assigned from birth, a garden with imported trees, and there was still no guessing how fast the earth could change, how indistinct the most familiar people could grow, how casually a curse or rebellion could fester, how a rainstorm or a fall or quirk of birth could scramble history, how untidily power could grow in one's grasp, though it might vibrate prettily as a string concerto.

Hardly more than a decade later, Elena put her mother in a wheelchair and went out to see the tearing up of the gardens of Ainahau to make room for a hotel. The peacocks had been sold and some of the salvageable plants given away for low prices at an auction. The legislature had decided that royal tokens were no longer of much interest, not since the United States had made Hawaii a territory. Archibald Cleghorn had died, and though he had worked to dedicate the garden for public use, the legislature voted against its upkeep.

Elena tucked a blanket up higher, near her mother's chin. She ironed everything, including blankets, to fill her days, hoping some of the ukulele power would return.

"Nurse," said her mother. "What are they doing? Let's go home!"

"I'd like to watch," said Elena. "It's a place where a princess used to live. I thought one day we would live in a place like that. You and I would have a garden that was like that one over there. Because Daddy seemed to be making lots of money. He brought a new kind of music here. And for a while, my hands did amazing things."

"How nice!"

"Not so nice, actually, Mama." The breeze was lifting the palm leaves on the trees as men with pickaxes headed into the estate to pull up what remained of the garden. A wrecking ball was set up near the house.

"O! What's that noise?"

"They're taking down the house, Mama. No one lives there anymore."

"No, no," said Amelia. "Not that noise! Not that noise! I'm hearing something else!"

Elena sighed, and could picture Kaiulani observing the end of her history, and Hawaii's history. If only she could turn her gaze upon Elena with her infirmed mother, to see that the story of the ukulele family, a history that had begun not long ago as an adjunct to royal dreams, was also at something of an end. Now the strings were invisible, and the garden would be tossed here and there, so that even the ghosts would not find it.

"Are you hearing a ukulele, Mama?" she asked. "A *braguinha*? Is it your stomach singing?"

"Shh! Shh, nurse!" said her mother. "Lord Almighty! Listen!"

That is what I shall do, thought Elena. I shall hold up my burdensome hands, and the moment I identify the song on the wind, it will pass on, leaving me to listen for the next one.

The harmony behind each of those songs will be constant. It will be: Plant no gardens; plant no gardens. A trousseau has no merit. Every plan is cursed, the heedless way we live now.

Vikram Chandra

Dharma

Vikram Chandra will be familiar to connoisseurs of magical realist literature as the author of the extraordinary novel Red Earth and Pouring Rain. *Born in Delhi in 1961, Chandra now divides his time between Bombay and Washington, D.C., where he teaches at George Washington University. His short fiction has appeared in* The New Yorker *and* The Paris Review; *he has won the David Higham Prize for Fiction and the Commonwealth Writers Prize for Best First Published Book.*

"Dharma," a tour de force of contemporary ghost fiction, is reprinted from Chandra's recent collection, Love and Longing in Bombay. *This book consists of five powerful stories interconnected by their enigmatic narrator, relating the tales as he sits in a smoky bar on the Bombay docks.*

—T. W. and E. D.

Considering the length of Subramaniam's service, it was remarkable that he still came to the Fisherman's Rest. When I started going there, he had been retired for six years from the Ministry of Defence, after a run of forty-one years that had left him a joint-secretary. I was young, and I had just started working at a software company which had its air-conditioned and very streamlined head offices just off the Fountain, and I must confess the first time I heard him speak it was to chastise me. He had been introduced to me at a table on the balcony, sitting with three other older men, and my friend Ramani, who had taken me there, told me that they had been coming there for as long as they had worked and longer. Subramaniam had white hair, he was thin, and in the falling dusk he looked very small to me, the kind of man who would while away the endless boredom of his life in a bar off Sasoon Dock, and so I shaped him up in my mind, and weighed him and dropped him.

I should have noticed then that the waiters brought his drinks to him without being asked, and that the others talked around his silence but always with their faces turned towards him, but I was holding forth on the miserable state of computers in Bombay. The bar was on the second floor of an old house, looking towards the sea, and you wouldn't have known it was there, there was certainly no sign, and it couldn't be seen from the street. There were old trophy fish, half a century old at least, strung along the walls, and on the door to the bathroom there was a picture of a hill stream cut from a magazine, British by the look of it. When the wind came in from the sea it fluttered old flowered curtains and a 1971 calendar, and I was restless already, but I owed at least a drink to the courtesy of my friend Ramani, who understood my loneliness in Bombay and was maybe trying to mix me in with the right circle. So I watched a navy ship, a frigate maybe, wheel into the sun, sipped my drink (despite everything, I noticed, a perfect gin sling), and listened to them talk.

Ramani had been to Bandra that day, and he was telling them about a bungalow on the seafront. It was one of those old three-storied houses with balconies that ran all the way around, set in the middle of a garden filled with palms and fish ponds. It sat stubbornly in the middle of towering apartment buildings, and it had been empty as far back as anyone could remember, and so of course the story that explained this waste of golden real estate was one of ghosts and screams in the night.

"They say it's unsellable," said Ramani. "They say a Gujarati *seth* bought it and died within the month. Nobody'll buy it. Bad place."

"What nonsense," I said. "These are all family property disputes. The cases drag on for years and years in courts, and the houses lie vacant because no one will let anyone else live in them." I spoke at length then, about superstition and ignorance and the state of our benighted nation, in which educated men and women believed in banshees and ghouls. "Even in the information age we will never be free," I said. I went on, and I was particularly witty and sharp, I thought. I vanquished every argument with efficiency and dispatch.

After a while my glass was empty and I stopped to look for the bearer. In the pause the waves gathered against the rocks below, and then Subramaniam spoke. He had a small whispery voice, a departmental voice, I thought, it was full of intrigues and secrets and nuances. "I knew a man once who met a ghost," he said. I still had my body turned around in the seat, but the rest of them turned to him expectantly. He said, "Some people meet their ghosts, and some don't. But we're all haunted by them." Now I turned, too, and he was looking straight at me, and his white hair stood clearly against the extravagant red of the sunset behind him, but his eyes were shadowed and hidden. "Listen," he said.

On the day that Major General Jago Antia turned fifty, his missing leg began to ache. He had been told by the doctors about phantom pain, but the leg had been gone for twenty years without a twinge, and so when he felt a twisting ache two inches under his plastic knee, he stumbled not out of agony but surprise. It was only a little stumble, but the officers who surrounded him turned away out of sympathy, because he was Jago Antia, and he never stumbled. The younger lieutenants flushed with emotion, because they knew for certain that Jago Antia was invincible, and this little lapse, and the way he recovered himself, how he came back to his ramrod straightness, this reminded them of the metallic density of his discipline, which you could see in his grey eyes. He was famous for his stare, for the cold blackness of his anger, for his tactical skill and his ability to read ground, his whole career from the gold medal at Kharakvasla to the combat and medals in Leh and NEFA. He was famous for all this, but the leg was the center of the legend, and there was something terrible about it, about the story, and so it was never talked about. He drove himself across jungle terrain and shamed men twenty years younger, and it was as if the leg had never been lost. This is why his politeness, his fastidiousness, the delicate way he handled his fork and knife, his slow smile, all these Jago quirks were imitated by even the cadets at the Academy: they wished for his certainty, and believed that his loneliness was the mark of his genius.

So when he left the *bara khana* his men looked after him with reverence, and curiously the lapse made them believe in his strength all the more. They had done the party to mark an obscure regimental battle day from half a century before, because he would never have allowed a celebration for himself. After he left they lolled on sofas, sipping from their drinks, and told stories about him. His name was Jehangir Antia, but for thirty years, in their stories, he had been Jago Antia. Some of them didn't know his real name.

Meanwhile, Jago Antia lay on his bed under a mosquito net, his arms flat by his sides, his one leg out as if at attention, the other standing by the bed, and waited for his dream to take him. Every night he thought of falling endlessly through the night, slipping through the cold air, and then somewhere it became a dream, and he was asleep, still falling. He had been doing it for as long as he could remember, long before para school and long before the drop at Sylhet, towards the hostile guns and the treacherous ground. It had been with him from long ago, this leap, and he knew where it took him, but this night a pain grew in that part of him that he no longer had, and he tried to fight it away, imagining the rush of air against his neck, the flapping of his clothes, the complete darkness, but it was no use. He was still awake. When he raised his left hand and uncovered the luminous dial it was oh-four-hundred, and then he gave up and strapped his leg on. He went into the study and spread out some maps and began to work on operational orders. The contour maps were covered with markers, and his mind moved easily among the mountains, seeing the units, the routes of supply, the staging areas. They were fighting an insurgency, and he knew of course that he was doing good work, that his concentration was keen, but he knew he would be tired the next day, and this annoyed him. When he found himself kneading his plastic shin with one hand, he was so angry that he went out on the porch and puffed out a hundred quick push-ups, and in the morning his puzzled *sahayak* found him striding up and down the garden walk as the sun came up behind a gaunt ridge.

"What are you doing out here?" Thapa said. Jago Antia had never married. They had known each other for three decades, since Jago Antia had been a captain, and they had long ago discarded with the formalities of master and batman.

"Couldn't sleep, Thapa. Don't know what it was."

Thapa raised an eyebrow. "Eat well then."

"Right. Ten minutes?"

Thapa turned smartly and strode off. He was a small, round man, not fat but bulging everywhere with the compact muscles of the mountains.

"Thapa?" Jago Antia called.

"Yes."

"Nothing." He had for a moment wanted to say something about the pain, but then the habit of a lifetime asserted itself, and he threw back his shoulders and shook his head. Thapa waited for a moment and then walked into the house. Now Jago Antia looked up at the razor edge of the ridge far above, and he could see, if he turned his head to one side, a line of tiny figures walking down it. They would be woodcutters, and perhaps some of the men he was fighting. They were committed, hardy, and well trained. He watched them. He was better. The sun was high now, and Jago Antia went to his work.

The pain didn't go away, and Jago Antia couldn't sleep. Sometimes he was sure he was in his dream, and he was grateful for the velocity of the fall, and he could feel the cold on his face, the dark, but then he would sense something, a tiny glowing pinpoint that spun and grew and finally became a bright hurling maelstrom that wrenched him back into wakefulness. Against this he had no defense: no matter how tired he made himself, how much he exhausted his body, he could not make his mind insensible to his phantom pain, and so his discipline, honed over the years, was made useless. Finally he conquered his shame, and asked—in the strictest confidence—an Army Medical Corps colonel for medication, and got, along with a very puzzled stare, a bottle full of yellow pills, which he felt in his pocket all day, against his chest. But at night these pills too proved no match for the ferocity of the pain, which by now Jago Antia imagined as a beast of some sort, a low growling animal that camouflaged itself until he was almost at rest and then came rushing out to worry at his flesh, or at the memory of his flesh. It was not that Jago Antia minded the defeat, because he had learnt to accept defeat and casualties and loss, but it was that he had once defeated this flesh, it was he who had swung the *kukri*, but it had come back now and surprised him. He felt outflanked, and this infuriated him, and further, there was nothing he could do about it, there was nothing to do anything about. So his work suffered, and he felt the surprise of those around him. It shamed him more than anything else that they were not disappointed but sympathetic. They brought him tea without being asked, he noticed that his aides spoke amongst themselves in whispers, his headquarters ran—if it was possible—even more efficiently than before, with the gleam of spit and polish about it. But now he was tired, and when he looked at the maps he felt the effort he had to make to grasp the flow of the battle—not the facts, which were important, though finally trivial—but the thrust and the energy of the struggle, the movement of the initiative, the flux and ebb of the chaotic thing. One afternoon he sat in his office, the pain a constant hum just below his attention, and the rain beat down in gusts against the windows, and the gleam of lightning startled him into realizing that his jaw was slack, that he had been staring aimlessly out of the window at the green side of the mountain, that he had become the sort of commander he despised, a man who because of his rank allowed himself to become careless. He knew he would soon make the sort of mistake that would get some of his boys killed, and that was unacceptable: without hesitation he called the AMC colonel and asked to be relieved of his command for medical reasons.

The train ride to Bombay from Calcutta was two days long, and there was a kind of relief in the long rhythms of the wheels, in the lonely clangings of the tracks at night. Jago Antia sat next to a window in a first class compartment and watched the landscape change, taken back somehow to a fifth-grade classroom and lessons on the crops of the Deccan. Thapa had taken a week's leave to go to his family in Darjeeling and was to join up in Bombay later. Jago Antia was used to solitude, but the relief from immediate responsibility brought with it a rush of memory, and he found the unbidden recall of images from the past annoying, because it all seemed so useless. He tried to take up the time usefully by reading NATO journals, but even under the hard edge of his concentration the pain throbbed in time with the wheels, and he found himself remembering an afternoon at school when they had run out of history class to watch two fighter planes fly low over the city. By the time the train pulled into Bombay Central, he felt as if he were covered not only with sweat and grit, but also with an oily film of recollection, and he marched through the crowd towards the taxi stand, eager for a shower.

The house stood in a square plot on prime residential land in Khar, sur-rounded by new, extravagant constructions colored the pink and green of new money. But it was mostly dark brown, stained by decades of sea air and monsoon rains, and in the late-afternoon sun it seemed to gather the light about it as it sat surrounded by trees and untidy bushes. There was, in its three stories, in the elegant arches on the balconies, and in the rows of shuttered windows, something rich and dense and heavy, like the smell of gun oil on an old hunting rifle, and the taxi driver sighed, "They don't build them like that anymore."

"No, they're drafty and take a fortune to keep up," said Jago Antia curtly as he handed him the money. It was true. Amir Khan the housekeeper was waving slowly from the porch. He was very old, with a thin neck and a white beard that gave him the appearance of a heron, and by the time he was halfway down the flight of stairs Jago Antia had the bags out of the car and up to the house. Inside, with Amir Khan puffing behind him, he paused to let his eyes take to the dark-ness, but it felt as if he were pushing his way through something substantial and insidious, more clear than fog but as inescapable. It was still much as he had left it many years ago to go to the Academy. There were the Victorian couches covered with faded flower prints, the gold-rimmed paintings on the wall of his grandparents and uncles. He noticed suddenly how quiet it was, as if the street and the city outside had vanished.

"I'll take these bags upstairs," he said.

"Can't," Amir Khan said. "It's been closed up for years. All just sheets on the furniture. Even your parents slept in the old study. They moved a bed into it."

Jago Antia shrugged. It was more convenient on the ground floor in any case. "It's all right. It's just for a few days. I have some work here. I'll see Todywalla too."

"What about?"

"Well, I want to sell the house."

"You want to sell the house?"

"Yes."

Amir Khan shuffled away to the kitchen, and Jago Antia heard him knocking about with cups and saucers. He had no intention of using the house again, and he saw no other alternative. His parents were dead, gone one after another in a year. He had been a distant son, meeting them on leave in Delhi and Lucknow while they were on vacation. Wherever they had met, far away from Bombay, he had always seen the old disappointment and weariness in their eyes. Now it was over, and he wanted not to think about the house anymore.

"Good, sell this house." It was Amir Khan with a cup of tea. "Sell it."

"I will."

"Sell it."

Jago Antia noticed that Amir Khan's hands were shaking, and he remembered suddenly an afternoon in the garden when he had made him throw ball after ball to his off side, and his own attempts at elegant square cuts, and the sun high overhead through the palm trees.

"We'll do something for you," said Jago Antia. "Don't worry."

"Sell it," Amir Khan said. "I'm tired of it."

Jago Antia tried to dream of falling, but his ache stayed with him, and besides the gusts of water against the windows were loud and unceasing. It had begun to rain with nightfall, and now the white illumination of lightning threw the whole room into sharp relief. He was thinking about the Academy, about how he had been named Jago, two weeks after his arrival. His roommate had found him at five o'clock on a Saturday morning doing push-ups on the gravel outside their room, and rubbing his eyes he had said, "Antia, you're an enthusiast." He had never known where the nickname Jago came from, but after the second week nobody except his parents had called him Jehangir again. When he had won the gold medal for best cadet even the major-general who was commandant of the Academy had said to him at the reviewing stand, "Good show, Jago." He had been marked for advancement early, and he had never betrayed his promise. He was thinking of this, and the wind flapped the curtains above him, and when he first heard the voice far away he thought it was a trick of the air, but then he heard it again. It was muffled by distance and the rain but he heard it clearly. He could not make out what it was saying. He was alert instantly and strapped on his leg. Even though he knew it was probably Amir Khan talking to himself, flicking away with a duster in the imagined light of some long-gone day, he moved cautiously, back against the wall. At the bottom of the hallway he paused, and heard it again, small but distinct, above him. He found the staircase and went up, his thighs tense, moving in a fluid half-squat. Now he was truly watchful, because the voice was too young to be Amir Khan. On the first landing, near an open door, he sensed a rush of motion on the balcony that ran around the outside of the house; he came to the corner, feeling his way with his hands. Everything in the darkness appeared as shades, blackness and deeper blackness. He darted a look around the corner, and the balcony was empty, he was sure of it. He came around the corner, back against the wall. Then he heard the move-ment again, not distinct footsteps but the swish of feet on the ground, one after another. He froze. Whatever it was, it was coming towards him. His eyes ached in the darkness, but he could see nothing. Then the white blaze of lightning swept across the lawn, throwing the filigreed ironwork of the railing sharply on the wall, across Jago Antia's belly, and in the long light he saw on the floor the clearly outlined shape of shoes, one after another, the patches of water a sharp black in the light, and as he watched another footprint appeared on the tile, and then another, coming towards him. Before it was dark again he was halfway down the stairs. He stopped, alone with the beating of his heart. He forced himself to stand up straight, to look carefully about and above the staircase for dead ground and lines of fire. He had learnt long ago that professionalism was a much better way to defeat fear than self-castigation and shame, and now he applied himself to the problem. The only possible conclusion was that it had been a trick of the light on the water, and so he was able to move up the staircase, smooth and graceful once again. But on the landing a breath of air curled around his ankle like a flow of cool liquid, and he began to shiver. It was a freezing chill that spread up his thighs and into his groin, and it caught him so suddenly that he let his teeth chatter for a moment. Then he bit down, but despite his straining he could hardly take a step before he stopped again. It was so cold that his fingers ached. His eyes filled with moisture and suddenly the dark was full of soft shadows. Again he heard the voice, far away, melancholy and low. With a groan he collapsed against the banister and slid down the stairs, all the way to the bottom, his leg rattling on the steps. Through the night he tried it again and again, and once he made it to the middle of the landing, but the fear took the strength from his hips, so that he had to crawl on hands and knees to the descent. At dawn he sat shaken and weak on the first step, his arm around the comforting curve of the thick round post.

Finally it was the shock in Thapa's eyes that raised Jago Antia from the stupor he had fallen into. For three days he had been pacing, unshaven and unwashed, at the bottom of the stairs, watching the light make golden shapes in the air. Now Thapa had walked through the front door, and it was his face, slack, and the fact that he forgot to salute that conveyed to Jago Antia how changed he was, how shocking he was.

"It's all right," Jago Antia said. "I'm all right."

Thapa still had his bag in his right hand and an umbrella in the left, and he said nothing. Jago Antia remembered then a story that was a part of his own legend: he had once reduced a lieutenant to tears because of a tea stain on his shirt. It was quite true.

"Put out a change of clothes," he said. "And close your mouth."

The water in the shower drummed against Jago Antia's head and cleared it. He saw the insanity of what had gone on for three days, and he was sure it was exhaustion. There was nothing there, and the important thing was to get to the hospital, and then to sell the house. He ate breakfast eagerly, and felt almost relaxed. Then Amir Khan walked in with a glass of milk on a tray. For three days he had been bringing milk instead of tea, and now when Jago Antia told him to take it back to the kitchen, he said, "Baba, you have to drink it. Mummy said so. You know you're not allowed to drink tea." And he shuffled away, walking through a suddenly revived age when Jehangir Antia was a boy in knickers, agile and confident on two sunburnt legs. For a moment Jago Antia felt time slipping around him like a dark wave, but then he shook away the feeling and stood up.

"Call a taxi," he said to Thapa.

The doctors at Jaslok were crisp and confident in their poking and prodding, and the hum of machinery comforted him. But Todywalla, sitting in his disorderly office, said bluntly, "Sell that house? Na, impossible. There's something in it."

"Oh don't be ridiculous," said Jago Antia vehemently. "That's absurd."

Todywalla looked keenly at him. Todywalla was a toothless old man with a round black cap squarely on the middle of his head. "Ah," he said. "So you've heard it too."

"I haven't heard a damn thing," Jago Antia said. "Be rational."

"You may be a rationalist," Todywalla said. "But I sell houses in Bombay." He sipped tea noisily from a chipped cup. "There's something in that house."

When the taxi pulled through the gate Thapa was standing in the street outside, talking to a vegetable seller and two other men. As Jago Antia pulled off his shoes in the living room, Thapa came in and went to the kitchen. He came back a few minutes later with a glass of water.

"Tomorrow I will find my cousin at the bank at Nariman Point," he said. "And we will get somebody to come to this house. We shouldn't sleep here."

"What do you mean, somebody?"

"Somebody who can clean it up." Thapa's round face was tight, and there were white crescents around his temples. "Somebody who knows."

"Knows what exactly? What are you talking about?"

Thapa nodded towards the gate. "No one on this street will come near this place after dark. Everyone knows. They were telling me not to stay here."

"Nonsense."

"We can't fight this, *saab*," Thapa said. After a pause: "Not even you."

Jago Antia stood erect. "I will sleep tonight quietly and so will you. No more of this foolishness." He marched into the study and lay on the bed, loosening his body bit by bit, and under the surface of his concentration the leg throbbed evenly. The night came on and passed. He thought finally that nothing would happen, and there was a grey outside the window, but then he heard again the incessant calling. He took a deep breath, and walked into the drawing room. Thapa was standing by the door, his whole body straining away from the stairs. Jago Antia took two steps forward. "Come on," he said. His voice rustled across the room, and both of them jerked. He read the white tightness of terror around Thapa's mouth, and as he had done many times before, he led by example. He felt his legs move far away, towards the stairs, and he did not look behind him to see if Thapa was following. He knew the same pride and shame which was taking him up the stairs would bring Thapa: as long as each saw himself in the other's eyes he would not let the other down. He had tested this in front of machine guns and found it to be true. So now they moved, Thapa a little behind and flanking, up the stairs. This time he came up to the landing and was able to move out, through the door, onto the balcony. He was moving, moving. But then the voice came around a corner and he stood still, feeling a rush in his veins. It was amazing, he found himself thinking, how localized it was. He could tell from moment to moment where it was on the balcony. It was not a trick of the wind, not a hallucination. Thapa was still against the wall, his palms against it, his mouth working back and forth, looking exactly where Jago Antia was. It came closer, and now Jago Antia was able to hear what it was saying: "Where shall I go?" The question was asked with a sob in it, like a tearing hiccup, so close that Jago Antia heard it shake the small frame that asked it. He felt a sound in his own throat, a moan, something like pain, sympathy. Then he felt the thing pause, and though there was nothing but the air he felt it coming at him, first hesitating, then faster, asking again, where shall I go, where, and he backed away from it, fast, tripping over his heels, and he felt the railing of the balcony on his thighs, hard, and then he was falling.

The night was dark below. They plummeted headfirst from the belly of the plane into the cool pit at a thousand feet, and Jago Antia relished the leap into reality. They had been training long enough, and now he did not turn his head to see if the stick was tight because he knew his men and their skill. The chute popped with a flap, and after the jerk he flew the sky with his legs easy in the harness. The only feature he could see was the silver curve of the river far below, and then quite suddenly the dark mass of trees and the swathe of fields. There were no lights in the city of Sylhet, but he knew it was there, to the east, and he knew the men who were in it, defending against him, and he saw the problem clearly and the movements across the terrain below.

Then he was rolling across the ground, and the chute was off. Around him was the controlled confusion of a nighttime drop, and swiftly out of that formed the shape of his battalion. He had the command group around him, and in a few minutes they were racing towards their first objectives. Now he was sweating freely, and the weight of his pistol swung against his hip. He could smell the cardamom seeds his radioman was chewing. In the first grey, to the east, the harsh tearing noise of LMG fire flung the birds out of the trees. *Delta Bravo I have contact over.* As Jago Antia thumbed the mouthpiece, his radioman smiled at him, nineteen and glowing in the dawn. *Delta Bravo, bunkers, platoon strength, I am going in now.* Alpha Company had engaged.

As the day came they moved into the burning city, and the buildings were torn by explosions and the shriek of rockets skimming low over the streets and ringing off the walls. Now the noise echoed and boomed, and it was difficult to tell where it was coming from, but Jago Antia still saw it all forming on his map, which was stained black now with sweat here and there, and dust, and the plaster knocked from the walls by bullets. He was icy now, his mind holding it all, and as an excited captain reported to him he listened silently, and there was the flat crack of a grenade, not far off, and the captain flinched, then blushed as he saw that Jago Antia was calm as if he were walking down a golf course in Wellington, not a street shining with glass, thousands of shards sharp as death, no, he was meditative and easy. So the captain went back to his boys with something of Jago Antia's slow watchfulness in his walk, and he put away his nervousness and smiled at them, and they nodded, crouched behind cracked walls, sure of each other and Jago Antia.

Now in the morning the guns echoed over the city, and a plummy BBC voice sounded over a Bush radio in the remnants of a tailor's shop: "Elements of the Indian Para Brigade are said to be in the outskirts of Sylhet. Pakistani troops are dug in . . ." Jago Antia was looking at the rounded curves of the radio on the tailor's shelf, at the strange white knobs and the dial from decades ago, at the deep brown wood, and a shiver came from low on his back into his heart, a whisper of something so tiny that he could not name it, and yet it broke his concentration and took him away from his body and this room with its drapes of cloth to somewhere else, a flickering vision of a room, curtains blowing in a gusting wind, a feeling of confusion, he shook his head and swallowed. He curled the knob with the back of his hand so that it snapped the voice off and broke with a crack. Outside he could feel the fight approaching a crisis, the keen whiplash of the carbines and the rattle of the submachine guns and the heavier Pakistani fire, cresting and falling like waves but always higher, it was likely the deciding movement. He had learnt the waiting that was the hardest part of commanding, and now the reports came quickly, and he felt the battle forming to a crescendo; he had a reserve, sixty men, and he knew now where he was going to put them. They trotted down the street to the east and paused on a dusty street corner (the relentless braying scream of an LMG near by), and Jung the radioman pointed to a house at the end of the street, a white three-storied house with a decorative vine running down the front in concrete, now chipped and holed. "Tall enough," Jago Antia said: he wanted a vantage point to see the city laid out for him. He started off confidently across the street, and then all the sound in the world vanished, leaving a smooth silence, he had no recollection of being thrown, but now he was falling through the air, down, he felt distinctly the impact of the ground, but again there was nothing, no sound.

After a while he was able to see the men above him as he was lifted, their lips moving serenely even though their faces were twisted with emotion, they appeared curved and bent inwards against a spherical sky. He shut and opened his eyes several times, searching for connections that seemed severed. They carried him into a house. Then he was slowly able to hear again, and with the sound he began to feel the pain. His ears hurt sharply and deep inside his head, in a place in which he had never felt pain before. But he strained and finally he was able to find, inside, some part of himself, and his body jerked, and they held him still. His jaw cracked, and he said: "What?"

It was a mine on the corner, they told him. Now he was fighting it, he was using his mind, he felt his strength coming back, he could find his hands, and he pushed against the bed and sat up. A fiercely moustached nursing-assistant pushed at his shoulders, but he struck the hands away and took a deep breath. Then he saw his leg. Below his right knee the flesh was white and twisted away from the bone. Below the ankle was a shapeless bulk of matter, and the nursing-assistant was looking for the artery, but as Jago Antia watched the black blood seeped out onto the floor. Outside, the firing was ceaseless now, and Jago Antia was looking at his leg, and he realized that he no longer knew where his boys were. The confusion came and howled around his head, and for a moment he was lost. "Cut it off," he said then. "Off."

But, said the nursing-assistant, holding up the useless bandages, but I have nothing, and Jago Antia felt his head swim on an endless swell of pain, it took him up and away and he could no longer see, and it left him breathless and full of loss. "No time. Cut it off now," he said, but the nursing-assistant was dabbing with the bandages. Jago Antia said to Jung: "You do it, now. Quickly." They were all staring at him, and he knew he could not make them cut him. "Give me your *kukri*," he said to Jung. The boy hesitated, but then the blade came out of its scabbard with a hiss that Jago Antia heard despite the ceaseless roar outside. He steadied himself and gripped it with both hands and shut his eyes for a moment, and there was impossibly the sound of the sea inside him, a sob rising in his throat, he opened his eyes and fought it, pulled against it with his shoulders as he raised the *kukri* above his head, against darkness and mad sorrow, and then he brought the blade down below his knee. What surprised him was the crunch it made against the bone. In four strokes he was through. Each was easier. "Now," he said, and the nursing-assistant tied it off. Jago Antia waved off the morphine, and he saw that Jung the radioman was crying. On the radio Jago Antia's voice was steady. He took his reports, and then he sent his reserve in. They heard his voice across Sylhet. "Now then," he said. "Finish it."

The room that Jago Antia woke up in had a cracked white ceiling, and for a long time he did not know where he was, in Sylhet (he could feel an ache under his right knee), in the house of his childhood after a fall from the balcony, or in some other room, unknown: everything seemed to be thrown together in his eyes without shape or distinction, and from moment to moment he forgot the flow of time, and found himself talking to Amir Khan about cricket, and then suddenly it was evening. Finally he was able to sit up in bed, and a doctor fussed about him: there were no injuries, the ground was soft from the rain, his paratrooper's reflexes had turned him in the air and rolled him on the ground, but he was bruised, and a concussion could not be ruled out. He was to stay in bed and rest. When the doctor left Thapa brought in a plate of rice and *dal*, and stood at the foot of the bed with his arms behind him. "I will talk to my cousin tonight."

Jago Antia nodded. There was nothing to say. But when the exorcist came two days later he was not the slavering tribal magician that Jago Antia was expecting, but a sales manager from a large electronics company. Without haste and without stopping he put his briefcase down, stripped off his black pants and white shirt and blue tie, and bathed under the tap in the middle of the garden. Then he put on a white *dhoti* and daubed his forehead with a white powder, and meanwhile Thapa was preparing a *thali* with little mounds of rice and various kinds of coloured paste and a small *diya*, with the wick floating in the oil. Then the man took the *thali* from Thapa and walked slowly into the house, and as he came closer Jago Antia saw that he was in his late forties, that he was heavyset, that he was neither ugly nor handsome. "My name is Thakker," he said to Jago Antia before he sat cross-legged in the middle of the living room, in front of the stairs, and lit the *diya*. It was evening now, and the flame was tiny and flickering in the enormous darkness of the room.

As Thakker began to chant and throw fistfuls of rice from his *thali* into the room Jago Antia felt all the old irritation return, and he was disgusted with himself for letting this insanity gather around him. He walked out into the garden and stood with the grass rustling against his pants. There was a huge bank of clouds on the horizon, mass upon mass of dark heads piled up thousands of feet high, and as he watched a silver dart of lightning flickered noiselessly, and then another. Now his back began to ache slightly, and he shook his head slowly, overwhelmed by the certainty that he no longer knew anything. He turned around and looked up the path, into the house, and through the twilight he could see the tiny gleam of Thakker's *diya*, and as he watched Thakker lifted the *thali* and walked slowly towards the stairs, into the shadow, so that finally it seemed that the flame was rising up the stairs. Then Thapa came out, and they stood in the garden together, and the breeze from the sea was full of the promise of rain. They waited as night fell, and sometimes they heard Thakker's voice, lifted high and chanting, and then, very faint, that other voice, blown away by the gusts of wind. Finally—Jago Antia did not know what time it was— Thakker came down the stairs, carrying the *thali*, but the *diya* was blown out. They walked up to meet him on the patio, under the faint light of a single bulb.

"It is very strong," he said.

"What is it?" said Jago Antia angrily.

Thakker shrugged. "It is most unmovable." His face was drawn and pale. "It is a child. It is looking for something. Most terrible. Very strong."

"Well, get it out."

"I cannot. Nobody can move a child."

Jago Antia felt a rush of panic, like a steady pressure against his chest.

Thapa said, "What can we do?"

Thakker walked past them, down the stairs, and then he turned and looked up at them. "Do you know who it is?" Jago Antia said nothing, his lips held tightly together to stop them from trembling. "It is most powerful because it is a child and because it is helpless and because it is alone. Only one who knows it and who is from its family can help it. Such a person must go up there naked and alone. Remember, alone and naked, and ask it what it seeks." Thakker wiped away the white powder from his forehead slowly, and then he turned and walked away. It was now drizzling, fat drops that fell out of the sky insistently.

Out of the darkness Thakker called. "You must go." Then a pause in which Jago Antia could hear, somewhere, rushing water. "Help him."

At the bottom of the stairs Jago Antia felt his loneliness like a bitterness in his nostrils, like a stench. Thapa watched from the door, remote already, and there seemed to be nothing in the world but the shadows ahead, the creaking of the old house, the wind in the balconies. As Jago Antia walked slowly up the stairs, unbuttoning his shirt, his pulse was rushing in his head, each beat like an explosion, not out of fear anymore but from a kind of anticipation, because now he knew who it was, who waited for him. On the landing he kicked off his shoes and unbuckled his belt, and whispered, "What can you want from me? I was a child too." He walked slowly around the balcony, and the rain dashed against his shoulders and rolled down his back. He came to the end of the balcony, at a door with bevelled glass, and he peered through it, and he could dimly make out the ornate curves of his mother's dressing table, the huge mirror, and beyond that the bed now covered with sheets, he stood with his face against the cool pane. He shut his eyes. Somewhere deep came the poisonous seep of memory, he felt it in his stomach like a living stream, and his mother was looking at him, her eyes unfocussed in a kind of daze. She was a very beautiful woman, and she was sitting in front of her mirror now as she always did, but her hair was untidy, and she was wearing a white sari. He was sitting on the edge of her bed, his feet stuck out, and he was looking at his black shoes and white socks, and he was trying to be very still because he did not know what was going to happen next. He was dressed up, and the house was full of people, but it was very quiet and the only sounds were the pigeons on the balcony. He was afraid to move, and after a while he began to count his breaths, in and out. Then his father came in, he stood next to his mother, put a hand on her shoulder, and they looked at each other for a long time, and he wanted to say that they looked like their picture on the mantelpiece, only older and in white, but he knew he couldn't so he kept himself still and waited. Then his father said to his mother, come, and they rose and he walked behind them a little. She was leaning on his father, and they came down the stairs and everyone watched them. Downstairs he saw his uncles and aunts and other people he didn't know, and in the middle of the room there was a couch and on it lay his brother Sohrab. Sohrab had been laid out and draped in a white sheet. There was a kind of oil lamp with a wick burning near Sohrab's head, and a man was whispering a prayer into his ear. There was a smell of sandalwood in the air. Then his mother said, "Soli, Soli," and his father turned his face away, and a breath passed through the room, and he saw many people crying. That was what they always called Sohrab. He was Soli, and that was how Jehangir always thought of him. His mother was kneeling next to Soli, and his father too, and he was alone, and he didn't know what to do, but he stood straight up, and he kept his hands by his sides. Then two men came forward, and they covered Soli's face, and then other people lifted him up, and they took him through the door, and for a long time he could see them walking through the garden towards the gate. His mother was sitting on the sofa with her sisters, and after a while he turned around and walked up the stairs, and above there was nobody, and he walked through the rooms and around the balcony, and after a while he thought he was waiting for something to happen, but it never did.

Jago Antia's forehead trembled against the glass and now he turned and walked down the corridor that ran around the house, through darkness and sudden light, and he walked by a playroom, and then his father's study, and as he walked he felt that it was walking beside him, in front of him, around him. He heard the voice asking its question, but his own desperate question seemed to twist in his throat and come out only as a sound, a sort of sob of anger. It went into the room that had been his room and Soli's room, and he stopped at the door, his chest shaking, looking at the floor where they had wrestled each other, the bureau between the beds on which they had stacked their books and their toys. The door creaked open under his hand, and inside he sat on this bed, in the middle, where he used to, and they were listening to the Binaca Geet Mala on the radio, Soli loved his radio and the Binaca Geet Mala. He was lying on the bed in his red pyjamas and the song went *Maine shayad tumhe pahale bhi kahin dekha hai*, Soli sang along with it, Jehangir was not allowed to touch the radio, but when Soli was away he sometimes played with the knobs, and once he switched it on and heard a hiss and a voice far away speaking angrily in a language he didn't understand, it scared him and he ran away from it, and Soli found his radio on, and then there was a fight. Jehangir lost the fight, but Soli always won, even with the other boys on the street, he was fearless, and he jumped over walls, and he led them all, and at cricket he was always the captain of one side, and sometimes in the evenings, still in his barrister's clothes, their father watched their games in the garden, and he said that Soli had a lovely style. When he said this the first time Jehangir raised his head and blinked because he understood instantly what his father meant, he had known it all along but now he knew the words for it, and he said it to himself sometimes under his breath, a lovely style, a lovely style. Now Soli raised himself up in bed on an elbow, and Amir Khan brought in two glasses of milk on a tray, and then their mother came in and sat as she did on Soli's bed, and tonight she had *The Illustrated Weekly of India* in her hand, folded open to a tall picture of a man with a moustache and a bat, and she said, "Look at him, he was the Prince." So she told them about Ranjitsinhji, who was really a prince, who went to England where they called him nigger and wog, but he showed them, he was the most beautiful batsman, like a dancer he turned their bouncers to the boundaries with his wrists, he drove with clean elegance, he had good manners, and he said nothing to their insults, and he showed them all he was the best of them all, he was the Prince, he was lovely. After their mother left Soli put *The Illustrated Weekly* in his private drawer, and after that Jehangir would see him take it out and look at it, and sometimes he would let Jehangir look at it, and Jehangir would look at the long face and the pride in the stance and the dark opaque eyes, and he would feel a surge of pride himself, and Soli would have his wiry hand on his shoulder, and they would both say together, Ranjitsinhji, Ranji.

That summer one Sunday afternoon they were dozing in the heat when suddenly Burjor Mama came in and tumbled them both out of bed, roaring what a pair of sleepyhead sissy types, and they laughed with delight because he was their favorite uncle. They knew his arrival meant at least two weeks of unexpected pleasures, excursions to Juhu, sailing trips, films, shows, and sizzling forbidden pavement foods. Their mother came in and hugged him close, and they were embarrassed by her tears, Burjor was her only younger brother and more precious for his profession of soldiering, she was exclaiming now how he was burnt black by the sun, what are they doing to you now, and he was really dark, but Jehangir liked his unceasing whiplike energy and the sharp pointed ends of his handlebar moustache. Barely pausing to thump down his hold-all and his suitcase, he gathered up the whole family, Amir Khan included, and he whisked them off for a drive, and he whistled as he drove. On the way back Jehangir, weighted down with ice cream, fell asleep with his head in his mother's lap, and once for a moment he awoke and saw, close to his face, his mother's hand holding her brother's wrist tenderly and close, her delicate fingers very pale against his skin with the strong corded muscles underneath.

And Jago Antia, walking down the corridor, walking, felt the sticky sleep of childhood and the cosy hum of the car and safety. And then he was at the bottom of a flight of stairs, he knew he had to go up, because it had gone before him, and now he stumbled because the pain came, and it was full of fear, he went up, one two three, and then leaned over, choking. Above him the stairs angled into darkness and the roof he knew so well, and he couldn't move, again he was trembling, and the voice was speaking somewhere ahead, he said, "I don't want to go," but then he heard it again. He knew his hands were shaking, and he said, "All right you bastard, naked, naked," and he tore at the straps, and then the leg rolled down the stairs to the bottom. He went up, hunching, on hands and knees, his lips curled back and breathing in huge gasps.

Burjor Mama bought them a kite. On Monday morning he had to report in Colaba for work, and so Jehangir's mother brought up his pressed uniform and put it on the bed in the guest room. Jehangir lay on the bed next to the uniform and took in its peculiar smell, it was a deep olive green, and the bars on the front were of many colors but mainly red and orange, and above a breast pocket it said, B. MEHTA. Jehangir's mother sat on the bed too and smoothed out the uniform with an open palm, and then Burjor Mama came out of the bathroom in a towel. As he picked up the shirt, Jehangir saw under the *sadra*, under and behind his left arm, a scar shaped like a star, brown and hard against the pale skin. Then Jehangir looked up and he saw his mother's face, tender and proud and a little angry as she looked at Burjor. After breakfast Soli and Jehangir walked with him to the gate, and he said, "See you later, alligators," and in the afternoon they waited on the porch for him, reading comics and sipping at huge glasses of squash. When the taxi stopped at the gate they had run forward, whooping, because even before he was out they had seen the large triangle of the kite, and then they ran up without pause to the roof, Soli holding the kite at the ends, and Jehangir following behind with the roll of string. Jehangir held the roll as Soli spun off the *manjha*, and Soli said, watch your fingers, and Burjor showed them how to tie the kite string, once up, once down, and then they had it up in the air, it was doing spirals and rolls, and Soli said, "Yaar, that's a fighting kite!" Nobody was flying to fight with nearby, but when their father came up he laughed and watched them, and when they went down to tea Soli's fingers were cut from the *manjha*, and when Jehangir asked, Burjor Mama said, "It's ground glass on the line."

Now he came up the stairs, his stump bumping on the edges of the stone, and his palm scraped against something metal, but he felt the sting distantly and without interest. The next day Soli lay stretched across the roof, his mouth open. Jago Antia pulled himself up, his arms around a wooden post, and he could see the same two-level roof, Amir Khan's old room to one side, with its sloping roof coming to the green posts holding it up, beyond that the expanse of brick open to the sky, and then a three-foot drop with a metal ladder leading to the lower level of the roof, and beyond that the treetops and the cold stretch of the ocean. He let go of the post and swayed gently in the rain. Soli walked in front of him, his hands looping back the string, sending the kite fluttering strongly through the sky, and Jehangir held the coil and took up the slack. It flew in circles above them. "Let me fly it," Jehangir said. "Let me fly it." But Soli said, "You can't hold this, it'll cut you." "I can hold anything. I can." "You can't, it'll hurt you." "It won't. I won't let it." And Jehangir ran forward, Soli danced away, light and confident, backwards, and then for a moment his face was surprised, and then he was lying below, three feet below on the ground, and the string flew away from him. Jago Antia dropped to his knee, then fell heavily on his side. He pulled himself through the water, to the edge, next to the metal stairs, and he peered down trying to see the bottom but it seemed endless, but he knew it was only three feet below. How can somebody die falling three feet?

He heard the voice asking its question, where shall I go, and he roared into the night, "What do you want? What the hell is it you want?" But it wouldn't stop, and Jago Antia knelt on the edge and wept, "What do you want," and finally he said, "Look, look," and he pushed himself up, leaned forward, and let himself go, and he fell: he saw again Soli backing away, Jehangir reaching up trying to take his hand away from the string, Soli holding his hand far up, and Jehangir helpless against his strength. Then Soli smiling, standing, and Jehangir shouting and running forward and jumping, the solid impact of his small body against Soli's legs, Soli's look of surprise, he's falling, reaching wildly, Jehangir's hand under the bottom of Soli's shorts, he holds on and tries, holds and pulls, but then he feels the weight taking him over, and he won't let go, but he hasn't the strength, he's falling with Soli, he feels the impact of the bricks through Soli's body.

When Jago Antia stirred weakly on the roof, when he looked up, it was dawn. He held himself up and said, "Are you still here? Tell me what you want." Then he saw at the parapet, very dim and shifting in the grey light, the shape of a small body, a boy looking down over the edge towards the ocean. As Jago Antia watched, the boy turned slowly, and in the weak light he saw that the boy was wearing a uniform of olive green, and he asked, "Where shall I go?" Jago Antia began to speak, but then his voice caught, because he was remembering his next and seventh birthday, the first party without Soli, and his parents holding him between them, soothing him, saying you must want something, and he looking up at their faces, at the lines in his father's face, the exhaustion in his mother's eyes. Burjor Mama sits on the carpet behind him with head down, and Amir Khan stands behind, and Jehangir shakes his head, nothing. His mother's eyes fill with tears, and she kisses him on the forehead, "Baba, it's all right, let us give you a present," and his heart breaks beneath a surging weight, but he stands up straight, and looking at her and his father, he says, "I want a uniform." So Jago Antia looked at the boy as he came closer, and he saw the small letters above the pocket, J. ANTIA, and the sun came up, and he saw the boy clearly, he saw the enormous dark eyes, and in the eyes he saw his vicious and ravenous strength, his courage and his devotion, his silence and his pain, his whole misshapen and magnificent life, and Jago Antia said, "Jehangir, Jehangir, you're already at home."

Thapa and Amir Khan came up the stairs slowly, and he called out to them, "Come, come. I'm all right." He was sitting crosslegged, watching the sun move in and out of the clouds.

Thapa squatted beside him. "Was it here?"

"He's gone. I saw him, and then he vanished."

"Who?"

Jago Antia shook his head. "Someone I didn't know before."

"What was he doing here then?"

"He was lost." He leaned on both their shoulders, one arm around each, for the descent down the stairs. Somehow, naked and hopping from stair to stair, he was smiling. He knew that nothing had changed. He knew he was still and forever Jago Antia, that for him it was too late for anything but a kind of solitude, that he would give his body to the fire, that in the implacable hills to the north, among the rocks, he and other men and women, each with histories of their own, would find each other for life and for death. And yet he felt free. He sat on the porch, strapping his leg on, and Amir Khan brought out three cups of tea. Thapa wrapped a sheet around Jago Antia, and looking at each other they both laughed. "Thank you," Jago Antia said. Then they drank the tea together.

Honorable Mentions: 1997

Addison, Linda D., "e-toy-oc, the trickster" (poem), *Animated Objects*.
Aiken, Joan, "Quando Tu Va," *Scaremongers*.
Alkalay-Gut, Karen, "Sympathy for the Devil" (poem), *The Alsop Review* (web site).
Allyn, Doug, "Copperhead Run," *Ellery Queen's Mystery Magazine*, June.
Annandale, David, "Via Influenza," *Northern Frights 4*.
Antczak, Stephen, "Good Vibrations," *Terminal Frights*.
Archambault, Gary, "Falling Awake to the Here in Now Brightly," *The Silver Web* 14.
Arnzen, Michael A., "The Piano Player Has No Fingers," *Palace Corbie Seven*.
———, "Stigmata," *Terminal Frights*.
Ashley, Allen, "State of the Ark," *The Third Alternative* 11.
———, "In Search of Guy Fawkes," *Back Brain Recluse* 23.
Asplund, Russell William, "Balkan Siege," *Realms of Fantasy*, Aug.
Avery, Simon, "Anonymity Walks," *The Third Alternative* 11.
Aycliffe, Jonathan, "The Scent of Oranges," *Midnight Never Comes*.
Bailey, Dale, "Quinn's Way," *The Magazine of Fantasy & Science Fiction*, Feb.
Baker, Kage, "Facts Relating to the Arrest of Dr. Kalugin," *Asimov's SF*, Oct/Nov.
Baker, Nicholson, "China Pattern," *The New Yorker*, Mar. 3.
Baker, Virginia, "The Country Store," *Tomorrow* 24.
Barker, Clive, "Men and Sin," *Revelations*.
———, "A Moment at the River's Heart," *Ibid*.
Barker, Trey R., "Jake Leg Blues," *Terminal Frights*.
———, "Here There Be Hangin's," *Night Terrors 5*.
Barnett, Paul, "Imogen," *Shakespearean Whodunnits*.
Barrett, Lynne, "Hush Money," *Marilyn: Shades of Blonde*.
Beagle, Peter S., "Choushi-wai's Story," *Giant Bones*.
Beaulieu, Natasha (trans. by Yves Meynard), "Laika," *Tesseracts 5*.
Behrendt, Fred, "In the Times After," *Return to Lovecraft Country*.
Bell, Marvin, "The Book of the Dead Man (#76)" (poem), *AGNI* 44.
Bender, Aimee, "The Rememberer," *The Missouri Review*, Vol. XX, No. 2.
Bennett, Nancy, "The Chameleon," *Nasty Piece of Work 2*.
———, "Sachets" (poem), *Stygian Articles* 9.
———, "Sickness" (poem), *Nasty Piece of Work 5*.
———, "Within" (poem), *Stigmata*, Vol. 6, Number 1.
———, "Women on Board," *Urges* 4.
Berman, Judith, "Lord Stink," *Asimov's SF*, Aug.
Biguenet, John, "The Vulgar Soul," *Granta*, Sum.
Bishop, Michael, "Cyril Berganske," *Omni* (web site), May.
Blattberg, Benjamin Jacob, "The Pack," *24:7 Magazine* (web site), Win.
Block, Lawrence, "Headaches and Bad Dreams," *EQMM*, Dec.
Blosser, Fred, "Forrest Whateley," *Crypt of Cthulhu lammas*.
Blumlein, Michael, "Paul and Me," *F&SF*, Oct./Nov.

Blumlein, Michael, "Snow in Dirt," *Black Swan, White Raven.*
Boston, Bruce "Curse of the Berserker's Wife" (poem), *Talebones 6.*
Bowes, Richard, "Drink and the Devil," *F&SF*, Feb.
——, "In the House of the Man in the Moon," *Bending the Landscape: Fantasy.*
——, "Streetcar Dreams," *F&SF*, Apr.
Bowman, Catherine, "In the Garden Again" (poem), *The Peregrine Reader.*
Bradbury, Ray, "Madame et Monsieur Shill," *Driving Blind.*
——, "Nothing Changes," Ibid.
Braunbeck, Gary A., "In Hollow Houses," *Things Left Behind.*
——, "Kite People," *First Contact.*
——, "The Marble King," *Elf Magic.*
——, "The Sisterhood of Plain-Faced Women" (novella), *Things Left Behind.*
Brenchley, Chaz, "Dog Days," *Peeping Tom 28.*
Brennan, Joseph Payne, "Adrian," *Whispers*, final issue.
Brite, Poppy Z. and Faust Christa, "Triads," (novella) *Revelations.*
Brooke, Keith and Brown, Eric, "Under Antares," *Interzone 126.*
Brotherton, Mike, "Pearl," *Tales of the Unanticipated #17.*
Burleson, Donald R., "Connect the Dots," *Return to Lovecraft Country.*
——, "The Temple of Yig," *Singers of Strange Songs.*
Burstein, Michael A., "The Spider in the Hairdo," *Urban Nightmares.*
Burt, Steve, "The Mason's Leech," *Midnight Never Comes.*
Butot, Michele, "An Ode to Lilith" (poem), *Canadian Women Studies: Female Spirituality Issue*, Win.
Cacek, P. D., "Baby Dolls," *Leavings.*
——, "Heart of Stone," Ibid.
——, "Under the Haystack," Ibid.
Cadger, Rick, "Of Weather Signs and Absolution," *The Third Alternative* 11.
Cadigan, Pat, "Another Story," *Dying For It.*
——, "This Is Your Life (Repressed Memory Remix)," *Dark Terrors 3.*
Campbell, Ramsey, "Between the Floors," *Destination Unknown.*
——, "Kill Me Hideously," *Dark of the Night.*
——, "The Word," *Revelations.*
Cancilla, Dominick, "The Window Box," *Wetbones* 1.
Carr, Michael, "A Dog's Night," *F&SF*, Dec.
Carroll, Jonathan, "Asleep in Wolf's Clothing," *The Time Out Book of New York Short Stories.*
Carson, Anne, "TV Men: Antigone (Scripts 1 and 2)" (poem), *The Paris Review* 142.
Case, David, "Reflection," *Dark of the Night.*
Castro, Adam-Troy and Oltion, Jerry, "Crucifixion 2," *Terminal Frights.*
Cave, Hugh B., "Killing Time," *The Urbanite* 8.
Cerda, Martha, "It's Their Fault," *Señora Rodriguez and Other Worlds.*
Chadbourne, Mark, "Above, Behind, Beneath, Beside," *Scaremongers.*
——, "All Things Considered, I'd Rather be in Hell," *Peeping Tom 27.*
Chapman, Stepan, "Inside Out," *Hawaii Review*, Spr./Sum.
Cherches, Peter, "Man in Chair With Book," *The North American Review*, Mar./Apr.
Chesbro, George C., "Unmarked Graves," *EQMM*, Sep./Oct.
Chetwynd-Hayes, R., "The Fundamental Elemental," *The Vampire Stories of R. Chetwynd-Hayes.*
Chislett, Michael, "Let Down Your Hair," *All Hallows* 16.
——, "St. Asphodel and St. Jonquil," *Midnight Never Comes.*

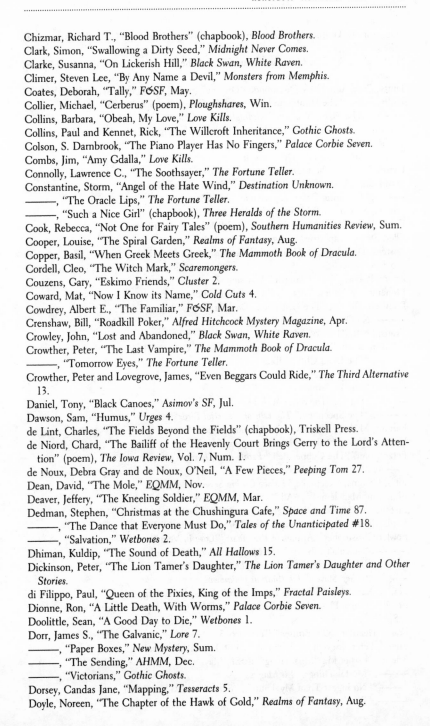

Chizmar, Richard T., "Blood Brothers" (chapbook), *Blood Brothers*.

Clark, Simon, "Swallowing a Dirty Seed," *Midnight Never Comes*.

Clarke, Susanna, "On Lickerish Hill," *Black Swan, White Raven*.

Climer, Steven Lee, "By Any Name a Devil," *Monsters from Memphis*.

Coates, Deborah, "Tally," *F&SF*, May.

Collier, Michael, "Cerberus" (poem), *Ploughshares*, Win.

Collins, Barbara, "Obeah, My Love," *Love Kills*.

Collins, Paul and Kennet, Rick, "The Willcroft Inheritance," *Gothic Ghosts*.

Colson, S. Darnbrook, "The Piano Player Has No Fingers," *Palace Corbie Seven*.

Combs, Jim, "Amy Gdalla," *Love Kills*.

Connolly, Lawrence C., "The Soothsayer," *The Fortune Teller*.

Constantine, Storm, "Angel of the Hate Wind," *Destination Unknown*.

———, "The Oracle Lips," *The Fortune Teller*.

———, "Such a Nice Girl" (chapbook), *Three Heralds of the Storm*.

Cook, Rebecca, "Not One for Fairy Tales" (poem), *Southern Humanities Review*, Sum.

Cooper, Louise, "The Spiral Garden," *Realms of Fantasy*, Aug.

Copper, Basil, "When Greek Meets Greek," *The Mammoth Book of Dracula*.

Cordell, Cleo, "The Witch Mark," *Scaremongers*.

Couzens, Gary, "Eskimo Friends," *Cluster 2*.

Coward, Mat, "Now I Know its Name," *Cold Cuts* 4.

Cowdrey, Albert E., "The Familiar," *F&SF*, Mar.

Crenshaw, Bill, "Roadkill Poker," *Alfred Hitchcock Mystery Magazine*, Apr.

Crowley, John, "Lost and Abandoned," *Black Swan, White Raven*.

Crowther, Peter, "The Last Vampire," *The Mammoth Book of Dracula*.

———, "Tomorrow Eyes," *The Fortune Teller*.

Crowther, Peter and Lovegrove, James, "Even Beggars Could Ride," *The Third Alternative* 13.

Daniel, Tony, "Black Canoes," *Asimov's SF*, Jul.

Dawson, Sam, "Humus," *Urges* 4.

de Lint, Charles, "The Fields Beyond the Fields" (chapbook), Triskell Press.

de Niord, Chard, "The Bailiff of the Heavenly Court Brings Gerry to the Lord's Attention" (poem), *The Iowa Review*, Vol. 7, Num. 1.

de Noux, Debra Gray and de Noux, O'Neil, "A Few Pieces," *Peeping Tom* 27.

Dean, David, "The Mole," *EQMM*, Nov.

Deaver, Jeffery, "The Kneeling Soldier," *EQMM*, Mar.

Dedman, Stephen, "Christmas at the Chushingura Cafe," *Space and Time* 87.

———, "The Dance that Everyone Must Do," *Tales of the Unanticipated* #18.

———, "Salvation," *Wetbones* 2.

Dhiman, Kuldip, "The Sound of Death," *All Hallows* 15.

Dickinson, Peter, "The Lion Tamer's Daughter," *The Lion Tamer's Daughter and Other Stories*.

di Filippo, Paul, "Queen of the Pixies, King of the Imps," *Fractal Paisleys*.

Dionne, Ron, "A Little Death, With Worms," *Palace Corbie Seven*.

Doolittle, Sean, "A Good Day to Die," *Wetbones* 1.

Dorr, James S., "The Galvanic," *Lore* 7.

———, "Paper Boxes," *New Mystery*, Sum.

———, "The Sending," *AHMM*, Dec.

———, "Victorians," *Gothic Ghosts*.

Dorsey, Candas Jane, "Mapping," *Tesseracts* 5.

Doyle, Noreen, "The Chapter of the Hawk of Gold," *Realms of Fantasy*, Aug.

Duchamp, L. Timmel, "The Apprenticeship of Isabetta de Pietro Cavazzi," *Asimov's SF*, Sep.

Duff, Valerie S., "The Nymphs, Seeing Circe at the Table" (poem), *The Antioch Review*, Spr.

Duffy, Carol Ann, "Mrs. Quasimodo's Divorce" (poem), *Acid Plaid: New Scottish Writing*.

Duffy, Steve, "The Hunter and His Quarry," *Ghosts and Scholars* 23.

———, "The Marsh Warden," *Midnight Never Comes*.

Duhamel, Denise, "Barbie in Therapy; Barbie in Therapy Part II; Barbie's Final Trip to Therapy" (poems), *Kinky*.

Duncan, Andy, "Saved," *Dying For It*.

Dyson, Jeremy, "The Maze," *Destination Unknown*.

D'Ammassa, Don, "Bad Soil," *Singers of Strange Songs*.

———, "Restoring Order," *Space and Time* 87.

Edghill, Rosemary, "May Eve," *The Fortune Teller*.

Eidus, Janice, "The Mermaid of Orchard Beach," *The Celibacy Club*.

Eller, Steve, "Tapestries," *Stygian Articles*, Final issue.

Epstein, Daniel Mark, "The Belled Buzzard of Roxbury Mills" (poem), *The American Scholar*, Aut.

Errera, Robert, "Sweet Mouth," *Wetbones* 2.

Etchemendy, Nancy, "Want's Bridge," *New Altars*.

Etchison, Dennis, "The Last Reel," *Dark Terrors* 3.

———"No One you Know," *Rage*, Oct.

Evans, Scott, "The Wooden Room," *Lore* 7.

Evenson, Brian, "Among the Living," *The Din of Celestial Birds*.

———, "The Dead Child," Ibid.

———, "A Difference in Ideology," Ibid.

———, "The Jar," Ibid.

———, "Prairie," *The Silver Web* 14.

———, "The Specimen," *The Din of Celestial Birds*.

Farrant, M. A. C., "Jigsaw," *The Malahat Review*, Sep.

Fenlon, Karen, "Striking Shona," *Peeping Tom* 28.

Fetzer, Bret, "The Copper Bell," *Petals and Thorns*.

———, "A Princess in Pieces," Ibid.

Files, Gemma, "Keepsake," *Palace Corbie Seven*.

Finnegan, Madeleine V., "All Meat is Prey," *Peeping Tom* 28.

Fletcher, Jo, "Dark of the Night" (poem), *Dark of the Night*.

Ford, Michael Thomas, "Angel Baby," *Brothers of the Night*.

Fowler Christopher, "Armies of the Heart," *Love in Vein II*.

———, "Dracula's Library," *The Mammoth Book of Dracula*.

———, "The Grande Finale Hotel," *Dark of the Night*.

———, "Wage Slaves," *Destination Unknown*.

Fowler, Karen Joy, "Standing Room Only," *Asimov's SF*, Aug.

Francis, Diana Pharoah, "All Things Being Not Quite Equal," *Dreams of Decadence*, Spr.

Fraser, Heather, "Old Bruises," *Tesseracts* 5.

Friend, Peter, "Seventeen Views of Mount Taranaki," *Aurealis* 18.

Friesner, Esther M., "Miss Thing," *F&SF*, May.

———, "Mortal Things," *Elf Magic*.

———, "No Bigger Than My Thumb," *Black Swan, White Raven*.

———, "Prey," *Asimov's SF*, May.

Friesner, Esther M., "Silent Love," *Dying for It.*

Fuqua, C. S., "Undertaker II: Drowning," *Cyber-Psychos* AOD 7.

Gagliani, William D., "Icewall," *Robert Bloch's Psychos.*

Gaiman, Neil, "The Daughter of Owls," *Tales of the Unanticipated* #18.

———, "The Price" (chapbook), *Cats and Dogs.*

———, "Reading the Entrails: A Rondel" (poem), *The Fortune Teller.*

Gardner, James Alan, "All Good Things Come From Far Away," *Tesseracts 5.*

Garton, Ray, "Hair of the Dog," *Hot Blood: Kiss and Kill.*

———, "Second Opinion," *Cemetery Dance*, Fall.

Geddes, Cindie, "Symbiosis," *Epitaph 2.*

Gibson, Stephen, "The Murderess," *Epoch*, Vol. 46, Num. 2.

Gilford, Henry, "Hamlet on My Mind" (poem), *The Sewanee Review*, Win.

Glasby, John, "Return to Y'ha-nthlei," *Lore 7.*

Glassco, Bruce, "True Thomas," *Black Swan, White Raven.*

Goldstein, Lisa, "Down the Fool's Road," *F&SF.* Oct./Nov.

———, "Fortune and Misfortune," *Asimov's SF*, May.

Goonan, Kathleen Ann, "Lullaby of Birdland," *Destination Unknown.*

Goingback, Owl, "Shaman Moon," *The Essential World of Darkness.*

Gordon, John, "Black Beads," *The Mammoth Book of Dracula.*

Gorman, Ed, "Emma Baxter's Son," *Cemetery Dance*, Spr.

Gould, Jason, "Thornboys," *Nasty Piece of Work 4.*

Grant, Charles, "Haunted," *Robert Bloch's Psychos.*

Grey, John, "The Spiders Beneath" (poem), *Pluto's Orchard 1.*

Griffin, Marni Scofidio, "Imbroglio," *The Urbanite 9: Strange Places.*

———, "Outside the Gates," *Midnight Never Comes.*

Guthridge, George and Berliner, Janet, "Notes Toward a Rumpled Stillskin," *F&SF*, Apr.

Gwynn, R. S., "Black Helicopters," *The Hudson Review*, Sum.

Hadas, Rachel, "On Myth" (poem), *Yale Review*, Vol. 85, Num. 4.

Hamilton, Steve, "The Silence," *Pirate Writings* 14.

Hardison, Jim, "The Wish," *Stygian Articles* 9.

Hardy, K. S., "A Plague of Birds" (poem), *Talebones* 7.

Harris, Marc, "Aging Gracefully (In the Cafe)" (poem), *Nasty Piece of Work 5.*

Harris, Steve, "Minimum Visibility," *Scaremongers.*

Hayhurst, Joanne, "Inca Girl" (poem), *Poet Lore.*

Hemmingson, Michael, "Shadowplayers," *Snuff Flique.*

Hershmann, Morris, "A Private Vengeance," *The Fatal Frontier.*

Hill, David W., "5Q389," *Talebones* 6.

Hill, Joe, "The Lady Rests," *Palace Corbie Seven.*

Hirsch, Connie, "The Céilidh," *Elf Magic.*

Hodge, Brian, "The 121st Day of Sodom," *Hot Blood: Kiss and Kill.*

———, "The Dripping of Sundered Wineskins," *Love in Vein II.*

———, "Little Holocausts," *Dark Terrors 3.*

———, "Madame Babylon," *Hot Blood: Crimes of Passion.*

———, "Some Other Me," *Hear the Fear: Death Equinox Program Book.*

Hoffman, Nina Kiriki, "The World Within," *F&SF*, Sep.

Holdefer, Charles, "Why I Wear a Hat," *Southern Humanities Review*, Sum.

Holder, Nancy, "Blood Freak," *The Mammoth Book of Dracula.*

———, "Syngamy," *Gothic Ghosts.*

Holladay, Cary, "The Rapture of the Deep," *Southern Humanities Review*, Win.

Hook, Andrew, "Making Faces," *Nasty Piece of Work* 5.

Hopkins, Brian A. and Wilson, David Niall, "La Belle Dame Sans Regret," *Terminal Frights.*

Houarner, Gerard Daniel, "A Blood of Killers," *Tomorrow* 3.

———, "Spider Goes to Market," *Tales of the Unanticipated* #18.

———, "Truth and Consequences in the Heart of Destruction," *Inside the Works.*

———, "The Question Man," *Wetbones* 1.

Howarth, G. W., "The Chinese Scholar," *Midnight Never Comes.*

Howkins, Elizabeth, "The Caretaker" (poem), *The Silver Web* 14.

Hughes, Rhys H., "Number 13," *Ghosts and Scholars* 23.

Hughes, Ted, "Tiresias" (poem), *Partisan Review*, Vol. LXIV, Num. 4.

Hutchinson, David, "The Trauma Jockey," *Interzone* 117.

Jackson, Shirley, "The Good Wife," *Just an Ordinary Day.*

———, "Jack the Ripper," Ibid.

———, "The Mouse," Ibid.

Jacob, Charlee, "Body and Soul," *Stigmata*, Vol. 6 Num. 1.

———, "Emetic Finger," *Stygian Articles* 10.

———, "The Piano Player Has No Fingers," *Palace Corbie Seven.*

———, "The Piano Player Has No Fingers #2," Ibid.

Jaffe, Maggie, "Lilith" (poem), *Bridges*, Spr.

Jeapes, Ben, "Wingèd Chariot," *Interzone* 118, Apr.

Jensen, Jan Lars, "Domestic Slash and Thrust," *Tesseracts* 5.

Johnson, C. W., "Drowned Love," *Realms of Fantasy*, Oct.

Jones, Gwyneth, "Balinese Dancer," *Asimov's SF*, Sep.

Jordan, Ceri, "There the Great City Stands," *Not One of Us* 17.

Kadleckova, Vilma (trans. by M. Klima and Bruce Sterling), "Longing for Blood," *F&SF*, Jan.

Keller, Jennifer, "The Wasp People" (poem), *Talebones* 6.

Kelly, Michael, "Father's Love," *Creatio ex Nihilo*, Jun.

Kernaghan, Eileen, "The Watley Man and the Green-Eyed Girl," *Transversions* 7.

Ketchum, Jack, "The Work," *Funeral Party* Vol. 2.

Kiernan, Caitlín R., "Emptiness Spoke Eloquent," *Secret City: Strange Tales of London.*

Kihn, Greg, "The Great White Light," *Hot Blood: Crimes of Passion.*

Kilpatrick, Nancy, ". . . . and Thou," *Stigmata*, Vol. 6 Num. 1.

———, "Teaserama," *The Mammoth Book of Dracula.*

Kincaid, Paul, "Last Day of the Carnival," *Back Brain Recluse* 23.

King, Stephen, "Autopsy Room Four," *Six Stories.*

———, "Everything's Eventual," *F&SF*, Oct./Nov.

———, "General," *Screamplays.*

Knight, Jesse F., "To Capture a Perfect Wave," *Midnight Never Comes.*

Koja, Kathe and Malzberg, Barry N., "Orleans, Rheims, Friction: Fire," *F&SF*, Aug.

Kratochvil, Jiri (trans. by Jonathan Bolton), "The Story of King Candaules," *Daylight in Nightclub Inferno: Czech Fiction.*

Krawiec, Robert, "The Uninvited Guest," *Lore* 7.

Kress, Nancy, "Johnny's So Long at the Fair," *Dying For It.*

———, "Steadfast," *Black Swan, White Raven.*

Laidlaw, Marc, "Babydoll," *Wetbones* 1.

Lamsley, Terry, "The Lost Boy Found," *Dark Terrors* 3.

———, "The Power of the Primitive," *Cemetery Dance*, Spr.

———, "The Snug," *Midnight Never Comes.*

Lamsley, Terry, "Volunteers," *The Mammoth Book of Dracula.*

Lane, Joel, "Keep the Night," *The Third Alternative* 12.

———, "Making Babies," *The Urbanite 8: Fabulous Creatures.*

———, "The Mouths," *The Main Street Journal* 3.

———, "The Plans They Made," *Scaremongers.*

———, "The Spoils," *The Silver Web* 14.

———, "Your European Son," *The Mammoth Book of Dracula.*

Lane, John, "My Dead Father Hands Out Advice; My Dead Father Visits My Mother; My Dead Father on Vacation" (poems), *Tar River Poetry*, Fall.

Langford, David, "The Case of Jack the Clipper," *Interzone* 126.

———, "Serpent Eggs," *The Third Alternative* 14.

Lannes, Roberta, "Dark Horse," *The Mirror of Night.*

———, "Good Girl," *Dark of the Night.*

———, "In the Mirror of Night," *The Mirror of Night.*

———, "Melancholia," *The Mammoth Book of Dracula.*

———, "The Shy Fruit of Pathos," *The Mirror of Night.*

———, "Sleeping Beauty Takes a Frog Prince," Ibid.

———, "When Memory Fails," *Love in Vein II.*

Lansdale, Joe R., "The Big Blow" (novella), *Revelations.*

Larkin, Morgan, "The Reclamation," *Stygian Articles*, Final issue.

Lease, Joseph, "Housekeeping," *The Virginia Quarterly Review*, Spr.

Lee, Rand B., "The Green Man," *F&SF*, Aug.

Lee, Tanith, "After I Killed Her," *Asimov's SF*, Jul.

———, "Cain," *Dying For It.*

———, "The Lady of Shalott House," *Realms of Fantasy*, Oct.

———, "Old Flame," *Realms of Fantasy*, Feb.

Leech, Ben, "The Harrowing Stone," *Scaremongers.*

Lees, Tim, "The God House," *The Third Alternative* 12.

Lepovetsy, Lisa, "The Piano Player Has No Fingers," *Palace Corbie Seven.*

Levy, Robert, "Thoughts of Benjy," *Tomorrow* 24.

Lewis, D. F., "The Gaze Strip," *Nasty Piece of Work* 2.

———, "The Piano Player Has No Fingers #1," *Palace Corbie Seven.*

Libling, Michael, "A Bite to Eat in Abbotsford," *Destination Unknown.*

Ligotti, Thomas, "The Bells Will Sound Forever," *In a Foreign Town, in a Foreign Land.*

———, "His Shadow Shall Rise to a Higher House," Ibid.

———, "A Soft Voice Whispers Nothing," Ibid.

———, "When You Hear the Singing, You Will Know It Is Time," Ibid.

Lima, Frank, "Maria Magdelena's Extreme Unction" (poem), *The Massachusetts Review*, Vol. XXXVIII Num. 3.

Little, Bentley, "The Murmerous Haunts of Flies," *Murmerous Haunts.*

———, "The Piano Player Has No Fingers," *Palace Corbie Seven.*

Little, Geradine Clinton, "Sunday Morning Bells," *Women in a Special House and Other Stories.*

Lodi, Edward, "And I Saw That It Was Dead," *Terminal Frights.*

Long, Mark Steven, "Temporary Town," *Intertext* (web site), Vol. 7 Num. 1.

Longhorn, David, "Last Wishes," *All Hallows* 16.

———, "The Ptolemaic System," *Ghosts and Scholars* 23.

Low, Janice, "Secrets," *AHMM*, Jul./Aug.

Lupoff, Richard A., "The Doom that Came to Dunwich," *Return to Lovecraft Country.*

MacEwan, Pat, "The Macklin Gift," *F&SF*, Jun.

Mackay, Colin, "Mary King's Close," *Midnight Never Comes*.

MacLeod, Ian R., "The Golden Keeper" (novella), *Asimov's SF*, Oct./Nov.

———, "The Roads," *Asimov's SF*, Apr.

Manchino, Albert J., "Evening Primrose" (novella), *Noctet: Tales of Madonna-Moloch*.

Masterton, Graham, "Roadkill," *The Mammoth Book of Dracula*.

Matheson, Richard Christian, "The Film," *Rage*, Jan.

———, "Whatever," *Revelations*.

McAuley, Paul J., "The Quarry," *Dark of the Night*.

———, "The Worst Place in the World," *The Mammoth Book of Dracula*.

McBride, Sally, "Hello Jane, Good-Bye," *Northern Frights 4*.

———, "There is a Violence," *Tesseracts 5*.

McClintock, Malcolm, "Kelso at the Voodoo Museum," *AHMM*, Feb.

McCord, Howard, "Waiting for the Elf" (poem), *The Peregrine Reader*.

McCormick, Mike, "Dead Man's Fuel," *Secular Psalms: Conjunctions 28*.

McDonald, Ian, "Jesus' Blood Never Failed Me Yet," *Albedo 14*.

McEwan, Ian, "Us or Me," *The New Yorker*, May 19.

McGuire, D. A., "This House Has Secrets Still," *AHMM*, Oct.

McInerny, Ralph, "Copy Dog," *EQMM*, Feb.

McMichael, Doris, "Mustn't Tell on Mama," *Talebones 7*.

McNaughton, Brian, "The Art of Tiphytsorn Glocque," *The Throne of Bones*.

———, "Malpractice," *Weirdbook 30*.

———, "Mr. Entwhistle's Sovereign Snuff," *Lore 7*.

———, "The Return of Liron Wolfbaiter" (novella), *The Throne of Bones*.

———, "Reunion in Cephaline," *Ibid*.

———, "Ringard and Dendra," *Ibid*.

———, "Water and the Spirit," *Lore 7*.

Melko, Jr., Paul J., "Bolt," *Talebones 6*.

———, "Doreen," *Not One of Us 17*.

Merwin, W. S., "The Chinese Mountain Fox" (poem), *Yale Review*, Vol. 85, Num. 1

Metzger, Th., "The Fly Room," *Love in Vein II*.

Meyard, Yves, "Within the Mechanism," *Tomorrow SF*,

Minnion, Keith, "Dead End," *Night Terrors 3*.

Monahan, Brent, "The Shadow Knows," *Monsters from Memphis*.

Monteleone, Thomas F., "Between Floors" (chapbook), Subterranean Press.

Moon, Lilith, "Nevermore," *All Hallows 14*.

Mooney, Brian, "Endangered Species," *The Mammoth Book of Dracula*.

Morlan A. R., "Buddy Holly Night in the Bone God's Lair," *Phantasm*, Spr./Sum.

———, "Duet on Thin Ice," *Night Terrors 4*.

———, "This is the Way We Wash Our Clothes, Wash Our Clothes . . . ," *Night Terrors 5*.

Morrell, David, "If I Should Die Before I Wake" (novella), *Revelations*.

Morris, Mark, "Holes," *The Third Alternative 14*.

Morton, Lisa, "Children of the Long Night," *The Mammoth Book of Dracula*.

Murakami, Haruki, "Another Way to Die," *The New Yorker*, Jan. 20.

Murakami, Ryu, "Fish Day Memories," *Michiko Kon: Still Lifes*.

Murphy, Derryl, "Cold Ground," *Arrowdreams*.

Myers, Jennifer McIlwee, "An Acceptable Sacrifice," *Tales of Lovecraftian Horror 7*.

Navarro, Yvonne, "Four Famines Ago," *Terminal Frights*.

———, "Motherdead," *Vampire Dan's Story Emporium*, Sum./Fall.

Newman, Kim, "Coppola's Dracula" (novella), *The Mammoth Book of Dracula*.
———, "The End of the Pier Show" (novella), *Dark of the Night*.
———, "Patricia's Profession," *Rage*, Jul.
Nickels, Tim, "The Last of the Dandini Sisters," *The Third Alternative* 12.
Nickle, David, "The Pit-Heads," *Northern Frights* 4.
Nicoll, Gregory, "For the Dead Travel Fast," *Terminal Frights*.
———, "Subway Accident," *Singers of Strange Songs*.
Oates, Joyce Carol, "In the Insomniac Night," *Black Swan, White Raven*.
———, "The Last Man of Letters," *Playboy*, Dec.
———, "Starr Bright Will Be with You Soon!," *Hot Blood: Crimes of Passion*.
O'Connell, E. Jay, "The Listening Box," *Pirate Writings* 14.
O'Driscoll, Mike, "The Ones We Need, the Ones We Leave Behind," *Back Brain Recluse* 23.
Ojouner, Terry, "Take One," *Peeping Tom* 26.
Ormerod, Jane, "Camel," *Psychotrope* 5.
Osier, Jeffrey, "Horizon Lines," *Horizon Lines*.
Owen, Barbara, "How Things Are," *EQMM*, Dec.
Pardoe, Rosemary, "The Sheelagh-na-gig," *Midnight Never Comes*.
Parks, Richard, "Knacker Man," *Robert Bloch's Psychos*.
Perry, Clark, "Deep Down There," Ibid.
Phillips, Walt, "Friday Morning Poem" (poem), *The Silver Web* 14.
Piccirilli, Tom, "Bedlam," *Inside the Works*.
———, "Bridge of Brothers," *Monsters from Memphis*.
———, "Curs," *Hot Blood: Crimes of Passion*.
———, "The Dog Syndrome," *The Dog Syndrome and Other Sick Puppies*.
———, "Inside the Works," *Inside the Works*.
———, "Recovery," Ibid.
———, "Where the Swamp Folk Go When the Need Comes," *The Dog Syndrome and Other Sick Puppies*.
Pinn, Paul, "Black God Fever," *Scattered Remains*.
———, "The Boiling Point of Solutions," Ibid.
———, "Phlon XI," Ibid.
Pinn, Paul, and Johnson, Alexander, "The Flayer," *Nasty Piece of Work* 6.
Ponder, Jeremy, "The Monster," *Plot* 8.
Prentice, Chris, "Taken, Given" *Dreams of Decadence*, Spr.
Pryor, Michael, "Time to Burn," *Aurealis* 18.
Ptacek, Kathryn, "Skinned Angels," *Dark Terrors* 3.
Pugmire, Wilem H., "Zombie Danse," *The Urbanite* 9: *Strange Places*.
Quinlan, Nigel, "Golden Thread," *Albedo One* 13.
Rainey, Stephen Mark, "Bloodlight," *Love in Vein II*.
———, "Shudder Wyrm," *Singers of Strange Songs*.
Rath, Tina, "Father O'Flynn and the Fressingfold Friezes," *Midnight Never Comes*.
———, "Rubies and Diamonds" *All Hallows* 16.
Rathbone, Julian, "Fat Mary," *Dark Terrors* 3.
Read, William I. I., "The Dentures of Count Dracula," *All Hallows* 16.
Reed, Robert, "Graffiti," *F&SF*, June.
———, "Mind's Eye," *Asimov's SF*, Oct./Nov.
Resnick, Laura and Chwedyk, Kathy, "She of the Night," *Urban Nightmares*.
Reynolds, Alastair, "A Spy in Europa," *Interzone* 120.
Richerson, Carrie, "Nuestra Señora," *Gothic Ghosts*.

Richerson, Carrie, "The Quick and the Dead," F&SF, Dec.

Riedel, Kate, "The Babysitter," On Spec, Win. 96–97.

Robson, Justina, "Deadhead," The Third Alternative 11.

Roche, Thomas S., "Razorblade Valentines," Hot Blood: Kiss and Kill.

Rogers, Bruce Holland, "With His Own Wings," Elf Magic.

Roibin, Sean Mac, "Anatomy of Resistentialist Induced Matricide," Albedo One, 14.

Rosenman, John B., "Trophies," Hot Blood: Kiss and Kill.

Routhier, William, "Graceland," InterText (web site), Vol. 7 Num. 3.

Rowen, Ted, "The Snake Bites Twice," AHMM July/Aug.

Royle, Nicholas, "Auteur," Ambit 150.

——, "Futility Room," Dark of the Night.

——, "The Pied Piper of Hammersmith," Time Out, Oct. 29–Nov. 5.

——, "Simple Ballet," Kimota 7.

——, "Vist," The Third Alternative 13.

Rusch, Kristine Kathryn, "Falling," Realms of Fantasy, Feb.

——, "The Hook," Urban Nightmares.

Russell, Jay, "Sous Rature," Dark Terrors 3.

——, "Waltz in Vienna," Dark of the Night.

Russo, Patricia, "Rat Familiar," Lore 7.

——, "Le Sang des Fées," Tales of the Unanticipated #18.

Sahu, Cathy, "The Book of the Servant," AHMM, Nov.

Sallee, Wayne Allen, "The Gagging," Lathered in Crimson 2.

Salmonson, Jessica Amanda, "The Spirit Elk," Weirdbook 12.

——, "Young Lady Who Loved Caterpillars," Bending the Landscape: Fantasy.

Santos-Febres, Mara (trans. by Nathan Budoff and Lydia Platon Lazaro), "Mystic Rose," Urban Oracles.

Saplak, Charles M., "Creeper in the Shroud," The Urbanite 9: Strange Places.

Sarafin, James, "In the Furnace of the Night" (novella), Asimov's SF, May.

Sargent, Stanley C., "The Black Brat of Dunwich," Cthulhu Codex 10.

Sanders, William, "The Undiscovered," Asimov's SF, Mar.

Sawyer, Robert J., "Gator," Urban Nightmares.

Schinker, Nick, "Since My Last Confession," EQMM, Sep./Oct.

Schow, David J., "Bagged," Rage, Nov.

——, "Dusting the Flowers," Love in Vein II.

Schow, David J., and Spector, Craig, "Dismantling Fortress Architecture," Revelations.

Schweitzer, Darrell, "The Silence of Kings," Weirdbook 12.

——, "Still There" (poem), Cthulhu Codex 11.

Serken, E. S., "The Childish Things," Night Terrors 3.

Shannon, Lorelei, "Gabriel's Gargoyle," New Altars.

Shippey, Tom, "The Low Road," Destination Unknown.

Shirley, John, "Cram," Wetbones 2.

Sigler, Scott, "Number One with a Bullet," Monsters from Memphis.

Silverberg, Robert, "Call Me Titan," Asimov's SF, Feb.

Simpson, Jacqueline, "Three Padlocks," Ghosts and Scholars 23.

Smale, Alan, "Feathers," Night Terrors 5.

Smeds, Dave, "The Trigger," Realms of Fantasy, Feb.

Smith, James Robert, "The Reliable Vacuum Company," Singers of Strange Songs.

Smith, Michael Marshall, "Dear Alison," The Mammoth Book of Dracula.

——, "Different Now," Scaremongers.

——, "Save As . . . ," Interzone 115.

Smith, Michael Marshall, "Victoria's Secret," *Dark of the Night*.

———, "Walking Wounded," *Dark Terrors 3*.

Smith, Thomas, "The Heart Is a Determined Hunter," *Gothic Ghosts*.

Snyder, Midori, "The Reverend's Wife," *Black Swan, White Raven*.

Sobolik, Kurt, "Scene" (poem), *Not One of Us* 17.

Solomon, Julian, "Ursa Major," *Puck* 1.

Somtow, S. P., "The Ugliest Duckling," *Urban Nightmares*.

Springer, Nancy, "Elvis Lives," *Tarot Fantastic*.

———, "Hexefus," *The Fortune Teller*.

———, "Transcendence," *F&SF*, Oct./Nov.

Stableford, Brian, "The Great God Pan," *F&SF*, Jun.

———, "Quality Control," *The Mammoth Book of Dracula*.

———, "Seers," *Gothic Ghosts*.

———, "True Collectors," *The Fortune Teller*.

Steinfeld, J. J., "The Most Remarkable Filmmaker the World Has Ever Known," *The Antigonish Review*, Spr.

Stone, Robert, "Bear and His Daughter," *Bear and His Daughter: Stories*.

Strieber, Whitley, "The Open Doors" (novella), *Revelations*.

———, "Under the Old Oak Tree," *Evenings with Demons*.

Stuart, Kiel, "Chimaera Ho," *Stygian Articles*, Final issue.

Sutton, Mark, "The Sound of Fury," *Monsters from Memphis*.

Swanwick, Michael, "Mother Grasshopper," *A Geography of Unknown Lands*.

Sweeney, Matthew, "The Box" (poem), *The Bridal Suite*.

———, "The House" (poem), Ibid.

———, "In a Field" (poem), Ibid.

Sykes, Jerry, "Call Me Walt," *Cemetery Dance*, Fall.

———, "Cracked Rear View," *Love Kills*.

Tanner, Jason A., "Buzzards Last Day in the Big Q," *Odyssey* 1.

Taylor, Lucy, "Chattel," *Tarot Fantastic*.

———, "Ceilings and Sky," *Love in Vein II*.

———, "Pain Threshold," *Painted in Blood*.

———, "Painted in Blood," Ibid.

———, "The Story Box," Ibid.

Tem, Melanie, "Aunt Libby's Grave," *Dark Terrors 3*.

Tem, Steve Rasnic, "Andrew," *Palace Corbie Seven*.

———, "Sharp Edges," *Dark Terrors 3*.

Tennant, Peter, "The Giving of Names," *Scaremongers*.

Tessier, Thomas, "La Mourante," *Hot Blood: Kiss and Kill*.

Thatcher, B. Franklin, "Lightning Boy," *Talebones* 9.

Thomas, Ashley, "The Sea and the Statues," *Peeping Tom* 28.

Thomas, Jeffrey, "Black Walls," *Black Walls, Red Glass*.

———, "One Big Happy Family," *Dark Dixie II*.

———, "Red Glass," *Black Walls, Red Glass*.

———, "The Red Machine," Ibid.

———, "Servile," *Cthulhu Codex* 11.

Thomas, Michael, "Nightwatch," *F&SF*, Mar.

Thomas, Scott, "The Apple Track," *Penny Dreadful* 4.

———, "Girls Who Like Nails," *The End* 5.

Thon, Melanie Rae, "The River Woman's Son," *Ploughshares*, Spr.

Thurlow, Clifford, "The Healing," *The Third Alternative* 13.

Tiedemann, Mark W., "Along an Ellipse of Tears," *Tales of the Unanticipated* #18.

Tripp, William T., "Sleight of Blood," *Night Terrors* 5.

Turzillo, Mary A., "Brit Lit One" (poem), *New Altars*.

Tuttle, Lisa, "The Extra Hour," *Destination Unknown*.

———, "Soul Song," *Interzone* 119.

Urban, Scott H., "Another Babynapping," *Cyber-Psychos AOD* 7.

Utley, Steven, "Once More, with Feeling," *Dying For It*.

VanderMeer, Jeff, "Detectives and Cadavers," *Back Brain Recluse* 23.

———, "Quin's Shanghai Circus,"*Interzone* 124, Oct.

Vaz, Katherine, "Undressing the Vanity Dolls," *Fado and Other Stories*.

Velde, Vivian Vande, "Remember Me," *Curses, Inc. and Other Stories*.

———, "The Witch's Son," Ibid.

Volk, Steven, "The Latin Master," *Midnight Never Comes*.

Vonarburg, Elizabeth (trans. by Howard Scott), "Readers of the Lost Ar," *Tesseracts* 5.

Wade, Susan, "A Recent Vintage," *F&SF*, May.

———, "The Sixteenth Card," *Tarot Fantastic*.

Walsh, Pat, "The Rune Stone,"*All Hallows* 15.

Walther, Paul, "It's Steady Work," *Space and Time* 87.

Walton, Diane L., "Bury Me Not on the Lone Prairie," *On Spec*, Sum.

Watkins, Graham, "Comeback," *Hot Blood: Kiss and Kill*.

Watson, Ian, "The China Cottage," *Destination Unknown*.

———, "The Last Beast Out of the Box," *F&SF*, May.

Watts, Peter, "Bethlehem," *Tesseracts* 5.

Webb, Don, "Boy," *Stealing My Rules*.

———, "House of Cards," *Tarot Fantastic*.

———, "It Sounded Angular," *Wetbones* 1.

———, "That Old Time Religion," *Stealing My Rules*.

Weighell, Ron, "The Mouth of the Medusa," *Midnight Never Comes*.

Wells, Martha, "Bad Medicine," *Realms of Fantasy*, June.

Wendig, C. D., "Bourbon Street Lullaby," *Not One of Us* 18.

West, Michelle, "By the Work, One Knows," *Zodiac Fantastic*.

What, Leslie, "In His Pants," *Talebones* 6.

Whitbourn, John, "Bury My Heart at Southerham (East Sussex)," *Midnight Never Comes*.

White, Alison, "The Looker," *EQMM*, Aug.

White, Jon Manchip, "The Flask," *New Millennium Writings*, Win.

Whorton, Jr., James, "The Dog," *Mississippi Review* (web site).

Williams, Conrad, "Bloodlines," *The Mammoth Book of Dracula*.

———, "Failure," *Scaremongers*.

———, "The Windmill," *Dark Terrors* 3.

———, "Yolk," *Peeping Tom* 25.

Williams, Gavin, "The Special Favour," *Scaremongers*.

Williamson, Chet, "Jacob Horst and the Dark Grocer," *Whispers*, Final issue.

Williamson, Jack, "The Hole in the World," *F&SF*, Oct./Nov.

Williamson, J. N., "It Does Not Come Alone," *Terminal Frights*.

———, "The Piano Player Has No Fingers," *Palace Corbie Seven*.

Williamson, Neil, "Shine, Alone After the Setting of the Sun," *The Third Alternative* 11.

Winston-MacAuley, Marnie, "Fade Out," *Realms of Fantasy*, Aug.

Winter, Douglas E., "The Zombies of Madison County" (novella), *Dark of the Night*.

Wisman, Ken, "Blizzard," *Whispers*, Final issue.

Yasgur, Batya Swift, "Photographs," *Cemetery Dance*, Spr.

Yolen, Jane, "Godmother Death," *Black Swan, White Raven.*
————, "Lost Girls," *Twelve Impossible Things Before Breakfast.*
————, "Song of the Cards" (poem), *Tarot Fantastic.*
————, "A Southern Night," *Robert Bloch's Psychos.*

THE PEOPLE BEHIND THE BOOK

Horror Editor ELLEN DATLOW was fiction editor for OMNI Magazine and OMNI Internet for more than seventeen years and is now editor of the *Event Horizon*. She has edited numerous anthologies including *Blood Is Not Enough*, *Alien Sex*, *Little Deaths*, *Off Limits*, and *Twists of the Tale: Stories of Cat Horror*. She has won five World Fantasy Awards for her editing. She lives in New York City.

Fantasy Editor TERRI WINDLING has been an editor of fantasy literature for almost two decades, winning five World Fantasy Awards for her work. She has published more than twenty anthologies, including *The Armless Maiden* and *Sirens* (with Ellen Datlow). As a fiction writer, her books include *The Wood Wife* (winner of the Mythopoeic Award), *The Moon Wife* (forthcoming), and *The Changeling* (for children). She edited *Good Faeries/Bad Faeries* by British artist Brian Froud, and writes a regular column on folklore for *Realms of Fantasy* magazine. As a painter, she has exhibited in a number of museums across the U.S. and abroad. She divides her time between homes in Devon, England, and Tucson, Arizona.

Packager JAMES FRENKEL edited Dell Books' science fiction and fantasy in the late 1970s and early 1980s, was the publisher of Bluejay Books in the 1980s, and has been a consulting editor for Tor Books for more than ten years. Along with KRISTOPHER O'HIGGINS and a legion of student interns, Frenkel edits, packages, and agents books in Madison, Wisconsin.

Media Critic EDWARD BRYANT is an award-winning writer of science fiction, fantasy, and horror. He has had short fiction published in numerous magazines and anthologies. He has won the Hugo Award for his fiction. His work also includes writing for television. He lives in Denver, Colorado.

Comics Critic SETH JOHNSON is a freelance writer who has written for newspapers and done work in the game industry. He lives in Madison, Wisconsin.

Artist THOMAS CANTY has won the World Fantasy Award for Best Artist. He has painted illustrations for innumerable books, ranging from fantasy and horror to suspense and thrillers. He is also an art director, and has designed many books and book jackets during a career that spans more than twenty years. He has painted and designed the jackets/covers for every volume of *The Year's Best Fantasy and Horror*. He lives outside Boston, Massachusetts.